The Knight Son

J.B. Vosler

**The New
Atlantian Library**

Habent Sua Fata Libelli

The New Atlantian Library

Manhanset House
Shelter Island Hts., New York 11965-0342

bricktower@aol.com • tech@absolutelyamazingebooks.com
• absolutelyamazingebooks.com

Library of Congress Cataloging-in-Publication Data
Vosler, J.B.
The Knight Son, The Sons of Jacob Series, Book IX.
p. cm.

1. FICTION / Thrillers / Psychological. 2. FICTION / Romance / Suspense.
3. FICTION / Mystery & Detective / International Mystery & Crime
Fiction, I. Title.
ISBN: 978-1-955036-73-3, Trade Paper

July 2024

The Knight Son

Sons of Jacob

Book IX

J.B. Vosler

Contents

MAP OF EUROPE

THE SONS OF JACOB Saga

BOOK I: "Shadow of the Phoenix"

This novel introduces MARTIN HENDERSON, who has survived a deadly fire only to return three-and-a-half years later as an assassin for EDWARD MORNINGSTAR, a Pentagon aide who sees himself as a Biblical Jacob. Henderson, once a brilliant entrepreneur, is now compelled to do whatever Morningstar asks – including murder – as a result of Morningstar's threat against a notable little girl, LILI PLATACIS. Henderson had sworn to protect Lili, and, when she is then taken, Henderson vows to bring down not only Morningstar, but his entire operation. In the meantime, Henderson's former lover, Senator Cynthia Madison – MADDI – has also become a Morningstar target, and it's up to Henderson to save her.

BOOK II: "The Maker's Prophecy"

The delusional Morningstar, who thinks he is Jacob, is well on his way to world domination. He has "adopted" twelve sons, who are his soldiers and will do whatever he asks. Henderson has made it his goal to stop Morningstar, and is doing what he can to undermine his efforts. Meanwhile, a deadly virus has been unleashed in Columbia, South Carolina, and Maddi's brother, ANDREW, as Medical Director of a downtown clinic, is the first to see its effects. When a more aggressive strain of the same virus shows up in Chicago, L.A., and Texas, Henderson knows Morningstar is somehow behind it. Maddi is once again threatened, and he must figure out a way to keep her safe from Morningstar's relentless pursuit.

BOOK III: "The Rise of the Avenger"

An entire village is massacred outside the town of Bariloche, Argentina, and Maddi is pulled into action at the request of one of her dearest friends, SIR ARTHUR KAUFFOLD, a former ambassador. She puts together a coalition to travel to the region. Morningstar learns of it, and sends two 'sons' to Bariloche to stop her. She succeeds not only in defending the coalition, but in averting a war with Argentina, thanks to the intervention of her former lover, HANK CLARKSON, the Deputy Director of Homeland Security. Meanwhile, Henderson has gone to Russia to undergo a revolutionary surgery designed to give him a completely new face. He then vows to seek revenge against Morningstar.

BOOK IV: "Strike of the Cobra"

A vicious assassin, COBRA, has killed a former IRA operative outside Donegal, which has thrown the Irish Republic into chaos. Cobra, also known as Dan, is one of the sons of Jacob, and has been instructed by Morningstar to carry out multiple killings in an effort to disrupt the UK and France. Maddi discovers that she is being stalked by someone from the UK, and insists on flying to London to find him. Henderson, who has undergone surgery and has changed his name to MATT, goes to D.C. to introduce himself to Maddi as Martin's cousin. He learns she has gone to the UK, and – when he learns why – follows her there. Hank does the same, and the two men are forced to work together to keep her safe.

BOOK V: "A Battle for Justice"

MARK JUSTICE, a British Private Inquiry Agent, seeks help for debilitating headaches, only to learn that he has an evil alter ego. Maddi had sought his help to find her stalker, and he has now become obsessed with her. She has left London to meet up with Henderson at his Latvian estate, their first reunion after four long, desperate years. Hank follows them, but then sees Maddi's devotion to Henderson, and decides to leave. But before he can, he learns that his CIA agent son, ROGER CLARKSON, has been taken by Cobra. He and Henderson are again forced to work together to try to not only keep Maddi safe from Morningstar, but to find Roger and save him from Cobra. It is then that Hank learns a terrible secret about Henderson.

BOOK VI: "The Morning Star"

A Nazi-era warship has been under the protection of a small group of families since its discovery in the late 1940's. Calling themselves "The Morning Star," a translation of the vessel's name, the group's mission is twofold: to understand its technology, and to keep it from falling into the wrong hands. When a powerful neo-Nazi threatens them and tries to steal the warship, the group is called into action. Led by Henderson's father, WALTER, they must do all they can to protect the vessel. Morningstar learns of the group, and assigns his son, SIMEON, to infiltrate their organization, which is about to meet in Paris. Meanwhile, Henderson and Hank arrive in Paris to save Roger from Cobra, and are led on a deadly game of cat-and-mouse. Maddi follows them, and saves Roger, but is devastated to learn that Henderson has been taken by the infamous killer.

BOOK VII: "The Vesper Bell"

Both Walter and Maddi have been lured to Lyon, expecting to meet Henderson in the town square. Instead, they are kidnapped by Cobra and taken to a remote dungeon, where they find Henderson close to death. Cobra travels to Scotland, stumbles upon an exact replica of his childhood school, and decides to bring his prisoners there. They are soon joined by Inspector Pritchard, Walter's wife Dora, his mistress Nenita, and psychiatrist James Samuels. When a fire begins to consume the old school, Cobra is prepared to leave them to die. Through the heroic efforts of Maddi's brother Andrew, and CIA agent Roger Clarkson, all seven are saved. Cobra escapes, however, and Henderson falls into a coma. As Maddi is about to go with him to the hospital, she reveals to Hank the stunning truth that Matt Henderson is actually Martin.

BOOK VIII: Part I of "The Revelation"

Maddi has spent the last five months waiting for Henderson to awaken from a coma. The time alone has forced her to revisit a past that has haunted her for twenty-two years. That past has attained new life, and will soon become a credible threat to her future. As Henderson struggles to regain consciousness, and Maddi fights her demons, Morningstar sees an opportunity to take down his two greatest adversaries in a cruel, creative fashion. He has uncovered a secret, and will use it to threaten both Maddi and Henderson, as well as the child, Lili. Meanwhile, Hank Clarkson has been assigned to bring Henderson to DC. But a sudden war in Latvia forces him to accompany the Hendersons to their castle by the Baltic Sea. As he alters his plans to accommodate the war, Maddi and Henderson slowly, painfully begin to unravel truths that will change their lives forever.

BOOK VIII: Part II of "The Revelation"

Morningstar, eager to put his Master Plan into effect, calls upon the international assassin, Cobra, to kill a troublesome adversary. Cobra's counterpart, Mark Justice, obsessed with the need to stop him, reaches out to psychiatrist James Samuels, forcing Samuels to choose between his devotion to justice and his obligation to duty. Meanwhile, as the war in Latvia rages on, a war with the past is being fought on three fronts by Maddi, Henderson, and a young Philadelphia police officer who is intricately tied to Maddi. This officer is eager to bring Maddi's old transgressions to light, but with each step he takes, he uncovers an unsettling fact about his own history. As Maddi tries to outrun her troubled past, and Henderson wrestles with a death wish, Morningstar sees a way not only to stop them from interfering in his efforts, but to end Madison's meddling for good.

"Pay no attention to the man behind the curtain!"

~ L. Frank Baum, *The Wonderful Wizard of Oz* ~

PROLOGUE

Trust God, for He will never let you down. Charles Sturgill sneered as he leaned against the stone façade outside the Augusta, Maine Statehouse. A stiff, bitter wind blew back his hair and he wrapped his overcoat firmly around his heavy frame as he contemplated the Biblical quotation. Though he had believed those words when he had spoken them repeatedly to his congregation during his twelve years as pastor of the Portage Church of God, they now just seemed like a mockery. He had let it go, all of it…the church, the congregants, the quote…three years, eight months, and six days ago, when his only son – his only *child* – was kidnapped by Chinese militants.

It had changed him…a lot. The past three years had taken not only his child, but his hope. It had aged him. Though he was only forty years old, his dark brown hair was now mostly gray, and he had become thick and flabby. He was still a commanding six-two, but his shoulders felt heavier, his back weaker…causing him to stoop, which made him look and feel much smaller, much older.

The trip to China had been full of optimism. He and ten members of his congregation had left the comforts of America to show Chinese indigents the pathway to God. Not only had Charles been taught that it was God's mission to reach out to those who may otherwise never hear The Word, but his wife had learned of a distant ancestor from the Yunnan Province, and, as a result, she had felt a unique and powerful tie to the country.

3

Their delegation had departed from Augusta, Maine on August 19th, 1976 for the small village of Baisha, and had spent the next three weeks helping the villagers to build a hospital and a school. It had been Charles who had arranged the day trip for his five-year-old son, Jamey. The young boy, always eager and undeniably bright, had expressed an interest in learning more about his mother's ancestors, the Akha villagers who lived in the mountains. Though any tie Beatrice might have had to them had been centuries ago, Jamey had nonetheless been eager to know them better.

Charles had asked the guide who had been with them from the start, Jan-Ping, to lead him, Beatrice, and Jamey to one of the more remote areas in the Yunnan Province. Bea had begged off, claiming she wasn't feeling well, leaving just Charles and Jamey to go. But Jamey had wanted to go alone. *"Please Daddy, can it be just me and Jan-Ping?"* Though Charles had been leery, he had come to trust the guide, and felt it would be good for the boy to have a stab at independence. His wife hadn't felt the same. *"It isn't safe, Charles,"* she had said when he had brought it up to her. *"Sure, it is, Bea"* he had told her, *"God will watch over him."* It was a hard tenet to argue, so she had finally given in and, on a hot, humid morning outside the village of Baisha, they had waved goodbye to their only son. The day was September 9th, 1976... the very same day that Chairman Mao Zedong would die. It felt as if the two events had been mystically tied. But Charles knew they hadn't. Chairman Mao's death had been hopeful...the loss of Charles' son had been anything but.

Jamey and Jan-Ping had been expected back by three that afternoon. By five, Charles had begun to worry, and by seven, he and Beatrice had worked themselves into a state of panic. But Chairman Mao's death had caused the entire country to be in a state of turmoil, and there was no one to listen when Charles tried to make his case to the local authorities; no one to care about a small boy who had gone missing while their revered Chairman Mao was lying in state. Three weeks later, emotionally wrecked, Charles and Beatrice had been forced to leave the country without their son.

Months passed, during which time Charles made several trips to China, doing all he could to find the boy. China's government wasn't hospitable at that time, and though it got easier once diplomatic relations were restored in 1979, by then, the trail had grown cold. Finally, two days ago, on May 13th, 1980, after receiving a certified letter from the State Department stating that Jamey had officially been declared dead, he and Beatrice had buried their only son, not with a body in a casket, but with a simple, subdued memorial service at their home in Portage, Maine. They didn't celebrate his ascension to God. They didn't celebrate anything. They merely took a box, filled it with photos, keepsakes, and the certified letter, and stuck it in the ground, ending forever the life of their little boy.

Trust God, for He will never let you down. Charles spit on the Statehouse steps as he thought of those words. They were nothing but platitudes… a silly phrase to comfort fools in need of hope. He knew that now. He knew that the promises offered in the Good Book were worthless. *As thin as the paper they're printed on.*

He shivered and began to pace in front of the Statehouse. His life as a pastor was over, now replaced by his role as an Augusta State Senator. He had been elected two Novembers ago following a rigorous campaign against a long-standing incumbent. He no longer worshiped at the altar of God, now devoting his time and energy to the lectern of power at the Augusta Statehouse. He had left the church a bitter and broken man, and had thought about leaving his marriage along with it. But his wife – who hated him for allowing Jamey to go alone that morning – refused to divorce him, clinging to some tired sense of loyalty to vows made to God; a God that no longer existed, as far as Charles was concerned. And Charles couldn't bring himself to leave her, either. But in his case, he knew it had nothing to do with God. His tie to Beatrice was his only tie to Jamey. Leaving her seemed like the final nail in the coffin. He didn't love her…he didn't love anything. He felt nothing, other than a burning anger for where his life had led him.

Which was why the call he had received early that morning from a brash Pentagon aide had gotten his attention. *"My name is Edward Morningstar. I work directly under General Alexander Daniels at the Pentagon, and I have a proposal for you."* The aide had promised to tell him more when they met. So here he was, on a cold morning in May – just two days after laying his son's memory to rest – waiting outside the Augusta Statehouse for a stranger from the Pentagon.

Spring typically came slow to Maine; this year, 1980, was no different. The air from Canada was cold, and the gray branches of nearby oak trees had yet to show signs of life. Charles wrapped a wool scarf over his neck and chin, then blew into his hands as he continued to pace the sidewalk. *Where the hell are you, Morningstar?*

He was about to forget the meeting and go back inside, when a black sedan pulled up. A tinted window lowered a third of the way, and a quiet voice said, "Representative Sturgill?"

Charles leaned close to the car. "Morningstar?"

The back door opened and Charles slid inside. The aide reached across, pulled the door shut, and the car pulled away. The man was young; he looked to be in his mid-twenties. He had short black hair – military cut – and his suit was tailor-made. He wore a diamond ring on his right hand, and when he crossed his legs, Charles noted a pair of expensive Louboutin shoes. Charles guessed that women found the man attractive; or at least commanding, which was often more important.

They drove for over ten minutes without a word. When Charles could stand it no longer, he cleared his throat and said, "What's so important that it couldn't be said over the phone?"

The man chuckled as he leaned forward, tapped on a partition, then slid it partway open. "Pull over at the park up ahead, Simpson."

The driver nodded and eased the government car into the right lane. After another minute, he pulled into a park just south of Augusta's downtown square and parked in a lot with a picnic table and a grill. Morningstar said through the half-open partition, "Step out and stretch your legs, Simpson."

The man did as he was told, leaving Charles alone with the mysterious Morningstar. Charles swallowed. "What's going on here? I've got a committee meeting in—" he checked his watch "—twenty minutes. Can we hurry this up?"

Morningstar grinned. "Certainly, Senator. As I said on the phone, I have a proposal for you."

"What sort of proposal?"

"I'm aware of what happened to your son several years ago, and I'm prepared to help you make it right."

Charles bristled. "What the hell are you talking about? How do you know about my son?"

The man narrowed his eyes. "You will soon learn, Senator Sturgill, that I know everything."

Charles cleared his throat. "Well, unless you can give me back my boy, there's no way to 'make it right.'" He sighed. "I've pursued it every way I could. Their government shut me down, then my government shut me down. What do you have to offer that the U.S. Government couldn't provide?"

The man leaned back, crossed his legs, and let out a chuckle. "Revenge."

Charles' eye twitched and he rubbed it. He liked the thought of it. If he couldn't have Jamey, retribution might be a nice consolation. "What sort of revenge?"

"First things first, Mr. Sturgill." The man pulled out a cigar and clipped off the end, letting it fall to the floor. He cracked a window, lit the cigar, and took a few puffs to get it started. "I have three things to offer you." He took a drag and exhaled, blowing smoke out the window. "The first is money; one million dollars, to be exact."

Charles felt his throat tighten. He said nothing.

"The second is power. The kind of power that men like you only dream about."

Men like me…what the hell? Charles fidgeted as he fought to hide a sneer.

"The third thing I can give you is retaliation…for what happened to your son, your family, and your faith."

Charles flinched. "What do you know about my faith?"

Again, Morningstar chuckled. "I know quite a bit about you, Mr. Sturgill." Another puff on the cigar. "For example, I know that you were once a pastor at the Portage First Church of God." He paused. "And I know that you left, not with a whimper, but with a wail. The entire church got to hear your disappointment in God, and your disenchantment with the church that God had guided you to lead." He shook his head and frowned. "Not too well received, I'll bet."

Charles said nothing. The man was right; it hadn't been well-received…but it had felt good…as if he was flipping off the entire Baptist religion.

Morningstar continued. "I also know that you and Beatrice sleep in separate bedrooms these days."

Charles bristled. "I'm out of here!" He went for the handle but Morningstar grabbed his arm. "Come come, now, Sturgill. No surprise there. She's as bitter as you are…and there's nothing colder at night than a bitter woman."

Charles said nothing. Again…it was true.

"Another thing I know about you, Sturgill, is that you've got some pretty powerful connections." He paused. "If I'm not mistaken, it was your uncle, the Federal Court Judge, who managed to keep you out of Vietnam…am I right?"

Charles jerked his arm from Morningstar's grasp, then shoved open the door. He had one foot on the gravel, when Morningstar said, "That judge and his wife were killed last night in an…ahem…unfortunate accident outside DC."

Charles stopped. He turned to look at Morningstar. The man's expression hadn't changed. Charles closed his eyes and shook his head. "I…I didn't know."

Morningstar nodded. "Of course, you didn't. No one knows. Except me. The press is just now learning of it." He paused. "Such a tragedy. They had only the one child, didn't they?"

"Yes…Jerome."

Morningstar grinned. "Ah yes, Jerome. The bright little Jerome Knight. I believe he's quite accomplished, not only academically, but athletically, isn't he?"

Charles nodded, grief overwhelming him as he thought of the promise of his own son, Jamey. "Yes. A bit of a prodigy, I think they told me once."

Morningstar nodded. "Yes, that's the one. Only fourteen years old. And now, there's no one to raise him. Such a shame."

Charles was having a hard time breathing. Jamey would have been nine by now…*and every bit as remarkable, I'm sure.*

Morningstar grinned. "How ironic, Sturgill. You and Beatrice are parents without a child, and Jerome is a child without any parents."

The outside air had turned colder. Charles pulled his leg back inside the car and closed the door. He turned to face the man. "What are you saying, Morningstar?"

The man sighed and took a long, slow drag on his cigar. He exhaled, and Charles choked back a cough. The man grinned as he held the cigar in front of him, eying it as if it was an impressive work of art. Finally, he lowered it and looked directly at Sturgill. "What I'm saying, Charles, is that I'll hand you the world if you'll raise Jerome Knight as your own."

PART I

"A crown is merely a hat that lets the rain in."

~ Frederick the Great ~

CHAPTER 1

Washington, DC

Jerome Knight was cold. Though the Situation Room in the White House was temperature-controlled, he found himself shaking as he listened to Secret Service Director Sam Allen review what they knew so far about the assassination of President James Wilcox, which had occurred less than an hour ago. Knight knew most of it already. Wilcox, in North Dakota for his re-election campaign, had finished a grueling day of campaigning. He had just settled in to watch TV, when apparently a gunman – a recent hire on the hotel's staff – had walked in and had killed four Secret Service agents, as well as the President himself. *"How on earth could such a thing happen?"* Knight had asked more than once. Allen had simply shaken his head. Though it would be easy to place blame squarely on the shoulders of the Secret Service, no one knew better than Knight how hard they worked and how careful they were with every decision regarding the safety of those under their watch.

So, who should I blame? he wondered as he jotted down thoughts for a speech to the American people. A White House cameraman was setting up in a small room not far from where they were sitting. Knight could hear him as he coordinated with staffers on the best angle for the camera. Knight sat back and sighed. The entire situation was unbelievable. *What will I say to them?* he wondered, as he did his best to stay focused on the stocky Secret Service Director. If he could just keep his mind on what Sam Allen was telling him, then he wouldn't have to

11

think about the elephant in the room. *I am now the President of the United States of America.* It was unfathomable. To think that only a few short months ago, he was the junior senator from the great state of Florida. A respectable role, to be sure, but nowhere near the role he had just been handed as a result of the President's assassination. What made it even harder was that Wilcox was one of those rare Presidents who was actually loved and admired by most of America. He had had his detractors, but they were few.

Which means that I have very big shoes to fill.

He checked his watch. It was midnight...and a terrible night, to be sure. Only a few hours ago, the nation had been forced to digest the loss of one of its more notable senators, Cynthia Madison, who had died in a plane crash somewhere in Latvia. Now they were learning that their leader – *their President* - had been killed just a few hours later by some maniac while on a campaign tour out west. Knight would be expected to somehow address it...to somehow make sense of both tragedies for the people of America, and for those around the world. Both Madison and Wilcox had been highly-regarded on the world stage. Madison's unique appeal had charmed dignitaries, while Wilcox had somehow tamed China, and had made at least a modicum of progress toward peace in the Middle East.

Knight had thought about waiting; putting off the speech until morning. After all, it was late, and it was possible that many Americans weren't even aware of the tragedy. But an advisor had recommended against it. *"Yes, it's late, but America's leader has been senselessly killed, and the people need to hear from you. They need to know that you're ready to lead them... not only as their President, but in the effort to find and punish the person behind this act."*

Knight had been unable to argue the point. While Madison had died in a tragic accident, the President's death had been anything but. He had been shot pointblank through the heart, then the head. There were no eyewitnesses; every agent had either been killed, or had been standing far enough away that they hadn't seen or heard a thing. The technical aspects of the hit had been impressive. The hotel's video feed had apparently been tampered with to create the impression to anyone monitoring it that all was well. Which was why it had taken so long for the agents sitting outside the President's suite to respond. The assassin had carried out the murders so quickly that there had been no time for an agent to even send out an alert. The most challenging aspect of the entire hit was how the shooter had gotten a gun past so many Secret Service agents. Every member of the hotel staff had been frisked any time they got within thirty feet of the President.

"You'll need to say something soon, sir."

Knight was pulled from his thoughts by the words of the former President's Chief of Staff, Anthony Dixon. Knight knew Dixon, but not well. After all, Knight had only been a part of the Wilcox Administration since March. Five short months to learn the inner workings of the White House and all of its staff. But Dixon would be invaluable. No one knew DC like Tony Dixon. For the last twenty-five years, he had served in one administration after another; both Democrats and Republicans. He was one of those rare individuals who had somehow managed to navigate beyond the mistrust that each party held toward the other.

Knight looked up at him and nodded. "Certainly, sir."

Dixon, whose red, puffy eyes betrayed his grief, said, "Please, call me either Tony or Dixon. You are 'sir,' I am not."

Knight sighed. "I've written down a few thoughts…do you want to maybe look at them and tell me what you think?"

Dixon nodded. "Certainly, sir." He picked up the sheet of paper and read it through quickly. "It's good, sir. You might want to add something about tomorrow, and how the sun will rise and the trains will roll…you know, sort of reassuring everyone that life will go on as planned."

Knight nodded and quickly added the comments. He looked down at his clothes. He had been in bed when he had been told of the assassination. He had thrown on slacks, a button-down shirt, and a pair of shoes. He wasn't even wearing socks. "Should I put on a jacket and tie?"

Dixon considered it. "You know, sir, I don't think so. You're harried; you look it. It's honest."

Again, Knight nodded. He was glad to have Dixon at his side. The aide was supposed to have gone with Wilcox on the re-election tour, but had stayed back at the last minute to prepare for a summit with the Japanese Prime Minister, which was to take place in three days. Knight frowned. "Will Takahashi still come to the U.S.?"

Dixon frowned. "Do you think he should?"

Knight considered it. His first real decision as President. "Yes. Reinforcing the narrative that matters of importance aren't left to a single man or woman…that international diplomacy will continue on uninterrupted."

"Write that down, Mr. President. It's good."

"Mr. President." Knight flinched, but he nodded as he jotted the lines on his sheet of paper. He cleared his throat. "How do we bury him… the President, I mean? How long does he lay in state…that sort of thing?"

Dixon frowned. "I'm working on that. You might want to say that details are being finalized, and that the White House will release regular updates for the next several days."

Knight wrote the comments on his paper and sighed. The words he had written seemed inadequate. How does one calm a nation after their leader was killed so violently? *Especially when this nation barely knows me.* He had never campaigned for his role as Vice-President. He had simply been chosen when the sitting VP, Jim Conner, had stepped down unexpectedly.

But Knight was no stranger to the role he had been handed. He had been groomed since he was fourteen years old to someday serve as an American leader. But he had imagined that the role would be that of a senator, or maybe a cabinet member. Never in a million years had he anticipated that he would be President of the United States. It seemed unreal. But even more than that; he felt unworthy of the role. Unlike nearly every other President in the history of the Republic, Knight had not had the proper training. He had never been voted on by the nation. Yes, the people of Florida had given him overwhelming support in a surprise victory six years ago, but Florida didn't represent the nation. Would Americans accept him? Would they have confidence in a man who had served only five months in the White House? 'Seat time' his Uncle Sturgill used to call it. *"You can't expect to know what you need to know until you've put in the seat time, Jerome."* He chuckled humorlessly. Though Sturgill had been referring to things like understanding Julius Caesar's strategy in the Battle of Pharsalus, or appreciating the nuances of the Mandarin language, the point was the same.

Knight suddenly was aware that Sam Allen had quit speaking. All eyes were on him. Dixon cleared his throat. "Are you ready, sir?"

Knight took a deep breath and sighed. He looked down at his notes. Jotted with an ink pen in a nervous, choppy hand, they were disorganized, at best. He nodded. "Sure. I'm ready." But as he walked up to the waiting camera and saw the man behind it begin to count down to zero, he realized that he was about as far away from ready as any man could be.

CHAPTER 2

Kemi, Finland

Cobra stretched his long arms in the air, doing his best to quell his uneasiness as he looked out on a rickety dock in the middle of nowhere. He was in a border town outside Kemi, Finland, and the journey that had taken him there had been a wild one, to say the least. His original mission had been to kill Hank Clarkson, who had been staying at the Henderson estate outside Uzava, Latvia. Starting in Scotland, Cobra had traveled by train, car, and bus to get to the estate. Once there, he had instantly been awed by the majesty of the place. The fact that it was his father's castle and that he hadn't even known it existed had burned a hole right through him. He had decided then that the castle must become his. He had said as much to Morningstar, who had told him he would give him the castle once he succeeded in killing Hank Clarkson.

Unfortunately, Hank had been driving away from the compound when Cobra had arrived. Cobra had been on foot, and rather than chase the man, which would have been impossible without some sort of vehicle, Cobra had decided to explore the castle, so he could make plans for the estate that would soon be his. As for Hank, Cobra had had every reason to think that the man would return to the castle before night's end, and he could kill him then.

That had been nearly twelve hours ago, and a lot had happened since. For one thing, Clarkson hadn't returned to the castle, at least not while Cobra was there, which meant that Cobra had had no chance to kill him.

Not only that; Cobra had gotten into a bit of a bind at the compound, and had been forced to call Morningstar to save him. Never in his life had Cobra required someone's help to stay alive. And now, because of it, he had become solely reliant on Morningstar.

But not for long, he thought, as he flinched at the first rays of sunrise coming through the only window. The piercing sunlight forced him to look away, and he cursed as he rubbed his temples and took in the small six-by-eight room.

He thought again about the night that had passed; the night that had seemed rather tame...until he had spotted Martin Henderson about to hang himself from a tree outside a second-story window of the castle. *The only reason that man isn't dead is because I saved him.* He chuckled at the irony. He had saved the man that, just months ago, he had been fully prepared to kill. Why? *Because I'll be damned if he's going to be the one to take his life. That is up to me...and not until I'm done with him.*

Cobra had big plans, not only for Martin, but for his father, the mighty Walter Henderson. And those plans required that both men were alive, so they could witness the downfall of one of the most prestigious families in modern history.

Walter had fathered two sons; one was the well-known Martin, the other was the bastard child, Mark Villamor. Mark had had the misfortune of being born to a Filipino mistress, who had insisted that she wanted nothing to do with the Henderson wealth. Cobra sneered. *She sure as hell didn't ask the boy, Mark, for his opinion.* Cobra, who had become a protector for Mark, had taken the slight personally, and now felt obligated to claim that wealth in the name of Mark Villamor. But quite a lot had happened since Cobra had stepped off that bus in Uzava, Latvia just over twelve hours ago; quite a lot indeed...

To call the town sleepy would be an understatement. Uzava was barely even a town. A few shops around a center square...that was about the extent of it. He would start by finding a place to eat, where he could also charge his phone...Henderson's phone that Cobra had taken from him months ago in Paris. For some reason, the phone he would have preferred to use was gone... lost during one of his annoying but far too frequent blackouts. This was the only phone he had.

He walked into a small café and ordered a sandwich and a beer. The place was practically empty. He plugged the phone into an outlet not far from his table. When he finished the meal, he unplugged the phone and shoved it in his pocket.

He wasn't ready to retire for the night, so he decided to walk in the direction of the Henderson compound. He didn't expect to reach it; not that night, anyway. According to his map, it was a full fifteen kilometers from Uzava. He guessed that he would find some sort of lodging along the way. He could sleep for a few hours, then start fresh in the morning. But the longer he walked, the more he realized there was no lodging. There wasn't even a house or a shed. He kept walking. It was late, the sun was setting, and a light rain had begun to fall. The air had cooled considerably, and Cobra found himself miserable and cold as he walked southwest toward the coast.

After about twenty minutes, he was glad to hear the sound of an engine. He looked behind him. An old pickup truck was coming; Cobra waved it down. The truck slowed and Cobra climbed inside. Though the driver tried to make conversation, his English was poor, Cobra's Lettish even poorer. After about twenty minutes spent mostly in silence, Cobra raised a hand and said, "Stop here, please."

The driver frowned. "Here? You sure?"

Cobra said nothing as he grabbed his backpack and stepped out of the truck. The rain was coming harder, and he shielded himself with his jacket as he shut the door. The man shrugged, then quickly drove off.

Cobra took a quick glance at a map that Morningstar had sent him. According to the map, the wheat field he was standing next to was about a mile north of the Henderson estate. Ignoring the rain, which had begun to fall even harder, he stayed on the road for another half-mile. He was wearing a reasonable disguise, and no one would expect to see the international assassin, Cobra, in that godforsaken country.

He thought again about his assignment. He was to kill Hank Clarkson. He didn't know why; it didn't matter. As he rounded a bend in the road, he pulled a photo of the man from his pocket. Holding the flap of his jacket over it to keep it from getting wet, he looked at it long and hard. It wasn't the first time he had seen Hank Clarkson; the man had been in the tunnel with his dying son not so many months ago. Cobra laughed at the memory, then tucked the photo in his pocket. He was about to cross the road to a thick grove of trees to get a reprieve from the rain, when he was nearly run over by a black BMW.

18

He tried to get a look at the driver. All he could tell was that the man sat low in the seat and had dark hair. Cobra cursed under his breath. 'Likely some Henderson lackey running an errand for his boss.' But then he spotted a second car, another BMW. Again, he tried to see the driver. This man was bigger, heavyset, with dark, curly hair. Again, Cobra looked at his photo of Hank. He would bet money that Hank was the man behind the wheel of that second car.

'So, where the hell is he going?' he wondered as he watched the taillights fade out of sight. 'Should I try to chase him?' Cobra was on foot; there was no way he could go after the man. He would simply need to wait for Hank to return.

He checked his watch. It was 7:05. He had less than an hour of daylight. With his backpack over his shoulder, he crossed the road to the grove of trees and continued south and west toward the sea. He used the trees to shield him from the pouring rain. As he neared the area that Morningstar's maps had indicated as the well-hidden Henderson compound, he was stunned to feel his phone – Henderson's phone – vibrate. He answered, and was even more surprised when he heard Cynthia Madison saying emphatically how much she loved him; well, actually how much she loved Henderson...it was his phone, after all. Cobra chuckled and said, "Why, hello Cynthia...remember me? Weather's nice here in Latvia." She didn't reply. The call ended abruptly and he laughed. 'I must have shocked the poor woman into silence.'

He slid the phone in his pocket and crept deeper into the trees, where foliage was thickest. He found a shallow ravine in which to hide, and, when he was confident he couldn't be spotted from either the road or an overhead satellite, he pulled out copies of the maps that Morningstar had emailed to him. If they were accurate, then the forest he was hiding in, as well as the field to the south of it, bordered the north end of the estate. If he stayed under the thick canopy of leaves, he should be able to maneuver parallel with the compound, and remain almost invisible to any overhead satellites. His goal was to get onto the estate by the time the time daylight faded in the west.

He continued to follow the trees west and south, trembling as he came to an incredibly deep ravine. It reminded him of a similar ravine he had seen in Lyon, France, not that long ago...a ravine he had nearly fallen into. Giving himself a wide berth, he hiked around it and continued west until he reached a large body of water. He felt certain it was the Baltic Sea. The timing was perfect. Dark shadows covered the craggy coastline; he should be able to run from the trees to the sea with little chance of being spotted. Holding his backpack over his head, he sprinted into the sea and immersed himself nearly completely under the waves. He swam south to what he had calculated was the coastline of the Henderson estate. That calculation was confirmed when he saw a stately fleet of boats tied to a freshly-painted dock. 'Let me guess,' he thought with a sneer, 'the Henderson Armada.'

Again, the shadows aided him as he crept onto dry land, ready at any moment to explain to a guard or a soldier that he had been thrown overboard in the storm and had washed ashore. No one came for him, however, so he slung his pack over his back and crawled into a stretch of thick brush. Moving slowly, and doing his best to identify cameras in the trees, he crept through the brush in the direction of the castle. The rain was coming harder, and soon he was covered in mud. He didn't mind. Though the wet dirt made him even colder, it was an excellent form of camouflage.

Eventually, he came to what looked like a courtyard. He continued on, and, after a few minutes, he spotted a large outbuilding. He crept further so he could see the front. From what he could tell, there were few windows and only one door. There was a guard at the door holding an AK-47. Cobra could see the castle not too far away, about a hundred yards beyond the building. Staying low in the brush, and continuing to watch for cameras in the trees and on the lampposts, he maneuvered to a thick grove of evergreens at the north end of the courtyard.

His legs had started to cramp. He stumbled to a row of tall boulders and was able to stand between two of them without being seen. As he cautiously stretched his legs, he looked around. The castle was closer now, and even in the pouring rain, he could see its magnificence. Toward the front was a long drive that weaved its way through well-groomed trees to what was clearly a moat. From what he could tell, a barricade on the other side would serve as a drawbridge when it was lowered. He was stunned. That castle could have been plucked straight out of the seventeenth century with its tall parapets and imposing ramparts. Brightly lit lanterns recalled days of old when actual flames had filled the glass; when knights had stood boldly atop the balustrades lying in wait for enemy invaders. 'I need to see inside,' he thought, his imagination captured by its splendor. Never had he seen such a place. His anger was ignited as he imagined the life the boy Mark could have had; a life that had been denied him, all because he didn't have the right mother. The Boston mansion, which Cobra had visited when he was seventeen, was impressive, but this castle was beyond anything he might have ever envisioned. 'I must have this place,' he thought as he crept closer. Never could there be a more fitting symbol to hold over the Hendersons as he brought them to their knees and made them pay for their betrayal of Mark's birthright; for having denied Mark – and Cobra – what was rightfully theirs.

He walked toward the front of the castle, each step carefully planned to avoid the cameras that he could see, as well as those he might be missing. Skulking was one of his finer skills, and he moved stealthily among the trees, aided by shadows from an occasional lamppost. Suddenly, he stopped. One of the cars he had seen earlier was returning to the castle. He was close enough to see inside as the car stopped at the moat to wait for the barricade to lower to a bridge. It was the first man, not Hank Clarkson. 'So, where's Hank?' He would wait there for the man to return.

As he waited, he imagined his reign over the remarkable castle. His first step would be to place Walter and Dora into servitude, not with force, but with what he liked to think of as gentle persuasion. How would he do it? By imprisoning their dear Martin. Eventually, he would kill the man; eventually, he would kill them all. But not until he had what he wanted. 'And what is that?' he asked himself. He grinned. 'An admission from all three that they failed me...that they failed Mark Villamor.'

He was pulled from his fantasy by the sound of a clock somewhere inside the castle. He counted the chimes; it was ten o'clock, and still no Hank Clarkson. Which meant that Cobra would have to find somewhere on that estate to hide and wait.

He kept moving, soon coming to the south end of the castle. He rounded the corner and was surprised to see a small but well-groomed garden. It looked mystical, its only lamppost iridescent in the rain, creating an amber haze over rocks, trees, and flowers. He could still see the drive, and was about to take refuge between two of the taller rocks to wait for Hank's return, when he heard the scuffle of feet above him. He looked up, stunned to see Martin Henderson – still disguised as Matt – standing on a windowsill with a rope around his neck. 'Dear God, he's going to jump!'

Cobra immediately got to work. 'Oh no you don't, brother...I have plans for you, and they require that you are alive,' he thought as he quickly climbed the tree to the limb on which the end of the rope was attached. He had nearly reached the knot, when Martin jumped from the windowsill. In a split second, Cobra pulled his knife from his backpack and slashed the rope just as it had *been about to pull taut. Henderson fell about twenty feet to the ground. Cobra clung to the tree, shocked by what had just happened. He barely took a breath as he waited to see if the man would get up. Henderson didn't move. Had the fall killed him?*

Finally, after a full minute, Cobra hurried down the tree and, with his knife ready, he crept closer to the body. He knelt down and, with a shaking hand, he felt for a pulse. There was a faint throb from the artery in Henderson's neck; he was alive.

Cobra heard commotion in the room upstairs, and he quickly took cover behind several of the taller rocks. He looked up, surprised to see Walter's face. Despair was written all over it. Walter yelled for help, then Cobra watched as, one by one, the staffers, then the Hendersons themselves, rushed out of the castle to where their beloved Martin lay. The entire castle seemed to have emptied to come to the aid of their prince. Cobra took the opportunity to run to a back entrance, ready to join the other saviors should he be spotted. He knelt out of sight behind a bush by the door. As another staffer ran out that same door, Cobra grabbed it before it could close, and stepped inside. He slid into the first open door he came to and darted underneath a table. He looked around. He was in a dining hall, and the room was massive. He thought of the many soldiers who had dined at those long tables, their thick arms raising mugs of beer as they were fed a fatted calf, all the while regaling themselves with tales of bravery and debauchery. He could feel the power of that room, and the anger boiled inside him as he realized all that he – that Mark – had been denied.

Now that he had managed to get inside the castle, what should he do? He couldn't stay long; the parade of staffers and overseers would soon bring their prince inside to tend to him. He listened; there wasn't a sound. At least for the moment, he was alone. He slid from under the table and snuck to a huge kitchen with four oversized ovens and a large ten-foot counter covered with various items for cooking. 'I'm hungry,' he thought, and he found a loaf of bread, a jar of peanut butter, and a jar of jam. He could hear the commotion outside as he made himself a sandwich.

"Don't move him! He may have broken his neck!"

Cobra chuckled as he opened one of four refrigerators, grabbed a gallon of milk, and poured himself a glass. He opened several drawers until he found a notepad and a pen. He walked to one of the colossal tables in the hall and sat down. He set his backpack beside him, took a bite of his sandwich and a gulp of milk. Then, he wrote:

"Dear Father,

Your disregarded bastard son
has saved the life of the other one.
The one whose glory never dies
Regardless of his sins or lies
But lest you think I did this deed
For some misguided holy creed,
The reason that I saved your son
Is so that when each day is done
You'll have no choice but to decree
That Martin owes his life to me.

Love, Mark"

Cobra chuckled as he read it aloud. He left it on the table and finished his sandwich, leaving his crust next to the poem. He had just slurped the last of the milk, when suddenly he heard a siren, and bright red lights began flashing both inside and outside the castle. He grabbed his backpack and sprinted to the back door. He saw a dozen staffers running toward the entrance. He stepped back and ran down a different hall, turning into the first room he came to. He looked around and chuckled. It was an office; Walter's office. What Cobra wouldn't give to spend time in that room...to see what was important to his father...what had landed on the shelves of that private space. A quick glance revealed little, other than a family portrait of Walter, Dora, and Martin, taken when Martin was just a boy.

He was seized by anger, and nearly immobilized by his hate. 'Move, Cobra!' he thought, and ran to a huge bay window that faced the courtyard. He opened one of the windows, but before he jumped through, he reached over and shoved the portrait of Walter's family to the floor. He laughed triumphantly as the glass broke into pieces, then he jumped through the opening and closed the window behind him. The rain was coming even harder. Holding his backpack over his head to protect him from the downpour, and staying in the shadows, he sprinted to the trees at the north end of the estate.

He could hear footsteps behind him. He ran as fast as he could to the ravine he had spotted earlier at the northernmost edge of the compound. He held his breath, then jumped over the side, clinging to a tree root to keep from falling all the way to the bottom. As he did so, he felt his backpack come loose from his shoulder. He tried to catch it before it fell, but failed in his efforts. He swallowed as, several seconds later, he heard it hit the bottom of the ravine.

'Shit,' he thought. Nearly everything he owned was in that backpack. All he had left was his phone – Henderson's phone – and his photo of Hank Clarkson. He felt for a root or a rock on which to rest his feet, and was relieved when his right foot touched on the edge of a sturdy piece of stone. He stood on that stone and clung to the root for what felt like hours as he endured the harsh rain on his face. He wasn't sure what had initiated the alarm. Was it the fact that Henderson had clearly been cut down from the tree, which meant that an unidentified stranger was loose on the compound? It didn't actually matter what had triggered it. Once Walter read the poem, he would know instantly that Cobra was somewhere on the property. Which meant that he needed to get away from there as soon as possible. But he was stuck in that ravine, with no conceivable avenue for escape. Even when CIA agent Roger Clarkson had him cornered in Kensington Park, he had had a way to escape. But now, unless something changed, it was only a matter of time before they found him.

He heard the barking of dogs and he cursed. As much as it pained him to do so, he pulled out Henderson's cellphone and tried to recall Morningstar's number. He was stunned when he saw 'Jacob' in the contact list. 'Could it be?' he wondered. 'It's worth a try.' He pushed 'send.' The call was answered after the first ring.

"Why, Joseph, so good to hear from you. Are you ready to come home?"

Cobra flinched. "It's not Joseph. It's me, Cobra. Morningstar, you need to get me out of here...now!"

There was a pause. "Tell me your situation."

Cobra told him where he was and that the dogs would find him soon. The call ended. Within minutes, a black man in a black suit with an obvious glass eye was staring down at him in the ravine. Cobra recognized him from Dalgety Bay.

"Gad," Cobra said, as he stared up at him.

The man offered a barely perceptible nod. "Climb out...now."

"They're watching...and they have dogs."

"I've distracted them, but not for long. Now c'mon, climb out."

Using tree roots and rocks, Cobra was able to climb up the side and over the ledge. Gad didn't lift a finger to help him. Cobra followed him toward the back of the compound, impressed with the speed and evasiveness of the man... especially in the pouring rain. They reached the sea, and Cobra was surprised to see a small fishing boat hidden among the many larger boats that made up the Henderson fleet.

Gad jumped into the boat and motioned him aboard. "Stay down!" he whispered as he turned on the engine and motored out to sea.

Just then, Walter and two guards reached the shore. Had Walter read his poem? Was he aware yet that it was his wicked son who had saved the Precious One? He sneered. If so, he would likely shoot him on sight.

He ducked lower, and Gad ducked down as well, zigzagging the boat further away from the shoreline. Cobra waited for a torrent of bullets; none came. He heard one of the soldiers yell, "Shall I shoot them, sir?"

He was shocked when he heard Walter reply, "No, let them go."

The gesture overwhelmed him. Was it intentional; one last honorable deed for the son he had dishonored so greatly? Or was it simply strategy; the boat was moving so erratically and so fast that it would be impossible to hit their target, especially in the pouring rain. Cobra would never know. But he refused to feel anything other than hate toward his father, and concluded it was merely a tactical decision by a wise general in a time of war.

Gad steered the rickety vessel across the ocean, the waves spilling over the side of the small boat. After hours on the salty sea, they came to a rickety dock. Cobra spotted a weathered sign that said, "Hoburgen."

"Where the hell's Hoburgen?" he asked, as Gad hurried him from the boat.

"It's an island near Sweden. Now, keep quiet."

Gad led the way to another boat, this one much larger, which was docked about a hundred yards from where they had landed. A thick man with even thicker hands shoved them both into the hold of the vessel, and Cobra had to wonder how far Morningstar's reach actually extended. Had he somehow orchestrated an escape that involved not only a soldier son in Latvia, but a crew of Swedish sailors, as well?

He and Gad spent the next hour crossing to the mainland. They docked and stepped onto the pier. Cobra saw a sign, "Nykoping." They were quickly ushered onto a tugboat, which took them north along the coast of Sweden. After what felt like a lifetime, they landed at the small town of Kemi, Finland, on the northernmost part of the Gulf of Bothnia...

And that was how Cobra had ended up in a youth hostel in a forgotten town on the north Baltic Sea. After their arrival, Gad had walked him through spitting rain to the hostel, and had then taken his leave. *"Where are you going?"* Cobra had asked. The man had sneered. *"Back to that godawful country."* That had been it. Gad had left, leaving Cobra alone in a dreary room that smelled like fish and had only a single window and a bed that squeaked.

Not only that; he no longer had any resources. He had lost his backpack when he had jumped into the ravine, and his disguise had been ruined by the rain. Though Gad had left him with 100 euros cash – or maybe because of it – the painful reality was all too clear; Cobra was now reliant on Morningstar, at least in the short term. It was unnerving for the infamous assassin, and he wasn't about to let it stand for long. *I'll get out of here, then I'll reclaim the upper hand with that bastard.*

During the nine-hour journey to Kemi, Gad had said little, and the sailors had said nothing at all. It had given Cobra time to think...to plan for his life – for Mark's life – not as a poor, forgotten boy from the Philippines, but as a wealthy and powerful Henderson. Though his father had failed to bequeath him such a life, Morningstar had promised it in the form of that castle. And now, having seen it, Cobra knew he had to have it. But he also knew that it would take the power of a government to deliver such a well-fortified estate. Only Morningstar had such power, and Cobra had every intention of holding him to his promise.

He opened the window, stuck out his head, and breathed in the air, choking on the smell. The sun had risen higher in the sky, and he was able to see more of his surroundings. There wasn't much to see; Kemi was cold and lonely and, in spite of the chill in the air, it reminded him of the wretched boarding school outside Baclayon. *Time to get out of here and get what's due to me.*

He was about to close the window when he stopped. There they were again; the same two girls he had seen standing by the pier when he and Gad had arrived at the hostel the night before. They looked to be about seventeen, their innocence on full display as they leaned wantonly against the pier. Cobra wondered if they lived somewhere nearby. He chuckled as he watched them. They were young, they were attractive, and – best of all – they were alone.

Keeping his eyes on the two girls, he pulled out his phone and dialed Morningstar. Without waiting for a hello, he said, "You promised me the castle; I'm expecting you to deliver."

Morningstar said tersely, "I believe that our original agreement stated that I would give you the castle once you confirmed to me that Hank Clarkson was dead."

Cobra sneered. "He was leaving the castle as I was arriving. I don't know if he even came back. And I certainly can't go back there to find out." Cobra paused. "So how do you expect me to kill the bastard when I'm not even sure where he is."

Morningstar chuckled. "That is your problem to solve, Dan."

The call ended. Cobra stared at the phone. For the first time in his entire relationship with Morningstar, the man finally had something that Cobra actually wanted; something he couldn't get on his own. And Hank Clarkson was the key. Which meant that Cobra somehow had to find Hank...and kill him.

He looked again at the girls standing by the pier. *But there's no reason I can't have a little fun before I do.*

CHAPTER 3

Somewhere in the southern part of Latvia

Homeland Security's Deputy Director, Dr. Hank Clarkson had been driving almost non-stop for the past thirteen hours. He was tired, he was angry, but most of all, he was heartbroken over all that had happened since seven p.m. the night before. A woman he had loved for much of his life had nearly been killed in a plane crash, and it was now up to him to make her well. But it hadn't been sheer misfortune that had caused that plane to crash. No, it had been intentional. And every time he thought of it, he would feel a fury like nothing he had ever known in all his forty-four years.

He had yet to stop, other than for a quick fill-up at an all-night gas station somewhere in southern Latvia. During that stop, he had helped his passenger into the bathroom so she could relieve herself, then he had done the same. He had helped her back to the car, then had walked into the station and had bought three trac phones, two gallon-jugs of water, plastic cups, and a handful of granola bars. He had quickly gotten back on the road. His passenger, Maddi, who was laying down in the back seat, had barely said a word the entire journey. She was awake; he had confirmed it many times as he had looked over his shoulder at the woman who had now become his sole responsibility. But a part of her was missing; that much was clear. The plane crash that had allegedly ended her life had taken a vital piece of her with it.

It had been her bodyguard's idea to pretend that she had died in the crash. Though Secret Service Agent Tom Cravens, the only other passenger to survive the crash, had been incensed when Hank had told him that the crash had been intentional and that Maddi had been the target, he hadn't been surprised. After all, there had been at least six attempts on Maddi's life over the past year. Cravens had insisted that he and Hank must do whatever they could to convince those responsible for the crash that they had succeeded. *"Otherwise, they're just gonna keep trying, Hank."*

Hank had been unable to argue the point, though for the life of him he could not imagine why anyone would want to kill Maddi. She embodied the very essence of goodness. Maybe that was the problem. In her effort to right the wrongs of the world, she had often been forced to go up against some very bad and very powerful forces.

He sighed as he again looked over his shoulder. Though Maddi's eyes were open, they were empty. Her stare had no substance; her face was completely blank. By all accounts, his passenger might as well have been dead. "Are you okay, Maddi?"

She looked at him and his heart broke. She gave a faint nod. "I'm fine, Hank."

But she wasn't fine…not at all. Not only had she been banged up by the crash, but her soul seemed to have left her. It was as if an empty shell was stretched out in the back seat of the 1984 blue Audi.

Getting that car had been Hank's first challenge. He had arrived at the site of the plane crash in a borrowed Henderson BMW. He knew the Hendersons would be looking for their car, so immediately after leaving the crash site, he had driven south in search of a replacement. The rain, which had been torrential during the aftermath of the crash, had finally eased, replaced by a cool, crisp night with a nearly-full moon. The light from that moon had been a godsend as they had driven frantically over dark backroads along the coast of Latvia, then inland on route A9. Somewhere west of the town of Barbele, Hank had spotted a lot with about ten cars lined up in a row. But he couldn't just grab a car and leave the Henderson BMW on the lot; GPS on the BMW would make it far too easy for someone to determine that Hank had been there, and the owner of the lot would then be alerted to one of his cars having been stolen. Though Hank couldn't be sure that someone was looking for him, he guessed that the disappearance of an American agent would initiate some sort of manhunt. Which meant that the first thing he had needed to do was get rid of the BMW.

He had passed a lake less than a kilometer from the car lot. He had turned around and had driven the BMW back to the lake. He had parked about a foot from the water, had helped Maddi out of the back seat, and had propped her against a large oak tree. He had then walked back to the car and had shifted it into neutral. He had walked behind it and had shoved it into the lake, hoping the water would disable the GPS. More importantly, he hoped that by the time it was pulled from the lake, any trace of Maddi would be gone.

As if at a vigil, he and Maddi had stood under an omnipresent moon, watching silently as the car was swallowed by the deep black water. He had then pretty much carried Maddi to the vacant car lot. He had found the blue Audi sitting toward the back; an older model that he guessed wouldn't have GPS. He had stolen license plates from a wrecked Czechoslovakian Skoda sitting a few cars away, and had slapped them on the front and back of the Audi. With any luck, the nondescript car would give them at least a few days of obscurity as Hank worked to come up with a way to get across Latvia's border. He couldn't use his ID; it would instantly reveal his location to those who might be looking for him. As for Maddi, she had no ID...it had been lost in the crash.

He rubbed his eyes. He was exhausted. He thought again about all that had happened to put him behind the wheel of a stolen car, driving east across Latvia to nowhere in particular, with a woman in his back seat who was supposedly dead. It had started when he had walked into the Henderson garage to borrow one of the BMW's for a much-needed ride to clear his head. As he had been about to approach an inner office where the keys were kept, he had overheard one of the drivers talking on his cellphone to a man, Jacob, whom he had also referred to as his father. From what Hank had been able to piece together, the man on the other end of the phone had told the driver to go to a site north of Liepaja to make sure that Senator Cynthia Madison died in a plane crash that was to take place in the next few minutes.

Horrified, Hank had waited for the driver to leave, had grabbed a car, and had followed the driver out of the compound. When the driver had stopped at a round-about, Hank had shot his tire to slow him down, and had driven to the site himself. He had been stunned not only to see a plane crashing to the ground less than a hundred feet in front of him, but to discover that Maddi and one of her bodyguards had somehow survived the crash. Hank had told the bodyguard, Cravens, about the conversation he had overheard. Cravens had insisted that the only way to keep Maddi safe was to convince the world that she had died, *"...so that whoever keeps trying to kill her will think that he has finally succeeded."*

Hank sighed as he ran a hand through his hair. He could only imagine what he must look like. He hadn't slept, he had spent over an hour in the pouring rain, and he was being eaten alive with worry about a woman he had loved for most of his life.

Again, he looked over his shoulder. Maddi hadn't moved. She laid there just as she had since they had swapped the BMW for the Audi; her body splayed across the back seat, her head on the armrest, her injured leg propped on his jacket. Her hair was tangled, her body bruised, and she was covered in mud. She looked terrible. But the extent of her tragedy was evidenced mostly by her eyes. Still blue, still beautiful...but more vacant than he had ever seen them.

He shook his head. *I wonder how Henderson's doing.* Hank had originally come to Europe to question and possibly arrest Matt Henderson for his role in January's bioterror attacks. Hank knew that Matt hadn't had a hand in those attacks; he hadn't even been invented yet. Matt was actually Martin Henderson, who had adopted the disguise to elude the authorities, who were looking for him because of his role as the assassin, Phoenix. That had been another hard pill to swallow; the esteemed Martin Henderson had become an assassin. It was unthinkable. Hank had known Martin for several years; they had even been friends at one time. Though Hank and Henderson had had their differences – he had, after all, stolen Maddi's heart – there was no way that Henderson could have done the things he was being accused of. So, Hank had decided that he would do all he could to keep the authorities from prosecuting Henderson for crimes Hank felt certain he hadn't committed.

But then came the war. Just as Hank had been about to take Henderson into custody and fly him to the United States, Putin had had the gall to attack Latvia. The Baltic country had been a part of the former USSR, and the Hendersons, who owned a castle along Latvia's west coast, had felt duty-bound to travel to the castle to enlist their army to aid in its defense. Hank had been forced to join them, and had spent hours sitting in Henderson's childhood bedroom watching the man as he had slipped deeper and deeper into despondency. For whatever reason, Maddi had walked out on Henderson, and it had left the man in utter despair. His misery had permeated the walls, the ceiling, the very chair that Hank had been sitting on, which was why Hank had been about to take one of the Henderson cars for a much-needed escape.

So what will Henderson do when he learns that Maddi is dead? He sighed. *It will destroy him.* Though Hank could ease the poor man's pain by letting him know that Maddi hadn't died – that she was only faking it to hold off the vultures until he or Cravens could figure out who was behind the crash – he couldn't do it. Maddi's life would be in danger the minute anyone learned that she had survived the crash.

As far as determining who was behind the crash; it would be a challenge. For one thing, the world had bought into the fact that the plane crash was an accident. Hank had gathered that much from the few radio blurbs he was able to pick up on his journey through Latvia. For another thing, there were only two men who knew the truth about the crash – he and Cravens – and both of them were hamstrung by the need to keep secret the fact that Maddi had survived.

He flinched. *No, there's one more man who knows the truth behind the cause of that crash; the driver from the Henderson estate.*

Hank had been tempted to call Walter and let him know that one of his drivers was a potential murderer. But he couldn't; not without telling him why he suspected the man, which would inevitably lead him to either lie to Walter about what he had overheard, defy Walter when he insisted that he return to the castle, or reveal to Walter that Maddi was still alive.

I can't even tell Jenny, he thought with a sigh. Though he trusted his ex-wife completely, he couldn't be sure that her cellphone was secure, or that her London hotel room hadn't been bugged. Especially if the authorities had begun to search for Hank. But he knew he would need to call her soon, if for no other reason than to ease her mind about why he had disappeared so abruptly. He couldn't tell her that Maddi was alive, but he could at least reassure her that his sudden disappearance had nothing to do with Maddi's death, or his fondness for her. He sighed. *But even that is a lie.*

Cravens was in the same boat. If he elected to investigate the crash, which Hank felt certain he would, then he would need to do it on his own, not as a Secret Service agent. Otherwise, he, too, would be forced to lie to those who trusted him.

Hank had decided he should talk to his own boss, Jason Hanover, before the world learned of Maddi's 'death.' So, as he had driven breakneck speed away from the crash site, he had pulled out his cellphone and had dialed the man. It would be the last time he would use that phone. He had told Hanover, 'something had come up,' and that he would need a few days off. Needless to say, the call hadn't gone well...

"What the hell are you talking about, Hank? You can't just take a day off like some clerk at a convenience store. There's a lot of shit going down right now, and you are responsible for watching over an alleged terrorist. Besides, you're supposed to be helping the Hendersons with the battle in Latvia."

"Hanover, there's been an accident. I'm sure you'll hear about it soon. It's terrible. Really bad. I've got to get out of here. You can fire me; you can even haul me in front of some court and put me in jail...I don't care. I need some time."

There was silence, then, "Are you okay Hank?"

"I don't know." Hank heard phones ringing in the background; the news was about to break. "I gotta' go. I'll call you later."

He had hung up and had smashed his cellphone several times against the dash. He had then pitched the pieces out the window as he had continued the drive south. Soon after that was when he had made the pitstop at the gas station, where he had purchased the three trac phones. If Walter's insistence that a simple call to his ex-wife would have put her in danger, then Hank would be well-advised to use impossible-to-trace trac phones to make any calls from then on.

After the pit stop, he had driven for about an hour or so, going back and forth on whether to make the next call...to Jenny. After another few minutes, he had pulled off the road, had grabbed one of the trac phones, and had stepped out of the car. With a shaking hand, he had dialed the number he knew so well...

"Hello?" Jenny's voice sounded tired.

"Jenny, it's Hank."

He heard a gasp. "Hank! Where are you? Are you on your way to London?"

"No, and I can't talk long. You're about to hear some awful news. I can't talk about it, but know this: I love you, Jenny Clarkson. I love you more than

anything on this earth," he paused, "...but I'm going to need to be away for a little while."

"What—what are you saying, Hank? What's going on?"

Hank flinched. "You can't tell anyone about this call, Jenny...no one. That is imperative. Your faith in me is about to be tested. Please believe in me. I love you."

He had hung up before she could ask any more questions. He had destroyed that phone as well, leaving him with two trac phones.

Now, many hours later, he was still trying to figure out how to get out of Latvia. He would need IDs; one for him, and one for Maddi. He sighed as he passed a small farmhouse in the middle of nowhere. He didn't have the first clue how to obtain fake ID's, especially in a foreign country he knew little about. What were his options? "I don't have any, dammit!" he muttered as he smacked the steering wheel.

"What's wrong, Hank?"

His eyes widened. It was the first time since they had left the crash site that Maddi had seemed the least bit engaged. He looked over his shoulder and gave her a weak smile. "Nothing. Just trying to figure out our next move."

There was a pause. "Didn't Cravens give you a number for a friend of his?"

Hank's eyes widened. "You're right, Maddi...he did!"

Hank patted his pockets in search of the crumpled sheet of paper that Cravens had handed him as Hank had been about to drive off with Maddi. *"This guy's an old friend. He lives in Spain, just south of Madrid. He'll help you. Tell him I sent you."*

Hank found the paper in his jacket pocket and read the name aloud.

"Angelo Recito, fisherman. +44-20-8985-458."

Again, he pulled to the side of the road. He grabbed one of the trac phones and, laying the paper on his lap, he dialed the number.

It rang several times. Hank was about to hang up, when he heard a gruff, "Que?" on the other end of the line.

Hank cleared his throat. "Um...is this Mr. Recito?"

There was a pause. "Quien este?"

"My—my name...mi nombre...es Hank Clarkson."

"Ha! I go now."

"Wait! Wait. Tom Cravens gave me your name."

A longer pause. "How you know Tom Cravens?"

"He—he's a bodyguard to my...to my friend."

"And?"

"She is in trouble. He told me to call if I need help."

"So...you need help?"

"Yes. We're on the run, we're in Latvia, and we need to get across the border."

"Latvia? Why would anyone be in Latvia? Never mind." Hank could hear the man breathing, but he didn't speak for a full thirty seconds. Finally, he said, "Okay, I help you. But we must start that you call me Angelo."

CHAPTER 4

Washington, DC

What to do, what to do? Claire Porter was pacing. She didn't often pace, especially in the middle of the night, but then again, rarely had she been in a more difficult situation. Not only had her client, the endearing Cynthia Madison, been killed in a plane crash in Latvia, but the President of the United States had been assassinated just hours later...*and Maddi had known it was going to happen!* Well, she hadn't actually known it; she hadn't said *"The President is going to be killed."* She had simply asked Claire to warn Hank Clarkson about a man named Morningstar, but only if a Secret Service agent died in the near future. Then, hours later, a Secret Service agent *did* die...actually, four of them, while trying to protect the President.

Claire didn't know Hank Clarkson. She knew *of* Hank because of her therapy sessions with Maddi. She knew that Maddi had been incredibly fond of him; that Maddi had even loved him, though no longer romantically. She knew he worked for the government, but she didn't know the branch, and that he had a son, Roger, who worked for the CIA. That was it. She was expected to somehow deliver a message to a man who could be anywhere in the world. Which was why Claire had spent the last several hours pacing her apartment, stopping only to refill her cup of tea.

She had left Evansville soon after learning of Maddi's death. She had already had a flight out of Indy for later that afternoon, and had gotten home soon after ten p.m. last night. Without even unpacking her bag, she had plopped down in her favorite chair with a cup of Earl Grey tea. Her hope was that the tea would calm her enough that she would be able to sleep. But that wasn't what had happened; not at all. One cup had led to another, then another, and so on.

I need to sleep, she thought, as she made another swipe around the living room. She had a busy day tomorrow, which was actually today. Fridays were always busy. But as she glanced at a cuckoo clock and saw that it was nearly three a.m., she knew it would be futile to try to sleep now. She felt certain that the minute she closed her eyes, all she would see would be images of Maddi, scared beyond belief as she looked out her window at the ground coming straight for her. It was a horrible thought and had left Claire so unsettled that she couldn't even eat. A rarity, for sure.

But Maddi's cryptic message had unsettled her almost just as much. Not only because it now seemed prescient, but because it held a warning for Hank Clarkson that was chilling. It involved a man named Morningstar, whom Maddi had said little about other than that he was terrible, and that Hank needed to watch his back...*but only if a Secret Service agent died.* Claire pulled out a scrap of paper. She was glad she had written it down, or most of it, anyway. Maddi had been talking so fast...

"Claire, I need a favor. A good friend of mine, Hank Clarkson, is on his way back to the States. It's quite possible, in light of what you've just told me, that I won't get a chance to talk to him. Will you give him a message?"

"I...I will, but...why me?"

"Because, it involves something I wouldn't want anyone else in DC to know. Tell him to watch his back. Tell him it has something to do with a secret committee he was on...and that several of the members...have died. It's...it's probably nothing. Just let him know that a terrible man, Morningstar—" she had hesitated. *"I'm sure it's nothing, unless someone shoots a high-ranking Secret Service agent in the next day or two."* Claire had heard what had sounded like a forced laugh. *"Please, just tell Hank to...to watch his back..."*

Claire laid the paper on her chair and walked into the kitchen. *What do I do?* She was about to refill her tea, when she chose instead to walk to a window that faced Rock Creek Park. Though it was the middle of the night, random street lights allowed her to see a grove of tall white pines that stood like sentries in the empty park. It was one of the reasons she had chosen the apartment. It was good for Claire to see trees; especially pines. They were resilient. Resiliency was often needed after a long day of counseling troubled souls.

She stared at the trees, hoping for inspiration. Not only inspiration; but strength...strength to do what she had intended to do when she had flown to Indiana in the first place. She was to share with the Evansville Prosecutor that Maddi had killed a police officer twenty-two years ago.

As a therapist, Claire was what was known as a Mandatory Reporter. It meant that if ever a client revealed to her that he or she had committed a capital offense, then, regardless of counselor-client confidentiality, she would be obligated to report it. Maddi's killing of Evan Jackson in an alley in 1982 most definitely qualified as a capital offense.

But once Claire had learned that Maddi was dead, she had instantly felt relieved of her burden; she would no longer need to share the horrid details of Maddi's horrid past. *What good would it do now?* she had conjectured as she had stood on those oversized courthouse steps. *Maddi's dead. Let her past die with her.*

But now, as Claire stared at the evergreens in the distance, she wondered if that had been the right thing to do. After all, there was a family out there who had been misled about the final hours of the life of their police officer son, husband, brother, or father. Didn't Claire owe it to them to set the record straight? Though Maddi could no longer make amends for what had happened, those people, whoever they were, still needed to know the truth. Claire frowned. *Do they?*

Yes, she thought with a frown. Maddi's death hadn't changed the fact that the capital offense had occurred, or that Claire was still obligated to report it. But it also hadn't changed the fact that, more than anything on earth, Claire didn't want to report it. She didn't want to destroy the reputation of one of the finest women she had ever known.

She walked to the kitchen for tea. As she again filled her cup and threw in two sugar cubes, she frowned. *So what are you going to do, Claire?* She shook her head and sighed. She clearly had two equally challenging dilemmas. The first was that she needed to warn Hank Clarkson – who could be anywhere – that he needed to watch his back. The second was that she needed to fulfill her obligation to report a capital offense to the proper authorities.

She sipped her tea. *I'll start with the warning to Hank.* Maddi had said that he was on his way back to the States. Because of the nature of his work, Claire could only guess that he would be coming back to Washington. That had been two days ago, which meant that he should be in DC by now. But DC was a big place; where would Claire even start? She had a friend at the Department of Justice; maybe he could help. She nodded. That was what she would do. She would call her friend, find Hank Clarkson, then deliver Maddi's message...Maddi's final request for Claire.

She choked on her tea. *Then what, Claire...then what are you going to do?*

Again, she thought about the Prosecutor in Evansville. Though she didn't want to do it, she knew that she had to...she had to call his office and reschedule her appointment. She nodded reluctantly. *Once I deliver Maddi's warning to Hank, I'll call the Prosecutor and schedule to see him as soon as possible.*

She set the tea on a table by her chair and stared out the window. She had made up her mind. She would deliver Maddi's warning to Hank, and then – and only then – would she reach out to the Prosecutor.

But before I do anything, I need to cancel my day at the office. There was no way Claire could serve her clients properly without sleep. She would use the morning to make three phone calls. The first would be to her friend at the DOJ. Then, once he told her how to reach Hank, she would make a call to Hank to warn him to 'watch his back.' *What if I can't find Hank?* She frowned. She would cross that bridge when she came to it. As for the third call, it would come only after she had spoken to Hank, and it would be to the Evansville Prosecutor. She shook her head and sighed. *Only after I have fulfilled Maddi's final request, will I throw her legacy to the wolves.*

CHAPTER 5

Columbia, South Carolina

Andrew Madison stared at the ceiling. It was still dark outside. He turned to look at a clock by the bed. Three a.m. He had tried to sleep, seeking the relief of at least a few hours where he didn't have to face all that had happened. But sleep wouldn't come. In a matter of hours, he had lost his entire family; not his wife or son, but his other family...the family that had been there from the beginning. His mother, Jeannie, and his sister, Maddi. It had just been the three of them for most of his life, ever since the murder of his father when Andrew was only twelve years old. Though he and Jeannie had no longer been close, he had still loved her, and he had held out hope that she would eventually regain her sense of self...that she would quit drinking and redeem the relationships she had allowed to sour so badly. But now, all that hope was gone.

Yet somehow, in the midst of her final hours, she had managed to leave behind a letter to him and Maddi, as well as a tape recording on a small device that Andrew had found lying next to her dead body. He hadn't read the letter, nor had he listened to the tape. He had intended on waiting for Maddi to do that with him.

He closed his eyes and gripped his hands as he fought another pang of grief.

His first thought after finding the letter was that it was likely an attempt by Jeannie to clear her conscience of the years of neglect following the death of her husband; the fact that, rather than face her grief head on, she had turned to alcohol for solace. He had assumed the same thing for the tape recording.

But then had come the Pentagon agents. Those two agents poking around so soon after Jeannie's death hadn't just alarmed him; it had angered him. And their claim that she had been working with terrorists was nothing short of laughable. The claim had, however, given both the letter and the tape a whole new significance. Had Jeannie confessed some bizarre tie to a terror group in either the letter or the tape? Or had there been something else she had either known or been a part of; something so awful that the Pentagon had felt a need to manage what should have been the simple interment of a tragic woman who had drunk herself to death. Andrew knew that he would eventually have to read the letter and listen to the tape. But he would be forced to do it alone. There was no one else now; Maddi was gone.

The loss of his sister had been far more profound than the loss of his mother. He and Maddi had been close; closer than most siblings, if for no other reason than the fact that for a good part of their lives, they had only had each other. Their father was dead, their mother was an alcoholic. Andrew, five years older than Maddi, had taken on the role of protector.

Which made her death in a plane crash in a country halfway around the world all that much more difficult to take. He had been unable to protect her. Though she had been out of the country for months, she and Andrew had talked on the phone almost daily. The absence of those phone calls would be harder on him than anything else. Maddi had had a way of making a simple phone call feel like a hug. She had been uplifting, reassuring, comforting, without even realizing she was doing it.

He felt a sudden urge to cry, and he tightened his jaw against it. He silently slid out of bed and walked to the door of the bedroom. There was no sense lying in bed awake, and he didn't want to wake Amanda.

As he stood at the doorway, he looked at Amanda. She was sleeping soundly, likely grateful for the fact that their son, Adam, was finally sleeping through the night. It had allowed her some much-needed rest. Andrew was overwhelmed as he looked at the mother of his child; she and his son were the only family he had left.

He left the room and walked the few steps to Adam's bedroom. After peering in and seeing that the boy was sleeping soundly, he walked to the living room. He sat on the couch and stared out the window at the darkness. Streetlamps created a soft yellow haze to the night, offering vague outlines of the buildings and trees of downtown Columbia. South Carolina at the end of summer was awash in green, though in the darkness it merely looked like a deeper shade of black.

He rubbed his eyes, fighting again the urge to cry. He had fought that same urge for the past twelve hours, certain that once he started, he might never stop. Having gotten past it one more time, he looked over at Adam's car seat, which was sitting on the floor by the door. They didn't normally bring the car seat into the apartment, but Andrew had felt it wise to do so tonight. Why? Because it was where he had hidden the letter and the tape recorder that he had taken from his mother's house soon after he had found her dead on the floor.

The Pentagon agent's claim that Jeannie was involved with terrorists was preposterous. Jeannie could hardly comb her hair. There was no way she was savvy enough to carry on an association with a terrorist organization. But there had to be some reason that the Pentagon had showed up at Jeannie's house within hours of her death. And it was that – along with his grief – that was keeping him awake.

First of all, how had Jeannie wound up on their radar? Other than being Maddi's mother, which was notable due to Maddi's success in the Senate, why had the Pentagon given two shakes about an alcoholic who was living alone in Indiana.

Second of all, how had they known she had died? Andrew hadn't seen a cellphone anywhere near her body, and the landline was in the kitchen. Which meant that she couldn't have called anyone as she was taking her last breaths...*so how did they know?*

His chest began to pound. It was the question that had unsettled him since he had left his mother's house. The only way that the Pentagon could have been aware of her death was if someone had told them. *And the only way that someone could've known that she had died...was if they were there.*

He gripped his hands into fists. No matter how hard he tried to come up with a different explanation, there wasn't one: Jeannie couldn't have been alone when she died. Which meant that it was possible that whoever had tipped off the Pentagon had played a role in her death. He rubbed his temples as he tried once again to come up with a different explanation. Maybe one of the neighbors had stopped by and had found her dead. He shook his head. *They wouldn't have called the Pentagon; they would have called the local police.* And there had been nothing to suggest that the police had been there or were on their way. So, what other possibilities existed? He flinched. There were none. The fact of the matter was that the Pentagon had shown up out of nowhere, just an hour or so after Jeannie's death. Someone had called them, and that someone was either directly involved in Jeannie's death, or he knew who was.

Andrew stood and walked over to where the car seat was sitting on the floor, mindful of the fact that whatever had happened to his mother hadn't gone down the way it had been portrayed. Jeannie didn't drink herself to death, or if she did, she wasn't alone at the time. And whoever had been with her hadn't called the police. No, they had felt it best to call the Pentagon.

He stared down at the car seat. Hidden inside it was a letter and a tape. He narrowed his eyes. *And I'll bet anything that the reason the Pentagon has involved itself in my mother's death is contained in at least one of them.*

CHAPTER 6

Washington, DC

Knight frowned as he stared at the TV screen. It was nine in the morning; he had been in the Oval Office since six. He was on his third cup of coffee, and had declined breakfast as he waited for updates on the fourth shooting in the past six days. From what the authorities could tell, there was no connection between the shootings. One had taken place outside Newark, New Jersey; another in Montana; a third in Iowa. The one that was unfolding that morning had occurred at a convenience store in Topeka, Kansas. A man – white, mid-thirties, dark hair, dark eyes – had walked into the store and had started shooting randomly at a line of people standing at the counter. He had managed to kill a young couple, as well as the man behind the counter, and had injured several others. He had run from the store, but according to the report that Knight was watching now, he had just been gunned down at a rest stop thirty miles south of Topeka.

Knight rubbed his eyes, then stood, and walked to a coffee pot on a nearby table. He poured another cup and carried it back to his desk. He didn't like this part of the job. Though he had accepted that his role as America's leader involved solving the problems of the day, random shootings without purpose seemed like something completely out of his league. He had prepared for orderly discussions regarding political challenges; not a search for sanity in a nation of 300 million people.

But that was what he had gotten, and it had started on his very first night in the office, with the murder of an American President. One big difference: the Wilcox assassination hadn't been random. Wilcox had been watching TV when a hotel staffer had come upstairs, had walked into the President's room, and had somehow shot him dead. Either before or after that, the same man had shot and killed four Secret Service agents. How could such a thing happen? The Secret Service were some of the most highly trained soldiers in the country. How could a gunman manage to get past them, let alone kill them? Even worse; they had yet to find the killer, which infuriated him. How had U.S. authorities managed to find a crazed Topeka, Kansas shooter, but they couldn't find the man who had shot and killed an American President?

Even worse was that there appeared to be no motive for the assassination. The killer had left no message, no indication of why he felt the leader of the free world needed to go. Even if he had claimed some bizarre need to impress a celebrity – as in the case of the attack on Ronald Reagan in 1981 – there would at least be an explanation for the horrible act. But as of now, they had nothing.

For the first few days after the assassination, Knight had given frequent updates to a nation in mourning. The updates had gone from several times a day to once a day, and now he rarely even touched on their progress. Only when he was questioned by a reporter did he try to address the status of the investigation. It was well-known that the odds of finding the killer decreased by the day, and now, forty-five days later, Knight had pretty much lost hope that they would ever find the man.

He sipped his coffee. There was one thing the assassination of the President and the random shootings had in common: the weapon of choice was a gun. Though the gun used to kill the President was like nothing that had ever been seen by the FBI's forensic investigators, it was a gun, nonetheless. The fact that the random shootings that were now consuming the country also involved guns meant that the topic of firearms had once again become front and center. Newscasters, talk show hosts, even late night comedians were all saying the same thing. *"If we didn't have such easy access to guns in the country, none of this would be happening."*

Knight wasn't so sure. After all, criminals would always find a way to get a gun. They had done so since the founding of the country. Guns had played a role in American society since the landing of the settlers in the early 1600's. Though most of the time, the weapons had served to either secure food or as a means of self-defense, there had always been the random few who had used guns to maliciously kill their fellow man.

With the adoption of the second amendment, the right to those guns was pretty much enshrined in the constitution. Knight himself had always been a staunch supporter of gun rights; he felt that the right to own and bear arms was a vital deterrent to a government run amok. But how long would he or those who shared his view be able to defend it when guns were causing such chaos around the country?

"Guns don't kill people; people do." How many times had he said those words? And, though he still believed them, he knew that they would hold little solace for a country not only in mourning for a President, but in mourning for one another. The victims of the shootings weren't prominent men or women who had possibly angered a group of constituents...they were ordinary citizens who had simply been going about their business. A mother of three who had been out for a jog; a businessman on his way to work; a group of teenagers on their way to a football game...*and now a store clerk and a young couple who had simply been buying a gallon of milk.* It was frightening as it felt more and more like no one was safe from such madness. Knight needed to somehow reassure the American people that he was doing all he could to fight what had been described by the press as a murder epidemic.

He had spoken with leaders of his party, who were also struggling with the messaging as they tried to hammer out some sort of legislation that would curtail gun purchases to only those who were mentally fit to have them. It was a slippery slope. What were the criteria to declare a man or woman 'mentally fit?' Who would decide? Psychiatrists? Family doctors? School counselors? There were many in his party who felt like the only thing to do was to forbid any sort of gun ownership; they had gotten to the point where they even wanted to ban hunting rifles. And he understood their reasoning. A hunting rifle was just as effective as an AR15 when it came to killing people. But how could such a law be enforced? Many law-abiding citizens felt that the freedom to hunt game was as American as apple pie. One thing was certain: the issue was far more complex and challenging than nightly newscasters made it seem.

But they weren't the only ones trying to simplify a complex issue. It seemed to be the curse of Washington...take complicated problems and come up with simple solutions. Not only simple, but ineffective. Answers that made it seem like legislators were doing their job, when in reality they were just kicking the can down the road.

That had been the most disturbing thing that Knight had discovered in his forty-five days on the job. No matter who he spoke to; be it the leader of the Senate, the Speaker of the House, or his most trusted advisors...not one of them was coming at him straight. Each one had an agenda, and it was never focused on what was best for America. Party leaders wanted more power, and his advisors wanted him to score political points. *To hell with actually getting anything done.*

He leaned back and ran his fingers through his thick hair. Though it was a far cry from the long brown hair he had had as a young man – the hair he desperately missed – it was still thick, and he smiled as he imagined Emma Melnikov running her hands through it. He shook the thought away, amazed that he could still be infatuated by the woman after sixteen years of being away from her. *Stay focused, Knight.*

There was a knock on the door.

"Come in," he said, as he sat up straighter in his chair.

"Sir, there's a call for you...on your private phone."

Knight nodded. His 'private phone' was a reference to a cellphone that had been designed to receive the calls of only one man: Edward Morningstar. The same man whom Knight often referred to as either father or Jacob. But never publicly. Their relationship was a well-kept secret. Why? Knight wasn't exactly sure.

He had only recently begun giving the phone to a Secret Service agent to carry. Morningstar hadn't liked it, but Knight had found that carrying the phone had become burdensome. *"I sometimes forget it, Jacob...or I leave it somewhere that I shouldn't."* He had assured Morningstar that the agent who carried it for him had no idea who was on the other end. *"He just answers it for me, Jacob. That's it."*

The agent handed him the phone. He nodded. "Thank you, Simmons. That will be all." He waited for the agent to leave the room. Quietly, he said, "Yes sir?"

"Good morning, Mr. President. I thought I would call to see how you were handling the events of this morning."

"You're referring to the shooting in Kansas, sir?"

"Yes, son."

Knight cleared his throat. "It's a tragedy, sir. And to be honest with you, I'm not quite sure how to handle it. After all, I can't really stop crazed killers from acting on their impulses."

There was a pause. "No, but you could get rid of the weapons they're using to carry out such carnage."

Knight's eyes widened. "Get rid of the weapons?" He shook his head. "With all due respect, sir, I can't very well take hundreds of millions of guns away from the law-abiding citizens of this country."

There was another pause; this one longer. "Perhaps not. We'll talk later, son."

The call ended. Knight stared at the phone. Was that what he thought it was? Had Morningstar just suggested that Knight *confiscate* the guns of every American? He shook his head. *Surely not,* he thought, as he stared once again at the TV. *There is no way in hell that anyone would advocate such a thing.*

But as he stared at the screen and watched a commentator interviewing a frightened citizen, he knew it was possible that, within the next several days, he would be asked to do that very thing.

CHAPTER 7

The Henderson Compound, Latvia

Martin Henderson pulled the blanket over his face as angled rays of sunlight found their way into the ancient castle window of his bedroom. Though in his old life he would have been up and about well before daybreak, these days he chose to sleep through not only those first rays of the morning sun, but its full rise over the Baltic Sea less than a mile from where he slept.

Sleep had become a refuge. A place where Maddi wasn't dead, Lili wasn't dead, and he, Martin Henderson, wasn't wanted for his role in a bioterror attack that he had never been a part of. A place where his life was promising, his hopes restored, his spirit renewed.

But the sun's fierce rays were making it impossible for him to stay in that welcoming world of sleep, and though he longed to hide in his bed with the blanket over his head, he couldn't; he had too much to do. He lowered the blanket unceremoniously. *Just get up, Henderson.*

He stretched his long arms in the air as he slid out of bed and stumbled to the window. His knees ached, his back ached...every part of him ached. Mornings were toughest. No matter how much he exercised, or how many massages he was given, the first steps of the day were always fraught with pain. Though he was only forty years old, he felt as if he was eighty.

He stood at the window and looked out over the garden below. He had always loved that window. The old castle wall had been preserved on that side of the manor, leaving the window and the wall around it with the feel of old-world Latvia. Thick stones cemented together with slaked lime and sand, the gray rocks stained a rustic brown from years of heartache and war. He had often imagined a knight standing in the very same spot where he was standing now, looking out over the garden below as he prepared to do battle with some unnamed foe.

He opened the double-paned glass and breathed in. It was mid-October, and the smell of fall was in the air. How many times had he stood at that window and watched the seasons come and go over the course of his forty years...dreaming of adventure as a young boy in the summer, planning his future as a young man in the fall. That window had been a source of magic for as long as he could remember. *Until I jumped out of it in an attempt to kill myself.*

He flinched. He had never believed in suicide, and he had certainly never seen himself as a man who would be capable of such a thing. He had always viewed it as a coward's way out. But then, somehow over the course of the last several years, he had become the coward. Too much had happened; too much had gone wrong. A fire that had disfigured him, the crimes he had been forced to commit because of it, the losses, first of Lili, then of the only woman he would ever love. Ending his life had seemed like the only answer to end the pain that had seeped so deeply into his soul.

Fortunately – or unfortunately – he had been saved from his attempt. He wasn't sure how. His parents had said little about what had happened that night. There was a tacit understanding that it was never to be discussed. All they had told him was that the rope he had used had come loose from the tree limb that had been holding it. The very same tree limb he was looking at now. He didn't see how the rope could have simply 'come loose.' He had tied that rope over that limb a hundred times, and never had it failed...not once.

He had tried to find the rope to see if it had frayed; it was, after all, thirty years old, but it was nowhere to be found. He guessed it had been thrown away. *That's what I'd do if my son tried to hang himself from a tree outside his bedroom window.*

He shook his head and sighed. Regardless of how he had survived his attempted suicide, he had vowed to never do it again. For one thing, he had humiliated himself. He was, after all, a world-class assassin. After killing so many others, then failing to kill himself, well, it was downright ludicrous. Then again, it was also enlightening. He had beat death so many times that he had begun to think, for whatever reason, he was meant to be alive. He couldn't imagine why God, the Universe, or whatever it was that held sway over lives and loves and losses would want him to live. He was a soulless man who had done terrible things. What use could there be for a broken world to have such a broken man for one more day?

Vengeance, came a thought out of nowhere. *A way to even the score before I go.* Was that it? Could it be that he had been saved simply so that he could take down his bitter rival? That maybe he, Martin Henderson, was the only one who could?

He shook his head. How on earth could he take down Edward Morningstar; he could barely get out of bed. His heart hurt, his head hurt... every part of him ached for his losses, and for the loss of who he used to be. *I barely have the energy to breathe.*

Regardless, he would need to find a way, if for no other reason than that the devotion to bringing down Morningstar had given him purpose. It had given him a reason to get up in the morning, to eat, to run, to engage in the world.

It had taken him weeks to come up with it...to uncover a feeling that could shove aside his longing for Maddi, the heartbreaking yearning that would cripple him every time he thought of her smile, her laugh, her love. It had come to him quite by accident, on a cold morning in early September. A feeling so strong that he had had to stop what he was doing. It had been a welcome change from the despair he had grown so used to. *What is this?* he had wondered at the time. A voice inside him had said, *"Hate."*

It hadn't been a new thing for Henderson to feel hate...he had felt it toward Morningstar for years. The man had ruined his life, and Henderson despised him for it. But hate took a toll on a man, and no one knew it better than Henderson. So, because of that, he had done his best to not indulge it. But suddenly, it didn't matter. If he wanted to nurse a self-destructive hatred, why not? *What else have I got to do?*

The hate had energized him; it had given him purpose. But first, he had had to regain his strength. Not only had he been in a coma for five months, but he had spent another month just lying in bed, mourning the loss of the woman who had defined his very existence. But with the help of his physical therapist, a thick, muscled woman whom he referred to as Helga, he was soon able to walk without the help of a cane.

Once he had regained the ability to walk, he had decided to run. It had started with a slow, halting jog, but, after only a couple of weeks, he had progressed to two-hour runs up and down the coast of the estate. And though he would have preferred to have run miles away from that castle in either direction, he was told by his father that he couldn't leave the compound. *"Matt Henderson is a wanted man, son."*

His father wasn't wrong. The man Henderson had chosen to become in an effort to hide who he had been was now wanted for his role in the Lassa fever attacks. Matt Henderson hadn't even existed at the time, but it didn't matter. Two months ago, evidence had been planted – most certainly by Morningstar – that had implied that Matt had aided and abetted the Phoenix in the Lassa fever attacks. The U.S. Government had responded to that evidence by sending an agent from Homeland Security, Hank Clarkson, to Scotland to bring Henderson home. But instead of going to America, they had been forced to come to Latvia and fight a war.

He thought of Hank and smiled. *Poor guy.* Hank had been given the undesirable assignment of keeping an eye on a despairing man. It had to have been torture. *Which is probably why he left when he did.* Henderson hadn't seen him since the day of Maddi's plane crash. He had asked Walter about it, but Walter had refused to say much, other than that Hank's assignment had come to an end. Henderson knew that was a lie; Henderson was Hank's assignment. He wondered if perhaps Hank had tried to kill himself, too. Could it be that while Henderson was jumping from a second-story window with a rope around his neck, Hank was driving a car off some cliff in an effort to end the pain; the endless agony that Henderson knew so well? He sighed. *More power to him. If Hank's dead, then he's in a far better place than I am.*

Henderson continued to stare out the window. The leaves of the trees were a pleasant yellow-red. Normally, he would embrace those colors as they hung in the air against a bright blue sky. But the truth of the matter was that he embraced nothing, he felt nothing...other than hate. Which was better than what he had been feeling; an agony so deep that it felt like a hand around his neck...like the breath was being squeezed out of him from a despair that seemed to know no bounds. Which was why, in an act of desperation, he had tried to end his suffering. He had failed. His attempt to hang himself from the tree that had defined his childhood had fallen short.

Walter had apparently been the first to find him. Apparently, he had gone up to Henderson's bedroom to check on him, having left him just minutes before after telling him of Maddi's death. He had seen the open window and had run to the sill and looked over the side. *"That was when I saw you lying on the ground, son."* He had alerted the staff and the entire castle had run out to the garden, where they had found Henderson at the base of the tree with a rope around his neck.

And when he had awakened and had realized that he had failed, his shame was every bit as deep as his longing for Maddi. He was a failure... even at killing himself.

The surprise had been to learn that the President of the United States had been assassinated just hours after Henderson's suicide attempt. His father, Walter, and President James Wilcox had been friends – good friends – and Henderson could only imagine the pain that had gripped his father. Not only had his son tried to end his own life, but one of his dearest friends had been shot dead in a hotel bathroom.

The President's murder had been investigated extensively. The conclusion was that he had been killed by a well-trained assassin while soaking in a tub at the end of the day. Several of his Secret Service agents had been killed as well, which was quite a feat, in and of itself.

As for the crash that had killed Maddi, there was still no explanation for why an MI6 transport plane had crashed just as it was about to land. According to Walter, no one had survived. Which was no surprise. A plane hitting the ground at several hundred miles per hour – even in landing mode – would destroy everything on board.

Henderson had asked several times to be taken to the site, but his father had urged against it. *"Not yet, son. You're not ready."* Henderson had no idea what that even meant. He would never be ready. But that didn't mean that he didn't need to see it, if for no other reason than to have a physical place to mourn the loss of the woman he loved. Maddi had died within miles of his home. It represented her last physical presence on earth. But for whatever reason, he had listened to his father...probably because the man was usually right. *I'll go there soon,* he thought as he turned from the window and walked to the bathroom.

He washed his face and brushed his teeth, then walked to his dresser and grabbed a sweatshirt and a pair of sweats. He pulled them on, put on his gym shoes, and walked to the door of his bedroom. He would start with a ten-mile run. Once he was finished with that, he would get to work.

Work consisted of reconnaissance. For the past two weeks, he had spent most of each day working on a way to take down Morningstar. Though with Henderson's skills, he could have easily killed the man, he knew it wouldn't stop him. Morningstar had conducted his affairs in such a way that even in death, his plans would carry on. As a matter of fact, Morningstar had told him that on countless occasions...

> "Keep in mind, Joseph, should you ever doubt me, or – God forbid – turn on me, not only will I kill you, but my legacy will live on long after I'm gone. This plan that I've put in place has a life all its own. There are others who know exactly what to do should I die unexpectedly...who are ready to jump in should I leave this earth before my work is done. Nothing will stop the plan. Do you understand me? Nothing. Don't ever think you can disrupt my God-given purpose, son. No one can stop me...no one..."

Henderson had failed to appreciate the depth of what the man was planning. It was only toward the end of their time together that he had begun to piece together Morningstar's vision for a new world where he would rule over every continent, every country, every person on earth. It was insane...Morningstar was insane. His blueprint consisted of rebellion and war in every major country around the globe. No one would be immune; not even the United States. There was no document to define his vision; no constitution to shape the new world he hoped to create. No, all he had was a sick dream and a misguided goal of a world that wasn't merely ruled by him, but was dominated by his cruel inclinations. Yes, he was crazy, and like so many crazed dictators over the years, he didn't care who got in his way.

As Henderson jogged down the stairs and out the front door of the castle, he bristled. *Which is why it is now my purpose in life to get in Morningstar's way.*

CHAPTER 8

Washington, DC

Edward Morningstar yawned as he stared at the TV. He hated Sundays. The politicians were out of town, the press was chasing street crime, and the city itself was dormant, lying in wait for Monday. This particular Sunday was no different. And, as his lovely concubine, Janet, became more pregnant and less desirable, he found himself with little to do.

Which was why he had elected to watch the TV coverage of the shooting in Topeka, Kansas. He hadn't been surprised by the shooting. For one thing, it and the other shootings confirmed what he already knew: America was sick. Of course, men were shooting one another. Left behind by the last gasps of a dying nation, they needed an outlet for their pain and their poverty...not only of means but of spirit. The United States was failing, and the world was failing right along with it.

Which is why God has chosen me to fix it.

And God had chosen wisely. Morningstar had received God's vision four-and-a-half years ago in a rotted-out hotel room in downtown DC, and, within a few years, the well-connected Pentagon aide had forged a secret family of soldier sons who were now slowly but surely transforming the entire world order. First had been Judah (Knight), who, through Morningstar's careful tutelage, had become President of the United States. Then had come Simeon (Jim Roberts), who had helped to pull Joseph (Henderson) from the fire that had nearly killed him. As for the other sons; Asher, a former CIA agent, had been killed back in January – by

Henderson, no less – and had yet to be replaced. Dan (Cobra) had been tasked with finding and killing Hank Clarkson, who was one of the few remaining men who had the potential to hurt Morningstar, and Levi (Josh Adams) was buried in the Pentagon basement, well-positioned to stop any attempt to undermine Morningstar's efforts. Reuben (Pocks) was in London, likely nursing a wounded soul over his role in bringing down the plane that had been carrying Cynthia Madison, while Simeon and Naphtali (Leroy Cooper) were hunting for a powerful warship in France. Issachar (Todd Jackson) was cooling his heels in DC, doing what was needed to compel young men to kill, and Gad (Marcus King) would soon lure Henderson to Lithuania, where he could capture him and bring him back to the States. Zebulun (Vladimir Karev) was in hiding after having done what no man had ever done before; kill a sitting U.S. President...*and* get away with it. Last but not least was Benjamin, true heir to the Morningstar bloodline, who was currently nestled in Janet's womb. All had played their parts well. But it was Morningstar who oversaw their efforts; it was Morningstar who made the plan work. Using assassinations, wars, and the fostering of internal strife, he had put in place the machinery that would soon allow him to reshape planet earth.

And it can't come soon enough, he thought as he watched the TV anchor. The man was practically crying as he told of the lives that had been lost in the Kansas convenience store. From Morningstar's perspective, those lives were merely collateral damage for a far more important purpose. A few lives sacrificed for the sake of the whole. His call to his son, Judah – Jerome Knight – had been intended to convey that...and to lay the groundwork for the next part of his plan.

But Knight would need persuading; Morningstar had heard it in his voice. To actually take America's guns would be a huge undertaking. Especially since Knight had always been a staunch defender of the second amendment. But Morningstar felt certain that he could appeal to Knight's sense of compassion and fairness. A few more shootings, and the new President would come around. *He won't have a choice,* Morningstar thought with a grin, *...the American people will demand it.*

Though Morningstar would have liked to have taken credit for such a scheme, the idea for the shootings had come from his most recently acquired son, Issachar. Todd Jackson had been a Philadelphia police officer just over a month ago, but then, for whatever reason, the man had developed a hatred for Cynthia Madison that had nearly rivaled his own. He wasn't sure why; all he knew was that it had something to do with Jackson's father, an Evansville police officer who had been shot in a back alley some twenty-odd years ago. And somehow, the fair-haired Cynthia Madison had played a role. Morningstar had also learned that her wealthy grandparents from England had managed to fly over and somehow cover up the entire affair. If Madison was still alive, Morningstar would tell the world of her family's treachery. But as it stood, it was no longer necessary; the woman was dead. *She's out of my hair forever.*

Morningstar had seen an opportunity in Todd's loathing of Madison. He hadn't yet decided to kill her by crashing her plane, so in an effort to undermine the woman, he had assigned Todd to drive to Madison's mother's house and record her admitting her daughter's role in whatever had gone down with the cop. But things hadn't gone as planned. Rather than record the woman acknowledging her daughter's complicity, Jackson had killed her. Not only that; he had somehow implicated Morningstar on the tape. To top it off, he had lost the recorder when leaving the house. Fortunately, Jackson had come up with a plan to resolve the mess; a good one, as it turned out. He had suggested that Morningstar send one of his minions to the house to find the recorder and take charge of the scene. Morningstar had given Levi the task, and had then advised Jackson to leave the house, the town, the state of Indiana at once. *"You need to lay low, Issachar. I'll do what I can to erase you from the scene at Madison's house, but I think it's best if you disappear for a while."*

Jackson had driven nine hours to DC without stopping. Morningstar had given him the address of his well-hidden warehouse, and he had arrived late that night. The two men had talked, and it hadn't taken long for Jackson to indicate his desire to be a part of whatever Morningstar was planning. *"What can I do to help you, sir?"*

Morningstar had sighed. *"I need to crush the will of American resistance."*

"The will, Jacob?"

"Yes, you know...the potential for incitement by an unruly mob, that might spur a far larger mob to fight back against my leadership. Using guns, for example."

Jackson had thought about it, then had nodded slowly. *"I know a way to remove that will,"* he had said with a grin. *"The best way to fight against the people is to make them fight against themselves."* And that was when mission "crazed shooter" was launched. According to Issachar, he would, *"...whip up enough hate and anger to compel desperate young men – who are already on edge in this messed up country – to do crazy things to express their rage."*

Morningstar had been intrigued. *"What are you saying, son?"*

Jackson had looked him in the eye. *"I can make men become shooters."*

And Issachar had done it. Through well-placed advertisements on appropriate websites, and hateful rhetoric spouted on social media, Jackson had provided the fuel that would ignite the hatred and anger of misguided twenty-something men. The first shooting had taken place six days ago, in Newark, New Jersey. A twenty-eight-year-old gunman had walked into a subway station and had started firing. He had killed a family of four, along with a teacher and a former marine. It had rattled the nation. There had been three shootings since, and each one seemed to underscore the horrible toll that America's love affair with guns was having on the nation.

The shooting that morning in Topeka had thrown the citizens into a near-panic. It was beginning to feel as if no one was safe. A few more shootings and Morningstar should have America – and Knight – right where he wanted them.

Morningstar stood and walked to the window of his Starlight Hotel suite. It was noon and the sun was high in the sky. He watched as a car pulled up to the hotel. An older couple got out, and he sneered as they walked hand in hand into the hotel. *About the same age as Madison's grandparents, I would guess.*

He pulled a gold locket from the pocket of his robe and rubbed it between his fingers. The locket had been sent to him by Gad. Though the young man had been forced to leave the Henderson compound after helping Cobra escape, he had been there when he was needed. Just before Cynthia Madison's plane had been expected to crash not far from the estate, Morningstar had instructed Gad to go to the site and verify that she had, in fact, been killed in the 'tragic accident.' *"Bring me proof."* And Gad had done it. He had driven to the site and had found the sole survivor, Madison's bodyguard, standing near the wreckage. According to Gad, the man had been staring down at the locket, a blue sweater, and Madison's Senate ID badge. *"It's all that's left of her,"* the bodyguard had muttered. Gad had feigned compassion, then had secreted away the locket without the agent knowing. He had overnighted it to Morningstar, who had carried it with him ever since. It was his trophy; his confirmation that one of his biggest obstacles had finally been removed.

He grinned as he inspected the locket. About the size of a quarter, it appeared to be made of solid gold. Inside was a stunning blue gemstone opposite a photo of an older couple. He guessed that they were Madison's grandparents from England; the wealthy grandparents that had paid off a police department in Evansville, Indiana to keep their granddaughter out of trouble. He massaged the gold fittings and smiled. *Just one more clue to tie Madison to the misdeeds of that day, and to whatever her wealthy grandpa had tidied up for her.* Not that he would need it; Madison was dead.

As for his other foe, Matt Henderson, who was actually Martin, Morningstar could only imagine the pain that the man was having to endure. He had lost the love of his life. Not only had Morningstar secretly compelled Madison to walk out on Henderson in Edinburgh, but she had then died tragically in a plane crash as she had been on her way back to him. Morningstar laughed. *That poor boy is probably ruined.*

But Morningstar had no way to learn how Henderson might be taking his lover's death. The Hendersons had been tightlipped about the status of their nephew who was actually their son. All Morningstar knew was that he was hidden away on their highly fortified compound.

Morningstar had instructed Levi to try to get a team of soldiers into the area, so they could eventually kidnap the man, but the more he thought about it, the less he liked the plan. He could too easily be tied to a military buildup, which wouldn't give him the distance he required. So, yesterday, while watching Putin struggle to distance himself from the war in Latvia, he had come up with a different plan. It would rely on Gad. The young man had proven himself not only to be reliable, but resourceful, as well. Why not put him in charge of retrieving the annoying Matt/Martin Henderson.

It should be simple enough. Henderson was wanted by both the Pentagon and Homeland Security for his role in the Lassa fever attacks. Though America had no extradition treaty with Latvia, they did have such a treaty with the country to the south: Lithuania. It had been put in place in 2001...*just in time for me to take advantage of it.* All Morningstar had to do was find a way to lure Henderson to Lithuania. Once there, Gad would be waiting with a team of U.S. soldiers to capture Henderson and bring him back to America.

The fly in the ointment was Hank Clarkson. He had been sent overseas nearly two months ago to bring Henderson back to DC. But Cobra had told Morningstar that he had seen Hank leave the compound on the very day that Madison's plane crashed, and that he hadn't seen him come back. Morningstar had followed up on it, and had learned that the man hadn't been back to the compound since. His disappearance was troubling. Why had he left? Where had he gone? What was he up to? Morningstar had reached out to the Director of Homeland Security, Jason Hanover, for information on the man, framing his questions as inquiries related to Clarkson's mission to bring Matt Henderson back to the States for questioning. Hanover had seemed reluctant to share much about his Deputy Director. All he had said was that Hank had taken a leave of absence. Morningstar had pushed the point. *"A leave of absence? Now? In the middle of a war?"* Hanover had replied evenly, *"Yes, Morningstar. The man had a personal matter to take care of. I'm sure he had no control over its timing."*

Morningstar bristled just thinking about Hanover's insolence. Fortunately, it wouldn't matter. Morningstar had given his son Dan, also known as the Cobra, the task of killing Hank. One thing Morningstar had learned about Cobra; he was a determined assassin.

He looked down at the wilted mums that lined the walkway outside the hotel and frowned. Cobra wasn't answering any of his calls. Every one of them had gone to voicemail. Morningstar had been stunned the first time he had tried to call Cobra. Using the number that Cobra had called from when he had been desperate to escape the Henderson compound, Morningstar had dialed and had gotten a taped message. But it wasn't Cobra's voice on the other end; it was the painfully hoarse voice of Martin Henderson. And the message had been touching. "It's me. If you're her, leave a message." Though Morningstar had been tempted to leave some sort of clever quip, he had refrained. It was best to not be recorded if it wasn't necessary. Cobra would recognize the number and call him back.

But Cobra had yet to do so. As a matter of fact, Morningstar hadn't talked to Cobra since that dramatic escape back in August. He bristled. *I'm sure he'll call me once he kills Clarkson...if for no other reason than to claim the Henderson castle as his own.*

Morningstar nodded. *It will all be fine.* If nothing else, Cobra was reliable. He would kill Clarkson, thereby removing the last member of

Morningstar's secret War on Terror Commission. *There'll be no one left to stop me.* Madison was already dead, and Henderson no longer had any power, more or less caged in his castle by the sea.

He shook his head and sighed. He still had concerns. What if Henderson talked before Gad could bring him in? What if Zebulun was captured and tortured, and was forced to reveal his ties to Morningstar? Finally, what if Hank Clarkson figured out that the last member of the War on Terror Commission – other than Morningstar and Hank – had been killed during the President's assassination? What if it finally dawned on him that what had started as an eight-member committee, was now down to two? It would lead him to only one conclusion; Morningstar, for whatever reason, was having the members killed. Once Clarkson arrived at that conclusion, he would know that he was next, and would initiate an investigation. The last thing Morningstar needed was a federal agent – or a federal agency – investigating his life. *Which is why Hank Clarkson must go...and soon.*

Morningstar flinched. Hank's disappearance sat like a thorn in his side. Where was he? Was it possible he had already figured out that the deaths of the committee members weren't a coincidence? If so, was he setting a trap? Morningstar shivered as he stared down at the rumpled flowers outside the hotel. *I'll be damned if I'm going to be taken down by some lackey from the Department of Homeland Security.* Yes, he would feel a whole lot better once he knew that Cobra had done his job.

CHAPTER 9

London, England

Cobra stretched his legs as he stepped off the train at Kings Cross station in downtown London. He smiled and said aloud, "Ah...it's good to be home." Other than to change trains on his journey to Latvia, Cobra hadn't been in London for over half a year. His trip to France back in March had started a cascade of events that had taken him from Paris to Lyon, then to Dalgety Bay, Scotland. From there, he had been forced to travel north and west in an attempt to stay one step ahead of the pesky CIA agent, Roger Clarkson, who had been on his tail following the events at the Bay. After indulging himself with the murder of an old woman not far from the ill-fated schoolhouse, Cobra had hiked across Scotland, with the CIA agent right on his heels. He had finally lost him when he had hopped a ferry to the Isle of Lewis, but not before he had managed to snap a photo of the man's beloved, the beautiful Tonna Kauffold, as she was changing trains at a station in Inverness. He had been stunned to see her there, and would have liked to have spent a bit of time with her, but Roger had reappeared out of nowhere, and Cobra had been forced to jump onto a merchant fleet tanker heading out to sea. He had hidden in the hold as the tanker had traveled north on the Norwegian Sea. The journey had given him time to recover, but he knew the agent would be looking for him, so he had taken another ferry to Iceland, and had laid low in the remote nature reserve of Hornstrandir. He had split the summer months between Iceland and the Orkney Islands at the northernmost point of Scotland. Three months ago, after deciding it was safe, he had returned to the Scottish mainland, where he had kept out of sight in a small fishing village outside Glasgow. It was then that he had experienced another infuriating loss of time, which had lasted a full month. He had been shocked when he had awakened in Edinburgh, with no recollection of what he had done during that month-long hiatus. It was soon after that that Morningstar had tasked him with the hit on Hank Clarkson. He had traveled from Scotland to Latvia, by way of London, using trains, a rental car, and a bus. But he had spent less than a day in the god-forsaken country before he had needed to be saved by Morningstar, which had irked him to no end. He had been whisked to Finland, where he had spent over a week trying to figure out how to find and kill Hank Clarkson. He had distracted himself by carrying out his customary pursuit, which was to terrorize women. He had spent several days getting to know two young girls in Kemi, and had then killed them in his typical fashion. Though he had had no cape, and no incisors with which to leave his signature, he did manage to carve the name Cobra into the forearm of one of the victims. *Mustn't let my artwork go unrecognized.*

After that, he had decided it was time to get out of there and go back to London, where he could get a new ID and some much needed cash. He had lost his backpack during his escape from the Henderson estate, leaving him with nothing but a photo of Hank Clarkson, and the cellphone that had once belonged to his half-brother, Martin. But he had needed cash to get to London, so his first task had been to rob a well-to-do traveler at a rest stop not far from Kemi. He had managed to steal 600 euros from the man, and had used it to buy clothes, food, and a cheap ID, which he had wrangled from a guy in nearby Tornio. The ID wasn't the best, but it was good enough to get him passage on the trains that would carry him back to London.

Which was where he was now, standing by the tracks at London King's Cross. But the journey, which should have taken a week, had taken three, and somewhere in there he had experienced another loss of time. He had no recollection of what happened for a full two weeks; all he knew was that it was now Sunday, October 10th, and over six weeks had passed since he had escaped the Henderson compound after saving Martin from his self-inflicted demise. *And I've yet to receive any sort of thank you for the deed,* he thought with feigned annoyance. He chuckled. He wondered who had found his poem. Assuming it was Walter, had he shared it with anyone? *Who all knows that it was the bastard son who saved the Chosen One?*

He followed signs to the center of the station. It was oddly quiet at King's Cross train station. Then again; it was late. He stepped outside and looked around at the familiar landmarks; vagrants loitering on the streets and alleyways, drunkards leaving the bars with boisterous, yet unfelt glee. He breathed in, basking in the smells of diesel and rubbish and grinned. *Jolly Old England...yes, it's good to be home.*

The walk from the station to his flat on the River Thames was a short one; about twenty minutes or so. Though he was wanted by every police force in the UK and beyond, he wasn't worried. It was late at night; he would be hard to see. Besides, the simple disguise he had acquired in Finland should be adequate to dissuade any eager police officer from suspecting that the man walking along the wharf so late at night was the Cobra. After all, he hadn't been in London for over half a year.

It was eleven p.m., as evidenced by the heartwarming chimes of Big Ben. As he made the walk along dark streets and even darker alleys, he felt inclined to sing an old English ballad, *"Allen's Farewell to his Love."* "Farewell love, farewell love, I am going to leave thee..." An old man on the corner glared at him and Cobra hissed back at the man, who jumped timidly behind a row of trashcans. Cobra laughed.

Another few minutes brought him to the door of his flat, which was hidden in the banks of the River Thames in what one might call the sketchier part of London. It didn't feel sketchy to Cobra; it felt like home. Unlike many who might wander the streets at night, Cobra was never afraid. He possessed skills that made him a formidable opponent, even to the vilest of those who typically roamed London's underbelly.

He grinned as he stared at the door. Had anything been disturbed? There were ways for him to tell; a subtle change in the way the metal chain hung on the door, the positioning of the nearby rock that hid his key. Yes, Cobra felt certain that he would know if someone had invaded his lair. After a brief inspection, he felt confident that no one had, and he bent over and lifted the rock. He dug up the familiar key which he had buried in the dirt, and slid it in a padlock on the door. He pulled off the lock and stepped inside. It was pitch black. There was no electric, so he pulled matches from his pocket and lit a lantern he kept on a table by the door. A wave of light filled the small room, and he smiled. Everything was just as he had left it.

Though the flat was small and had little in the way of decor, it was his, and it held his most cherished mementos. Photos of his victims, along with a few of their treasures hung on a corkboard on the wall. A trunk underneath a narrow bed held his clothes, his shoes, and a book of poems that comprised his journeys over the last six years. He also had a laptop, which he would connect to the internet by way of a hotspot on his cellphone.

What he didn't have was money; at least not in his lair. It was in a bank downtown, under the name M. Villamor. Over the years, Cobra had been paid handsomely by men like Morningstar to do what he would have been glad to do for free: kill people. And, because his needs were small, he had amassed quite a sum. He would go to the bank first thing in the morning. Until then, he had quite a lot to do.

He started by walking to an all-night convenience store, where a man whom he had used many times in the past was working the counter. All Cobra had to do was pull away his glasses and let the man look in his eyes. The man gave an almost imperceptible nod, as Cobra grabbed a cola from a rack and put it on the counter. He handed the man two euros, along with a folded note that promised 1,000 euros for a new ID. *"I will be an investment broker from Stockholm. Use the name Oskar Berg."*

Once he had the ID in the works, he walked back to his lair and began his research on Hank Clarkson. He already knew the basics: Hank was a physician, a Deputy Director of Homeland Security, and – according to Morningstar – had once dated the now-deceased senator from America, Cynthia Madison. Most significantly, he was the father of the CIA agent who had hounded Cobra incessantly since March. But Cobra would need to know more about the man if he hoped to hunt him down and kill him. He began by reviewing old newspaper articles and archives from Hank's former medical society. The information was surprisingly dull. Hank's life had been the typical, tedious life of a middle-aged doctor from a boring town in America. He had married Jenny Wilson in the seventies; she currently worked as a loan officer at a bank in Strongsville, Ohio. They had been married for only ten years when Jenny had filed for divorce, claiming 'irreconcilable differences.' He chuckled when he came across photos of Hank with Cynthia Madison at Washington DC galas, out to dinner in New York City, and on vacation in some exotic locale. *Irreconcilable differences, indeed.*

Suddenly, he frowned. Madison's tragic death would have surely troubled Hank, in spite of the fact that she had become obsessed with Henderson. Was it a coincidence that Hank had gone missing so soon after Madison's death?

He kept going, surprised when he saw that Hank had played football – the American version – while in college, and that he had aspired at one time to play professionally. It would appear that the timing of his marriage and the birth of his son had likely interrupted that dream. The decision to go to medical school had come a few years later. He had been in practice for nearly ten years when, in 2000, he had suddenly left practice to work for an insurance company, Marker Health, Inc. Cobra pulled up the company's website. There wasn't much to see. Just the same old song and dance about how Marker Health promised to work diligently on behalf of the ailing and infirm. Cobra sneered. *What a load of crap.* He was about to log off, when he noticed a photo at the bottom of the page. It was a photo that was similar to so many he had seen over the years; the handsome Martin Henderson was standing in front of a group of what looked like stakeholders. He read the script underneath. His eyes widened. Martin Henderson had *founded* the company that Hank had ended up working for. Two men in love with the same woman who ended up working at the same company? *An intriguing coincidence*, thought Cobra, though he could find nothing more about either of them on the website. He guessed that when the world had believed that Henderson had died in the hotel fire four years ago, Marker Health had been forced to move on without him. *But what about Hank? Where did he go?*

It was only two years later, in January of 2003, that Hank landed the job at the Department of Homeland Security. The fact that he was given the high-ranking Deputy Director position suggested that Cynthia Madison's DC ties had likely played a role. Hank's trip to Edinburgh was on the Homeland website, but only to say that there had been new information regarding the Lassa fever attacks that had taken place back in January, and that he was traveling to the UK to investigate. Following that entry was a single line: *Deputy Director Clarkson has taken a leave of absence.*

He frowned. *So...where is Hank spending his time away from work?*

Cobra typed in the website address for every major airline, hacking into their manifests from August 26th to the present day, October 10th, in search of the name Hank Clarkson. Where had Hank gone after he had left the Henderson estate? Had he flown back to DC? If not – and Cobra could find no evidence to suggest that he had – then that meant that he had likely stayed in Europe. But if the man had originally been sent to the UK to follow up on new information regarding the Lassa fever attacks, it was likely he hadn't planned on staying long. Which meant that he wouldn't have brought much cash with him...right? *So, what is he using for money?* Had Hank been born into wealth? Was it possible he was funding his 'leave of absence' by using money from a family trust of some sort? Cobra's eyes lit up. *If so, then maybe I can track the funds.*

The first thing he needed to determine was whether Clarkson had come from money. Cobra scrolled back to the days before Homeland, before Marker Health, before medicine; even before Jenny. From what he could tell, Hank had been born and raised in Strongsville, and certainly not to a family of means. His father had been a paralegal at a local law firm, and his mother had taught second graders in a nearby elementary school. What was curious, however, was that Cobra saw no evidence that any of Hank's family still lived there. His parents were dead, and he had apparently had no brothers or sisters. Nonetheless, Hank had recently made several trips to Strongsville. There were receipts at three different restaurants, and several gas station receipts, as well. *But no hotel bills,* he thought with a grin. So, where did he stay?

Cobra began to chuckle. The answer was obvious. There was only one reason that a man would go back to a town like Strongsville when he no longer had family there. *Love.* He chuckled. The most likely option was his ex-wife, Jenny. Was she the reason for his trips home? Had they maybe rekindled their relationship? He sat back and grinned. *If that's the case, then I'd bet money that Hank has either reached out to that woman for cash... or will do so soon.*

CHAPTER 10

The Henderson Compound

Henderson reached for his pistol as he was startled awake from a deep sleep. There was no pistol. Hiding a gun under his pillow was a discarded vestige from his days as an assassin. *Old habits die hard,* he thought, as he cast a quick look around the dark bedroom. His eyes fell on a clock by the bed. *Four a.m. ...what woke me?*

He waited for his eyes to adjust, then sat up. The room was nearly pitch black, the only light coming from a lone lamppost outside his window. He waited; it felt as if someone else was in the room. He reached over and switched on a lamp. He looked over every inch of that room; no one was there. He turned off the lamp, preferring the darkness. He slid out of bed and stumbled to the window.

He stared out at the lamppost, transfixed as its misty haze enshrouded the garden below. It was strikingly beautiful; he was amazed he could appreciate it as such. He rarely noted beauty anymore.

Then, suddenly, he heard her.

"She isn't dead," the sweet voice said, and he felt an instant ache in his chest. The voice had come from the young girl, Lili, and, though he knew that – like Maddi – Lili was dead, sometimes, in the deepest part of darkness, it felt like she was actually talking to him. She wasn't; she couldn't be. Morningstar had killed her soon after Henderson had left him; soon after Henderson had made it clear that he would no longer be the man's hired gun.

Morningstar had warned Henderson that he would do it; that he would kill Lili if he ever stopped killing for him. So Henderson shouldn't have been surprised when he received the photo of Lili lying dead in the snow. But he had been. Not only surprised, but devastated. Lili had been a remarkable child, gifted in so many ways. The fact that Henderson was responsible for her death had nearly destroyed him. But she wasn't the only one he had put in harm's way. He had essentially killed Maddi, as well, along with a score of world leaders who might have made the world a better place. He may not have always been the one to pull the trigger, but there was no question that he had been responsible for killing each and every one of them.

He ignored the sweet voice, not even bothering to remind it that Lili was dead. *What good would it do?* he thought, as he continued to stare at the lamppost. And the voice's claim that Maddi wasn't dead wasn't new, either.

"She didn't die in that plane crash, Uncle Mart. Ask her best friend."

Henderson's eyes widened. That part of the message was new. *Ask her best friend.* After a minute, he shrugged it off, just as he had the last fourteen or fifteen times that Lili had spoken to him. It had started just before his suicide attempt, and had continued nearly every day in the weeks that followed. And always it was the same. *"She didn't die in that plane crash, Uncle Mart."* It had been unbearable.

But it had been over a month since he had heard from her. *So, why now?* he wondered. It didn't matter. She wasn't real. Early on when she told him that Maddi hadn't died in the crash, out of hopeful desperation he had pursued it. He had asked Walter to tell him details of the crash, results of the investigation, the how and why of what was believed to have happened.

Walter's reply had been short and to the point. *"They think it was caused by weather, and that every person aboard was killed instantly. Now let it go, son."*

Henderson flinched. *"...let it go, son..."* He would never be able to let it go.

He turned from the window and walked to his closet. He grabbed sweats and a sweatshirt from his dresser and pulled them on. He walked into his bathroom and switched on the light. He flinched; the bright light felt intrusive after the comfort of darkness. He brushed his teeth and combed his hair; the black hair, now shoulder length, that he continued to dye in an effort to keep the myth of Matt Henderson alive.

He left the bathroom and slid into his running shoes. He walked quietly from the bedroom to the stairs, and crept down them to the front door. He gave a quick nod to a security guard who was standing next to the doorway, then stepped outside. It was still dark. He was glad. He had always enjoyed running in the dark.

He crossed a bridge, turned right, and ran toward the south end of the castle. The air was cool and crisp and it almost made him smile. He crossed back over the moat by way of a narrow foot bridge that was hidden in a thick row of trees, and was able to see the small garden that sat below his bedroom window. As he ran past it, he nodded at the lone lamppost as if he was nodding at a friend...a light in the darkness; the only light he knew. He continued on past the courtyard, then past the barracks, to a stone path that led to the sea. In the distance, he could see the sky turning a soft violet as the sun began to appear on the horizon. He breathed in the salty mist from the sea and it inspired him; he pushed harder, reaching the coastline in less than five minutes. He ran north along the coast for several miles until he reached the end of the estate, demarcated by a thick row of trees that covered the entire northern perimeter of the compound. He turned around and ran hard in the other direction. The sky was growing lighter, and he felt his spirits lift with the rising sun. He dug his heels into the sandy shoreline, pushing harder with each step until he came to the southern border of the property, defined by a trickling stream that flowed effortlessly into the sea. On the other side was another row of nearly impenetrable brush. How he wanted to keep going; to keep running hard and fast to wherever that coastline took him. But he couldn't; he had to turn around. He bristled. *I'm a prisoner on my own estate.*

He made the same loop four more times, finishing as the sun rose over the sea and lit up the entire compound in rays of buttery light. He stopped and watched the sun as it rose higher in the sky, thinking of Maddi and a sunrise they had shared four years ago in a hotel room in Providence. He choked back tears and pounded his thigh with his fist as he stood on the sand and stared at the ocean. *How can she be gone?* he wondered for probably the hundredth time, recalling her smile when he had told her that he liked croissants for breakfast. *"Of course you do,"* she had said with a laugh.

He wondered about her final moments. Had she known she would die? If so, had she thought of him…of that morning in Providence…maybe said a quick goodbye, or even an 'I love you' as she was taking her last breath? He grimaced, his heart so heavy he wasn't sure he could make it back to the manor. Then, suddenly, he knew: *I need to go to where she died…I need to go to the site of the plane crash…and I need to do it soon.*

His father had told him he wasn't ready; he shouldn't leave the estate. He got it; he was a wanted man. But if he didn't go soon, he felt certain he would implode.

He walked down the path to the castle and strode inside, this time through a back door that led to the kitchen. He walked into the oversized mess hall, and smiled at a servant who handed him a plate with bacon and eggs. "Thanks, Carlis."

The man smiled. "Not at all, Mr. Henderson."

Another servant poured him a glass of juice as he sat and wolfed down the breakfast in a few quick bites. He left the kitchen and walked upstairs to his bedroom. He shed his sweats, and, just as he was about to step into the shower, he was suddenly brought to his knees by a horrific pain in his temples. It was followed by an array of red and blue lights flashing in front of him. *Calvin,* he thought. *James Calvin, the man whose face I so ignobly stole from his dead body, has come back to visit me.* The deceased Iraqi war hero hadn't known that he was giving his face to a killer so the killer could hide the awful things he had done…the awful man he had become. Calvin had simply agreed to be an organ donor.

Joke's on him, Henderson thought as he continued to grit his teeth against the pain. *What words of wisdom are you going to impart upon me now, Corporal?* That was what he had done ever since Henderson had co-opted his face. Calvin would give him a glimpse into his life, usually with the goal of teaching him something, or inspiring him to do better, to be better…to be more like Calvin. *And I've failed miserably.*

He opened his eyes, surprised to see that he was no longer kneeling on the bathroom floor; now he was lying on a desert and every part of him was in agony…

"Just let me go! Save yourself…and go! That's an order, Lieutenant!"
"I will not, sir! Now grab onto my arms."

Calvin looked up at the man who was trying to save him. Not only was he his lieutenant, he was also his best friend. Together, they had grown up on the unholy streets of Detroit, endured the rigors of boot camp, and were then sent to Iraq – together – to fight a senseless war. "Leave me, Bill. Just go."

"I won't leave you, Calvin...so shut up and grab my arms."

Calvin lifted his arms to try to grab onto his friend, but his right arm fell back onto his chest. "I think it's broken."

Bill, who had clearly been injured himself, pushed away a scalding tire, along with the front bumper of the trunk. Ignoring the blood spurting from a hole in his chest, he reached down and, with the strength of two men, lifted Calvin from the fiery debris. He carried him a good distance away from the truck, then laid him as gently as he could behind a military jeep. He fell down beside him, just as the truck they had been driving burst into flames.

Calvin coughed. He looked up at his lieutenant. "You saved me, Bill."

The man who had been his best friend for as long as he could remember coughed several times, then simply smiled. "Well, you certainly aren't capable of saving your own ass, Calvin..."

The lights faded and the pain in his temples eased. He opened his eyes, reassured as he saw the four walls of his bathroom. There was no desert, no exploding transport truck, just him alone...with a bathtub, a toilet, and a sink.

He stood slowly, processing the memory. It was odd to think that he hadn't heard from either Calvin or Lili in over a month, then suddenly had heard from them both within hours of one another. And in each instance, the message was the same. Not only the survival of someone from a deadly crash that no one should have survived, but the acknowledgement of a best friend who had been present at the time.

He frowned. *But how does this relate to Maddi?* She had *not* survived the fatal crash, and she certainly hadn't had a best friend anywhere nearby.

He shook his head. Perhaps there was something else from the crash that had survived...a letter, a book. Suddenly, his eyes widened. *The journal...what happened to my journal?* He had given Maddi his journal back in March, when he felt certain he would die saving Roger from Cobra. As a matter of fact, his guilt not only from all that he had done, but his discovery that he had genetic ties to the murderous Cobra had left him ready to die if it meant that Roger could live.

But I didn't die. And, according to Maddi, she had read only the first few pages. But she had held onto it; she had told him that they would read it together. He felt his throat tightening; he swallowed and took a deep breath.

Had the journal been destroyed in the crash? *Of course, it was. Nothing could have survived the impact...or the explosion and the fire that surely followed.* But what if it wasn't? What if that journal had somehow survived? He flinched. It would ruin him. Not only did it reveal his identity as the assassin, Phoenix, but it also told of every terrible crime he had committed over the years...the burglaries, the bombings, the assassinations. That journal was an unequivocal indictment of Martin Henderson.

He thought again about Lili's message, *"Ask her best friend,"* and Calvin's message of how a best friend had saved Calvin. Does a 'best friend' somehow offer insight, either into the location of the journal, or maybe into Maddi's final moments? Henderson had been tortured by what he imagined her last seconds to have been. Would a best friend somehow give him a glimpse into what had happened at the end? Both Lili and Calvin were trying to tell him something...what was it? Did it concern the journal...or maybe even Maddi herself? Maybe her last words before she died?

He shook his head as he used the bathroom sink to pull himself up from the floor. *You're desperate, Henderson...that's all this is...a desperate man's attempt to find something real to hold on to.* He didn't care; it was better than nothing...his first shot at something tangible.

So, who is Maddi's best friend? Though he would have loved to think that it was him, he knew better. He hadn't been a friend to Maddi; as a matter of fact, in many ways, he had been her worst enemy. Because of her fondness for him, she had lost everything. He nearly choked on his self-loathing.

So, who was Maddi's best friend?

Actually, the answer was easy. *Hank...Hank Clarkson.*

He sighed deeply as he stepped into the shower. He allowed the steaming hot water to soothe him as he continued to ponder the visit from the two ghosts.

After about five minutes, he stepped out of the shower, dried off, then walked to his closet and slid into a pair of jeans. He grabbed a sweater, pulling it over his head as he walked barefoot to the window. He looked out on the garden, now awash in the light of an unrepentant sun, and sighed. Hank was Maddi's best friend; he likely knew her better than anyone. *And one of these days, I'll need to talk to him again...if for no other reason than to see the woman I love through that man's devoted eyes.*

CHAPTER 11

Somewhere in Germany

The sun was streaming through the window of the car, blinding Hank Clarkson as he drove down the A-24 highway. He combed his fingers through his thinning brown hair and pulled down the visor. He was exhausted. His head hurt, his eyes were tired, and his heart was broken as he imagined the despair of the woman in the back seat. He looked at his watch. It was almost noon in Germany; the date was October 11th. He and Maddi had been on the run now for over a month-and-a-half.

He checked on his passenger, smiling sadly as he saw Maddi half-asleep in her make-shift bed in the back. It had become her home. She could stretch out and stare at the sky in her refuge in the back of the old black Saab that he had picked up just south of Grodno, Poland. It wasn't luxury by any means, but it had served them well. It was the second car he had stolen since they had left Liepaja.

Getting out of Latvia had been tricky. Fortunately, Cravens' friend, Angelo, had helped them. Per Angelo's instructions, Hank had driven two hours east to Bauska, a small town about twenty kilometers north of the Lithuanian border. With some effort, he had found the feed store where Angelo had told him that someone would be waiting to help him. *"Go to back of store. Tell him Angelo send you."* Hank had parked in front of the feed store, had left Maddi in the car, and had walked to the door. He had opened it, and a small, stooped man, dressed in overalls and wearing a long, thick beard, had come from the back. With dark, Asian eyes, their brightness dulled only slightly by age, and deep creases on weathered cheeks, the old man had reminded Hank of a wise sage from books he had read about Chinese warlords from the twelfth century A.D. The man had looked at Hank over a pair of dirty spectacles. *"Kto ty?"* he had asked, to which Hank had replied, *"Angelo sent me."*

The man had narrowed his already-narrow eyes and had motioned for Hank to follow him. They had walked into a room no bigger than a closet. The floor had been covered in sawdust, with the smell of manure hanging heavy in the air. The man had taken a seat on a rickety stool, and in broken English, had asked Hank to tell him what he needed. After Hank had laid it out, the man had asked him to describe the woman traveling with him. *"She's five-eight, weighs about 130 pounds – maybe 120 by now – with blue eyes and blonde hair that stops just above her shoulders."*

Five minutes later, Hank had left the store carrying a brown paper bag. Inside was 1,000 euros cash, two pairs of glasses, a mustache for Hank, and a shoulder-length brown wig for Maddi. Hank had pocketed the cash, then had pasted on the mustache. He had pinned back Maddi's hair and had covered it with the wig. He had handed her the glasses. *"We'll need to wear these,"* he had said. She had said nothing, but had put them on.

Once the disguises were in place, Hank had carried Maddi into the store and into the back room. The man had snapped their pictures. An hour later, they had left the store carrying a credit card, as well as passports for a Frank and Flora Wilkinson from Billings, Montana. Hank had tried to pay the man, but he had waved him off, saying, *"Angelo will handle it."*

The passports had gotten them across the border not only of Latvia, but of Lithuania and Poland, as well. They had changed cars in Poland – which was where he had found the Saab– and had spent two days recovering in a youth hostel outside Warsaw. During that time, Maddi's ankle had swelled considerably, and her cuts had become angry and red. Hank had gone to a local medical clinic, where he had feigned an illness to get antibiotics. He had then gone to a drugstore, where he had bought antiseptic and bandages. He had gone back to the hostel and had started Maddi on the antibiotics. He had treated her wounds and changed her bandages faithfully every two to three hours. He had also wrapped ice in a towel, and had intermittently held it to her ankle. Somewhere in-between, he had stolen an hour or two of sleep.

They had left the youth hostel two days later and had headed west through Poland. At one point, when he was certain Maddi was asleep, he had turned on the radio to the BBC. It was the first time he had dared to listen for more than a few seconds to anything; he was desperate for news. He had been stunned to learn that President Wilcox had been assassinated only a few hours after Maddi's crash. Which had explained the flags at half-mast that he had seen early on in their journey. He had heard various foreign leaders express their sorrow at the tragedies that had befallen America; the loss of a well-known and well-loved senator, along with the callous murder of a highly-regarded President. Though Hank had done his best to keep Maddi from learning of the Wilcox assassination, he knew it would be impossible to keep it from her for long. Finally, after another day on the road, he had decided to tell her. She hadn't said a word, simply shrinking even further into herself. She and Wilcox had been friends; good friends...allies in an unforgiving town. Not only had she lost everything, but a great man she had admired and loved had been taken as well.

Somewhere west of Warsaw, she had said, *"What should my name be? I've been Cindy, Cynthia, or Maddi for 37 years...what will we call me now, Hank?"* He had sighed, too unnerved to come up with a name. After a few minutes, he had shrugged and said, *"Agnes,"* and they had shared a much-needed laugh.

They had passed into Germany on day eight of their journey.

He had driven further down the highway and, during a brief stop at a gas station, he had seen that Maddi's cuts were getting worse. She was chilled, and had begun to refuse food or water. She needed a hospital. But it would have to be out of the way and small...so small that it wouldn't bother with some of the particulars that a larger facility might be forced to address. After several hours of driving on back roads through northern Germany, he had come to a town, Hagenow, with a hospital at the far edge of town. Knowing that Maddi's wig wouldn't survive a hospital stay, he had stopped at a convenience store and had bought brown hair dye. He had carried her into the bathroom and had dyed her hair in the sink. If she stayed with the glasses, she would still pass for Flora Wilkinson. He had driven her to the hospital, where he had hoped the care was good, and the scrutiny not so good. He had carried her in and had shown her ID. No one had questioned it. There had been a few forms to fill out regarding her past medical history, but that was it. An hour later, an x-ray had shown that her ankle was broken and needed surgery. They had performed the surgery the same day, and had kept her in the hospital on IV antibiotics for three weeks. Hank had stayed in the hospital room with her the entire time. He had slept there, eaten there, bathed there. Once her fever had finally broken, they had removed the IV and had given her oral antibiotics. Hank had then moved her to a nearby hotel. Like the hospital, the hotel was small and nondescript, and had asked little in the way of ID. Even though there was only one camera in the lobby, Hank and Maddi had made sure to stay with their disguises whenever they left their room. It took another two weeks for the fracture to heal well enough for Hank to feel comfortable traveling, and, at his insistence, the doctor had removed her cast. *"It is sooner than I like, sir. She mustn't walk on it for another week, at least."* Hank had promised the man that he would make sure to keep her off the ankle, and they had left Hagenow. Finally, Maddi was on the road to being healed...on the outside, at least.

But the hospital and hotel had taken nearly all his cash, including the money the Asian in Bauska had given him. He had put what he could on the credit card, relieved when it was approved. But he had hardly any cash left. He was tempted to call Angelo for more, but felt he would be pushing his luck. The man had already done plenty; money, ID's, a plan to make Maddi disappear once they got to Spain. It was enough, especially for a stranger, even if he was a friend of Tom Cravens.

It was now noon on Monday, the 11th of October; they had been on the road for 46 days. He needed cash. As he sped down highway E26 toward A261, which would take him to Germany's western region, he batted around how he might get a hold of some money. *I could always rob a gas station,* he thought with a chuckle.

His stomach growled and he sighed. They hadn't eaten since leaving Hagenow, and he looked back at Maddi. "Are you hungry?"

She nodded. "I could eat."

Hank pulled off at the next exit. He found a café and, after spending five euros on two cups of coffee and two muffins, he counted the cash he had left. Less than 200 euros. He had no choice but to call Jenny. She was a banker, after all. She could wire him money...right? But could she wire it to a foreign bank? And which bank would he choose? The only bank Hank had any knowledge of was Deutsche Bank. It was the bank that the U.S. Government often used when overseas transactions were required.

They finished their meal, and he helped Maddi back in the car. He tried to get up the nerve to call Jenny. He didn't even know where she was. Had she gone home to Ohio? She had been in London the last time he had spoken to her. He flinched. *That was over six weeks ago, Hank!*

He drove for another hour, then looked over his shoulder at Maddi. She was sound asleep. She appeared to be sleeping easier now that the ankle was on the mend. He turned off at the next exit, pulled into a rest stop, and took out one of the trac phones. He stepped out of the car and walked several feet away. His hand was shaking as he dialed Jenny's number. He was overcome when he heard her voice.

"Hank? Is that you?"

He cleared his throat. "Yes. I...I can't talk long. Where are you?"

"Home...in Strongsville. Just finishing some last-minute packing."

"Good. I need your help." He paused. "Is there any way that you could wire ten thousand dollars – make that euros – to a Deutsche Bank account. But you can't use my name. Send the transfer to Flora Wilkinson. Put it in your name." He paused. "And maybe use your maiden name, if you can."

"Who is Flora Wilkinson, Hank?"

"Don't worry, Jenny...she's not real. I can't say anything more."

"Hank...are you okay?"

Hank closed his eyes. *I am the furthest thing from okay.* He cleared his throat. "I'm fine, Jenny. Except that I miss you more than you could ever know."

There was a pause. "I miss you, too, Hank." Another pause. "I'll...I'll need time to get the money together."

Hank flinched. He was asking a lot from his ex-wife. "I'm so sorry, Jenny. I'll pay you back...every cent of it."

"Don't be ridiculous, Hank. What's mine is yours...and all that. I'll just have to move some money." She paused. "I'm sure you don't remember, but it's my last week at the bank."

He flinched. He hadn't remembered. "Will you be able to do this?"

"I think so, but I'll need an account number so I know where to send it."

He frowned; he hadn't thought of that. "Okay. Give me a day to open an account in Flora's name."

"I thought you said she wasn't real."

"She's not. Please, just trust me, Jenny." But he could hear it in her voice; she didn't trust him...not completely. And how could she? He had betrayed that trust before...in a big way. How could she not struggle to believe that he wouldn't betray it again. "Jenny, please know that I love you...so much. You have to believe that." He waited; she said nothing. He went on. "Keep the transaction as private as possible," he hesitated, "...and Jenny, I love you. I don't love anyone else the way I love you."

Again, he waited. He could hear her breathing. Finally, she said, "Call me with the account number." The call ended.

Hank grimaced and closed his eyes. He took a deep breath, then walked to the edge of the parking lot. He smashed the phone with a rock, hitting it more times than was necessary. He kicked the pieces in the brush, then ran back to the car. When he got to the door he stopped. He gripped the handle, his eyes closed, his jaw tight. He couldn't let Maddi see him like this. He couldn't let her feel his misery. She had her own misery. He took a deep breath, then opened the door and slid behind the wheel.

He was about to start the car, when a quiet voice said, "I'm sorry, Hank."

He rubbed his eyes and looked over his shoulder. "Sorry for what, Maddi?"

"For all that you're being forced to do for me."

He turned in his seat so that he was facing her. Fighting an awkward urge to cry, he said, "Maddi, I'm doing this because I have a love for you that will never die. It isn't romantic; I know that now, but it's deeper than anything I have ever felt."

She smiled, silent tears falling onto sunken cheeks. "I understand, Hank. I feel the same. I don't know how this journey ends, but I will forever be indebted to you."

He smiled. "As I am to you."

He turned around and started the engine. He eased onto the road and quickly picked up speed. The late afternoon sun was shining in his eyes, challenging the tears that he had somehow managed to hold back. He went to pull down the visor; it was already down. As they eased onto highway E26 and headed west, he thought of Jenny...worried, alone, and completely unsure of him...and of herself. He sighed. *You don't have to worry, Jenny. I love you. I have always loved you. I don't love Maddi more...I love her different. I know that now...and hopefully, when all of this is over, I will figure out a way to make you understand.*

CHAPTER 12

London, England

By early Monday morning, Cobra had secured his new ID, and, using a credit card with the same name, had spent the rest of the morning buying clothes for his new disguise. Soon he would be Oskar Berg, a financial advisor from Stockholm, Sweden. But not today; today he would wear a different disguise; a disguise he had worn many times, and had become quite comfortable with. Today he would be M. Villamor.

He draped the newly-purchased clothes across his bed, then pulled the M. Villamor clothing from his trunk. He smiled at the ease with which he could go back and forth between a notorious killer and two respectable men of means. How easy it would be to simply choose one of those two identities forever, and leave behind the nonstop running from the police, from Interpol, from the bothersome CIA agent. He pulled on a pair of pleated pants and sneered. "Then again, what fun would that be?"

He had taken a shower in a nearby public bathroom, and now felt refreshed as he slipped into a beige silk shirt and a charcoal suitcoat. He lifted a pair of contact lenses from a box in the trunk, touched them to his eyes, then blinked to set them in place. He combed his hair, pulled it in a ponytail, and stuffed it under a brown wig, which he also took from the trunk. He put on a pair of clear glasses and stepped in front of a small mirror, admiring the clean-cut M. Villamor. He leaned closer, staring at the eyes. Though the lamp gave off little light, their green hue was quite apparent. It wasn't the norm for Cobra, whose two eyes were actually a different color from one another; one was gray, the other was blue. Heterochromia was the scientific term. The feature had become one of his most notable traits...*which is why I must hide it.*

He stepped back and adjusted his tie. He was ready. He reached under the bed and dragged out a pair of tall black boots that he had obtained from a man he had killed years ago. *It's not like he was going to need them,* he thought with a chuckle. He pulled them on, then grabbed an ID for M. Villamor from inside the trunk. He slid it in a leather wallet, slipped the wallet in his jacket pocket, and left the apartment. He locked the door behind him and returned the key to its hole beneath the rock.

It was eleven a.m. by the time he left the wharf to walk the five blocks to Victoria Street, where his London bank was located. What he was about to do would be a longshot. For one thing, he didn't know for sure that Hank and his ex-wife had rekindled their romance. For another, even if they had, he couldn't be sure that Hank would reach out to her for cash. But he had no other way to find the man. *It's worth a shot,* he thought as he walked through the massive double doors of the bank.

Because of the large amount of funds that he kept there, he was given VIP treatment, and was soon greeted by the bank's President, a tall, sophisticated man by the name of Gerard Cook. Cobra played his role well, and was soon sitting across from Cook in his oversized office that looked out over downtown London. After a few formalities, Cobra cut to the chase. He alluded to a possible purchase he hoped to make in Dubai. "But first, I'll need to withdraw a thousand euros cash."

"That is never a problem, Mr. Villamor." Gerard called for a teller to come up. When she arrived, he passed on the request. He then waved the teller out of the room.

Once she was gone, Cobra leaned in and said, "Now, on to the purpose of my visit." He paused. "I am here as a courtesy, to make you aware of a multimillion-dollar investment that I'm currently looking at in the Al Shindagha area of Dubai near *Khur Dubay,* which, as you know, is commonly referred to as Dubai Creek."

Gerard's eyes widened. Clearly intrigued, he buzzed his secretary and asked her to bring two glasses and a bottle of his finest bourbon. As the two men shared a glass of Old Forester, Cobra gave the man only enough information to make the deal seem plausible, then pivoted to the actual purpose of his visit. "I can see that you're interested, Gerard, and of course,

I'll want to finance the entire effort through your bank. However, there's a bit of a hiccup," he paused, "...and I may need your help."

Gerard, who had been sitting back in his chair with his hands behind his head, leaned forward and nodded. "Certainly, Mr. Villamor. What do you need?"

Cobra hesitated. "There is a bank in America, in Ohio of all places, that I have learned is being used to try to interfere with my Dubai purchase. It's a local bank, which I'm sure the potential buyer is hoping will allow him to keep his intentions under the radar until the purchase has been finalized. The bank, First National, is located in downtown Strongsville. You'll not see any of the usual names involved in this transaction. I believe they're using a loan officer to source the cash."

Gerard frowned. "That is unusual."

Cobra nodded. "But clever. I have no proof to offer you. Should you choose to assist me, you will have to take my word on the matter."

Gerard nodded. "You have always been straightforward in your dealings with this bank, Mr. Villamor." He paused. "So, how may we help you?"

Cobra nodded. "Your bank, Deutsche Bank, is one of the busiest overseas banks in the world. It is where we must start. After all; if a small bank in America is trying to invest in a multimillion-dollar project in Dubai, it will need to utilize the services of a global bank." He paused. "I'm wondering if there's a way that you could keep an eye out for a large transaction from First National bank in Strongsville, Ohio, to Deutsche Bank or one of its subsidiaries either here or in Europe."

Gerard turned up one eyebrow. "That would be highly irregular, sir." He paused. "For one thing, I'd need to know the ABA routing number for the U.S. bank."

Cobra frowned. "I'm sure a bank of your stature could obtain that number."

"Yes, but to use it to track a monetary exchange 'somewhere overseas,' as opposed to actually being part of that exchange...well, it wouldn't be right, sir."

Cobra nodded. "Yes, I guessed that that might be the case. And I completely understand." Cobra scooted back his chair and made a move to leave.

Gerard stopped him. "Please, wait, Mr. Villamor. Though I don't condone what you have suggested, I am curious. What is the name of the loan officer who is moving the money on the American side of this exchange?"

Cobra had to fight not to grin. "Jenny. Jenny Clarkson." He thought back to the biography he had read on Hank and the woman he had once been married to. *Hank's no dummy. He'll know that Jenny is being monitored for any contact with him.* He added quickly, "...or maybe Jenny Wilson. You should probably look for both."

CHAPTER 13

Washington, DC

Jerome Knight was nervous, which was odd considering the crowd he was about to address. He had been President for over six weeks now and had spoken to this same group of reporters on many occasions. But this time was different. This time, instead of sending out consoling words for the loss of a revered president, or expressions of grief for a senator who had died the same day, or even outrage for the number of shootings that had taken place across the country, this time he was being challenged to actually do something about it. The White House Press Corps were angry...and so was the public. America had had its fill of armed attacks.

From what authorities could tell, the targets were random. And yesterday, the target had been three innocent Americans at a convenience store.

It was raining; he could hear it beating against the windows as he stood at the door to the James S. Brady Press Room in the West Wing of the White House. The very name of that room had come about because of a shooter trying to kill President Reagan in 1981. Knight frowned as he scanned the empty faces. Suddenly, he stopped. A reporter in the second row, a woman by the name of Mary Stowe, had been absent for the last two briefings, but now, clearly, she was back. Black hair, blue eyes, pale skin. Though he had never met her personally, for some odd reason, he felt as if he knew her. He shifted uncomfortably. He didn't know her...not at all. She just happened to resemble a woman whom Knight had once known quite well…a woman whom Knight had once loved…deeply. He coughed; he felt like he couldn't breathe. He coughed again, then took a sip of water. *Get a hold of yourself, Knight.*

He focused on the other reporters in the room. Every one of them seemed upset…angry. And why wouldn't they be? Citizens were being wiped out randomly, one, two, even three at a time. The next target might easily be one of them. Knight could see it in their eyes as they looked up from their notepads. They weren't interested in platitudes or false promises. No, they wanted – they *needed* – answers. Something concrete…a real plan. They needed to hear that all was well…that he had a solution to all of the carnage. The shootings, on top of the assassination of a U.S. President, were a reminder that the world had become unsafe…untenable…unkind.

Again, he caught the eye of the dark-haired reporter. *Quit staring at her, Knight.* But he couldn't. Every time he looked at her, he saw the face of the woman he had loved…the face of Emma Melnikov. *Focus, Knight.*

He cleared his throat as he walked to the lectern, his six-three frame imposing, his dark eyes even more so. He made a point of looking away from Mary to the other side of the room. He was hoping to see another set of eyes to lock onto, another smile to distract him. But no one was as alluring as the woman who looked like Emma.

The Secret Service had gone to great lengths to secure the room. It was what they always did, but there was a new urgency to the task. Only six weeks ago, they had lost a President; they weren't about to lose another one. So, the protection was tight; so tight that Knight felt like he might suffocate. An agent stood on each side of him, and there were four more manning the corners. No one had been allowed to bring bags or backpacks into the room; they had been forced to leave their jackets outside, as well. He got it. James Wilcox had been assassinated on their watch. No one should be able to kill the most powerful man in the world while he is bathing at the end of a long day. The realization had left not only the Secret Service, but all of America more afraid and less confident in a country that had once seemed safe.

He was about to walk to the lectern, when the words of a man he valued greatly echoed in his mind. *"Don't ever forget why you're there, Jerome. Don't ever lose sight of the goal."* That was his challenge. To somehow go from Comforter-in-Chief to Commander-in-Chief, and to bring the country with him.

He looked out at the faces of the men and women of the Press Corps. His hands had begun to sweat. The goal that had been told to him from the beginning suddenly seemed far larger, far less achievable than it had early on. What he was about to set the stage for would shock not only the reporters in that room, but all of America. As a matter of fact, it would shock the entire world; especially the world.

Could he do it? Could he follow through on his mission? He sighed. It shouldn't be that hard...after all, it had been planned for him from the beginning....

"If you want to lead men, my son, you must first be able to conquer." The statement had come from his mentor, Edward Morningstar. "We have been ordained to save this great nation, Jerome...you and I...and we will do it." Knight had learned the tenets of purpose from Morningstar...the simplicity of greatness, the clarity of power...all in preparation for what was to come. Morningstar would often quote Machiavelli, a leader he revered more than most. "Be clever but strong, both a fox and a lion." He would then add his own take, "...and most importantly...trust no one." Morningstar's final mantra, also taken from Machiavelli, had become gospel, every bit as significant as the Ten Commandments or the Constitution. "Remember, Jerome, it is safer to be feared than loved..." to which he had added, "...and it is better to rule than to be ruled." He had repeated these tenets, ingraining them in Knight's mind over and over, insisting that Knight not only be able to say them back, but that he find a way to embody them. Knight had done it; he had internalized those doctrines with the vigor that comes with reverence and devotion.

Then, on Knight's twenty-second birthday, Morningstar had pulled away. "The time has come, Jerome. From now on, you must pretend to know me only as a friend of your uncle's. No one can ever know how deeply we're tied to one another."

Knight had asked, "Why?"

Morningstar's answer: "It could weaken your hand, son. You must stand alone when the time comes. But know this: I will be standing behind you... the wise king to the gallant knight. Go, Jerome, go and be a knight for your king."

The Biblical names of Jacob and Judah had been introduced four years ago; Knight wasn't sure why. All he knew was that, for whatever reason, the mission had gone from Morningstar's vision of a stronger America, to a purpose that Morningstar had begun to portray as Biblical...as being handed down by God Himself.

One of his aides leaned forward and said, "Sir, it's time."

Knight nodded. *Here 'goes.* He took a quick sip of water, then leaned into the microphone. "Once again, we are gathering with a heavy heart. Another shooting has left an already-troubled nation troubled even more." Knight's hands were shaking; he gripped the lectern. "We are only just beginning to learn the details of yesterday's shooting; I promise to keep you updated as I'm made aware." He paused. "But know this...it will not stand. Americans are being murdered, taken too soon, just as James Wilcox was taken too soon." *"Don't refer to him as President, my son...that is your title now..."* "I promise to avenge their lives, just as I continue to avenge his."

He saw Mary Stowe nodding, and he forced his eyes to look down at his notes. *Don't look at her, Knight...don't get distracted.*

"Though my time with Jim Wilcox was cut short, I learned what I needed from him. He welcomed me, taught me, guided me through the corridors of DC. He showed me what truth and integrity look like, and how it was possible to unite even the most bitter rivals." Knight waited for nods of approval; there were none. "I promise to do all that I can to lead this nation through the struggles it now faces; the violence, the anarchy, the loss of faith in everyone and everything. I vow to make these deaths have purpose. I will honor each of these victims in every action I take, with every word I say, and through every deed I carry out as your President."

He leaned forward and gripped the lectern even tighter. "This morning, I have submitted a legislative proposal to Congress that will address not only our gun laws, but the mental health needs of our nation." He nodded. "I'm referring to it as the "Keep America Safe" agenda, and it will involve the addition of 10,000 peace officers, who will position themselves on nearly every corner of America. In this way, I hope to eradicate the sense that Americans must have guns in order to defend themselves. We must then find a way to take guns from those who shouldn't have them, and ensure a system that addresses the mental anguish that compels young men to kill." He narrowed his eyes as he looked out at the rows of reporters.

"We have mourned as a nation, now we must heal as a nation. Then, together, we will rise up and put an end to this cancer that has taken over our very soul."

In the back of his mind, he could hear the voice of his teacher, the man he called father, the king he called Jacob. *"Let them know exactly who you are, Judah; how different you are from your predecessor."*

He cleared his throat. "I will close by saying this: We are about to enter a new day for America; a time of strength and willful defiance against the forces of evil that have crept into the crevices of this country. This is our nation; we are the United States of America, and we will now embark on ridding first our country, then the world, of the pervasive sin of apathy. It is indifference that brought civilizations to their knees; a lack of passion that allowed evil to infiltrate the hearts and souls of the faithful. Well, no more. We, the people of the United States of America, are about to stand strong as we lead all nations to the restoration of their glory in the eyes of God."

He waited. There was silence. The expressions on the faces of the reporters showed concern rather than comfort. Mary Stowe raised her hand; he waved her off. "There will be no questions, Em—." He turned and left the room. *Get out of here, Knight...get out of here now!*

He walked quickly toward the Oval Office. It was done. He had laid down the marker. He would soon set America on a path of righteousness, and the doubt in the eyes of a few would turn first to relief, then to triumph as they saw the truth of his vision. His task was clear; his purpose well-understood. It was up to him, Jerome Knight – *Judah* – to save America from itself, and pave the way for Jacob and his Sons.

TEN DAYS LATER...THURSDAY, OCTOBER 21st, 2004

CHAPTER 14

London, England

Cobra was still sleeping when the call came in on Thursday morning from his banker friend, Gerard. He stretched his arms as he grabbed his cellphone – a burner phone that he had picked up ten days ago – from its charger by his bed. "Yes?"

"Mr. Villamor, it's Gerard Cook."

Cobra's eyes widened. He sat up and threw his legs over the side of the bed. "Hello, Gerard."

"Good morning, sir. I have information for you."

"Finally. It took you long enough. It has been ten days."

"Yes sir, I'm sorry for the delay. But we just got a hit. Not on Jenny Clarkson, but on Jenny Wilson from the bank in Ohio that you mentioned." He paused. "I was able to put out a tracker for the routing number of the bank, on the pretense that I was anticipating a transfer of funds to one of our more illustrious customers. Apparently, the transfer wasn't made until yesterday morning. It was held overnight to allow for confirmation, but it reached the bank this morning."

"Which bank...what location?" Cobra said, trying not to sound too eager.

"It's a smaller affiliate, outside Hamburg, Germany."

"Who was the transfer directed to?"

There was a pause. "Flora Wilkinson...from Billings, Montana."

Cobra frowned. *Who the hell is she?* "And you say this transaction was completed this morning?"

"Yes. It went through less than an hour ago." There was a pause. "The only odd thing, sir, was the amount."

"The amount?"

"Yes sir. Just ten thousand euros." Another pause. "I would think that a buyer looking at a project in Dubai would need to move a far greater amount of cash."

Think Cobra! "Um...yes. Well, I'm guessing this is just a test run."

"A test run?"

"Yes. To make sure that it went through okay."

There was another pause, this one longer. "It has occurred to me, Mr. Villamor, that a bank the size of the bank in Ohio will struggle to move such large amounts of cash."

Again, Cobra was forced to come up with an explanation. "I...I agree. I imagine they'll begin with these smaller transfers. They will then coalesce the funds into the account at the Hamburg branch to be used to make their bid."

Silence. Finally, "Perhaps. So are you prepared to make a counter bid, sir?"

Cobra had gotten what he needed from Gerard Cook, and was losing his patience with the man. "Very soon, Gerard. But first, I need to know the identity of my competitor."

"Do you think it is this Flora Wilkinson?"

"No. I'm guessing that whoever it is, he – or she – is using an alias."

"Why do you believe that someone would go to such trouble?"

Cobra was forced to expand on the lie. "As I said, I think whoever it is, is trying to blindside me." He paused. "Quite clever, actually, but also quite perturbing. The good news is that I have several men in Germany who are well-versed in such things. I'm going to have one of them follow up on this exchange. I should be able to determine the player or players involved from the information that you have so capably given me."

Another pause. "Can you tell me, sir, why it's so important that you expose this competitor?"

Cobra cleared his throat. With as much patience as he could muster, he said evenly, "It's not so much that I need to expose him, Gerard...it's that I need to be ready to do battle with him." He paused. "I believe it was Julius

Caesar who said, *'The greatest enemy will hide in the last place you would ever look.'*"

There was a pause. "Uh...certainly, Mr. Villamor." He cleared his throat. "Please let us know how we can be of service."

"Yes, of course, Gerard." Cobra ended the call before the man could pester him with any more concerns. After all, he didn't have time for such stupidity. He now had a probable location for Hank Clarkson. And if he wanted to find him – and kill him – he needed to get to Hamburg, Germany as soon as possible.

CHAPTER 15

Hamburg, Germany

Hank stared at the bank across the street. He had chosen the branch outside of Hamburg because of its size. It was smaller than most of the Deutsche Bank branches and, though it was affiliated with one of the largest banks in the world, his hope was that tellers at a smaller branch would assist an American traveler with less scrutiny.

Though Jenny had warned him that it might take 'a few days,' it had actually been over a week since he had reached out to his ex-wife. The thought that it had taken her that long to come up with 10,000 euros had sat in his gut like bad sushi. Jenny wasn't a wealthy woman. And though she had likely been responsible enough to have extra cash on hand, 10,000 euros – the equivalent of over 12,000 American dollars – was likely more than she had immediately available. *So, how is she getting the money?* he wondered. He shook his head. She would probably be forced to borrow from her 401K. He grimaced. *I'll pay her back the minute I get home.*

He and Maddi had needed to stay in Hamburg until the money arrived, which meant that they had been there a full nine days. Every afternoon, they had gone into the bank to ask about the *'U.S. transfer.'* And every day it was the same. *"Nothing yet, I'm afraid."* He hoped today would be different. Their money was all but gone.

He had been careful with the little bit of cash they had left. They had needed 100 euros to open the bank account, which had left them with about seventy-five euros to last them for what had turned out to be over a week. They had lived on granola bars, canned beans, and tuna. There had been no money for gas, so they had parked the car in a hiking preserve outside town, using it only to drive to the bank and back. The gas tank sat at empty. Hank's stomach growled. *My stomach sits at empty.*

He stared at the bank and sighed. He was almost afraid to go in. What if the money still wasn't there? Even worse; what if Jenny had become so fed up with Hank's evasiveness that she had decided against sending the cash. He shook his head. Jenny wasn't made that way. She might be fed up with Hank, but she would most definitely come through with the cash. Why? *Because I asked her to.*

But the bank would close soon. If they wanted to get the money today, then they needed to go in now. He frowned. The entire situation made him nervous. What if the delay wasn't from Jenny having to scrounge up cash, but was because the U.S. government was now monitoring the transfer? What if they had confronted Jenny soon after Hank's call, and had hijacked the entire exchange? What if they were letting the transfer go through, thinking they would find Hank, but would then discover that Maddi had survived the plane crash? *Stop it, Hank.*

He continued to stare at the bank. He and Maddi had first walked into that bank nine days ago and, disguised as Mr. and Mrs. Wilkinson, had opened an account in Flora's name. The idea to involve Maddi as the recipient had been a risk. But it had been the only way to create distance between Hank and Jenny. Fortunately, no one had batted an eye. 'Flora' had had proper identification, and had chatted on about how they had made a last minute decision to extend their European vacation, but were running low on funds. *"We're expecting a sizeable transfer in the next few days."*

Maddi had handed the teller the 100 euros, had signed some papers, and the account was opened. They had left the bank and had considered getting a hotel room, but with only 75 euros, Hank was worried the money wouldn't last. He had, instead, driven to a convenience store, where he had bought supplies to get them through the next few days in what would become essentially a camping trip. It was now day number nine, and their supplies were pretty much gone.

That first night, after driving to the hiking preserve, they had slept in the car, but had been lucky to find an empty cabin the following day. Though it was small – no beds, no kitchen – it did have a fireplace. Hank had brought in logs from the forest and they had slept in front of it, using their coats – which they had picked up at a once-around shop in Poland – as beds for the past eight nights. They had showered in a public camping facility, and had occupied the remainder of the daylight hours with short walks and quiet conversation. Maddi had had little to say. She had been through too much. Not only had she survived a crash that should have killed her, but she had left her entire world behind. Hank guessed that it would take quite a while before Maddi would be willing to talk about all that had happened.

They had found a day-old newspaper on one of their walks, and Maddi had read it from top to bottom. It had been a mistake. The assassination of America's President had left a mark on the world, and Maddi had told Hank that her inability to be present during such an unsettled time made her feel as if she was derelict in her duty. *"I'm playing hooky when I should be helping the nation recover from the death of its leader."* Hank had assured her that the decision to fake her death was far more than 'playing hooky,' and that it had been the only option they had had. *"Besides, your presence in DC wouldn't have kept the President from getting shot."* Though Maddi had nodded in agreement, she had said nothing more for the rest of the day.

At Maddi's suggestion, they had taken one of the days to drive into town and go to the local library. *"I want to do a bit of research, Hank."* He had asked for specifics, which she had refused to give, saying, *"Don't worry...I won't go to any sites or use any passwords that might reveal who I am."* They had spent several hours there, during which time Maddi had sat exclusively at a computer, while Hank had found a copy of Michael Grant's *"The Fall of the Roman Empire,"* that had kept him busy for at least a few hours. They had left the library, surprised to see that the sun had begun to set. When they had gotten back to the cabin, Hank had asked Maddi if she had uncovered anything interesting in her research. Her reply: *"No...not really."*

Also at Maddi's insistence, they had taken a day to go to the Hamburg Museum on Holstenwall. She had expressed an interest in a collection of Nazi-era coins, and they had spent over four hours poring over various coins from 1932 to 1945. Maddi hadn't shared her reason for wanting to see the coins, only that her grandfather had told her once, *"...if you ever come across coins from the days of Hitler, pay special attention. They hold great value...and great power."* She hadn't elaborated; Hank hadn't asked.

There had been only one moment during their time at the museum when she had actually become excited. She had been looking at a particular coin from 1939, and her eyes had grown wide. *"I can't believe it's here,"* she had muttered under her breath. *"Can't believe what is here?"* Hank had asked. *"Oh, nothing,"* she had replied. That was it. Nothing more was said about it. They had driven back to the cabin soon after.

The rest of the days had been spent walking the park, with neither of them having much to say. Occasionally, Maddi had asked what Hank thought her future would hold, and he had replied with a simple shake of his head. *"It's hard to say, Maddi...but I'm sure it will be fascinating and fulfilling."* Did he really believe that? No, but what else could he say?

Each day, the advent of winter became more real, as the few leaves still on the trees were forced to the ground by pre-winter gales blowing in from the north. He and Maddi would put on their coats and head for the hiking trails, making sure to walk fast enough to stay warm. Those were the times when it almost felt how it used to. The ease of being with Maddi had amazed Hank from the start. Though he knew now that it wasn't romance that tied them so deeply to one another, they were, most definitely, connected on a level that he doubted either one of them understood.

He stared at the bank as he again checked his watch. It was almost four; they needed to hurry. He looked over his shoulder and nodded. "Okay, Maddi, with any luck, today's the day. You, Flora Wilkinson, will walk into that bank and withdraw 10,000 euros – plus the initial 100 – from the account we set up last week." He paused. "Let's go over it one more time. If they ask, the cash is being wired from your estate back home. Though we reside in Montana, you've maintained ties with the bank where your parents kept their money...in Strongsville, Ohio." He added, "As I said before, I'll be right beside you in case something goes wrong."

Maddi nodded. He watched her as she smoothed down her brown shoulder-length hair, which he had originally dyed in Hagenow before she had gone to the hospital. She had touched it up only once; the morning that they had set up the bank account. She seemed confident; ready for the task. She put on her glasses and stepped out of the car. Still limping, with most of her weight on her good leg, she crossed the street and walked into the bank. Hank was at her side. She went up to a teller who had helped them in the past and smiled. "Hello, Hannah. Shall we try one more time?"

The woman smiled in reply. In rough English, she said, "Good afternoon, Ms. Wilkinson. I think I may have good news."

Thank God, Hank thought, fighting the urge to shout with joy.

"Excellent," Maddi said as she handed Hannah her ID.

The woman took it and typed on her keyboard. She stared at the screen and frowned. She continued to type and continued to frown. Maddi didn't move; but Hank found himself shifting back and forth, doing his best to not appear nervous. Finally, the teller's eyes lit up. "Ah, yes. Here it is. How much do you need, Ma'am?"

"Ten thousand euros, plus the hundred-euro deposit that opened the account."

Hannah's eyes widened. "That is the full amount, Ma'am."

Maddi nodded. "Yes, we shouldn't need to trouble you for any more cash during our stay."

Hannah frowned. "So, we are closing the account?"

"Yes please."

Again, Hannah nodded. "How would you like the bills?"

"Tens, twenties, fifties, and hundred-euro bills, please. Equally distributed."

The woman opened her drawer and began counting out the cash. All the while, Hank stood behind Maddi, ready to grab her and run out of the bank if there seemed to be any indication that something wasn't right.

Suddenly, the woman stopped counting.

Maddi said, "Is everything okay?"

The woman frowned. "Please, give me one moment, Ma'am."

Maddi nodded casually. Hank was impressed with her ability to play it cool. He said nothing, but quietly took her by the arm. It was a silent warning. He could feel Maddi tense, but she didn't visibly react in any way.

Finally, the woman walked from the back, and Hank was pleased to see that she was still by herself. She was carrying a stack of hundred-euro bills. She smiled at Maddi. "I ran out of hundreds."

Maddi smiled, but said nothing.

The woman handed the money to Maddi, counting it into her palm one bill at a time. "Anything else, Ms. Wilkinson?"

Maddi nodded. "No, thank you, Hannah. You've been very helpful."

Maddi tucked the money in her purse, and she and Hank walked casually out of the bank and across the street to their car. Hank got in the front seat, while Maddi slid into the back. Hank's hands were shaking as he pulled out the keys and started the car. He gripped the steering wheel and looked over his shoulder. "You good?"

Maddi chuckled. "I am now...I'm loaded."

Hank laughed and eased out of the parking spot. He drove down the street to a gas station. He filled the tank using some of their newly-acquired cash, then drove straight to the highway, where he headed south on route A261. It was late afternoon, and the sun was in his eyes. He lowered the visor. After about an hour, he looked over his shoulder; Maddi was asleep. He was half-listening to a radio station that played old seventies songs from America and the UK, when a song came on from 1975. He smiled. The song made him think of Jenny. Nineteen-seventy-five was the year that they had started their long and rocky romance. That romance had led to marriage and Roger, not necessarily in that order. It had ended due to Hank's incessant desire for Maddi, but had picked up again only a few short months ago. And now, he was glad to see that even his protracted journey with a woman he had loved for much of his life hadn't disrupted his newfound love for his ex-wife.

He longed to call her. Other than his call to request the money, he hadn't talked to Jenny since that first call eight weeks ago. He knew she was worried. But, what could he tell her? *I've spent the last eight weeks caring nonstop for the woman who came between us, Jenny...no worries.* He shook his head and sighed. He didn't want to lie, but he couldn't tell her the truth. Not even a woman as understanding as Jenny could accept such a situation. *What a mess I'm in.*

Again, he looked over his shoulder. *But not as awful as the mess she's in...*

"Have you ever wondered, Hank, what it would be like to disappear?"

"What do you mean, Maddi? Like a vacation?"

They were sitting in her living room having coffee, the sunrise visible through an open window. *"No, I mean really disappear...you know, vanish."*

Hank frowned. "I can't say that I have." He pulled her closer and kissed her forehead. "Do you want to disappear?"

"Sometimes." She pulled away. "Sometimes I just want to run away and never come back."

Hank frowned. "Why?"
"I don't know...maybe start over; become someone else."
"You're pretty remarkable the way you are."
She laughed and punched him playfully in the arm. "But not as remarkable as I'd be if I were the Invisible Woman..."

Hank rubbed the back of his neck. *Well, Maddi...you got your wish.*

He sighed as he stared at the road in front of him. Clouds were gathering; a storm was coming. Hank enjoyed a good storm. It was like a tantrum; a way for God to clear the air. Perhaps a storm could clear his muddled mind. Only eight weeks ago, he had pulled his ex-girlfriend from a plane crash that had been designed to kill her. He had then whisked her away so the world would think she had died. In the process, he had left his own world behind: his job, his role in overseeing a fugitive, his duty to help the Hendersons navigate a war with Russia, and – most notably – his ex-wife, who had come back into his life after years of them being apart.

But the hardest part was knowing that whoever had tried to kill Maddi was still out there. He had spent hours trying to imagine who might have been behind the crash. Why had they wanted Maddi dead? What would they do now that they thought they had succeeded? And the most troubling question of all: Was her attempted murder tied in any way to the Wilcox assassination? Both tragedies had occurred on the same day. A coincidence...or some horrible plot in play?

He was surprised to see his oil light come on. *Dammit!* he thought. They would need to stop at a gas station. He checked the time. Six p.m. The nearest town, Oldenburg, was only ten kilometers away. They could stop there; check the oil and find something to eat...maybe even get a room in a decent hotel so they could sleep on a bed for a change. But they couldn't stay long. They still had to get through France. Angelo's address was south of Madrid, which meant that Hank still had a country-and-a-half to go; a full two or three days at least.

They came to the exit and, as he eased off the highway, he glanced again at Maddi. He tried to imagine what would happen to her once they got her to wherever her new life was about to take her. Hank would return to the U.S., but what about her? She couldn't go back; she was dead. And he, her former lover, had become her only link to the world. If it wasn't so tragic, it might be funny. He had been given an overwhelming task.

Somehow, he had to get Maddi to a place where she could start over without anyone learning that she had survived. And he had to do it without telling a soul, all while maintaining his role at Homeland Security. More importantly, he had to try to hold onto his relationship with his ex-wife, who had been through far too much in their time together ...*because of my ties to the passenger in this car.*

He sighed as he pulled off the exit and looked for a hotel. In the next few days, he would need to come up with a way to make it all work. Why? *Because the very survival of the woman in the back seat of this car – a woman I have loved for much of my life – depends on it.*

CHAPTER 16

The Henderson Compund

Henderson sighed as he once again greeted the morning outside his old-world bedroom window. He couldn't imagine a better view for watching the seasons pass, and now, as he stared out at the almost leafless limbs of his favorite tree, and saw the angled light over the horizon, he knew... winter was coming. October would soon end, and what would follow would be fleeting days that rolled into long, dark nights. Was he ready? Was he ready for the cold that could cut a man to his very soul? He shrugged. *What does it matter?* In a way, he welcomed it...days that eased so quickly into night that one could hardly see the sun; when darkness dimmed daylight almost in an instant, like a snuffer dousing a flame. *At least I'll be less mocked by the sun.*

He had had no more visits from his ghosts, either Lili or Calvin, but the impact of their messages hadn't left him. Each one had stressed the value of a friend, and how that friend had somehow aided in a person's survival against all odds. Lili had claimed several times now that Maddi was alive, and Calvin had told of his own survival after a fiery blast. Henderson knew for a fact that Maddi wasn't alive; no one could have survived a plane crashing headlong into the ground. Not only that; his parents would never have told him she was dead if there was any chance she wasn't.

As for Calvin, he had, in fact, survived. And his best friend had been the reason why. Had Calvin been trying to somehow relate that to Henderson's survival from the suicide attempt? From what Henderson had been told, there had been no friend involved in his survival; the rope had simply come loose. Not only that; Henderson didn't have any friends...not any more.

He stretched his arms, and was reminded instantly that not only had he come out of a coma two months ago, but he had spent a good portion of the last four years being attacked and beaten in his role as a Morningstar assassin. He had fought off scores of men during his time as a hired killer, and his body still felt every fist, every lead pipe, every gunshot. But he had gotten used to it. As a matter of fact, he saw it as a sort of atonement. *My penance for all that I've done and the many people I've hurt.*

He walked to the bathroom, relieved himself, then washed his face and brushed his teeth. He was about to put on sweats to go for his morning run, when he decided against it. *Too much to do.* Instead, he threw on a pair of jeans and a sweater, and left his room. He jogged downstairs, hurrying out the front door before he could be stopped by either Dora or Walter, who would inquire how he was, how he had slept, if he was hungry. Though the questions were well-intentioned, he didn't want to hear them. He just wanted to be left alone.

He succeeded in leaving the mansion without being stopped, and he crossed over the moat by way of a bridge. He circled around the north end of the house, and crossed again by way of another bridge that was hidden in a clump of trees further north of the manor. As he walked, he breathed in, the crisp fall air almost making him smile. He crept through the trees, sneaking past the barracks where the Henderson army was monitoring every step of Putin's war. Though Henderson had made himself available to assist in that war, he had little stomach for it. Not anymore. He had been through too much; he had seen too much. Did it really matter who were aggressors or who were victims? *At the end of the day, we're all aggressors... and we're all victims.*

He picked up his pace, and was now jogging along a barely visible path to the sound of waves beating against the shore. He neared the Baltic Sea, seeking comfort in the trueness of the tide; the reassuring rise and fall of the ocean. *As predictable as sunrise,* he thought, as he climbed a rocky crag and stood tall against the gales sweeping in from the sea. Constancy: that was what he needed now, and things like the changing of the seasons and the certainty of the ocean tides seemed to provide it.

As he looked out over the bright blue of the Baltic Sea, he was soothed by whitecaps reflecting the sun. He watched for several minutes, astounded at the power of the sea. He had thought about drowning himself...many times. It would be so easy. But after the fiasco of trying to hang himself, he had decided that he would probably float ashore before he could actually take in enough water to drown. All it would do was create more heartache for his parents. *And I've created enough of that already.*

He climbed down the crag and jogged another hundred yards until he came to a clump of trees. He squeezed between two tall oaks, their lush green leaves now a scant yellow/red. He stopped. He could smell fall...wet, musty leaves that lay dead on the ground; the chill in the air as autumn marched rapidly toward winter. For just a moment, it took him back...to childhood...to trick-or-treat...to caramel apples and ghost stories by a fire. But then that fire became an inferno and, as he fought the sensation that he was smothering under a heavy beam, he quickly moved on.

After another hundred yards, he came to a cabin that was almost completely hidden by trees. The twelve-by-twelve cottage sat nestled between evergreens and oaks, and would likely be invisible to anyone passing by. That was the plan, anyway. He and his friends had built the cabin nearly twenty-five years ago, and, as he thought of it now, never had he felt more alive. It was hard to think of those days...when he had still been hopeful, when he had still been kind. His friends, Albins Platacis and Danil Latkovskis had helped him build the cabin in 1978, soon after Henderson's fourteenth birthday. They had just formed their alliance as a band of brothers, and had decided that they would need a place from which to launch their missions. The Three Musketeers, they called themselves. The cabin had been the perfect hideout for three young boys eager to plot deeds of heroism. And, in a sense, Henderson was using it now for the very same purpose. But instead of heroism, he was plotting revenge.

He flinched as he unlocked the cabin and walked inside. He breathed in, the earthy scent of old logs reminding him of the many times that he and his friends had conspired ambushes in that small but perfect room. Over time, the Three Musketeers had become the Latvian Freedom Fighters, and their usefulness had quickly become apparent. Though Latvia acquired its independence from Russia in late 1991, Russian insurgents – led covertly by Vladimir Putin's army – continued their efforts to undermine that independence. It had become the mission of Henderson and his friends not only to suppress such uprisings, but to try to stop them before they began.

Which was why there had been such an elaborate electronic grid in the cabin. Though much of the technology was outdated, the wiring that had been put in place twenty-five years ago had allowed for Henderson – with the help of Mikus, one of the castle's older technicians who had been a friend to Henderson all his life – to update and modernize the entire cabin. But recruiting Mikus to help him had been tricky. Henderson was, after all, claiming to be Matt, Martin's cousin. But he had sensed for the past month that Mikus knew the truth. That fact had quickly been confirmed when he had asked the old man to keep the existence of the cabin a secret: *"No one can know this cabin is here, Mikus."* Mikus had agreed with a chuckle and a nod. *"Don't worry, Marty...your secrets are safe with me...they always have been."*

Between the two of them, they had set up one of the most elaborate tracking systems on the entire European continent. But for Henderson's purposes it would need to be even better. Technology was useful, but it was also easily identified by anyone with satellite access. So, he had researched options to deflect satellite tracking and, with Mikus's help, they had come up with a plan. They had started with a casing known as RAM (radiation absorption material), which they had spread over the entire cabin. They had enclosed it with a unique mesh netting, which would deflect and scatter any radio waves or satellite signals. Finally, at the old man's suggestion, they had shielded the walls and ceiling with aluminum, not only to keep out the cold, but to add one more layer against NSA technology or its counterparts around the globe.

Once the cabin was protected from any and all surveillance, Henderson had put up a dish that was capable of linking him to a long-range satellite that had been put in place by the U.S. Army two years ago. It had allowed him to tie into any network on earth. He only knew of the satellite because of Morningstar; the irony had made him laugh. *He has given me the means by which to ultimately take him down.*

Lastly, because it was not unheard of for him to spend entire days, and even the occasional night at the cabin, he had filled the cupboards with bottled water, canned beans, packets of tuna, and granola bars. He had lied and had told his parents that he was camping; that sleeping under the stars somehow made him feel better.

Why had he gone to such trouble? There were two reasons. The first was that it had taken his mind off of Maddi, at least for brief moments throughout the day. The second reason – which had become an obsession – was to have a place from which to launch his attack on the man who had ruined his life: Edward Morningstar.

For the past two weeks, he had spent hours in his chair, ergonomically designed by 'Helga' to support his broken body, and had learned all he could about the day-to-day operations of the well-connected Pentagon aide. His goal wasn't to try to understand him; he had already mastered that task as the man's protégé for four years. No, he needed to learn the intricacies of his plan; his endgame....*and how I can stop him...forever.*

Though he was fully aware of the evil that Morningstar had perpetrated over the years, there was little he could truly hold over the man's head... except for one carefully-obtained piece of evidence. Henderson had acquired it soon after the Lassa fever attacks in January. It was video feed from an airport bathroom in Dallas, Texas, that showed Morningstar changing into the disguise he had worn when he had poisoned a bus station full of people. Henderson had copied the video onto a flash drive, which he had hidden in a lockbox in a small savings and loan in Boonsboro, Maryland, about an hour from DC. He had gone so far as to taunt Morningstar with the tape. But as damning as it was, Henderson knew that the video alone wouldn't be enough. Morningstar knew it, too. Morningstar had powerful friends. In the face of such evidence, the man would lie and obfuscate, and those who didn't want to believe it would obfuscate right along with him. Especially the Chairman of the Joint Chiefs, Morningstar's boss, Alexander Daniels. The man trusted Morningstar like a son. If Henderson hoped to take him down, he would need more than just the flash drive.

He had originally thought he could stop Morningstar by eliminating his sons. Starting with Clint Molinaro, "Levi," he had picked them off one at a time. Molinaro, who had been Henderson's assistant in his old life before the fire, had been hired by Morningstar to kill Maddi, which had made his murder easier to justify. Henderson's next target had been a man in South Carolina, "Asher," who had also been sent to kill Maddi as she sat at the bedside of the ailing Amanda Madison, Maddi's sister-in-law.

But then things had gotten complicated. Henderson, whose longing for Maddi had become unbearable, had begun to obsess about seeing her again. Concluding that she would never be able to get past the scars that had disfigured the left side of his face, he had elected to try one more surgery, this one far different from the eight he had already endured. The face transplant had been successful, and he had pivoted from seeking revenge on Morningstar, to grasping the possibility of a renewed relationship with Maddi. He had chosen an identity as Matt Henderson, a distant cousin who had died at the age of two. His mistake had been to assume that by changing how he looked on the outside, he could change who he was on the inside.

But his obsession with his newfound shot at life had left the Morningstar sons free to flourish. And flourish they did. Killings, kidnappings, even war had been propagated by the Sons of Jacob while Henderson had indulged his new identity. Then, by some crazy quirk of fate, Henderson's half-brother, Cobra, had kidnapped Hank's son, Roger, a CIA agent who had been tasked with capturing Cobra. Henderson, feeling honor-bound to save Roger, had offered himself to Cobra instead, and had been drugged, beaten, and poisoned. It had ended up consuming six months of his life, which had given Morningstar even more time to put his evil plan in place. Which meant that Henderson now had to dismantle a complex and well-executed blueprint that had progressed to the point where the world was on the brink of war.

But Henderson was hamstrung by his inability to leave the estate. Not only had his father forbade it, but Morningstar had likely put the names and descriptions of both Martin and Matt on every fly list, boat list, and border list that existed around the world. Which meant that however Henderson hoped to stop Morningstar, he would be forced to do it from that ergonomic chair in his cabin in the woods.

He sighed and ran his hands through his thick black hair. It was an impossible task. Though he had been working almost non-stop for the past two weeks, all he had accomplished was to track Morningstar's actions over the past year. What he really needed to learn was what Morningstar was planning for the future; what the sons were up to. And to do that, he would need to be free to roam...free to travel to those places where Morningstar's soldiers were doing the most harm. But first, he would need to find them. They would likely use disguises to carry out their crimes, and would also be inclined to leave the minute they had completed their task. It was, after all, what he had been taught to do. So how would he find them? His only option was to use his technical ability to somehow intercept Morningstar's correspondence with one of them. *Once I do that, I'll have an inside track on their next move.*

His second task – the greater, by far – would be to find a way to then try to undermine their loyalty to Morningstar. If he could gain an ally in at least one of them, he might be able to destroy Morningstar from within. But to do so, he would need to confront the man, face-to-face, which would require him to travel.

He leaned back and sighed. *I can't travel...I can't even leave my own goddamn house.* But there was no question about it: the sons were the path to the father. *Which means, sooner or later, I must leave here...and I must leave Latvia.*

He walked to a small table at the back of the cabin and started a pot of coffee. He looked out one of only two windows as he waited for it to brew. He and his friends had designed the windows so that they would have a view of the coastline. *"We must be able to spot an enemy coming at us by sea,"* they had concluded, with all the bravado of their fourteen-year-old selves. The thought of it made him smile, but the smile was short-lived. All good thoughts and feelings were short-lived.

He turned back to the pot of coffee, poured himself a cup, then carried it to his desk. He sat and angled the three screens in front of him as he powered up his computer. He would start with a greeting to Morningstar; a pop-up on Morningstar's computer with a subliminal message that said "Morningstar is a monster." It would appear in a flash, then leave. Morningstar wouldn't actually have time to read it, but it would register somewhere in his mind, and would, at least, unsettle him.

He logged in using four different passwords, and was about to enter his greeting to Morningstar, when his cellphone rang. It wasn't the phone he had carried for years; that phone had been taken by Cobra back in March. This was a flip phone his father had given him a few weeks ago. Henderson didn't even know the number.

"Hello," he said, distractedly.

"It's Walter. Where are you?"

"Out for a walk. Why?"

"I have something I need to discuss with you."

Henderson frowned. Walter rarely called him. Whatever it was that he felt he needed to discuss must be important. "Okay. I'll be home in a few minutes."

He quickly sent Morningstar the subliminal message, then shut down the computer. He turned off the coffee pot, but left his nearly-full cup on the table. He would be back once he talked to Walter.

He ran out the door and jogged the two miles back to the castle. His father was waiting at the back door. "Come with me, son."

Henderson followed him into his office. Though it was a bright morning outside, the drapes were closed, leaving the room dark with only a lamp in the corner to offer any sort of light. "What's up, Dad?"

Walter frowned. He looked older in the shadows; his black hair had turned mostly gray, and his eyes looked tired. "Have a seat, son."

Henderson sat in a stiff chair across from Walter, who sat behind his desk. The older man ran a hand through his hair and sighed. "There's something I need to ask you about."

"What is it, Dad?"

"Two months ago, on that terrible night when you...jumped...I found a letter. Apparently, you had written it thinking...you wouldn't come back." He cleared his throat. "Anyway, you talked about Morningstar. Were you referring to Ed Morningstar?"

Henderson had forgotten about the letter. He tried to remember what it said. "Do you have it...the letter, I mean?"

Walter unlocked the top drawer of his desk. He pulled out a scrap of paper and handed it to Henderson.

Henderson took the paper, gripping it with trembling hands as he recalled the utter despair he had felt as he had written what he had expected would be his final words...

Morningstar has secrets. He carries burdens of sin that would shame the devil himself. Lassa fever, Argentina, Al-Gharsi...A desperate man pulled the trigger, but Morningstar pulled the strings. Morningstar has secrets. Stop him. Stop Jacob...and stop his sons...

Henderson simply stared at it, saying nothing.

Walter cleared his throat. "How do you know him, son?"

He forced me to join his family of outlaws and kill innocent men. "It's complicated, Dad. Let's just say...for a period of time, I had an inside track on him."

Walter narrowed his eyes. "These are some hefty allegations."

Henderson frowned. "Yeah, well, I may have jumped the gun on this. Can you keep it to yourself...at least for now?" Henderson folded the note and slid it in his pocket. "But I'm curious...why didn't you say something sooner?"

"I was waiting for the right time."

"And is that time now?"

Walter leaned back. "Yes. I received a call late last night from a woman in America; she says her name is Claire...Claire Porter. Have you heard of her?"

The name seemed familiar. "I can't place her. Why?"

"Apparently, she was Maddi's therapist." He paused. "She called because, as she put it, there was something I needed to know."

Henderson narrowed his eyes. Now he remembered her. He had tracked Maddi to her office on a cold morning back in January. He nodded. "Go on."

"She asked if I knew that...my son – you – were alive."

Henderson's eyes widened. "And what did you say?"

Walter sighed. "I told her that I was going to hang up."

"And?"

"She pleaded with me not to. She said that she had information for... my son. Information from Maddi...that she could only share with him."

"What did you tell her?"

Walter shook his head. "I had no choice but to reaffirm that you died in a hotel fire four years ago." He flinched. "I don't know what you did the past four years, son," he held up his hand, "...and I don't want to know, but Phoenix is a wanted man...for far worse crimes than whatever Matt is wanted for. Keeping your identity secret is the right move, wouldn't you agree?"

Henderson offered a solemn nod.

Walter went on. "She insisted I take down her number in case I reconsidered."

Henderson shook his head. "It's weird that she would call you."

Walter nodded. "That's what I thought. I asked her how she justified betraying a client's confidence. You know what she said?"

"What?"

"That it was an appropriate thing to do when someone might be in danger."

Henderson frowned. "That's intriguing."

"I asked her to elaborate. She refused. She insisted on talking only to you."

"What do you think I should do?"

"What do you want to do?"

"I'd like to speak to her." Henderson paused. "Clearly, I or someone close to me must be in some sort of danger."

Walter shook his head. "I don't think you should call her. You risk quite a lot by letting one more person know who you are."

"But she already knows."

Walter sighed. "So she says, but the whole thing sounds suspicious. I'm having one of my men look into it...into her." He paused. "But there's one other thing she said that I found curious."

"What's that?"

Walter stared at his son, his blue eyes nearly black in the dim light from the lamp. "She said that what she needs to tell you involves a man named Morningstar."

CHAPTER 17

Oldenbburg, Germany

Cobra looked around at the pathetic bar where he had spent the last seven hours. He had arrived in Oldenburg, Germany at three in the morning, and had been too exhausted to drive any further. So, he had found a bar that was about to close, and had hidden in a small broom closet until it opened again an hour ago, at ten a.m. He had managed to sleep for about five hours, which should be enough to get him through at least the next several days. As he looked around the tavern, he chuckled at the loyal patrons who couldn't seem to start their day without a shot and a beer.

"What a sad and surly lot
A bare-breasted lady and a thin-haired sot
They drink their pilsner with a shot
And make believe they are who they're not
They lie about the fish they caught
Then lie some more 'bout wars they fought
They stay until their souls are bought
By he who dwells in the sewer rot."

He chuckled as he walked to the far end of the bar. *My wit knows no end.* He sat on an old stool that had clearly seen better days, and rested his elbows on the bar.

A barkeep walked over to him. "Was kann ich ihnen besorgen?"

Cobra frowned. "Kaffee," he said, using the German pronunciation that he had mastered somewhere along the way.

The barkeep nodded and went to get him a cup of coffee. Cobra pulled out his laptop and set it on the bar. He was still on the trail of Hank Clarkson. A week-and-a-half ago, at around nine a.m., Clarkson's ex-wife had wired 10,000 euros to a Deutsche Bank somewhere outside Hamburg, Germany. The minute Cobra had learned of it, he had taken a train out of London, had changed trains in Paris, and had reached Hamburg at ten at night.

He had gotten a room for the night, and had visited the bank first thing the following morning. He had worn the disguise he had purchased in London, Oskar Berg, Financial Advisor, and, claiming to be an EU bank regulator, had asked about an exchange that had taken place the day before involving Flora Wilkinson and a U.S. bank. The teller, backed up by her manager, had insisted that she couldn't discuss such a thing without a written notice from either the customer, or the President of the European Council. Something about *a client's right to privacy.* Cobra had wanted to kill every last one of those tight-lipped bankers. But he had held off. It would do him no good to become the target of an investigation while using his new ID.

So, he had used a different tack. He had asked the teller to look at the photo of Hank that he had kept from his journey to Latvia, and simply confirm or deny that a man resembling him had escorted a Flora Wilkinson to their bank the prior morning.

The woman had considered it. Quietly, quickly, she had said, *"It could be him. But if it is, he was wearing a beard, a mustache, and a pair of glasses."*

Cobra had thanked her. It was good enough. He now had three very important pieces of information. One: Hank had most likely been in that bank less than twenty-four hours ago. Not only had Cobra's London banker confirmed that 10,000 euros had gone to Flora Wilkinson from Jenny Wilson by way of that bank, but the teller had verified that a man resembling Hank had been there with the mysterious Flora. Two: Hank was likely wearing a beard, a mustache, and glasses. Three: if it was Hank, then he wasn't traveling alone. He was with Flora Wilkinson. Was that her real name? It didn't matter. Her ID had clearly passed the rather steep standards of an overseas bank, which implied that if she was wearing a disguise, then she had gone to a lot of trouble to obtain it. Who was she?

Was Hank trying to protect her? If so, why? Or, had he simply used her to obtain the cash, so that he didn't have to expose his own identity? He sighed. So many questions, so few answers.

Once satisfied that he was on the right track, he had left Hamburg and had taken a bus heading west. Whenever the bus made a stop, he would flash his photo of Hank to area merchants, making sure to add that the man was likely wearing a beard, a mustache, and glasses. He had gotten nowhere.

Finally, after a full day of no success, Cobra had left the bus and had walked to a diner. After finding a booth and ordering coffee, he had opened his laptop and, using hacking skills he had acquired after one of his longer lapses of time, he had hacked into all bus stations, airports, and car rental companies in Germany. Neither Hank Clarkson nor Flora Wilkinson was listed on any of the manifests.

The following day, after spending the night in a cheap hotel, he had hopped another bus, which had taken him into Germany's western region. It had stopped at a town outside Osnabruck, where he had stayed at another cheap hotel. He had gone through the same routine of asking shop owners and gas station attendants if they had seen the man in his photo. They had not. Feeling desperate, he had resorted to hacking into interstate highway video footage; another trick he had learned during one of his lapses of time. It had been tedious, to say the least. For one thing, there was a preponderance of tape, and most of it was of low quality. So, he had simplified the task by looking only at video from rest stops and gas stations between Hamburg to the north, and Stuttgart to the south. That was when he found his first hit. Four days ago, a man resembling Hank had stopped at a gas station outside Oldenburg. Cobra had immediately taken a train to Oldenburg, and had arrived at three a.m. It had been too late to get a room – middle-of-the-night check-ins draw far too much attention – which was how he had wound up in the bar.

He stifled a yawn as he waved his empty cup at the barkeep. "Mehr Kaffee," he said with a crisp German accent. The barkeep poured him another cup. Cobra laid a ten-euro bill on the bar. He sipped the coffee, trying to come up with his next move. He had gotten close to finding Hank with the hit at the Hamburg bank, and, because of highway video footage, he was fairly certain that Hank had stopped in Oldenburg. Clearly, Hank was heading south. Or was he? Was he even in Germany? Cobra scoffed.

For all he knew, Hank had left Europe and was now hiding away on some distant continent. *I could very well be wasting my time.* But it was all he had. Either he continued tracking the man who resembled Hank; the man who had been to Hamburg, then to Oldenburg; or he give it up and forget ever taking possession of the castle in Latvia. He flinched; losing the castle wasn't an option. *I'll keep going.*

In one frame of the video footage, Cobra thought he saw a shadow in the back seat of Clarkson's car. He had rewound the tape to look at the seconds before and after, but could tell nothing other than the make of the car. If it was Hank, then he was driving a dark-colored Saab. Good information, for sure. But what about the shadow? Was it his banking cohort, Flora Wilkinson? If so, why was she traveling in the back of the car instead of the front? Cobra's only conclusion: *Flora is on the run.*

He looked out the window of the bar. It was hard to see; the hazy glass was covered with half-a-century of spattered liquor and cheap cigar smoke. But he could see enough to know that he was a half-block from a gas station. He could also see several shops, a diner, and a convenience store on the way to the gas station. He sipped the coffee and sighed. As he had done for the past two days, he would start at the first shop, show the shopkeeper his photo of Hank, mention the beard, the mustache, and the glasses, and keep going until he reached the gas station.

He finished his coffee, then left the bar and started walking. He stopped at the first shop. He would use the same ruse that he had for the past two days: He, Oskar Berg, Financial Advisor, was trying to find the man in the photo so he could inform him of an inheritance that would be turned over to the bank if it wasn't claimed by the end of the month. Cobra had learned long ago that people responded far more favorably to the notion of helping someone than they did if they thought they might get an innocent man in trouble with the law.

He walked into the shop and went up to a clerk who was marking tags. "Good morning, Ma'am," he said in crisp, clear German. He flashed his ID. "My name is Oskar Berg. I represent the Suisse National Bank in Stockholm." He showed her the photo of Clarkson. "I'm looking for this man so I can inform him of a recent inheritance. Please consider that he may have grown a beard and mustache, and that he could be wearing glasses." He paused. "My challenge is this; if the man doesn't claim the inheritance by the end of the month, he will lose it. Have you seen him?"

The woman looked closely at the photo, then shook her head. "Nein."

Cobra thanked her, then left the shop. He went through the same spiel at the next three shops. No one had seen anyone resembling the man in his photo. He walked into a convenience store at the end of the block and again recited his speech. The man at the counter looked long and hard at the photo. In German, he said, "I may have seen him a few days ago. Only he looked a bit more ragged than he does here."

Cobra's eyes widened. "Did he happen to say where he was going?"

The man frowned. "No. But as you can see, we have construction at the end of this road. The man asked me the easiest way to get around it to the A261 highway."

Cobra thanked the man, and asked him if he had seen what make of car the man was driving. The man shook his head and Cobra left the station. He walked two blocks to a rental car company and rented a light blue 2004 Toyota. He handed the clerk his fake ID, along with a credit card bearing the same name. The card was tied to a Swiss bank account, and there was five thousand dollars of credit on the card. It was standard for Cobra IDs. Not too much money, but not too little. The card went through, and the man handed Cobra the keys. "Happy driving," he said with a grin.

Cobra smiled. "Happy driving, indeed."

He found the car and got in. It was nothing fancy. *It will do,* he thought. The A261 highway traversed Germany from north to south. The man at the convenience store had said that Hank, if it was Hank, had asked how to get to the A261 highway. Which meant that he was either heading north or south. He had spent the last two months heading south; it wasn't likely that he would suddenly start heading north. It was a safe bet that if Cobra followed A261 south, the odds were better than fifty-fifty that he would run across his target. It was a long shot, but Cobra had learned long ago that long shots – along with a bit of persistence – nearly always paid off.

> *"Dressed in black, I stake my claim*
> *For fear and darkness are the same*
> *And as I feel him skulk away*
> *I laugh, for I will catch my prey*
> *Persistence is the key, I've found,*
> *No matter if he's underground*
> *Or if he's changed his name and face*

Or moved to some exotic place
I'll find him if I stay on track
And then I'll kill him, dressed in black."

He chuckled and turned on the engine. "I'm coming for you, Clarkson."

CHAPTER 18

Washington, DC

"Last night's shooting in Little Rock, Arkansas marks the sixth in just two months of lone gunman attacks. This time, the victim was a young mother of two who had walked outside to see the sunset. The shooter, a middle-aged man with ties to the military, yelled that mankind was doomed before he fired randomly in the direction of her house. Coming on the heels of so many other shootings, Americans are desperate for a solution. President Knight has vowed to address the issue, but will his "Make America Safe" initiative be enough to satisfy a citizenry desperate for answers? Especially considering Knight's long-standing support of the second amendment."

The sun had just begun to rise over the DC skyline as Edward Morningstar sat in the back of a cab and listened to the breaking news on the radio. He grinned. *Things are coming along nicely.* The taxi pulled to the curb, and he paid the fare. He grabbed his briefcase, stepped out, and walked the half block to the Morgan Building. He wasn't a tall man, but his steps were long and confident, and he covered a lot of ground with just a few strides. His telltale limp, an unpleasant relic from childhood, slowed him only a little as he made his way to a flight of stairs. When he reached the top step, he stopped; he could smell rain in the air. He liked rain...it was like a purging from God. *And who doesn't love a good purging.*

It was late October, and the air was cold. *Winter is on the way.* Inspired, he raised a hand in the air as he quoted Shakespeare. "O, that that earth, which kept the world in awe, should patch a wall to expel the winter flaw!" He chuckled and pulled his overcoat tighter around him as he jogged the rest of the way to the door.

He had a meeting to attend. The Bentley Group, a secret cabal comprised of seven of the most influential men in the country, met nearly every Monday morning at eight. Though their meetings were always consequential, today's meeting would be even more so. Morningstar was about to update them on the status of what had become a very chaotic world. *Thanks to me,* he thought as he crossed the lobby to the elevator. With the help of a secret army of soldier-sons, he had skillfully orchestrated several high-profile murders, and had even brought about a threat of war that had thrown the countries of the west into a full-fledged panic. But the biggest coup of all had taken place just two months ago on America's own soil. A menace had come out of nowhere and had assassinated the President of the United States...*while he was watching TV in the tub.* Morningstar chuckled as he hurried to the elevator.

Because of the upheaval, the Bentley Group's favorite arms dealer, Silverton, was selling weapons at a record pace. Though he could pat himself on the back for much of it, he had to give credit where credit was due. It was his sons who had carried out most of the killings, and it was Zebulun – a fiercely devoted Russian expatriate – who had managed to get close enough to Wilcox to put a bullet through his brain.

Morningstar didn't know how Zebulun had pulled it off; he didn't need to know. He was confident of one thing, however; the weapon he had used – a yet-to-be-released prototype – would be impossible to trace. According to Silverton, who was the maker of the prototype, the gun left no casings, no grooves in the shells; nothing to tie it to a weapon or a shooter, which meant that there was nothing to tie it to Morningstar. And there were only two prototypes in the entire world; one in DC, the other in Israel. The gun he had used had been 'borrowed' from the DC vault by Silverton employee Bernard Kuntz, who just happened to be one of Morningstar's stooges. Kuntz had given the gun to Zebulun, who was to use it to kill Wilcox, then get it back to Kuntz as soon as possible. *"The gun holds seven bullets. Make 'em count, Zebulun."* Morningstar had yet to receive confirmation that the gun had been returned, but felt certain it had. After all, it had been over two months since the hit.

He and Zebulun had spoken only once since the assassination, when Zebulun had called to tell him that it was done. Morningstar had instructed him to lay low for a couple of months, while the country carried out what Morningstar had rightfully predicted would be a full-scale manhunt in search of the President's killer.

And of course, there had been the weeks of mourning for the loss of the beloved President. Not only had Wilcox been one of America's more popular leaders, but he had been gunned down in cold blood, which hadn't happened since JFK in 1963; it was a big deal. Though Morningstar had forced himself to publicly mourn along with the rest of the nation, he had failed to see what all the fuss was about. Wilcox had always seemed weak to him; too willing to compromise. *We need strength, not diplomacy,* he thought as he stepped into the elevator.

Fortunately, Jerome Knight was just the man to deliver it. But Knight was relatively new to the inner workings of DC. He had only become Vice-President about six months ago and, already the youngest VP to ever hold the job, Knight had been forced to step in and fill the shoes of the highly regarded James Wilcox. But Knight was doing well; as well as could be expected, anyway. Morningstar felt confident that in another month or two, Knight would have the country's full support. He possessed a sense of purpose that was rare for a man his age, and his command of words and his commitment to action, along with his firm sense of honor, would soon inspire and heal a nation that had been mired in tragedy.

Or so we hope, Morningstar thought as he stood alone in the elevator. He pulled out an access key and slid it in a slot overtop a row of buttons. He was quickly taken to the top floor. The doors opened and he stepped into a windowless, well-appointed room. He breathed in the blended scents of strong coffee and expensive cigars. He smiled as he saw the six men sitting around the table. They were waiting; waiting for his guidance. There were no longer bodyguards manning the door; the need for them had vanished once the Vice President, James Conner, had 'resigned' from the group – and the Vice-Presidency – seven months ago. Though Morningstar had been responsible for Conner's ouster, there were times when he missed the man. Conner had been the only one with enough backbone to challenge him. But Conner's departure couldn't be helped. The only way to propel Knight to be Leader of the Free World was to force the VP to step down. Then, helped along by a well-placed word and a stellar resume, Knight had become the logical choice to replace him. Once Knight had become VP, all that was needed was for the President to be removed from office. *And, lo and behold, the poor man was assassinated.*

Morningstar walked to the back of the room, took off his overcoat, and hung it in a closet. He walked to a buffet and poured a cup of coffee. He carried it to his chair and sat down. "Good morning, gentlemen." There were a few mumbled greetings. He set his briefcase on the table and pulled out a document. "Let's start by reviewing how things stand." He put on reading glasses and skimmed the document. "Germany has increased arms purchases by twenty percent. And, thanks to a relationship forged by our newest member," he nodded at DC's fifth circuit judge, Matt Carson, "... Silverton Industries has sold them nearly all of those guns." He adjusted his glasses. "The UK has ordered three new fighter jets, Spain has purchased six missiles, and France has requested two top-of-the-line infantry tanks." He looked at the men and grinned. "And here's the kicker: The United States has just ordered a doubling of arms for every branch of government; Army, FBI, CIA, Special Forces, Secret Service. The nation is on high alert, which has implemented a need for a whole lot of weapons." He chuckled as he removed his glasses and slid them in his pocket. "Best of all, my friends, our greatest obstacle, the lovely senator from Indiana, is no longer here to stop us." He grinned. "Such an unfortunate accident."

The men at the table shifted uncomfortably. Morningstar returned the document to his briefcase. "Gentlemen, I'm guessing that we have increased sales by nearly forty percent, which amounts to...." he pretended to calculate ".... oh, I don't know, about a million apiece?" He laughed and reached for a cigar from a box on the table. He lit it, then leaned back and blew a perfect smoke ring into the air.

Judge Carson said, "That's all good and well, Morningstar, but we might have a problem."

Morningstar flinched. He focused on his cigar, ignoring the comment. *Somebody always has to kill my buzz.* The room was silent as he blew another smoke ring in the air. Finally, he said, "And what might that be, Judge?"

Carson cleared his throat; he was nervous. Morningstar grinned. *It's good that they're afraid.* The Judge's voice shook as he said, "Um, my friend in Germany...he's been in contact with a member of the Mossad."

"So?"

"Well, as you know, Morningstar, Silverton has been working with the Mossad to create a new type of assault weapon."

Morningstar tensed. They all knew all about the prototype. They hoped to make a mint once the item was released. But none of them knew that Zebulun had used it to kill the President. "I thought it was still in production."

"It is. But apparently its signature has appeared on a high-profile hit."

Morningstar adjusted in his seat. "What signature? The point of the prototype is that it *has* no signature."

Carson nodded. "That's what I thought, but somehow it was identified."

"By who?"

"Whoever investigated a hit done a few days ago...here in DC."

Morningstar relaxed. *Wilcox was shot two months ago...in North Dakota...it isn't him.* Nonetheless, his legs had begun to shake; he quickly crossed them. "Who was killed?"

"Some lowlife attendant at a gas station."

"And we're sure it was with the prototype?"

Carson nodded.

Morningstar flinched. *Shit Zebulun! What the hell did you do?* He had begun to sweat. He pulled a handkerchief from his jacket pocket and wiped his forehead. "How on earth would someone gain access to the weapon?"

Carson shook his head. "I don't know. My contact in Mossad swears their gun hasn't left Tel Aviv. And, since there's only two – one in Israel, the other here in DC –" Carson swallowed nervously, "—I concluded that ours must be the one. So, yesterday, I checked with a confidante at Silverton. He went to the vault." He swallowed again. "The prototype is gone."

Morningstar gulped the coffee. The shaking in his legs had gotten worse, and he put his hands on his lap to try to calm them. "Well, they just need to get it back. I still don't see the big deal. Some lowlife gas station attendant gets killed by a new type of weapon...so what?"

Carson shifted in his seat. "Um...apparently sir, that same gun was used two months ago...to assassinate the President of the United States."

CHAPTER 19

Washington, DC

Short, stocky Vladimir Karev – *Zebulun* – was standing tall, one foot on the ledge of the ferry that was carrying him across the Potomac. *Like George Washington crossing the Delaware on Christmas night in 1776,* he thought as he puffed out his chest. It had just started raining. He watched as raindrops hit the water and formed tiny spouts, reminding him of the geysers on Kamchatskiy Krai. That krai, on a far-removed Russian peninsula in the Sea of Okhotsk, was just one of the places where Zebulun's father had been sent – banished – by the tyrant, Putin. Vladimir grinned. *But my payback has begun.*

Ignoring the rain, he removed his hat, still trying to adjust to the short hair and shaved face that Jacob had insisted on once he had completed his hit on the leader of the free world. Other than when he had crept into the States five months ago, he had had a beard for as long as he could remember. He stroked his bare cheeks and sighed; he felt naked. But the cause was just. He had been called on by one of the wisest men he had ever met to perform a task that would etch his name forever in history books.

He was surprised he was still a free man. It had been two months since he had killed James Wilcox, and, though the hit had been planned to perfection, it shouldn't be so easy to kill the President of the United States...let alone get away with it.

And he hadn't expected to. He had accepted the assignment as a suicide mission, never dreaming he would not only pull it off, but would escape untouched. *"No matter what happens, Zebulun, you must never tell who you are, why you are here, or who you know in America. Got it?"* Zebulun got it. He felt no need to give up Morningstar, the man who had inspired the hit. But he remained stunned that he had so easily killed the most powerful man in the world...*while he was watching TV!*

Ironically, Wilcox had made it easy. He was running for re-election, and had chosen to 'tour the heartland.' And, though security was unbelievably tight, it was never as good on the road as it was while the man was tucked away inside the hard-wired safety of the White House. So, Zebulun had planned the hit around the travel schedule of the President, the details of which had been a well-kept secret...*except to a uniquely-placed Pentagon aide.* The stop in North Dakota, which had seemed like a last-minute decision when it was announced, had been planned well ahead of time. And, though the President's advance team had already begun securing the hotel and all stops leading to and from, Zebulun had been one step ahead of them.

He had snuck into America in early June, holed up in the bilge of a European tanker. He was carrying a visa, forged by a friend of Jacob's who worked in the State Department. He had had to cut his hair and shave his beard, but it had been worth it. The visa, identifying him as Zeb Kabinov from Estonia, had allowed him to evade the long arm of Russia's Putin, who had issued an alert at every major airport, seaport, and train station around the world in search of his AWOL soldier, Vladimir Karev. Describing Karev with long black hair and a heavy beard, the alert offered a million-ruble reward; about sixteen thousand dollars American. Not an oversized amount as far as rewards went, but enough that a motivated American might think twice were they to see a bearded man with long black hair arriving at an east coast shipping port.

Once he was safely in the U.S., he had grown his hair and beard, and, going by his actual name, had been the one to kill the President. A bearded Vladimir Karev had done the hit, while a clean-shaven Zeb Kabinov had walked away scot-free.

But in order to succeed with the assassination, Zebulun had been faced with two challenges. The first was to get close enough to the President to kill him. That challenge had been met by moving to North Dakota in late July, nearly a full month before the President's tour. He had secured a post as an IT specialist at the same hotel where Wilcox would be staying. He had been hired with little fanfare, thanks to a powerful resume supplied – once again – by Morningstar's mole in the State Department.

By the time he had interviewed for the job, he had regrown the beard. Though it wasn't nearly as long as it was in his Vladimir Karev ID, it was long enough to allow him to use the old ID, hopeful that Putin's reach didn't extend to a hotel in Fargo, North Dakota. How perfect to pin the assassination of the American President on a man who was also wanted by Putin. Both governments could unite in their efforts to find him. *My own version of Perestroika,* he thought with a chuckle.

Morningstar's State Department friend had given a him an impressive dossier, which he had mastered quickly. *"I am Vladimir Karev. My parents emigrated from Russia in late eighties when I was just a boy. They moved to Chicago to live near family. I was educated in Chicago's public schools. I learned auto mechanics at a trade school. I couldn't find work in Chicago, so I traveled to my cousin's home in Oregon. I took computer courses to boost resumé, then learned of job at hotel from my cousin's best friend, who lives here in North Dakota. Though I have only been here a few months, I hope to make a life in North Dakota, where the sky is as big as my native Siberia."*

The hotel had done a basic search prior to hiring him, the details of his life having been created and reinforced by Jacob's plant in the State Department. By the time Wilcox had arrived, there had been no question as to Zebulun's legitimacy. He, Vladimir Karev, was the bearded IT guy who had moved from Oregon about a month ago.

The second challenge had been to find a gun that could evade the security of the Secret Service. It just so happened that Jacob had had the very weapon Zebulun would need. Shaped like a small notepad, the device could be converted to a pistol with the flip of two hidden switches, which would be programmed to respond to the thumb and index fingerprints of the user. Jacob had made it clear that he wanted the weapon used only once. *"Then you must go back to DC and return the gun to Kuntz."*

On August 26th – eight weeks and four days ago – the President had come to North Dakota as planned, and Zebulun, a member of the staff of the five-star Hotel Donaldson, had moved into action. He had tucked 'the journal' in his back pocket, had made sure that his hotel ID was in place, and had lined up for inspection by the Secret Service agents. He hadn't flinched when they had pulled the journal from his back pocket and had thumbed through it. For legitimacy, Zebulun had made entries about his new life in North Dakota. They had handed it back to him and he had returned it to his back pocket, hiding a grin at how easily he had fooled them.

Two days before, he had disabled a camera at the service entrance, replacing it with a continuous loop of an empty entryway. He had enabled a remote-control device that would allow him to turn on the replacement feed whenever he wanted, so he could go in and out without being seen by the agents who were monitoring the exits. He had done the same to the hotel's closed-circuit TV system, pulling in a loop of feed that showed an empty perimeter whenever he needed to navigate the premises.

The President had spent the day greeting well-wishers and had retired early. Once Zebulun was certain that Wilcox had been tucked in for the night, he had turned on the empty video feed, had come in through the service entrance, and had stood in the hallway, waiting for the call that he knew would come. Morningstar had told him about a peculiar habit of the President's. Any time Wilcox was on the campaign trail, he would soak in a tub at the end of each day and watch news coverage of his visit. So, the day before, during a routine inspection of the President's quarters, Zebulun had loosened a wire in the bathroom TV set, which would cause the picture to fade in and out. As expected, the call came within minutes of Zebulun reaching the service entrance. He had trotted up to the suite and had knocked, surprisingly calm...

The door was answered by a tall Secret Service agent who quickly frisked him. The agent found the journal in Zebulun's back pocket. He pulled it out, flipped through it, then handed it back to him. Zebulun said nothing as he calmly put it back in his pocket. He was escorted to the bathroom. The agent knocked on the door.

"Yes?"

"Sir, it's Watkins. I have the serviceman here to fix the TV."

"Send him in."

The agent escorted Zebulun into the bathroom, while two other agents stood outside the door. As expected, Wilcox was soaking in a tub, covered in bubbles, watching TV. There was an agent standing next to the tub. Zebulun had become familiar with the man; his name was Hal Kennedy and, for whatever reason, Jacob had told Zebulun to make sure that whatever he did, he killed him, too.

The President cleared his throat. "I'd stand and shake your hand, but it might be a bit awkward." He smiled; it was a warm smile.

Zebulun smiled back and nodded. "Yes sir."

He walked to the TV, made a fuss of tightening the loose wire, then checked the TV screen. "I think that does it, sir."

Wilcox nodded. "Technology has outpaced me, I'm afraid," said the leader of the free world. Zebulun almost felt guilty for what he was about to do. But then he reminded himself that every leader was corrupt...even those with warm smiles.

He grabbed the journal from his back pocket, clumsily dropped it, then bent over to pick it up. He stood slowly, at the same time pushing the two hidden buttons with his thumb and finger, which instantly turned the journal into a high-powered, short-range weapon. Before Agent Kennedy had time to react, Zebulun shot him in the forehead, then shot the agent who had escorted him into the room. He was surprised that the gun's firing mechanism was so loud, especially since it was such a revolutionary weapon. He would need to move quickly. He aimed the gun at the President, smiled, and said, "Enjoy the show, sir." He fired a shot into Wilcox's heart, then his head, tucking behind a shower door just as the two agents who had been standing at the door ran into the bathroom. He shot them both, then ran to a laundry chute in the back of the bathroom. He jumped through the chute and fell to the basement, where earlier in the day he had piled dirty sheets to break his fall. He left the hotel through a service entrance and ran to a back alley. He turned over a rusted trashcan where he had taped a .38 Special to its underside, grabbed the gun, and jammed it in his pocket. He slid aside another trashcan which covered an opening to a tunnel that led to the sewer. He jumped into the tunnel, pulled the can over the opening, and crawled to the main sewer. He swam through the muck until he reached a manhole two blocks away. He knew the manholes were likely being watched, so, using a thin wire, he shoved a small lens the size of a pea up through an opening in the cover. He scanned the area. He saw several police cars race by, and spotted two officers patrolling on foot. He slid the manhole cover aside two inches, pulled out the .38, and aimed it at one of the officers. He fired and, before the second officer could register what had happened, he killed him as well with a single shot to the forehead. He jumped out of the manhole, replaced the cover, and ran half a block to a locked shed, where he had stored a cooler and a change of clothes. He undid the lock and slid inside. He pulled a damp towel from the cooler and wiped the sewer filth from his face and hands. He yanked off his Vladimir Karev ID and threw it into a metal trashcan. He stripped out of his hotel uniform, threw it in the trashcan, then slid into a pair of khakis, a button-down, and a windbreaker that he had hidden in a trash bag. He cut his hair and shaved his beard, catching the shavings in the towel. He put on a pair of clear glasses, then rubbed on a skin-toned paste to cover the rough skin where the beard had been. He pulled the fake Zeb Kabinov ID from under a floorboard and put it in his wallet. He stuffed the .38 Special in his back pocket, and put the prototype pistol – now once again a journal – in another pocket. He threw the towel with hair and beard clippings into the trash can along with everything else, and set it on fire. He walked away calmly, listening to an iPod that he had pulled from a pocket of his jacket. He grinned. 'Only I, Zebulun, could kill the most powerful man in the world and walk away untouched, with Musette de Beethoven playing in my ears...'

Zebulun smiled. He had done it. But not only that; he had gotten away with it.

A cold breeze blew in off the Potomac, and he pulled his coat tighter around him. The rain had slowed, but the mist hit his cheeks with a sting that reminded him of his father when he was angry. He patted the prototype weapon in his pocket and grinned. It was now his only protection. He had tossed the .38 in a lake outside Fargo.

But he wished he had had that .38 two days ago, when he had been forced to shoot a gas station attendant. The man, picking up on Zebulun's accent, had maligned his native Russia, and Zebulun had had no choice. *I, alone, am permitted to disparage my mother country.* He doubted that anyone would miss the low-life attendant. Even if they did, the gun that Zebulun had used to shoot him – the same weapon that had killed a President – was, according to Morningstar, completely untraceable.

The rain was picking up. He leaned against the side of the boat and hiked his collar. He slid his hands in his pockets and grinned. What he had done had been truly spectacular. He had killed America's leader, but here he was, a free man, floating down the Potomac River in the very heart of America.

The cold, wet air took him back to his homeland; the homeland that the attendant had mocked so carelessly. He chuckled. *That will teach you to belittle my country. Russia forged me with its cruel and heavy hand. It gave me the will not only to kill you, gas station attendant, but to kill your beloved President, as well.*

CHAPTER 20

Columbia, South Carolina

Andrew Madison stared down at his hands; they were shaking. It was nearly eight-thirty in the morning, and he was expected at the downtown clinic any time. But he couldn't leave his townhouse; not yet. He was waiting for someone. He had received a call just moments ago from a man who claimed to be working on behalf of the Pentagon. *"I need to speak to you, Dr. Madison...now...in person."*

Andrew had told the guy to go to hell, but the man had been persistent. *"Trust me, Doctor, you will want to hear what I have to say."* Andrew had asked why, and it was the man's response that had left him standing anxiously at the door. *"I have information that could bring harm not only to you, but to your entire family."*

Andrew's wife, Amanda, and his infant son, Adam, had already left when the call came in, which was good. Amanda was anxious enough without having to worry about some nefarious Pentagon plot. She had barely survived the Lassa fever virus; it had nearly ended her pregnancy. Her fear that something might happen to Adam kept her on edge much of the time. *A heavy-handed bureaucrat is the last thing she needs.*

Though Andrew had been stunned by the call, it hadn't been entirely unexpected. His run-in with the Pentagon two months ago, and again two weeks ago, had led him to believe that he hadn't seen the last of them. As a matter of fact, he felt certain they wouldn't stop until he gave them the tape recorder that he had sworn to them he didn't have.

The visit two weeks ago had gotten his attention. The Pentagon aide – the same man who had come to his mother's house soon after her death – had shown up by Andrew's car as he had been getting ready to leave for work. The aide had been pushy and overbearing, insisting that Andrew give him the recorder, *"...or I'll send in an army of agents to find it."* Again, Andrew had denied knowing anything about it, and, the minute the aide had left the parking lot, Andrew had driven to the clinic. Without Amanda even knowing he was there, he had taken both his mother's letter and the tape recorder from Adam's car seat in the back of her car. Sneaking from the parking lot to a nearby park and staying hidden among the trees, he had jogged downtown to a bank he had never used and had locked the two items in a safe-deposit box. He had jogged back to the clinic the way he had come, and had hidden the key in a pile with several others in the console of Amanda's car.

And now he was glad he had. As he leaned against the frame of the front door of his townhouse, he had to work to hide his anger. *I should be left alone to grieve,* he thought as he thought back on all that had happened. It had started two months ago, when he had found his mother's dead body on her living room floor. First had been the Pentagon agents showing up out of nowhere, then had been an autopsy, which had been overseen by the Pentagon. Why had there needed to be an autopsy? The coroner had concluded that Jeannie had simply drank herself to death. *I could've told them that,* he had thought at the time. He knew he would get nowhere by trying to challenge the Pentagon, however, so once they had completed the autopsy, he had buried his mother and had tried to move on.

And then there was Maddi. As her only surviving relative, it had been up to him to handle everything with her, as well. There had been no body to bury, so he had arranged for two memorial services: One in McCordsville where they had grown up, and one in DC where most of her friends lived. That one had been the toughest. Never had he seen so many people with so much love and regard for one person. The only notable absence was Hank. Andrew had no idea why Hank had chosen not to come; he had concluded that it was simply too painful. *I get it,* he had decided when he had had time to reflect. It had been all Andrew could do to get through it.

Not only had there been memorials to arrange, but there had been houses to sell and belongings to disburse. Jeannie hadn't had much; she had brought little with her when she had moved back to McCordsville. Maddi hadn't had much, either. Though she had lived in her DC house for over six years, she had been far too busy to accumulate much. Andrew had kept a few of her items; a guitar, some music boxes, a few of her favorite books. And Amanda had insisted on keeping a quilt that Andrew had found in her living room. Her secretary, Phil Jenkins, was still combing through her senate records, and had agreed to use his discretion regarding their dispensation.

That should have been the end of it, but it wasn't. Over the last two months, the same Pentagon agent that had come to his mother's home on the day of her death had either called Andrew or physically confronted him four times, and always it was the same. *"You need to give me that tape recorder, Dr. Madison."*

For some reason, Andrew had yet to tell Amanda any of it. He wasn't sure why; maybe it was to save her the worry, or maybe he was hoping the whole thing would just disappear. *Obviously, it isn't going to,* he thought, as he readied himself for the agent's visit. He had called the clinic and told them he would be late, blaming it on a broken water pipe so that Amanda wouldn't worry. He had then sent her a text, assuring her that he would take care of the pipe before he came in to work. He hated to lie, but it was the only way to keep her from knowing what was really going on.

Why don't I just tell her? he wondered as he waited at the door. He thought about the tape. He still hadn't listened to it. What if his mother really had been involved with terrorists? He shook his head. *There's no way.* So, why not listen to it? Why not hear it and then hand it over to the agent? He sighed. For two reasons. The first was that he couldn't be sure that his home, his car, his office hadn't been bugged by the Pentagon agent. He even wondered about the sanctity of the bank vault where the lockboxes were kept. After all, he was dealing with the Pentagon. There was no telling how far they might be willing to go. If Jeannie had done something wrong, he didn't want them to be able to confirm it by hearing her confess it on the tape.

The second reason was that he wasn't sure he could bear to hear Jeannie's final words. His fear was that she had, in fact, been drunk, and all he would hear would be a slurred recording of her making excuses for her life. Even worse, was the fear that – as preposterous as it seemed – she *had* been involved in something treasonous, or at least illegal. He didn't want either of those to be his last impression of his mother.

It had taken him weeks to even read the letter. But finally, when he could stand it no longer, he had driven to the bank and, in the privacy of the vault, had taken it from the safe-deposit box. He had opened it with an unease that reflected the many years of disappointment he had felt toward his mother and her behavior. As he had pulled the letter from the envelope, a gold coin had fallen onto the table. He had guessed that it was a sobriety token; a way for Jeannie to let him and Maddi know that she had tried so hard over the years to get past her affliction. He had stared at the coin for a solid minute, then had shoved it in his pocket, which was pretty much where it had stayed ever since. She had referenced it only once in the letter, simply instructing Andrew to protect it. *"It was given to me by your Grandfather Madison, with instructions that you hold onto it, as it may prove to be vital at some point in the future."* Andrew had felt that to be a bit dramatic, but had honored Jeannie's wishes and had kept the coin with him as a reminder of all that his mother had been through.

As for the letter, he had expected that it would be an apology for all that Jeannie had done to disappoint him and Maddi, or had failed to do as their mother. And that was pretty much how it had started. But what he had found refreshing had been her willingness to own it...all of it...along with a heartfelt acknowledgement of her love for him and Maddi, her regret that she might never know Adam, and her wish that he and Maddi could move forward knowing that they were deeply loved. She had added that she was trying one more time to get sober, with the hope that she could someday meet Adam, but that she was afraid the effort might kill her. *"If I die, I need you both to know how much I love you and how sorry I am for all I did wrong."* It had moved him to tears, and he had been tempted to stop right there. But he had pulled himself together and had read the rest of the letter. That was when things had gotten interesting. The longer she had written, the shakier the writing had become, and it had broken his heart to imagine her struggling to put the words to paper. But she had done it, and Andrew had felt a sense of pride for her efforts.

She had disclosed in a few short paragraphs the truth behind the murder of his father, officer Stewart Madison. Though it had been blamed on a jewelry heist gone bad, Jeannie had relayed her version of how he had *actually* been killed. Andrew didn't know if he should believe it. After all, his mom had spent the last thirty years either drunk or on the way. Had she concocted some conspiracy theory during that time that had allowed her to view her husband's death in an entirely different light? Perhaps, but the premise was fascinating. She claimed that Stewart had been murdered not by thieves cornered during a jewelry heist, but by a secret group of vigilante police officers who had been upset over Stewart's discovery of their less-than-honorable pursuits. She had finished that part of the letter with a special note to Maddi. *"There is more to the story, but I don't have the time or energy to lay it all out here. Some of the answers lay in that locket you wear, Cindy. Keep it safe, and use it to learn the truth the next time you go to the Darlington estate."*

The Darlington estate was a reference to an estate that had been owned by Andrew's grandparents; his father's parents. They had been quite wealthy, and had left the estate to Andrew and Maddi when they had died. Neither Andrew nor Maddi had had a chance to do much with it, however, and had requested that the devoted staff look after it until either he or Maddi could find time to fly over and take steps to oversee its operation. He shook his head and sighed. *I guess that task is now up to me.*

As for the locket; Andrew had searched all of Maddi's belongings and hadn't found it, so he had reached out to the State Department, asking their representative if a locket had been found at the scene of the plane crash. *"I'm sorry, sir...all we have is a sweater and her Senate ID badge."* Andrew had asked for the ID badge; it had arrived six days ago, and was lying on a table in the den, next to a photo of Adam.

Though he had given quite a bit of thought to his mother's theory, he had finally concluded that it didn't matter how his father died. He was dead, Jeannie was dead, Maddi was dead. *And I am alive...and needing to move on.*

He wondered if the Pentagon agent, whom he now referred to as 'khakis,' was bringing the 'army of agents' he had promised in his visit two weeks ago. He flinched. An entire team of government agents with instructions to do 'whatever it takes' to find the recorder. *Let 'em look,* he thought...*they'll never find it.*

There was a knock on the door and he jumped.

"Who is it?" he barked, as he stared through the peephole.

"Josh Adams. Pentagon."

Andrew could see at least three agents standing behind the man he recognized as Adams. He opened the door and stepped back, allowing Adams and four other agents to storm into the room. Adams handed him a folded piece of paper. "Search warrant" he mumbled as he started opening drawers.

Andrew stood back and watched as the five men upended furniture, pulled mattresses from the beds, and threw drawers onto the floor, dumping their contents with little regard. They opened every cabinet in the living room and the kitchen, and even pried floorboards loose in the bedrooms. He was glad Amanda wasn't there to see it. He wouldn't leave until the men were gone and he had restored order to his home. But, as he watched them, seemingly desperate in their efforts, he couldn't help but wonder...*What the hell is on that tape?*

CHAPTER 21

The Henderson Compound

Henderson had left his father's office and had gone back to the cabin. He had stared at the coarse tongue-and-grooved walls, more aware than ever that he would never get to Morningstar by sitting in that cabin. *I need to get out of here...away from this estate,* he had finally decided two hours later. He had pitched the coffee, locked the cabin door behind him, and had hiked back to the castle. He had climbed the stairs to his bedroom, knowing that Walter would never approve of him leaving. He had changed into sweats and had gone for a run. Afterward, he had gone back to his room, where he had spent the rest of the afternoon lying on his bed trying to figure out what to do about the call from Claire Porter. The call had surprised him. Not only because of her boldness in telling his father that his son was still alive, but the very fact that she had called Walter in the first place. Why him? *And how did she get his number?*

Walter was right; the caller could be trying to fool them by claiming she was a DC therapist who had had Maddi's confidence. Henderson had checked out Claire Porter once already; back in January. She was, in fact, a DC therapist, and she had, in fact, been Maddi's therapist. *But what if the woman who called is just pretending to be Claire Porter?* He shook his head. *She knows far too much to be lying.*

But why call Walter? She had said that she was hoping to speak to his son, and that her message involved Edward Morningstar. Why did she feel the need to talk to Martin Henderson? Was it because of his connection to Maddi? It had to be; she couldn't have known of his ties to Morningstar. No one was aware of those ties.

I need to talk to her, he finally concluded as the late day sun eased its way into the room. He sat up and threw his legs over the side of the bed. It was the only plan that made sense. Not only talk to her, but follow whatever lead she might offer. She had said the name Morningstar. Had Maddi told Claire something about Morningstar that could help Henderson stop him from carrying out whatever plan he had in mind?

He shook his head. Regardless of what Claire might know or say, for Henderson to do anything about it, he would need to leave the compound. And to do that, he would need a car, a phone, and some cash. He could simply take those items, but it would be far easier if he could obtain his father's blessing. *Fat chance,* he thought with a sigh. Walter had been adamant that under no circumstances was Henderson to leave the estate. *I need to find a way to make him let me go.*

He closed his eyes and thought of all the things he might say to make his father understand why he needed to leave. He flinched. *I could tell him about my past, my history with Morningstar...and why I'm the only man who can bring the man down.* He shook his head, then stood slowly, moving his legs that had become stiff and sore. He couldn't tell his father about Morningstar; that truth was too awful.

After a minute or two of stretching, he began to pace. Half an hour later, as a grandfather clock somewhere in the mansion rang out four chimes, he nodded. He knew what he needed to do...what he needed to say to make Walter understand.

He walked into the bathroom, took a quick shower, then ran a comb through his hair. He changed into jeans and a sweater, slid into a pair of hiking boots, and left the bedroom. He walked downstairs and went straight to Walter's office. He knocked, hoping against hope that he was still there.

"Come in."

He walked in and, with an outstretched hand, said, "I'd like the number."

Walter hesitated. He reached in his pocket and handed over the therapist's number. "Can you at least wait until my men have completed their research?"

Henderson nodded. "Fair enough." He sighed. "And I'll need a better phone than the burner you gave me."

Walter frowned. "Why?"

Henderson narrowed his eyes. "Because if I do decide to call her, I'll need a phone that I can use in places where phones don't often work."

Walter shook his head. "Your current phone works anywhere on the estate."

Henderson frowned. "That's just it, Dad. I need to leave the estate."

Walter shook his head dismissively. "No. Absolutely not. We've already discussed it. You know the risks."

"Yes, I know the risks, but I can't stay here forever." Walter said nothing; he simply stared at him. Henderson cleared his throat and, with a boldness he didn't feel, he added, "I'm going to leave here, Dad...either with your blessing, or without it."

Walter frowned. "Why? Why is it so important that you leave now?"

Henderson let out a sigh. "I have something I need to do...something I should have done long ago. And I can't really do it from here. I've tried, and I can't."

Walter looked at him. His eyes were filled with sadness as he stood and put his hands on the desk. He said pleadingly, "Talk to me, son. Please, just let me in."

Henderson took a deep breath. *Perfect timing.* He wouldn't tell Walter everything, but he would tell him enough so that he could begin to see the monster that Henderson had become. "Dad, the best way I know to put it is this: after the fire, I...I lost my way. I got tangled up in...in a mess." He hesitated. Could he say the next part? He cleared his throat. "And because of it, there were victims...crimes that I was a part of...that have...brought me shame." He took another deep breath. "The very knowledge of those crimes would destroy you...it would destroy Mom." He sighed. "Though in most instances, the outcome might be viewed favorably by those who cherish freedom," he frowned, "...in no way does that make it right." A pause. "Because there were times when the outcome was just the opposite... it was terrible."

Walter didn't move. He simply stared at his son with eyes that told of the remarkable love he had for him, in spite of all that Henderson had put him through over the last several months...or the last several years when Walter didn't even know he was alive. Henderson went on. "Of all the victims," he closed his eyes. *Tell him, Henderson... just get it over with,* "...the most important one," his voice broke. He looked at Walter, then looked down at the floor. "...the one that you and I know – knew – best," he whispered, "...was Lili. Lili Platacis."

Walter said nothing, but his eyes had narrowed.

Henderson winced, then tightened his jaw. He couldn't break down now. "I...I didn't directly have a hand in getting her kidnapped and killed, but...but indirectly, I played a role...a central role." He added quickly, "I didn't mean for it to happen...but it did...because of me." He swallowed. "And I'll have to live with that every day for the rest of my life." He squared his shoulders and said defiantly, "But that doesn't mean that I have to let the bastard who did it get away with it."

Walter stared at his son for what seemed like hours. Finally, with tears in his eyes, he walked around the desk and hugged him. The absolution was more than Henderson could bear. He quickly pulled away. "Dad, don't—"

Walter raised his hand. "Stop." He sighed. "Listen, Martin, I don't know what went on with you or with Lili; I don't need to know. But someone else took that little girl and killed her. You did not. It's an important distinction. Remember that."

Henderson wanted to believe him, but he couldn't. He cleared his throat. "Lack of intent is no pardon, nor should it be." He sighed, then said resolutely, "But it doesn't matter. The only thing that matters now is to make it right." He paused. "I've got a feeling that I'll soon be forced to account for my past, either by my government, or by the man who actually pulled the strings. But before I do, I have to make things right." He stared at his father. "Now do you understand why I need to leave?"

Walter shook his head. "No, no son, I don't. You can't change the past. The sins of our past are a curse we must all live with. No one knows that better than me." He took a deep breath, then rested his hands on Henderson's shoulders. "I started over...you can, too. I can help you...Dora and I can help you make amends."

Henderson shook his head. "No, not this time, Dad. I have to do this myself."

Walter let out a sigh. Slowly, he walked behind the desk and opened a small wooden box that sat on top. He pulled out a satellite phone and tossed it to Henderson. "Top of the line," he said evenly. He took a set of keys from his pocket and unlocked a drawer. He grabbed a stack of hundred-euro bills, along with a plastic card, and handed both to Henderson.

Henderson shoved the money in his pocket, then looked at the card. It listed him as M. Helmanis, a Latvian consul, and had an ID number and an email address with a contact name from Latvia's central government. He frowned. "What's this?"

"I have one for each of us. Keep it. It might open a door or two." He paused. "And whatever you do, son, don't leave Latvia."

Henderson frowned. "Why?"

"There's no extradition treaty between Latvia and America...not yet, anyway. But that isn't the case for the surrounding countries."

Henderson nodded and tucked the card in his wallet, along with Claire Porter's phone number. "Thanks, Dad," he managed to say as he shook his father's outstretched hand. He walked around the desk and hugged him. "Where's Mom?"

"She took a bunch of pies to the troops stationed in Uzava."

Henderson grinned, his heart breaking at the thought of Dora's kindness contrasted with his own lack of it. "Tell her I had something I had to do... that I'll be back soon."

His father nodded. "We're going to Riga for the night. I have business there in the morning. She won't realize you're gone until we get back tomorrow afternoon."

Henderson sighed, then turned and left the office. As he was about to close the door behind him, Walter said, "I love you, son. That will never change...never."

Henderson said nothing as he closed the door and traced his steps back to the foyer and up the stairs. He walked into his bedroom and closed the door. *Go, Henderson...get out of here.* He grabbed his backpack, threw in a change of clothes and his laptop, and went downstairs to the garage. He walked in and nodded at a couple of drivers standing by the door.

They both straightened, and one of them said, "Do you need a ride, sir?"

Henderson shook his head. "No. Thank you." He walked into the inner office and grabbed a set of keys. He walked out to one of the BMWs, opened the door, and slid inside. He gripped the steering wheel, surprised to see that his hands were shaking. It would be the first time he had driven a car since March. Not only that; it would be the first time he had left the compound since arriving there in August.

He pulled out of the garage and, as he drove up to the first gate, a security guard gave him a nod. "Out for a drive, Mr. Henderson?"

He nodded and forced a smile. The man lowered the gate. As Henderson hugged the curves to the outer gate, he couldn't stop thinking about Claire's message to his father. *"...what she needs to tell you involves a man named Morningstar."*

He reached the end of the drive and stopped. His plan was to turn left and travel north through Uzava to the highway that would take him east to Riga. Latvia's capital was big enough that it would give him anonymity, as well as contacts and transportation; a way to travel that didn't involve a Henderson BMW with GPS.

He took a deep breath and stared at the road in front of him. He eased forward. But instead of turning left, he turned right. He had something he needed to do first.

He picked up speed, glad to see that he had lost none of his skills behind the wheel. As he drove, he thought of Lili. She had been a remarkable little girl. Not only had she been filled with the joy of childhood, but she had been gifted with kindness, and a vision for what the world needed. He tightened his jaw and stepped on the gas.

He looked around at the trees, the sky, the road ahead...suddenly aware that for the first time in months, he was free...physically, at least. He was no longer stuck in a bed or caged in a castle. *So, what do I do with this freedom?* The first thing he would do would be to call Claire. He couldn't wait for his father's men to verify her identity; he felt certain that she was exactly who she claimed to be: Claire Porter, Maddi's former therapist.

Why call her first? Because not only could Claire give him information that might help him take down Morningstar, but there was probably no one on the planet who knew as much about Maddi as Claire. Though he didn't know what all Maddi had shared with her, Maddi had gone to her for the very purpose of sharing.

Claire knows – knew – Maddi as well as or better than anyone.

She could fill in the blanks that seemed to gnaw at him. She could tell him how Maddi had felt about him...about their brief time together... about how much she had known about his days as the Phoenix and the things he had done...or if she had forgiven him for staying silent for all those years. Lastly, she might be able to put to rest his fear that, like so many others, he had ruined Maddi; that he had destroyed her by making her love him. As he drove south along route P111 and saw signs for Liepaja, he felt his heart pounding in his chest. He nodded. It was time. *I will call Claire from the very spot where Maddi took her last breath.*

CHAPTER 22

Washington, DC

Morningstar paced his hotel suite, his anger boiling over as he etched a circle in the carpeted hotel room. Though a press briefing was being played live on his TV set, he was barely listening. The meeting with the Bentley Group hadn't gone as planned. The news about the missing prototype was a loose end; Morningstar hated loose ends. He had expected the pistol to be back with Silverton by now; after all, it had been over eight weeks since Zebulun had shot the President. His orders had been clear: *"The minute you get back to DC – if you get back, my brave son – return the gun to Bernard Kuntz."* What would compel his wise and obedient Zebulun to use such a weapon to kill a gas station attendant? Surely, he recognized the risk?

But there was a far larger problem than just the carelessness of one of his sons. Somehow, the untraceable prototype had been traced. *How?* He smacked the wall. *That was the point of the damn thing; it was supposed to be untraceable!*

He needed to talk to someone at Silverton; he needed to talk to Kuntz.

Bernard Kuntz had been with Silverton for over six years; the same amount of time that Morningstar had been a member of the Bentley Group. He had met Kuntz at an outing for high-ranking Pentagon officials at a secluded resort in the Pocono Mountains. Kuntz had been on the service staff, and Morningstar had taken a liking to the disarming Mennonite from Pennsylvania. The two men had talked, and Morningstar had picked up on the boy's rebellious desire to not only get away from home, but to get away from what he had referred to as the backward thinking of his church. *"What better way than to work for an arms manufacturer?"* Morningstar had said to the boy when they had had a chance to talk. In spite of the fact that Kuntz had been raised as a pacifist, he had jumped at the offer. Morningstar had arranged for him to be hired in the service department at Silverton's Philadelphia branch. There he could live in the city, escape his mountains and his Mennonite faith, and immerse himself in the secular world. For Morningstar, the unobtrusive man would be his eyes and ears within the company.

And Kuntz had done well, delivering inside knowledge that Morningstar couldn't have gotten any other way. It wasn't long before Morningstar moved him to DC, making him a liaison between Silverton and the Pentagon. After another few years, Kuntz had been put in charge of innovation; specifically, new weapons designs for Silverton Industries. Kuntz would let him know when a ground-breaking weapon was being created, and the only thing Kuntz required was a handsome payout in quarterly installments. Morningstar had no idea what the man did with the money; he didn't care. The arrangement worked well for everyone.

He rarely contacted Kuntz personally. As a matter of fact, the call he was about to make would be only the second time he had spoken with the man since Kuntz had started working for Silverton. The first time had been to relocate the young man to DC. This time, he would arrange a meeting. There was an old warehouse on the south side of town that was completely off the grid...no security cameras, few lights, and too many trees to allow for adequate satellite surveillance.

He checked his watch. *9:30...I'll have Kuntz meet me there at noon.*

He had been unable to go back to work after the Bentley Group meeting; he was too shaken by the news about the prototype weapon. So, he had called in sick, and had gone back to the hotel where he and his girlfriend Janet now spent most of their time. Janet worked for the State Department, and he had told her to call in sick, as well. Though she was seven months pregnant and was no longer the alluring siren he had met over nine months ago, she was carrying the future heir to his realm...she was carrying Benjamin. Which made her desirable in a whole different way.

She was resting in the bedroom, while Morningstar paced the living room and tried to come up with a solution to the prototype dilemma. He stopped at the window. Their hotel room overlooked a courtyard, but this time of year there was little to see. The trees were bare, the flower pots empty...nothing but dry earth awaiting next spring's planting. He bristled as he stared at the barren plots of dirt. *Why did Zebulun defy me?* Morningstar couldn't tolerate disobedience. He had been specific with his instructions. *"Return the prototype to Kuntz the minute you get back to DC. Why hadn't he done it? And why did he then use it to kill a gas station attendant?* Didn't he know that the discovery of the prototype could lead authorities not only to the assassination of Wilcox, but to Silverton Industries? Such a connection would be disastrous...not only for Zebulun, but for Morningstar and his Bentley Group. Silverton had worked with the Bentley Group for far too long and with far too much success to allow Zebulun's bungling to disrupt the relationship now.

The TV was still on. A newscaster suddenly interrupted a roundtable discussion of Knight's "Make America Safe" initiative. Morningstar turned and looked at the TV. The volume was low, but he heard enough. The words "Beaumont, Texas" followed by "crazed gunman" were all he needed; he raised a triumphant fist in the air. "Good work, Issachar!" Another shooting...another setback for the second amendment.

He walked to a corner desk. As he sat in an oversized leather chair and watched the news coverage, he nodded. Things were going well... remarkably well, as a matter of fact. He couldn't let the incident with the prototype dissuade him. He had to protect Silverton and he had to protect the Bentley Group. *Think, Morningstar. How can you fix this?* He leaned back and crossed his feet on the desk. With his eyes closed, he made a silent supplication to his Maker. *Tell me what to do, God.*

He waited. Within minutes, an idea began to take shape...a plan that would not only take care of his current problem, but would allow him to advance his agenda even further. After another few minutes, the details became clearer. Finally, in a flash of inspiration, he jumped up from his chair and called into the bedroom, "Janet, get in here! I have a task for you."

He could hear her groan as she got up from the bed. She waddled out from the bedroom, one of his button-down shirts covering her belly, making her look almost as good as she had before she got so big. Strands of fiery red hair had fallen over one eye, and, as she brushed them away, she grinned. "What d'ya need, baby?"

He stood and walked toward her, ignoring the urge to take her again, instead giving her a peck on the cheek as he said, "Just a few forged documents, babe."

Chapter 23

Columbia, South Carolina

Andrew said nothing as the men finished trashing his townhouse and walked to the door. They had found nothing, and the frustration on the face of the khakis-wearing Adams was palpable. During their search, Andrew hadn't moved from his chair in the living room. As he heard the men filing out the door, he stood and walked to the entryway. Tall and already quite lean, Andrew had only become leaner over the past two months. His clothes hung loosely on his lanky frame, and he tugged at his pants to keep them from falling below his waist. He put one hand on the frame of the door as he watched the agents leave. He shook his head and sighed. *Good riddance.*

Adams was the last to go, his wrinkled shirt now untucked over his tight, high-riding khakis. He crossed the hall and was about to get into the elevator, when he turned and looked at Andrew. "Ya know, Madison, you might wanna watch your back."

Andrew frowned. "Why?"

Adams grinned. "Let's just say that we're not the only ones interested in that recorder." He paused. "Maybe if you give it to me, I can protect you."

"From what?"

The man grinned. "Bad people...people far worse than me."

Andrew could feel his throat tighten.

Adams went on. "Aren't you the least bit curious why I'm so determined to find that recorder?"

"No. I don't care."

Adams grinned. "Sure, you do. But I wonder...have you even listened to it? I'll bet you haven't. You're afraid of what's on it." He paused. "Evidence of your mom's collusion with some overseas terrorist organization," he grinned, "...or, better yet, the slurred words of an alcoholic who's about to die."

Andrew ran at him and was about to punch him, when one of the agents appeared out of nowhere and grabbed him by the wrist. "No, you don't, buddy."

Andrew tried to wrestle his wrist from the man's hand. "You mean this asshole gets to come into my home, tear it apart, and then insult my dead mother?"

The man chuckled as he gave Andrew's wrist a hard squeeze before letting it go. "That 'asshole' can say or do whatever he wants. He works for the United States government."

Andrew was shaking, but said nothing. It wasn't his first run-in with an arrogant bureaucrat. But it was the first time that one of them had said something so hurtful...and so true.

Adams laughed. "You still don't get it, do you Madison?"

Andrew glared at him but held back from saying anything.

"It's not just your mom we're looking at." Adams stepped into the elevator. As the door was about to close, he added, "Your sister was working for them, too."

CHAPTER 24

Washington, DC

"Certainly, Mr. President."

Mr. President. Knight nodded at the aide as he stood and left the room. Though Knight had been raised to believe that he might someday be a leader within America's government, he had never seen himself as President. *I wonder if the Pope – as a young man – ever thought that he would be the Pope.* Interestingly, the Pope oversaw a vastly larger 'flock' than a U.S. President, but the President seemed to have a far greater impact.

The morning presser was over, and, at least for the moment, he was alone. He cherished that alone time. For one thing, it was rare. For another, it was the only time when he could truly be himself. He knew of a place in the White House – a room his predecessor had shown him – that was far-removed from the demands of the Oval Office. Though less than a hundred feet from that office, it felt like a hundred miles from DC and the many challenges that faced the nation...that faced him.

He stood from his desk, then stole through a side door down a narrow hallway to the secret room. He nodded at a Secret Service agent standing outside the door of the small room. The agent had insisted on keeping watch, especially since Knight had begun to visit the room so frequently. Knight felt his shoulders relax as he walked into the brightly colored room with the tall window. He looked out on a simple garden with a few trees, a couple of flowerpots, and a stone path that seemed to lead to nowhere. Inside the room were two yellow chairs that sat on each side of the window, with a small table in-between, and a maple writing table with a stool that stood along one wall. The walls themselves had been painted a soft blue, and for whatever reason, whenever he walked in, he would catch the scent of pine. It reminded him of the mountains in Maine, which only added to the magic of that secret hideaway. It was a modest room with a modest purpose; to allow a man to feel invisible. It had none of the symbols of power like those in the Oval Office, nor did it boast of historic relics, like those that stared at him from the hallways of the house where only a relative few had lived before him. That room let him escape, and he went there as often as he could...in an effort to feel normal.

But Jerome Knight was anything but normal. He had been given a multitude of gifts. He was smart, athletic, and not altogether unattractive. Though he strove for excellence in all that he did, he had developed a humility based on life experiences, and a sense of humor based on loss. He was well-liked, well-respected, and well-to-do. He had been told that those attributes were why he had been chosen to replace Jim Conner when the man had stunned the world by stepping down from his role as VP just months before his boss's reelection. *"I want Jerome Knight,"* Wilcox had apparently told his Chief of Staff. Conversant in four languages, Knight could speak to any constituency, be they immigrants or refugees, Blacks or Hispanics, east coasters or Midwesterners. He was able to convey a sincere regard for every one of them and the problems they faced. He had shown it to the people of Florida, and, for whatever reason, Wilcox had felt that he could show it to the people of America. But, according to Wilcox, there had been more that had made him such a desirable pick for VP. He could stand toe to toe with the most formidable congressman, his six-three frame a towering presence when he needed it to be. Two hundred pounds of mostly muscle made him a force to be reckoned with, whether it was on a Lacrosse field two decades ago, or with a senator in DC, where a little intimidation went a long way.

He walked to a mirror hanging over the writing table, and couldn't help but laugh. *I, Jerome Knight, am President of the United States.* It was beyond humbling; it was almost absurd. He stared at the image, the stranger who had somehow become leader of the free world. He barely recognized the dark eyes staring back at him, or the dark hair that didn't even touch his ears. The haircut was a far cry from how he had worn it when he was younger. At Morningstar's insistence, he had cut it when he had turned twenty-two...to prepare him for his future. Like the lead in a Broadway play, he had been coached for the role of a lifetime...he had been groomed to be king.

But, before that – before he had had to give up himself and his dreams for the sake of the mission – his dark brown hair had fallen to his shoulders, the natural wave making him look almost gothic; or at least that was how Emma had seen it. *"You're like Alaric the First, who defeated Attila the Hun in the mid-400's."* He had liked being compared to Alaric the First; brave and fierce, yet kind...that was the man he might have been. It was that man who had known and loved Emma Melnikov...

"I didn't think you'd be able to keep up." Emma laughed, her black hair flowing over her shoulder as she looked back at Jerome, who was two bike lengths behind her. Her legs were moving rhythmically, pedaling up the hill with ease.

He, on the other hand, was working hard. He was fit, but she was more so. It was the off-season for Lacrosse and he had done little exercise for the last six weeks. He wasn't about to let her beat him, however. "I'm...right...behind you...Emma."

She pedaled faster and Jerome struggled to keep up. When she reached the top of the hill, she stopped and pulled the bike to the side of the road. She parked it next to a bench, then sat and waited. As he struggled up the last rise, he watched her. She was looking to her left at a garden full of rose bushes. She turned to him and grinned. She motioned toward the garden as her hair fell over her shoulders in a sea of black. Had she known the park would be there? Likely. Had she known that Jerome would be spent from the climb up the hill? Also, likely.

He was almost to the top, and she feigned a yawn as she yelled, "Don't worry, Romer, I'll wait for you!"

His Lacrosse teammates had given him the nickname Romer partly because of his name, Jerome, and partly because he roamed the Lacrosse field like a cheetah. The nickname had stuck. He smiled as he said between breaths, "I'm...only pretending...to be...wiped out." She laughed again and he could barely finish the last ten feet of the climb. Another two minutes and he was standing in front of her, his hands on his knees as he gulped in air. "I...didn't want...to embarrass you, Emma."

This time she laughed with every part of her; her head fell back and her shoulders shook as she grabbed her knees and said, "Stop. You're killing me."

He grinned. "I'll prove it to you." He took a deep breath, then stood and lifted her in his arms. He carried her to a spot behind the roses, laying her gently on moss-covered ground. He fell on top of her and grinned. "I was with you the entire time."

She framed his face with her hands, then pulled him close. "No, you weren't. But, as I said, I will wait for you..."

Knight flinched. How long had it been? How many years had passed since that day when he had looked in her eyes, touched her skin, and felt his heart beat out of his chest – not from exertion – but from a love he knew he had no business feeling. How long had it been since she had told him she would wait for him? And she would have. She would have waited if he had given her the chance. His jaw tightened as he combed his fingers through his clipped hair. *My hair...and my life...cut far too short.*

He had been told by Morningstar that the current haircut, his for over fifteen years, was more suitable for the role he would eventually play...*the role I'm now playing.* He couldn't deny that the shorter cut accented his forehead and strong chin. He had been amazed at the respectability he had acquired with just a clip of his hair.

He put a hand to his jaw; square and solid...*like Arnold Schwarzenegger,* he thought with a chuckle. That was how a press agent had described him. But he was far different from the man who had governed California; a Republican married to a Democrat. Knight wasn't a compromising sort of man. There was right and there was wrong; it was that simple. He and Emma hadn't agreed politically. At the time, he had thought it wouldn't matter. He knew now, it would have. *A deal-breaker...that's what it would have been.*

Though Morningstar encouraged a wife for Knight, he hadn't felt Emma to be suitable. For one thing, she was from Russia. Morningstar wanted someone more ethnically safe: Fair-haired, American-born, easily shaped to whatever was needed as he moved forward with his political career. Once Morningstar had forced him to tell Emma goodbye, the man had gone so far as to set him up with different women. And, out of respect, Knight had tried to make it work. But after a third try with a blue-blooded girl from Connecticut, he had put his foot down. It was one thing to make him leave Emma; it was quite another to force him into a relationship he didn't want.

Which now made him one of the most eligible bachelors in America. He chuckled humorously as he stared at the dark eyes looking back at him. They were like his mother's. Not Beatrice Sturgill, whose pale gray eyes were empty and lifeless; no, they were like those of his *real* mother, Glenda Knight, whose deep brown eyes had reassured him...they had made him feel warm, inside and out.

But the eyes he was looking at now didn't seem warm...they seemed blank. He missed his mother. He was fourteen when she died, and, though it was 23 years ago, he could still remember her and the certainty of her hug. But he had come to terms with it; he would never know that hug again. He would never know any hug. Not from his mother, and not from the only other woman he had ever loved...*Emma.*

He turned away. None of it mattered; he hadn't been put on this earth to enjoy what others enjoyed...the comfort of a mother's touch, or the closeness of a woman lying next to him. No, Jerome Knight had been born for a different purpose. And though he didn't like it, he would learn to live with it...each and every day. Because as Jacob had told him, time and time again, "*...the future of the world depends on it.*"

CHAPTER 25

Liepaja, Latvia

Henderson's journey to the site of Maddi's plane crash was harder than he had expected. Not only was he overwhelmed by the thought of her lying dead in that empty field with no one to hold her, but he underestimated the connection he would feel to the ground on which she had laid. Though it had been over two months since the crash, there were still pieces of debris in the grass, and he tightened his jaw as he bent down and picked up a piece of metal from the plane. He massaged it slowly in his hand, overwhelmed by the coldness of the steel. That jagged shard of metal was the only tangible item he had to tie him to the woman he loved. No love letters, no jewelry; nothing but a sliver of steel from a wrecked plane.

As the sun slowly faded in the distance, he stared at the ground, trying to imagine Maddi's final seconds. Had she felt pain? Had she been frightened? Had she known she would die? *Did she think of me in her last few seconds of life?*

He had no idea how long he stood there staring at the grass, but a bitter cold wind and the fading sunlight forced him from his trance. He pulled out his phone. He dialed the first four digits of the number that Claire had given his father, but hung up before completing the call. Why? Out of respect for his father's wishes? Or was it something else? A refusal to even speak while on such hallowed ground...as if uttering a single word would shatter the silence and destroy his tenuous tie to Maddi.

As daylight eased deeper into dusk, he finally made himself leave the field and get back in his car. He put the key in the ignition, sliding his other hand in his pocket to touch the piece of metal he had taken from the site. He laid back and closed his eyes. After a minute, he put his hand on the wheel and started the car. As he drove away from the site, he noticed a row of shops and a busy tavern less than a hundred yards from the field where Maddi's plane had crashed. Had anyone in the bar seen the crash? Had they run out to try to help? Had they heard screams? He flinched. *Or did they hear only silence?* Though he was tempted to stop at the bar and ask, his father's words echoed in his mind. *"Never forget that you're a wanted man, son."*

He took a last look at the row of houses, then turned left out of the field. He got back on route P111 and drove ninety kilometers north to a tavern that sat off the road near Uzava. As he pulled into the small lot outside the pub, he looked up at the sign and smiled. "Sniegotā pūce." *The Snowy Owl.* As a young man, he had spent hours in that tavern, talking strategy – and girls – with Danil and Albins. They had chosen the bar for its privacy. Only the locals knew of it, which meant that he and his friends could feel secluded and safe as they discussed the challenges of the day.

He hiked his hood over his head and put on sunglasses. He walked in and immediately went to a booth in the back. It had been their booth, and he could almost see Albins brushing his blond hair from his forehead as he waved for Henderson to hurry. *"We 'ave a lot to do, ya laggard."* He choked back tears as he took a seat in the booth. A waiter walked over, and, in Lettish, asked him if he wanted a drink.

"Tikai kafija." *Just coffee.*

The waiter walked away. Henderson looked around. He felt comfortable there. He had once known friendship and adventure in that pub, and, though it had now become a symbol of all he had lost, it also reminded him that, for a time in his life, he had known happiness.

The coffee came and he sipped it slowly, planning the call he was about to make to Claire. He was curious how she knew about Morningstar. Had Maddi shared something about the Pentagon aide, something so alarming that the therapist felt the need to risk the safety of a wanted man – of him – thousands of miles away?

He pulled his laptop from his backpack, typed Claire's name into a search engine, and read through a brief summary. He saw little that he didn't already know. Claire Porter was a therapist in DC. Her office was located near Dupont Circle, and she had been there for about fifteen years. He looked at the phone number on the site, then pulled out the scrap of paper with the number she had given Walter. They were different. *Is the number she gave Walter to a private cellphone? Or are the two numbers different because she isn't really Claire?* His father had asked that he wait to call her until his men had verified her identity. Could he wait? Should he call her at all? What if it was a trap? What if she was working for the U.S. government and was trying to trap Phoenix into revealing his true identity? Or, maybe she was a charlatan who had somehow learned the truth about him and was intent on blackmailing him for his former crimes. He shook his head. The secret had been kept far too well for that to be the case. Besides, Claire – if that was who she was – had gone to a lot of trouble to find Walter, and she had said the name that mattered...*Morningstar.*

He could always call her office. He could mention her phone call to Walter and gauge her reaction. If she had been the one to call Walter, she would likely own up to the call. Then, it wouldn't matter what phone she had used.

He memorized the office number from the website and logged off. He checked the time. It was after five. He took a quick look around. A few patrons had begun to trickle in for a drink before they drove home for the day. He kept his head down and looked away from the door. He couldn't risk staying there much longer.

The waiter came by again. "Tas viss pēc tam?" *Will that be all, then?*

Without looking at the man, Henderson nodded. "Ja, paldies." *Yes, thank you.*

The waiter walked away. Henderson closed his laptop, slid it in his backpack, and tossed it over his shoulder. He laid five Latvian lats on the table and walked out the door. He got into the BMW and drove to a rest stop a few miles further north. The lot was empty. He turned off the car. Like the field where Maddi had died, and the tavern where he and his friends had shared many a laugh, that rest stop was meaningful. It was where he had stopped after picking up Maddi in Riga. He closed his eyes, overcome by the memory of their first moments together after four long, painful years apart. He had been so nervous...so scared. And Maddi had been stunned...and so incredibly beautiful. He swallowed. *Make the call, Henderson.*

He pulled out the sat phone, surprised to see that his hand was shaking. *It's just a phone call.* Again, he checked the time. *Five-thirty in the afternoon in Latvia...ten-thirty in the morning in America.* He dialed the number he had memorized – the number to Claire Porter's office – and waited.

It took only two rings for her to answer. "Claire Porter. May I help you?"

Her voice was comforting; he felt a lump in his throat. *Keep it together, Henderson.* He tried to say something; he couldn't speak.

"Hello?" she said.

"Um...yes. I'm calling on behalf of Walter Henderson." He paused. His voice was hoarse; a remnant of the fire. He tried his best to hide it. "I—I understand you're looking for his son?"

There was a long pause. "This wasn't the number I gave. This is my office."

Henderson nodded. *There's my proof it was Claire Porter who called Walter.*

She said softly, "Are you Walter Henderson's son?"

Henderson rubbed his forehead. "I'm...I'm sorry, Ma'am, but Martin Henderson was...killed...in an explosion four years ago."

Another pause. "We both know that he wasn't. I'll ask again...are you him?"

Henderson sighed. "No. As I said, he's dead. May I ask why you care?"

"I need to speak with him."

"Why?"

"Because I have important information – a warning – that I was asked to give to Dr. Hank Clarkson."

Henderson sat back and frowned. *This is about Hank?* "Why not contact Dr. Clarkson yourself, Ma'am?"

Silence.

"Ma'am?"

"Be—because I've tried, sir. Apparently, he's not been heard from – by anyone – since August 26th...the day that Cynthia Madison died."

Chapter 26

Morningstar was giddy. With the help of his brilliant Janet, he had put together a plan that would not only solve the issue of the missing prototype, but would end the search for the Wilcox assassin. In spite of his frustration with his son's decision to hang on to the prototype weapon – *and then use it to kill a gas station attendant* – Morningstar didn't want to lose Zebulun. The man had proven to be one of his finest soldiers. Evidenced by the very fact that he had actually succeeded in killing the President. How many men throughout history had tried to kill a sitting U.S. President? So very few had succeeded. Zebulun was one of a rare breed. And, though Morningstar would need to discipline him for hanging onto the prototype weapon and then using it to kill again, he would offer him praise, as well. *I'm such a good father.*

He had intentionally held off speaking with him; it was imperative that no one ever link the two of them, whether Zebulun was implicated in the assassination or not. He was, after all, a hired killer. The further away Morningstar stayed from him, the better.

He heard papers rustle in the bedroom, and he grinned. Janet was doing what she did so well; creating phony documents with 'facts' to back them up. She had put together a second office at the hotel, and kept everything she needed in a lock box under the bed. It was a good thing. As the pregnancy had advanced, she had been forced to spend more and more time away from her office at the State Department.

He was glad that both of them had called in sick. They were much more productive when they were able to physically work together. He chuckled. *We can't be bothered with the day-to-day problems of the Pentagon or the State Department when we're preparing to take over the world.*

He had just gotten off the phone with Kuntz, his contact at Silverton. The two had agreed to meet at noon at the warehouse on the south end of town. Morningstar had spoken with Bentley Group member Carson, the judge who had a direct link to the Mossad. Carson had reassured him that his contact within the Mossad, as well as the one at Silverton, had kept his inquiries about the prototype weapon under wraps. Once Morningstar tidied things up, he would have Carson call both men and thank them for being valuable partners in the war on terror. He would then have him assure them that the Silverton prototype had been found, and, because of their help, the perpetrator had been caught. Neither one would ever have to know the truth. But the next few hours were critical. His meeting with Kuntz had to go exactly as planned; otherwise, he and the Bentley Group could kiss Silverton Industries goodbye.

Janet called to him from the next room. "Hey babe, I want you to look at these documents and tell me what you think."

He grinned. *I'll tell you what I think.* He walked into the room, shoved piles of paper onto the floor, and slid under the covers beside his very pregnant, very enticing woman. The entire world would soon be theirs; it was time to celebrate...again.

CHAPTER 27

Columbia, South Carolina

Andrew had somehow managed to clean up the townhouse and get to work by 11:00 a.m. Though both he and Amanda worked at the clinic, Andrew's role was administrative, which meant that he had a private office where he could be alone. He had hidden out in that office since returning from the ransacking of his house. Amanda had stopped on her way to a treatment room, and, after spending less than ten seconds with him, had known that something was wrong. He had done his best to lie – again – and tell her he was just worried about the plumbing. *"Seems like a lot of angst over pipes,"* she had said with a chuckle. He had simply nodded and grinned. *"Yeah, I guess so."*

Pentagon agent 'Khaki Adams' had suggested that Maddi had had terrorist ties...which was preposterous. But combined with what the man had said two months ago – that his mother had also been tied to terrorists – the entire situation was starting to get under his skin. After all, if he was dealing with terrorists, it was hard to say who was safe, and who wasn't. He wasn't worried for himself; he was a big man who knew how to handle a rifle. He was worried for his family...*the only one I have left.*

Which was why he had spent the last fifteen minutes sitting at his desk and staring at the wall. He needed to find a way to guarantee that Amanda and Adam were safe. He had thought about sending them away, but there was nowhere to send them. Amanda's parents had died when she was in college, and she had no brothers or sisters. Hank was an option; he and

Maddi had been so close for so long that Andrew felt Hank would be glad to help. But a phone call had resulted in a message on his voicemail, with a follow-up call from his ex-wife, Jenny, telling him that Hank was still overseas. She had seemed a bit shaken herself, and he had been tempted to ask if everything was okay. But he didn't want to pry. After all, Hank and Maddi had been in a relationship for years. Who knew what Hank was going through after Maddi's death, and, in turn, what his ex-wife might be going through. *"I'll try again later,"* was all he had said, though he doubted he would. There wasn't time. He needed to get his family to safety, and he needed to do it soon. Jenny had been kind enough to give him her cellphone number. *"Call me if you need anything, Andrew...anything at all."*

He shook his head and sighed. He wouldn't call her; he wouldn't call anyone. No one could help him protect his family. There was only one option: he would need to be the one to leave. It would be far easier for him to lay low than it would be for a mother and child. Besides, it was his mother, Jeannie, and his sister, Maddi, who had been accused of having ties with terrorists. Any threat – from either the government or the terrorists – would be directed at Andrew, not Amanda or Adam...*right?* He didn't know that; he couldn't know that. *So, I'll get them protection,* he decided. It would be easier than sending them away. But it wouldn't change the fact that he needed to go. Better to have the terrorists or the government focused on him rather than his family. But convincing Amanda that it was best for Andrew to leave, with her and Adam under the care of a hired gun, would be another matter.

Just get it over with, he thought, as he massaged his mother's medallion. As instructed in the letter, he now carried that coin with him at all times. It was like some unspoken symbol of the family he used to have. He continued to rub it between his thumb and fingers as he waited for Amanda to slide into the office for another break.

It was 11:30 before she came back. She walked in, and he jumped up and closed the door. She looked at him and frowned. "Okay, Andrew, what's up?"

He took a deep breath. "Amanda, have a seat."

She hesitated, then sat down cautiously, not taking her eyes off of him.

He stood over her, his towering frame making her seem small... vulnerable. "I have something to tell you. Something I should've told you long before now."

She sat there waiting, her dark eyes looking expectantly at his. He looked away. How many times had he done this to her? How many times had he kept her in the dark in an effort to 'protect her,' only to tell her later, after he had already done so much damage by keeping it from her in the first place. *Too many.*

He cleared his throat. "There's...something I didn't tell you...about the day I found Jeannie...dead."

She said nothing. He went on. "As you know, I found a letter on the bar."

She nodded.

"But there was something else in that room."

She frowned.

"A tape recorder was lying next to her."

"A tape recorder? What was on it?"

He shook his head. "I don't know."

Her eyes widened. "You don't know what's on the tape recorder?"

"No, I was...afraid to listen to it." He paused. "Anyway, I had told you that two men showed up at Jeannie's house while I was there, but I didn't tell you why."

"You said they were there because of a call from a concerned neighbor."

He looked down. "That was a lie."

She narrowed her eyes but said nothing.

"They were from the Pentagon. They told me they were surveilling Jeannie."

Amanda frowned. "The Pentagon? Surveilling Jeannie? Why?"

He swallowed. "They...they suspected her of having...terrorist ties."

"That's ridiculous!"

"I know. That's what I told them. They had insisted that I stay in McCordsville, but I knew I couldn't. My sanity wouldn't have allowed it. They also insisted that I take nothing from the house. I didn't tell them that I had the recorder."

"They didn't frisk you?"

"No. I'm guessing they felt bad for me. After all, I was standing over my dead mother's body."

Amanda nodded, but said nothing.

Andrew went on. "The problem is, they've called me several times now, both here and at home, insisting that I hand over the recorder." He frowned. "And this morning, they actually came to the house."

She frowned. "So, no broken pipe?"

"No. They had a search warrant, and they—"

"A search warrant?"

"Yes...and they tore the place apart." He added, "but don't worry, I cleaned it up." He paused. "As they were leaving, the guy in charge said that Maddi had been involved with terrorists, as well."

Amanda bristled. "That is just absurd!"

"I know. Here's my concern. I'm pretty sure they're going to keep coming."

"So, why don't you just give them the recorder?"

"Because I need to know what's on it before I turn it over."

Her eyes flashed. "Then listen to the damn thing!"

He nodded. "I will...tonight. I plan on getting it from its hiding place when I leave here." He paused. "But before I do I need to know that you and Adam are safe."

She frowned. "Safe from what?"

He shook his head. "I'm not sure."

"Andrew, what are you trying to say?"

He sighed. "Amanda, this...situation...isn't good." He paused. "It's not safe. *I'm* not safe. So, I'm going to leave...today. I'm not going to tell you where I'm going, and I'm leaving my cellphone here." He took his phone from his pocket and laid it on the desk. "We'll use trac phones from now on."

Her jaw dropped. "Trac phones? This is crazy, Andrew. We shouldn't have to skulk around like criminals just because of a threat from some government agent!"

He frowned. "It's not just the government I'm worried about." He hesitated. "Amanda, what if – I don't think it's true – but what if Jeannie really was somehow mixed up with terrorists...and what if she implicated one of them on that recorder?"

"There is no way, Andrew." She stood and looked him in the eye. "Go... listen to the tape. If there's something on it, then, fine...hide until you can figure things out." She turned and walked to the door. She stopped and looked over her shoulder. "But if there's nothing on it, then hand it over to the Feds and be done with it. Deal?"

He walked over, took her in his arms, and forced her to look at him. He could feel her shaking. "Amanda," he lowered his voice to a whisper, "I can't be sure they're not listening to us...here, now, or at home. I need to get far away from here before I listen to that tape." He paused. "But, even if there are no terrorists, something tells me that whatever's on the tape has the potential to get somebody in a whole lot of trouble."

Amanda looked up at him. There were tears in her eyes as she whispered, "I can't argue the point. They're obviously going to a lot of trouble to find it."

He hugged her tight and neither one said a word. Finally, she looked up at him. "Where will you go? How long will you be away?"

"Like I said...I can't tell you. I actually don't know. But I'll do my best to stay in touch." He walked her to a chair. She sat and put her head in her hands. He knelt in front of her. She looked at him and he grabbed her hands. He whispered, "I don't want to do this, Amanda, but the thought that something on that tape might put you and Adam in danger is a risk I'm not willing to take." He paused. "I'm going to call someone to watch over you...an ex-cop I met a couple of years ago."

"Andrew, I don't need you to—"

He placed his fingers gently over her lips. "Stop. I'm doing it. You won't even know he's there." Again, he hugged her. He didn't want to let her go. With a deep sigh, he stood and walked to the desk. He packed his laptop into his backpack.

"You're leaving *now*?" She was still whispering, and her voice was shaking.

He couldn't look at her. Keeping his eyes on his backpack, he said quietly, "I'll stop at home to pack, but I'll be gone before you get there." Still not looking at her, he added, "It's the only way, Amanda." He took a trac phone from his pocket and laid it on his desk. "Use this to call me... but only if it's an emergency. I'll do the same."

He put on his jacket, threw the backpack over his shoulder, and walked to the door.

She stood and ran to him. She grabbed him by the arm and forced him to look at her. "Andrew, wait. I don't want you to go. I don't think you *need* to go. We can solve this...together."

He tightened his jaw. "I don't think you understand, Amanda. It's not safe for me here...or for you and Adam if I stay." He turned and put his hand on the knob. He stood there, unwilling to move. Without looking at her, he whispered, "Whatever my mom and Maddi got themselves into is big...and I feel certain that whoever's threatened by it would think nothing of killing me – or those close to me – to make it go away."

CHAPTER 28

Washington, DC

Go on, Claire...you know it's the right thing to do.

Claire Porter stared at the chart on her desk. A simple folder, it was a relic in the era of computerized records. Claire didn't like computers; she didn't trust them. *Just a way for someone to get into your business,* she thought as she contemplated what she was going to do. She brushed a hand through her cropped strawberry-blonde hair, then crossed her hands and laid them in her lap as she stared at the file. She had cancelled her morning appointments, and was considering cancelling the rest of the day. She was determined to put her dilemma to rest – today – one way or another.

It was just like two months ago when she had done the very same thing. Cancelled her morning, suddenly in a hurry to put something to rest that she had sat on for far too long. *And yet, here I am...still not sure that I can do this.*

But it wasn't the only thing that was bothering her. She had vowed that she wouldn't call the prosecutor until she had delivered Maddi's warning to Hank Clarkson. But she had been unable to find Hank, so, in a fit of desperation, she had reached out to Walter Henderson, thinking that – just maybe – between him or his son, they might know how to reach Hank, or at least how to get a warning to him.

But the call she had received from the Henderson representative just an hour ago had been troubling. She hadn't been sure of the wisdom to call Walter in the first place, and, the fact that the call back was from some underling instead of his son had left her unsettled. *He doesn't believe me. Or, even more unsettling…he doesn't know his son is alive.* She scoffed. *He has to know.*

She knew that she shouldn't have called Walter with such a bombshell, but she hadn't known what else to do. Maddi's message, which at the time had seemed rambling and incoherent, had seemed anything but once the President – and his Secret Service agents – were assassinated. *It was basically what she had warned me about!*

Maddi had mentioned Hank, as well as a Secret Service agent and a man named Morningstar. More importantly, she had asked Claire to tell Hank to watch his back. So, Claire had started by trying to find Hank. She had reached out to her friend at the Department of Justice, and was told that Hank worked for Homeland Security, but that he hadn't been seen since the plane crash. Days later, she had attended Maddi's DC Memorial, thinking she would surely see him there. But after looking at hundreds of faces, she had seen no one that resembled the photo that she had pulled from the Homeland Security website. She had become alarmed. What had happened to him? Did it have something to do with Maddi's warning? Or had he vanished out of a simple need to grieve her death? Either way, he was missing, and she was left with a troubling message – a warning – that she needed to share with someone.

"So, why on earth did I decide that that someone should be Walter Henderson and his dead-but-not-dead son?" She had said the words aloud, and she shook her head as she also answered aloud. "Because you had nowhere else to turn, Claire."

It was true. Because of the nature of Maddi's message, Claire wasn't sure who to trust. Maddi had implied that several high-level agencies and at least one VIP were involved in the warning to Hank. A secret committee, a man named Morningstar, *…and a Secret Service agent responsible for the safety of a U.S. President!* When she couldn't find Hank, she had decided to turn to the only person she knew who could operate on such a stage; the man whom Maddi had loved, lost, then found again…Martin Henderson.

But she had had no way to reach him. Luckily, she was able to get a number for his father, Walter, from her friend at the Department of Justice. Walter's name had come up in a conversation that Claire and her friend were having about Russia's attack on Latvia. *Thank god Walter Henderson is over there to try to keep this thing from escalating,"* her friend had said. Further questioning had revealed that he knew Walter quite well. Claire had then told him of the life-or-death nature of her information, and of her need to speak with Walter. Though her friend had been hesitant, he had finally agreed to give Claire the most recent cell number he had for Walter. *"But you mustn't share it with anyone, Claire...understand?"* Claire had promised that she would make the call, then destroy the number. *"He'll either help me, or he won't."* After receiving the call back from a Henderson aide, and not from either Martin or Walter, she felt that she had her answer. *He is not going to help me.*

She sighed and looked toward the window, hoping to see her newest friend, the Exigent Cardinal, perched on one of the leafless tree limbs. He wasn't there. It was probably too cold and too wet. *I guess I'm on my own with this one.*

She frowned. Could it be that Walter truly believed his son to be dead? Or, did he know he was alive, but had no idea how to reach him? That seemed plausible. After all, it had taken Martin four years to contact a woman he was deeply in love with. *So, what if I never find him?* she thought, with a bit of panic. Who would she give Maddi's warning to? The police? No, they would never believe her. Besides, what would she say? *"My former client, who is dead, gave me a cryptic message before she died regarding one of the President's Secret Service agents, a secret committee, Hank Clarkson, and a man named Morningstar."* Again, she scoffed.

She had tried to figure out who Morningstar was, but had hit a brick wall there, as well. There were over fifty Morningstars in the metro DC phone book. Not only that; she guessed he was probably unlisted. *Or it might even be a code name.* After all, the name Morningstar had had many connotations throughout history. The Son of God, the devil, a star that signified hope, a star that signified death.

She sighed and walked back to her desk. She sat and stared at Maddi's chart sitting conspicuously on top of her desk. She had vowed to herself that she wouldn't reach out to the prosecutor until she was able to pass on Maddi's warning to Hank. *So what do I do now?* she wondered as she stared at the chart. She took a deep breath and nodded. *You take care of this now, Claire, as you might never find Hank.*

She continued to stare at the chart. She had to make a decision – today – about how she would dispense with Maddi's case. She had tried to address the same thing back in August...on the day that Maddi died. She had thought that Maddi's death had been the end of it, but she was wrong. Nothing had changed; nothing at all.

Claire was comforted by the fact that at least no one else was being punished for Maddi's crime. *"Too little evidence,"* Maddi had told her the first time they had discussed it. Though two men had been jailed, it wasn't for Evan Jackson's murder; it was for armed robbery, *"...and a slew of other crimes."* Claire's research had revealed that one of the prisoners had died while incarcerated, and that the other one was in Pendleton Penitentiary just outside Indianapolis. What would the revelation that someone else was responsible for killing Jackson do for either of them? Nothing.

But you still need to report it, Claire. There's a family out there that needs to know the truth about their loved one. She shook her head. *I doubt it.* From what Maddi had told her, it was hard to imagine that Evan Jackson even had a loved one. *It doesn't matter, Claire...his family has a right to know.*

Which left her where she was now...sitting at her desk, staring at Maddi's file, contemplating what to do. It was why she had cancelled her morning appointments, and why she was considering cancelling her afternoon. She was tired of thinking about it...tired of losing sleep to a decision that would leave her empty no matter how she chose to handle it. She had made up her mind that by the end of the day, she would either call the Prosecutor, or bury the entire incident forever.

She stared down at the file. It was surprisingly thick considering how little time Maddi had spent under Claire's care. They had started therapy in late December, and Maddi had had her last appointment in early March, just before she left for London. But in that short time, Claire had learned quite a bit about Maddi, and nearly all of it was contained within that chart. Maddi's loves and losses, her family struggles...*and her killing of a cop twenty-two years ago in Evansville, Indiana.* Claire was either going to put the file in her briefcase to take with her when she met the Prosecutor, or she was going to burn it in the hearth across the room.

She looked over at the fireplace. Flames were raging, ready to consume a file full of secrets...like hungry teeth waiting to devour each dirty detail. A simple toss of the chart into the fire would make it all disappear. She sighed. *But would it?*

Certainly not in Claire's mind. The entire matter had haunted her now for nearly a full eight months.

Again, she looked at the chart. Sitting next to it was a scrap of paper with a phone number she had scratched down way back then; the number for the Vanderburgh County Prosecutor's office. She looked from the scrap of paper to the chart, from the chart to the flames, from the flames to the scrap of paper. *Which is it, Claire? What're you going to do?*

A cuckoo clock on her desk struck the quarter hour. As she looked at the clock, she frowned. It was 11:45. *What if they've gone to lunch?* She shook her head. *They won't leave until noon...so, you better hurry up, Claire.*

She grabbed her phone, pulled the paper closer, and let out a deep sigh. She dialed the number. She waited, staring at the fire. *I don't like it...but I'm almost certain it's the right thing to do.*

CHAPTER 29

Washington, DC

The newscaster seemed almost smug as he recounted another tragic shooting that had taken place less than two hours ago.

> *"It looks like the gun rights activists are going to have to finally give it up. I'm standing here in Beaumont, Texas, at the scene of another shooting, the seventh in three weeks. It has left a father of four dead, his only crime; taking his children to school..."*

Knight clicked off the TV and tossed the controller onto his desk. A firestorm was brewing...and he hated it. His legislative recommendations would soon be dealt with in Congress, and, though the House Speaker had promised quick action, Knight doubted it would be quick at all. The debate over guns had gone on for decades with little to no success; a divided House and Senate weren't likely to do any better.

But it wasn't the only strategy he had put in place to try to address what was quickly becoming a crisis. A week ago, he had formed a special commission to evaluate and assess the laws that were already on the books regarding the buying and selling of guns in America. Unfortunately, the group had yet to meet. He sighed as he ran his hand through his hair. It was just one of his frustrations with Washington; nothing happened quickly, and it always took at least a dozen meetings.

He pushed the intercom. "Greg, get me Studebaker...the senator from Iowa."

"I believe the Senate is in session, sir."

Knight frowned. "Have him call me when they take a break."

"Yes sir."

Knight hung up and leaned back in his chair. Iowa's senator, Steve "Suds" Studebaker, had been put in charge of the commission. One of the shootings had happened in his hometown of Sioux City, and Knight knew the senator was eager to see that something got done. *So, why haven't you at least called a meeting?* Maybe Knight could inspire him to have the committee meet in the next day or two, so he would have something to tell the nation when he spoke to them in his prime-time address Wednesday evening. That address would need to be one of Knight's best. The nation was tired of platitudes. He had to put a stop to the shootings, or at least look as if he was trying to, if he was to have any hope of moving forward with his agenda.

My agenda. He sighed. The agenda, put forth to him from his first days with Morningstar, had been intentionally vague. But as Knight had acquired more power, the agenda had become more specific. And, though he wasn't necessarily in favor of it, he did believe in the man behind it: Edward Morningstar. *But if I don't get these shootings under control, the country will have little patience for what I hope to do.*

The first shooting hadn't received much attention. The rare, random shooting had unfortunately become commonplace in America. But then there were more...six more in less than three weeks. Why so many? And why so random? It was almost as if they were planned...as if the randomness wasn't really random, at all.

Suddenly, he frowned. *Had someone orchestrated these killings?* He narrowed his eyes. *No...no one would do such a thing.* Even if someone for whatever reason decided that random killings by different shooters across America was a good idea, how would he do it? How would he inspire so many shootings by men with no ties to one another? Who would stand to gain from such a thing? He thought of the anti-gun crowd and flinched. How better to rid the country of guns than by causing widespread panic... from guns. But would someone be so depraved as to make their case by inspiring gun owners to kill their fellow citizens? He shuddered; surely not.

He was saved from considering it further by a knock on the door. "Come in."

It was Agent Simmons. He was holding the cellphone that received calls from one man only...Morningstar. "You have a call, sir."

Knight took the phone and nodded. "Thank you, Simmons." He waited for the agent to leave, then answered with a hushed, "Yes, Father?"

"Did you see the news?"

Knight frowned. "About another shooting? I did, sir...it's terrible."

"Yes, son, it is. I wonder if maybe you should at least consider what we talked about a couple of weeks ago."

Knight frowned. "What was that?" he asked, though he knew the answer.

There was a pause. "Maybe it's time to take away the peoples' guns."

Knight swallowed, then cleared his throat. "With all due respect, Father, that would be unconstitutional. And it seems like a bit of an overreach, don't you think?"

A pause. "Remember our conversation several years ago?"

Knight tensed. He remembered it...far too well. As the two men had watched Australia take guns from its citizens in 1996, Morningstar had said, *"Their country will be so much easier to govern."*

Morningstar went on. "Think about it, son. You're the President *because* of an incidence of gun violence. There was a day when the second amendment made all the sense in the world, but now, with so much tragedy, maybe it's time for a break. Not a repeal of the amendment; maybe just a brief 'time-out' until you can get things under control. It would certainly make the next step of our plan much easier to put into place... don't you think?" Another pause. "At least consider it." The call ended.

Though the comments had been delivered as proposals, Knight knew exactly what Morningstar – Jacob – was saying: *"Take their guns, Judah, and do it soon."*

He thought again about who might have something to gain from the tragedies. There was only one group who would get what they wanted: the anti-gun lobbyists.

Then, out of nowhere, came another thought. *Or someone who wants to solidify my power...by removing guns from those who might stand in my way.*

He thought again of what Jacob had just said. *"It would certainly make the next step of our plan much easier to put into place."*

Knight's head had started to hurt. He stood and paced the office. *There is no way, Jerome...*he frowned...*no way that anyone, least of all the man who raised you and loves you like a son, would stoop to such a level.* He quickly dismissed it.

But, as he continued pacing, he knew, deep down...in that place one rarely allows himself to go...it was at least possible.

CHAPTER 30

Washington, DC

Morningstar hung up his cellphone and slid it in his pocket, grinning at his effectiveness. Subtle but firm, that was how he handled things with his discerning son, Judah. The young man would do what he asked; Judah always did what he asked.

He stepped out of his car, grumbling as he reached for a scarf from the back seat. The rain had stopped, but the wind had picked up, leaving the air far colder than it had been. He cursed as he wrapped the scarf over his neck and chin. He checked the time. *Almost noon...hurry up, Kuntz.*

Morningstar had arrived at the abandoned warehouse just minutes ago, careful to hide his car – a gray Ford Taurus that he hid in his warehouse for times such as these – behind a row of evergreens not far from where he was to meet Kuntz. The car was titled under Simeon's legal name, Jim Roberts. Morningstar chuckled as he crept through the trees. *Just one more layer to protect me, in case the car is ever spotted where it shouldn't be.*

He pulled his overcoat tighter around him as he jogged to a spot behind a thick maple where he could hide as he waited. Five minutes later, he spotted Kuntz sneaking around the back of the warehouse, a hat tucked low over his forehead, his collar hiked to his neck. Kuntz had once told him that he didn't mind the cold. *"There's a lot of it in the mountains, there is."* Morningstar had just laughed, trying to imagine what it was like to live in the middle of nowhere.

The man approached, and Morningstar stepped from behind the tree, making sure to stay in the shadows. He waved, stifling a laugh. Kuntz's odd dress and even odder mannerisms had made Morningstar chuckle on more than one occasion. But it had kept Kuntz from being suspected. *He's as innocent as the driven snow.*

The sun, now at its highest point, was blocked by the angled roof of the warehouse, creating a thick patch of shadow that followed Kuntz as he walked toward him. Kuntz wasn't a tall man by any means, and it looked as if he had lost a few pounds since the last time Morningstar had seen him. His beard had grown and he had acquired a mustache to accompany the jet-black hair he wore just above his ears. *Perfect.* The man took a final drag on a cigarette – clearly a new habit – and threw the butt to the ground as he stuck out his lower lip and directed the smoke away from him. *I'll bet the congregation would have a hard time with that one.* Kuntz blew out the last of the smoke as he walked up to Morningstar and nodded. "Boss," he said, with the accent that had always amused Morningstar. "So, what d'ya know now?"

"The weapon has been traced."

Kuntz frowned and tugged on his beard. "It is impossible."

"Yeah, so I've been told."

"I tell you, now, it is not traceable. To what...*event*...was it traced?"

"Oh, you know, just a little thing called a presidential assassination."

Kuntz's eyes widened and he shook his head. "Not good."

"I'll say. And now it's missing, Kuntz."

"I know."

"It would certainly be a shame if the missing weapon was somehow tied to Silverton...or to you. I'm guessing the assassination of a president would be a pretty big deal." He moved closer, now only inches from the man's face. Kuntz had begun to tremble and Morningstar could feel his fear. He moved even closer as he slid a hand into his coat pocket. "Probably a death sentence, don't you think?"

Though Kuntz was two inches taller than Morningstar, he seemed much smaller as his jaw trembled and his eye twitched. But he didn't back away. He glared down at Morningstar and said in a low voice, "With all due respect, sir, the secret of the weapon isn't mine alone." He moved closer. "You know of it as well."

What a fool. Morningstar pulled out a knife and stabbed it into Kuntz's chest, pushing until the entire blade was buried. He felt the warm blood on his hands and he stepped back, staring at a bold red stain that spread like a bull's eye beneath the man's coat. "Thanks for giving me a reason to kill you, dumbass."

Kuntz fell to the ground. Morningstar pulled the blade from his chest and wiped it with a handkerchief. Kuntz's eyes were wide as he gasped for air. He put his hand to his chest and tried to speak.

Morningstar leaned closer. "What is it, Kuntz? You wanna take it back?"

The man raised up and whispered, "I'm...not the only one...who...knows what you're doing." He took a final breath and fell to the ground. He was dead.

Morningstar stared at him, doing his best to push the words from his mind. Was it true? Had Kuntz told others about the weapon...about Morningstar? Had he known what Morningstar and the Bentley Group were up to? Had he shared it? Or was Kuntz simply trying to die with a final jab at the man who had just killed him. *That's it...a desperate man's last gasp.*

But, as Morningstar stood and scanned the area, he couldn't help but wonder: *Who else knows?* Other than those in the Bentley Group and a few of his soldier sons, no one else knew what the group was up to. *Right?* Morningstar was the well-respected aide who had been with General Daniels for decades. *Right?*

He kicked the body in an effort to put the thoughts to rest. He pulled a pair of brass knuckles from his pocket and put them on. He leaned forward and, using his closed fist, beat the poor man's face – including his jaw and his teeth – over and over again, in an effort to blur the distinction between Kuntz and the man Kuntz was about to become. After he had bloodied the entire face to hamburger, he looked down at the dead Bernard Kuntz. The similarity between him and Zebulun had been fortuitous. *Again, God watches over me.* He lit a match and burned the tips of Bernard's fingers and thumbs, removing any trace of the man's prints. He grimaced. Though he had smelled burning flesh on many occasions, he had never gotten used to it. He pulled his scarf over his nose as he finished burning the last of the fingertips.

When he was done, he pulled out a replica of the Vladimir Karev ID that Zebulun had used to get his job at the hotel in North Dakota. He slid it in Kuntz's pocket. For all intents and purposes, Bernard Kuntz had just become a Russian émigré; he had just become an assassin. But not just any assassin; the man lying dead on the ground would soon be 'proven' to be the President's killer, Vladimir Karev. America had found its assassin. *No need to look any further.* Not only that; Putin would no longer need to look for his AWOL soldier. *Zebulun is finally free.*

He pulled a pair of surgical gloves from his pocket and put them on. He walked over to where Kuntz had tossed his cigarette butt to the ground. He found it with little difficulty, and slid it in his pocket. He walked back and frisked Kuntz to be sure there was nothing that could identify him. He found a driver's license and a Silverton ID badge and put them in his pocket, as well. He would eventually place all three items on another dead body in a far-away shed, strike a match to it, and leave the death of *that* Bernard Kuntz for the authorities to sort through.

Still wearing the gloves, he took a baggy from inside his jacket pocket which held three folded documents. Janet had wiped them clean of prints, but, as he took them from the bag, he ran a soft cloth over each one. *You can never be too careful.* The first document showed detailed reconnaissance of the hotel in North Dakota where the President had been shot. A second document was a well-worn summary sheet of the prototype weapon, with all references to Silverton removed, and a competitor's name, Wilson Weaponry, attached instead. A third document – a last-minute stroke of genius by his lovely Janet – discussed the Lassa fever bioterror attacks from January, and identified Phoenix *and* Matt Henderson as not only the architects, but the perpetrators of the attacks. Though Morningstar had already planted that seed, there was nothing wrong with driving the point home. According to the document, Kuntz had been the one to obtain the vials of Lassa fever, and was hoping to blackmail Phoenix with his knowledge of the assassin's role in the attack. Morningstar's goal was two-fold; to suggest that the man lying dead on the ground, Vladimir Karev, had acquired access to the prototype weapon that had been used to kill the President, and to imply that he had also helped Phoenix and Matt Henderson carry out the Lassa fever attacks back in January. Then, once 'Karev' had indicated his plan to betray Phoenix, it would be clear to anyone investigating the fake Karev's death that the assassin, Phoenix, had had no choice but to kill the poor boy.

It felt good to put the screws to Martin Henderson, aka Matt Henderson, aka Phoenix, aka Joseph. The man was being protected by his powerful father, and Morningstar resented him for it. *I'll get him back here...if it's the last thing I do.*

And that document would start the ball rolling. Except this time, he had outdone himself. Far more than simply suggesting that Matt *might* have played an accessory role in the January terror attacks, the document tied him directly to the site of each attack. Janet had manufactured flight manifests, credit card purchases, and cellphone data to create a record that showed that Matt Henderson had been in each of the three cities at the very time when the attacks had taken place. It wasn't like anyone was going to find information that contradicted those details. Matt hadn't even been created when the Lassa fever attacks took place. Morningstar's hope was that the evidence would be enough to show irrefutably that Matt had aided and abetted a terrorist. Then, maybe Morningstar could get U.S. authorities – Hanover – to override Walter's plea for his nephew to stay in Latvia to help him fight a war.

Still wearing the gloves, Morningstar folded the documents and placed them inside Kuntz's coat pocket. He took the man's cellphone from another pocket and used it to dial Silverton Industries. He recognized the high-pitched voice of the receptionist, as she said mechanically, "Silverton Industries; how may I help you?"

Morningstar lowered his voice. "Is this Jane?"

"Yes, who is this?"

He did his best to mimic the unique accent. "It is Bernard Kuntz. I don't feel well." He coughed for effect. "A cold, I think. I need a few days off."

"I'll let 'em know upstairs. Bring a note when you come back."

"Will do," Morningstar ended the call and put the phone in his own pocket. He took the knife he had used to kill Kuntz, wiped it clean of prints, and set it next to the body. He grabbed a roll of tape from his pocket. On one side was a printed letter "P." He had created the tape while Henderson was still under his control. The roll contained Phoenix fingerprints; tiny smudges he could leave wherever and whenever he wanted to suggest that the rogue assassin had been present at the scene of a crime. It was the same spool he had used when he had carried out the bioterror attacks, pasting Phoenix fingerprints on each of the Lassa fever vials. He chuckled. *Just another way for me to control the outcome.*

He unrolled a small piece of the tape and held it against the handle of the knife in the place where a fingerprint would logically be if a man had just stabbed someone. He smudged a corner of the print, as if someone had tried to wipe it clean. He put the roll in his pocket and grinned. *My, my, Phoenix...you do get around.*

The entire plan was brilliant. With one fell swoop, he had not only removed suspicion from Zebulun, but had ended the hunt altogether. The President's killer was no longer in hiding; he was lying dead outside an abandoned warehouse in Washington, DC. Not only that; the man had been stabbed by another assassin, Phoenix, which would reignite the search for Henderson...for Phoenix. And, finally, one of the documents that Morningstar had tucked in Kuntz's coat would reinforce that Matt Henderson had been a willing participant in the Lassa fever attacks, which would force Hanover to bring him back to the States...*so that I, the Pentagon's liaison for the January bioterror attacks, can finally interrogate – and then kill – the bastard.*

He backed away from the fallen Kuntz, checking the area to make sure he hadn't been seen. But it wasn't necessary...he knew he hadn't. He had had Levi disable any cameras or satellites in a five-mile radius, and had made sure to stay in the shadows throughout the exchange. He took off the gloves, shoved them in his pocket, and ran back to his car. He slid behind the wheel, and, as he drove from behind the grove of trees, he glanced in the rearview mirror, chuckling as he saw the warehouse fade from view. *Now it's time to alert the authorities.* He pulled a burner phone from his pocket and dialed.

"911. How may I help you?"

"There's been a murder. Just off of route 95. Behind the old Cutler Warehouse."

"Your name, sir?"

Morningstar ended the call without a reply. *And now, we wait.*

CHAPTER 31

Washington, DC

Levi, Josh Adams, was spent. He had just gotten back from Columbia, South Carolina, where he had faked a warrant in order to violate Andrew Madison's constitutional rights. And, though he hated what he had done, he knew...it was for a good cause. He sighed as he pulled a burger and fries from a paper bag. *But was it?*

He set the fries on his desk and dug into the burger. The search for the missing recorder was weighing on him. He had no idea what was on that tape, but whatever it was, Morningstar needed to have it, and for some reason, it had become Levi's job to get it. *It wasn't even me who lost the damn thing.*

He sighed as he propped his Sperry-clad, size nine feet on his desk. His khakis were a bit too short, and they pulled up, revealing puffy, pale ankles. There was an empty can of Mt. Dew on the desk, and another in his hand. He took a sip. He was getting tired of Morningstar's insistence that he find something that Andrew swore he didn't have. Levi believed Andrew.

"Well then, where is it, Levi?" Morningstar had asked, when Levi had called him and told him it wasn't there. *"I don't know, sir...maybe it fell out of Issachar's pocket on his way to his car and he ran over it."* Morningstar had insisted that Levi keep looking. Unwilling to spend another minute in South Carolina, Levi had brought in a low-level Pentagon employee to keep an eye on Andrew; it was the best he could do. If the agent found the

tape, Levi would take the credit. If he didn't, Levi would say nothing about him. *Kind of how Morningstar handles me.*

He sighed as he took a bite of the burger. The man, Morningstar, was a conundrum. In one instance, he had been the sainted knight that had been willing to offer Levi a high-level job when no one else would. On the other hand, he had asked Levi to skirt the law on numerous occasions. He laughed. *My savior...and my pimp.*

Levi had worked for the Pentagon for nearly four years, his qualifications consisting of top-rate computer skills, a knowledge of the Middle East, and – most importantly – a quiet, unassuming nature. But those skills had almost gone unnoticed due to a messy past. He had been a wild young man and his rap sheet – with two felonies – had nearly undone his efforts to land a job with the U.S. Government.

The felonies were nothing more than teenage idiocy, but he had had a hard time convincing anyone else of that fact. The first felony had occurred soon after his eighteenth birthday. He had stolen a blanket from a Florida hotel room during spring break his freshman year of college and had carried it across the state line to his home state of New York. He had been caught – to this day he didn't know how – and he had learned quickly that taking stolen property across state lines was a big deal.

The second incident was a bit touchier. It involved another spring break, only this time it was his junior year. He had gone with a group of guys to Panama City, and there had been an incident with alcohol, girls, and an accusation of rape. One of the girls had identified Josh as her attacker and, though he had done nothing of the sort, Josh's lawyer had been unable to get her to recant. Josh felt certain that he couldn't survive a trial, so a deal was made and the charge was reduced to assault. Josh agreed to the lesser charge in exchange for an apology to the girl. Josh's lawyer had managed to get the record sealed, claiming his future would be significantly compromised if the girl's allegations were ever made public.

When Josh decided he wanted to do technical analysis for the U.S. Government, he knew the felonies would come to light. He was prepared to defend his behavior as 'the foolishness of youth,' and had been reasonably confident as he had walked into his first interview with the FBI task force representative. He had extended his hand to the interviewer, who had introduced himself as Agent Smith. Smith was a thick, muscled man about six-four, with dark, ugly eyes and a broad forehead. He had given Josh's hand a quick shake, and had motioned for him to sit in a metal chair on the opposite side of a narrow table. Smith had thumbed through Josh's folder and, after only a few seconds, had sneered, *"Is this a joke?"* Josh had begun to sweat in his J.C. Penny suit. *"Is what a joke, sir?"* The man had tossed the folder on the table. *"You're a felon, asshole."* Josh had nodded. *"Yes, I guess I am. But don't you want to know what happened, sir?"* The guy had walked out the door, muttering, *"I don't give a shit what happened."* Josh had sat there for several minutes; his anger mixing with disgust for the ugly FBI interviewer who had likely never gone anywhere for spring break and probably hadn't ever bedded a girl in his life. Finally, when it was clear that he had bombed the interview, Josh had stood and walked out of the room, un-tucking his stiff shirt and removing his tie. *"You're the asshole,"* he had said as he had walked away from the building.

But he wasn't ready to give up on the U.S. Government, and decided to try again, hopeful that the next guy would be more understanding. Steering clear of the FBI, he interviewed for a position within the Pentagon's Computer Investigations task force. He had walked into the meeting dressed in the same suit and tie, but with far less confidence as he prepared to face down his felonies. An older man had walked into the room, hiding an almost imperceptible limp. This man, though far shorter than the FBI agent, was, for some reason, far more intimidating. *"Have a seat, young man."* Josh had done as instructed, sweat beading on his forehead. The man, who hadn't bothered to introduce himself, had picked up Josh's folder and had thumbed through it. *Here 'goes,* Josh had thought, as he had prepared himself for a quick end to the interview. After an agonizing minute or two of the man flipping back and forth through the folder, the man had sat across from Josh and had said, *"So, tell me Josh, did you have a good time?"* Josh had frowned. *"I'm sorry, sir?"* The man didn't change his expression. *"These little excursions...during the spring of your freshman and junior years of college; were they entertaining?"* Josh had shifted nervously in his chair. *"Um, yes sir, they were. Well, except for the girl. I never raped her, sir."* The man had leaned back in his chair, and a slow grin had appeared on his face. His gray eyes had danced back and forth as he said, *"I don't care if you did. Rape is in the eye of the beholder, don't you think?"* Josh had been stunned by the remark, not knowing whether to be grateful or offended; he chose grateful. The man had then introduced himself as Edward Morningstar, and had explained that his boss, General

Alexander Daniels, was looking for an analyst to aid with Middle East reconnaissance. What would be the first attack on the World Trade Center had taken place about seven years earlier and Josh's training, a major in Middle Eastern Studies with a minor in computer science, was a perfect fit. *"I'll tell you what, Josh. I like you. And because I like you, I'm going to hire you."* He had then moved even closer and whispered, *"We'll just keep this little history of yours between us."* He had then stood and extended his hand. *"Josh Adams, welcome to the Pentagon."*

That was four years ago and Josh had stayed faithful. Wary, but faithful. He had been hired in spite of two felonies, with no explanation other than *'...let's keep it between us.'* Why would a high-ranking Pentagon aide be willing to overlook such a thing? It all became clear within months of his hiring. Josh was soon pulled in to do other types of surveillance for Morningstar; things that had little to do with the Middle East or the safety and security of America. And at first, he had been willing to perform such tasks without question. After all, Morningstar had given him a pass.

And the events of the last six months had only reinforced his dedication. Josh's mother had died from cancer when he was only a boy; he was raised by a distant father and an overprotective older sister. Six months ago, the sister moved out west with her boyfriend, and, only a few weeks later, his father passed away from a heart attack. Josh had been devastated. He was suddenly alone in the world. Though he had done his best to hide it, Morningstar had noticed a change and had asked him about it. Reluctantly, he had told him what had happened. *"I'm sorry sir, if it has affected my work. I'll do my best to not let it interfere."*

Then Morningstar had made an unusual offer. *"Don't worry about it, son. I'll tell you what. Consider me your father now. I'll look after you. I've done so these past four years, haven't I?"*

"Um, yes sir, you have."

"Good. Now, you'll continue on as you have within the Pentagon with only one change."

"What's that, sir?"

"You'll now have a code name."

"A code name, sir?"

"Yes, you will now be known as Levi...and I will be your father, Jacob."

And that's how it had been for the past six and a half months. For the most part, Josh liked his new role. Not only had Morningstar replaced the father who had died; he was better at the job. And Josh – as Levi – was let in on Morningstar secrets that were far bigger than Middle East reconnaissance. Morningstar knew the truth. Not what everyone professed among the Washington think-tanks and media elite; but the *real* truth about war and power, and changes that were about to take place. Morningstar had every intention of being a part of those changes, and he had made it clear that he wanted Levi to join him in his efforts. Being included had felt good; it still felt good. But as he leaned forward and grabbed a handful of fries from the bag on his desk, he flinched. *I just need to make sure that I watch my back.*

CHAPTER 32

Washington, DC

As the tall, hefty Charles Sturgill hurried toward the Capitol, he thought again about how much he hated the weather in DC. Not that he hated the cold; he was from Maine, after all. But something about the bitter winds coming off the Potomac made him shudder. Far different from the determined gales that blew in from the North Atlantic which forced strong-willed waves against the shoreline, DC's winds were weak, gutless wafts that caused little more than ripples in the waters of the Potomac.

Much like America in the modern world, he thought with a sneer. And that was why he was there...why he had come to DC. It was time for the United States to rise up, not with a whimper, but with a roar, and show the world what it was made of.

Especially China. Charles hated China. And not just because they had become arrogant and bullying. No, Charles hated China for far deeper reasons; reasons he could barely think about without falling apart. But soon he would have his revenge. After twenty-four years, the time had finally come.

He walked through the Capitol doors and nodded at the security staff he had come to know so well. The fifty-eight-year-old senator had been in DC long enough to go through three different security details; he even remembered when there was hardly any security. Though there had always been someone standing guard, the checkpoints now seemed like Fort Knox compared to those of the past. He had come there in the early eighties, just as the nation was trying to re-define its role in the world. The country had passed through the antiwar era, finally saying good riddance to Vietnam and all that had come with it. Fortunately, because of his family's connections – Charles' mother was a member of the prestigious Knight family from New Hampshire – Charles had managed to avoid Vietnam. He felt no shame in it; it had never been his fight. He had always been more of a pacifist, if the truth be told.

But not anymore.

Much had changed since the sixties and seventies, both with the country and with Charles. And the changes were similar. Lofty idealism had been replaced by painful reality, followed by cynical anger. Both he and America had become older, wiser...and far more bitter.

Charles reached the Senate Chamber and walked inside. He had never forgiven them; the people of China...the country itself. It was why he had agreed to work with Morningstar. It was why he had agreed to raise up Jerome as his own.

But now it was time for payment. He hadn't gone through the last two-and-half decades just to be cast aside, his need for revenge forgotten in the fog of time that had passed as one or two years became twenty-four. He had raised Jerome Knight to become the Leader of the Free World. *I have fulfilled my end of the bargain.*

Though he had been warned against ever calling Morningstar, the time had come; he was willing to risk it. He and Beatrice had waited decades – had sacrificed their very lives – to secure the retribution that had been promised by Morningstar.

For years after the kidnapping, Charles had made it his own personal mission to find his son. America and the world had gotten behind his efforts; at least for the first few months, but then other crises had come along and pretty soon the tragedy of a kidnapped American missionary's boy – even a nephew of the notable Judge Knight – faded from the headlines. In an act of desperation, Charles had asked for help from his uncle's best friend, Judge Carl "Cab" Colvert. The judge was able to persuade a diplomat to accompany Charles on a final trip to the Yunnan Province. But the Chinese had blocked them every step of the way, and, in December of 1979, he was forced to give up. The diplomat had promised that he would stay with it, however, and a month later he had called Charles with the name of the man who had likely been responsible,

Pyong Pang. *"He's been implicated in other kidnappings of young boys, and, based on the timing and location, I'm almost certain he's your guy."* But Pang had allegedly been killed in a raid, *"...along with most of the boys he had kidnapped,"* the diplomat had said. *"A government crackdown early this year forced kidnappers to...um...get rid of their cargo."* Two weeks later, Charles received a memo from the State Department which confirmed that a boy fitting Jamey's description had been found in an alley, dead from malnutrition and exposure. They had enclosed a photo, though to this day Charles hadn't had the nerve to look at it.

He had insisted on flying over to pick up his son's dead body but had been forbidden by both governments. *"There is no need...he has been cremated...there are too many people in China to keep corpses for very long."*

That was it. After four years, Jamey had been all but forgotten by the press and the U.S. Government, and, on a cold morning in January of 1980, the State Department had issued a final memorandum stating their assumption that the boy was dead *"...and no further resources will be allocated to the search."*

Charles remembered it as if it had happened yesterday; the cold wind rustling his hair as he walked down the snow-covered drive to the mailbox. The sting from the metal as he pulled open the mailbox door and found the official envelope stuck between magazines and bills. The gray day as the sun brooded behind ever-present clouds, refusing to shed light on words that stung far worse than the bitter gusts of cold air. Even now, twenty-four years later, it was enough to piss him off all over again. He gritted his teeth as he pulled a handkerchief from his pocket and wiped his forehead. Charles had been broken by it. It was weeks before he would even leave his house. And he hadn't stepped foot in a church ever since.

That was when Morningstar had come into the picture. He had approached Charles on a cold day in May, only days after he and Beatrice had laid his son's memory to rest, when the trees were bare and the gray of winter seemed as if it might last forever. It had been four years since Jamey's disappearance, and four months since the memo had arrived stating that the case was closed. Charles had become angry and withdrawn. The Pentagon aide had known exactly what to say to persuade Charles to work with him, and, though the man had unnerved him even then, their conversation in the back of that black sedan in the spring of 1980 had marked the first day of their less-than-honorable pact. That was twenty-four years ago, and Charles had done what had been asked of him. *Now it's your turn, Morningstar.*

But it was the phone call two days ago that had compelled Charles to finally call in the favor. He had heard from his embassy friend – now an ambassador – that a second man may have been involved in Jamey's kidnapping. He had uncovered a memorandum buried deep in a forgotten logbook which suggested that Lin Chu, a high-ranking member of China's military elite, may have played a role in Jamey's kidnapping back in '76. Charles, as Chairman of the Senate Foreign Relations committee, was familiar with Lin Chu. Though Chu wasn't directly in charge of China's military, he was the man responsible for its recent rise in status. He had been given the role two years ago, and had proven himself to be remarkably capable.

Because of Charles' role on the Foreign Relations Committee, he was in a unique position to investigate the man. *"Be careful, Charles,"* the ambassador had told him. *"This guy has powerful friends."* Charles was well aware of that fact, which was why he would leave the bulk of it to Morningstar. The Pentagon aide would have a far better chance of infiltrating the Chinese to get to the truth, and then bring pain to the man who had ruined his life. *I'm sure there's someone over there Morningstar can blackmail.*

Charles picked up the phone and dialed the number that had been given to him decades ago, wondering if it still even worked. He was surprised when a young man's voice answered. "Josh Adams, technical analyst. May I help you?"

Charles frowned. "Um, yes, young man. This is Senator Charles Sturgill, chairman of the Foreign Relations Committee. I have a matter I need to discuss with Edward Morningstar and was told that this number would connect directly to him."

There was a pause. "I see. Can I take your number, sir and I'll have him contact you?"

"Fine, but there better not be a delay. I'm a busy man, you know."

"Yes, I'm sure you are, Senator. He's currently away from his office, but I'll call him right away. Either he or I will call you back in the next few minutes, sir."

Charles gave him the number, then waited impatiently, pacing his senate office as he looked at framed photos on the wall. He stopped now and then to recall the moment when each picture had been taken. After twenty-two years in the Senate, Charles had quite a few photos. He stopped in front of a picture of him and the recently-assassinated President Wilcox standing arm and arm in front of the Capitol. *One hell of a guy, that man was.*

His phone rang and he answered quickly. "Hello."

"Charles?"

He recognized the voice; it had changed very little from the last time the two had talked. "Yes, is this Edward Morningstar?"

"Yes, it is. What can I do for you, Charles?"

"I think you know exactly what you can do for me. I have upheld my end of the bargain. Now it's your turn."

There was a pause. "Charles, I've not forgotten our agreement. But I thought Pyong Pang was dead. What is it you would like me to do?"

"I have just learned that there may have been a second man involved... he's a pretty big deal. I can give you his name now, if you'd like."

"No. Not over the phone. I'll send my assistant to meet you."

"How soon? Like I said, I've been waiting twenty-four years for this."

"How about this afternoon? The gentleman who answered the phone, Josh, works directly for me. I'll have him come to your office at 4:00. Will that work?"

Charles checked his ledger. There was a vote in twenty minutes – at 2:15 – and a committee meeting at four-twenty. Four o'clock was good. "Sure. My office."

"Good. Give him the name and we'll make sure to address your needs."

Charles hung up the phone. *By god, you better, Morningstar. I didn't raise the leader of the free world for nothing.*

CHAPTER 33

Washington, DC

Morningstar hung up from talking to Charles and chuckled. *What an ass.* But a deal was a deal, and he had every intention of fulfilling his end of the bargain. He made a quick call to Levi. "Get over to Charles Sturgill's Senate office at four p.m. today. He has something for you." He ended the call. His desk phone rang. He answered with a curt, "What!"

"Edward, it's Daniels."

Morningstar cleared his throat. "Oh, hello sir. What can I do for you, sir?"

"I just got off the phone with Sam Allen at the Secret Service."

Morningstar grinned. "Yes sir?"

"It appears that they may have found the assassin who killed the President."

"That's great news, sir. Who is it?"

"Some guy named Vladimir Karev. He's an expatriated Russian who went AWOL from Putin's army a few years ago."

"Russian. Interesting. Was he working alone?"

"Hard to say; we're looking into it. There were documents found with him. The CIA's Phoenix was mentioned."

"Really?" Morningstar fought to contain a chuckle.

"Yes, in association with Matt Henderson." There was a pause. "Matt's a nephew to Walter Henderson of Boston. Pretty farfetched to think that a Henderson would be involved in all this." There was a pause. "That's a good family, Edward."

Yes...the best. "I know, sir. I'm shocked, as well." He paused. "As you may recall, sir, Homeland Security tried to bring Matt to the U.S. for questioning two months ago, but was shut down by Walter, who insisted that he needed his nephew's help to fight Putin in Latvia." He paused. "Would you like me to overrule that request and get Matt back to the States, sir?"

He heard a sigh. "Let me talk to Hanover at Homeland."

"I would be glad to call him, sir."

A pause. "You know, Edward, that would be great. I'm kinda tied up with this bullshit in Fallujah." Another pause. "But go easy on the Hendersons; especially Matt. He's been through a lot, what with that weird coma and all."

Poor boy. "Yes sir, I will." Morningstar paused. "Can you tell me a bit more about the evidence that ties this man, Vladimir Karev, to the Wilcox assassination?"

"One of the documents shows detailed surveillance of the hotel where Wilcox was killed." He paused. "Another is a schematic of a unique weapon that supposedly can't be traced. A prototype, they're telling me." He paused. "I just received confirmation that it's the same weapon that was used to kill Wilcox."

Morningstar paused for effect. "How did you confirm it if it can't be traced?"

"I was told that it doesn't leave a traditional signature, but it leaves some sort of residue where the bullet enters. I guess you have to be looking for it to find it."

Some sort of residue? Morningstar narrowed his eyes. *So that's how an untraceable gun was traced.*

Daniels went on. "A representative from Wilson Weaponry – the company cited as being responsible for the creation of the weapon – has denied knowing anything about it. The FBI is looking into it."

Again, Morningstar grinned. *Perfect.* He cleared his throat. "I'm wondering, sir, if the whole thing could be a set up. I mean, that's a lot of incriminating evidence found on one guy. What's he got to say for himself?"

"That's just it. He was found stabbed and beaten to a pulp behind an abandoned warehouse off route 95."

"Who killed him?"

"They just ran the prints." Another pause. "It's Phoenix, Morningstar; the CIA's prized assassin." A sigh. "I'll be damned, Edward. The same guy responsible for the Lassa fever terror attacks just killed the asshole that shot the President."

Morningstar chuckled. "A little bit of good in every man, I guess."

"Yes, I guess so. Though Phoenix is an embarrassment to the CIA, he appears to have done us a favor with this lunatic."

"Maybe he's trying to make amends."

Daniels laughed. "Yeah, maybe so. There's gonna' be press all over this. Can you take care of that, too...after you talk to Hanover?"

"Certainly, sir."

They ended the call. Morningstar grinned. *It couldn't've gone any better.* He dialed another number. A receptionist said, "Homeland Security. May I help you?"

"Yes. This is Edward Morningstar at the Pentagon. I need to speak with Director Hanover at once."

"Yes sir."

Morningstar tapped the end of a pencil on his desk as he waited. He soon heard a gruff voice say, "This is Hanover."

"Hello, Director Hanover. It's Edward Morningstar from the Pentagon, your liaison in the bioterrorism case."

The Homeland Director was curt. "If you're calling about Hank Clarkson, all I can tell you is that he's still out on leave."

Insolent bastard. Morningstar cleared his throat. "I'm not calling about Hank." He paused. "I just got a call from General Daniels. They think they've found the President's killer."

"You're kidding! Who is it?"

"A guy named Vladimir Karev."

"A Russian? Was he working alone?"

"They're still digging through the details. Here's the thing. He was brutally murdered...and they're almost certain it was Phoenix who killed him."

A pause. "The President's assassin was killed by *the Phoenix*?"

"So they say. So now there's an even greater urgency to find Phoenix."

"We've been looking for him for nearly a year, Morningstar."

"I know. But I think I might have a lead. Matt Henderson's name was found on a document in Karev's jacket. It suggests that Matt was directly involved in the Lassa fever attacks last January."

A pause. "I still say that's impossible, Morningstar. My deputy director interrogated the man; he said there was nothing to those allegations." Another pause. "You're talking about a member of one of the most prestigious families in the country. I know for a fact that Matt Henderson is one of the good guys."

Morningstar rolled his eyes. "Then maybe the whole thing's a setup. Regardless, Daniels feels it is now imperative that we get Matt back to the States for a proper interrogation." He quickly added, "...not to suggest that your deputy didn't do a proper interrogation in the first place; it's just that...you know...sometimes a little pressure needs to be applied."

The response was fierce. "First of all, we don't condone torture in this government! Second, Matt Henderson is innocent until proven guilty. Is that clear?"

Morningstar bristled. *I can't wait to bury this ass.* "Certainly, Director. I couldn't agree more. I promise you that I won't let anyone do anything inappropriate to him." Morningstar had to put his hand over his mouth to keep from laughing.

"I'll see what I can do."

"Get him back here, Hanover. The general insists."

A pause. "As I said, Morningstar, I'll see what I can do."

They ended the call. Morningstar laughed. Never had he manipulated America's leaders so effectively. There was no doubt that he would soon have Henderson not only back in America, but the man would be placed completely under Morningstar's oversight. *Which means that within days I'll have Martin Henderson – Joseph – back home where he belongs. Then I can kill him.*

CHAPTER 34

Riga, Latvia

Henderson had left the rest stop in Uzava and had driven east, not even sure where he was going. In a matter of hours, quite a lot had changed. Claire Porter, a therapist from DC, had told him not only that she knew he was alive, or that she had information about Morningstar, but that she needed his help to find Hank. Why? Because she had a warning for Hank, and that Hank – the man who had befriended Henderson when he probably shouldn't have, and who had loved Maddi for much of his life – had gone missing...*on the same day that Maddi died.*

The conversation had pretty much ended once Henderson had learned that Hank had disappeared. He had shied away from telling her that he was Martin, in spite of the fact that she had insisted that she would speak only to Martin Henderson. He knew – sooner or later – he would call her back...*with the truth.*

Why hadn't he done so during that call? Because with Claire's warning in mind, Hank's disappearance felt ominous. Henderson had been fully aware that Hank had left the compound; what he hadn't known was that the man hadn't been seen since. Though it was possible that he had wandered off and killed himself, it wasn't likely. Hank had far too much intestinal fortitude to end his life in such a way. Not only that; he had told Henderson that he had gotten back with his ex-wife, and that it was 'better than ever.' Which meant that someone else was likely involved in his disappearance. Henderson needed to find out who it was – and why – before he revealed anything to Claire.

He had stopped several times on his journey east, pulling off the road to either hike among the trees that covered the lowlands between Uzava and Riga, or sit by one of the many lakes in the low-lying area, which was where he was now. Anything to help him think. The questions were piling up. What warning did Claire need to share with Hank? Did it have anything to do with Hank's disappearance? What did Claire know about Morningstar? Finally, how had something that Maddi had confided in Claire compelled the therapist to not only call Walter halfway around the world, but to take the bold step of revealing to him that his son hadn't died after all?

He shook his head and sighed. The sun had set; he needed to keep moving. He climbed the hill to his car that he had parked behind a row of thick evergreens, and slid behind the wheel. He pulled onto route A10 and headed east, no longer sure where he was going or what he was going to do. His biggest concern had changed from seeking revenge against Morningstar to finding Hank.

The moon was high as he reached the capital city of Riga. He drove to a hotel at the north end of town. He knew of the hotel from his days as a Freedom Fighter; it was a place where he could lay low; where a man would be left alone.

He pulled into the hotel parking lot and found a spot in back to park the car. He opened the dash and took out a pair of driving gloves. *Just in case,* he thought, as he walked into the hotel. Checking in as M. Henderson, he requested the top floor and paid up front in cash. He used the stairs instead of the elevator, and kept his head down as he walked to his room. *Old habits die hard.* He walked in and threw his backpack on the bed. There was little to unpack; he had left the estate with nothing but a change of clothes, a laptop, and the satellite phone that his father had given him. He turned to the window. The drapes were open; he closed them, leaving the room in total darkness. He was about to turn on a lamp, when he decided against it. *Better to keep it dark.* Again, old habits.

Because he felt certain that Hank would neither kill himself nor run away in despair, his disappearance was worrying. His last known location had been the Henderson estate. Walter had told Henderson that Hank had left the compound because his assignment had ended. So why wouldn't

Hank have gone back to DC? And how had he left the compound? Did someone pick him up? No, the estate's location was a well-kept secret. Walter would never have permitted it. So, did a Henderson driver take him to the airport? Did Hank drive himself? Once he had arrived at the airport, how would he have left? All flights had been grounded going in or out of Latvia. *So how on earth did Hank get out of Latvia...assuming that he did...and where did he go?*

Henderson leaned over and, using the light from his phone, opened the top drawer of a table by the bed and pulled out paper and a pen. He wrote: *ask Dad how Hank left the compound.*

He leaned back and stared at the ceiling. There were water stains along one corner, and streaks where the paint had faded. *Another five-star hotel,* he thought with a sigh. *I'm back...Phoenix is back.* He closed his eyes. He needed to rest.

Just as he was about to fall asleep, he heard a voice. A girl's voice. *Lili.* He covered his ears; he didn't want to hear from Lili. Her repeated insistence that Maddi was alive did nothing more than remind Henderson that she wasn't. "Go away, Lili."

"I need you to listen to me."

She sounded so clear; so present. He opened his eyes, half-expecting to see her on the bed. There was no one. *Of course, there's no one...she's dead, you idiot!*

Her voice was firm; even. *"You need to find the manifest; not everyone died."*

Henderson's eyes widened. He sat up and threw his feet over the side of the bed. In spite of himself, he said, "What?"

"Check the manifest. Not everyone died in that plane crash."

Henderson tried to recall what his father had told him about the accident. *"It happened north of Liepaja. No one survived."* That had been it. No details; nothing. And Henderson hadn't wanted details. He had refused to read newspaper articles or watch TV. But now he wished he had. He wished he had learned all that he could about the crash that had taken Maddi away from him. Instead, he had trusted his dad's version of events. *Would Walter lie to me?*

He was about to add that to his list of questions, when his sat phone rang. He frowned. *No one knows this number.* His hand was shaking as he answered with a whispered, "Yes."

"It's me...Walter."

Just the man I need to talk to. "Did someone survive the plane crash, Dad?"

There was a pause. "What are you talking about?"

"The crash. Maddi's...accident. Did someone survive?"

Another pause, this one longer. Finally. "Yes."

Henderson felt as if he had been kicked in the gut. He jumped up from the bed and began pacing the floor. "Who was it? And why didn't you tell me?"

Another pause. "Because I thought it would only make it worse if you knew."

"If I knew what?"

He heard a deep sigh. "That Maddi's bodyguard, Tom Cravens survived."

Henderson was having trouble breathing. "I need to talk to him."

"I don't know how to reach him."

"Then I need to talk to his boss." He paused. "Do you have his number?"

"Son, I—"

"Please, Dad...I just need to know what happened...how she was...at the end." He was shaking, and he took several deep breaths in an effort to calm down.

"The poor man was likely questioned a million times about the accident, son."

Henderson was about to explode. "I just need to hear it...from him." He hesitated. "I...I need to know what she was doing...her last words." He finished with, "I need to know how she was when she...died."

There was a pause followed by a deep sigh. "I have Sam Allen's private cell number. We spoke several times after the accident." Another pause. "Ready?"

Henderson grabbed the pen. "Yeah."

Walter gave him the number, then said, "Where are you, son?"

"In Riga. I needed a place to think things through...to put a plan together." He hesitated. "Did you know that Hank was missing? That he hasn't been heard from since the day of Maddi's crash?"

"How did you hear that, son?" A pause. "Did Ms. Porter tell you that?"

Henderson narrowed his eyes. "She did. I called her, Dad...I couldn't help it." He added, "...but I didn't tell her who I was."

"Did she tell you anything else?"

"No, she insisted on talking only to Martin." He paused. "I called her office, Dad, instead of the number she gave you. But unprovoked, she admitted to having called you. I think that proves that her call to you was legitimate. Have your men found out any more about her?"

"No...not yet."

Henderson frowned. He glanced at the jotted note on the table next to him and said quickly, "Dad, how did Hank leave the estate?"

"He took one of our cars."

"To where?"

A pause. "Originally, it was to have been a simple ride in the country. He was going crazy being cooped up at the castle. I could see the toll it was taking on him, so I told him to go for a drive to clear his head."

"Did he come back?"

"No."

"Didn't you find that odd?"

"Yes."

"Don't all of the cars have GPS?"

"Yes. We tried to track the car he had taken. We got nowhere." Walter paused. "Which means that he had to have disabled it."

Henderson frowned. *Why would he do that?*

Walter continued. "Son, there's a reason I'm calling you." He paused. "I just got a call from Jason Hanover."

Henderson's eyes widened. "Was it about Hank?"

He heard a sigh. "Sort of. Do you remember why Hank had come to your Edinburgh hospital room in the first place?"

How could I forget. "Yes...to take me – to take Matt – back to America to question him about his knowledge of the January bioterror attacks."

Another sigh. "Well, apparently a document has surfaced that offers proof that Matt not only played a supportive role in those attacks, but was present at every single one."

"Does it say anything else?"

"I don't know. But it implies that Matt worked directly with the Phoenix."

Henderson laughed. "Well...we both know that that can't be true."

"Yes, but someone's certainly going to a lot of trouble to make it seem like it is."

Morningstar. "Don't worry, Dad, I'll take care of it."

"Here's the thing, son. Hanover was calling me as a courtesy. He wants you back in the States...immediately."

I can't go to America...not now! Especially not as a suspected terrorist. "Clearly, that can't happen."

A pause. "I told him that you had left the compound for a few days, and that I didn't know where you were or how to reach you." A pause. "It's the Department of Homeland Security, son. They have a lot of resources at their disposal."

So do I. "I understand, Dad. Like I said, I'll take care of it."

"Martin, don't take matters into your own hands. You aren't equipped for it."

Oh, but father, I am...I'm so amazingly well-equipped. "Don't worry, Dad. I won't do anything reckless...I promise."

He heard another sigh. "I love you, son. And I finally have you back. Please, don't put your life at risk."

Henderson let out a laugh. "As you know, Dad, my life means very little to me." He hesitated, then added, "but I'll be careful." He ended the call before Walter could say anything more.

He stared at Sam Allen's number...the number of the man who could tell him about Tom Cravens, the only survivor of Maddi's plane crash. Though Henderson was tempted to call him, it would have to wait. He was now not just wanted for questioning; he was being hunted by America's Department of Homeland Security. And not for his knowledge of a crime...*but for the crime itself.*

He stuffed Sam Allen's number in his pocket and stood and grabbed his coat. He needed to get out of there. Walter had just spoken to Hanover, which meant that a warrant had already been issued. He threw his backpack over his shoulder and was about to open the door, when he heard footsteps in the hall.

There was a firm knock. With a strong Lettish accent, a man yelled through the door, "Mr. Henderson, I need to talk to you."

Shit! He ran to the window and lifted the pane, allowing a rush of cold air into the room. He looked out. He was on the third floor, but there was a tall oak less than three feet away. With the backpack over his shoulder, he climbed onto the ledge.

"Mr. Henderson! Are you in there?"

He heard a jiggle of the doorknob, followed by a key in the lock. He jumped for the closest branch, reaching it easily as he grabbed a nearby limb to steady himself. He crawled to the center of the tree and shimmied partway down, ignoring the rough bark as it scraped his forearms and hands. He pulled the gloves from his pocket, and was putting them on, when he heard commotion at the window he had just come from. He dropped his backpack to the ground and looked up. He could see two officers – they looked like Riga police – peering out the open window. *The United States Government has enlisted the help of the Latvian police?* From what he could tell, they hadn't spotted him. He crawled further down the trunk of the tree. When he was within ten feet of the ground, he jumped, picked up his backpack, and sprinted into the woods. He ran without looking back, unsure where he was going; just knowing that he had to get as far away as he could from that hotel and from Riga.

In a matter of hours, his entire life had changed. He was once again on the run, only this time it was black-haired Matt they were looking for. Hank was missing; he had taken a Henderson car over two months ago, had disabled the GPS, and hadn't been heard from since. Finally, Secret Service Agent Tom Cravens had survived a plane crash that no one should have survived. But most stunning of all, was that Lili – a young girl who had died almost a year ago – had just told him that very same thing.

CHAPTER 35

Riga, Latvia

Gad – Marcus King – hadn't expected any excitement on his late-night jaunt through Riga. And he most definitely hadn't expected to see Matt Henderson.

Just minutes before, he had been stretched out on a lumpy mattress in a dingy hotel room, lamenting the fact that the stale room had been his home for the past two months. Because of the need for him to save Dan – Cobra – he had been forced from the Henderson estate with nowhere to go. But he hated Riga. He was eager for a change and could hardly wait for Morningstar to send him somewhere else.

But not Lithuania, he thought with a sneer. Not only was he being asked to go to another drab country, but he had been given an impossible task once he was there. *"Lure Henderson to Lithuania so he can be taken by a few of our soldiers, son."*

That assignment had been given to him two weeks ago, and Gad had spent the time since trying to come up with a plan. The task was complicated by the fact that Gad was a wanted man. It was almost a guarantee that the Henderson security team was looking for him. Walter had been suspicious of him from the minute he had spotted him as a driver for the estate. And if Walter or any of his soldiers had figured out that it was Gad who had helped Cobra escape the compound, they would have all the more reason to be suspicious. He chuckled. *And I'm sure they got the message when I didn't show up for work the next day.*

But how hard would the soldiers look for him? What lengths would they go to find him while they were in the midst of a war? Were they looking for him now? Had they put out some sort of APB? He didn't know, but one thing was clear; he couldn't risk one of them catching him. If they did, he felt certain they would kill him.

As for luring Henderson to Lithuania, he had yet to come up with a plan. Henderson was no dummy. He would know that to leave Latvia would be to put his freedom in jeopardy. Which meant that Gad would have to come up with a very compelling reason to make the man risk his own safety and leave Latvia.

Gad had begun the late night walks soon after arriving in Riga. The darkness gave him cover, as well as an excuse to leave the stuffy hotel room. He found that walking helped him think. But always, he was careful. He wore a hoody, carried sunglasses in his pocket, and brought his backpack on every single walk. In it was his wallet, his gun, two cellphones, and the few items of clothing he owned. Morningstar had made it very clear over the years that whenever Gad left a hotel or a hostel, he should leave as if he was never coming back. *"Even if you're just leaving for an hour or two, take everything with you. You never know when the place might be searched."*

The wallet held two ID's; his old one, which he had taken from a Henderson driver whom he had killed on his first day at the compound, and a newer one that Morningstar had told him to get as soon as he got to Riga. The older ID listed him as Carlos DeMarco. The newer one showed him to be an Estonian soldier by the name of Adrus Sepp. Though he had been tempted to destroy the DeMarco ID, he had held onto it...just in case. *One never knows when he might need to leave a false trail.*

As for the phones; one was a direct link to Jacob, and the other was a trac phone that he had purchased soon after arriving in Riga. He used it whenever he needed to talk to someone off the grid. It was how he had managed to get the second ID. It was also how he had learned his way around Riga; where to get a gun, where to find women, how to score weed. He couldn't use Jacob's phone for those pursuits.

He had just wandered over to a city park in Old Town and was about to stroll among the trees, when, by the light of a nearly-full moon, he spotted a man leaping from a third-story window to an oak tree a few feet away. Curious, he crept closer and looked up, stunned to see that the man clinging to that tree was the same man who Gad had drugged, then transported from Lyon, France, to Dalgety Bay, Scotland...the same man who had laid in his bedroom the entire forty-eight hours that Gad had spent at the Henderson estate...the same man who Morningstar had instructed Gad to lure to Lithuania. *Why is Matt Henderson climbing out of a third story window...in Riga?*

Intrigued, but fully aware that if Matt saw him he would likely report him to the Henderson security team, Gad quickly knelt down behind a clump of bushes near the tree. He needed to find a way to take advantage of the situation. Clearly the man was in trouble. Gad chuckled. *I should just grab him and take him to Morningstar.*

He shook his head. Bad idea. Henderson wasn't just some rich boy who lived in a castle. From what Gad had been told, he was one of the best assassins ever, and he was also highly skilled in hand-to-hand combat. It wasn't likely that Gad could simply grab the man, let alone keep him long enough to deliver him to Morningstar.

He heard commotion from the same window the man had just jumped out of, and he looked up to see what all the fuss was about. He saw two armed officers leaning out the window. They were obviously looking for Matt, and, from what Gad could tell, they had yet to spot him in the tree. *I should just yell that he's up there.*

Gad stooped lower in the bushes. He couldn't do that either. Morningstar wanted Matt Henderson; he had made that very clear. If the Latvian police were to take him, it was impossible to say how or when Morningstar would get the man.

Gad was glad he was wearing the dark hoody. He pulled the hood low over his forehead and put on the sunglasses. He watched the man creep further down the tree, surprised when he saw him stop and drop his backpack to the ground. What was it that Morningstar had always told him? *"When you see an opportunity, son, you must pursue it at once; there is rarely time to second-guess yourself."*

Without a moment's pause, Gad ran to the tree and looked up. Henderson was still a full twenty feet above him, and was staring up at the window, not down at him. Gad was about to grab the backpack, when, suddenly, he stopped. *Why steal the backpack when I can use it, instead?*

He slid his own backpack from his shoulders and pulled out his trac phone. As he did so, he spotted his pistol gleaming in the moonlight. How good it would feel to just shoot the man. In Gad's opinion, Matt

Henderson had taken up far too much of Jacob's time. But a shootout would surely end up with one of them dead. Especially with the armed officers not far away. Gad wasn't ready to die, and he couldn't kill Henderson; that was Morningstar's job. *Jacob would destroy me if I offed that asshole.* He chuckled. *So, I'll just follow him, instead.*

He slid the trac phone into Henderson's backpack, slung his own backpack over his shoulders, and fell back behind the bushes. Within seconds, the man jumped to the ground, grabbed the backpack, and sprinted into the trees. Keeping his distance, Gad sprinted after him. He grinned. *And if I lose the bastard, I'll just give him a call.*

CHAPTER 36

Washington, DC

Charles looked again at the clock on the wall. *Four p.m. on the dot...let's go, Josh.* He had been waiting since 3:45 for the Pentagon analyst. Morningstar had promised the man would come at four; Charles didn't appreciate someone being late for a meeting.

He was pacing his office, his large frame lumbering back and forth like old Marley carrying chains of remorse as he sought a chance to make amends. But, unlike Dickens' Marley, he wasn't the one who needed to pay; he was the one who was owed. *But the chains are there, nonetheless.*

He stopped at a window to look out at the faded remnants of fall. Orange and yellow mums lined the walkway, and fallen leaves of the same colors covered the ground. Nothing but yellows, oranges, and browns in a backdrop of dreary gray. He hissed; he hated Washington, DC.

There was a knock, and his secretary poked her head in the doorway. "You have a visitor from the Pentagon, sir."

"Send him in."

Josh was a young man – likely in his late twenties – with a heavy build and light brown hair and glasses. He was wearing wrinkled khakis, his shirt was only partway tucked in, and his North Face jacket was unzipped and a size too small as it failed to cover his oversized belly. Charles was amazed that the crisp, disciplined Morningstar would allow his representative to dress so casually. "You must be Josh."

The man extended his hand. "Yes sir. I'm to pick up a list of names?"

"Only one name." Charles walked to his desk and grabbed a folded piece of paper from inside a binder. He handed it to Josh. "Be careful with this, young man. It represents over two decades of hard work."

Josh nodded. "I understand, sir. I'll deliver it immediately."

"Thank you."

Josh turned and left, leaving Charles to contemplate what he had just done. If the information he had received from his ambassador friend was correct, then twenty-eight years ago his boy Jamey had been taken not only by Pyong Pang, but by the man whose name was on that paper. Even writing the name had cut Charles deep in his soul...in a place he thought he had walled off completely. Clearly he hadn't, and the resurgence of that hatred was boiling within him like a cauldron of black tar. The name on that paper was a compilation of nearly thirty years of hate that had eaten him alive, cost him countless hours of sleep, and spurred him to a need for revenge that had pretty much defined his entire existence. And he was close; finally, he was close.

He looked at a picture on the wall. It was an old photo, taken before the digital age, tucked inside an old wooden frame. It seemed out of place amid the professional photos of presidents, congressmen, and world leaders. But it was centered among them; a simple truth surrounded by a regalia of hypocrisy. The boy in the picture had just turned four; the photo had been taken at his birthday party. He was wearing a hat, and icing from his birthday cake was smattered on his face. He was laughing, and the camera had caught him just as he had realized that someone was taking his picture. His eyes had lit up as he had turned to the lens, and it looked to Charles like Jamey was nodding at him. Charles nodded back. "It won't be long now, son."

He fought tears as he stared a minute longer, surprised he could still feel such grief after so many years. When Jamey was kidnapped, Charles felt as if he had died; that feeling hadn't changed. Though he walked among the living, he was dead, his life taken from him by the thieves who stole his boy.

"Marley was as dead as a doornail."

The clock rang out the quarter hour. He sighed and reached for his briefcase. He had a committee meeting to attend. He walked to the door, then stopped and looked back at the picture. As though Jamey was waving goodbye, Charles gave a wave and said again, "It won't be long now, son."

CHAPTER 37

Somewhere in Eastern Europe

The edict came down from the Kremlin at 1:36 a.m. in Uzbekistan, 11:36 p.m. in Eastern Europe, and 9:36 p.m. in the UK. Tim Johansson, U.S. intelligence officer, buzzed on coffee and cigarettes, had been monitoring his screen from a bunker in the Turkestan mountains for the past four hours and had nearly missed it. But it was the unique combination of words that had caused him to take note: *The Russian Bear will recover her cubs.* Nothing flashy, but the message was worth looking into. Was Russia going after a prior holding...a *Soviet* holding? Tim dialed into the frequency and waited. Within minutes, he heard a staticky comment that caused his heart to race. *"Our...men are ready...Baltics, sir."* Tim had no idea who 'sir' was; it didn't matter. 'Baltics' left little room for interpretation. The states surrounding the Baltic Sea: Estonia, Latvia, and Lithuania, were countries much like Uzbekistan, which had left Russia in the early nineties. They had once been a part of the vast Soviet Union, and their departure had been a symbol of its fall. Though there were already threats of war breaking out in Latvia, there had been no direct proof that Putin was behind the attacks; only circumstantial evidence that had implicated Russia. Putin had denied any involvement. Was this discovery the proof the west had been looking for?

Johannsson couldn't tell for certain where the order had originated, but data points suggested strongly that it had come from the Kremlin. Was it Putin? Or had a subordinate come up with the idea in a fit of unparalleled hutzpah? Either way, Tim felt the objective was clear: Russia was about to make good on its threat to take back Estonia, Lithuania, or Latvia...or maybe all three. *This is big; I have to report it.*

Tim Johansson had worked with the National Security Administration for the past four years; prior to that he had worked for the CIA. He was never a part of the action; always a part of the reconnaissance. He didn't mind; it was far better to track those who might be dangerous than to be in danger himself. Besides, his long, lanky frame and his weak joints were more suitable to a spectator's role. He had been the teenager who had locked himself in the basement with each release of "Mortal Kombat" along with a distant army of strangers, united in their quest to kill an enemy that flitted across their TV screens in the middle of the night. It had been a logical progression to go from video games to satellite reconnaissance, and no one was better at it than he was. His current assignment, the monitoring of chatter between Russia and Iran, had been his task for the past two years, when hints of a nuclear Iran had begun to appear just after the 9-11 attack. Though the politicians were willing to waste time on sanctions, Tim knew: it was too late. Not only did Iran already have the nukes, they were soon going to try to use them.

It was also no secret that Russia had sided with Iran off and on over the course of the last several years. So, the NSA had set up a special satellite designed specifically to monitor communications between the two countries. Fortunately for Tim – and likely the reason he had been given his current assignment – he was fluent in both languages, and was able to tell immediately the difference between idle chit chat and truly sensitive information. He made constant sweeps of Iran and Russia, and the exercise had proven useful. Only months ago, he had intercepted part of a phone call, followed by an email exchange to a Russian operative which had included diagrams of an estate in Western Latvia. The operative had been in Estonia, and was given information detailing the location and security capabilities of a hidden compound just outside Uzava. Within twenty-four hours, an assault was carried out against the security team at that very same compound, killing thirty men before it was over. Tim had alerted his supervisor to the phone call prior to the assault, but the man had ignored him. Once the attack was underway, the supervisor notified the CIA, telling them of his intercept of the call to the Russian operative; the CIA had immediately flown a team to the site. Johannson had heard nothing more about it, except that they had arrived too late. More importantly, he had never received the proverbial pat on the back for intercepting the email, or for his attempt to warn his supervisor. It was okay...he was used to being overlooked.

But then, only days after the assault at the compound, he had been contacted by a representative from the Pentagon. This man was different; he seemed to understand how vital Johannson's work was to national security. He had asked him to continue his reconnaissance, *"...and call me if you hear anything more. I'll be sure the higher-ups take note."* He had overnighted him a sat phone that would connect only to him, and was told to use only that phone to call him. *"Speak of this to no one. I promise you that I will act directly on your information, and I will get it to the men who matter...no one will interfere."*

Just an hour ago, that same Pentagon aide had called to tell him that the man suspected of assassinating the U.S. President was believed to have been Russian. *"This makes the work you're doing that much more important, Johansson."* The entire intelligence community had ramped into high gear, which had placed him center stage – covertly, of course – as America sought more and better intelligence.

Johannson wasn't surprised to learn that Russia was involved. *"One plus one equals two,"* he had told his supervisor when he was asked about it. *"After all, Wilcox was pushing to sanction Russia for cozying up with Iran."* As far as he was concerned, the Latvian estate attack, the assassination of Wilcox, and the Russian communique he had just intercepted were all connected...all part of the same master plan. They pointed to one thing and one thing only: a sizeable Russian land grab in the coming days or weeks. Johannson's work had suddenly become vital, especially to the Pentagon. *It's about time,* he thought, as he stared at his monitor, recalling images from "Mortal Kombat." *It will be like version III,* he thought, *...and it all comes down to me.*

He was due to report to his London supervisor at ten p.m. their time; two in the morning in Uzbekistan. But there was someone else he would contact first; the man from the Pentagon who had assured him that his efforts would not go unrecognized. He looked at his watch, which had a dual setting for America's eastern standard time. *Four-fifty-five p.m. in DC... I'll bet the guy's getting ready to leave work.* Johannson made sure he had his facts in order, then picked up the sat phone. He dialed and waited for the call to go through. An impatient voice answered. "Yes?"

"It's Tim Johansson, Mr. Morningstar. I have information."

CHAPTER 38

Washington, DC

Levi took a drink of his soda as he checked his monitor. He was tracking the communique he had embedded only minutes before, hoping to see something to indicate that his data had done what was intended. The goal? To further lure Russia into a war with the West.

Morningstar had been trying to do that since August, but Putin had continued to deny any role in the attacks on the NATO country of Latvia. The West wasn't willing to counterattack as long as Putin denied it, unless they had proof that he was, in fact, behind it. Levi laughed. *So, I just gave them the proof that they need.*

Morningstar's instructions had been clear. *"Plant satellite intel that suggests that Russia is going to attack its prior Soviet holdings of Lithuania and Estonia, to augment its attack on Latvia."* And it had been simple. The NSA was constantly monitoring chatter from Russia. All Levi had needed to do was transmit a memo that said *"The Russian Bear will recover her cubs."* Once he had sent it, he had waited a few minutes and had sent a memo that said, *"Our men are ready in the Baltics, sir."* Within the next twenty-four hours, he would release an encrypted message with an easily cracked code: *"Takeover of L, L, and E to begin within 72 hours."*

Morningstar had framed the entire project as a brilliant solution to an ongoing problem: America's weakness in the Middle East and Eurasia. *"Iran and Russia have become cozy. We keep pushing diplomacy, which you and I know is bullshit. If we rattle the chains of the mighty Putin, it's likely he and Iran's Supreme Leader will ratchet up the rhetoric just enough to get our government off its ass."* Levi couldn't agree more.

Nonetheless, tinkering with a catalyst to war bothered him. Like so many of Morningstar's requests of late, it wasn't moral, it wasn't ethical, and it most certainly wasn't legal. Levi certainly didn't see himself as a beacon of decency, but the last thing he needed was one more criminal act on his record.

Which was why – starting four days ago – he had begun keeping records...of everything. He took a snapshot of every text, he copied every email, he recorded every phone call, and he scanned all memos from the man who called himself Jacob. He kept it all in a secure, password-protected location on his computer. The only way it would ever be found was if he wanted it to be...*or if I'm dead.*

He was on his fourth can of Mt. Dew, and he took another sip as he stared at the screen. It was nearly five p.m. in America, which meant that it was almost ten p.m. in the UK, midnight in Riga, and two a.m. in Uzbekistan, where an NSA analyst should have uncovered the communique by now. Levi was getting antsy.

He leaned back, doing his best to relax. If things went as planned, he was about to ignite a war, or at least the threat of it, and the burden weighed heavily on him. But he could justify what he was doing...for the most part, anyway. Yes, he was violating his oath to his country and to God, but he felt it was necessary; maybe even heroic. Morningstar had reinforced that last point nearly every day. *"What you're doing, Levi, will change the world."* That is what Josh had always wanted to do...to make a difference...to leave the world better than he found it. And, thanks to Morningstar, he was about to get the chance.

Or was he? Was he making the world better, or was he putting it on a path of destruction from which it might never recover? He shook his head. *No...this war is necessary to keep America strong.*

His stomach growled. He hadn't eaten since the burger and fries he had picked up on his way from the airport; he was hungry. He was trying to decide if he wanted to go out for a sandwich and a beer, or if he should just order pizza and keep working. He had more or less decided on pizza, when his private cell rang. "Adams, here."

"Levi, it's Jacob."

Levi leaned forward and clicked on a recorder attached to the phone.

Morningstar's voice was enthusiastic; almost animated. "You've done it, my son. Your data was discovered and will soon be acted on. Keep watching your monitor; things are about to get very interesting. Good work, Levi."

"Thank you, fa—Jacob." Levi was still having trouble calling the man father. It was hard enough calling him Jacob.

"No, thank you, Levi. I'll let you know when to plant the next communique."

They ended the call and Levi turned off the recorder. He leaned back and stared at the monitor. He was unnerved by what he had just done. *I may have just started World War III.* He leaned forward, turned off his computer, and grabbed his coat. Pizza was out. The desire for a beer had suddenly become overwhelming.

CHAPTER 39

Somewhere in the southern part of Germany

Hank was tired and his heart was aching. It really hadn't stopped since that moment when he had seen Maddi's plane crashing into the ground. Whether it was for Maddi's predicament, for his own life that he had put on hold, or for Jenny and the agony she must feel as she wondered where he was, it was hard to say. *Perhaps all three,* he thought as he sped blindly down the highway.

It was late; nearly eleven p.m. in Germany. The moon was hidden behind clouds, the only light coming from the occasional streetlamp along the highway, or the headlights of a passing car. He saw an exit sign indicating that Stuttgart was two hundred kilometers away, and he glanced at a map he had bought in Oldenburg. *Only four hours to France's border.* He yawned and forced his eyes to stay open.

During their journey south, they had stopped at two small towns, Oldenburg and Sankt Goar. Though the stop in Oldenburg had been intended to provide them with some much-needed rest, there had been a convention in town, and the clerk at the only hotel with a vacancy had seemed far too curious about who they were, what car they were driving, and why they were there. As a result, they had left Oldenburg after just a few hours. They had driven further south, and, fortunately, the *Hotel Krone* in Sankt Goar had been far more discreet. All the receptionist had asked for was a driver's license and a form of payment. Though the hotel wasn't the finest that Hank had ever seen, they had ended up staying several days, and Maddi had spent a good deal of that time asleep. Though there had been a second bed in the room, Hank had spent most of the time in an overstuffed chair, sleeping a few hours here and there. He had spent the rest of the time watching Maddi sleep. How many times had he done that through the years; watched Maddi sleep and wondered what was going on in her mind. But this time, he felt like he knew. She was dreaming...of the past; a past that she was no longer a part of. *And it's not like there's a future for her...not yet anyway.* His job was to help her find one; a link between the old Maddi and the new. *A human conveyor belt between yesterday and tomorrow.*

At Maddi's insistence, after they had checked out of the hotel, they had spent the day at the local library. He had tried to talk her out of it, but she had insisted the research was important. *"Did you know, Hank, that the Sankt Goar French played a significant role in the Resistance during World War II?"* He had shaken his head, unsure why it mattered, seeing as how they were traversing the entirety of Europe in an effort to get Maddi to safety. She hadn't elaborated, and Hank was once again relegated to finding something to read. This time he chose an anthology of ancient Greece. They had been starving by the time they left the library, so they had stopped at a local diner. It had been almost nine p.m. by the time they left Sankt Goar.

That had been over two hours ago; they had been on the road ever since. He turned on the radio, but could find only static. He switched it off. He was still driving the Saab; they had had it for well over a month; he needed to change cars. As they drove down highway E41, he kept his eyes open for a car lot that was set back from the road and had minimal lighting. *I'm getting way too good at stealing cars,* he thought with a chuckle. *Thank you, Barry Slater.*

Never had Hank thought more about his cousin, Barry, then he had the past eight weeks. The cousin, his mother's sister's son, was three years older than him, and had grown up far different from how Hank had been raised. Barry's father, a mechanic, had taught Barry everything he would ever need to know about cars; how to fix them, how to detail them, how to steal them. Hank grinned as he thought of the tall, lanky Barry, hovering over the engine of an old Buick in his father's garage. *"Hank, here's how ya start a car without a key. Ya gotta have the right wires. Though cars use different wiring harnesses, they all work pretty much the same. Once ya find the right wires, ya just tie 'em together, then poof...ya got yerself a car."*

Hank hadn't spent a lot of time with his cousin. Once his mother found out that Barry was teaching him how to hotwire cars, she had pretty much put a stop to their time together. He laughed. *Who knew how vital your education would be, Barry.*

He slowed as he spotted a car lot about a hundred and eighty kilometers north of Stuttgart. He pulled off the highway, crossed a bridge that took them over the Neckar River, then turned left into the lot. He parked the car toward the back, doing his best to avoid any cameras. He didn't see any, but was nonetheless careful as he stepped out of the car. Just like he had done the last two times he had stolen a car, he crept through the lot in search of a vehicle that was old enough to not have GPS. The older cars were also easier to hotwire; something else his cousin had taught him. As he stole through the darkness, he had to laugh. In a matter of weeks, he had gone from a respected Deputy Director for America's Department of Homeland Security, to a kidnapper and a car thief. Thankfully, Maddi had succeeded in getting the money from the bank, or he would have had to add bank robber to the list.

He came to an old green Peugeot and stopped. Built in 1985, Hank was certain it wouldn't have GPS. Though he had never hotwired a Peugeot, he guessed it wouldn't be much different than the other two cars he had stolen.

He ran back to the Saab to check on Maddi. She was asleep. He grabbed a flashlight from the glove box, then stole back to the Peugeot. He opened the driver's side door and looked around. The car appeared to be in reasonable shape. He lifted the hood; everything looked okay. He needed that car to get them through the rest of their journey; he didn't have it in him to steal a fourth car.

He reached under the steering wheel and found the different-colored wires. As he had done with the last two cars, he put the appropriate wires together, and was pleased when he heard the engine begin to purr. He ran back to the Saab, checked to make sure that he had left nothing behind, then wakened Maddi and walked her to the Peugeot. He helped her into the back seat, and she immediately fell asleep; he was glad. He didn't want to explain to her how he knew so much about stealing cars.

As he had done twice before, he found another car in the lot that had license plates, and took those plates and put them on the Peugeot. He backed it out of the lot, then put it in park and ran to the Saab. He pulled it into the spot where the Peugeot had been, wiped it free of prints as best he could, then ran back to the Peugeot. He slid behind the wheel, then pulled out of the lot and onto the highway. He checked his watch. It was 11:20 p.m. The entire exchange had taken less than fifteen minutes.

What time is it in Ohio? Five-twenty in the afternoon. He sighed. He missed home...he missed Jenny. Normally, she would just be getting home from work, and, if he was visiting, they would be thinking about what they should have for dinner. *"Let's have steaks, babe...and share a bottle of Bordeaux."*

He squeezed the steering wheel, suddenly feeling as if he was about to explode. He needed to talk to her; to hear her voice. She had to be thinking the worst about the fact that he had been away so long; especially since it had occurred in such close proximity to Maddi's presumed death. He wanted to relieve her of that burden....to reassure her that, though he was now Maddi's sole protector, it was Jenny who owned his heart. But he couldn't tell her that; he couldn't tell anyone.

Again, he picked up the map. He looked at a line he had drawn from Stuttgart, Germany, to a location just south of Madrid. That was where Angelo had told him to come. Did Angelo live there? Or was it a safehouse where Maddi could stay, at least for a while? So many questions, which would hopefully be answered once he reached Madrid. According to the map, he had about twenty-four hours to go. *Then what?*

Hopefully, Angelo would give Maddi a permanent ID. Something with a backstory that was infallible, and a paper trail that would convince even the most rigorous investigator that Maddi was whoever Angelo said she was. He chuckled. *Something with a bit more substance than Flora Wilkinson from Billings, Montana.*

Once Hank knew that she was safe, he would find a way to stay in touch with her...a way for her to reach him if necessary. What would that look like? A special phone that only rang when Maddi's life was spiraling out of control? He shook his head and sighed. *I'm sure Jenny would love that.*

As for Jenny, what would he tell her? How would he explain the last nine weeks of his life? When he had called her that first night, he had implied that he would be gone for a short time. Clearly, that hadn't been the case. And the fact that he had spent every second of that time with Maddi would be even harder to explain.

And what do I tell Hanover? His boss was probably ready to fire him; he might have already done so. Hank couldn't tell him the truth. No one – not even the Director of Homeland Security – could know that Maddi was still alive. Why? Because the minute one person knew, the risk was too great that others would learn of it. Hank had been in DC long enough to know that no secret was kept...ever. Which meant that he would need to come up with a story so good that no one would even think to question it, or feel the need to verify that it was true. A story that would convince both his boss and his ex-wife that his absence had had nothing to do with Maddi or her sudden death in a plane crash just miles from where he had been.

Good luck with that one, Hank. He sighed and ran a hand through his hair. The need to talk to Jenny had become overwhelming. He was about a hundred and forty kilometers from Stuttgart. He saw an exit sign with a gas station up ahead. *They'll have a phone booth.* He could call her from there, then he wouldn't have to use his last trac phone. A phone booth... in the middle of nowhere. Who would even think of intercepting such a call? *The U.S. government?* He shook his head. *No...I'm not important enough to inspire that sort of effort.*

He turned off the highway, pulled into the gas station, and idled behind an outbuilding. It was late; the place was empty. The moon was hidden by clouds, and a single lamppost was the only light as he searched for a phone booth. He spotted one among the shadows at the south end of the station and inched the car forward. He stopped in front of it and fumbled through his pockets for coins. He needed to do it; he needed to talk to Jenny. But what would he say? *"Hey babe, I'm driving nowhere in a hurry for no special reason, shirking all my obligations, but I love you."*

He smacked the steering wheel and looked down at the coins in his hand. He shoved them in his pocket and drove away. He couldn't call her; he couldn't call anyone. He looked over his shoulder at Maddi. She was still asleep. She almost looked dead. *It's as if we've both died...as if I disappeared every bit as much as she has.* He drove back to the highway, his very soul feeling as if it had been shaken dry. He barely noticed the moon easing from behind the clouds.

Suddenly, a voice came from the back seat; a voice he had barely heard since the entire sordid drama had begun.

"Hank...I just remembered something from before the plane crashed."

He frowned, thinking that any memory of the crash was likely not an uplifting one, nor would it be reliable. "Maddi, I—"

"Hank, listen to me. I think Cobra was in Latvia...I'm almost certain that I spoke to him just before the plane hit the ground."

Dear god...she's delusional. "Maddi...think about it. Why would Cobra be in Latvia? And how could you have spoken to him just seconds before you crashed?"

Maddi sat up and leaned over the console beside the driver's seat. "I called a number that I thought was...Henderson's." She shifted awkwardly. "I...I wanted to tell him goodbye." She cleared her throat. "But Cobra answered, which meant that he had Henderson's phone." She frowned. "Now that I think of it, he must have taken it when he kidnapped him back in March, right?" She didn't wait for Hank to answer. "Anyway, he told me he was in Latvia. I think we should tell someone, don't you?"

"Like who?"

Her voice quieted. "The Hendersons."

Hank let out a deep sigh. "Maddi, it's been over two months since that plane crashed to the ground. Don't you think that if Cobra was going to do something, he would've done it by now?" He paused. "Besides, we can't reach out to anyone...least of all the Hendersons."

Maddi looked at him long and hard. Finally, she nodded but didn't say a word. She leaned back against the seat.

Hank meant it. Regardless of what Maddi might remember or who those memories might help, there was no way they could reach out to anyone. Maddi was dead, and she needed to stay dead.

He frowned. *She's just imagining that she spoke to Cobra...right?* But as they barreled down highway A-1 toward Stuttgart, Germany, he couldn't help but wonder, *...but if she's not, then why was Cobra in Latvia?*

* * *

Cobra had been on the road now for over twelve hours, and had yet to spot a Saab of any color, let alone a black one. Which seemed odd. After all, there had to be plenty of Saabs in Germany, right? He had periodically pulled off the highway to ask various gas station clerks if they had seen a darkly-colored Saab, or the man in his photo. He had gotten nowhere. He had finally stopped for the night at a hotel about two hours north of Stuttgart. As he was about to complete the check-in process for the less than auspicious *Hotel Krone,* he decided on a whim to ask the man at the counter whether he had seen the man in his photo.

The man had shaken his head. But Cobra had seen a flash in his eyes; the man was lying. He laid a 100-euro bill on the counter. "No way you've seen this man?" he said in German as he slid the money closer. "He probably has a mustache and beard, and he could be wearing a pair of dark-framed glasses. Maybe take another look."

The man looked again, then nodded. In a voice that was almost a whisper, he said in German, "He was here...for three days. He left this morning around ten a.m."

Cobra's eyes widened. Still speaking in German, he said, "Did you happen to see what he was driving?" The man shook his head.

Cobra took the key from the counter. He was about to walk away when he said, "Tell me, sir...was he alone?"

The manager shifted uncomfortably. "I—I don't know...I never ask."

Cobra sneered. *Flora was with him.* He was about to reach across the desk and force the man to fess up, when he shrugged and walked to the stairs. What did it matter? He would find Hank soon enough, and then he could hear it straight from him how he was tied to the mystery woman.

He climbed the stairs to the second floor and walked to his room. It was nearly midnight; he was exhausted. Assuming the guy was telling the truth, then Clarkson was only about a day ahead of him. *I should keep going,* he thought with a yawn. But there was no way he could keep driving without at least a couple of hours of sleep. He unlocked the door to his room and walked in. It was unbelievably small, and it smelled like a mixture of mold and sweat. He practically gagged. But the bed was inviting, and he fell onto it, not even bothering to take off his clothes.

* * *

Hank's eyes were heavy. It was one a.m. Except for the few hours of sleep he had gotten at the hotel in Sankt Goar, he hadn't slept since leaving Hagenow. He was exhausted. *I need to sleep.* But he didn't want to get another hotel. For one thing, it was a risk to continue checking into hotels. For another, he was eager to complete his journey. *A few hours of sleep... that's all I need.*

He was about 90 kilometers north of Stuttgart. He left the highway and drove to a poorly-lit rest stop. He pulled behind a small brick building, making sure that he was far away from the only source of light; a single lamppost at one end of the lot. He turned off the engine and got out of the car. He needed to pee, but he didn't want to go inside and leave Maddi alone, so, just as he had done a hundred times over the course of the past eight weeks, he walked to an area of thick brush and relieved himself. The whole time, he made sure to keep the green Peugeot in his sight. When he was done, he ran to the car and slid behind the wheel. He leaned the seat back so that he was at least a little reclined, then closed his eyes. Should he set an alarm on his phone? He shook his head. *No...I'm sure I'll wake up before sunrise.*

* * *

Cobra awoke to an alarm on his phone. He checked the time. Three a.m. He needed to get back on the road. He sat up, then stood and walked into a bathroom with a stained tub and a toilet with no seat. He relieved himself and splashed water on his face. He grabbed the only towel in the bathroom and dried his face.

He walked to the bed and opened his backpack. He took out his laptop and logged into the same site where he had obtained the video footage the night before. Again, he focused on rest stops and gas stations. Though looking at the video feed was a tedious process, it had provided the lead that had gotten him within a day of his target, which meant it was clearly worth the effort. He was about to log off, when he saw video of a man running from a car to an area of thick brush behind a rest stop. He watched as the man ran back to the car. Cobra grinned; he recognized him. Though the man was bearded and his hair was a mess, Cobra would bet money that it was Hank Clarkson. He frowned. *But why didn't he just go into the rest stop to pee?* He chuckled. *Because he needs to keep an eye on his car...and whoever the hell is inside.*

Cobra rewound the video feed and froze the image. Tall, muscular, dark curly hair. In spite of the beard, the mustache, and the glasses, there was no mistaking that it was Hank Clarkson. But it wasn't a black Saab he was driving. It was a Peugeot; Cobra couldn't tell the color. Why had Clarkson changed cars so many times? *Because he, or the person traveling with him, is on the run.* He checked the location. It wasn't far from Sankt Goar. He checked the time on the video. *One-fifteen a.m. ...today. Holy shit...that was less than two hours ago!*

He slammed shut the laptop. Not only had he learned that the man he was looking for was now driving a Peugeot and was definitely not alone, but he had also learned that Hank Clarkson, the man he needed to kill, was only about 100 kilometers ahead of him.

CHAPTER 40

Washington, DC, Camden, Maine

"You must let her go, Jerome."

"What are you talking about, Edward?"

Morningstar walked with Jerome among the flowers of the garden outside Sturgill's Maine estate. They had just celebrated Jerome's twenty-second birthday, and Morningstar had asked Jerome to join him on a walk. Morningstar rarely came to visit. As a matter of fact, Jerome hadn't seen him for over two years. Morningstar stopped, then turned to face him. "I need you to tell Emma goodbye."

Jerome stared at his mentor. "What?"

"You must tell Emma Melnikov goodbye."

"But why?"

"She isn't right for what will soon be asked of you."

Jerome's eye was twitching. "What do you mean...she isn't right?"

"Her heritage is wrong."

For the first time in his life, Jerome wanted to punch Morningstar, the man who had become like a father to him. "What the hell is that supposed to mean?"

Morningstar narrowed his eyes. "There's so much you don't understand, Jerome. So many events that you will eventually be a part of that simply cannot include a Russian émigré."

"Jesus, Edward. She's second-generation!"

"It doesn't matter. Her parents are Russian. They speak the language...they attend Russian Heritage meetings."

Jerome tightened his jaw. If he thought he could get away with it, he would have decked Morningstar then and there. "How do you know so much about them?"

"It's my job."

"It's your job to know about my girlfriend's family? What the hell, Edward?"

Morningstar stopped at a bench that was situated among a wide array of hydrangeas. He sat and indicated that Jerome should sit, as well.

Jerome stiffened. "I'll stand, thank you."

Morningstar sighed. "Jerome, I don't think you understand what will soon happen to you."

Jerome paced, not wanting to hear it. He was being asked by the man he respected most in the world to give up a woman he loved with every part of him. Regardless of the messenger, nothing was going to convince him that it was the right thing to do.

Morningstar went on. "Jerome, you are being groomed to someday be a leader. And I'm certain that, on your watch, difficult challenges will face this country that you will be asked to address. Don't ask me how I know; I just do." He paused. "Haven't I been right about everything up to now?"

Jerome sighed. That much was true. Morningstar had predicted every major event of the last decade. But asking him to give up Emma was simply more than Jerome was willing to do. He was overcome by a surge of emotion, and had to clench his jaw to keep from crying. "But I...I love her, sir."

Morningstar nodded slowly. "I know, Jerome. But she has to go..."

Knight sat up in his massive four-poster bed, sweat covering him as tears streamed down his face. He looked at the clock. *Two a.m.* It was same thing nearly every night. One of two nightmares, both from his past, waking him, making him wonder how on earth he had gotten to where he was. It was either him learning that his parents had died when he was fourteen years old, or it was the memory of the goodbye that he had been forced to give to the love of his life, Emma Melnikov.

He pulled off the covers and slid his feet over the side of the bed. His silk pajamas were drenched from sweat. He stood and ripped them off, leaving them unceremoniously on the floor as he walked naked to the bathroom. What did he care? It wasn't like anyone could see him, right?

Wrong. There were cameras everywhere. And, though he didn't think that they spied on him in his bedroom, it wouldn't surprise him. He doubted there were many moments when he was truly alone.

He strutted into the bathroom, almost daring the watchers to see his manhood. *Not bad, eh?* Was he bitter? Perhaps, but not toward those who had been assigned to keep him safe. He understood their job and was grateful for their efforts. He was just tired of living in a cage.

Truth be told, he had lived most of his life in a cage. He had spent decades preparing for the role he was now playing. And he had prepared well. But he felt like an actor; merely going through the motions of Commander-in-Chief...as if he was playing a part, a character in a movie that he could walk away from in another day or two and go back to the life he was meant to live...a life devoted to Emma.

He turned on the shower, letting the hot water run until the entire bathroom was covered in steam. So many nights it was the same...he would awaken from the dream and stumble into the comforting warmth of the shower. He was probably the cleanest President in history. He chuckled. *Some men are remembered for their courage in a crisis; I'll be remembered for my hygiene.*

He stepped into the shower and allowed the scalding water to numb him. He closed his eyes and put his face directly under it, rinsing off the sweat, drowning the memory of his beautiful Emma. She hadn't wanted him to go. She had loved him. With all her heart and soul...she had loved him. "Dammit!" he cried as he pounded the wall with his fist. "I loved you, too, Emma...and I always will."

* * *

Emma Melnikov Cannon turned over in her king-sized bed and sighed. What had awakened her? She looked at a clock by the bed. *Two a.m.* She sat up and looked around the room. Was there an intruder? *Not in the house,* she thought with a sigh...*but there's one in my heart.* She frowned. *Get out of there, Romer.*

Quietly, so as not to wake her husband, she stood and grabbed her robe from a chair by the bed. She wrapped it around her and walked to the window. The curtains weren't closed; she never closed them. She loved the outdoors and ushered it in every chance she got. A steady rain was falling, but the cold air had turned each raindrop to ice, and they beat against the window like bullets from a machine gun.

Why tonight? Why is he in there tonight? After all, it had been sixteen years since Romer – Jerome Knight – had left her...sixteen years since he had told her goodbye. He hadn't wanted to go; it was clear by the pain in his eyes. So why had he left? *Who cares, Emma? It was a lifetime ago.* But tonight, for whatever reason, the memory was as clear as the day he walked away. Was it because his incredible face was suddenly all over her TV? His voice calm and reassuring as he tried to comfort a nation that had been through far too much over the last two months. She had spent the last sixteen years forgetting him, making him nothing more than a secret from her past. No one – not even her husband – knew that she had once dated the man who was now President of the United States...and she intended on keeping it that way.

She had tried to forget him; to move on...even going so far as to marry a man she wasn't actually in love with. Though she loved Michael; she wasn't *in love* with him. And she had been satisfied with the bargain, content with her simple life and her safe, reasonable marriage. Until tonight. These memories out of nowhere were unsettling, to say the least. And she knew they had only just begun. Now that he was President, she saw him everywhere...on TV, in the newspaper, even on her computer screen when she turned it on first thing in the morning. It was making her crazy. Her contentment with her life with Michael was quickly starting to change to contempt for that life, and for Michael. Why couldn't she love Michael the way she loved Jerome?

She sighed, her guilt crushing her as she looked over her shoulder at the good man she had grown to despise...and all while he snored blissfully unaware.

She had been married to Michael Cannon for fifteen years. In that time, they had fallen into a routine. The marriage hadn't been a bad one, but it held little passion. They had sex, but they rarely made love. They had a child, Galina, named after Emma's mother, and she had been worth the compromise...or at least, Emma had thought so. *She is why I stayed.*

But Galina was a gifted pianist, and had recently signed a contract with a celebrated Maine orchestra. She had left ten weeks ago, her care given over to Michael's aunt, who had agreed to accompany her as they traveled the world. Galina, only fifteen, would finish her high school years mostly overseas, going from country to country as she played piano and learned about the world. The aunt, a teacher most of her life, would fill in the gaps of Galina's high school education. Which meant that Galina was gone... she had essentially left home. Though she would come back from time to time, it wouldn't be for long, and when the tour ended, it would be time for her to go to college. *Which means that, from now on, it is only Michael and I.*

Other than Michael and Galina, Emma was essentially alone in the world. Her mother had died a year ago from cancer, and her father, Adrik, had died the year before from a heart attack. She had a cousin, Irina, in Eastern Europe, but hadn't seen her in years, and she had no brothers or sisters. Emma was alone...the only one left of the fearless Melnikovs from Chelyabinsk.

She sighed as she listened to the wind beating against the glass. She welcomed the gales as they blew in from the sea; it was one of the things she loved about Maine. *"The squalls on this coast are just like the gales from the Black Sea; they cut all the way to your soul,"* her mother used to say.

A strong gust sent a tree branch careening against the window. Emma closed her eyes, eager to feel the power of the wind. *With wind comes passion.* How Emma longed for passion...

"Don't ever do that to me again, Romer." Emma was half-crying, half-laughing as she looked at her drenched lover standing outside her door in the rain.

"Don't worry, baby, I knew I would make it."

"No, you're lucky you made it. Men have died trying to tackle that river."

"Yes, Emma, but they aren't me."

He grinned and her knees grew weak. She took him by the hand and pulled him into her apartment. "No, and they don't have me to soothe them when it's over."

She dragged him to the bed and pretended to throw him on top of it. He fell dramatically across the cover and she jumped on top of him. She leaned over to kiss him and he stopped her. "Wait."

"What do you mean, wait?"

"I have an idea."

He stood and lifted her into his arms. He carried her through the door and down the steps.

"Where are you taking me?"

"Just wait."

He walked outside, ignoring the rain, and she laughed as she clung to his broad shoulders. "We're getting wet, Romer."

"I like getting wet...or haven't you noticed?"

He carried her past the building and down a hill to a small clearing. He hiked across it to a grove of trees, then marched on until they reached the edge of the Kennebec River. He took her to a part of the river where the water spilled into a small causeway, and laid her gently on the wet earth beside it. He pushed a strand of hair from her forehead, kissing her as a gentle stream trickled nearby. The rain pelted them with a warm, steady rhythm, as Jerome fell on top of her, kissing her with a passion that filled her soul. "Now, where were we...?"

Emma clung to her nightgown, the pain of remembering tearing at her chest. She covered her mouth, afraid she might cry out and awaken Michael. She took deep breaths, finally calming down as she wiped away a tear. This time she refused to look over her shoulder; she didn't want to look at Michael as she wept for another man. She put a hand on the sill, trembling as each raindrop hit the pane. Though it hurt to remember him, for some reason, tonight, she wanted to...she *needed* to.

She had felt of late as if she had died, or at least a part of her...especially now that Galina had left her. Her daughter's departure had revealed a place inside her, a vital piece of her soul, that felt as if it had been snuffed out... a part of her life that had been unlived. She had made her peace with it; she had accepted that she must accept her choices, that to hunger for a man she couldn't have wasn't just a waste of time, but was hurtful to those she loved. But suddenly, tonight, she didn't care. *If I can't have Jerome, at least I can imagine him.* She felt as if – just maybe – remembering those moments when she had been deeply, relentlessly in love might kick-start that part of her that had faded away. *And then maybe I can let it...let him... go.*

And so, she would indulge herself...tonight. *What harm can it do,* she thought, as she raised her hand to the glass. With her shame tucked away in the safety of darkness, she looked out the window and sighed. *Now, where were we?*

CHAPTER 41

Washington, DC

Morningstar leaned back in the sofa in his hotel suite. Though it wasn't even three a.m., he had been unable to sleep. The name that Sturgill had given to Levi had left him stunned. Not only had he recognized it, but, unlike the little-known Pyong Pang, who had originally been thought to have kidnapped and killed Sturgill's son, Lin Chu was far more notable, at least to anyone involved with the armed forces. Though Chu had worked behind-the-scenes, he was basically in charge of the Chinese military. Not only that; he was the same man who, at Morningstar's request, had overseen the kidnapping of Lili Platacis nearly a year ago. *What are the odds?* he thought, as he stared out at the darkness. He chuckled. *Clearly, Lin Chu has a knack for kidnapping.*

But if Sturgill's claim about Lin Chu was true – and Morningstar had no reason to think that it wasn't – then in spite of the fact that the man had brilliantly executed Lili's abduction ten months ago at Morningstar's request, the man deserved whatever fate was about to befall him. He had directly or indirectly been responsible for killing Sturgill's boy; an American child. But it meant that Morningstar would soon be obligated to satisfy Sturgill's thirst for vengeance by killing the very man who at one time had done Morningstar's dirty work.

He frowned. *It isn't good to go around killing one's accomplices.*

His first step had been to instruct Levi to learn all that he could about Lin Chu. *"I want to know where he sleeps, where he eats...I even want to know when he takes a shit, Levi...you got it?"* Levi had responded with a languid, *"Sure."* It was enough; Levi was lazy, but he got the job done.

But it wouldn't be easy. Though Lin Chu's work had been monumental with regard to the Chinese military, he had managed to keep a remarkably low profile. It was one of the reasons that Morningstar had chosen him to kidnap Lili. But it meant that Levi would have his hands full as he worked to learn details about the man.

It wasn't like Morningstar was upset by the discovery. It would actually play into his hand quite nicely. Which could only mean one thing. *God has made it so.* Morningstar had planned on removing Chu from his post eventually; it wasn't wise to keep a man who knew Morningstar's secrets in power for too long. But because of Lin Chu's significant role in China's military, Morningstar had put it off, saving it for the end when there would be few who could fight his efforts. But Sturgill's discovery had moved up the timeline...*and it will now take place with the willful aid of a United States Senator.* Morningstar laughed. *You can't make this shit up!*

But not just anyone could kill a gifted military leader. It would require the skills of a unique assassin. Fortunately, he had such an assassin in his arsenal. The only problem was that the assassin, Dan – aka Cobra – was busy killing Clarkson.

Morningstar frowned. He had yet to receive a call from Cobra. But the fact that Hank Clarkson hadn't been heard from since late August suggested that Cobra had likely succeeded in killing him. But if that was the case, then why hadn't Cobra called? There was no question that he was eager to get his hands on the Henderson castle, and would demand that it be handed over to him the minute he completed his task. Which could only mean one thing: *Cobra hasn't yet killed Hank.* Morningstar couldn't pull Cobra into a new assignment until he had completed the old one.

But one thing was certain: Cobra would have to be the one to kill Lin Chu. The hit would require the skills of a unique sort of killer; a hardened soul incapable of remorse...an assassin who wasn't just ruthless, but could alter a crime scene in such a way that no one would have any idea of the true motive behind the crime. Though Cobra wasn't Morningstar's most trusted son, he was without a doubt the only one who could pull off such a hit.

But Morningstar had another problem to consider: He was running out of incentives to lure Cobra into doing what was needed. The latest one had been the Henderson castle; how would Morningstar top that? He rubbed his chin as he stared at his private cellphone that was laying on the coffee table. *I'll come up with something.*

He reached for the cellphone and dialed the number for Cobra. After several rings the call went to voicemail, and Morningstar was once again forced to listen to the raspy voice of Martin Henderson. "It's me. If you're her, leave a message."

Morningstar was about to end the call without leaving a message, but was suddenly irate. He had had enough of Cobra's evasiveness. Evenly, he said, "Call me, prick...or the deal is off." He sneered. *That should do it.*

Surprisingly, he didn't have long to wait. Within minutes, his private cellphone rang. "Hello?" Morningstar said, doing his best to sound calm.

"You rang, asshole?"

Morningstar couldn't help but laugh. "Why didn't you answer your phone...or should I say, Henderson's phone?"

There was a pause. "Not that it's any of your business, but I'm careful with that phone." He laughed. "As it had once belonged to my dear half-brother, I never trust who might be on the other end."

"I see. Listen son, I need you to do something for me."

The voice was cold. "I'm about to kill Clarkson. What more could you want?"

Morningstar stiffened. What he had suspected was true. "You're *about* to kill him? I figured you already had. What have you been doing for the past two months?"

There was a pause. "Don't push it, Morningstar. I'm not an enemy you want to have." Another pause. "As for Clarkson, he's cleverer than I thought. But I'm right behind him, now. He'll be dead within the next twenty-four hours."

Morningstar narrowed his eyes. He went through the timeline. If Cobra killed Hank by tomorrow night, then Morningstar could get him to China by the weekend. He nodded. *It will work.* "Okay. But make it quick, and make the kill a clean one. Clarkson is, after all, a government official." He paused. "Then, when you're done with him, I'll need you to do one more thing for me."

"I don't work for you, Jacob."

Morningstar bristled. *Keep your cool.* He took a deep breath. "I'm prepared to offer you quite a lot if you'll assist me with one last assignment."

"My obligation to you is over, Jacob. The castle you're about to give me will represent the end of our relationship."

"I can give you even more than that."

"What more could you give me than a castle by the sea, Jacob?"

Morningstar frowned. *Think, dammit.* Suddenly, he smiled. *When in doubt, tell the man the truth.* "Your task involves the assassination of a high-level Chinese leader. Once you do this, Dan, you will become the most infamous killer of all time."

Evenly, the man said, "I'm already the most infamous killer of all time."

Morningstar flinched. "Perhaps. But what if I told you that the death of this leader will lead to war...maybe even World War III. And there will be only one man who will be immortalized for having caused it. Just like with the assassination of Archduke Ferdinand, the death of this man – at your hand – will be one of the most historic and monumental events of the modern world."

Another pause, this one longer. "I'll consider it." The line went dead.

Morningstar chuckled as he slid the phone into the pocket of his silk robe. Cobra would do it. At the end of the day, men like Cobra killed for one reason only; the glory of the kill. *What greater glory than being the man who started World War III?*

Morningstar stood and walked to the window. As he looked out at the dark night, he nodded. Slowly, cleverly, he was putting all of his chess pieces into play. *And the next move will be one of the most important on the board,* he thought as a clock on the wall sounded three low chimes. Again, he nodded. *It's time...time to take America to the next level.*

He pulled out his phone and dialed. Without waiting for a hello, he said, "Issachar, put it into play." He ended the call before Issachar had a chance to reply. His newest son would know what to do. The plan had been put in place months ago.

Soon after Issachar had come up with the brilliant idea of turning young men into shooters, Morningstar had challenged him. *"Though your idea is truly innovative, my son, I can't help but think that it may not be enough."*

"Enough? What do you mean, Jacob?"

Morningstar had rubbed his chin. *"You mentioned not long ago that the best way to wage a fight against the people is to make them fight against themselves."* He had then looked Issachar directly in the eye. *"Can you take it a step further?"*

Issachar had narrowed his eyes. *"A step further, sir?"*

Morningstar had nodded. *"You know; do something – involving guns – that will scare the American people shitless."*

Issachar had frowned. *"I suppose I could, sir."* He had paused. *"Like what?"*

Morningstar had patted the man on the shoulder. *"I can't help but think that this country is a powder keg, son...just waiting to explode. Brother against brother...that sort of thing."*

Issachar's eyes had widened. *"You mean like a civil war?"*

Morningstar had chuckled. *"Not exactly. More like an insurrection."*

"An insurrection?"

"Yes. Challenge the very nidus of power, my son."

Issachar had taken a deep breath. *"As in...Washington, DC?"*

Morningstar had grinned. *"Yes. It's an election year, my son, and the country is ripe for such a thing. I have to think that an act against the leaders who rule our nation would be enough to put this country in a state of panic, wouldn't you agree?"*

Issachar had laughed nervously. *"Um...yes, I think you're right, Jacob. If the American people felt that their very government was under attack, they would tolerate quite a bit from a leader, especially if he offered a way to ease those fears."*

Morningstar had slapped him on the back. *"Exactly, my son."* He had stood and walked to the window. Without turning away from it, he had added, *"So, can you convince someone to carry out such a deed?"*

Issachar had considered it. *"I believe I can, Father. Hopeless men are not that hard to find."* He had looked at Morningstar and nodded. *"I'll get right on it, sir."*

And get right on it, he had. While he was cultivating angry young man across the country to become shooters, he was also cultivating one very demoralized Capitol police officer. A man whose fortunes had waned; who was bitter and desperate and at the end of his rope. Somehow Issachar had become aware of this, and would now take steps to use that bitterness to further Morningstar's agenda.

Morningstar chuckled as he continued to stare out the window. *It won't be long now,* he thought with a nod. Though it was the middle of the night, the moon was bright, allowing him to see the less-than-inspiring garden beneath the Starlight Hotel room window. *I don't know how much longer*

I can stomach this place, he thought, as he watched a gust of wind blow dozens of leaves to the ground.

But in spite of the bleakness, he had to admire the power of the cold north wind. Another gust sent the leaves flying, and he felt a rush of energy surge through him. He laughed at the wind's boldness, knowing that, within weeks, he would be every bit as powerful as that wind. He looked up at the moon and said loudly, "So persecute them with thy tempest, and make them afraid of thy storm!" The psalm, one of his favorites, now felt like his own personal refrain, and he trembled as he looked down at the leaves swirling beneath the window...as if they were responding to his command. It was stunning at how far he had come in four short years. What had started in a stale hotel room in downtown DC, had morphed into an actual blueprint, not only for how to dismantle America, but for how to take over the entire world.

But the coup de gras would be when son Dan took on – and took down – the Red Dragon. The fall of China's military machine would be a stunning display that would cut that proud country to its core. But Morningstar wouldn't stop with China. Russia and all of Europe would soon succumb to his authority. It had already begun. The war in Latvia would soon spread to all of the Baltic States. All of Eastern Europe would soon be destabilized...*and ripe for the taking,* he thought with a laugh. But it would take more; it would take the power of the magical warship, *Der Morgenstern,* a vessel that could raze ten city blocks with a single blast. *And soon I will have it,* he thought, as he gripped his hands into fists. *Once Naphtali and Simeon find that ship, my military might will be unstoppable.*

As he stared out at the blackened sky, he raised his fists in the air, overcome by all he had done. So many had tried before him and had failed; Genghis Khan, Josef Stalin, Adolf Hitler. *But they didn't have what I have,* he thought with a nod. *I am the messenger of God Himself, His born-again Jacob here on earth...His kingmaker, who will soon be Lord over all the world.*

He laughed. "And it all begins here...in America...with the Grand Insurrection."

PART II

*"All men are fools, and all men are knights
where women are concerned."*

~ George R.R. Martin ~
"A Knight of the Seven Kingdoms"

CHAPTER 42

Washington, DC

Capitol Police Officer Carl Mavis pulled out his handkerchief and once again wiped sweat from his brow. The handkerchief, given to him by his mother the day he left Iowa to go to Washington was old and tattered, but he didn't care. He kept it with him to remind him of where he had come from...to remind him of who he was.

He checked the time. *Eight-twenty-nine.* The House Select Committee to Reconsider Gun Laws in America would start their meeting at any moment. Carl tugged at the collar of his uniform. As he lowered his hand, his fingers touched on two medals that he had earned during his sixteen years with the Capitol Police Force. The first had come about in 1989, when Carl had single-handedly stopped an armed intruder who had somehow gotten inside the Capitol during a joint session of Congress. The second had been given to him after the 9-11 terrorist attack, when Carl had led several frightened Congressmen and women to safety in the secret building underneath the Capitol. Carl was proud of those medals.

Which was why he was struggling with what he was about to do. *It's okay, Carl...family comes first.* He swallowed as he thought of his two children, Billy and Jane, fourteen and twelve, respectively. Happy kids, good at school, strong in their Christian faith. He teared up, then wiped his eyes as his thoughts turned to his wife, Margie, who at that very moment was receiving chemotherapy in a cold, sterile treatment room that abutted the downtown clinic. The chemo had been a long shot, but with their kids so young, Margie had chosen to go ahead with it. Carl shook his head as he thought of how hard it had been for her. Twenty pounds thinner and losing her hair, she barely had the strength to brush her teeth. There had been newer, better alternatives, but Carl had been unable to afford them. Even with help from the church and a local charity, the out-of-pocket costs had been too high. He put his hand on his pistol and set his jaw. *Which is why I must do what I'm about to do.*

Because of his seniority within the department, he had been given a role inside the chamber, where he was to oversee the safety of the men and women who presided there. He looked around the vast chamber. Besides four other officers, it was mostly empty; the compromise he had made with the stranger who had promised him one million dollars cash. *"I cannot bring myself to...do this...to the entire chamber,"* Carl had told the man, hopeful he would accept the compromise. After a quick phone call, the tall man with the light brown hair had smiled. *"That works for us."*

Carl didn't know who 'us' was; it didn't matter. One million dollars would solve a lot of problems. His wife would be able to obtain the best treatment money could buy, and his children would have a far better future. *"So, who will oversee the cash...once I'm...gone?"* he had asked, his voice trembling. *"I will,"* the stranger had said. He had then held up the list of requests that Carl had given him and had nodded. *"I promise you, Carl, that I will make sure that all of these requests are honored."*

"How can I know that you will do this?"

The muscled man with the firm jaw had smiled. *"One, because I'm a cop like you. And two, because what you're doing for us is so much bigger than a simple shooting. You are about to change the world, Carl."*

And that had been the end of it. After all, what choice did Carl have? He was watching his wife die a horrible death, and he knew – once she was gone – he would likely die himself from either grief or shame...*or both.* And if he didn't die, he would most certainly be incapable of carrying on. Either way, the children would be parentless...adrift in a heartless, hopeless world. At least this way, Margie would have a chance at life, and his kids could go to the very best private school. They could then go on to impressive colleges without incurring mounds of debt. As it stood now, Carl could barely feed his family, let alone provide them the advantages that would give them a shot at happiness in the cruel, bloodthirsty America that Carl had once been willing to give his life for.

He shifted awkwardly as he watched the committee members take their seats. If he was honest with himself, he had to admit that America wasn't to blame for his financial failures. Carl had been paid well over the years, and the Capitol Police had provided plenty of perks that Carl had managed to take advantage of. But like everything else in the country, the perks had changed; they had been bilked by regulations and belt-tightening, to the point where they were almost worthless. The biggest change had been with healthcare. The premiums were no longer as cheap, and the deductible was higher, with out-of-pocket expenses practically unaffordable.

But that wasn't the only reason that cash was tight. Over the past four years, Carl had managed to gamble away a good portion of their money. The addiction had come on slowly, with the occasional bet on a baseball game or a horse race. Pretty soon, he was placing bets on anything and everything; who would win a local election, how soon it would be before the first snowfall. By the time he recognized that he had a problem, it was too late. He had given up not only their life savings, but their 401K, and the kids' college fund, as well. He had been forced to sell one of their cars, and take out a second mortgage on the house. He clutched the pistol at his side. *"Which is why I must do this terrible thing...to make my family whole, and to atone for how badly I wronged them."*

The strike of a gavel jerked him to attention. His assignment was simple. Just after eight-thirty, as the sixteen-member committee focused on the task at hand, Carl was to pull out his pistol and start shooting. And though the tall stranger had promised 'the best lawyers that money can buy' to keep Carl from incurring the death penalty, Carl knew exactly what would happen the minute he fired that first shot. After a few seconds – during which time, his fellow officers would process that one of their own had lost it – one of them would shoot him dead. *It is what I would do,* he thought with a stiffened jaw. Which meant that within the next five minutes, Carl Mavis from Salt Lake City, Iowa, would surely be dead.

Was he ready? He took a deep breath and held it. He pulled out his pistol and, as he aimed it at the chairman of the committee, he nodded. *I am.* And then he pulled the trigger.

CHAPTER 43

Washington, DC

President Jerome Knight's breaths were heavy but even as he checked his watch. He had been running for forty minutes, and was making good time; as a matter of fact, it was the fastest he had run in years.

He had been unable to go back to sleep after the dream about Emma, and had spent the rest of the night looking through old photos of his time at the university; his time with Emma. Finally, as the sun had begun to rise, he had put away the photos, and had donned a pair of sweats. He had informed his Secret Service team that he wanted to go for a run, and had been driven to a park at the far end of town.

He was just about to make another lap around, when out of nowhere, two members of his team of agents grabbed him and shoved him into the back of a black sedan that had come out of nowhere.

As they pushed his head to the seat, he said, "What is this? What's going on?"

One of the agents frowned. "There has been a shooting, sir."

Knight tried to get up; they wouldn't let him. "Dear God...not another one."

The agent bent over and looked him in the eye. "At the Capitol, sir. During a committee meeting."

Knight's eyes widened. "How many injured? Any dead?"

The agent shook his head. "I'm not sure, sir."

"Who was the shooter?"

"A Capitol Police officer, sir."

Knight stared at the man. "What on earth? Why?"

Again, the agent shook his head. "I'll have more information soon, sir."

They sped back to the White House, and Knight was immediately taken to a bunker below. Within minutes, he had called a meeting with his cabinet leaders, and, still in his sweats, had ordered the Capitol and the White House locked down, with U.S. Military standing guard. All normal business had come to a halt. He monitored the TV as his agents gradually filled in the details of the morning's attack. Five members of a sixteen-member select committee had been hit before the shooter – a thirty-seven-year-old Capitol Police officer – had been shot dead by a fellow officer. Fortunately, none of the victims had died, but two were fighting for their lives at a nearby hospital. The shooter, who was apparently struggling financially, had been with the Capitol Police for over sixteen years. His wife had been battling stage four cancer for the past year-and-a-half, and he had two children, both in middle school.

"Why would a man leave his family at a time when they needed him so badly?" Knight asked one of the agents.

The man shook his head. "I don't know. We're trying to learn more, sir."

The nation as a whole had reacted how Knight would have expected; horror, followed by fear. It felt as if the very fabric of the country was coming apart...as if far too many men had lost their minds.

As for Knight, he just felt old...and tired. One calamity after another. *When will it end?*

His phone rang; the private phone that he kept for calls from Morningstar. He motioned for his agents to clear the room, then answered with a hushed, "Yes sir?"

"Hello Judah."

"Hello, sir. I was expecting your call."

"The events of this morning have changed things, son."

Knight flinched. "What do you mean, sir?"

"It has moved up the timeline. We must act quickly." There was a pause. "As those around me are fond of saying, never let a crisis go to waste."

Knight shifted uncomfortably. *What does that mean?*

Morningstar continued. "People are scared, Judah. The incident in the Capitol is being referred to as an attempted coup." There was a pause. "Are you aware that they found a type-written manifesto in the cop's locker?"

Knight had been informed, though he had yet to hear what it said. "Yes sir. Did it explain why he did it?"

"His hope was that his actions would inspire the rest of the country to rise up and take on a government that had become far too big and far too powerful."

Knight shook his head. *Great. Just what we need. A call to arms.*

Morningstar went on. "Combine it with everything else that has been going on, son, and you've got a population that is scared shitless...and demanding action."

"What do you think I should do?"

"What we talked about yesterday." There was a pause. "Actually, what we've talked about all along, son." He paused. "It is time to take the first step."

Knight's stomach turned. He didn't want to take the first step. "How soon?"

"Today...within the next hour or so. Are you ready?"

Knight frowned. Of course, he wasn't ready. "Certainly, sir."

"Good. I've paved the way. You will have the Pentagon's full support. I'll let you know when it's time for the step that will follow."

The call ended and Knight shoved the phone in his pocket. He shuddered as he tried to guess what Morningstar had meant by paving the way.

He ran his hands through his hair and sighed. There was no denying that the attack at the Capitol had given Knight a somewhat plausible excuse to do what he was about to do. The fear of a possible insurrection was bigger than random shootings around the country. An attack on the Capitol was an attack on America itself. Every citizen would feel the repercussions, and they would be scared to death.

But is it enough to make them willing to give up their guns? He shook his head. *Quite the contrary.* If anything, it would make many of them even more determined to hold onto the weapons they had. He let out a sigh. There would never be a way or a time when Americans would be willing to give up their guns. He had known it since the first time that Morningstar had brought it up, soon after Australia had passed their mandatory buy-back in 1996. Knight had even said as much.

"It will never happen here, Father. Americans will never give up their guns. It is too ingrained in who they are...in who we are as a country."

Morningstar paused. "Nonsense. If Australia can do it, then we can."

"Australia is a much smaller country, Father." Jerome hesitated. "And there is some argument as to whether it was even necessary."

Morningstar narrowed his eyes. "Of course it was necessary. A shooter had just killed 35 Australians. The people had had enough."

"But Americans have already suffered far greater tragedies, and yet it still isn't enough."

Morningstar stiffened. "It is necessary, Jerome, if the man in charge says it is necessary. That is the whole point."

Jerome flinched. He cleared his throat. "May I speak freely, Father?"

Morningstar hesitated, then nodded. "Certainly, son."

"I don't know when you think this could happen, or who might be in charge when it does, but I cannot think of any incident or series of incidents that would compel Americans to give up their guns." He paused. "Any act that might inspire such a thing from some, would inspire just as many to hold onto their guns out of fear. This is America, Father. We were founded by a rebellion that was made possible by our possession of guns."

Morningstar sighed. "Son, let me put it to you this way. Three things will be needed to make this happen. The first is chaos, which, if things continue as they have for the past several years, is easy to imagine. The second is fear. Also easily imagined."

"What is the third, Father?"

Morningstar looked him in the eye. "A willing leader. A man who is strong enough and loves his country enough to do what is needed to keep it safe."

At the time of that debate, Knight had had no idea that the leader Morningstar was referring to would be him. Suddenly, he frowned. *Did Morningstar know it would be me?* He shook his head. Of course, he didn't. How could he have known that the Vice-President would step down, or that Wilcox would choose Knight to fill his spot, or that the President would then be assassinated. He quickly dismissed it as he checked the time. Almost nine. He had been in that bunker for less than twenty minutes, but it felt like twenty years. There seemed to be no way to stop the madness that had engulfed the country, and now that madness had resulted in what looked like a possible rebellion. It was unbelievable. *And there is nothing I can do about it.*

He thought of Morningstar's order. *Or is there?* Could he find a way to take America's guns? *At least then I would look like I was doing something.* He frowned. There was no way it could work. Americans would never tolerate such a thing, either voluntarily or involuntarily. They would give up their very lives if they had to. *"From my cold, dead hands."* Wasn't that how NRA President Charleton Heston had put it.

But Jacob has told me to do it, Knight thought with a frown. Which meant that – in spite of Knight's awareness that such an order would never work – he would do it. Why? He shook his head and sighed. *Because my father has asked me to.*

He took a deep breath, then stood, and walked to the bathroom. He splashed water on his face and, as he reached for a towel, he caught a glimpse of himself in the mirror. The man he was looking at seemed like a stranger; someone he barely recognized. His hair was lighter, his eyes darker, and the lines in his forehead were far deeper than they had been when he had been elected Florida's senator six years ago. He had thought then that he had fulfilled Jacob's plan. He had become a leader and he had been effective. He had put forth legislation that favored a more aggressive America, and had managed to spearhead most of it through the Senate chamber.

But the unexpected resignation just six months ago of Vice-President Jim Conner had changed everything. Knight had been tapped to replace him, and his life had been upended ever since. Thinking about it now, it was as if Jacob had known that Wilcox would choose him; as if he had expected it all along. *As if it had been planned.* Knight flinched as he stared in the mirror. So much of what had happened seemed to play perfectly into Morningstar's plans...*as if it had all been prearranged.*

He shook his head dismissively. *There's no way.* First of all, President Wilcox had belonged to no one; not the party bigwigs, not the fat cats on Wall Street, not even the lobbyists who would someday be in a position to reward him handsomely for his time in the White House. *And certainly not some aide from the Pentagon.* Wilcox had recognized the corruptness of all of them; those unelected bureaucrats in the Intelligence Community and the State Department who had been in Washington so long they even smelled like sleaze. Wilcox had been his own man; he had made his own decisions. Knight felt certain that it was why he had been assassinated; he had refused to play in the poisoned sandbox that was Washington, DC.

But he couldn't ignore the coincidences. *First, I win – overwhelmingly – a senate seat that I was never supposed to win; then, out of the blue, Conner resigns, and I'm given his spot as VP. Finally, Wilcox is assassinated, which makes me President of the United States...all in less than six months.* Knight rubbed the back of his neck. In hardly any time at all he had gone from near obscurity to the leader of the free world. *How spectacular,* he thought, *...and how utterly implausible.*

He didn't want to think about it. But suddenly, he couldn't *stop* thinking about it. How had it come about? Luck? He shook his head. He didn't believe in luck. But how else could one explain it? An answer shouted back at him. *Morningstar.* Again, he shook his head. *Stop it, Jerome.* Yes, the man was powerful. He had vision, along with nerves of steel. It was how he had become one of the more influential leaders in the Pentagon. Though he was merely an aide, he had access to the most powerful general in America's army; the Chairman of the Joint Chiefs of Staff, Alexander Daniels. *And Daniels would never buy into anything like this.*

Knight wiped his face with the towel, then left the bathroom. He walked back to his desk, thinking about Daniels. Though Knight didn't know him well, he felt certain that the man who had commanded America's military for the last decade would never condone any less-than-honorable actions by his senior aide. Which meant that if Morningstar had, in fact, done something illegal, he would have had to have done it without Daniels knowing. But how on earth could a Pentagon aide conjure up something big enough to compel an American VP to step down. Better yet, how could a Pentagon aide arrange for the assassination of a U.S.

President? Knight shook his head. *There's no way it could be done...and there's no way that the man who is like a father to me would even dream of such a thing.*

Then again, what did Knight actually know about Morningstar? He was aware that the man's father had been a decorated captain of the Green Berets, but that was it. Did he have any siblings? Had he ever been married? Had he ever even been in love?

Knight thought of Emma, and Morningstar's callous insistence that Knight tell her goodbye at the tender age of twenty-one. He sighed. *No... it's obvious that he has never been in love...otherwise he never would have forced me to leave her.*

As for the sons; Judah knew little about them, as well. He didn't even know how many there were. Though he had been told that the Sons of Jacob would someday change the world, any knowledge he had of a specific son had come about completely by accident. Not long ago, he had overheard Morningstar on the phone with someone he had referred to as Simeon, and had heard him call the man "Son." He had given Knight the nickname Judah four years ago, obviously furthering the notion that he, Morningstar, was Jacob. How many sons were there? Twelve, consistent with the Biblical Jacob? What did they do? Were they powerful like Knight? Or did they lurk in the shadows, only half-a-step away from being scions of the underworld?

He had asked Morningstar about it, but had instantly been shut down. *"Judah, you are never to speak of them again. Is that clear?"* Knight had asked why, to which Morningstar had replied, *"Plausible deniability."* That had been the end of it.

But suddenly, he was curious. How many were there? Who were they? Were they men like him? Parentless, adrift, in need of guidance? He guessed that they were. *Who else would agree to such a role?* He flinched. *Don't think about it, Jerome.*

Morningstar had told him to keep his mind on his responsibilities. *"You have plenty to do without worrying about your brothers. Stay focused on the mission, son."*

"And what is the mission?" Jerome had asked.

"When I give the word, Judah, you must prepare America for the changes that are about to take place."

Knight frowned. He had just been given the word.

An agent walked in and laid a binder on his desk. "What we know so far, sir."

Knight picked it up, staring at the cover. It was solid black, and again, he thought of Emma. Her hair was *"...black as coal."* How many times had he told her that? He smiled sadly. *Emma.* He was amazed at how strong his feelings were for her after so many years apart. Jacob had told him his love would fade; he was wrong. It was about the only time he had been wrong, but Knight would have given anything for him to have been right. Knight's love for Emma hadn't faded one bit; if anything, it had grown stronger. And it hurt...physically...worse than anything he had ever felt.

He continued to stare at the binder, frowning as he thought of the old Jerome Knight; the man who had loved Emma with every part of him. His life had been so much simpler then. No nation to run, no crises to solve.

I miss you, Emma. Did she miss him? Did she even think of him? Though part of him prayed that she did, another part – the better part – hoped that she didn't. *I would hate for her to feel the pain that I feel every night as I lay awake alone.*

Suddenly, he felt his throat tighten. Emma would have no idea of what would soon take place. *How could she?* The world was about to change – dramatically – and the thought that she would be unprepared and unprotected weighed on him. *Let it go, Jerome...leave her behind.* That was what Morningstar had told him to do, and that was what he had done. But it had never felt right. It had never made sense to leave behind the only woman he had ever loved. And for what? For the sake of appearances? For the sake of power? Why had he gone along with it?

He sighed. *Because Morningstar told me to.*

Knight had always done what Morningstar had told him to do. But there was no denying that after sixteen years, he still wasn't over Emma. *"Leave her behind, my son."* Though it had hurt him to his soul, he had done it; he had listened to his father.

I have always listened to my father.

He called for an agent. Simmons walked in. "Yes sir?"

"I need to get upstairs. I need to be seen. The country needs to see their Commander-in-Chief in command of the situation."

The agent hesitated. Then, after a deep sigh, he nodded. He motioned for a second agent, and the two of them led Knight down a long hallway to the elevator. They took it to the first floor and walked to the Oval Office.

As they entered, Knight handed Simmons the Morningstar cellphone. "Let me know if I get a call." The agent nodded and tucked the phone in his pocket. He followed Knight into the Oval Office.

Knight was scheduled to meet with his security advisors. The meeting would be brief. Not only was the greatest fighting force in the world – the U.S. military – preparing for a potential war with Russia, but at the same time, America's citizens were killing one another with weapons that no one actually needed. And now, on top of it all, a man – a Capitol police officer – had initiated what could only be described as the first step of a revolution. What more was there to say?

He walked over to the Resolute Desk and stood behind it. He nodded at an aide, who opened the door and welcomed a group of advisors into the room. He motioned for them to sit, then listened as they summarized the morning's attack. The Capitol police officer had acted alone, but had left a manifesto that implied there were others. *"This is only the beginning,"* it had said. Every major military branch and the FBI were working diligently to try to find any co-conspirators before they could act.

The committee finished its summary, and Knight dismissed them. Next would be his Press Secretary, Pete Hastings, who would go over the day's message. Knight frowned as he thought of what that message should be. *'Get ready, America...life as you know it is about to change forever.'* Though that would be accurate, Knight had already chosen the words he would use. As Hastings walked in, his gray suit pressed and ready for the cameras, Knight stood and shook his hand. "Good morning, Pete."

"Good morning, Mr. President. I'm glad to see you here...in the Oval, sir."

Knight nodded. "I'm glad to be here." He paused. "Are you ready?"

"Yes sir. I'll open with a statement regarding the attack at the Capitol."

Knight hesitated. "Pete, things are going to go a bit differently today."

"Differently, sir?"

"Yes. Just minutes ago, I spoke with a high-ranking Pentagon administrator who is about to arrange for all available military personnel to station themselves in every major city throughout the country. He will also notify the National Guard and all local police so they can prepare."

Pete tugged at his collar, visibly shaken. He cleared his throat. "Prepare for what, sir?"

"A significant change in policy. And, because of it, instead of you starting off the presser this morning, I'll go first. You can follow to take questions."

"I'll have no idea what to say, sir."

"You've been in that position before, Pete. You'll do fine." He paused. "Just say 'I'm not at liberty to say,' if something gets really tricky. Does that sound okay?"

Pete frowned. "May I ask what is going on, sir?"

Knight sighed. *Do not let him see that you have any doubts about this.* "I'm going to open with the following message: 'Ladies and gentlemen of the press, I'd like to inform you that, in light of a verified plot to carry out an insurrection in this great country of ours, as of noon today, I am issuing two executive orders. The first will be to declare that we are now in a state of emergency. The second will be to instruct the U.S. military to begin the process of a mandatory buyback of all firearms...registered or unregistered.'"

Pete's jaw dropped. "With all due respect, you can't do that, sir."

"Certainly, I can, Pete. I'm the President of the United States in a time of war, not only overseas, but on our own soil." He swallowed, working hard to appear confident with a decision that he was not confident with at all. As he smoothed down the lapels of his jacket, he cleared his throat and said, "I can do it, Pete...and I will."

CHAPTER 44

Somewhere in Eastern Europe

Tall, lanky Tim Johansson stretched his long legs in front of him, awaiting orders from the Pentagon. Finally, he was working on something worthwhile. Russia's takeover of Latvia could happen at any time, and the Pentagon's Edward Morningstar had made him the point man. *"The minute you see movement from the Russian military, let me know. Only then, do I want you to inform your supervisor."* Morningstar had added, *"And maybe tell a couple of your friends in reconnaissance; let them know the good work you've done. You deserve the credit. Besides, I would hate for something bad to happen simply because they were unaware."*

Why had Johannson been willing to take orders from this stranger? He sighed. *Because he's the only one who recognizes what I'm capable of...the skills I bring to the table.* He had been monitoring the skies over Lithuania, Estonia, and Latvia for months now from his nook in the Uzbekistan mountains. It was time he received the recognition he deserved. And he had been particularly diligent over the past twelve hours...ever since he had intercepted the message that Russia was about to make a play for the Baltic States. But he had yet to hear anything more.

He was tired. He hadn't slept in over twenty-four hours, and he was beginning to feel it. He sucked down another cup of coffee, and played with a pencil on his desk, rolling it between his fingers, then tapping it on the corner of a blotter; anything to stay awake. His uncovering of the Russian plot would surely get him recognized. It was about time. He had been with the NSA for four years now, and it would be the first time since he started that his efforts would be appreciated. Morningstar had even promised him a commendation when the matter was resolved. He looked around at his dingy surroundings; the small, gray room with no windows, the old metal desk with only one working drawer, the ancient lamp that offered barely a sliver of light. He frowned as he thought of the number of times he had been passed over for some young techno-wizard who didn't possess half his knowledge. It would feel good to finally get the credit he deserved.

He was currently watching a series of blips along Russia's western border. He continued to follow them, almost missing a sudden increase in activity just outside Ludza, Latvia. He looked closer. *There it is! The build-up has begun!*

He dialed up the satellite to that region, stunned when he heard a garbled message in a coded dialect often used by Russia, "...take-over...in 72 hours." His hands were shaking as he pulled out his phone and dialed. He got a terse, "Yes."

"Mr. Morningstar, it has begun."

There was a pause. "Thank you. Alert your supervisor at once."

The call ended and Tim chuckled nervously. He had done it. He had just averted World War III. His legs were shaking, and he puts his hands on his knees. He stared at the monitor. *Or did I just set the whole goddamned thing in motion?*

CHAPTER 45

Washington, DC

Morningstar chuckled. He had played Johannson like a fiddle. Not only would the man eagerly alert his supervisor to the threat from Russia's military, but he would surely tell others, and, pretty soon, the entire East Europe reconnaissance team would know that Russia had escalated its efforts to take over the Baltic states.

He checked the time. It was nine-fifteen in the morning. *Time to put another piece of this puzzle into play.* Now that Johannson was making his move, and now that Knight was finally ready to follow through on the plan that had been put together years ago, it was time to take the next step. He dialed the Department of Homeland Security. The secretary answered with a solemn, "Department of Homeland Security. May I help you?"

Morningstar sneered. "It's Edward Morningstar from the Pentagon. I need to speak to Director Hanover at once."

"I'm sorry, sir. He's in a meeting."

Morningstar frowned. "Have him call me the minute he comes out."

"Yes sir."

Morningstar ended the call. Though he knew that the shooting at the Capitol would dominate the Director's time, he was eager to get news on Matt Henderson. He had told the Director yesterday afternoon that Matt was no longer simply a valuable witness to a crime; he was now wanted for that crime. Hopefully, the Director had acted on it. It would be so much easier to have the U.S. Government bring Henderson to America, as opposed to Levi somehow luring the man to Lithuania.

Morningstar stood and paced his office as he waited for the call back. Fortunately, he didn't have long to wait. He had only gotten in three quick laps around the small office, when his phone rang. "Yes?"

"Morningstar, it's Hanover."

Morningstar leered. "Good morning, Director. Two things. First, I'm guessing your meeting was about the shooting at the Capitol?"

"Yes. I'm expected to report to the President later this morning."

"Good. Hopefully, it's just a one-and-done and that will be the end of it." He waited for a reply; Hanover said nothing. Morningstar went on. "Number two: Have you arranged for Matt Henderson to be brought to the States for interrogation?"

There was a pause. "No. We don't know where he is."

Morningstar bristled. He tugged at his collar. "You don't know where he is? I can tell you exactly where he is...he's hiding out at that damn castle!"

Another pause. "Morningstar, you need to get a hold of yourself. I called Walter Henderson immediately after your call yesterday. He told me that Matt had left the compound and that he didn't know where he had gone."

"And you believed him?"

"Yes. The man has no reason to lie to me."

Other than to protect his son from accusations of treason. He sighed. "So, what are you doing to try to find him?"

"We are fortunate to have the cooperation of the Latvian police. They're reluctant to be too aggressive, however. The Hendersons have done a lot for Latvia."

Morningstar rolled his eyes. "So I've heard." He paused. "Let me know when you find him. I want updates every hour."

A longer pause. "I'll call you when I have something, Morningstar."

The call ended. Morningstar stared at his phone. *I hate that son-of-a-bitch.* He slammed down the receiver and pulled out his private cellphone. He dialed; it was answered after the first ring. Without waiting for a hello, he said, "Where are you?"

Gad whispered, "On a train to Vilnius, Lithuania."

Morningstar frowned. "I thought I told you to get down there two weeks ago."

"You did, sir. But I needed time to put together a plan."

Morningstar bristled. "You needed time, did you? Dammit, Gad, because of your delay, the guy is on the run."

Gad chuckled. "Don't worry, Jacob. I've left him with a calling card."

"A calling card? What the hell are you talking about?"

"I was able to put a burner phone in the pocket of his backpack. Once I'm in Vilnius and I've worked out a plan, I'll give the asshole a call."

Morningstar was steaming. "What makes you think he'll take your call, Gad?"

Another chuckle. "I'll be so persuasive, he won't have a choice, Jacob."

Morningstar stiffened. *Cocky son-of-a-bitch.* "By god, you better be, Gad!"

Morningstar ended the call. Though he was irritated with Gad, the man had yet to let him down. As a matter of fact, Gad had proven on many occasions to be not only resourceful, but remarkably clever. Morningstar began to relax. Gad would succeed; he always succeeded. Morningstar chuckled. *Leave it to one of my sons to complete the task that the United States Government is incapable of taking care of.*

CHAPTER 46

Camden, Maine

Something had changed. The rain had stopped, but it wasn't a weather pattern that was holding Emma Melnikov Cannon's attention as she stared out at the Maine coastline less than a mile away. She had spent the morning in the bedroom and, when Michael had asked if she was okay, she hadn't lied when she said, *"I'm just not feeling well."* He had seemed to accept it. He had thrown on a pair of sweats and had gone for a jog. But when he returned, she hadn't left her spot in front of the window.

"Do I need to call someone, Emma? Do you need a doctor?"

Emma had chuckled silently. *If only it was that simple,* she had wanted to say. But instead, she had said nothing. It wasn't Michael's fault that she was in love with another man. But it was different this time. Over the course of the last twenty-four hours, Romer hadn't just entered her thoughts, he had taken over her very soul. She couldn't seem to shake him; she couldn't make him leave. It was as if he had said goodbye only yesterday, and she was reeling from it just as much.

But I'm married...we have a child! Emma stood and, with her hands on the sill, she stared out the window as blustery gales blew against the glass. *Yes, but the child is gone now...traveling abroad for the next two years, then going off to college.*

Dawn had brought little relief. Late October days in Maine were harbingers of winter...cold, dark, and lonely. As she looked out at the bitter gray morning with hints of more rain, she began to see that, for whatever reason, her love for Jerome hadn't faded...not one bit. *You're being silly, Emma; you've moved on.* And she thought she had. She had married, had had a child, and had convinced herself that she had left Romer behind. But she knew now that she hadn't, and it was making her sick inside. *Go for a run, clean the house...do something!* But she couldn't. It was as if her legs were broken. All she could do was kneel by the window and stare out at the rain.

She heard commotion in the kitchen. *Michael must be making breakfast.* A few minutes later, she heard footsteps and cringed. Then she felt guilty. He was a good man...*he doesn't deserve this.* He had done nothing but love her, and her inability to love him back suddenly angered her. She had known true love; she had known it with Romer, and it infuriated her that she couldn't feel it for her own husband. *Damn you, Michael, why can't you make me love you?*

He knocked on the door. "Emma, are you feeling better?"

No, I feel terrible. I'm living a lie, and I'm dragging you and Galina down with me. "I'm fine, Michael. Just a bit under the weather."

"Are you hungry? I'm making eggs."

"No, I'll get something later."

She heard him walk away. Michael wasn't a hoverer.

Her daughter, Galina, wasn't a hoverer, either. She was also remarkably perceptive. Her travels with the orchestra had been well-timed...she would have sensed the lie. Emma frowned. It had been tough for her to let Galina go on tour. In spite of sending her with Michael's aunt to serve as her legal guardian while away, Emma couldn't help but feel as if she had abandoned Galina. Emma couldn't have gone; she had a job that she loved, and responsibilities at home. But oh how she mourned the loss of her child... the little girl who had worshiped her and loved her like no one ever had. Regardless, Galina was gone...and when she returned – *if* she returned – she would be a grown woman. *And I am quickly becoming an old woman.*

Emma walked to a full-length mirror in the corner of the room and stared at her thirty-seven-year-old body. It wasn't bad; she still had strong, lean legs, and her skin remained soft and smooth. *But I'm certainly not twenty-one anymore.* Never had she felt so old...or so lonely. *You've seen it, haven't you, mirror? The lie on my face as my husband makes love to me and I pretend to love him back. The look in my eye as I awaken from sleep and long for the arms of another man.*

Another round of tears crept down her cheeks, and she didn't even bother to wipe them away. Her heart ached, both for Romer and for Michael. The thought of hurting Michael made her feel sick inside. He had been good to her; he was kind and loving, and, if he knew what she was feeling, he would be devastated. She began to shake. *Which is why I need to let this go!*

She walked back to the window and knelt in front of it. She would stay in that bedroom until she put Romer away; it was that simple. She frowned. *It's not simple at all. He's not just some board game I can throw in a box and set on a shelf.*

But she had done it before, so, why was this time different? *Because he's everywhere!* Her lover from the past was now the President of the United States, and his face was on every TV screen and every newspaper across the land. She shook her head. *President Knight.* It was laughable. Romer was hers; not the entire nation's. It was as if America was the woman that had stolen him away from her. She smiled sadly as she thought of her young Romer somehow transformed into the elegant, almost regal President Knight...*not even close.*

She had been surprised – and selfishly relieved – that he had never married. He was such a desirable man. Handsome, smart, powerful. How had some beautiful, well-heeled woman not come along and snatched him up? Though Emma wanted to think that it was because he had never gotten over her, she doubted that was the case. He was, after all, the one who had said goodbye to her. So, what was it? Was he too busy? Was he worried that he wouldn't be able to devote the proper time to a wife in the midst of what had become a demanding political life? She frowned. Was that the reason he had left her in the first place? It didn't matter. He had done it. He was gone.

She fought a sudden round of tears as she pounded her fists on the sill. *So, why can't I get you out of my head, Romer?*

She thought back to the day he left. He had given her no reason for why he was leaving; no explanation for suddenly walking away from a love that had been so deep, so meaningful...*so honest.* But she had sensed that he had been sad about what he was doing...no, not sad, he had seemed angry...as if he hadn't wanted to do it. She closed her eyes and sunk lower in front of the window. *So, why did you, Romer?*

She sighed. It didn't matter. He had crushed her very soul, and it was Michael who had saved her. He had taken her in and had loved her when her spirit had been decimated. And her life with Michael had been good; not great, but good. They had built a life...together. They shared a history, a fifteen-year anthology...the milestones as Galina was born, and grew, and became a young woman. The challenges as they paid down the mortgage, paid off the car, set aside money for college. Emma *loved* Michael; maybe not in the right way, but she loved him, and knew he loved her back.

Again, she pounded the windowsill as she stared out at the darkening sky. With a desperation greater than anything she had ever felt, she whispered, "You left me before, Romer...so, why won't you leave me now?"

She looked at the clock. Her eyes widened. *Nine-forty...I'm late for work!* She shook her head. *There's no way I can go to work...not like this.* She had been kneeling at that window since two a.m., yet was no closer to ridding her mind – her heart – of Romer than she had been when she started.

Again, Michael came to the door. "Feeling any better, Emma?"

She swallowed. "Um...no, no I'm not. Could you please call my office and let them know that I won't be coming in today?"

"Sure, babe." She heard him walk away, and, still kneeling, she put her head in her hands. An observer might think she was praying; she was doing anything but. *God must be so disappointed in me.*

She couldn't help it; she couldn't stop the feelings that had hijacked her heart. For whatever reason, on this cold, dreary morning, she could no longer pretend. Not anymore. Romer had come to stay. She had never stopped loving him, and these agonizing hours stuck in her bedroom confirmed it. He had left her while they were still in love – she was sure he had felt the same – and, at least for her, nothing had changed...the love was still there. *But he left you, Emma. He's gone.* But he hadn't wanted to go; she could tell by the way he had said goodbye. Something else had made him leave. She wondered if he still thought about it...that final moment when he had touched her cheek, then had turned and walked away.

She looked over her shoulder and saw in the mirror a woman, kneeling, with long black hair covering her face, her eyes...as if hiding her from the truth. *I'm living a lie, and I'm forcing Michael to live it with me.* Still looking in the mirror, she stood and walked toward it. She stared at her image, wondering if, just maybe, it might not be a kindness to let Michael go. *"To pretend to love is the worst sort of lie."* It was something her mother had told

256

her. She looked long and hard at the face staring back at her...the wrinkles that had started at the corners of her eyes and across her forehead. They were telling of the journey she had traveled...the journey she had forced Michael to travel with her. The agony, not of leaving a man she loved, but of being left by him. And the heartache of making another man endure it.

She took a deep breath. It was time to learn the truth. Her love for Romer only mattered if Romer felt it, too. If they were still in love with one another, then at least there would be a justification for her to say goodbye to Michael. But if she was the only one who felt it – if the love was hers alone – then she would need to keep it buried, if for no other reason than the pain it would cause would never be worth it. *Emma, Romer wouldn't have left you sixteen years ago if he had still loved you.* But something told her that he had...that he left her while still very much in love with her.

She moved closer to the mirror. Her eyes were dry now, the deep blue sharp and distinct. *"Almost indigo,"* Romer used to tell her. Her hair had never been dyed; it was still as fiercely black as it had been when she was twenty-one. She brushed a loose strand over one shoulder as she nodded slowly, and said, "Emma, it's time."

CHAPTER 47

Strongsville, Ohio

Andrew Madison pulled his car into the quiet subdivision and turned off the engine. He looked around. It was just after ten a.m. on a Tuesday and the street was quiet. The small Tudor house he was parked in front of looked unremarkable, yet welcoming as he grabbed his bags and stepped out of the car. But he was cautious, nonetheless.

Now, where did she say that key would be? He walked along a sidewalk to a stone path that led to a set of steps. He climbed them and was standing on a small front porch. He did his best to act like he belonged there. *"Under a flower pot at the edge of the porch."* He looked for the pot. There were three pots sitting together at the far end of the porch; he walked over to them. He found the key under the last of the three and walked to the door. He unlocked it and walked inside. An alarm began to beep. *Put in the code!* He plugged in the four-digit code he had been given; the beeping stopped. He slid the key in his pocket, then closed and locked the door.

Except for a cardboard box here and there, the place was empty. Jenny Clarkson, Hank's ex-wife, had put the house up for sale months ago, but had had no luck selling it, *"...not for the right price, anyway."* She had offered it to Andrew the minute he had called her and had told her what was happening. *"I need a place to hide, Jenny."*

He wasn't sure what had compelled him to call her. Her offer of help after he had called looking for Hank had seemed sincere, but he barely knew her. Then again, he knew *of* her because of Hank and Maddi's relationship. *Maybe I feel closer to her because of Maddi and Hank.* He laughed. *That's ridiculous. It was Maddi who had come between them.* Regardless; he had called her and, true to her promise, she had helped him. *"I have a house in Strongsville, Ohio, that's currently sitting empty."*

The house was perfect for a couple of reasons. Not only was no one there, but the odds of a Pentagon agent tying Andrew to a house in Ohio were slim, at best. *There's no way they'll have this place bugged.* It was the first time since he had left his mother's house that he felt confident that if he listened to whatever was on that tape, it wouldn't be overheard by some agent hiding away in the basement of the Pentagon. His house, his car, his office, even the bank vault...none of it had felt safe. But this empty house in a nondescript suburb of Strongsville, Ohio felt totally safe.

The journey from Columbia, South Carolina to Strongsville had taken him nearly twenty-four hours. Before he had left his office, he had grabbed the key to the safe deposit box from the console in Amanda's car. He had driven to their townhouse to pack a bag, and from there had gone to the bank, where he had opened the safe deposit box. He had grabbed the recorder, and had made a quick stop at the daycare to check on Adam, who was napping. After a silent goodbye from across the room, he had left and had gone to a convenience store, where he had purchased a blanket, a case of water, apples, and about ten granola bars. By the time he left Columbia, it had been four in the afternoon, which meant that he had hit not only Columbia's rush hour, but Charlotte's as well. He had headed straight up route 77. Sometime after midnight, he had stopped at a motel in Beckley, West Virgina, to get a few hours of sleep. He had awakened at four a.m., and had finished the drive to Ohio.

He looked around, shivering as he searched for a place to set up shop. She had told him that she had kept the electric on to protect the pipes from freezing, but had left the thermostat at fifty degrees. He was pleased when he found a small room in the back of the house with windows facing east. They let in heat from the morning sun, making the room several degrees warmer than the rest of the house.

He walked over and lowered a set of blinds. In spite of the sun's warmth, he couldn't risk anyone seeing him there. He set his backpack on the hardwood floor of what he guessed had been a den. Leaving on his jacket, he opened the sack of items he had bought at the convenience store and pulled out the blanket. He laid it on the floor. He opened his backpack and took out the tape recorder. Using the backpack as a pillow, he laid on the blanket, set the recorder on his chest, and crossed his legs.

I wonder what Amanda is doing? He checked the time. *Ten-twenty-five.* She would have dropped Adam at the daycare on her way to work, and would now be knee-deep in patients. His heart ached as he thought of her. The only other time he had left her had been back in March, when he had been asked – no, pretty much ordered – to attend a meeting of the secret Morning star organization. She had been very pregnant at the time, and he had hated to leave her. But at that time he hadn't been afraid for her safety...or for his own. Now, he was afraid for all three of them.

Which was why he was glad he had called his cop friend to look after Amanda and Adam. The cop had been a patient of his soon after Andrew had come to Columbia. Andrew had discovered a tumor in the man's liver and, though Andrew had simply been doing his job, the man, Bill, felt certain that Andrew had saved his life. As a result, he had offered his help on many occasions. This was the first time that Andrew had taken him up on it. *"I'll need them watched twenty-four hours a day, Bill. Is that possible?"*

The former officer hadn't even hesitated. *"For you, Andrew, I'll make it work. I have another retired cop who can take the day shift."*

He sighed and stared at the recorder on his chest. After months of trying to imagine what was on that tape, he was finally about to hear it...he was finally about to hear his mother's last words. Was he ready? He sighed. *I guess I better be.*

With a shaking hand, he pushed the rewind button, waited for it to go to the beginning, then pushed 'play.'

But instead of hearing what he had expected to be his mother's final words to either apologize for the tragedy of the last thirty years, or to comfort him and Maddi as she died unceremoniously alone, he heard the voice of a man. *"You tell it to me first, Jeannie...then, together, we'll hear it straight from the bitch's mouth."*

CHAPTER 48

Washington, DC

Levi got the call from his Pentagon stooge at 10:54 a.m. "Yeah?"

"It's me...agent Thompson."

"What have you got?"

"I followed him...all the way to Ohio."

Levi frowned. "Ohio? What the hell is he doing there?"

"I don't know. He's at a house...in Strongsville. Got here about an hour ago. What d'ya' want me to do?"

Levi sat back in his chair and stretched his legs. It was odd; Andrew had suddenly left town – had left his family – and had driven all the way to Ohio. "Whose house is it, Thompson?"

"It's listed under Jenny Clarkson. But she hasn't been here in over a week."

Levi frowned. *Jenny Clarkson...any relation to Homeland's Dr. Hank Clarkson?* "Find out what you can about her."

"Okay. Then what?"

Levi frowned. Why had Andrew left town so abruptly? Yes, Levi had been rather heavy handed when he had ransacked the guy's house, but had he actually scared him into running away? *Only if he has the damn tape!* He narrowed his eyes. "Just watch him, Thompson. Don't let 'im leave."

There was a pause. "How will I keep him here if he decides to leave?"

"I don't know...arrest him, I guess."

"Arrest him? For what?"

Levi sighed. "For carrying stolen goods across state lines."

"What stolen goods?"

Levi frowned. "I don't know. Throw a TV in his car. Anything. Just don't let 'im leave."

"Okay. How long do I need to keep an eye on him?"

Levi rubbed his chin. Morningstar had told him to get the tape...and now he knew exactly where that tape might be. He chuckled. *Maybe I can be a hero after all.* "I'll tell you what. I'll meet you in Strongsville...tonight, if I can find a flight."

"Tonight?"

"Yeah. Text me the address. Whatever you do, don't let 'im leave."

Levi ended the call. He grinned as he shoved his phone in his pocket. If he was lucky, he would have the recorder by midnight. He would give it to Morningstar first thing tomorrow morning, and he would finally be a hero. *But before I give it to him, I'll listen to it...and find out just what it is that Morningstar is so afraid of.*

CHAPTER 49

On a train to Riga, Latvia

Henderson had been on the run since leaving the hotel the night before. He was exhausted. Though he hadn't seen anyone behind him, he was certain he was being followed. He hadn't sensed anyone's presence since around daybreak, but he knew better than to stop now. Those police officers who had come to his hotel room weren't going to give up. Clearly, they had agreed to cooperate with the U.S. government, which surprised him. The Hendersons had a long and illustrious relationship with Latvian law enforcement. But something – or someone – had clearly convinced them that it was more important to find a perceived fugitive than to worry about the contributions of his family. Which meant that his father had been right; America's Homeland Security had a long reach.

Henderson's advantage, at least early on, had been the cover of darkness, helped along by a cloud-covered moon, and miles and miles of untouched forest. But then had come the threat of sunrise, and he had been forced to come up with a plan. He had needed sleep and a new identity. Fortunately, in spite of all that he had done wrong during his four years with Morningstar, he had made a few friends along the way. One such friend, Emil, was located near a town east of Riga...Koknese, Latvia...at the junction of routes A6 and E22. The small town wasn't even on most maps. About an hour before dawn, Henderson had managed to hitch a ride with a trucker who had taken him most of the way there. He had arrived at the man's house at seven a.m., just as the sun was starting to rise. The isolated farmhouse had been quiet; Henderson hadn't been sure anyone was home. Though he would have normally tried to call the man first, his contact information was in his old phone, which Cobra had taken from him months ago. So he had shown up unannounced, with a completely different face, and had quickly learned that someone was, in fact, home. Before he could even knock, the man had rushed through the door, had pushed his face to the ground, and had shoved a knee in his back. The only thing that had kept Henderson from getting his head blown off was that he had known the code words; the expression the two men had used when they had done business in the past. *"Putin will...soon name...St. Petersburg... St. Putinburg,"* he had muttered as Emil had pressed a gun to his head. Emil had eased up, but he had continued to hold the gun to Henderson's temple. *"Who are you?"* he had asked, his familiar voice a comfort. *"Phoenix. I saved your ass in Riga two years ago."* The man had hesitated, but then had laughed. *"That you did, my friend...that you did."* He had lowered the gun, and had stood and helped Henderson up from the ground. He had stared at him for what had felt like a full minute, then had walked him into his house, shoving away two goats and a chicken that had strutted out from a back room. Still holding the gun, but no longer aiming it at him, he had asked, *"Why do you not look the same?"*

Henderson had sighed and, with as much detail as he could, he had summarized the last ten months of his life. He had explained how a transplant had given him another man's face, and had shown Emil the few scars that remained on his neck and forearms. Emil had stared at the scars; he had even run his fingers over them, as if to prove to himself that he was actually the same man. Henderson had then told him that he was being hunted by America's Homeland Security for a crime he had had no part in. *"I need a way to move around without being identified."*

Without a moment's pause, Emil had nodded and said, *"Wait here."* He had disappeared for several minutes, leaving Henderson to fight off the goats. He had come back carrying a bag, along with a contraption that Henderson had recognized as a forging machine. Emil had handed him the bag. *"Bleach your hair; put on the mustache and glasses."*

Henderson had opened the bag, frowning as he had looked past a pair of black-framed glasses to a blonde mustache and a bottle of bleach. The bleach would strip away the black dye in his hair, which would leave it essentially the same color that it had been as the Phoenix. He had sighed.

"I can't go back to blond, Emil. I need another color." The man had shaken his head. *"It is all I have."* Henderson had hesitated. That black hair had kept him safe for the past eight months. But dark-haired Matt wasn't any safer than blond-haired Phoenix. And Henderson looked quite a bit different from how he had looked as the Phoenix. He no longer had the scars that had defined the international assassin, nor did he have the classic Henderson jaw.

He had put a hand to his face – the face that had been given to him by the dead corporal, James Calvin – and had nodded, praying that the mustache, the glasses, and the altered jawline would be enough to keep him from being identified. He had then carried the bag with the bleach into the bathroom, and had stripped the black dye from his hair. He had put on the mustache and the black-framed glasses, and had walked out of the bathroom. Emil had snapped his picture, had printed it using a portable printer, then had processed it through the forging device. He had handed him the finished passport. *"It is a bit basic, my friend, but it will fool border or airport agents. You are now Aiden Balkus from Lithuania."* The two of them had then built a biography for Aiden, with Emil electronically inserting enough history in various institutions to make it appear authentic should anyone go to the trouble of looking. Once he had completed the transformation, Emil had offered him breakfast.

That had been over eight hours ago. Henderson rubbed his eyes as he leaned against the seat of the train. He had left Emil's soon after breakfast, and had hitched a ride to Viesīte, about sixty kilometers south of Koknese. Though Emil had offered to let him stay at his home, Henderson had felt that he would be putting Emil in danger. *"They're still looking for me, Emil… and they're not going to stop."* He had checked into a hotel outside Viesīte, had slept for about four hours, and had left the hotel. That was just under an hour ago; it was now six p.m.

The train would take him back to Riga. He had spent most of the train ride scrolling through his laptop, finally doing what he should have done after Maddi's plane crash: reading articles about the crash. It had been torture. The tributes to Maddi had been overwhelming. He was glad he had a seat to himself as it had been all he could do to not fall apart as he read tribute after tribute. At one point, an article even mentioned the DC hotel explosion, *"….and Senator Madison, along with the notable Martin Henderson, saved many that night. Mr. Henderson actually died from his efforts...*" It had been unbearable, but he had made himself read every account, every horrid detail, not only of the crash, but of the aftermath. Cravens' survival hadn't been mentioned in earlier stories; it had taken nearly a week for it to make the news. But then it had been on the front page of every major paper. *"Secret Service Agent Survives Harrowing Ordeal."* Cravens had told reporters – reluctantly, from what Henderson could determine from the articles – that he had been standing when the plane had gone down, and had been thrown from the wreckage before it burst into flames. *"Otherwise, I'd have suffered the same fate as the rest of those poor souls."*

Henderson took a deep breath and sighed. He checked his watch. Six-ten. The train would arrive in Riga in about twenty minutes. He closed the laptop and shoved it in his backpack. His first task would be to talk to Cravens...the last man to see Maddi alive. But he had no idea how to find him. He would start by calling the man's boss. He pulled out the sheet of paper on which he had written Secret Service Director Sam Allen's number. He looked around the small compartment. *Too many people.* He would make the call once he reached the city.

The train arrived at the Riga train station at six-thirty sharp. Now that he had a reasonable disguise, it should be safe for him to move around the city. He got off and walked to a nearby café. He found a table in back, ordered coffee and a sandwich, then dialed Allen's number.

A deep voice said, "Allen here."

Henderson's hands were shaking. Doing his best to hide his scratchy voice and imitate his father's, he said quietly, "Sam, it's Walter Henderson."

A pause. "Hello, Mr. Henderson. I hope things are going okay in Latvia?"

Say as little as possible. "It's why I called." He paused. "Sam, I need a favor."

"Whatever you need, Mr. Henderson."

Henderson rubbed the back of his neck. *Here 'goes.* "I'm trying to assess the Russian army's influence along our western border," he rubbed his hand on his pants, "...and I'm reviewing the attack on my security team that took place in March. I was hoping to talk to one of your agents who had come to the compound to investigate."

He heard a sigh. "Cravens and Cross. I haven't sent anyone else to Latvia since the nineties." He heard him clear his throat. "But um...Cross is...uh... dead; he died in a plane crash...and Cravens isn't available, I'm afraid."

Henderson flinched. *Cross was killed in the same crash that killed Maddi.* He cleared his throat. "I'm so sorry, Director, but I really need to talk to Agent Cravens."

"As I said, Mr. Henderson, he's not available."

"Do you know how I might reach him?"

Another pause. "Um, Mr. Henderson...I'm sure you recall that Agent Cravens was in an accident a couple of months ago; the same accident that killed his partner."

Henderson paused for effect. "I know, Sam...but I really need to talk to him."

Silence. Finally, "Listen, Mr. Henderson...I don't want to be disrespectful or anything...but Cravens has been through quite a lot."

"I understand, Director. I promise not to trouble him for more than a few minutes."

More silence. Then, "Here's the thing, Mr. Henderson," he sighed, "... Tom Cravens hasn't been heard from since he was released from the hospital...about three days after the plane crash."

CHAPTER 50

Liepaja, Latvia

Damn, it's cold out here. Secret Service Agent Tom Cravens pulled his coat tighter around him as he stopped to rub his low back. It hurt worse than usual. He had suffered with a bad back ever since an assassination attempt on a Vice-Presidential candidate back in '92. The attempt had failed, but only because Cravens had tackled the guy on the top row of a set of bleachers, both men falling over ten feet to the ground. He had never been the same. *And this cold weather isn't helping.*

Neither was the plane crash he had miraculously survived nine weeks ago.

He pushed his fist into the small of his back as he stole down a dark alley in the heart of Priekule, Latvia. The city, about twenty miles southeast of Liepaja, was on the bottom rung of a circular path he had been travelling for the past two months. Starting with Pavilosta to the north, then heading east, he had covered nearly five hundred miles since his release from the hospital three days after the plane crash that had killed everyone but him and Maddi. He was disgusted; not only with his situation, but with all that had happened since the crash.

It had started with his three-day stint in the Liepaja hospital. Other than repairing a gash in his forehead, there was little they had needed to do. He had been permitted to leave only after some unnamed bureaucrat had said it was okay; a bureaucrat he was certain was taking orders from some other bureaucrat halfway around the world. The delay had been unfortunate, to say the least. Cravens had been eager to interrogate a man who had followed Hank to the site of the plane crash; a man Hank had been certain had been sent to ensure that Maddi had been killed in the crash. Fortunately, Maddi had been taken from the site before he had arrived. The man, whoever he was, had walked over to Cravens, and together, they had stared at the wreckage. Cravens had had to fight his disgust as the man had feigned concern. Cravens would never forget him. Not only because of what Hank had alluded to, but because of his eyes...one of them was clearly made of glass. Though the man had made a point of never looking directly at him, Cravens had noticed the odd blue eye almost immediately. *And I will know it if and when I see that man again.*

But because of the hospital stay, he had lost three days, and in that time, the man had vanished. Though Hank had given Cravens very little information about the man, Cravens was working on the assumption that he was a driver at the Henderson estate. After all, that was where Hank had been staying as a result of his obligation to look after Matt Henderson. Hank had told Cravens that he had overheard the driver on the phone, and that the guy had been sent to prove to whoever he was talking to that Maddi had died in the crash. There was only one conclusion to draw from such a statement: whoever the driver had been speaking to had known in advance that Maddi's plane was going to go down.

And the man's actions at the crash site had done nothing to make him think any differently. Driving a black BMW, he had stopped about a hundred yards from the downed plane and had walked up to Cravens. He had told Cravens that he worked at a nearby estate, and had been driving by when he had seen the accident.

Cravens, holding true to the plan that he and Hank had devised before Hank had whisked Maddi away, had told him that everyone else had died, and had made sure to show him the three items that Maddi had left behind to 'prove' she had died: her blue sweater, her senate ID badge, and a locket that had been given to her by her grandparents. The man had seemed to believe him. Before he left, he had reached down and picked up the three items and had handed them to Cravens. But when Cravens went to send the items to the State Department, all he had was the sweater and the ID badge. Had the man stolen the locket? It was hard to say, though Cravens certainly wouldn't put it past him. The man had left quickly; he had seemed eager to get away from there. Cravens had written the car's license plate number on a scrap of paper, and he rubbed that paper now as he jogged to a semi that had stopped to give him a ride.

"Where are you going?" the man asked in Lettish.

Cravens understood the language far better than he could speak it, "Liepaja."

The man nodded. Cravens settled into the passenger seat. They pulled away.

He had spent the last two months trying to track down the driver of that black sedan. The man represented Craven's only clue as to who was behind the plane crash. He knew that the car had belonged to a nearby estate, and he guessed it was the Henderson's. What he didn't know was if the driver was still there. Though Cravens had been tempted to call Walter Henderson and ask him if he had a driver with a glass eye, he realized that if he did make such a call, he was jeopardizing Maddi's safety. He would need to explain that Hank had overheard the man, and that the man had implied that the plane crash had been planned. Which would lead to two obvious questions: Who planned it, and where was Hank? An investigation would ensue, which would likely expose both Hank's and Cravens' roles in covering it up. It might also lead to the conclusion that Maddi hadn't died in the crash.

Cravens could concoct a lie and say that Hank had come to the site after overhearing the driver, and, upon learning that Maddi was dead, had simply driven off into the night. But he couldn't count on Walter leaving it there. Walter would feel compelled to find Hank, if for no other reason than to learn more about a driver in his employ who was clearly a criminal. And to find Hank, would be to find Maddi.

Nor could Cravens call his boss for help...for all the same reasons. It would cast doubt on the cause of the plane crash. And any mention of the source of his concerns – Hank – would lead his boss to also feel compelled to find Hank. He was, after all, the man who had overheard the driver's damning phone call.

So, Cravens had taken it upon himself to try to find the driver on his own. Starting in Liepaja, he had walked the streets in search of a black sedan and/or a wiry black man with a blue glass eye. He had noted the license plate of every black car that had driven through town. After several days with no success, he had left the city and had hitched a ride heading north, where he had hid in the brush outside the Henderson estate.

Though the estate was a well-kept secret, Cravens had been to the compound back in March, following an attack on the Henderson security team. He felt that he had memorized enough landmarks to at least get close to the place. His goal was to wait in the brush until he spotted the man with the glass eye, or at least the car he had driven. But after three days of seeing plenty of BMW's, but none with a license plate that had the numbers he had written down, or a driver that looked like the man he had seen at the crash site, he had decided that maybe Hank had overheard the man not at the Henderson estate, but at a diner or a nearby gas station. So he had once again hitched a ride, this time with a produce driver, who had dropped him at the first town he came to. Cravens had taken it from there. From Pavilosta to Regi, then on to Kuldiga, he had spent his days looking for either the black sedan or the man with the glass eye, and had spent his nights trying to justify the fact that he had been one of only two survivors of a crash that no one should have survived. He hadn't had luck with either one. Now, two months later, he had come full circle and was on his way back to Liepaja. Why? *Because that is where it began.*

He brushed a hand through his scraggly beard. He was surprised he had allowed it to get so long. He had never had a beard. Not only had his wife detested facial hair, but whiskers made him itch. His hair had grown out as well, and, as he ran his hand through thick gray tangles, he frowned. *Maybe it's time I clean up a bit.*

They neared Liepaja and the driver stopped south of town. "Good enough?"

"Yes." Cravens mumbled a thank you and stepped out of the truck. The sun was setting as he walked toward the same hotel where he had stayed the last time he was there. On the way, he stopped at a department store and purchased a cheap suit, along with a pair of clippers. He left the store and walked to the hotel. The place seemed deserted, except for a desk clerk who nodded at Cravens as he walked through the door. Cravens was glad to see that it was the same clerk who had manned the desk the last time he had been there; the man spoke English. Cravens checked in using the same fake name he had used before, and then – as he had also done before – he pretended to fumble through his wallet for identification. He shrugged. "I must have lost my ID," he said as he slid the man a twenty-euro bill.

As he let go of the cash, he noticed that he was down to his last hundred euros. His boss had wired him 1,000 euros the day he had left the hospital, after Cravens had told him that he had lost his wallet in the crash – which wasn't true – and that he needed the cash to do some traveling…which was sort of true. *I'm hoping the travel will help me wrap my mind around all that happened.* Cravens hadn't wanted to use his credit card; it would leave a trail for anyone who might be looking for him.

Allen had seemed to accept Cravens' explanation, and had honored his request. He had wired him the cash with an understanding that he would make a full accounting of every dime once he was back in the States. It was the last time the two had spoken. Cravens didn't want to have to call him for more money…it had been too long. Allen would insist that he come home; he would *order* him to come home. He stared at the money and frowned. *I'll just have to make it last.*

The desk clerk slid the twenty-euro bill in his pocket. "Forty euros for the night." Cravens handed him the cash; he handed Cravens a key.

Cravens walked to his room, glad when he saw that it faced the back of the hotel. He was carrying Walter's briefcase that he had picked up in Lyon back in March, stunned that it had survived the plane crash, along with a cheap duffle bag that he had picked up at a sundry shop soon after his release from the hospital. Inside it were two shirts, two pairs of pants, and a few pairs of underwear. He washed the items every few days, depending on what town he was in. Essentially, that was all that was left of Tom Cravens.

He tossed the clippers on a chair, draped the garment bag over the back of it, and set the duffel bag and briefcase on a table. He laid his cellphone – that had miraculously survived the plane crash – on a table by the bed, then hung his overcoat on a hook on the door. As he was about to walk away, he noted for probably the twentieth time that the coat still smelled of smoke. There was also a tear in the sleeve, and he brushed his fingers over it as he sighed and shook his head. *I should throw this coat away.* But he didn't know if he could. Though it was a reminder of an awful event that had changed his life forever, it also served as inspiration for what he needed to do. He had to find the man responsible for that crash; he had to find Maddi's would-be killer.

He narrowed his eyes. *I'll cut my hair and shave off my beard, and maybe I'll even put on the new suit I just bought, but I don't think I can ever get rid of that coat.*

The room was dark, but he didn't bother turning on a lamp. He sat in the only chair, shoved a pillow against his low back, and rested his feet on a nearby table. It didn't take long for the aching to set in, so he kicked off his shoes and slipped out of his shirt and pants. Though it wasn't even seven p.m., he slid under the covers, adjusting the pillow on the uneven mattress as he turned on his side, hoping to relieve the pressure on his back. He closed his eyes, but immediately regretted it, as he saw it all again; the crashing of the plane, the dead bodies of Cross and the pilots, Maddi's empty eyes as Hank ushered her away. And, like every other time when he remembered the events of that day, he suffered the guilt of having survived. There was no sense to it; no logic as to why he would live and a man like Cross would die. Why had it turned out that way? Cravens had asked the question so many times that he no longer noticed as it clawed away at the lining of his skull.

But an even more unsettling question was how someone had managed to sabotage an RAF plane. The Royal Air Force would have kept tight reins on who was permitted to go on and off of that plane. And, though Cravens was aware that it had needed mechanical work prior to their departure, he felt certain that the men chosen to work on such an aircraft would have been cleared at the highest levels. Which had led him to wonder more than once if maybe the crash really had been an accident, and if Hank had maybe imagined the conversation he had overheard. But always Cravens would come back to Hank's words as they had stood by the broken aircraft: *"The man following me had been told that this plane was going to crash."*

Cravens winced as he turned slightly and felt his back go into spasm. He let out a groan, finally giving up and sitting on the edge of the bed. After a minute, he stood and grabbed a pack of cigarettes from the pocket of his suitcoat. He walked to the only window. The sunlight was nearly gone, but as it sunk behind the trees, he could see its reflection on the Baltic Sea. He pulled up a chair and took a seat. He opened the window half an inch, letting in the cold air, as well as the sound of the waves against the shoreline. He pulled out a cigarette, lit it, and stared at the trail of smoke as it wafted out the window. Though he had been trying to quit for the past three years, he no longer saw much point in it. After all, he had survived a plane crash that should have killed him...a crash that had killed nearly everyone else on board. He took another drag. *Why did I live when so many people – really good people – died?* No, he could no longer think of a reason not to smoke. Besides, who was he quitting for? His ex-wife? She had hounded him incessantly about the 'nasty habit,' but he had never found the willpower to quit. The Secret Service? They had turned a blind eye to it, his boss saying time and again, *"As long as you can pass the physical, I don't give a shit what you do, Cravens."* Amazingly, he had managed to pass, with a little leeway from the doctors at the base. So, if he wasn't quitting for his ex-wife or the agency, then who the hell was he quitting for? A quiet voice inside his head said, *"For yourself."*

He took a long, deep drag, relishing the feel of it as it burned his throat. "Well, to hell with that." His partner was dead, his protectee was gone, and the only two people who knew what had taken place in that muddy field on a rainy afternoon were out of his life forever. *"No matter what, Maddi, I can't call you...you can't call me. You understand?"* She had said nothing, but he had seen it in her eyes; they both knew they would never see each other again. He shifted in the chair, his large frame already growing stiff from the hard wood. He would miss her...the woman he had grown so fond of. He shook his head and sighed. *There was no other option.*

He took another drag, suddenly grinning at the cigarette as if he was chatting with an old friend. He had relegated himself to half or quarter-sized cigarettes for so long that to smoke a whole one felt like heaven. "I missed you, Marlboro," he said with a chuckle. He could almost hear a reply. *"I missed you too, Cravens."*

He leaned back and rubbed a hand over his stubbly face. As he stared out the window, he heard a clock somewhere ring out seven chimes. The sun was gone, but the rising moon cast yellow-white shimmers on the rough waters of the Baltic. He wished he sailed. Then he could just rent a boat and put out to sea. He chuckled. *Knowing me, I'd probably get seasick.* Besides, what fun would it be to sail alone?

No, what Cravens did best was to look after others. Be it his ex-wife, Betty, his old dog Chet, or even the pet bird that Betty had finally made him get rid of, Cravens was meant to watch over those he loved. Which was why his job had suited him so well. He looked after his protectees as if they were family. An assault on one of them was an assault on him. He looked past the sea to the shadows in the distance and frowned. *And someone has deliberately tried to kill a member of my family.*

He massaged his beard and brushed back strands of overgrown hair. *It's time,* he thought, ...*after two long months of woeful self-pity, it's time to clean myself up and get to work.* He raised the window higher, letting more cold air into the room as he stood and put his hands on the sill. He leaned out and said to no one in particular, "I'm coming for you. I don't know who you are or why you tried to kill Maddi...but I'm coming for you."

CHAPTER 51

Washington, DC

Knight was staring at a TV in the Oval Office. He had announced his gun confiscation edict less than two hours ago, but already, the media was having a field day. The decision had dominated the news, interrupted only briefly by the attack from a lone gunman who had shot up a naval base in Virginia. *Well-timed,* he had thought – with shame – when he had heard the news. But there was no question; the attack would be helpful, as it lent further justification for his earth-shattering decree.

Not only was the decision to seize America's guns not playing well with the media; it wasn't playing well among Washington's policymakers, either. Politicians from both sides of the political aisle had erupted in outrage, one side declaring he had gone too far, the other suggesting he hadn't gone far enough. Each side claimed that Knight had created a constitutional crisis, and demanded that he either recant, or at least allow the lawmakers to have a say in the decision. The only silver lining was that the outrage of those senators had resulted in something that hadn't happened in quite a long time in DC; it had brought together legislators from both sides of the aisle. That team of senators had already written a challenge, which they would soon file in a DC court. *I have fostered bipartisanship,* he thought with a chuckle.

Knight had stuck to his guns – literally – insisting that a possible war in the Baltics, the shootings taking place around the country, and the potential for a coup had created a state of emergency that had given him not only every right to act as he had, but an obligation to do so. And, in spite of the controversy surrounding it, the confiscation had started off well. There had been scattered protests in the streets, but no riots, at least not yet. Knight had used the hour before the speech to call up the National Guard, along with reservists and retired military, instructing them to man central locations such as police and fire stations, courthouses, and city halls in all major towns across the country. And, under the leadership of his Attorney General, the Department of Justice was utilizing tools they already had in place to track extremist groups before they could pull together any sort of organized rebellion.

Knight had gone so far as to designate today, October 26th, "Gun Liberation Day." On this day only, he would allow citizens to hand over their weapons without consequence, regardless of whether or not the guns were licensed. But he had made it clear that, starting tomorrow, searches would begin in homes around the country. Soldiers would go from house to house, using force, if necessary, to make the citizens comply. Anyone who failed to give up their guns would be arrested on the spot.

At Morningstar's urging, he was able to convince a plurality in both the Senate and the House to cancel the upcoming election, which was to take place in a week. It was a big deal to move an election. In the history of the republic, it had never been done; not even during the Civil War. It required Congressional approval, and, within an hour, majorities in both houses had voted to move it to the first Wednesday in January, on the 5th. It seemed fitting, as America's very first presidential election had occurred 216 years earlier, on the first Wednesday in January, 1789. *"It will feel like a fresh start,"* Knight had argued. Congress had ultimately agreed. Though each side claimed that holding an election now would be chaotic and unsafe, the truth was that it would give the opposition more time to try to defeat Knight, and it would give Knight's party more time to move past his controversial decision. Prior to today, Knight had been considered a shoo-in for reelection. But Morningstar had warned him that gun confiscation could change that. *"Give them time to get past it, son, and see the wisdom in what you've done."* Knight was glad he had listened. He would now have over two months to convince America that what he had done was right.

But did he believe it was right? No...not completely, anyway. Though he had been forceful and confident as he had issued the order, he felt neither forceful nor confident. His prior support of the second amendment had given his critics plenty of ammunition to target him as a fraud. *"Hypocrite in Chief"* had been the banner on one of the popular cable news channels. And they were right. Knight knew it...in his heart. Seizing the guns was an overreach. The premise that the country was in a state of emergency was also an overreach; yes, there was an epidemic of gun violence in the U.S., and yes, there had been an actual attack on members of Congress, but did it rise to the level of a national emergency? Knight didn't think so. But it hadn't been up to him. It had been Morningstar's idea. *"You will need greater authority than that normally afforded a President, son. An emergency declaration is the only way."*

The fact that Knight had been able to wield such authority so quickly was nothing short of alarming. He was certain the country's founders had never intended for one man to have so much power. He had challenged Morningstar on the point...

> *"It's too much, Father...I can't defy the peoples' right to have guns."*
>
> *"Son, I know it goes against your beliefs, and I know it seems like a power grab. But surely you see that the American people no longer know what's best for them. They've been fooled for decades by deceitful politicians." He chuckled. "It's simple, son. First, you take their weapons...then you take their souls."*
>
> *"But Father, I—"*
>
> *"It's okay, Judah. Once we've achieved our goal, you can give them back their guns."*
>
> *Knight said quickly, "And what exactly is our goal, Father?"*
>
> *He heard the man laugh. "Why, restoring America's greatness, son."*

And that had been it. Though Knight didn't like it, he had done it. Why? Because Morningstar had asked him to. For twenty-four years, Morningstar had been like a father to him. He had raised him, had inspired him, and had taught him how to be a man. The least Knight could do was carry out his request.

And Knight had to admit; the timing was right. Though he knew there would be holdouts, he doubted there would be many. The American people were scared. And it wasn't just the threat of an insurrection or the current spate of random shootings that seemed to underpin their fear. Five years ago, a massacre at a school in Colorado had left the country shaken and stunned. Since then, there had been mall shootings, courthouse shootings, even a synagogue had been the site of an attack. The violence had gotten out of hand, and the prevailing winds had shifted. Many Americans were now not only willing, but eager to do whatever they could to rid the country of guns. His detractors would claim that once he disarmed the American people, the only ones with guns would be the criminals. Knight's reply – fed to him by Morningstar, and rehearsed many times over the last several hours – would be short and to the point. *"Then we'll know who the criminals are, now won't we."*

But the voices of dissent were already being heard. Led by the NRA, protests had begun to break out in every part of the country, especially in the South. Thankfully, just minutes ago, Knight had received an endorsement from a surprising source. An elder statesman of his party, Texas Senator Sam Lawford, who had also been a staunch advocate for the second amendment, had come to his defense. *"Though we feel strongly that the second amendment guarantees the right for all Americans to own and bear arms, with the intolerable rise in violence of late, we feel it is in the best interest of the country that we accede to the President's dictate."*

Knight shook his head. *Such well-worded horseshit.* Regardless, Lawford's support had been helpful. Not only was he highly respected in most circles, but he was from Texas; arguably the gun capital of the world. The man had breathed new life into Knight's dictate, and Knight watched, stunned, as things moved along in a more-or-less orderly fashion. He shook his head. Jacob had been right once again.

Knight continued to stare at the TV, watching as his National Guard went through the steps of repossession. And all the while, he could hear Jacob in the back of his mind. *"First, you take their weapons...then you take their souls."* From the look of things, he would be after the souls in no time.

CHAPTER 52

Somewhere in France

Cobra had been on the road since 3:15 a.m. Nearly fifteen hours, driving eighty kph through Germany, then through France, and he still hadn't spotted the Peugeot that he now suspected Hank Clarkson to be driving. He had stopped only three times; twice to relieve himself, and once to get a bite to eat. He was losing his patience. But about the time he was ready to hang it up and tell Morningstar to forget it, he would remember the castle. Then he would step on the gas, revitalized.

Which is why he had returned Morningstar's call so quickly. The man had had the nerve to imply that he would refuse to get Cobra the castle if he didn't call him back. So, as he was leaving Sankt Goar, and with Hank less than 100 kilometers ahead of him, he had called Morningstar. He had to admit; the hit on the Chinese military leader was intriguing. If he were to carry it out, it would be one of the more high-profile hits he would likely ever do. *Right up there with killing America's Secretary of State,* he thought with a chuckle. But traveling to China sounded exhausting. He shook his head and sighed. *I'll see how I feel after I kill Clarkson.*

He had purchased a CB in a store north of Paris, and was listening to it now in an effort to stay awake. Mostly it was just truckers talking back and forth about nothing. They spoke in English so that all of them would understand, making it easy for Cobra to only half-listen as he searched the highway for the Peugeot. It was amusing to hear them focus on such trivialities as traffic or weather or cops.

Then again; cops weren't actually a triviality. The police had disrupted Cobra's plans on more than one occasion. He grinned, suddenly curious how Inspector Pritchard had survived his near-death experience in the schoolhouse in Dalgety Bay. Cobra had had little time to look in on the man's recovery. All he had heard was that Pritchard was on an extended leave of absence. He laughed aloud. "Perhaps when this is over, Pritchard, I will take the occasion to pay you a visit."

It was six p.m.; traffic was heavy. Cobra had passed into France around six a.m., and he guessed it was another six hours to the southern border. Should he keep driving all the way to Spain? *Or should I make a beeline for the Mediterranean?* The CB was chattering in the background. He was about to switch it off and look for music on the radio, when suddenly, his ears perked up.

"There's a cop on the shoulder of A-2 near Gueret. He's pulled over a car, an older-model Peugeot, but as you know, that won't stop 'im from speed gunnin' us."

Cobra's eyes widened. He turned up the volume. *Could it be?*

Another trucker said, "Exact location?"

"About ten kilometers north of Gueret...route A-2."

Cobra grinned. *Perfect.* He was heading south on route A-2. He looked for road signs for Gueret. After about ten minutes, he came to a sign that said that Gueret was twenty kilometers away. Which meant that Cobra was only about ten kilometers from the pulled-over Peugeot. He stepped on the gas. If he hurried, he might be able to catch up to the car before it got back on the highway.

Suddenly, his jaw dropped. A different trucker was talking now; he had apparently just passed the pulled-over Peugeot. "They're pullin' a guy out of the car."

Cobra leaned forward, hoping to hear something about the man's description. Instead, he heard the trucker whistle as he added, "...and he ain't alone. He's got a woman with him. Though she's a bit skinny, she ain't bad to look at...not at all."

CHAPTER 53

Strongsville, Ohio

Andrew hadn't left his spot in the den. Though it had been torture, he had spent the last two hours listening to the tape. It had been slow going. He had stopped often, either to think about what he had heard, or to recover from the bittersweet pain of hearing his mother – sober and defiant – but in truly terrible trouble.

He didn't recognize the voice of the man on the tape, and he had yet to hear Jeannie say his name. Whoever he was, he was making Jeannie's final hours horrible. After the first comment about *"...hearing it straight from the bitch's mouth,"* there had been a click and the recording had stopped. At first, Andrew had thought that maybe that was it...that maybe that ugly comment was all he was going to get. But he had reluctantly pushed play, and after about a minute or so of silence, he had once again heard the man's voice, only this time, he had sounded far more threatening.

"Call her. If you won't tell me what happened, I guess I'll have to hear it from her." A pause. *"And no funny business, Jeannie. I can kill you in two seconds and be out of here before anyone has the slightest idea what happened."* Another pause. *"Call her...now, Jeannie."*

Jeannie's voice had been shaky. *"She's likely on her way home from work."*

"Don't you know her cell number?"

"No, as I said, we're not close."

"Call her home phone. If she's not there, call her office. I hear they're working late these days in our nation's capital."

Andrew had stopped the tape there and had yet to go on. It was unbearable. That man, whoever he was, had literally threatened Jeannie's life. Andrew felt like he was smothering from the weight of it, and at one point, he had needed to crack the window to get some air. The fact that he hadn't been there to help his mother was unforgiveable. *Who is this asshole,* he wondered for probably the twentieth time. Was he some crackpot who didn't like a law that Maddi had passed, or a position she had taken on some controversial issue? He shook his head. *Just keep going, Andrew.*

He pushed play.

He could hear Jeannie fumbling with what he guessed was a cellphone. After about fifteen seconds, she said, *"She's not home."*

"Call her office."

Again, he heard Jeannie fumbling with the phone. This time, the call must have gone through, as he heard Jeannie talking to someone he guessed was Maddi's secretary. His heart broke as he sensed the pride in Jeannie's voice for all that Maddi had accomplished. Jeannie ended the call and said evenly, *"She's out of the country."*

There was a pause. Andrew could hear the man lifting something from a table or a desk. *"Who's this?"*

Jeannie stammered. *"Um, some...distant cousins."*

The man laughed. *"Ya lyin' bitch. You don't think I've done my homework on the Madison clan? This is Andrew, isn't it? And it looks like Andrew has a family."*

Andrew tensed. He heard something slam against a table. *A framed picture of my family, perhaps?* The man went on, the anger in his voice undeniable. *"A family would be nice, wouldn't it?"* A pause. *"But I wouldn't know about that. My family was shot dead by your daughter."*

Andrew's jaw dropped; he shut off the tape. He stared at the recorder. Had he heard that right? The man had claimed that Maddi had killed his family. He shook his head. *The guy's nuts.* He cleared his throat, then resumed the tape.

"If I can't talk to her, then I'll talk to your son. Get him here...now."

Andrew winced, his guilt almost insurmountable. *This is when Jeannie called me.* He continued to listen.

He heard Jeannie sigh; she sounded tired. *"Andrew hasn't been here for years, Todd."*

Andrew's eyes widened. *Todd...the guy's name is Todd. Todd who?*
Jeannie added, *"...and he hates me...even more than Cindy."*

The man, Todd, yelled, *"I don't give a shit if he hates you or not. Get him here or I'll drive to wherever the man lives and kill his precious baby."*

Andrew closed his eyes, his anger – and his guilt – rising inside him. He stopped the tape, then stood and paced the room. He had told Jeannie that he didn't want to come. If it hadn't been for Amanda, he wouldn't have gone to her house at all. As it turned out, he had gotten the first flight out, but that hadn't been until the following morning. Obviously, it had been too late.

He took a deep breath, sat once again on the blanket, and pushed play.

Jeannie was talking, she sounded desperate. *"If I...can get him to...come here, will you promise to leave Adam alone?"*

Andrew couldn't help but feel pride in his mother. She wasn't only solidly sober, she was brave...*and was doing her damnedest to keep me and my family safe.*

He heard Todd say, *"Adam, how biblical. Yeah, sure. I'll leave Adam alone. As long as I get what I want."*

"And what is that, Todd? What is it that you want?"

"What I want, Jeannie Madison, is revenge." The man lowered his voice to a whisper. *"And I'll have it."*

That was it. The tape stopped. It sounded as if it had been started and stopped several times after that, but little had come of it. Andrew turned off the recorder and set it on the floor beside him. He was sitting opposite the windows in the den. The blinds were still closed. It was around noon, and the light from the sun was over the house, and was no longer streaming through the windows. It made the room much darker and much colder.

I need to pee. He had fought the urge for the last hour, but now he knew he needed to take care of it. The water had been shut off, which meant the bathrooms weren't working. He would need to go outside. He stood and walked to the window. Although the sun was high, a large maple was thoughtfully providing shade over a sizeable area of the backyard. *If I go now, I'll be hidden by the shade of that tree.*

He walked to the back door, opened it slightly, and looked outside. When he was certain that no one was there, he snuck past the door to a row of trees just beyond the window. He slid between them and the window, relieved himself, then ran back into the house. He closed and locked the back door, then returned to the den.

He sat on the blanket and grabbed a granola bar from the bag he had brought in from the store. He had already eaten two granola bars, as well as an apple. That was all he had had for the last twenty-four hours. He wasn't hungry. If he was being honest with himself, he would say that he was barely functioning at all. His mother had needed him; she had reached out to him...and he had failed her.

He was about to open the granola bar, when instead, he simply laid it on his backpack. He stared at the tape recorder. Though it had gone silent, he realized that he was only about halfway through the tape. Should he see if there was more?

He leaned back against the wall; he was exhausted. He was also ashamed of how badly he had failed his mother. But he felt a good deal of pride, as well, for his mother's courage...her pluck. Most of all, he was proud of her sobriety in a situation that would have made even the toughest man or woman break. Throughout the ordeal, that man...that *Todd*...had offered Jeannie multiple drinks, but she had said no...she had held tough every single time.

As he picked up the recorder, finally ready to go on, he let out a deep and mournful sigh. *As a matter of fact, she has proven herself to be far tougher, far kinder, and far more devoted than I have ever been.*

CHAPTER 54

Washington, DC

Knight had taken his lunch in the Oval Office. He was still fixated on the TV, watching as National Guard soldiers – America's soldiers – collected America's guns. Though newscasters were running nonstop coverage of the confiscation, they had also been forced to make time for the escalating violence in Latvia. Putin had sent troops to Latvia's eastern sector; he was definitely on the march. Knight had released a statement a few hours ago: *"In an effort to support Latvia, our newest NATO ally, we are supplying weapons and advisors to offer assistance in whatever way we can. At this point in this war, we have committed no soldiers to this fight. I'll say that again – we have committed no American soldiers to the war between Russia and Latvia."*

He had taken calls from the UK and Germany, their leaders supportive, not only of offering increased military support for Latvia, but of issuing sanctions to isolate Russia and its power-crazed leader. The surprise had been the support they had also offered Knight for his confiscation of America's guns. *"We've always been a bit unsettled by America's love affair with guns,"* the British Prime Minister had said. *That's only because we used our guns to beat you in the Revolutionary War,* Knight had wanted to reply, but had kept it to himself. The man's support would be helpful.

In the last hour, riots had broken out in Oklahoma and Texas, and he had called in not only the National Guard, but a contingency of reservists to the areas, as well. News anchors from the more conservative networks expressed concern that Knight was close to violating one of America's most ardent dictates: that the U.S. military would never be used against its own citizens. Their opinion anchors were revving up the populace, encouraging them to fight back. Knight had been tempted to shut down those networks, designating them as instigators and seditionists, but had stopped himself. *Defy only one constitutional amendment at a time, Knight.*

A knock on the door made him jump. "Yes?"

It was Secret Service agent Jerry Foster. Knight liked Foster. He was the only agent that Knight had developed any sort of relationship with since assuming the role of President. Like Knight, Foster had lost his family when he was a boy, and both men had been raised by an uncle whom they had barely known. The two had had many chances to talk during the last nine weeks, and, though Knight's full trust extended to no one other than Morningstar, Foster had come closer than anyone else in his DC world.

Knight smiled when he saw the agent's lanky frame in the doorway. "Come in, Foster."

The tall, lean Foster walked to the desk, his fair skin and red hair evidence of his Irish ancestry. The young man nodded cautiously, his cheeks reddening the way they always did when he was uncomfortable. "Mr. President, I...I know you have a lot going on, but your secretary received a call about an hour ago when you were on the phone with the Prime Minister. She debated even giving you the message and asked us to look into it first. I had almost dismissed it, but I was curious by the choice of words. The caller asked that we tell you...um...," he cleared his throat, "... *Emma seeks Romer.*"

Knight stared at the agent. "What did you say?"

"She asked the secretary to tell you that 'Emma seeks Romer.' She insisted that you would know who she was."

Foster looked away, embarrassed, as if he had invaded Knight's privacy. He had.

Knight couldn't move. He could barely find his voice. "Did...did she leave a number?"

"Yes sir." He handed Knight a memo-sized sheet of paper. He cleared his throat. "Do you need anything more, sir?"

Knight stared at the note. "No, that will be all. Thank you, Foster." He barely noticed the agent leave the office as he stared at the note. His hand was shaking.

EMMA CANNON. MAINE. 570-456-7890. VERIFIED FOR ACCURACY.

Knight knew what "verified for accuracy" meant. After the call had been received, one of the agents had investigated every part of Emma Cannon's life. They now knew everything about her; where she lived, where she worked, who she spent time with...*even the last time she made love.* He closed his eyes. Was Emma Cannon *his* Emma? *Of course, she is.* There had been no other Emma in his life. Especially not one who would refer to him as Romer. *And she still lives in Maine.*

But why would Emma reach out to him now? She was married. Had she maybe gotten a divorce? Or had her husband passed away? Was she simply saying 'hi' after sixteen years because she had seen him on TV?

He looked at the memo and was surprised to feel tears forming in the corners of his eyes. She hadn't forgotten him. *Emma seeks Romer...*

The camping trip had been a bust. Well, not a complete bust. He and Emma had made love off and on throughout the rain-drenched weekend. But their plans for hiking and mountain climbing had been put on hold. On the last day, they were wakened by the bright sun of a Northern Maine morning. "Finally," he said as he leaned over and kissed her awake. She reached for him. The sun came through the tent, nudging them to come out and start the day. Jerome sat up and threw on a shirt and a pair of shorts. 'Well, Miss Melnikov, are you ready for the hike of the century?'

She grinned. Her coal-black hair fell over one cheek, and Jerome wanted her all over again. 'You bet. But I'm afraid you're gonna' hold me back.'

He laughed as he slid out of the tent. He made a fire and cooked bacon and eggs. They ate, packed their gear, and then headed out for a day of hiking in the Baxter Mountain Range. The hike was uneventful, the fresh air invigorating as the sun rose higher in the sky. When it reached its highest point, they stopped for lunch on the side of a small canyon. The site was notable for the way its architecture was highlighted by the midday sun. They laid out a blanket and, just as Jerome was about to dig in his bag for sandwiches, he felt the soft tickle of her lips against his neck. He grinned and turned as she pulled him to the blanket. "What's this?" he asked.

She laid back on the blanket and grinned. "Emma seeks Romer...."

Knight stared at the paper. Should he call her? *No, Knight! You're preparing a nation for war! You don't have time for this.* But suddenly his hand was on the phone and he was dialing. His entire body was shaking and he chuckled. *You're the President of the United States of America...get your shit together, Romer.*

The phone rang once, twice... Knight was shaking so badly that he was forced to sit down. After the fifth ring, he pulled the receiver from his ear, ready to hang up. Suddenly he heard the familiar voice of the woman he had never stopped loving.

"Hello?" Her voice was cautious; unsure.

"Emma?"

There was a pause. Almost in a whisper, she said, "Yes."

"Is this Emma Melnikov?"

Another pause. "Romer?"

"Yes." He felt weak. "Yes, it's Romer."

Knight had no idea how much time passed, but it felt like an hour before a hesitant voice said, "Romer, I need to see you."

CHAPTER 55

Liepaja, Latvia

Cravens was once again sitting by the window in the dingy hotel room. Only now, his hair was cut, his beard was gone, and he was using the light of the moon to stare at a scrap of paper he had taken from his overcoat. It had the plate number of the black sedan that had shown up out of nowhere at the scene of the plane crash. What he wouldn't give to make a quick call to Walter Henderson, ask him about the man with the glass eye, and, if the driver was his, let him take it from there. But as he had reminded himself many times over the last two months, he couldn't tell anyone about the driver without providing some context, and the slightest suggestion that the crash had been anything but an accident would put Maddi at risk. Why? Because all of a sudden, what had been accepted as an accident, would now be deemed a crime. It would result in forensics experts, who might discover that Maddi hadn't died in the crash. It would also result in endless questions to Cravens, which he could hold off for only so long. Which is why he had searched every village in a five-hundred-mile radius for a glass-eyed black man driving a sedan...and why he was back in Liepaja.

He sighed as he rubbed his smooth chin. He had spent the last forty minutes in his hotel room's bathroom cutting his hair and shaving his beard; he felt naked. But he had been unable to put it off any longer. It was time for him to look like what he was: a U.S. Secret Service agent who was investigating a crime.

A clock somewhere rang out eight chimes and he sighed. *Time to go, Cravens.* He stood, stretched his arms, then unzipped the new suit from the garment bag. He stepped into the new pants, then put on a white shirt, followed by the new jacket. He stared in the mirror, rubbed the fading scar on his forehead, then ran a comb through his freshly-clipped hair. He nodded. He looked better without all that hair. *One might even assume that I didn't miraculously survive a plane crash a couple of months ago.*

He threw his clothes in his duffel bag and put his wallet, his cellphone, and a pack of Marlboro's in his pants pocket. He was about to leave the torn, sooty overcoat hanging on the door, when, at the last minute, he grabbed it and put it on over his suit.

He left the hotel, carrying his duffel bag in one hand, and Walter's briefcase in the other. It had been a miracle that the briefcase had survived the crash. It had actually survived quite a lot since Cravens had found the damn thing back in March. *I'll need to find an excuse, and an explanation, to get it back to Walter.*

His eyes lit up. Perhaps he could tie his questions about the glass-eyed driver to his need to return the briefcase. He nodded. Not a bad idea, but it would make even more sense if he was certain that the driver had, indeed, come from the Henderson estate. *I need some sort of proof.* As he walked toward town, he patted the wallet in his pocket, thankful his Secret Service ID had survived the crash. For the first time since leaving the hospital nine weeks ago, he would actually claim to be a U.S. agent.

It was dark outside...and cold. He hiked the collar of the overcoat as he walked to the nearest diner. He walked in, found a booth in the back, and ordered a sandwich and coffee. He made quick work of the meal, left a tip for the waitress, then walked from the diner toward the center of town. Though his back ached, it felt good to walk. He spent the time rehearsing the lie he would use to get the info he needed.

Within minutes, he had reached the center square, and he spotted a police station sitting next to a two-story courthouse. He nodded. *A good place to start.* There was a light coming from inside the building. He walked in and rang a bell on the counter. A young man who looked barely old enough to shave walked out from a back room, his gray uniform pressed, his officer's badge displayed proudly on his chest. The man smiled and said, "Sveiki?"

Cravens showed his Secret Service ID. Though he had acquired a working knowledge of the Lettish language, he wasn't great with it, and he hoped the officer understood English. "The name's Cravens. I'm with the U.S. Secret Service. I was sent over here to investigate the plane crash that took place two months ago."

The man stared at Cravens' ragged overcoat and frowned.

Cravens mumbled, "It was a long flight."

The young man narrowed his eyes.

Cravens nodded. "Fine. I'm the guy who survived."

The man's eyes widened. "I'm so sorry, sir. That must have been terrible."

You don't know the half of it. Cravens cleared his throat. "Can you help me?"

"I will try, sir." His English was actually quite good.

"What's your name, son?"

"Vitols." He pointed to his badge. "Officer Igors Vitols, at your service, sir."

"Well, Vitols, I have a lead from a Liepaja local, and I need your help... but it will need to be kept on the DL."

Vitols frowned.

"It needs to stay between you and me. Can you do that?"

The man nodded eagerly.

"Good. One of the pilots on that plane is suspected of having terrorist ties. We don't think it had anything to do with the crash...as a matter of fact, we're sure of it. But we've recently seen an increase in chatter, and we believe that the man's brother might be plotting something." He paused. "We also think this brother was present at the scene of the crash...but he left before anyone could question him. I was asked to look into it." He paused. "I have part of a license plate number; hopefully it's enough. It was taken from the plate of a car spotted near the crash site. Our suspicion is that the driver may have come to the site in an effort to save his brother."

"I will try to help you, sir. Tell me the number."

Cravens pulled out the scrap of paper and read off the number. Vitols wrote it down. "Give me a minute, sir." He walked back to an office, and Cravens could see him accessing a computer, his young, nimble fingers moving over the keys like a world class pianist. *Oh, to be a kid in this day and age.* Within minutes, he walked out, grinning as if he had just won the third-grade spelling bee. "I have it, sir."

"Great."

"The license plate belongs to a fleet of cars from nearby Uzava."

Cravens narrowed his eyes. "A fleet of cars?"

"Yes sir. They are listed to a family with the last name Henderson."

CHAPTER 56

Strongsville, Ohio

Andrew was exhausted...both physically and emotionally. He had spent much of the afternoon listening to the tape, though it had been slow going. And one thing had become quite clear: the hours his mother had spent with the man named Todd had been unbearable. As the tape had progressed, he could hear Jeannie's voice weakening; it had cut him to his core. But in spite of being completely spent, she had somehow found the strength to resist several more offers of a drink. The ability for an alcoholic to do that in the midst of a horribly stressful situation was exceptional, and Andrew found himself respecting his mother in a way he hadn't in over thirty years.

In spite of being nearly all the way through the tape, he had yet to hear any explanation for why the Pentagon was so desperate to get their hands on the damn thing. Though it was full of revelations, those disclosures would only be interesting to someone who knew Jeannie or her family. He looked at the tape and sighed. *Maybe whatever they're looking for is at the end.* Reluctantly, he clicked play.

Todd's voice sounded angry...and tired. *"One more time, Jeannie. Your daughter, Cynthia Madison, a sitting U.S. senator, had no choice but to shoot my father, Evan Jackson, in an alley twenty-two years ago...in cold blood... right?"*

Andrew dropped the recorder. He was shaking as he reached down and switched off the tape. It was the first time that the man's full name had been used. *Todd Jackson…Evan Jackson's son!* Andrew hadn't even known that Evan had a son. And it sounded like the young man, Todd, was no better than his father.

Andrew leaned against the wall and closed his eyes. He had been away at school when Maddi had gone through the Evan Jackson ordeal. He thought back to the events that had taken place over twenty years ago. He had never heard the details, but he knew enough. The man – his father's former partner on the force – had been far too old for Maddi. He had taken advantage of her, then had then left her in a cruel and heartless way. Andrew had been glad when his grandparents had stepped in. He wasn't sure how they had become aware of what was going on, but when Maddi had told him that she was going to stay with them for the summer, he had felt relieved. He knew she would get her head on straight after a month or two with their grandparents. And she did. Her life had changed dramatically.

But clearly there was more to it. Apparently, Evan Jackson had been murdered in a back alley, and for some crazy reason, Todd was convinced that it was Maddi who had pulled the trigger. *How could he even think such a thing?*

He pulled out his laptop and, using his phone as a hotspot, tried to find articles about Evan Jackson's murder. It was slow going, however, as the murder had taken place over twenty years ago. It took him several minutes to even find one article. He finally found an archived article from 1982 in an Indianapolis newspaper. It didn't say much. Just that Evan Jackson had died as a result of his *'…brave efforts to stop a robbery.'* Andrew ended the search knowing little more than he had when he started.

He reached for the unopened granola bar, tore off the wrapper, and leaned against the wall. He took a bite, chewing slowly as he stared at a single candle in the middle of the floor. Though it was still daylight, the room had grown dark as the sun had eased to the west. He couldn't turn on an overhead light; it might alert someone to his presence. He had found the candle and a pack of matches in a kitchen drawer, likely forgotten when Jenny had packed up the house. As he lost himself in the flame of the candle, he wondered again about Todd's insistence that Maddi was responsible for Evan Jackson's death. The article had said that he had died while stopping a robbery. Why would Todd think that Maddi had had something to do with it? A fling, yes…a murder? *No way.*

He took another bite of the granola bar and looked down at the recorder. He tried to guess how long Todd had been in Jeannie's house. There was little to mark the time. All Andrew knew was that it had been at least a night and the following morning...hours upon hours that Jeannie had spent in agonizing misery, both physically and emotionally. *How awful,* he thought as he rubbed the back of his neck, *"...to have endured such a thing for so long."* He reached for the recorder, annoyed when he saw that his hand was still shaking. *Time to finish this.* He clicked 'play.'

Todd sounded even angrier than he had before. *"Just say it, Jeannie. Say it and I'll let you go."*

Jeannie's voice sounded so weak...so tired. *"I...I won't say it, Todd, because...it...isn't true."*

Her voice had begun to sound different. At first, Andrew thought she was just hoarse from so long an ordeal, but suddenly he realized...*she's being strangled!* He stiffened and tossed the granola bar on the floor. He leaned forward, having to force himself to keep going. He could practically feel Todd's anger through the tape.

"We both know it is true! Now just say it!"

Jeannie was choking. *Dear God...that man is killing my mother!* His entire body had begun to shake, but he kept listening. Suddenly, Jeannie laughed. But the laugh quickly turned into another choking spell.

"What's so funny, bitch?"

Jeannie was whispering now; weak gasps accompanied by even more defiance.

"You...are, Todd. You're...just as bad...as your father was."

"What do you know about my father?"

"I know plenty about...your daddy, Todd. For example, I know that...he was skimming money from...dead cops...bilking their families...out of pensions that were rightfully theirs."

"Take it back!" Todd was screaming now.

"I will not...take...it...back, Todd." Jeannie had barely been able to say the last few words. Andrew could feel her spirit leaving her. Out of nowhere, he began to cry. He dropped the recorder to the floor and put his head in his hands, letting the tape continue to play. *If only I had come sooner,* he thought as he stared at the candle. It was more than he could bear. The one time his mother had actually asked for his help, he hadn't been there for her. *I am so sorry, Mom.*

He stood and walked to the window. He cracked the blinds and looked outside. It was unbearable to think that he had just listened to his mother being killed, being *murdered*...by a man who had made such irrational and baseless claims. He stared out at the shadows, which now covered the surrounding lawns. He jumped as he heard a car door slam nearby. *A neighbor bringing their child home from school?* He wondered if any of his mother's neighbors had heard the commotion in the small house that sat in a quiet cul-de-sac in McCordsville, Indiana.

Suddenly he tensed. There were muffled sounds on the tape. He turned and stared down at the recorder. Someone – Todd? – was rummaging around the living room. Andrew could hear the sound of a glass on a counter, followed by heavy breathing as the man knelt close to Jeannie and poured something – alcohol? – all over her. Andrew heard the man stumble and curse. Then he mumbled something; Andrew couldn't hear it.

Andrew walked over to the recorder, picked it up, and played it back. He put his ear to the tape, his heart sinking as he grasped the meaning of what he had just heard.

"It doesn't matter anyway, Jeannie. Jacob will soon use the power of the Pentagon to end your daughter...forever."

CHAPTER 57

Liepaja, Latvia

Henderson looked out the window of the train as it neared the city of Liepaja. It was dark and there was little to see, but he saw enough. He had hoped that his trip there the night before would be his last. But the news about Cravens had changed everything. The man had survived the crash, had recovered in a Liepaja hospital for three days, then had completely disappeared. Where was he? Why hadn't he gone back to the States? *And why didn't he at least tell his boss where he was going?*

Henderson had concluded – reluctantly – that his only option was to go back to Liepaja and trace Cravens' steps. But as the train neared the west coast town, he stiffened, feeling a renewed sense of grief as the train passed within a mile of the crash site. Though he hadn't actually seen the wrecked plane, he found it hard to believe that anyone had survived. *No one survives a plane crash.* One of the articles he had read had talked about the fact that the plane had been close to the ground when it crashed, which meant that it hadn't been going quite as fast, and it didn't have quite as far to fall. Still, to think that someone had lived through such a thing was unbelievable. *Almost like living through a fire that burned down an entire hotel.*

But it meant that Henderson was now looking for two men. Was it a coincidence that Hank and Cravens had disappeared at about the same time? Hank hadn't been seen since the afternoon of the plane crash, and Cravens hadn't been seen since leaving the Liepaja hospital three days later.

298

Hank had driven off in a Henderson car, which he had then apparently ditched. Finding him would be like looking for a needle in a haystack. But not so with Cravens. At least with him, Henderson had a place to start. *I'll go to the hospital where he was last seen.*

The night was dark, the air cold as he stepped off the train. He buttoned his coat and walked from the terminal to the center of town. He wasn't sure where the hospital was, and was about to ask a merchant on the corner, when he noticed a sign, "Liepajas Policijas Iercirknis" *Liepaja Police Station.* He flinched and quickly hid under the shadow of a tree. Twenty-four hours ago, he had barely escaped the Latvian police. He took a deep breath. *But now I'm wearing a disguise; I'm Aiden Balkus.*

He saw a light coming from inside the station. He stepped from under the tree and walked toward it. He went to reach for his Aiden Balkus ID. He stopped. Why would the police answer a random citizen's questions? He would be risking his freedom, and they might not even be willing to help him. *I need more clout.*

He hurried back into the tree's shadow, trying to come up with the words that would compel a police officer to give him information about the survivor of a plane crash. Suddenly, his eyes widened. *I'll use the consulate card.*

He grabbed his wallet and took out the card that his dad had given him. He stepped from under the tree and, using the light from a nearby lamppost, he held up the card. It bore the symbol of the Latvian consulate and had the name M. Helmanis imprinted just above a consul ID number. He memorized the name, then returned the card to his wallet. As a precaution, he pulled out the Aiden Balkus ID and hid it in the grass next to the tree. He would pick it up when he left the station.

He walked to the station and stepped inside. The place was empty. He approached the counter, and, in Lettish, he said, "Hello? Anybody here?"

A young officer walked out; he looked barely old enough to drive. He stuck out his chest and said proudly, "Sveiki?"

Henderson nodded. "Mans vards ir...Helmanis." *My name is...Helmanis.*

The officer nodded. "Igor Vitols, jusu ribica, kungs." *Igor Vitols, at your service, sir.*

Staying with the Lettish, Henderson said, "Officer Vitols, I'm here on behalf of the Latvian consulate, to look into a plane crash that took place just north of town about two months ago." He paused. "There was only one survivor, is that correct?"

The officer frowned. "I'm sorry, sir. I've been instructed not to speak of the accident, unless it is with a properly authorized agent."

Henderson pulled out his wallet and took out the card. He handed it to the officer. "I represent a Latvian family that lives not too far from here, the Hendersons. They were acquainted with one of the victims, and have asked our consulate to see what we can learn about the man who survived."

The officer looked long and hard at the card, then handed it back. He seemed to be deliberating on whether he should cooperate. "Do you have a photo ID?"

Henderson tensed. "I...I don't, sir. My family is fortunate to have drivers, so I never bothered to get a driver's license, and I've left my passport at home." He waited, sweat starting to form under the collar of his shirt.

The officer narrowed his eyes. After what seemed like hours, he finally nodded. "I don't suppose it would do any harm for me to talk to you about the survivor of that crash." He sighed. "Actually, sir, it was a miracle that he made it out alive."

Henderson nodded, trying to encourage him. "Yes. My thoughts exactly."

The officer seemed to be weighing his next words carefully. "Uh...it just so happens, sir, that that very man was here only moments ago."

Henderson's eyes widened. "Really? Where did he go?"

Vitols shook his head. "I don't know, sir."

"You don't know...or you won't say?"

Vitols took a step back. Indignantly, he said, "I don't know."

Henderson rubbed his chin and sighed. "Can you at least tell me why he was here?"

The man hesitated. "He was following a lead."

"A lead?"

"Yes sir. He had part of a license plate number. He said that it had something to do with terrorists and the plane crash. He wanted me to trace it."

Terrorists? "Were you able to?"

Vitols shifted uncomfortably. "Um...yes sir. The license plate belongs to a fleet of cars from...from the estate of the family you represent...the Hendersons."

CHAPTER 58

Somewhere in southern France

The flat tire couldn't have happened at a more inconvenient spot. Hank had been just a couple of hours from the southern border of France, when he had felt the car pulling to one side. He pulled off the highway to a small town outside Bergerac, and drove to the only place that appeared to be open; an all-night diner. He drove to the back and parked behind a dumpster so that the car wasn't visible from the street.

He shook his head as he got out to check the tire. Though it wasn't completely flat, it was well on its way. He frowned. The delay was poorly timed. He had already been stopped once, about an hour ago. He had been pulled over on the highway and had been told to get out of the car. The officer, a pushy young man, had made Maddi get out, as well. When Hank had questioned why he had been pulled over, the officer had told him that his right taillight was out. *"All this for a busted taillight?"* The cop had ignored him, and after nearly a full hour of sitting on the side of the highway, he had finally let him go with instructions to get the taillight fixed.

And now this? he thought as he stared at the deflating tire. He would either need a new tire or a new car. He would also need to fix the taillight, unless he wanted to confine his travels to daytime. Something told him that Barney Fife wasn't about to let that go.

He shook his head and sighed. He was less than a day away from Angelo's. He didn't want to steal another car. *I just want to get there and get this over with!* He walked to the trunk and lifted it, hoping to find a tire and a jack. He found neither.

He checked the time. Nine p.m. He walked from the lot to the road and looked around. Other than the diner, the town was dead. Even the gas station didn't appear to be open. He would be forced to wait until morning to fix the car.

He walked back to the car and checked on Maddi. She was asleep in the back seat. He locked the car and walked into the diner. He didn't sit down; he wasn't there to eat. A man walked up, and in impeccable French, he said, "May I help you?"

Hank replied in less-than-impeccable French, "I need a room for the night."

The man nodded and walked Hank to a picture window at the front of the diner. He pointed down the road to a partially-lighted sign that hung over a two-story building. In English, he said, "There. Only hotel in town. They should have a room."

Hank thanked the man and walked out to his car. He unlocked it and nudged Maddi awake. "Maddi, we need to walk about two blocks. Are you up for it?"

She gave a weak smile. "Of course, Hank, I'm fine."

He helped her out of the car and walked her to the hotel. A sign that was meant to say "Hotel Germain," was missing two lights, leaving it with no 'e' in hotel and no 'a' in Germain. It looked like it said "Hot l Germ in." *Can't wait to see what this place looks like.* They walked in and Hank was pleased to see that at least the lobby was clean. He handed a clerk his and Maddi's passports. "We need a room."

The man took the passports, looked at Hank, then at Maddi. He nodded and reached behind him for a key. "Number 65; second floor."

Hank paid for the room in cash and grabbed the key. As he was about to lead Maddi up the stairs, he stopped, and, in mangled French, said, "My car has a flat tire. Is there somewhere nearby I can have it fixed?"

The man nodded. In English, he said, "Leroux's. Two blocks down." He pointed in the direction of the highway. "Opens nine a.m."

Hank nodded and walked Maddi up the stairs. The going was slow; she was still recovering from a broken ankle. They reached the top of the stairs, and he looked for room 65. It was three doors down. He walked Maddi to the room and opened it. There was only one bed. If they were both to sleep, they would need to share the bed.

He closed his eyes and sighed. It was the first time in their long ordeal that Maddi wasn't simply an invalid that he would help to the bed without a word. No, Maddi was now the living breathing woman he had once been madly in love with, and there was only one bed on which the two of them could sleep.

Suddenly, he heard her chuckle.

"What's so funny?"

"Hank, I know how difficult this has been for you. Not only have you had to lie to your boss and your ex-wife…and not only have you needed me to pretend to *be* your wife in order to get money for this journey, but now you're going to be forced to sleep next to me; something we used to do under far different circumstances." She shook her head. "I won't make you do it, Hank. I can sleep in the chair."

Hank wanted to hug her…not out of some romantic desire, but out of his appreciation for how thoughtful she was and how difficult life had been for both of them, not only for the past two months, but for the past six years. But he didn't hug her. Instead, he simply shook his head. "Don't be ridiculous, Maddi. I'm not the one who recently survived a plane crash, and then had surgery in a sketchy hospital in the middle of nowhere." He paused. "I'm actually good at sleeping sitting up."

Suddenly, she ran to him and threw her arms around him. With tears in her eyes, she whispered, "Thank you, Hank, for being you."

He fought a sudden urge to cry. He hugged her back and said, "The… the same to you, Maddi."

She stepped back and looked at him. She smiled; it was her first real smile in quite a while. She turned and walked to the bed. "Are you sure you won't join me?"

He shook his head. "No, I'll be fine."

She nodded. "Suit yourself. But if you do wind up next to me in this bed, I promise I won't attack you in the middle of the night." Again, she chuckled, and again, he shook his head.

She fell onto the bed and was asleep within five minutes. As he made himself comfortable in a small cushioned chair, he watched her and sighed. She was right. Not all that long ago, he would have lain next to her and held her through the night after making love to her in the soft glow of moonlight. But those days were gone. She had fallen in love with Henderson, and Hank had fallen in love – again – with his ex-wife. He no longer cared for Maddi the way that he had back then. As a matter of fact, he had no words to describe the love he felt for her. It wasn't romantic, it wasn't friendship. It was as if they had discovered a whole new kind of relationship.

As he tried to put a name to it, his lids grew heavy, and he fell asleep to the not-unpleasant clang of a barge horn somewhere on the river. *I do love you, Maddi...and I know that you love me. For now, that is enough, as I am the only person alive who can embrace you as the woman you used to be. That tragedy alone is enough to make me forever devoted to you...and to this love – whatever it is – that we share.*

CHAPTER 59

Liepaja, Latvia

Henderson left the police station, grabbed the Aiden Balkus ID from where he had left it by the tree, then walked to the north end of town. The officer's news that a Henderson car had been at the crash site had left him stunned. He could come up with only one explanation...*the driver had to be Hank.* But how had Hank known about the crash? If what his father had told him was true, then Hank had left the compound in an effort to clear his head. Could he have simply stumbled upon the crash? If so, why would he have left without doing more for Cravens, or at least talking to a police officer? *And why wouldn't he have driven back to the estate?*

Henderson came to a park and found a bench next to a street lamp. Again, he pulled out the number for Maddi's therapist, Claire. He stared at the number. Claire's message for Hank had suddenly taken on a new meaning. She had been asked by Maddi to warn Hank. Could it have something to do with the plane crash? Henderson shook his head. What warning could Maddi have wanted to give Hank days before the crash that would explain him driving to the site, then leaving without a word? And why would Cravens need to sleuth around police stations to learn where the car was from? Wouldn't Hank have simply told him? He frowned. *Not if Hank left before Cravens had a chance to talk to him.* But why would Hank do that? He frowned. *I need to talk to Claire.* He pulled out his phone and dialed.

Claire answered after only one ring. "Hello?"

"Ms. Porter?"

"Yes?"

"It's me again...the Henderson representative."

There was a pause. "As I told you before, I am only going to speak to one man...Martin Henderson."

Henderson frowned. Should he do it? *I have no choice.* He held his breath as he said evenly, "I am him."

Silence. Then, "How can I be sure?"

What would Maddi have told her about me? No longer trying to hide his hoarse voice, he said, "Maddi and I met in DC, we fell in love in Providence, we were then separated in a hotel ballroom from a fire that basically left me dead." He waited.

Finally, "I feel as if I know you."

Henderson's throat tightened. From nowhere, he said, "I miss her."

Another long pause. "Me too."

Henderson tightened his jaw. Though he longed to hear every word Maddi had ever said to the therapist, it would have to wait. "I'm short for time and I need some answers. Can you tell me again why you were looking for Hank?"

He heard a deep sigh. "For reasons I can't go into, my last conversation with Maddi wasn't good." A pause. "As a favor to her – and believe me, Mr. Henderson, I owed her –" she paused, "...she asked that I find Hank and give him a message."

"Why couldn't she give him the message herself?"

Another sigh. "Well, for some reason, she couldn't reach him on his phone."

He nodded. *Of course she couldn't...my father confiscated it.* "Go on."

"Not only that, Mr. Henderson...I had put Maddi in a position where she wasn't likely going to be able to talk to him...not after another forty-eight hours, that is."

Henderson frowned. *What is she talking about?* "What position could you have possibly put her in?"

Another clearing of the throat. "I...I can't say. But, she told me that she was worried for Hank's safety."

"Did she say why?"

"Only that it had something to do with a secret government committee where several of the members had died, and it involved a man named Morningstar."

Henderson flinched. "But why did you call my father?"

"I was hoping that once I told him that I knew you were alive, he would let me talk to you." A pause. "I needed to find someone used to dealing with...these sorts of people...someone I could trust. You were the only man I could think of."

"Someone you could trust? Why?"

He heard a pause, followed by a deep sigh. "At the end of the phone call, Maddi said something odd."

"Go on."

"She said that none of it would matter unless someone shot a high-ranking Secret Service agent in the next day or two," she cleared her throat, "...then the President – and four of his Secret Service agents – were shot forty-eight hours later."

CHAPTER 60

Vilnius, Lithuania

Dr. James Samuels let out a sigh as he stretched his silk-sleeved arms in the air. He had been at the diner in downtown Vilnius for the past two hours, doing his best to justify his continued occupancy of the booth with an endless cup of coffee and two slices of pie. He had begun the evening in the library, but unfortunately, it had closed at nine p.m., and he hadn't yet completed his work. Thankfully, the librarian had allowed him to check out the book he had been reading. He was hopeful that the tome might offer an answer to a cryptic clue he had received about four weeks ago.

The clue had come from Mark Justice, and it had been in the form of a rhyme. Justice, the beleaguered alter ego of Cobra, had called him in a panic, insisting that if Samuels didn't act soon, then all of Eastern Europe would soon be in a world war.

It wasn't the first time that Justice had made such a claim. He had said the same thing two months ago, which is what had prompted Samuels to travel from London to Vilnius in the first place.

And it wasn't a trip that Samuels had wanted to make. After all, he had spent much of his life trying to forget what had happened to him, not just in Vilnius, Lithuania, but in Latvia as well.

So, why didn't I just go back home when nothing came of it? It was a question he had asked himself many times over the course of the last two months. And always, the answer was the same. *Because I might be in a position to forestall a world war.*

His first few days in Vilnius had been trying. Though he had been born and raised there, he hadn't been sure whether any members of his family were even alive, let alone residing in the same town where so much had gone wrong. So, he had checked into a hotel, and in-between efforts to find Justice or at least speak to him, he had spent the next week looking for his family. It was to no avail, however. He had even gone to a nearby synagogue to ask the rabbi – a man he didn't recognize – if any of his family was still attending. The rabbi hadn't recognized any of their names. It was as if the entire Samuels clan of Vilnius, Lithuania, had been wiped off the map.

He had tried several times to call Justice, but each time, the call had gone nowhere. He hadn't been surprised; Justice had told him that he was getting rid of that phone. But Samuels knew of no other way to find him, as it was impossible to predict when the man would identify as Justice, or when he would revert back to Cobra. Which had left Samuels with no other option than to simply wait for Justice to call.

In the meantime, he had reached out to Walter Henderson to warn him that Cobra might be coming his way. As it turned out, the call had been a day too late...

"Is this Walter Henderson?"

"Yes. So good to talk to you, Dr. Samuels. I'm sorry I didn't get back to you sooner. I received your messages, but I wasn't in a position to reply."

"I totally understand, sir. I hope this call finds you well."

There was a pause. "As well as can be expected, Doctor. Unfortunately, there continues to be a lot of upheaval here in Latvia."

Samuels nodded. "That is why I'm calling." He paused. "I received a call a few days ago from Mark Justice. He was traveling, though he wouldn't say where. All he would tell me was that Cobra was on his way to Latvia, and that he feared that Cobra might be trying to widen the scope of the war."

Another pause. "I see."

Samuels waited for Walter to say more; he didn't.

Samuels went on. "My concern is for you and your family, Walter. If Cobra is on his way to Latvia, it is quite possible that he is heading to your home, sir." He cleared his throat. "We both know what that could mean."

Another pause, a bit longer. "Actually, Doctor, he was already here."

Samuels' eyes widened. "Oh dear. Since I'm speaking with you now, I'm guessing that he caused no major disruption?"

He heard a deep sigh. "He's gone. He left last night. I saw him go."

Samuels was beside himself. "You saw him go? Does that mean that you let *him go?"*

"I didn't know it was him until after he was gone."

"If I might ask, sir, how then are you certain that it was him?"

Samuels heard Walter sigh. "He left me a poem."

"A poem? Oh, dear me."

"Yes, Doctor, it was rather unsettling."

"Are you comfortable sharing it?"

Another sigh. "Actually no, not at this time. It's...a bit personal."

Samuels frowned. "I understand. Do you have any idea where Cobra might have gone?"

"No. But I'm rather certain he won't be back here any time soon."

"If I may ask, what makes you so sure?"

A pause. "Let's just say that as he departed, my soldiers made it fairly clear that he wasn't to return."

Samuels nodded. "Understood." He paused. "I'm going to continue to pursue this, Walter. I've elected to spend another week or two here, so—"

"Where is here, Doctor?"

"Oh, I'm sorry, I should've told you that from the start. I'm in Vilnius, Lithuania. Latvia isn't permitting flights in or out, so I elected to fly to Vilnius once I knew that Cobra – and thereby Justice – was traveling to Latvia."

"I see. Then you're not too far from me. Perhaps we'll have a chance to meet...for dinner, perhaps."

"I would welcome that, Walter. Let me know where and when; I'll be glad to travel to that location." He paused. "I can be reached at any time by way of my cellphone. I'll look forward to hearing from you, Walter."

And that had been that. Samuels had stayed longer than two weeks, however; he had stayed a full month, during which time he had split his time, either looking for members of his family, or trying to find Justice. He had had no luck with either one, however, and by the end of September he had been fully prepared to journey back to London. But just as he had been about to check out of the hotel, he had received another call from Justice. Again, the man had been distraught, and again he had alluded to the fact that Samuels' intervention might very well avert a world war. But this time, as he had been about to end the call, he had given Samuels a clue; a somewhat curious rhyme...

"Latvia and Russia will never dance,
but with Lithuania, Putin might have a chance."

That had been four weeks ago, and upon hearing the reference to Latvia, Samuels had again reached out to Walter. This time, the call had been more fruitful...

"So sorry to trouble you again, Walter, but I thought I might share the substance of a call I just received."

"No trouble at all, Doctor. Please, tell me."

"The call was from Justice. He restated his concern regarding a third world war, but this time he added a clue at the end."

"A clue?"

"Yes. It was rather cryptic. He sounded scared; a bit paranoid, actually. I'm guessing that he's becoming more aware of Cobra's presence in his mind, and perceives it as someone following him." He paused. "Anyway, as we were about to end the call, he said – and I quote – 'Latvia and

Russia will never dance, but with Lithuania, Putin might have a chance."'

Samuels waited. Finally Walter said, "What do you think it means?"

"I have no idea, Walter. I was hoping you might be able to help me."

Another pause. "My best guess is that he is suggesting that Lithuania might prove to be more of an ally to Russia than anyone would expect."

Samuels scoffed. "That's absurd. Why, I can't think of a single Baltic State that would welcome the imperious Russian government into their lives."

"Nor can I, Doctor, but I have learned over the years that every one of the former Soviet republics has hold-outs among them...men and women who feel more attached to the ways of the Russians than they do to the customs of the West." He paused. "Our version of freedom isn't always as desired as we have been led to believe."

Samuels frowned. "Supposing that's the case, what are we to do?"

There was a long pause. "Are you up for a bit of sleuthing, Doctor?"

Samuels' eyes widened. "Why, yes...certainly, Walter. I would be honored to help in any way that I can."

"Good. Though Lithuania's army has been unwavering in their pledge to join the fight against Russia if called upon, I wonder if you could do some digging, Doctor, and maybe get a sense of how the people themselves feel about a possible invasion by Russia."

Samuels wanted to laugh. What on earth would make Walter think that Samuels was suited for such an inquiry. As if reading his mind, Walter added, "You're a psychiatrist, Doctor. You spend your days, and likely many of your nights, digging deeply into the thoughts and feelings of your clients. Combine that with your recent history with Scotland Yard's Chief Inspector, and I'll bet you could be very effective in gathering this information."

And that was how Samuels had ended up staying another full month in Vilnius. He had done what Walter had asked. Posing as a British envoy, he had done his best to cozy up to some of the more prominent members of Lithuanian society in an effort to understand their allegiances. The results had been mixed. Though most were adamantly opposed to any sort of Russian occupation, he had been surprised to find a distinct few who welcomed the Russians. Either they had family in Russia to whom they still felt quite attached, or they longed for the prestige of aligning with a larger, more powerful country. Either way, there were enough who sympathized with the Russians that Samuels had begun to see that what Justice had alluded to was at least possible. The research he was pursuing in the massive tome in front of him was an effort to provide a framework for what he had learned. He hoped that a review of Lithuania's long and convoluted relationship with Russia would provide context for his conclusions. His plan was to reach out to Walter the following morning.

He readjusted himself on the plastic seat, and pored once again into the thick annal, "The History of Lithuanian Resistance." The book consisted of over 700 pages of painstaking details regarding every battle Lithuania had ever fought with Russia, starting in the late 1700's. From what Samuels could tell, Lithuania had never been given a choice regarding its subjugation to Russia. As a result, on far too many occasions, it had been overtaken by an army and a country that was 200 times bigger and 300 times more brutal. He shook his head as he reread – for probably the tenth time – the timeline of the Battle of Jieznas, fought in 1918, soon after World War I. It was one of the earlier clashes of the Lithuanian-Bolshevik War. As historian Norman Davies put it, *the German army was supporting the Lithuanian nationalists, the Soviets were supporting the Lithuanian communists, and the Polish Army was fighting them all.* That quote, though referencing a battle that had taken place nearly a century before, seemed an apt summary of the complexity of modern day alliances within the Baltic States; what Samuels had come to refer to as a love/hate relationship with Mother Russia. More importantly; it lent credence to Justice's curious clue.

But still, he felt unsettled. Yes, he had found plenty of evidence to substantiate Justice's cryptic poem, but he couldn't help but think that he was missing Justice's main point. *There is more to his curious rhyme...and by god, I'm going to find it.*

He rubbed his forehead and stroked his beard, sipping the coffee the waiter had been kind enough to refill. Though his task felt mighty, indeed, Samuels had never shied away from a challenge. Not even when the most notorious serial killer in the modern world walked into his offices on West Calhoun Street, London...

> *A tall man in a bone-colored suit walked confidently into the room, and reached out a gloved hand. "You must be the renowned Dr. Samuels."*
>
> *Samuels stood and shook the man's hand. In spite of the gloves, Samuels noted that his grip was firm. He was lean, but not scrawny. He had shoulder-length blond hair, and smooth, pale skin. His eyes were a piercing blue, unlike any Samuels had ever seen. 'Almost artificial,' he thought, as he tried not to stare. Mark's suit had clearly been tailor-made; his entire visage was professional and polished. He seemed remarkably put together in an office where most who visited were anything but. Samuels hid his enthusiasm as he offered the man a chair. "Yes...and you are?"*
>
> *The patient took a seat. "I'd like to remain Mark if that is acceptable."*
>
> *Samuels nodded. "Certainly, Mark." He noticed that the man didn't remove his gloves. Scarred hands? A phobia of some sort? He smiled and said, "Now, what can I do for you, Mark?"*
>
> *The man crossed his legs. "I'm having headaches." He paused. "And not just your run-of-the-mill headaches, either. They're happening almost daily, and they are...debilitating."*
>
> *Samuels closed his eyes, and leaned back and combed through his beard. "Go on."*
>
> *"They cause me to forget things."*
>
> *Samuels opened one eye. "Really?"*
>
> *"Yes, sometimes for days at a time."*
>
> *Samuels had to fight a sudden surge of glee. "Tell me more, Mark."*

"I've had every neurologist in London examine me and they all say the same thing: 'You're fine, Mr. Justice.' But I'm certain they've missed something."

Samuels tried not to react to the fact that now he knew the man's full name: Mark Justice. "I see," he said evenly. "What makes you so certain?"

Mark shifted in his seat, rubbing his neck, tapping his fingers on the desk. Suddenly he pointed to the coin. "Now, isn't that a fascinating relic."

Samuels did his best to hide his frustration. 'Avoidance... he's trying to dodge whatever's coming next.' "Yes, it's from my father."

Mark nodded. "A silver shekel...from Israel's First Revolt... in 66 A.D., if I'm not mistaken."

Samuels' eyes widened. "You know your coins."

Mark cleared his throat. "Something I learned as a boy."

"I see. Please, tell me more."

Mark shook his head. "I'd rather not."

Samuels nodded. 'Steer clear of his childhood...for now.' "That's fine. Perhaps we should get back to your headaches." He smiled reassuringly. "You were telling me how the neurologists have missed something. Why do you think that?"

Again, Mark shifted in his seat. Samuels waited, knowing whatever came next would determine their path for several sessions to come.

Finally, Mark looked Samuels in the eye and said, "Because when the headache eases, I often wind up somewhere different from where I started."

'Oh, glorious day!' Samuels held his expression. He nodded. "Go on."

Mark cleared his throat. He reached in his jacket and pulled something from his pocket. He clutched it tightly, hiding it in closed fingers, unwilling to part with it. After another minute, he laid it on the desk, keeping his gloved hand over it like a child might cover a bad mark on a spelling *paper. He looked up at Samuels. His voice was shaking as he said, "Whatever I say...is kept...in the strictest confidence?"*

Samuels leaned forward, nodding reassuringly. "Absolutely."

Mark pulled his hand away. There was a nametag with dark red droplets spattered across the front. Mark turned away, disgusted.

Samuels stared at the tag. "Cora Winslow." Where had he heard that name? He racked his brain, trying to recall. Suddenly he remembered. He sat back, stunned. In his mind he could see the morning newspaper with the headline "Medic brutally murdered near London's East End." His eyes widened and he looked at Mark, who was holding his head in his hands. 'Dear god!' He took a deep breath and, using his most soothing voice, he said, "Please continue, Mark..."

That encounter had put Samuels on a path that had changed his life forever. Though he had understood at that moment that Mark Justice was also the notorious Cobra, he had found a soft spot in his heart for the man, and had spent the last seven months trying to find a way to save the alter ego, Justice, from Cobra's corrupt mind. He had failed miserably, and in doing so, had defied his obligation to the law, allowing the killer to roam free for a far longer time than he might have. Samuels cringed. *Who knows how many people I'm responsible for killing by letting that man go free?* He shook his head resolutely. *You mustn't think about it, Samuels.*

But as he resumed his review of the massive tome in front of him, he knew, not only was it true, but he would spend the rest of his life trying to make up for it.

CHAPTER 61

Vilnius, Lithuania

Gad was exhausted by the time he stepped off the train. He had spent the last ten hours on two different trains just to get from Riga, Latvia, to Vilnius, Lithuania. The journey had been uneventful, but his efforts to get some much-needed sleep had been thwarted by the antics of two young boys who had been sitting in the row in front of him on the first leg of the journey to Daugavpils, and had then appeared in the row behind him on the second leg to Vilnius. *What are the odds?* he thought as he sneered at the two boys, who were hugging what he guessed to be their mother's hem.

He had elected to travel to Vilnius once his efforts to follow Henderson had been unsuccessful. Though he had kept pace with him for the first several hours after the man had curiously jumped out of his third-story hotel window, Gad had lost him somewhere in the forests north of Riga. He guessed that Henderson's familiarity with the area had given him an edge, leaving Gad to give up the chase more quickly and more easily than he might have, fully aware that – now that his burner phone was tucked neatly away in the man's backpack – it would be simple to find him whenever Gad was ready. *I'll come up with some unassailable reason for that bastard to come to Lithuania...and then I'll just give the man a call.*

It was a shame he couldn't track the phone. But it was a burner phone; the very purpose of those phones was to be untrackable. Then again, the idea of actually calling Henderson had a nice ring to it. *"Hello, brother... I'd like to invite you to tea."* He chuckled as he walked from the train station

317

to the center of town. What he wouldn't give to see the look on the man's face once he figured out that Gad had gotten close enough to hide a cellphone in his backpack.

But luring the man to Lithuania seemed like an impossible task. Though Morningstar had ordered Gad to get him there two weeks ago, Gad had put it off. Why? Because, truth be told, he had been unable to come up with a strategy. Surely, Henderson knew, that unlike Latvia, Lithuania had an extradition treaty with the U.S., which meant that the minute he crossed into Lithuania, his freedom would be in jeopardy. What could Gad offer that would encourage the man to take such a risk?

"Just get him over the border, Gad, then arrest him...with the aid of a few American soldiers." That had been Morningstar's order, and Gad was doing his best to carry it out. He had reached out to the soldiers while he was on the train. Morningstar had given him a contact number for a brigade just south of the Latvia/Lithuania border, and, using General Alexander Daniels as his calling card, Gad had told them only that a prized U.S. target would soon be arriving in Lithuania, and – on behalf of the general – Gad would need four men to be ready to take the man into custody. He had met little resistance, which had reminded him of just how powerful Edward Morningstar really was.

He checked his watch. Almost eleven p.m. He lowered his hood and removed his sunglasses, certain no one would recognize him on the dark streets of Vilnius. He reached the center of town, and looked with disdain at a city that was basically asleep. He was tired and he was hungry. Hopefully, he could find a diner that was still open. But as he walked along the lonely streets, he was dismayed to see that the lights to every single establishment had been turned off for the night.

Suddenly, his eyes widened. About two blocks away, he spotted a lighted sign with the words, "All night café" written in both English and what he assumed was Lithuanian. He was glad for the English. He had no idea how to speak Lithuanian.

He walked to the diner and stopped outside the door. Though he doubted there would be anyone in that godforsaken town who would recognize him, Morningstar's adage rang through his mind. *"Wherever you go, keep your head down. Your glass eye is notable, Gad. You mustn't let yourself be identified... anywhere."* Gad took a deep breath and sighed. Reluctantly, he once again pulled his hood over his head and put on his sunglasses. He walked into the diner and went to the back, where he found a booth that faced away from the door. He sat in the booth and, with the hood still up and the glasses in place, he ordered coffee and a sandwich. He had no idea what sort of sandwich. Though the sign on the café was in English, the menu was not.

He sat back and took off the glasses. He was about to rub his eyes, when he spotted a familiar face in a booth on the other side of the diner. Gad immediately put his head down. Fortunately, the man was focused on some oversized book; Gad felt certain the man hadn't seen him. Gad sunk lower in his seat, put on his glasses, and stood the menu on the table so it covered his face. He snuck a glance around the menu, then slowly began to chuckle. *Well, look at you, old man. You're just the person who might be able to help me persuade Matt Henderson to come to Lithuania.*

CHAPTER 62

The Henderson Compound

Once again, Henderson had been forced to rethink his entire investigation. Claire's comments regarding the killing of a top-level Secret Service agent had changed everything. What had Maddi learned that would make her say such a thing? Claire had said that Maddi had made the statement glibly; as if she hadn't thought it would happen. He frowned. *But – for whatever reason – she suspected that it might!*

After the phone call, Henderson sat on the bench for another twenty minutes, trying not only to process what he had learned from Claire, but to come up with a plan regarding Cravens. The agent had learned that the car that had come to the scene of the plane crash was a Henderson vehicle. Henderson tried to put himself in Cravens' shoes. What would he do next? Henderson nodded. *He'll go to the estate.*

Henderson could easily go back and intercept him there, but he needed to do so without anyone knowing that he, Henderson, had returned to the estate. The U.S. Government was after both Martin and Matt, and though the estate was a well-kept secret, he guessed that the Americans were at least somewhat aware of its location.

He had pulled out his laptop and, using his phone as a hotspot, had done a quick search for info on Tom Cravens. Though the Secret Service agent had sat outside his door the entire time he was in the Edinburgh hospital, Henderson had caught a glimpse of the man only once, and it had been too quick for him to glean any details. So, after staring at several photos of the man, he took out his phone and dialed his head of security. "Dimitri, it's Matt. I think you'll soon see a heavy-set man, mid-fifties, with graying hair, trying to sneak in past the gate. Let him go. He's a friend."

"If he's a friend, then why is he sneaking in?"

"Because he doesn't want me to know that he's there." He paused. "But don't stop him or say a word to him. Make him think that he has succeeded." Another pause. "I'll be there shortly, but I, too, will be sneaking in through the main gate."

"Sir?"

"It's a long story. I'll tell you more when I get there."

He ended the call, and sighed. He was asking a lot of Dimitri.

He packed up his gear and walked into town. He found a twenty-four hour convenience store at the end of the block, with a section for hunters toward the back. He bought a knitted camouflage cap, as well as a pair of night-vision binoculars. He left the store and jogged to the nearest highway on-ramp, where he hitched a ride with a trucker heading north. The ride to the estate would take about forty minutes. He leaned back and closed his eyes, reviewing all he had learned about the plane crash and the hours surrounding it. Number one: Cravens, who had miraculously survived the crash, had vanished three days later, but had just been seen back in Liepaja. Number two: Cravens had questioned a police officer, who had told him that a car belonging to the Hendersons had been spotted at the scene of the crash. Number three: Cravens had told the cop that he was investigating a terrorist plot. Henderson frowned. Was that true? Were terrorists somehow involved in the crash that killed Maddi? He stiffened. *Heaven help the bastards if I learn that that plane crash was anything other than an accident.* Number four: Hank had taken a Henderson car for a drive, and, for whatever reason, had disabled the GPS and had disappeared. Had he been the driver of the car that Cravens had seen at the crash site? If so, why hadn't he stayed to help. *And if not, then where the hell is he?* Number five: Maddi had given Claire an ominous – and somewhat prophetic – message about how Hank needed to watch his back...*but only if a top-ranked Secret Service agent was killed.* What had Maddi learned? Did it have anything to do with the crash? And what had she wanted to warn Hank about? Was he in trouble? Is that why he left? Had he gone into hiding to steer clear of the very thing that Claire had been asked to warn him about? Number six: Claire had mentioned Morningstar. What role had he played? Had he been involved in a secret committee, and was he responsible for the deaths of several of its members? Had Maddi somehow learned of it? He closed his eyes, the next thought almost unbearable. *If so, had it been enough to get her killed?* He shook his head. *No, the crash was investigated thoroughly and was ruled a weather-related accident.*

But what if it wasn't? What if Maddi had uncovered a plot involving a secret committee that somehow involved Hank? What if Morningstar was behind the deaths of its members? *And what if Cravens knows more than he has shared...with anyone?*

The ride went quickly. When they were about a mile from the secret entrance to the compound, Henderson asked the man to stop.

"Šeit? Tur ir nekas, bet koki." *Here? There's nothing but trees.*

"Man patīk pārgājiens mežā." *I like to hike in the woods.*

"Pulksten vienpadsmitos naktī?" *At midnight?*

Henderson shrugged and edged to the door as the man stopped the truck. He stepped down, gave a quick wave, and waited for the trucker to disappear around the bend. When he was well out of sight, Henderson jogged to the hidden entrance. He put on the stocking cap, and adjusted the glasses and the blonde mustache his friend Emil had given him. It wasn't safe for him to come back home...not as Matt anyway.

Fortunately, the moon was hidden behind clouds, leaving the night darker than usual. Pushing his way through heavy groundcover and thick vines, Henderson reached the gate, all the while making sure to stay clear of the cameras. He knelt down, pushed a series of numbers on a hidden key pad, and waited for the gate to open. Anyone monitoring the compound would know immediately that the gate had opened. Henderson's hope was that Dimitri had taken charge of the monitors. As he jogged past the gate to the trees, he frowned. *I guess I'll know soon enough.*

He moved carefully; he knew where every camera was hidden. He hid behind a tree, took off his glasses, and pulled out the binoculars. He scanned the compound, starting with the front yard. Nothing. He looked south; still nothing. He followed the river north of the manor. He stopped. He saw him. Hiding behind a row of trees was a heavyset man with thinning gray hair. He zoomed in; it was Cravens. The man was close to a private side entrance; as if he had known where to go. *Of course he does, he's been here before.* According to Walter, Cravens had come there in March after the attack on the security team. As a trained agent, he had likely drawn a map of the place in his mind. *But why is he just standing there?*

But as Henderson continued to watch him, he began to understand. Cravens was waiting for someone to walk out that door so he could sneak in and talk to whoever had been driving the car that had shown up at the scene of the plane crash. Then and only then would he ask to speak to Walter. *It's what I would do.*

Henderson continued to watch him. Cravens wasn't moving. Periodically, he would reach in his coat pocket and pull out a cigarette. He would stare at it, then shove it back in his pocket. *Good move,* Henderson thought. A lighted cigarette would give away his presence at the compound.

A blast of cold air blew in from the sea and Henderson shivered. He needed to get inside. He shoved the binoculars in his pocket, put on his glasses, and crept toward Cravens, stealing past trees and bushes that he knew like the back of his hand. When he was less than ten feet away, he said, "Ya need a light?"

Cravens stood as still as stone.

Henderson moved closer. "I said, do you need a light?" He held up his hands in case the agent was carrying a gun. "Agent Cravens, it's me...Matt Henderson."

Cravens turned to look at him. Even in the dark, Henderson could see the toll the crash had taken on the man. His cheeks were drawn, his eyes empty. The sleeve of his coat was torn and Henderson frowned. *Surely, he wouldn't walk around in the same coat he'd had with him when the plane went down.* But as he got closer, he could smell remnants of diesel fuel and fire...smells that Henderson knew well.

Cravens frowned. "You don't look like Matt Henderson."

Henderson cleared his throat. "I'm wearing a disguise."

Cravens narrowed his eyes. "Why? Your family lives here."

Henderson nodded. "Yes, but I'm a wanted man."

"Didn't Dr. Clarkson clear you back in Edinburgh?"

"Yes, but apparently more evidence has come to light." He paused. "So, if you want to be a hero, Cravens, I'm yours. You can take me in right now."

Cravens frowned. "You're not wanted at your own family's home, are you?"

"No, but I don't want them to know I'm here."

Cravens frowned. "Why not?"

Henderson frowned. "Because I don't know what Walter might be hiding."

Cravens raised an eyebrow. "Why would Walter hide something, especially from you?"

Henderson shook his head. "I'm not sure...but I didn't know about you – that you had survived the plane crash – until twenty-four hours ago."

Cravens sighed. "I've been pretty quiet about it. It...it doesn't feel right."

Henderson nodded. "I understand."

Cravens sighed. "As for your presence here...on your family's estate... your secret's safe with me." He hesitated. "Regarding the claims that the U.S. authorities have made...I know for a fact that any charges against you are bullshit."

Henderson said nothing, but slowly lowered his hands.

Cravens rubbed the back of his neck. "How did you know I'd be here?"

"Because I just spoke with Officer Vitols...in Liepaja. He filled me in."

Cravens frowned. "Dammit...he wasn't supposed to say anything."

"I had a consulate card...he didn't really have a choice."

Cravens took a cigarette from his pocket. "Do you care if I smoke?"

"Not at all, but move over here so that no one inside sees the light from your cigarette." He led Cravens to an overhang around the corner.

Cravens lit the cigarette and took a long, slow drag. "That's quite a disguise," he said cautiously. "If I recall, didn't *Martin* Henderson have blond hair?"

Henderson flinched.

Cravens took another drag and exhaled slowly. "I know who you are, Martin. Dora let it slip one afternoon...soon after Dalgety Bay." He paused. "We had a lot of time on our hands while you were sick. I think it made her feel better to talk about it."

Henderson nodded. "I imagine." He sighed. "How much do you know?"

"Enough. You've been through a lot. I don't need to know any more." He sighed. "And I really don't know what to make of this mess."

"You mean the fact that a Henderson car was driven to the site of the crash right after it occurred, and that the driver simply left the site without a word?"

Cravens cleared his throat. "Uh...yeah."

Henderson stared at the last man to have seen Maddi alive. His hands had begun to shake; he shoved them in his pockets. A sharp wind blew in off the ocean; it was getting colder. He pulled out his phone. "Dimitri, it's Matt. I'm coming inside with that friend of mine. No one – not even Walter or Dora – can know we're here."

"Walter and Dora aren't here, sir. They've gone to Riga for the night."

Henderson had forgotten. It would work out well. Hopefully, he could learn what he needed before his parents got back. "Good. We're coming in through the north entrance, and I'm wearing a disguise. I'll meet you outside the security room." He ended the call and turned to Cravens, who had begun to shiver. "Let's go."

"Gladly." Cravens took two final puffs on the cigarette, then put it out against a tree. He slid what remained in his pocket.

They climbed the steps, Henderson unlocked the door and they went inside. They waited in the shadows near the Security Room. Dimitri appeared within seconds, his pistol raised. He walked up to Henderson.

Henderson removed the glasses and the mustache. "See, it's me."

Dimitri stared at him. "Why the disguise, sir?"

"The American government wants me. I'm not ready to go."

Dimitri grinned. "Code word, sir?"

"Saint Meinhard." It was a reference to an early Latvian leader.

Dimitri nodded and stood at attention. "I cleared the security room. I told the men to take a fifteen-minute break." He added, "How else can I be helpful, sir?"

"We'll stay in the den. Can you kill the cameras from here to there?"

Dimitri nodded. "Certainly sir."

Henderson waited for Dimitri to return to the Security Room, gave him a minute to stop the video feed, then led Cravens down the empty hallway to the den. Once inside, he locked the door, closed the curtains, and switched on a lamp. There was wood in the fireplace; he bent down and lit it. "Let me take your coat, Cravens."

Cravens removed the overcoat and handed it to Henderson, who carried it to a closet. He swallowed uncomfortably as he hung the smoke-covered coat on a hanger.

He walked to a small bar and poured two glasses of Scotch. He carried them to where Cravens was standing and handed him one of the glasses. The man looked even worse in the light. It had been over eight weeks since the tragedy, but in many ways, he looked like he had just walked away from it. Henderson offered him a seat on the couch, then sat across from him in a cushioned chair. He sipped his drink. "As I said, Cravens, I was told very little of what happened regarding the...plane crash." He hesitated. "I'm sure it was some sort of gesture to...protect me...but it ticks me off that I wasn't told that there had been...a survivor."

Cravens looked at him. It was clearly uncomfortable for both of them. Eight-plus weeks later, Henderson could see that it unsettled Cravens to even think about it...though that was likely all he had done.

Cravens sighed. "I'm not sure I did...survive it, I mean."

Henderson leaned back and stretched his legs, crossing them at the ankles in an effort to make Cravens feel more comfortable. He sipped his Scotch. "I get it."

Cravens stared at the fire, his fingers practically white as he gripped the drink. After another minute, he looked at Henderson. "Do you know how terrible it is to be...the only survivor?"

Henderson tightened his jaw. He had a pretty good idea.

Cravens went on. "I'm not really sure how it happened." He paused. "The only thing I can think is that I was standing at the time the plane went down, and because of it, I was thrown clear of the wreckage."

"Why were you standing?"

Cravens shook his head. "I...I don't remember."

The men sat in silence for another ten minutes. Finally, Cravens sighed and said, "I...came to...and crawled away as best I could. I was pretty beat up." Another pause. "It was raining, which is probably why I didn't burn to death." He cleared his throat. "I...I tried to...save them, but—" His voice broke and he stopped.

Though Henderson wanted more than anything to ask about Maddi, he knew that now wasn't the time. "Tell me about the license plate...the car at the scene."

Cravens looked at him. "For the longest time, I thought I might've imagined it." He shook his head and sighed. "I didn't tell the police about the driver or the car."

"Why not?"

"I'm not sure. I guess I needed to find out who he was and why he was there...for myself." He paused. "I told Vitols he had ties to terror; that was a lie."

Henderson nodded, relieved. *One less phantom evil for me to hunt down.*

Cravens went on. "But I felt certain that the driver had something to do with the crash. I needed to find out what he knew before I gave him up."

Henderson frowned. "What makes you think he had something to do with it? Couldn't he have simply been driving by?"

Cravens turned back to the fire. He seemed to be weighing his next words carefully. Finally, he looked at Henderson and sighed. "He wasn't simply driving by."

"How do you know?"

Cravens rubbed his forehead as he stared in his drink. Then, he swigged the entire thing in one gulp. When he looked at Henderson, his eyes were wide; almost as if he was afraid of what he was about to share. "Because... someone overheard him."

Henderson frowned. "Someone? Who?"

Cravens set his empty glass on the table. "Hank. Hank was there...and he knew that the crash was going to happen."

CHAPTER 63

Washington, DC

Morningstar's phone was vibrating. Not the phone he kept for private calls from his 'family,' but the one he used for work. He checked the time... just after five. He had left work less than half-an-hour ago. He sneered *Can't they give me at least a minute's peace?* He had stripped down to his underwear and had been sitting in the dark living room since walking in about ten minutes ago. Janet was napping in the bedroom, and he had just poured himself a drink. He sat up and, not bothering to turn on the lamp, he opened the phone. "Yes?"

"Good evening, Mr. Morningstar." The voice was shaky; tentative.

"Who is this?"

"Um...it's Emmett Wilson, sir. Remember...with the Secret Service?"

Morningstar frowned. *You mean formerly with the Secret Service.* "Yes, Emmett, how can I help you?"

"Um...sir," he cleared his throat, "I believe that it is I who can help you."

Morningstar's eyes narrowed. "And how is that, may I ask?"

There was a pause. "It's rather delicate, sir."

"I see. Let me call from a different line."

"Yes sir." Emmett gave Morningstar his number.

Morningstar grabbed his private phone from the pocket of his pants, which he had draped over the back of a chair. He dialed the number. "So, tell me, Mr. Wilson, how you can be of use to me."

"As you know, sir, I was recently let go from the Service over a...um misunderstanding."

Misunderstanding, my ass. You were caught stealing from one of your protectees, you dumbass. "Yes, trumped up charges, I'm sure."

"Definitely. You had asked me a couple of months ago, before I was let go, to monitor President Knight – when he was still VP – without letting anyone know."

It was true. Morningstar had asked the low-level agent to track Knight soon after he became Vice-President, not only to keep him safe, but to verify that no one knew of his ties to Morningstar. But he had let it go once he had learned that the agent had been caught stealing. "Go on."

"With all this free time on my hands, I decided to carry on with your request."

Morningstar frowned. He wasn't sure he liked where this was headed. "And?"

Another pause. "Sir, there's something I think you should know."

"What's that, *former* Secret Service Agent Wilson?"

Again, the man cleared his throat. "The President has just left for Maine, sir."

Maine? Why? "Is that so unusual, Wilson? After all, his uncle lives there."

"It's unusual, sir, when he doesn't clear it first...not with the Secret Service, not with the military, not with anyone." There was a pause. "Sir, it would appear that President Knight has just snuck away."

CHAPTER 64

The Baxter Mountain Range

Emma squeezed her hand around a small gold medallion. Given to her by her mother when Emma was five, she found that she often gained strength just from holding the coin. She kept it with her always; something her mother had asked her to do, and she would rub it when she felt nervous or afraid. *Like now,* she thought as she sat in a dark hotel room just off route 202, about thirty miles from Camden, Maine. Never had she been so anxious. And she had certainly underestimated what was involved in arranging a meeting with the President of the United States. *Particularly when you don't want your husband or your daughter to find out.*

From the moment they had made plans to meet, Emma's world had been turned upside down. She had expected it to some degree. So, her first step, even before making the call to Jerome, had been to tell Michael that she needed time away.

She hadn't gone into detail. All she had told him was that she was struggling and needed time away to get back on her feet. Michael had suggested that it was probably due to Galina being so far away. Emma hadn't argued the point; there was certainly some truth to it. *"Perhaps you're right, Michael,"* she had told him, unwilling to hurt him any more than she already had.

So, what is the real reason, Emma? She frowned. The real reason was that she now knew for a fact that she had never quit loving Jerome. And she needed to know if he felt the same. Did Jerome still love her? He had never married. Was it because he was still in love with her? And, if so, would it change things? What would she do if she was to learn that Jerome did, in fact, still love her? She had no idea.

But why now? she wondered as she stared out the curtained hotel room window. Why had she suddenly become so broken by her love for Jerome that she could barely eat or sleep? Was it because his face had been blasted across TV's and newspapers almost nonstop for the past two months? She nodded. *Probably.*

But her actions were nothing short of selfish. She had decided years ago that it was better to be content; to keep things as they were for her husband and her child, than to fulfill some self-centered need to find true love. *So... what has changed?* she wondered as she stared out the window of the old motel. She frowned. *The degree to which I have become unhappy.* Last night had told her that much. She felt as if she was losing too much of herself to the compromise. *I need to at least play this out...to get a bit of clarity about who I am, how I feel, and how Jerome Knight feels about me.*

Ironically, she didn't agree with a single policy decision that Jerome, as President, had made. *So, why isn't that enough? Why can't our political differences stop me from wanting that man?* She chuckled as she recalled a slogan from the eighteen hundreds. *"Politics makes strange bedfellows."*

She had said nothing to Michael about her feelings for Jerome; Michael didn't even know that she had once had a relationship with the current president. When Jerome left her, she had been utterly destroyed, and had erased every part of him from her life; at least the life she was willing to discuss with others. But it felt cruel to take a leave of absence from a man who had given her so much...who had given her Galina...without a better explanation for why she was leaving. *I can't help it...I can't stop...this.* For whatever reason, her love for Romer, a love that had clearly been there for the past sixteen years, had come to the fore...*and it is refusing to leave.* It stood between her and Michael like an immense white pine. Though they could look around it, they would never be able to get past it...*until I know for sure.*

Michael hadn't seemed surprised by the request...as if he had maybe expected it. As if her discontent that morning had told him all he needed to know. Not her reasons, but her need to resolve it – whatever it was – by herself. It had been one of his finer gifts; his ability to sense what Emma needed – even if it was something unfavorable to him – and his willingness to give it to her at his own expense.

But his understanding had only made it harder. The steps she was about to take might undermine the very understanding that Michael had been so kind to offer. *And it might all be for nothing.* What if her longing for Jerome was nothing more than nostalgia for the past? It wasn't unheard of to amplify feelings from long ago, only to discover that they were no longer there when forced into the unrelenting light of the present. If that was the case, then she certainly didn't want to hurt the one man who had shown her love and kindness when she had needed it most. More importantly, she didn't want to rip apart the only family she had. So, before she would let herself destroy everything she and Michael had built over the last fifteen years, she would find out. *I'm certain that I'll know how Romer feels about me the minute I see him.*

She was grateful that Jerome had responded as he had. She knew he was busy. She laughed. *Busy is for mothers who are trying to get dinner after working all day. Jerome is far more than just busy.* Nonetheless, he had agreed to meet her. It was as if he, too, wanted – needed – to know.

A Secret Service agent had quickly, thoroughly combed through every aspect of her life, as well as her husband's and her child's. She had expected it, at least to some degree, and had told Michael that she had been contacted by the White House to meet with the President concerning her work on green energy. It was plausible…she worked for a green energy company outside Camden. But the notion that the President of the United States would go to the trouble of meeting with a representative from a small energy company outside Camden, Maine, during a time when the country was in crisis both domestically and abroad; well, it was a bit far-fetched. But Michael hadn't challenged it. Again, it was as if he knew.

As for Galina; she was overseas with the Maine orchestra and had no idea what was happening. And though the Secret Service had likely investigated her, as well, there wasn't much to learn about a fifteen-year-old girl that a chat with friends and a school administrator or two wouldn't reveal.

It was nearly 6:00 p.m. when a car pulled up to the hotel thirty miles outside Portage, where Emma had gone after telling Michael that she needed time away. She had picked the hotel because it was far enough away that no one would know what she was up to, but close enough that she wouldn't have far to go if she changed her mind. She had checked in soon after noon, and had been there ever since, answering questions, securing information for the Secret Service agents investigating her life.

She was watching from the window when two agents climbed the stairs to her room on the second floor. They knocked on her door and she grabbed the red wool coat that her husband had given her for Christmas the year before, wincing as she thought of what she was about to do...of the betrayal she was about to carry out.

Too late to turn back now, Emma.

She shoved her mother's coin in her pocket and, with barely a word, she was escorted down to the car and helped into the back seat. It was dark; the sun had already begun to set, the fading light a symbol of all that she was leaving behind. She felt like she was smothering as they drove silently in the darkness. She was grateful when one of the agents turned and smiled. He had red hair and freckles, and his green eyes gleamed as he looked at her and said, "Are you okay, Ma'am?"

Emma recognized the voice. It had a subtle Irish brogue. He was the same man who had contacted her after her call to Romer. She gave a weak grin. "I—I think so." She hesitated. "May I ask your name, agent?"

He hesitated, then nodded. "I'm Agent Jerry Foster, Ma'am."

They drove to a private airfield outside Ashland, and pulled up beside an unmarked black helicopter. Foster helped her aboard and led her to one of only three seats. She strapped in and they were quickly airborne. Within minutes, they landed at a different airfield, and she was escorted off the helicopter. As she stepped onto the tarmac, she looked around, and was amazed that she recognized the area. She had been to that same location before...many times. They were near the base camp of Mount Katahdin.

She was led to another black sedan and was again helped into the back seat. She watched through tinted windows as they drove up the mountain to the same gorge where, twenty years ago, she and Romer had made love in the canyon. The moon was high by the time they parked the car halfway up the rise. Foster opened the door and, as her feet hit the ground, she breathed in and closed her eyes. The smell of pine was sharp, and the crisp autumn air gave her a chill. Her eyes filled with tears. She remembered it well. She and Jerome had come there often, and, in that way that only nature can, it was consuming her with the feelings of all that had happened back then.

She was led up the hill to a spot just yards from where they had picnicked in 1984. A small cabin was hidden among the trees, and again Emma felt tears sting her eyes. She and Jerome had used that cabin many times as a retreat from the cold, and she pulled her coat tighter as she felt her entire body begin to shake. She walked toward the cabin and the agents led her inside. She was surprised to see a white tablecloth, a bottle of wine, and two plates waiting for whatever was inside a picnic basket sitting nearby. There was a fire in the hearth and she walked over and put her hands over the flames to warm them. Tears began to fall down her cheeks, and she wiped them away, staring at the fire so the agents wouldn't see.

Where is he? she wondered as she did a quick glance around the cabin.

All at once she heard a whisper from the doorway. "Over here."

She turned to the whisper, then glanced at the agents. Foster remained stone-faced, though she could see the hint of a grin. She crept to the door, then cautiously stepped outside. He whispered again. She walked to an alcove only a few feet away; it was protected by a wall of tall boulders. There were agents on each side and one standing above, all three holding binoculars in one hand, a rifle in the other. She swallowed and laid a hand on the rock, the cold, rough surface reassuring. *This is real...this is actually happening.* She held her breath and slowly peered around the rock. Her heart stopped. Standing there, in a pair of khakis and a turtleneck beneath a thick wool jacket, was President Jerome Knight. She didn't know what to say. *'Hello sir,' would be good,* she thought, as she struggled to find her voice. She had seen his face a thousand times on TV; she knew the changes he had undergone after sixteen years of living. *But he hasn't seen me.* She was suddenly self-conscious and put a hand to her hair as if to brush away nearly two decades of growing older. He seemed to sense her concern. "Emma, you're even more beautiful than when I saw you last."

"You mean when you said 'goodbye'?"

He looked down and she flinched. *That was stupid, Emma! You can't rehash an old break-up.* "I'm sorry, Romer. That wasn't fair."

Slowly, he lifted his head, his brown eyes reflecting the moonlight over the canyon. "It's fair. I just don't know what to say. I was an idiot."

She felt her heart skip a beat. "I've...I've missed you."

He walked closer and she could smell him. It was the same as sixteen years ago, and she closed her eyes and breathed in, letting it fill her soul.

He took her hand and leaned closer as he whispered, "I missed you, too."

She felt him, the touch of his skin on hers, the warmth of his breath on her cheek. She looked up at him and it was as if no time had passed. Her knees felt weak and she thought she might faint. "I—I need to sit down."

He walked her to a wooden bench behind the rocks. None of the agents moved. It was likely as close as Romer ever got to being alone. He kept a hold of her hand as they sat down. "I'm glad you called," he said.

He smiled and she held her breath. *Was she glad she called?* "I'm...I'm glad I called, too...I think." She chuckled nervously. She saw him swallow; a nervous gulp that she recognized from the days when they had just started dating. *Though he's the most powerful man in the world, I can still make him nervous.* She breathed a sigh of relief; it was still there. The unstoppable attraction they had felt decades ago hadn't disappeared; if anything, it seemed even stronger.

"Have you been okay?" he asked, as he took her hand in his.

No. I've been living a lie...I'm in a passionless marriage and the only notable thing to come of it – my beautiful daughter – has left the country and will soon be gone for good. "I've been okay. And you?"

They both laughed. *Such a ridiculous thing to say, Emma!* He rubbed his chin. "I've been okay, too...kind of busy, but okay." He leaned closer and whispered in her ear, "I never stopped loving you, Emma...not for one second."

He had said it; what she had wanted to hear...he had said the words. It was why she had come; why she had called and asked to see him. Suddenly nothing else mattered. Her fifteen-year marriage, her daughter; all of it faded away as she looked in the eyes of the man she was still so deeply in love with. "I...I never stopped loving you, either."

He kissed her on the forehead and pulled her close. She hugged him and it felt like it always had; like they had never been apart...like they were meant to be together and had resumed their intended roles in the universe. As though the last sixteen years had merely been a detour and they were now back on course. They said nothing and Emma clung to him, listening to the beating of his heart. Never in her 38 years of life had she felt more at peace. She was with the man she loved and she knew – regardless of what happened – it was where she would stay.

Suddenly one of the agents leaned his head around the rock. "Excuse me, Mr. President, but your phone is ringing."

Romer said evenly, "Answer it, Simmons."

"I can't sir; it's your...*other* phone."

Emma felt it; like the storm that blows in after a perfect day on the water, she felt Romer change. Though he kept hold of her hand, he was pulling away. He looked down at her and said coolly, "I have to take that."

She nodded as he stood and left the alcove. She was alone. The agent on the ledge above her hadn't moved, and the guard by the rock said nothing as he stood as still as a statue. She tried to listen as Romer took the call, but all she could hear was the hum of his voice; the soft, soothing sound that had given her more joy than thirty lifetimes might provide. She stood and paced the six-by-six alcove, waiting for him to come back. *How many phones does a President have? Two? Three?* The minutes ticked by and she kept pacing, trying to imagine what would come next. Would she leave Michael? *I have to.* Would Galina understand? *No...she'll hate me.* Did it matter? *Certainly, but not enough to stop me from finally being honest with myself.*

* * *

Dammit! Knight thought as he took the phone from Simmons. The call from Morningstar couldn't have been more poorly timed. It was unsettling. More than unsettling, it was irritating as hell. Somehow Morningstar had learned that the girl he had forced Knight to say goodbye to sixteen years ago was back. His first words confirmed it.

"Leave her, Judah. Leave her, now."

Knight was seething. *Who told him?*

"Did you hear me, Judah?"

"Yes...yes, I did, sir."

"Good. Now take care of it. Things are about to get intense. I'm going to need you back at the White House," he paused, "...fully focused."

Knight said nothing.

"Judah? Do you understand what I'm saying?"

"Yes sir, I do."

"Good. Get back to DC. As I said, things are about to get intense."

Knight wanted to throw the phone into the cavern and tell the agents to get lost. Suddenly, being the leader of the free world was the last thing he wanted. He had almost gotten up the nerve to challenge Jacob, when the man added, "Judah, don't forget where that woman comes from."

The call ended. Knight squeezed the phone in his fist, ready to slam it into a rock, but he simply gritted his teeth as he slid it in his pocket. He had a mission to carry out, and Jacob was counting on him. His role in what was about to take place was pivotal, and he knew it. *But now I know... I love Emma more than anything; more than any mission.* What should he do? Why did he need to leave Emma in order to carry out the plan? He knew the answer. *Because Jacob said so.*

He walked slowly back to his beautiful Emma. He could see her shadow pacing on the other side of the rock. He stopped and watched. How many times over the past sixteen years had he imagined that walk, or envisioned that woman's smile, her hair, her very touch? *And now she's only a few feet away.* He closed his eyes; he couldn't do it. He couldn't turn her away. *But I have to...Jacob has ordered it.*

He took a step; he knew he wouldn't be able to look at her. He loved her. He wanted to lay with her and make love to her for hours...*like we used to.* His legs felt weak; he leaned against the rock. *Just get it over with.* He pounded his fist repeatedly against the rough stone, then rubbed his bleeding knuckles as he walked the few steps to where she was waiting.

* * *

Emma heard his footsteps and tensed, ready to pick up where they had left off. But the minute he came around the rock she could tell; things had changed.

"I'm sorry, Emma. Something has...come up. I'll have my men take you back to your hotel."

She said nothing, simply staring at him. If she could have found her voice she would have said, *"But what now...what's next?"* Instead, she tightened her jaw, fighting tears as she nodded and turned away. Foster, the red-haired agent who had been so kind, came up to her and smiled. But the smile was sad...as if he knew that that was not how it was supposed to end. "I'll walk you back to the car, Ma'am."

He led her away from the alcove, through the cabin, past the picnic basket meal that hadn't been touched. They walked out the door and down the rise toward the car that was waiting where they had left it. As they neared the car, she looked over her shoulder, hoping Romer would yell for her to come back. She saw him on the mountain, his silhouette in the moonlight reminding her of Brando in "On the Waterfront" ...stoic and alone. He waved; a short, quick wave that said little...or maybe it said a lot. He quickly turned away.

What just happened? Emma had no idea, but one thing she knew for sure; nothing would ever be the same.

* * *

Knight had seen the disappointment in Emma's eyes. But there was little he could do. He had been given a unique mission; a task that only he could complete. He had trained a lifetime for it; he had sacrificed his youth to follow through on the remarkable duty that was about to be asked of him. His feelings for a girl – a woman – paled next to the responsibility of restoring a nation to righteousness.

Suddenly, he frowned. Was he restoring a nation to righteousness? Or was he simply fulfilling the vision of one man's quest for power? For the first time in his life, he began to question the journey. *How could anything be 'righteous' when I'm not with the woman I love?* As he watched Emma being walked down the canyon and back to the car, he gave her a wave... an empty gesture for a heartless deed. He was making her leave...again. *Why can't I have her and still fulfill my destiny?* As he looked up at the moon and felt the cold mountain air chill him to his soul, he made up his mind; this time he would find a way to do both. He would find a way to honor Morningstar, and still have Emma in his life. *Now all I have to do is make Morningstar see that.*

CHAPTER 65

The Henderson Compound

Cravens sighed as he watched the moon creep once again from behind the clouds. He had been watching moonbeams filter in through the massive bay window of the guest bedroom for well over an hour, marveling at their precision as they seemed to shine directly on him, exposing him for the weak man that he was. He was holding onto a dreadful secret and, though he knew it would save Henderson to know the truth, Cravens had been unable to do it; he had been unable to alleviate that poor man's pain.

They had left the den around one a.m., the combination of the fire, the Scotch, and the lack of sleep finally catching up to them both. Cravens had told Henderson only the basics about how Hank had overheard the driver's phone call. He couldn't afford to tell him too much without giving away the fact that Maddi had survived the crash and had been whisked away – by Hank – to who knew where. Henderson had seemed to accept it, but that might have been only because they were both so tired.

Henderson had made a quick call to his security officer asking him to kill the video feed to the hallway, the stairs, and the upstairs bedrooms, and had then led Cravens to the room on the second floor.

Never had Cravens seen such a room; it was as big as his entire apartment in DC, and better furnished. Someone had built a fire in the hearth, and had laid out a pair of silk pajamas across a massive, four-poster bed. Henderson had pointed to a solid cherry armoire which stood against one wall, and had told him he could hang his clothes in there. He had then taken his leave. As Cravens had been about to take off his pants, he had felt a key in his pocket. It was to a locker at a bus station in Liepaja. He had left both his bag and his briefcase – Walter's briefcase – in the locker for safekeeping. He had yet to come up with a good way to return the briefcase to Walter.

He had changed into the pajamas, had hung his clothes in the armoire, then had practically fallen into bed. But, in spite of the warm fire and the unmatched accommodations, he had been unable to sleep. Like every night since the plane crash, the only thing he saw when he closed his eyes was burning metal and dead people. He could still smell the diesel fuel, he could still hear the blast as fire consumed what remained of the wrecked plane. And he could still see Maddi, shaken and bleeding, her eyes staring vacantly as he and Hank lifted her into the back seat of the car.

But what was working on him even more as he stared out the double-paned glass was his inability to alleviate the burden of a man who was clearly not well. *Henderson's in mourning...over a woman I know is still alive.* It was written all over the man; in his demeanor, his face, his eyes. Cravens had wanted so badly to tell him that Maddi was alive. He knew what she had meant to him; he knew what they had meant to one another. And, as he had sat by that fire in the den, he had almost done it...several times. But always he had caught himself. Why? *Because it would put her in danger.* Henderson would be unable to help himself; he would go looking for her. And anyone who was trying to find Henderson – the United States Government, for example – might then discover the truth...*Maddi isn't dead.*

He turned on his side and closed his eyes. He needed to sleep, and he would never have a more comfortable place to do it. But he couldn't sleep. The guilt was weighing on him too heavily. *Just tell him, Cravens...right now. Get up out of this bed and go tell that poor man that the woman he loves is alive.* He frowned. What would he say after that? *"...but I don't know where she is."* Henderson would push him, and he would eventually tell him that Hank knew her location, after which Henderson would hunt down Hank with a fervor that would surely lead to him finding him, which would put Hank in a terrible position. *How could Hank refuse to tell Henderson where she's hiding?* He shook his head. *But if Hank did tell Henderson, then Hank would be putting her at risk, just like I would be.* Could Henderson keep the secret? Absolutely. Could he stay away from her? Absolutely not. It was a no-win situation, and, by the time Cravens heard a clock somewhere in the mansion ring out two soft chimes, he had concluded that his original decision had been the right one; don't tell him. At least for now. It was the only way to ensure that Maddi stayed safe.

But it saddened him...in a place he rarely allowed himself to go. Not only for Henderson, but for Maddi. Never had he seen such unbridled love and devotion between two individuals. Wouldn't they both be freed from their agony if Henderson was to learn the truth. *No. The risk is too great; the risk is Maddi's life.*

Cravens sighed and pulled the blanket to his chin. As moonlight once again flickered between the clouds, he shook his head. *I'll leave it to someone else to tell him...I simply cannot make that call.*

CHAPTER 66

Boe, France

For about the tenth time, Cobra slowed his Toyota as he drove past the exit for the town of Boe, approximately 95 kilometers south of Bergerac, France. He thought he had spotted a dark-colored Peugeot just north of the exit, but by the time he had crossed three lanes to get to it, the car was nowhere to be found. He had been up and down that highway for the last several hours, certain that Hank and his Peugeot could not have driven fast enough to evade him. *Which means that he had to have pulled off at Boe.* But the town looked like a dead-end. Boe appeared to have little to offer other than a gas station and an all-night diner. Cobra looked at his gas gauge. He was getting low on gas; he was also hungry. He checked the time. Two a.m. He had been driving non-stop for nearly a full day; he could use a break. He pulled into the far left lane, made a U-turn, then drove back to the exit. *Whether Hank's here or not, at least I can get gas and a bite to eat, and maybe even find a cheap hotel and get some sleep.*

He eased off the exit and drove into Boe. He stopped at the gas station, annoyed to find that it was closed. *What kind of one-horse town is this place?*

He drove further into town. Other than the diner, the town appeared to have shut down for the night. He parked on the street in front of the diner and walked inside. He ordered a sandwich and a beer, then nursed a second beer as he pulled out a map to get his bearings. From what he could tell, he was about eight hours from Spain's border. Was Hank going all the way to Spain? He chuckled. *He's probably thinking that he and sweet Flora will hide away on some island off the coast.*

He folded the map and drank the last of his beer. He stood and walked to the counter. He handed the man twenty euros, told him to keep the change, and was about to leave, when he walked back to the counter. He pulled out his ID that showed him to be a Swedish financial adviser, then took out his photo of Hank and laid it on the counter. In flawless French, he said, "Have you seen this man? He might be wearing a beard, a mustache, and a pair of glasses."

The man stared at the photo, then nodded. In French, he said, "He was here. Maybe six hours ago. He was looking for a hotel."

Cobra's eyes widened. Keeping with the French, he said, "Did you direct him to one hotel in particular?"

The man narrowed his eyes. Cobra added quickly, "He is due a considerable amount of money, but I must find him before the end of the month or the inheritance becomes null and void." Still seeing doubt in the man's eyes, he added, "I'm in charge of the transfer of funds. I would hate to see it go to the tax collectors."

The man hesitated, then leaned over the counter and pointed out the window. In French, he said, "Down the street. The Hotel Germain. It is the only hotel in town."

Cobra smiled and thanked the man. He walked out the door to his Toyota. It was the only car on the road and, though he doubted anyone would recognize either him or the car, he felt it to be a bit too conspicuous. He got in, drove to a side road that abutted the hotel, and parked the car. As he looked up at the old hotel, he chuckled. *I'm close... I can feel it. I am very close to killing you, Hank Clarkson.*

* * *

Hank awoke with a start. He had heard something. He looked around the room, trying to get his bearings. A streetlamp outside the hotel offered the only light. He was still sitting in the cushioned chair, and Maddi was asleep on the bed; she hadn't moved. *What time is it?* He rubbed his eyes as he checked a clock by the bed. Three a.m. They had been in that room for nearly six hours. It was the longest that Hank had slept uninterrupted since their harrowing journey had begun.

Whatever he had heard had come from outside. He stood and walked to the only window. It faced a side street, and he was careful as he pulled aside the curtain and looked down at a narrow road outside the hotel. There was no traffic on either the side road or the main street, and he could see no late-night revelers; the town was dead. He spotted a car; a newer model light blue Toyota parked a few feet down from the window.

He frowned. Was he imagining it, or had he seen that same car behind him on the highway, just before he had turned onto the exit to Boe. He remembered it because the driver had crossed several lanes of highway at once. He shook his head. *I'm sure there are a lot of light blue Toyotas on the road, Hank.* But still he felt uneasy. He had a bad feeling about that car – so similar to the one he had seen on the highway – being parked outside the same hotel where he and Maddi were staying.

But even if he was right, and the person driving that Toyota was following him, what could Hank do? It wasn't like he and Maddi could just get in their car and lose the guy on the highway. The Peugeot had a flat tire and a broken taillight. They couldn't leave until the car was fixed. *And that can't happen until nine a.m.*

Suddenly, the driver side door of the Toyota opened and a man stepped onto the sidewalk. He stared up at the hotel. Hank quickly pulled back his head and let the curtain close. Who was he? Why was he staring at the hotel? *It's the middle of the night…in a town that shut down hours ago.* The hair on the back of his neck was standing straight up as he stared at the closed curtain. Something was wrong; he could feel it. He walked over and nudged Maddi. "We have to go…now."

Maddi came awake, but was groggy. "Did you fix the tire?"

Hank shook his head. "No. We'll have to improvise."

Maddi frowned, but didn't say a word as she rose from the bed and shuffled into the bathroom. A minute later she walked out and nodded. "Ready."

Hank grabbed their bags, then held her arm as he walked her out of the room. "Stay close to me. We'll need to go out the back."

Again, Maddi said nothing, simply nodding as she walked with Hank to the stairwell. They walked carefully down the stairs; Maddi's ankle was still stiff. They reached the ground floor and Hank held a finger to his mouth. He crept down the hall in search of a back door. He found it behind a storage room, and led Maddi down the hall and through the door into a very cold, very dark night.

She shivered and he instinctively put his arm around her. They circled around until they came to the alley where he had left the green Peugeot; it was still there, and the right back tire was now undeniably flat. He looked around for another prospect; another car to steal. A tan Saab was parked across the alley from it. He shook his head. *Too new…it will have GPS.* He spotted an older-model dark gray pickup truck about ten feet away. He walked Maddi to the truck, opened the door as quietly as he could, and helped her into the passenger seat. He closed the door, making sure not to slam it. He walked around the front of the truck and slid behind the wheel. Once again channeling cousin Barry's unique skills, he hotwired the truck.

"Where'd you learn to do that, Hank? I mean, you're really good at it," Maddi said with a grin. "I'm guessing they don't teach that at Homeland Security School."

He chuckled. "No, I have my cousin to thank."

Driving as slowly as he could, he eased from the lot to the alley behind the restaurant. He drove to the main road and turned left. He drove past the hotel and was able to see the man standing beside his Toyota. He was still staring up at the hotel. Hank continued to drive slowly along the main road. He could see the front of the Toyota in his rearview mirror, as well as a portion of the man who had been behind the wheel. He came to a stoplight and was forced to stop. The man didn't move.

He turned left onto a highway access road, quickly losing sight of both the car and the man who had been driving it. The highway was about a mile in front of him. As he drove to the exit, he fought the urge to gun the engine. Instead, he kept a slow twenty-kilometers-per-hour pace, never taking his eyes from his rearview mirror.

He eased onto the highway and picked up speed. As he drove toward Madrid, he tried to put the Toyota out of his mind. Maybe it was a coincidence. Or maybe it had been a different light blue Toyota. *There are probably a hundred light blue Toyota's on the road,* he thought with a nod. Besides, there was no way that someone could have followed him; he had been too careful. *Yes…it's just a coincidence.*

Then again, no one knew better than Hank, very few things in life were truly coincidences. He tried not to think of it as he and Maddi drove in silence on highway E41 toward their final destination.

* * *

Cobra stared at the sign that fronted the hotel. Something about the few missing lights caught his attention. He had seen a sign much like it years ago, when he had lived in Baclayon, outside Manila in the Philippines. Only then, instead of the missing letters causing the sign to spell only nonsense, the letters on the shop in Baclayon had gone from saying *Cutlery And Kilts,* to a sign that had said, *Cut_er__n _Kil__.* He laughed. He had felt it to be a command, and had followed through in what would become his own immutable style.

Nonetheless, the memory unsettled him. He didn't like to think of those days. For one thing, they had become confusing, as he was having a hard time figuring out which memories belonged to him, and which belonged to the child who had needed his help, Mark Villamor. Acting as the boy's savior had given them a closeness that often caused him to intertwine his memories with those of the boy. Either way, the memories were troubling. Mark Villamor had been abandoned, then abused at the hand of a brutal headmaster. Cobra had saved the boy, and, instead of gratitude for what he had done, he had been cast aside by the one man who had been responsible for all of it: Walter Henderson. He sneered, once again reminded of why he had driven all this way and invested all this energy: to kill Hank Clarkson, and thereby acquire a castle that should have been his in the first place.

He was pulled from his memories by the sound of an engine. It was three in the morning, and he had seen no evidence of anyone other than the few at the diner since he had arrived. He looked to his left and spotted a dark gray pickup truck driving away from him on the main street in town. Cobra tried to get a look at the driver; he couldn't...it was too dark. *Probably just one of the patrons at the diner.*

He was about to walk into the hotel, when he stopped. If Hank was at the hotel, then his Peugeot would be parked nearby. Cobra chuckled. *Perhaps I can sabotage it...just in case he tries to leave without me seeing him.* He crept around the back of the hotel, but was disappointed to see no green Peugeot. He walked to the other side, then crossed the street and walked down an alley, thinking maybe Hank had tried to hide the car. He found it a few minutes later, parked behind a dumpster in an alley behind the diner. He walked over to it, fully prepared to break a windshield or flatten a tire, but was pleased to see that it wouldn't be necessary; someone had beaten him to it. The right rear tire was nearly completely flat.

Cobra chuckled and walked back to the hotel. He now knew two things for certain: the first was that Hank was at the hotel. The second was that he couldn't get away quickly.

He strode through the front door of the hotel and spotted a clerk behind the counter. The old man was perched in front of a TV, unaware that Cobra had walked in. There was a row of numbered keys hanging from a corkboard next to the TV.

Cobra went up to the counter and cleared his throat.

The clerk looked over his shoulder and let out a sigh. He stood, stretched his arms, and grumbled in French. "Vous voulez une chambre ?" *You want a room?*

Cobra shook his head and showed the clerk the photo of Clarkson. The man narrowed his eyes. "Je ne révèle pas de détails concernant mes clients." *I don't reveal details regarding my customers.*

Cobra wasn't in the mood for obstinance, and he didn't have the time or the energy to go through his spiel about being a Swedish investment advisor. Instead, he grabbed the clerk by the collar, pulled out a gun he had picked up in Paris, and held it to the shaking man's temple. "où est-il?" *Where is he?*

The man stammered. "En haut. Chambre 65. J'ai une clé supplémentaire." *Upstairs. Room 65. I have an extra key.*

Cobra shoved the man backward, reached over and grabbed the key, then ran upstairs. He came to room 65 and grinned. He was close. Within minutes, he would kill Clarkson and be one step closer to claiming the Henderson castle as his own. With his gun raised and ready, he slid the key into the doorknob and silently opened the door. It took him only seconds to determine that the room was empty.

He felt the sheets; they were still warm. The bed had been slept in… and not long ago. But how had Hank left? His car was parked behind the diner with an obvious flat tire. Suddenly, Cobra remembered the gray pickup he had seen just minutes ago. "Dammit!" he said as he ran out of the room. He took the stairs two-at-a-time, then ran out the door of the hotel. He climbed into his Toyota, convinced beyond the shadow of a doubt that Hank Clarkson had been driving that truck, and that he was now less than ten minutes ahead of him.

CHAPTER 67

Nantucket, Massachusetts

Former Vice-President James Conner looked out at the sea as it crashed against his piece of the Nantucket coastline. He was troubled. He hadn't felt that way since leaving DC, and he didn't like it. *Why did you even come to me, Johnson?* But he knew the answer. *Because I'm the only one who can fix this.*

Less than an hour ago, Scott Johnson, Conner's former Secret Service agent, had pulled up to the mansion unannounced. For reasons that Conner wasn't aware of, Johnson had been let go from the Service soon after Conner had stepped down as VP, which meant that the man had needed to be vetted before even being allowed on the premises. Forty minutes later, Conner's butler had escorted the man into Conner's study. Johnson had waited for the butler to leave, and had then proceeded to share his suspicions that a top-level Pentagon aide by the name of Edward Morningstar had somehow been involved in a plot to bring down America.

"That's horseshit, Johnson!" Conner had said, adding, *"Morningstar's a lot of things, but a traitor to his country?"*

The agent had replied, *"I've been watching him, sir, and—"*

Conner had interrupted. *"Why have you been watching him?"*

Johnson had then made the statement that Conner couldn't get out of his head. *"Haven't you ever wondered, sir, why he was so adamant that you leave the Vice-Presidency when you did?"*

349

Conner couldn't deny it; the timing had been unsettling. Morningstar had more or less blackmailed Conner into leaving his role as VP and, within months, the President had been killed and the new VP, Jerome Knight, had taken over the job.

But Conner hadn't allowed himself to think too much about it. After all, Knight was a good man. It was unthinkable that he would involve himself – knowingly, at least – in a plot to gain power by having a U.S. President assassinated. Conner had concluded that it had simply been an unusual string of events which just happened to have benefitted Knight. Besides, Conner was glad to be rid of it all; he liked his new life away from DC. He hadn't missed – even for a moment – the grueling schedule of a reelection campaign, or the relentless hounding from the Press if he so much as sneezed when he wasn't supposed to. Yes, though Conner had been angered by the way in which he had been strong-armed out of his role as VP, he couldn't deny that it had worked out well for him.

But Johnson's assertion couldn't be ignored. Unemployed and motivated by the unexplained downfall of his protectee, Johnson had apparently spent the seven months since looking into the man who had so cavalierly removed Conner from his role in the Wilcox Administration. His conclusions were stunning …and improbable. Johnson claimed that he had discovered a secret email account belonging to a man who went by the name Levi. There were exchanges that suggested that Levi, acting under orders – Morningstar's? – had possibly falsified documents with the intent of pulling America into a war with Russia. Johnson admitted that Morningstar's name was nowhere on the email, but he was able to determine that Levi's account was indirectly linked to several of Morningstar's private accounts.

"That's not proof, Johnson," Conner had told him, to which the agent had replied, *"Maybe not, but it is one hell of a coincidence."*

Johnson had summarized what he had learned by saying that he felt certain that the same man who had forced Conner so unceremoniously from his role in the White House, had also taken steps to orchestrate a major war with Russia. Conner had listened, had laughed, and had then asked Johnson to leave.

But now, for whatever reason, he couldn't let it go. Though Morningstar was not above orchestrating a war or two – and no one knew that better than Conner – was he actually capable of throwing America into a world war? A war that could easily result in the destruction of mankind? *There is no way.* But Johnson's assertions had definitely piqued his interest. He needed to know more. And he needed something more convincing than a questionable email account that didn't have Morningstar's name anywhere on it. Morningstar could easily – and convincingly – argue that he knew nothing about the account...*even if he did.* More than once Conner had seen Morningstar clean up Pentagon scandals with the efficiency of a master, not caring how he did it or who he hurt, and never leaving even the slightest hint that he had been a part of it. *Which is why Johnson decided to come to me in the first place.* If the former agent hoped to take down Morningstar, he would need help...he would need the assistance of someone who was still close to power...he would need Jim Conner.

Conner sighed as he sipped his cognac and leaned back in his cushioned chair on the terrace of his Nantucket estate. The sun had set hours ago, and the moon reflected on the smooth water of Nantucket Sound, underpinning the quiet serenity of his life on the bay. He shook his head. *Why would I risk all of this to help an ex-Secret Service agent who might be full of shit?* That was the question he had been asking himself since Johnson had left. And, though he had nearly convinced himself to ignore Johnson's plea and go out to the patio and get in the hot tub with his wife, he couldn't let it go. He had never been one to fall on his sword, but the thought of a man like Morningstar ruining the country that Conner loved; well, he wasn't sure he could let that happen...not knowingly, at least.

He sipped his drink and frowned. He knew how Morningstar worked; if he thought anybody was on to him, he would try to scare them, and then, if that didn't work, he would have them killed. Conner had seen him do it more than once over the years. And, though at the time the victims had been rivals that he and Morningstar had shared, Conner suddenly shivered at the thought of becoming one of them.

Johnson had left over an hour ago. On his way out, he had said, *"This guy's a real ass, Conner, and you know I'm right."* Conner had said nothing. He had watched Johnson jog down the stairs to a waiting cab, and had then walked to the glassed-in veranda, where he had taken a seat in his favorite chair. He had been there ever since.

He looked out past a well-lit courtyard and stared at the majestic bay in the distance. He knew Johnson was right...he had known it for quite some time, if he was being honest with himself. He took another sip of cognac. But he had let it go, thinking that Morningstar was just one more corrupt bureaucrat. But a world war?

He shook his head and sighed. He would like to disregard it; let the bastard carry out his war games and do whatever he wanted to the country and the world. *As long as he leaves me alone.* But, he couldn't let it go. Conner hadn't always been a model citizen, but he was a loyal American. *"These colors don't run"* was etched in a plaque on the wall beside him, and, as he raised his glass to it, he vowed – as he had so many times over the past forty years – "I will live and die by those words."

He stared at the plaque, his heart heavy. His life was full; he enjoyed his slow, easy days and his alcohol-enhanced nights; he had no desire to change things. But the gauntlet had been handed off, and, though he didn't want it, it was now his. The minute Johnson had conveyed his suspicions, Conner knew they were valid. He had sat at the same table with Morningstar as they had arranged shady arms deals based on manufactured wars, and Morningstar had always seemed willing – almost eager – to take it a step further. Though the Bentley Group had been created with the goal of increasing America's influence in the world, it had also been formed with the worst of motives. The men who sat around that table in the Morgan Building's penthouse were crooked and greedy; it was their common bond. But they were also patriots who had grown tired of America's weakness on the world stage. It was the perfect combination to justify inciting wars, selling weapons, and raking in cash. But only Morningstar had ever shown a willingness to murder innocents for the sake of the cause. Conner wasn't sure what drove the man, but he didn't think it was money, and he knew for a fact that it wasn't patriotism. Morningstar wanted something far different from the Bentley Group. *He wants power.*

Conner pulled out a cigar and leaned back in his chair. *So, what do I do now?* To reveal Morningstar's motives could cause his own to come to light. After all, Conner wasn't innocent. He, too, had put lives at risk by fueling wars around the globe. But he had always had America's best interests at heart. The fact that he had made a mint from the exercises was simply one of those 'win-win' situations; the best kind. *Just let it go, Conner. Leave it for someone else to handle.*

Again, he stared at the plaque. *"These colors don't run."* Morningstar was plotting something that threatened America. Conner frowned. *How far are you willing to go, Morningstar?* He lit the cigar, listening as the waves hit the shore with unyielding force in the midst of high tide. He loved the sea; it was big and gruff like him, and more powerful than any army. *It doesn't bow to the whims of man.*

He would at least look into it. He swallowed the last of his cognac and was about to call to his wife for another, when, all at once, he thought better of it. He couldn't afford to get drunk. Not now; he had work to do. He had a country to save.

But what about his own crimes; the sins of his past? Perhaps he could find a way to bring down Morningstar without revealing the role that he, America's former VP, had played. It wasn't like any of the men who sat around that table in the Morgan Building would talk; they were too afraid. And Conner's former agents wouldn't talk; they were too loyal. The only man he had to fear was Morningstar himself.

He took a puff on the cigar and combed through his wild gray hair, crossing his thick legs in front of him. He adjusted his wool sweater over his oversized belly and stared out at the sea. His eyes flashed and he chuckled a bit uneasily as he said to no one in particular, "I never liked that prick anyway."

CHAPTER 68

Washington, DC

"Agent Foster, would you come in here, please?"

Knight had returned from Maine broken and depressed. He had gone to his desk in the Oval Office, had taken off his jacket, and hadn't moved from that spot for the past four hours. The faint glow from a single lamp was all he had allowed, letting the darkness command the room. Everything looked different...worse. Even the painting of George Washington was no longer an inspiration. Now when Knight looked at it, all he could think of was how George must have felt as he sacrificed everything for the sake of his country. What had he given up in order to oversee the birth of a nation? He frowned. *At least you got to stay with Martha, that much I know.*

He stared at a small note card, turning it over in his hands as the tall, fair Foster walked through the door. Foster's reassuring smile was firmly in place as he said, "Yes sir?"

"Have a seat."

"Yes sir." The man pulled a chair in front of the large oak desk and sat down, his legs squarely in front of him, his hands on his lap.

"Foster, I need your help."

"Certainly sir. Anything."

Knight leaned forward. "Here's the thing. What I'm about to ask of you is rather sensitive."

Foster narrowed his eyes. "I see, sir."

354

"I will need your full discretion. You can't speak of it to anyone...not even your supervisors." He paused. "Can you honor that request?"

The man hesitated, staring back at Knight. He nodded and said, "For you sir, I believe I can."

Knight nodded. "Good. What I'm about to ask of you will not threaten our nation's safety or its security in any way."

Foster shifted in the seat awkwardly. "That is certainly good to know, sir."

Knight looked intently at the young agent. "I need you to kidnap someone."

Foster's eyes widened. "Sir?"

Knight grinned. "Don't worry; I think she wants to be kidnapped." Foster nodded knowingly. "It's Ms. Cannon, isn't it, sir?"

Knight sighed. "Yes, and from now on we will refer to her only as Emma."

"Yes sir."

"You will need to take this message to her." Knight handed Foster the notecard that he had written just minutes ago. "Once she reads that note, I'm hopeful that she will agree to go with you. If she does, then you need to take her to someplace well-protected and safe, but off the radar. Do you know of such a place?"

Foster frowned and rubbed his forehead. "For how long, sir?"

Knight sighed. "I'm not sure. Hopefully, not too long. But it needs to be comfortable...just in case."

Foster nodded, saying nothing as he slowly massaged his forehead. All at once, his eyes lit up. "I know just the place, sir. The State Military Academy. I drove by it the other day when I was canvassing for your speech to the cadets at the Virginia Officers College. They had used the old Military Academy prior to moving to their new location." He frowned. "But no one has been there for quite some time, sir. It may be a bit rough."

Knight nodded. "Could you fix it up a bit?"

"Yes sir, I'm sure I could. How soon?"

"Very soon, Foster...within the next few hours." He paused. "Is it away from the mainstream? Off the grid, if you know what I mean?"

"Yes sir. It's about thirty miles from here, and there's only a single point of entry. It's well-protected with a security fence and a surveillance system."

Knight frowned. "A surveillance system?"

"Yes sir. But it's no longer in use. I think it's still operational, however, but I'll make sure that there is no outside access. I can even disable it completely, if you'd like, sir."

Knight leaned back and rubbed his chin. "Keep it on, but make it accessible only to you. Can you take care of it quickly, Foster?"

"Yes sir. Will she be at the same hotel where we picked her up earlier?"

"I'm hoping that she will be. Get the site ready first. Just the basics; we can do more to it later, if it becomes necessary. Then take one of the fighter jets and fly to the hotel in Maine. If she's there, hand her the note." He stood from behind the desk. "You need to do this alone, Foster. Can you do that?"

Foster nodded. "I'll request the rest of the night off, sir. Personal time."

"Good." Knight reached in his pocket, pulled out four hundred-dollar bills, and handed them to Foster. "Supply it with essentials. Food, water, a place to sleep."

Foster took the money. "How long do you think she'll be at the new site, sir?"

"As I said before, hopefully not for long."

"And then what, sir?"

Knight sighed. "I don't know, Foster, but one thing's certain. If Emma agrees to go with you, I will never leave her again."

CHAPTER 69

The Henderson Compound

Henderson had pressed Cravens hard before the two had retired for the night, but Cravens had offered little about what Hank had overhead that had compelled him to drive to the crash site. *"I don't know what he heard, he just showed up out of nowhere…and disappeared just as fast."* Cravens had insisted that it was far more important that they find the driver of the car that had come to the site after Hank. *"He's our ticket to understanding all of this."* He had then handed Henderson a scrap of paper on which he had written a partial license number for the car.

But the very notion that Hank had known of the crash before it had happened could mean only one thing: *the crash wasn't an accident.* The realization had been shocking. *"Dear God, Cravens…why haven't you told anyone?"*

The agent had sighed. *"Because I don't know who I can trust."*

Henderson could understand that, but was nevertheless stunned that Cravens hadn't shared his story with anyone. *"Have you at least tried to find Hank?"* he had asked. Cravens had shifted awkwardly in his chair, then had replied. *"Trust me, Henderson…Hank was as messed up about all this as anyone. I'm guessing wherever he went, he'll stay away until he's good and ready to face a life without Maddi."*

Henderson had then asked what he had felt to be the obvious follow up: *"Do you think there's any way that Hank could have been…involved? I mean, how else could he have known that the crash was going to happen?"*

357

Cravens had looked Henderson straight in the eye. *"There is no way that Hank was involved in that crash, Henderson. He learned whatever he learned too late to stop it, and now he must live with the consequences of that for the rest of his life."* He had added, *"We need to stay focused on the guy who was driving the second car."*

And that had been the end of it. Cravens had then asked to lay down. Henderson had put in a call to Dimitri to shut down the video feed from the den to the upstairs bedrooms, and had led Cravens to a guest room on the second floor. Once he had gotten Cravens settled in, he had walked down the hall to his own room and had tried to go to sleep. He had failed, unable to put the revelation out of his mind. *Someone killed Maddi...intentionally.*

Sometime after three a.m., he had called Dimitri, had had him once again kill the video feed, and had crept back down to the den. He had spent the hours since trying to connect what Claire had told him with what he had learned from Cravens. He had brought his backpack down with him, and about an hour ago, had pulled out his laptop. He had built a spreadsheet, listing Claire's information in columns, cross-referenced with the revelations from Cravens. At the end, he had typed what Claire had described as a hesitant comment from Maddi, that *"... none of it will matter unless a high-ranking Secret Service agent is assassinated."* Next to it he had written: *And then...he was.*

The only solid intersection between Claire's information and Cravens' revelations involved Hank: Maddi had wanted Claire to warn Hank about a secret committee, and Hank was the one who had overheard something that had compelled him to drive to the site of the plane crash...and then drive away and disappear for good. *What did you hear, Hank...and where did you go?*

Henderson closed the laptop and pulled a quilt over his shoulders as he stood and walked to the window. It was still dark, but the sun would rise soon. He sighed. *Maybe daybreak will shine some light on this mess.*

He looked over his shoulder at the fire; it had faded to embers. He walked over, picked up a log from a nearby stack, and tossed it on the cinders. He stoked the logs, staring at the flames as they started to rise. *And how is Morningstar involved in all of this?* Claire had said his name, but that was about it.

He stood there another few minutes, then went back to the couch. He opened his laptop and stared at the spreadsheet. Cravens was right. The only man – other than Hank – who could shed light on the events surrounding the crash, was the driver who had followed Hank to the site in a Henderson car. He nodded. *The driver is the key.*

He checked his watch. It was six-twenty. Jacques, the man in charge of the garage, came in at seven. Though Jacques could certainly tell him about the driver, Henderson couldn't reveal his identity to Jacques; Matt Henderson was a wanted man. And Jacques would have no reason to confide in the stranger, Aiden Balkus. *So, I'll have to find the information I'm looking for in the garage ledgers before Jacques gets here.* Which meant that he had less than forty minutes to find what he needed.

He called down to Dimitri, whose shift was about to end. "Dimitri, before you go, could you kill the feed to the garage?"

"Certainly, sir. Ivor is coming in at seven to take my place. Shall I make him aware of the situation, sir?"

Henderson thought about it. The last thing he needed was another staffer knowing he was there. "No. This should be my last request."

There was a pause. "How about if I stay until noon, sir. I'm not all that tired, and I'm not scheduled to work tonight. Will that be helpful?"

Henderson sighed with relief. "Yes, thank you, Dimitri."

He stood and walked to the door, waiting until Dimitri had had time to kill the video feed. Making sure that no one was in the hall, he stole to the garage. He listened at the door, then slid inside and walked to a center office. He went to the desk and rifled through drawers until he found what he needed: the logbooks that had been signed by the drivers. He pulled out the one for August and set it on the desk. He spotted a row of ledgers on a nearby shelf. Tall, thin books the size of journals were standing upright, categorized by the month of the year. He grabbed the ledger for August and opened it. It showed entries for each day of the month. He thumbed to the day in question; August 26th. He pulled out the scrap of paper with the partial license plate number that Cravens had given him, then skimmed the list until he found a number that fit. He opened the logbook and looked for the name of the driver who had been assigned to the car. On that particular day, it had been a man named Carlos DeMarco. He skimmed the logbook, looking for other names that may have been assigned to that same car on the day in question. There was only DeMarco's.

He pulled out his phone and dialed Dimitri.

The man answered with a crisp, "Yes sir?"

"Dimitri, for reasons I can't go into, I need to see biographies of each of the drivers. I promise you that what I'm doing is for the good of this estate. Are you comfortable getting me that information?"

There was a pause. "Certainly, sir. The biographies are on a flash-drive." He paused. "Where would you like me to bring it?"

"Set it in on the table in the den." He paused. "Thank you, Dimitri… and, again, keep it to yourself."

"Of course, sir."

He grabbed the logbook and the August ledger, and carried both to the den. He was glad to see a flash-drive sitting on the table. He checked the time. *Six-forty-five…I need to hurry.* He plugged the flash-drive into his laptop, waited for it to load, then scrolled to the letter D. He found Carlos DeMarco and read the biography. The twenty-seven-year-old had started out in America, but had come to Latvia when he was five. His mother was from Latvia, and they had come back so she could be with her father, who was ill. According to the summary, DeMarco had worked for the Hendersons for the past two years. A photo showed him to be black, and he wore glasses. He spoke three languages, and was listed as six feet tall. His time at the estate had been unremarkable. Henderson stared at the photo. He didn't recognize him.

He skimmed the rest of the names, pulling up photos of each one. There were ten in all, but not one of them was black except for DeMarco…*which should make him memorable to anyone who uses the drivers on a day-to-day basis…like Walter.*

He opened the ledger to see the locations where the car assigned to DeMarco had been driven on August 26th. The crash had occurred at around seven-thirty, which meant that the car would have left the compound sometime after six. He checked listings for the evening of August 26th. Four vehicles had been checked out after six. Two went to Uzava, one to Ventspils, and a fourth went to Riga. All heading north or east; not one going anywhere near Liepaja, where the crash had taken place. But the license plate that Cravens had written down confirmed that someone from the estate had been there. Which could mean only one thing: the driver hadn't logged the trip.

He pulled out his phone and dialed Security. "It's me again, Dimitri. I need the video feed for August that covers the garage exit and the surrounding area."

Within five minutes, Dimitri had brought another flash-drive to the den.

"Thank you," he said as Dimitri handed him the disc. "Remember, Dimitri –"

"I know, sir. I'll keep it to myself." He was about to walk out when he stopped. "You look so much like him, sir…so much like…Martin."

Henderson offered a weak smile, then waited for him to leave. He combed his fingers through his hair; the hair that looked so much like Martin Henderson's.

He plugged the flash-drive into his laptop. He opened it and went immediately to August 26th, slowing the feed as he reached the hours after six p.m. The angle of the camera allowed him to see only the last four numbers of a license plate. He hoped it was enough. He waited; no car had left the garage between six and seven. He kept going. He saw a car leaving at 7:03 and froze the screen. The numbers he could see matched what Cravens had given him, and, though he was unable to get a good look at the driver's face, he could tell that the man was black. There was no question now…*Carlos DeMarco drove that car to the crash site.* Had he been the man who Hank had overheard? He frowned. Hank had gotten to the site *before* the man driving that car. But so far, anyway, no car had left the compound after six p.m. except for DeMarco. *So, where is Hank?* He resumed the tape. Within a minute or two, he saw another car leave the garage. Henderson checked the log. That car wasn't listed. He played back the video and froze the screen. He wrote down what he could see of the license number. He went to the ledger. The car had been assigned to a Carlis Jansons. He clicked to the biographies he had gotten earlier and looked for a photo of Carlis. The man had a long, thin face, with shoulder-length blonde hair…*he shouldn't be too hard to spot.* He went back to the video feed, adjusting the resolution to try to make out the driver's face. *Is that you, Carlis?* The image still wasn't clear; he enlarged it.

He sat back, stunned as it came into view. There was no long face, no blonde hair. The man driving that car had dark curly hair, broad shoulders, and was wearing a regular jacket instead of the formal suitcoat worn by the drivers. Even with the poor resolution, Henderson recognized him. Hank Clarkson had *followed* DeMarco to the scene of the crash. But Cravens was adamant that Hank had come and gone *before* DeMarco arrived on the scene. Though Hank had left the estate after DeMarco, somehow he had beaten DeMarco to the crash site. There was only one route to Liepaja…only one road on which both DeMarco and Hank could have driven to the site. Had DeMarco stopped somewhere along the way? If so, why? Did it matter? He shook his head. *No, not really.* Regardless of the sequence of events, or the timing of DeMarco's arrival, Hank had known exactly where to go, and that he needed to get there in a hurry. *Hank knew all of it…and he hasn't bothered to tell a single soul.*

CHAPTER 70

Outside Camden, Maine

What time is it? Emma looked at a clock by the bed. *Three a.m.* She was at the same hotel, taken back there after the trip to the mountaintop. She had walked in the door and had immediately crawled under the covers. She hadn't left the bed, except to use the bathroom and get a glass of water, and she hadn't slept a wink. She had lost Romer once again. But this time was different; this time, she knew...*he didn't want to go.* So, she would do whatever she could to get him back. Regardless of what it took or how much she would need to give up, Emma had made up her mind. *I'm done with the lies of the past sixteen years.* She would either have Romer, or she would be alone; no other option made sense.

But what about Michael...what about Galina; what would happen to them? *They'll be fine...they'll hate me, but they'll be fine.* Galina would eventually forgive her; or at least she hoped so. *But what about Michael?* He had been her companion for a decade-and-a-half. They had weathered the loves and losses of Galina's far too brief childhood; they had gone through the changes in themselves. She loved him; just not enough. And, though she had done it for the past fifteen years, she could do it no longer; her eyes had been opened. *It's one thing to fool yourself when there's nothing to tell you any different...it's quite another to do it when the truth is staring you in the face.* The truth had looked her in the eye and she had been overwhelmed by it. The minute she had laid her head on Romer's shoulder – the instant she had felt his heartbeat – she had known: *I belong with this man.*

A sudden knock on the door made her sit up, her eyes wide, her heart racing. *Who would come here at this hour?* She reached over to turn on the lamp, but at the last minute, decided against it. She slid out of bed and threw on her robe. She walked to the window and slid the curtain a half-inch. Her eyes widened. Standing there in an overcoat with his cap pulled low over his forehead, was the agent from the mountaintop. *It's Foster. Something's happened to Romer!* She walked to the door and opened it. The agent immediately stepped in and closed the door. She reached for the light switch; he grabbed her hand. "No! Keep it dark."

Emma was frightened. "Why?"

"I think you're being watched."

Emma had begun to shake. "Wh—why would someone…watch me?"

"I don't know, Ma'am, but it's best we take precautions."

"What are you doing here?"

"I'm here on behalf of the President. He has asked that I give you this."

Foster handed her a notecard; she tore it open. She held it up to the window to take advantage of a nearby lamppost. The handwriting was familiar…after sixteen years it had changed, but not so much that she didn't recognize it.

"If you are so inclined, I would like for you to go with the agent who brought you this note. I trust him; you can trust him. Speak of this to no one. If you choose not to come, I will understand. I hope and pray I will see you soon. Love, Romer."

Emma stumbled to the bed, holding the note to her chest. Tears rolled down her cheeks…Romer was asking her to come to him. She looked up at Foster and smiled. "Just give me a minute to pack."

* * *

Emmett Wilson was bored. Though he hadn't questioned Morningstar's order to fly to Maine and keep an eye on the woman who had been taken from the mountain after her rendezvous with the President, he was starting to feel more like a lackey than a Secret Service agent. *I'm too qualified to just sit in this rental car and stare at a dark window,* he thought, as he took another sip of lukewarm coffee.

Though Morningstar had described the woman as a spy, Emmett had seen little to suggest that she was of much importance. *I mean this hotel is practically a Motel 6,* he thought as he stared at the window. But he didn't have the option of ignoring Morningstar's instructions. After all, he had been dismissed from the Secret Service. If he ever hoped to regain some semblance of respect, he would need to have the blessing of the Pentagon aide.

But if the bitch in that hotel room doesn't do something soon, I might just have to go upstairs and make her. Otherwise, I'm gonna' die of boredom. He laughed. *"Former Secret Service agent found dead in rental car. Suspected culprit: Boredom."*

He was about to light his fifth cigarette, when he noticed a dark figure hurrying toward the hotel. He checked his watch. *Three a.m....pretty late for a guest.* He looked up at the window of room 214, the room where Emma Cannon had checked in the day before, waiting to see if a light came on. There was nothing. After five minutes or so of staring at the dark window, he looked away. *Just a middle-of-the-night traveler.* He lit the cigarette, took a long, slow drag, and let it out with a sigh. He reached down and turned the radio on low, fidgeting with the dial until he found a station that played eighties music. He heard the familiar opening from Phil Collins' "In the Air Tonight," closed his eyes, and readied his hands for the classic roll of the drums. As he used the dashboard of the black Explorer to tap out the rhythm, he failed to notice a man and woman steal quietly out the back of the hotel, sneak down the street, and disappear into a black sedan.

CHAPTER 71

The Henderson Compound

Henderson had returned the logbook and the ledger to the office just minutes before Jacques had walked into the garage. He had run back to the den and had spent the next hour trying to put it all together. Somehow, Hank had left the estate after DeMarco, but had gotten to the crash site before him. Which meant that Hank hadn't only known that the crash was about to happen, but he had known exactly where to go. Which made Henderson even more curious why Cravens was so nonchalant about Hank. Yes, DeMarco would be worth talking to, but it seemed that most of the answers lay with Hank.

Cravens called from his upstairs bedroom around ten. Henderson had Dimitri cut the feed from upstairs to the den, then asked if he would round them up something to eat. After making sure the stairs and hallway were clear, Henderson called Cravens and told him to come to the den. Thirty minutes later, as they dined on steak and eggs, Henderson told Cravens what he had learned about Carlos DeMarco. He said nothing about his discovery that, even though Hank had left after DeMarco, he had arrived at the site before him. That would come later.

"So, the guy that drove the car to the crash site was named Carlos DeMarco?"

Henderson nodded. He had had Dimitri print out DeMarco's photo, and, as Cravens was taking his last bite of eggs, Henderson slid the photo over to him. "Do you recognize him?"

Cravens stared at the photo and shook his head. "That's not the guy I saw."

Henderson frowned. "It has to be. DeMarco signed out the car, and I saw him on video leaving the compound half-an-hour before the crash. He has to be our guy."

Cravens shook his head. "I'm telling you, that isn't the guy who came to the crash site." He looked at Henderson and sighed. "Do you feel like taking a walk?"

Henderson nodded, hiding a grin. *Cravens needs a smoke.* He pulled out his phone. "Dimitri, we're going for a walk out back. Can you turn off the feed to the hallway, as well as the cameras outside the north entrance?"

"Not a problem, sir."

Henderson took their coats from the closet and they put them on. He checked to make sure the hallway was clear, then they walked out the same door they had come in the night before. It was a cold, crisp morning, and they both hiked their collars as they hurried from the castle. When they were a safe distance away, Cravens pulled a cigarette from his pocket. "You want one?" Henderson shook his head. Cravens lit it and took a puff. "Here's what I know. In spite of what you saw on that video feed, the man who drove the Henderson car to the crash site wasn't Carlos DeMarco. Which means, whoever he is, it's quite likely that he killed DeMarco in order to take his place."

Henderson narrowed his eyes. "If you're one hundred percent sure it isn't him, then you're probably right." He frowned. "So, who is he?"

Cravens nodded. "That's the question, isn't it?" He took another drag on his cigarette, then turned to Henderson. "I know you're concerned about Hank's role in all of this," he shook his head, "...but I'm telling you, it's not important. Hank was devastated by the crash. He left with hardly a word, and I haven't heard from him since." He took another drag on the cigarette. "What's important is that the plane crash wasn't an accident, and that the driver pretending to be DeMarco knows who's behind it." He took another drag. "So, who might want to deliberately crash a plane?"

Henderson rubbed his chin and frowned. "My money would be on the guy who has been trying to kill Maddi for the past year."

Cravens nodded, but said nothing, still puffing his cigarette as he looked to the sea.

Henderson shook his head. "But how would he do it? I mean, he would have had to have done something to the plane before it took off." He frowned. "How on earth would someone be able to sabotage an RAF plane?"

Cravens turned to look at him. "That's what I've been trying to figure out for the past two months, Henderson."

CHAPTER 72

Washington, DC

Morningstar frowned as a Bergamo clock chimed the hour. *Three a.m.* The expensive clock had been a gift from General Daniels to mark twenty-five years of service. He stared at it now as he stifled a yawn. *You're welcome, General.*

He had come to his office, unable to sleep after the debacle with Judah and the Russian woman, Emma Melnikov. He sat at his desk and stared out the window at the darkness, sneering as he said the name aloud. "Melnikov...you can't get any more Russian than that."

He cracked his knuckles as he stood and paced the room. *I need to fix this...for good,* he thought. He had come too far to let Judah's foolish infatuation with a Russian émigré disrupt what he had so carefully orchestrated. Madison was out of his hair, both Henderson and Clarkson soon would be, and his latest addition, Issachar – the Philly cop, Todd Jackson – had brilliantly inspired a slew of random shootings and an attempted coup that had made America's citizens practically beg for their President to rid the country of guns. *Now...if only Judah can keep his pants zipped long enough for me put the final piece of this plan into place!*

He pulled out a cigar, ignoring the Pentagon's no-smoking policy as he lit it and put his feet on his desk. He was blowing a smoke ring when his private cellphone rang. *Who the hell would be calling me at this hour?* "Yes?"

"Jacob, it's Levi. I found the info you wanted on the Chinese officer."

"What the hell are you doing at work so early, Levi?"

There was a pause. "Uh...I couldn't sleep, sir."

Morningstar grinned. *He's trying to make up for not getting me that tape recorder.* "The Chinese Officer...you're referring to Lin Chu?"

"Yes sir."

"What can you tell me about him, son?"

"Well, sir, as you know, the man keeps a low profile."

Morningstar yawned. "Tell me something I don't know, Levi."

There was a pause. "The man has a child; a son. His name is Tai Chu."

Morningstar's eyes widened. That was a surprise. He wasn't aware that Lin Chu had a son. He took another drag on his cigar as he considered it. "You know, Levi, Tai Chu could prove to be useful to us. It's often easier to gain leverage over a man if you can gain leverage over his son." He nodded. "As a matter of fact, getting rid of Tai Chu might prove to be more valuable than removing Lin Chu."

Levi cleared his throat. "Um, here's the thing, sir. The son, Tai Chu, just like his dad, is pretty high up in the Chinese hierarchy." A pause. "He is actually the deputy chairman of China's Communist Military Commission."

Morningstar whistled. "Impressive. Then again, not all that surprising when you consider that his father pretty much oversees the entire Chinese military." He puffed the cigar. "Once I work things out with Dan, we'll be ready to move on it. In the meantime, find out Tai Chu's plans for the next week or so, as well as his father's."

Another pause. "Um, sir?"

"Jesus, Levi! What is it?"

"Tai Chu isn't exactly who you think he is."

"What do you mean?"

"He's white, sir...and he's thirty-three years old." A pause. "I think he might be Sturgill's kidnapped son."

CHAPTER 73

Ocaña, Spain

"Salir del coche!"

Hank tried to remember his Spanish. Actually, no translation was necessary, as the officer was practically pulling Hank from the gray pickup truck.

"Salir!"

Hank had begun to shake. He looked at Maddi and whispered, "Keep your head down, Mad—Flora."

He stepped out and put both hands against the truck. The sun had just climbed above the tree line, and shadows were hiding the officer's face. Hank swallowed as he looked over his shoulder and said, "What seems to be the trouble, Officer?"

The slight, dark-skinned policeman looked at Hank and glared. "You speak English, eh?"

Hank nodded. "Yes. I'm from the United States. What have I done?"

The officer narrowed his eyes. "I need to see your passport."

Hank reached into the truck and over the dash to the glove box. He grabbed the same passports that had gotten them through the borders of Poland, Germany, France, and Spain, and handed them to the officer. "Here you go, sir." He then told the same story he had told the officer who had stopped him outside Bergerac. "My wife is sick. I'm driving her to my friend's house outside Ocaña. He's a doctor."

The man looked past Hank to the passenger seat. Hank could feel his heart pounding as he watched the man look at the passport, then at Maddi, whose head was turned away from them, her dyed brown hair covering her face. The story was far-fetched, but it had worked in France; the mention of illness seemed to lessen the urge for an officer to take a closer look at the woman traveling with him. With impeccable timing, Maddi groaned, and the man flinched. "What's wrong with her?"

Hank shook his head. "I don't know. She's been vomiting and she's getting weaker by the hour. She has spots on her arms and legs; I'm afraid it's contagious."

The man stepped back quickly. "She should be...how you say... *cuarentena!*"

Hank panicked. "Yes...yes, my doctor friend is planning on doing that...once we get to his home, where he can take care of her."

The man shook his head. "It should have already been done."

Hank nodded. "It seemed like nothing when it started, sir." He paused. "It's gotten worse in the last several hours."

The officer frowned. "Okay. You were driving way too fast. I let you go, but slow down." He glared at Hank and, with one hand on his pistol, he said, "Find el doctor...and *cuarentena la señorita.* I will be watching, Senor."

Hank swallowed. "Th...thank you, Officer." The officer walked back to his car, and Hank slid behind the wheel of the truck. His hands were shaking as he fastened his seat belt and turned on the engine. He pulled out slowly, careful to not break any laws as he merged with the downtown traffic. The speed limit was listed as 90 kilometers. Hank had been going closer to 120. He rubbed his forehead as he thought of how close he had come to once again blowing the whole thing. *First, the broken taillight, and now this.*

He drove the speed limit and it felt like he was crawling. He watched the officer several cars behind him. He couldn't let him follow him to Angelo's home; Hank felt certain that Cravens' friend didn't want the police at his door.

Hank had called Angelo just two hours ago from a payphone and had gotten his address. *"8 Dingo Pass...about a kilometer south of town."* Hank had tried to find it on his map; the closest he had come was 3 Dingo

Pass, which they had just driven past. It was a rundown bait and tackle shop. *Where the hell is number eight?*

He continued to watch the officer in his rearview mirror, deciding that, if the man didn't turn around soon, Hank would simply keep going until he reached the highway. He didn't want to compromise the only man who could help them. And there was no question that they needed Angelo's help...badly. This was the second time they had been stopped by the police. It was only a matter of time before one of them was identified. Either Angelo helped them in the next few hours, or Hank would be forced to tell the world the truth. He cringed as he tried to imagine the fall-out from such a revelation. *"Homeland Security Deputy, Hank Clarkson, hides a well-known senator – presumed dead – in the back of a stolen vehicle for months..."*

He reached the south end of the village and slowed as he made a turn onto a narrow side road. He waited to see if the police car would slow as well, and was relieved when the officer pulled into a café parking lot. Hank drove on, took a left at the next turn, then another left, and followed the road for nearly a mile. He was looking for La Espana, a road which, according to his map, should take him to Dingo Pass from the opposite direction. He drove another few minutes, but couldn't find a street sign for La Espana. He was about to turn around, when he spotted a battered sign hidden among overgrown brush, with the words "La Espana" etched faintly in the wood. He frowned as he stared at the road beyond. It was little more than a trail of gravel dust with tufts of grass and weeds. He shifted into low gear and turned onto the road.

Suddenly he heard a chuckle. He looked over at Maddi. She had her head propped against the door and his heart broke. She looked terrible; her face was thin, her hair was limp and stringy. Her eyes – normally a bright blue, looked dull and gray. But she was smiling, and it almost made up for it. "What's so funny?" he asked.

She laughed again, the eyes showing a trace of who she used to be. "You're doing your damnedest to keep me safe, even sacrificing your own happiness. You're faking your way through checkpoints, in and out of gas stations and cafes, and you've stolen four cars now, though, amazingly, no one seems to have caught on. After all that, you're gonna get us busted because you have a lead foot."

She laughed again, louder, and Hank couldn't help himself; he, too, burst out laughing. As the late morning sunlight crept through the trees, Hank and Maddi shared the first bit of laughter they had known in months. In spite of all that had happened and all that remained ahead of them, Hank felt something he hadn't felt in quite a long while...joy.

CHAPTER 74

The Henderson Compound

Henderson was finding it hard to look at Cravens and not be angry that he had told no one that the plane crash had been deliberate. He had known it for over two months, and had yet to share it with anyone other than Henderson. Which meant that a full nine weeks had gone by with no one doing more than a routine investigation into the crash. He also found it unsettling that Cravens was so willing to dismiss Hank's involvement in the timeline of events. But Henderson had said nothing more about it. Cravens had made it clear that Hank was pretty much off limits.

After a quick call to Dimitri, they had walked back inside to the den. They had been there for over an hour, but little more had been said. The only new information Cravens had shared was that before their RAF plane had left Heathrow, it had been delayed due to some sort of mechanical issue. Had the mechanics that had worked on the plane somehow been compromised? That had to be the case, though neither Cravens nor Henderson could understand how. Any mechanic permitted to work on an RAF plane would have been carefully vetted.

"Is there any way to get their names?" Henderson asked.

Cravens frowned. "Only if we're willing to tell someone why we're asking."

Henderson nodded. "Which leaves us with only one option."

"What's that?"

"We need to pull in Walter."

Cravens narrowed his eyes. "Why? What can Walter do?"

"Well, for one thing, he can get a list of Heathrow mechanics who've received that sort of clearance. He can claim he needs it for an upcoming visit to the UK. We can work backward from there." He paused. "As for the driver of the car that showed up at the crash site, Walter has likely seen, and maybe even talked to the man."

Cravens seemed to consider it, then fervently shook his head. "No, we can't."

Henderson bristled. "Why are you so nervous for someone else to learn that the crash wasn't an accident?"

Cravens sat back in his chair. "Because the more people we tell, the more likely the killer will learn that he didn't get away with it...and will go into hiding."

Henderson considered it. Though he saw the logic, he felt it to be weak. "Walter is remarkably trustworthy. He won't tell a soul if we ask him not to."

Cravens sighed, then looked at Henderson. "On one condition."

"What?"

He hesitated. "That we say nothing about Hank."

Henderson was beside himself. *Why is he so adamant to protect Hank... and what is he protecting him from?* He shook his head and sighed. "Whatever you say."

Cravens nodded. "Thank you." He hesitated. "Um...by the way, I have something I need to give to Walter. Something I need to return to him."

Henderson frowned. "What is it?"

"I'd prefer not to say until I can hand it to him personally."

"Okay. Where is it?"

"In a locker at a bus station in Liepaja." Cravens pulled a key from his pocket.

Henderson's eyes widened. "You're wanting us to go to Liepaja... *now?*"

Cravens shifted awkwardly. "I think we should. I've had...the item... longer than I should have." He sighed. "This would be a perfect time for me to return it."

Henderson considered it, then nodded his head slowly. "Okay." He called Dimitri. "I need one more favor, Dimitri. I know you agreed to stay until noon, which I appreciate. I wonder if just before you leave, you could kill the video feed to the north entrance one more time, then maybe give us a ride to Liepaja?"

"Certainly, sir. That will work out well. I have business in nearby Grobina."

"Perfect. Pull your car to the front of the drive and wait for us by the gate." He ended the call, then turned to Cravens. "We'll leave here in about thirty minutes." He sat back and sighed. "You're not going to tell me what you're returning to Walter, are you?"

Cravens shook his head. "You'll know soon enough." He hesitated. "But it does present a bit of a problem."

Henderson frowned. "Why?"

Cravens let out a sigh. "Well, what I'm giving back to him involves a secret…a secret that I'm not supposed to know."

Henderson looked at him and, after a few seconds, he laughed. "It seems to me, Cravens, your whole life is filled with secrets that you're not supposed to know."

Cravens chuckled. "Yes, I guess that's true." He let out another sigh. "Speaking of which, I wonder if your dad will let us talk to that driver."

Henderson shook his head. "I checked the logbook; the guy's gone, Cravens." He sighed. "Just like Hank, he hasn't been seen since the night of the plane crash."

CHAPTER 75

Washington, DC

Charles Sturgill rubbed his eyes and glared at the ringing phone. *Who the hell is calling me at 4:30 in the morning?* He answered. "What!"

"Charles, it's Edward Morningstar."

"This better be good, Morningstar. I was asleep. Don't you ever sleep?"

"I think what I'm about to tell you will be worth losing a little sleep over."

Charles pulled himself to the side of the bed. His wife, Beatrice slept in the guest room. They hadn't shared a bedroom for years, her not wanting to listen to him snore, and him not wanting her next to him at all. "I'm listening."

"After twenty-eight years, I cannot only verify that Lin Chu played a role in your son's kidnapping, but I know the secret address of his home outside Beijing."

Charles' heart was racing. How long had he waited for this moment? For nearly three decades he had used every resource available to learn the truth about who had taken Jamey. Now, not only had he uncovered the name of a possible second kidnapper, but – through Morningstar – he had proof that that man had, in fact, been involved. To top it off, Morningstar had located the man's home address. *It took a conniving Pentagon aide to finally find the bastard.* "You've found Lin Chu?"

"Yes."

"Where is he?"

"Not so fast, Charles," he paused, "…we need to come up with a strategy."

"A strategy?"

"Yes." A pause. "As you know, Charles, the first kidnapper, Pyong Pang, is dead. But just so I'm totally up front with you, the guy left behind a wife and daughter." He paused. "We've found them, but I think we should leave them alone."

Charles frowned. *Are you kidding me? Pyong Pang took Jamey away from me and killed him.* "With all due respect, Morningstar, that's not your call."

There was a sigh. "Charles, we have only so much capital to expend on this vendetta of yours." He paused. "The second man, Lin Chu, also has a child…a son."

Charle's eyes lit up. "Even better. The children must pay for their fathers' sins. We will torture the daughter *and* the son…in front of the two fathers. Can you make it happen?"

"I can, Charles, but there's something you need to know before we do this."

"I can't think of a damned thing that would make me change my mind."

Another pause. "What if I were to tell you that Lin Chu's son, Tai, is white, and is now thirty-three years old."

Charles stared at the phone. He threw it on the bed and ran to the window, throwing it open as he gasped for air. He took a few quick breaths, then stumbled back to the bed. His legs were shaking; he rubbed his thighs to get them to stop. He stared up at the photo on the wall of him and his son, taken just before they left for that mission trip twenty-eight years ago. *Can it be? Is Jamey alive?*

"Charles? Are you still there?"

Charles picked up the phone. "Y—yes, I'm here."

"What do you want us to do? It's your call. I'm a man of my word and I will handle this however you like."

Charles shifted on the bed. Was the white man Jamey? *He has to be.* And Charles knew exactly how – and why – it had happened. Because of the high regard the Chinese placed on pale skin, and because of Jamey's Chinese ancestry, Lin Chu had seen in Jamey the perfect successor. What better future military leader than a white man whom they could claim was Chinese. Jamey hadn't been kidnapped to trade or kill, he had been kidnapped to be groomed for power. *Much like Knight,* came a thought out of nowhere.

Charles swallowed. He needed to see him. *But it's been almost thirty years!* He wrestled with a crease in his pajamas. Would Jamey even recognize him?

"Charles?"

He sighed. "I…I want…to see him…then I'll decide what to do."

"I guessed you would say that. There's only one problem. The father, Lin Chu is essential to a…uh…covert mission…that is currently being undertaken by the Pentagon. We're involved in trying to – how shall I say it? – reprogram him."

Charles frowned. He held the phone close as he said, "You're going to kill him, aren't you?"

A pause. "I'm hoping it won't be necessary. We just want to get him to alter the direction he's taking with China's military. Now that we know he has a son, it might be easier to use the son, Tai Chu, to convince him to rethink his aggressive posture." Another pause. "Would you like me to have Tai Chu brought to DC?"

"No. Don't you lay a hand on either him or his father…not yet, anyway." Charles rubbed the back of his neck. "I need to go to China."

"Why?"

"Because I need to see him…there." He closed his eyes; he was shaking.

He heard a sigh. "That complicates things a bit." A long silence, followed by a deeper sigh. "Here's what I'll do. I'll arrange the trip, but you will need an escort."

"Why would I need an escort?"

"Because, Charles, you're going into unfriendly territory, you're emotional, and your goal is to meet personally with a Chinese military leader's son."

"That boy is *my* son!" Charles yelled. He lowered his voice. "He's *my* son, Morningstar, and I don't need an *escort* to protect me while I meet my own son!" Suddenly it occurred to him…not only would he come face to face with his son, but he would likely come face to face with the man who took him. He rubbed his chin. "On second thought, I'll take you up on your offer. But I need this escort to be well-trained and off the grid, if you catch my drift. I'm a senator going to China on a fact-finding mission. My 'escort' is just a reliable man with a reliable weapon. Got it?"

There was a pause. "Yes, I believe I do." Another pause. "I'll have the man meet you in your senate office Saturday morning at 8:00 o'clock sharp. He'll pose as Secret Service and accompany you on your journey. Is that acceptable?"

"Yes, that sounds good. How will I know him?"

Another pause. "He'll have a nickname. He'll refer to himself as Viper."

CHAPTER 76

Ocaña, Spain

The small house – which was more of a shed – looked as if it had sat idle for the past several years, and Hank wondered if he had the right place. There were weeds covering the flower beds, and the grass was brown and patchy. He pulled a scrap of paper from his pocket and double-checked the address that Angelo had given him over the phone: 8 Dingo Pass. It matched what was written on a rusted mailbox that sat on a post by the road, and he pulled into a dirt driveway and stopped the truck. He looked at Maddi. "I'll go in first."

She nodded.

Not for the first time in their long journey, Hank wished he had his gun…the gun he had used to shoot the tire of the Henderson driver who had been on his way to kill Maddi. But Hank had tossed the gun soon after leaving the crash site, afraid that if he was stopped, the gun would create the need for an investigation.

He stepped out of the car, glad for the comfortable sixty degrees after the cold, damp air of northern Europe. He walked cautiously to the front of the old house and knocked three times on a faded wood door that was barely hanging on its hinges. He stepped back, scanning the area for signs of life. There was nothing; no cars, no toys, no pets. The place looked and felt deserted. Hank tensed at the sound of footsteps. The door opened about three inches, and an old man with leathered skin and long gray hair eyed him with a frown. He glared at Hank through a pair of scratched lenses, his forehead lined with wrinkles from years spent in the sun. "Quien està?"

Hank swallowed nervously. "No hablo Español."

The man bristled. "English?"

Hank nodded.

"What you want?"

"Um, I'm looking for Angelo. My name is Hank. He and I spoke earlier."

The man narrowed his eyes. "Who send you?"

"Tom Cravens."

He grabbed Hank by the arm and pulled him inside, then closed and locked the door. "Is she with you?"

"Yes, in the truck."

"Get her."

"Is it safe?"

The man yanked off his glasses. His gray eyes were cold as steel. "Get her!"

Hank tried to open the door, forgetting that the man had locked it. He fumbled with the bolt and threw open the door. He ran to the pickup truck and opened the passenger-side door. His heart stopped; Maddi wasn't there. He was about to yell for her when he heard her familiar laugh. "Relax, Hank. I just needed some air."

She was behind him, standing awkwardly, most of her weight on the ankle that hadn't been injured. Her coat was blowing in the wind, her dyed-brown hair flowing behind her. She was thin, almost haggard, but when she smiled, she looked like Maddi, and it broke his heart.

He frowned. "We need to get inside. Now." He walked over and gently took her arm. He walked her to the door and knocked. Angelo opened it and pulled them both inside. Again, he locked it, then whisked Maddi to what looked like a closet in the corner of the one-room shack. He switched on a light, and Hank could see a sink, a toilet, and a mirror on the wall. There was hair dye and scissors sitting on a small countertop, and a long skirt and a blouse were hanging from a hook by the mirror. He was able to see what looked like the brim of a hat on the floor behind the door.

"Hurry!" the man said, as he handed Maddi a pair of clear, dark-framed glasses. "Use hair dye and scissors. Make hair short...to here."

0

0

He pointed just below his ears. "Then put on clothes and glasses. Do it...now!"

Maddi walked into the room and closed the door. Hank could hear her opening the box of dye.

The man motioned to Hank. "We go over plans. There is boat to Island."

"What Island?"

"Corsica."

"How long will it take?"

"Two days. She arrive Friday afternoon." He paused. "Does she get seasick?"

"No."

"Good. Waters may be rough. I have money and passport. Her name will be Harriett Winthrop."

"She's going alone?"

"Do you want to go with her?"

Hank frowned. He hadn't really thought about it. Had he expected to go with her? Of course not. As much as he hated the thought of sending her off by herself, he had a woman he loved, along with a job and obligations waiting for him back home. *But I've never left Maddi.* He sighed regrettably. "No. I can't go with her."

The man nodded. "Of course not." He grabbed a small satchel from a nearby table and opened it, showing Hank a credit card and a stack of euros. "Two thousand each...cash and card." Hank stared at the items. Maddi's new identity; her new life in a sack no bigger than a handbag.

He heard water running in the bathroom; Maddi was likely rinsing out the hair dye. There was the clip of scissors, followed by the sound of a blow-dryer. He stood there silently, waiting. He felt unsteady; he could feel his legs shaking. He leaned against the table, doing his best to distract himself by looking around. There wasn't much to see; Angelo lived a simple life. *I wonder how Cravens knows him.*

He was about to ask, when the door to the bathroom flew open. Maddi had been transformed. Her shoulder-length hair was now barely below her ears. It was a darker brown, which made her pale skin look even paler. The clothes were a size too big, making her look thin, almost wispy. She was wearing the glasses, and held a small-brimmed hat in her hand which she immediately plopped on her head. It covered her ears and her forehead, and she grinned, that smile the only recognizable feature of the woman he had loved for the past six years.

"Now, who am I?" she said, playfully.

Hank gave a weak smile. "Your name is Harriett Winthrop...from London."

Maddi grinned and, with a feigned British accent, she said, "Jolly good, then."

Angelo reached over Hank's shoulder and pulled a camera from a shelf. The camera looked more expensive than the hut they were standing in.

"Take off hat...I need picture."

Maddi did as he asked and he snapped the picture. He used a cord to attach the camera to a specialized printer – which Hank guessed also cost more than the house – and printed out what would become the first full page of the passport. Maddi's photo had been perfectly imbedded in the page. Angelo then walked into the bathroom and, using the hairdryer and a special adhesive that he pulled from the pocket of his shirt, he secured the page into the passport. He held it to the light and looked it over. After a minute, he nodded, then handed it to Maddi. He turned to Hank. "Any questions?"

Hank had lots of questions. Where was she going? Who would look after her once she got there? Instead, he just shook his head and said, "No. Can I pay you?"

The man glared at him. "No! I do this for Cravens!" He handed Maddi the bag with the credit card and the money. She slid the passport inside, then threw the bag over her shoulder. Suddenly she frowned. "Aren't you coming with me, Hank?"

Hank sighed and looked down at the floor. "I...I have to go home, Maddi." He looked up. She was staring at him, her eyes brimming with tears. His heart ached.

She set her jaw firmly and nodded. "Yes...yes, Hank, you do."

He swallowed; he thought he might cry. *Man up, Hank.* "Think of it as an adventure, Maddi."

He was about to walk into the small room to grab her clothes, when Angelo said, "Leave them! I will burn them." He waved his hand. "She must go...now!"

Hank pulled his keys from his pocket and ran toward the front door.

Angelo said, "No! Not by car. My daughter take her...in buggy." He grabbed Maddi by the arm and shoved her toward a door at the back of the house. "Go...now! Buggy out back. It take you to coast!"

Angelo practically pushed Maddi out the door. Hank followed her. A small black buggy was sitting a few feet away, with an old workhorse in front of it. There was a young woman seated behind the horse; she was glaring at them over her shoulder. Maddi shook her head. "Hank, I—"

"Get in!" It was the daughter, who was every bit as overbearing as her father. She scowled at Maddi with dark eyes as she jumped down and opened the door.

Maddi looked at Hank and frowned. He turned to the daughter and was about to say something, when they heard the sound of tires on the gravel driveway out front. Angelo was standing at the doorway. He motioned to Hank. "You must go, too!"

The daughter motioned for them to get into the buggy. Angelo ran to Hank and slid a scrap of paper in his hand. "Take this. Go with her as far as coast. I take care of truck."

Hank shoved the scrap of paper in his pocket and tossed Angelo the keys to the truck. He then followed Maddi inside the buggy. There was little room; Maddi was forced to more or less sit on Hank's lap. He did his best to not hold her too tight. *Jenny would kill me if she saw this.* The daughter closed the door and the small space seemed even smaller, the only fresh air coming through two narrow slats on each side. The smell of horses and hay filled the cabin. The woman climbed onto the seat, and they felt a sudden jolt as she flashed the reins. The work horse broke into a trot.

Hank looked at Maddi and grinned. "Well, Harriett, here we go."

She forced a smile. "Yes...here we go."

Hank looked over his shoulder through the narrow slat at the hovel no bigger than a Henderson bathroom, where Maddi had shed her identity onto a dirt floor in a matter of minutes. He looked to the front of the house, surprised not only to see the same police car that had stopped him earlier, but another car driving by more slowly than it should be. He tensed. It was the light blue Toyota; the same car he had seen in Boe. It continued on past Angelo's house, just as the police car pulled into the drive. The same officer who had stopped him just minutes ago stepped out of the car.

As they trotted off, only partially hidden by orange trees which were scattered randomly on the open field, he could see the cop walking up to his gray pickup truck. Hank was glad that Angelo had made him leave with Maddi. Not only was that policeman a threat, but whoever was following them in the light blue Toyota was a threat, as well; he could feel it. Hank had no idea who he was or why he was tailing them; it didn't matter. Hank was just glad that they had gotten away when they had.

As for the policeman, Hank guessed that he was making sure that Maddi had gone into *cuarentena*. She hadn't, and Hank could only guess what that might mean for Angelo. Clearly, Hank had put the man in danger. He shook his head and sighed. So many people had been put in danger to keep Maddi safe. Had it been worth it? He looked up at her as she bounced awkwardly on his lap. She smiled at him and he sighed. *Of course it was…Maddi is worth whatever it takes.*

CHAPTER 77

Ocaña, Spain

Cobra was close. He had driven like a bat out of hell in search of the gray pickup, and had finally spotted it less than a mile from Ocaña. Fortunately, the truck had been stopped by a policeman, which had allowed Cobra to get even closer to the truck. He had waited on the side of the road, and had watched as the driver of the truck was questioned, and was then permitted to continue on with his journey. Cobra had followed him along the backroads south of the small village.

The policeman had followed the truck, as well, leaving Cobra no choice but to pull back and keep his distance. Finally, the cop had turned off and had pulled into a diner.

Now I have Hank all to myself, Cobra had thought as he had followed Hank down a series of desolate roads. He had seen him pull into a decrepit house in the middle of nowhere, and Cobra had pulled to the side of the road about half-a-mile from the old house.

He had been there for the past five minutes, readying himself to go into the house and kill whoever was there, including Hank. He would then take a photo of Hank's dead body so he could prove to Morningstar that he had finally killed the bastard.

But then he spotted the cop...the same cop who had stopped Hank a few miles back. Cobra hissed. *What the hell is he doing here?* If Cobra wanted to kill Hank, he would need to kill the cop, as well. It was far riskier to kill a cop then to kill some lowlife who was living in the middle of nowhere.

After a minute, he nodded and put the car into gear. *I have no choice.*

He pulled onto the road and was only a few yards from the house when his phone rang. "Yes," he mumbled, as he edged closer to the house.

"It's me…Jacob."

Cobra sneered. "Well-timed, asshole. I'm about to kill your boy."

There was a pause. "Excellent! Where are you?"

"Spain. About an hour from Madrid."

There was a pause. "Interesting. It's going to be a clean kill, I hope."

Cobra continued past the house, frowning as he stared at the cop car. A clean kill? Hardly, not with the policeman there. *Maybe I'll just blow up the whole damn house.* He chuckled. "No…but does it matter?"

A pause. "It does. The death of that man mustn't be messy. For one thing, he is too well known. For another, I can't allow you to be captured or killed…I have too much I need you to do." Another pause. "Either you kill him without leaving any sort of mess behind, or you wait."

Cobra sneered. "Then I guess I'll wait."

"I'm fine with that. It will free you up to make the hit on the Chinese military man that we discussed earlier."

Cobra bristled. "Oh no you don't. I want my castle. You have made it clear that the only way I get it is if I kill Clarkson."

There was a pause. "How about if I promise you the castle after the hit in China…whether you end up killing Clarkson or not."

Cobra considered it. "I need a timeline…a definite date of delivery."

A pause. "Whenever the damn hit is done, Cobra."

Cobra hissed. "No. No matter what, I want my castle…got it?" He paused. "How about we agree that you get me that castle by Christmas."

He heard a deep sigh. "Fine. You'll have the castle by Christmas, regardless."

"Good. Now tell me more about the hit."

"You'll be impersonating a U.S. Secret Service agent, so brush up on your American accent." He paused. "It will take a couple of days for me to get you a proper passport, and to cover over any discrepancies about where you've been for the past few weeks." He paused. "You'll fly to America, where you'll meet up with a senator. You will then fly with him to Beijing, where you will kill Lin Chu's only son, the deputy chairman of China's Communist Military Commission, right in front of him."

Cobra couldn't help but chuckle. "You intrigue me, Morningstar. Go on."

"The timeline is important." He paused. "You need to get to the States by Saturday, to China by Tuesday, and kill the vice-chairman on Thursday, November 4th, at eight p.m. in Beijing. Can you do it?"

Cobra scoffed. "Of course, I can. But why such a focus on the timing?"

"There's a celebration taking place on November 4th. It will give you cover."

"I see. Who's the senator?"

"His name is Sturgill. He's the surrogate father of the President."

"Of the United States?"

"Yes."

"Nice touch. If I decide to do this, where will I meet him?"

"In his senate office, Saturday morning at eight. Though your passport will say Daniel Frisk, you'll tell Sturgill that your name is Viper."

Cobra laughed. "Another nice touch. Go on."

"You must look respectable. Three-piece suit, short blond hair." A pause. "Wear blue contacts and black-framed glasses. No facial hair. No need to lighten your skin." Another pause. "Once you make the changes, I'll need you to send a photo to this phone. Within twenty-four hours, I should have a passport ready for your entry into America. I'll make sure you have it by Friday at noon, London time. It will be in a safe deposit box at London's downtown post office. You'll access it using a key that will be left in a brown paper bag outside the door of your River Thames flat."

Cobra stiffened. "How do you know where I live?"

He heard Morningstar chuckle and wanted to reach through the phone and strangle him. Morningstar said smugly, "Dan, I know everything. The sooner you realize that, the better." A pause. "When you get to America, the first thing you'll do is meet up with your brother in arms, a man I refer to as Levi. He'll be waiting on the south side of the Pentagon at 7:00 a.m., and he'll be wearing a dark red fedora. He'll give you a Secret Service standard-issue weapon, along with a badge identifying you as an agent. You will then proceed to the Capitol building, where you will be passed through with little more than a cursory exam. You'll go straight to Sturgill's office." Another pause. "Any questions?"

"What do I do with this Sturgill guy once I've killed Lin Chu's son?"

There was a pause. "Why don't you go ahead and kill him, too. Make it look as if he was into something he shouldn't have been, and that he killed himself out of guilt." Morningstar chuckled. "You can make the whole thing look like it was his idea. A murder-suicide sort of thing."

Cobra sneered. "Sounds intriguing. I'll begin my preparation just as you've outlined." He paused. "And I'm to let Hank go?"

There was a pause. "For now. I'll get him later."

Cobra frowned. Never in all his years of killing had he let a target go. Then again; the only reason he was killing Hank was to get the Henderson castle...and now he was getting the castle regardless...*and by Christmas!* "Fine. I'll do it. But remember, Morningstar...either I get that castle by Christmas, or you'll get a final resting place six feet in the ground. You got it?"

"Yeah, I got it."

"Good. I'll send you a photo as soon as I make the changes we discussed."

CHAPTER 78

Washington, DC

Morningstar was ecstatic. Cobra was completely on board, and would arrive in the U.S. on Saturday morning. Would America be ready for what would come next? Morningstar chuckled. *I'll make sure they're ready...or at least I'll have Judah make sure.* It was time to call Knight and have him carry out the next part of the plan.

He pulled out his phone and was about to dial, when he stopped himself. He set the phone on the desk and leaned back in his chair. He wanted to bask in the moment a bit longer. He couldn't help but laugh as he thought of what Cobra was about to do. His murder of Lin Chu's son, Tai, would destroy Lin Chu, making it easier for Morningstar to loosen Chu's hold over the Chinese military. It would destroy Sturgill, as well, finally ending Morningstar's ties to the man. Sturgill had done his job; he had raised a President. Nothing more was needed of the man.

He frowned. There was still the matter of Hank Clarkson. Why was he in Spain? The Homeland website hadn't changed his status; he was still listed as being on a leave of absence. Why? The curiosity was almost enough to make Morningstar want to call Cobra back and have him confront Clarkson just to learn what he was up to. He shook his head. There wasn't time to worry about it now; the plan in China was vital to Morningstar's strategy; Clarkson's death was not...*not yet anyway.* But eventually, Morningstar would have to kill him. Whatever was keeping Clarkson from DC wouldn't last forever, which meant that, soon enough, he would realize that the War on Terror Committee had disbanded, not out of disinterest, but as a result of the death of every one of its members…except for Hank and Morningstar. He would then launch an investigation…*and I don't have time for that bullshit.* He chuckled. *Maybe after Pocks takes the safe deposit box key to Cobra's lair, I'll have him fly to DC, wait for Clarkson to fly home, then kill him at the airport.* He shook his head. Pocks wouldn't do it…the man was a mess. His role in the death of Madison had left him completely unhinged. So, who? *Zebulun?* He shook his head. *No, too soon after the hit on the President.* Though Morningstar had taken the pressure off of Zebulun by killing Kuntz and cleverly implying that Kuntz was the assassin, it wasn't wise to expose Zebulun to such a risk…not yet. Suddenly, he grinned. *Issachar…I'll have my Philly cop blow a hole in Clarkson's head the minute he steps foot on American soil.*

He sighed. *But how will I know he's home?* He picked up the cellphone and dialed. Without waiting for a hello, he said, "Levi, you need to monitor all flights out of Spain, France, and Portugal for the next seventy-two hours. You're looking for Dr. Hank Clarkson." He hung up without waiting for a reply. It was a longshot, but it was worth a try. *The bastard has to come home one of these days.*

But now Morningstar was left with a new challenge. His vow to get Cobra the Henderson castle was no longer just a vague, loosely timed promise; now, it was a clearcut obligation that had to be completed by Christmas. And Morningstar had no doubt that, should he fail, Cobra would bury him – literally – just as he had promised.

He sat back and considered his options. Perhaps he could use the premise of Latvia's war with Russia to acquire the castle. He could have Janet pull together a document – a ceasefire between Moscow and NATO – that stated that now that Latvia had lost the war, the supervision of all national treasures, including the old Henderson castle, would be overseen by a neutral agency. Morningstar was certain Latvia would lose the war. It was part of his plan; he had put in place the tools to make it happen. The minute Russia claimed victory, Morningstar could suggest that Walter's poor oversight of the Freedom Fighters had led to a lack of confidence among the people of Latvia, and that the castle – which the Hendersons had been graced with overseeing for a generation – would now be managed by an impartial administrator. *And who will that impartial administrator be?* He laughed. "Me!"

He stood and paced the small office, imagining how it would be to oversee such a place...to live in such opulence in a castle by the sea. To rise in the morning to the sound of the waves...to hold sway over servants who would accommodate his every whim...to look out over ramparts and flowing gardens as he took stock of his kingdom...a kingdom that would soon consist of every nation state in the world.

He checked his watch. Six a.m. It was time to call Judah...time to set the final act into motion. He walked to the desk and picked up his phone. Just as he was about to dial, he stopped. There was a flaw in his plan. *Even if I do gain control of the castle, Cobra will simply take it from me the minute he comes back from China.*

He dialed Knight's number, then walked to the window. As he waited for him to answer, he watched moon shadows dance across the Capital dome. Suddenly he laughed. *Which is why I'll make sure that Cobra never comes back from China.*

CHAPTER 79

Washington, DC

Knight frowned as he stared at the ringing cellphone. It was the same phone that had been used just hours ago to force Knight to leave Emma...again. He didn't know if he could answer it, so angry was he with the man on the other end. It continued to ring. He checked the time. Six a.m. *Father's up early.*

Finally, he grabbed the phone from the nightstand. "Yes, Father?"

"The pieces are in place, Judah. It won't be long now. Do you understand?"

Knight hesitated. "Yes sir. I know what to do, sir."

"Good, my son. Make it so...today."

The call ended. Knight didn't move.

After a minute or so, he set the phone on the table and lay back on the pillow, staring at the ceiling of the dark bedroom. He had barely slept, anxiously awaiting Emma's reply to his note. Though they had left it that Foster wouldn't notify him until Emma was either situated comfortably in the abandoned warehouse, or was on her way back home, he found himself feeling like a schoolboy excited about a date.

A lamppost outside the window was the only light, and, as he stared at it through a break in the curtains, he sighed. *Either way, I need to get up and get busy.*

The call from Morningstar hadn't been a surprise. Knight had been expecting it, especially after what had happened the day before. But still he wondered, could he do it? *It's too soon. I'm not ready.* But he should be ready. As a matter of fact, he should be more than ready, especially after the many years he had spent preparing for this very moment. How long had it been? How long had he been nurtured like a seed in the dirt for this historic day when he would finally bear fruit? *Since I was a boy....*

"But I don't want to do this anymore."

"Shut up, you stupid boy. You're only fifteen. You don't get a say."

From a back room, a man's voice yelled, "Bea, don't talk to him that way."

She yelled back, "Fine, then you come out here and deal with his obstinacy."

The man who had been acting as his father for the past year walked from the back room, his large frame intimidating. But he smiled and Jerome felt better. There were times when he actually liked Charles; he was far kinder than Beatrice.

"Now what seems to be the problem, Jerome?"

"I want to go to a normal school...and hang out with other boys."

The senator frowned. "I'm sorry, son, but that option disappeared the minute your parents died."

Jerome looked away. "It's not fair." He tightened his jaw. "I...I miss them."

With an uncommon display of warmth, Sturgill sat beside him and laid his arm gently over his shoulder. "I know." He sat back and sighed. "But it's important that you learn now, Jerome, that little in life is fair." He stood and cleared his throat. "Now get back to work."

Jerome frowned. "I...I don't want to, sir. I'm tired of this. I want to go to a normal school and have normal friends and do all the things the other kids do."

The senator's eyes flashed. "Stop talking that like, Jerome. Your future is so much brighter than theirs. You'll be more successful than they will ever be. While they're playing video games or chasing basketballs, you're learning the importance of geopolitical warfare." He paused. "I bet they'd trade you places in a heartbeat."

Jerome knew they wouldn't. Though it was cool to learn some of the things he was learning, it would be far cooler to have a group of friends to laugh with... a handful of boys to grow up with and learn about life.

But he knew there was no use arguing, so he nodded and said, "I guess so."

The man patted him on the shoulder. "Good. Now, do what Beatrice is asking, and, whatever you do, don't get her upset." He leaned closer and whispered, "She can be such a bitch sometimes." They both laughed and the senator walked out of the room. He yelled, "Bea, he's ready for his Mandarin lessons."

Beatrice returned and stared down at him. "Can we begin, Jerome?"

Jerome nodded, but instead of opening his book and staring at the strange Chinese writing, he looked out the window at the trees, the hills, and the endless sky. What was happening out there? While he was learning Chinese, what were other boys doing? He knew the answer…they were pursuing adventures. Forts were being built, battles were being waged…with boys his own age.

But this was his life now. For whatever reason, he had been chosen to carry out a mission far greater than any other. At least that was what he had been told.

He looked up at Beatrice and forced a smile. "Yes ma'am. I'm ready…."

And Knight had done it. All the work, all the sacrifice, and now the moment had arrived. He was about to initiate what would prove to be one of the most significant events in the history of the United States. Finally, the country would get back on track; it would resume its path to greatness. America would lead the world once again. Knight had embraced the mission, and, though he had never imagined himself as the President, he had never doubted the role he would play. *Until now.*

In the blink of an eye, everything had changed. Emma had found him, and, because of it, the mission had taken on new meaning. Yes, he would still carry out his obligations, but now he knew…he needed her at his side. He hadn't stopped thinking of her since their meeting on the mountaintop. Whether he was prepping for a press conference, or was on the phone with an overseas leader, he found himself trying to imagine what she was doing…what she was thinking…who she was with.

As a result – and in spite of Jacob's instructions that he leave her behind – he had taken the first step to make her a part of his life. It was the only time he had ever defied Jacob, and it had been hard; far harder than he had expected. But it had been necessary. There was no way he could honor the man's directive that he leave Emma. Morningstar was wrong about her. *He just doesn't realize how much I need her.*

Knight shook his head. It was useless. No matter what he said or did, Morningstar would never see Emma as anything other than a Russian sympathizer. So, he would need to proceed with caution. Though he had always suspected it, it was clear now that Jacob had eyes and ears in the White House. How else had he known that Knight was with Emma on the mountaintop? But it had never mattered until now.

Which was why Knight had put his trust in Agent Foster. And the only thing the agent had asked in return was that Knight do well by the country. *"Don't ever lose sight of why you came here, sir. Don't let this city or that woman change you."*

Knight had smiled. *"I promise you, Foster…if Emma changes me at all, it will be for the better. Emma has always made me a better man."*

It was true. It was as if Emma unleashed his gentler conscience; a kindness that lay hidden deep within him. If Knight was to let her back into his life, she could take him from a President that had simply been infused with power, to a truly good leader…a wise man to oversee a great country.

But could he keep her a secret? Jacob seemed to know everything, not only about Knight, but about the entire world. It was as if the man was omnipotent. He had predicted each of the wars in the Middle East, and had somehow known that North Korea would launch its first ballistic missile when it had. *"Leaders like Kim-Jong-Il act out whenever there's a deficit of leadership, my son."* Morningstar had even anticipated the attack on 9-11. Though he hadn't known the exact date or the buildings that would be targeted, he had said on more than one occasion, *"America's a sitting duck. We've riled our enemies, and we've left our country unprotected from an attack by air."* It hadn't taken too many times of Jacob being right and the rest of the world being wrong before Knight had decided that he had backed the right horse.

But what does he know of love? From what Knight had seen, Morningstar had no partner, no girlfriend, no wife. What could he know of that wonderful, terrible struggle to breathe when you were lying next to the woman you loved? Or the crushing pain when she was away from you, even for a day? Morningstar didn't know those things because love wasn't important to him. The mission was all he cared about. But now Knight knew that he needed more in his life. He needed love; he needed Emma. And now, after seeing her and holding her on the mountaintop, he knew, not only did he not *want* to live without her…he couldn't; not anymore.

He looked out at the early morning darkness. He took a deep breath and sighed. The call from Morningstar was his signal to act. Knight would soon put forth a declaration that would change the lives of every American, and they weren't going to like it. But Jacob was right;

sometimes they didn't know what was best for them. *"They're like little children, Judah. They need a wise steward to show them the way."*

And Knight was to be that steward. He would lead them from the wilderness of their own complacency and make them hunger for their place in the world. Americans needed to be reminded of their unique role in the universe; their God-given path, their remarkable ingenuity, their uncanny ability to win every battle...*and to be right.*

He checked the time. *Six-ten.* Emma should have gotten his note by now. Was she on her way to the secret facility in Virginia? He prayed that she was. The very thought of seeing her again filled him with more joy than he had known in years.

"There's no time for love when the future of the world is at stake." That's what Jacob had told him sixteen years ago; it was likely what he would tell him now. *"Get over her son...she'll only hold you back."*

Knight knew better. Though he would keep her a secret for now, he would soon find a way to have her at his side as he, President Jerome Knight, imposed Martial Law on the United States of America.

CHAPTER 80

Strongsville, Ohio

Levi's flight had set down in Cleveland Hopkins airport sometime after five a.m. There had been no non-stop flights available, and he had been unwilling to use a military transport plane; he couldn't let Morningstar find out that he had let Andrew leave town with the tape recorder. Which meant that Levi had spent the hours from six p.m. Tuesday to five in the morning Wednesday shuffling through airports trying to get to Strongsville, Ohio. He had uncovered the truth about Lin Chu's son while sitting in an airport in Cincinnati at 3:00 a.m., and had called Morningstar at once, not even aware that it was so early. From what he could tell, Morningstar had interpreted his middle-of-the-night call as a measure of his eagerness, not as an intrusion.

But now Morningstar has given me yet another task. His boss wanted him to monitor flights out of Spain for the next seventy-two hours. *Doesn't he realize he has me working on about four tasks already?* Levi had made a quick call to a friend of his in aviation, and the man had sent him a link for real-time updates of the manifests of all flights leaving Spain, Portugal, and France. Once that was done, Levi had taken a cab from Cleveland Hopkins to Strongsville, and had had the driver drop him at the end of the street where Agent Thompson was parked outside Andrew's hiding place.

Which was where he was now, standing on the corner, staring at nice homes on an upscale avenue in Strongsville. He checked the time. *Six-*

fifteen. They would need to move quickly; the neighborhood would be waking up soon. He shivered; it was cold in northern Ohio. He adjusted his backpack, then buttoned his coat and tightened his scarf. He pulled up his hood as he scanned the street. There were only about three feet between the houses, which meant that a gunshot would awaken everyone on the block. *Hopefully we won't need our guns.*

Levi had done his research on the house. It belonged to a Jennifer Clarkson and had been for sale for months. It just so happened that she was the ex-wife of Homeland Security Deputy, Dr. Hank Clarkson; the very same man that Levi was supposed to be looking for on flights out of western Europe. A coincidence? *Who knows and who cares,* he thought as he hurried down the tree-lined sidewalk.

It was still dark outside, but there were plenty of lampposts lining the street. With his hood covering most of his head and face, Levi glanced in each parked car as he made his way down the street. Finally, he spotted Thompson sitting behind the wheel of a black, government-issued sedan, munching on a sandwich. *Could you make it any more obvious?* he thought as he leaned over and tapped on the window.

The startled agent looked up, nearly choking on a cheeseburger.

Levi blew on his hands. "Let me in."

Thompson unlocked the car. Levi ran around to the other side and slid into the passenger seat. He threw his backpack in the back seat. "Why didn't you get a rental car, Thompson?"

Thompson wiped his mouth with his sleeve. "Why would I do that?"

Levi shook his head. "Forget it. Have you seen anything?"

Thompson rubbed his eyes. He looked terrible. It was clear he hadn't slept, and he smelled like sweat and old food. "Nope. The guy hasn't left."

"Any alarms on the house?"

Thompson had just taken another bite of the sandwich. With his mouth full, he said, "Not that I could find."

Levi nodded. "Okay. Let's go."

Thompson's eyes widened. "Now?"

"Yeah. Before daybreak. I don't want him to see us and then hide the tape."

Thompson swallowed the bite of food and stuffed the rest of the sandwich into a paper bag. He tossed it in back and grabbed his coat.

He put it on, his long arms hitting the rearview mirror as he shimmied into the sleeves. "Okay, I'm ready."

The sun had yet to rise and the clouds were thick, keeping the tree-lined street in shadow. Levi was wearing a dark overcoat, as was Thompson. They would be hard to spot. *Good,* Levi thought, as he looked at Thompson's lanky frame, and thought of his own poorly-toned physique. They would be no match for Andrew in a foot race. *We need to get to him before he has a chance to run.*

"Wait a minute," Levi whispered as they stepped out of the car. He pulled off his scarf and walked to the back of the car. He looked around and, seeing no one, knelt down and wrapped the scarf over the license plate. *Just in case.* He then led the way as they crossed the street to the house. They did their best to act like they belonged in the old neighborhood with the well-groomed lawns. The truth of the matter was that they didn't belong there at all.

They reached the house, and Levi climbed a set of cement stairs. Cautiously, he walked onto the porch, testing each floorboard to see if it was loose before he put his weigh on it. He was pleased when he got to the door without a sound. He looked over his shoulder; Thompson was right behind him. Levi gave him a nod; the agent stepped forward and pulled out a bump key, which could open nearly any locked door. He slid it into the doorknob, jiggled it a couple of times, then smiled when he felt the lock release. He pushed open the door. A shrill siren began to sound.

"Shit!" Levi glared at Thompson as he pulled out his gun and ran inside.

Thompson shrugged. "I checked...there was no alarm listed for this house!"

Levi said nothing as they ran from room to room. There was no sign of Andrew. The siren had pierced the silence of the quiet neighborhood; Levi knew the police would be there any minute. Though he and Thompson could show their Pentagon IDs and claim they were there on behalf of the government, the last thing he needed was to have to explain to Morningstar that not only had he invaded a private home, but he had once again failed to get the recorder.

"Let's go!" he shouted to Thompson. They ran out the door, across the porch, and down the steps, sprinting to the black sedan. They could hear sirens in the distance. They climbed into the car. As Thompson pulled away, Levi could see neighbors looking out their windows. He smacked the dash. "Dammit!"

"What do you want me to do now?"

Levi could barely look at the man. "Pull over in that minimart up ahead."

Thompson pulled over and Levi jumped out of the car. He ran to the back and undid his scarf from the license plate. He got back in and said, "Now drive…slowly."

"Where?"

Levi checked the time. *6:40.* He was supposed to be at the Pentagon forty minutes ago. It would take forty-five minutes to get to the airport, at least two hours to get a flight, an hour of actual flying time if he was able to fly non-stop, then an hour to get to the Pentagon. *Noon at the earliest.* "How long's the drive?"

Thompson frowned. "To DC? About six hours if we don't hit heavy traffic."

Levi nodded. "Just drive."

The man widened his eyes, but didn't say a word as he obediently followed the signs to Interstate 80. Levi tried to imagine Morningstar's reaction if he ever learned what had happened. *He'd be pissed.* He smirked. *Maybe he'd fire me.* Though in the short term it would eliminate a few of Levi's concerns, he had seen enough to know…*Morningstar doesn't fire people…he makes them disappear.* So, no matter what, he couldn't tell Morningstar about Strongsville. *But he's going to wonder where I am.*

They drove east toward the Interstate, and he pulled out his phone. He stared at it while he rubbed the back of his neck. Finally, he dialed, not even giving Morningstar a chance to say hello. "Sir, it's me…Levi. I've arranged for the monitoring of flights out of Europe, and now I'm at the Library of Congress trying to find old papers that might at least mention Lin Chu's son. So far, I've found nothing, but I'll keep looking. I should be back at the Pentagon by about 1:00 p.m. or so."

Morningstar said "fine" and ended the call. As they pulled onto I-80 east, Levi sat back and looked out the window. In spite of the fiasco at the house in Strongsville, he now knew something he hadn't known before. *Andrew definitely has that tape.*

CHAPTER 81

Strongsville, Ohio

Andrew hadn't noticed him at first. He had thought that the black sedan sitting across from the Tudor house in Strongsville must have belonged to a family down the street. It wasn't until early that morning, when, on his way to the back door for another trip to his 'bathroom,' he had glanced out the front window and – with the aid of a nearby lamppost – was able to see a man sitting in the driver's seat. The guy was eating a sandwich, clearly in no hurry to leave. *I'm being watched.*

He had immediately run back to the den and had shoved his laptop and the blanket into his backpack, along with three empty water bottles and several granola bar wrappers. He had put on his coat, thrown the pack over his shoulder, and had gone to the back door. He had looked out a window and, when he was confident that the man out front didn't have a friend waiting in the back yard, he had snuck out the door, making sure to arm the house as he left. The early morning darkness had been a godsend as he had sprinted to a nearby grove of trees, which was where he was now, trying to catch his breath and come up with a plan to get away from there.

He checked the time. Six-thirty. He had been at that house for over twenty hours. He wondered how long the man out front had been sitting there.

With his hands on his knees, he watched the house. He had just started to breathe easier, when he saw two men sneaking up the front stairs. He slid further into the trees. His hands began to shake; he shoved them in his coat. He recognized one of the men. *Khakis.* The same guy who had overseen the raid on his house yesterday; the same guy who had been in his mother's living room the day she died.

The disturbing revelation that a man named Jacob had been willing to use the Pentagon to destroy Maddi had left Andrew sick inside. And the presence of the two agents outside Jenny Clarkson's house just now gave further credence to the claim. If what Todd said on the tape was true, then a Pentagon employee, Jacob, had been dead set on ruining Maddi's life. The question Andrew had yet to answer was how far he had been willing to go. Was Todd working for him? Had he gone to Jeannie's house on Jacob's behalf? It certainly sounded like it. If so, then that meant that the Pentagon had okayed Todd's brutality toward an innocent U.S. citizen. They hadn't suspected Jeannie of terror. Her only crime had been to be the mother of Cynthia Madison.

But why? What had Maddi done to invite such scrutiny from the Pentagon? That one was easy. Maddi had made a point of investigating the powerful in DC. It wasn't a reach to think that she had gone after the wrong man, and a Pentagon stooge had then been sent to 'shut her up.' But how far had they been willing to take it?

As for the recorder, it was now clear that Jacob was behind the Pentagon's search for it. Why? *Because he was mentioned on the tape.* But how did Todd even know Jacob? More importantly, how did Jacob know Todd? Had he somehow learned of Todd's crazy belief that Maddi had killed his father? And, if so, had Jacob used the power of the Pentagon to coerce the disgruntled Todd to do his dirty work for him?

The possibilities had left Andrew dumbfounded, and he had paced the den until well after the sun had gone down. He had spent the rest of the night trying to come up with a plan; a way to learn not only the connection between Todd and the mysterious Jacob, but how to find at least one of them so he could learn the truth of what happened…not only to his mother, but to his sister, as well.

At about three in the morning, he had logged onto his laptop and had spent over an hour searching every Pentagon website for an employee named Jacob…either first name, or last. He had found three. One was a janitor with the first name Jacob. Andrew had spent a few minutes looking at the man's biography, though he felt it unlikely that a janitor would be willing to or capable of destroying a powerful U.S. senator. The other two were women who both had the last name Jacob. One was a low-level secretary; the other worked in the cafeteria. Again, not likely candidates to follow through on the relentless pursuit of a powerful senator.

Andrew continued to watch the house. The two men had just walked inside, and the sound of the house alarm made him jump. *I need to get out of here.* He fled deeper into the trees, not sure where to go. *What about my car?* He couldn't go back for it; they would be watching it. But he had to get out of there. As evidenced by the reappearance of "Khakis," it was clear that the Pentagon would stop at nothing to find that tape. And now he understood why. *Todd Jackson has pretty much admitted that someone named Jacob was willing to use the Pentagon to destroy my sister.* Whoever Jacob was, it was obvious that he held a high position within the Pentagon. Which meant that Andrew was now a man on the run... not from a couple of nameless, faceless agents, but from the most powerful military establishment in the world.

CHAPTER 82

Washington, DC

Knight shook his head as he hung up the receiver of the phone – a phone he referred to as the bat phone – that sat on the old Lincoln desk in the Oval Office. The call he had just taken had been from Jason Hanover, Director of Homeland Security, and what the man had told him had left him stunned. *"I just got a call from one of the investigators of the plane crash in Latvia. He says he's got reason to believe that it may not have been an accident."* Knight had asked for details; Hanover had promised to get them as soon as he could. All he had told him was that the investigator had said that there may have been an almost imperceptible alteration to the fuselage.

"If it was imperceptible, how did he find it? And why did it take him so long?"

"I don't know, sir. He said it was something small…easily missed by even the best investigators. I think maybe he had suspected it from the start, but felt he didn't have enough data. He said his worry about it woke him up last night, so he went to the lab and reexamined the debris from the crash. I'm meeting with him later today."

"Who knows of this, Hanover?"

"Only the guy who just called me, and now you, sir."

"Good. Swear that man to secrecy, and tell no one until we know more."

"Yes sir."

"And keep me informed, Hanover."

407

"Trust me, Mr. President…if we find out that someone sabotaged that plane, you will be the first to know."

Knight frowned. *Did someone purposely bring down an RAF plane?* It was unthinkable. Not only would it imply a breach of security that would alarm the entire world, but its timing couldn't be more concerning. If what Hanover had just old him turned out to be true, then two great American leaders had been killed – *murdered* – within hours of one another.

He turned in his chair and looked out the window. The sun was rising, but thick clouds had left the sky a dark, dusky gray. A typical day in late October in the nation's capital. His eyes fell to a young tree, newly planted in the front lawn. It had been put there by the White House staff in honor of Senator Madison. *She should have been President,* Knight thought, as he stared out the window. She was far more qualified. But it hadn't happened that way. Like so much in history, what makes sense is rarely what occurs. Instead, the job had become his, thrust in his lap by the surprise resignation of a trusted VP, followed by the tragedy of a President's assassination. He had had little time to adjust to the role as he had guided the country through the loss of their leader, the threat of war, and the chaotic shootings that had forced him to confiscate the peoples' guns.

And now…in the middle of it all, I learn that Madison's plane may have deliberately been brought down. He massaged his forehead as he thought of the Secret Service agent who had survived the crash. Was he aware that it may not have been an accident? If not, maybe someone should tell him. He might be able to offer details that weren't clear to him on the day of the crash; information that he had buried away as the tragedy had overtaken him.

Knight pressed the intercom. "Beth, could you put me in touch with the agent who survived the plane crash that…that killed Senator Madison two months ago?"

"Right away, sir."

He stood and paced the office. How could someone pull it off? After all, the plane was Royal Air Force…security would have been tight. Which meant that if someone had, in fact, altered the fuselage, he would have needed help from someone in power…someone well-positioned, either in Britain's or America's government. Maybe the survivor? Could the agent that survived the crash be acting as a double agent? Knight shook his head. *There's no way that guy could know that he would survive a plane crash.*

His phone rang; he walked back to his desk and picked up the receiver. "Yes."

"Sir, a riot has broken out in Queens; I'm sending in the Guard."

"Thanks Cooper." Marty Cooper was Knight's National Security Advisor. Knight had put him in charge of handling resistance to the confiscation order.

Knight returned to his chair. He put his elbows on the desk, rested his head in his hands, and let out a sigh. He suddenly felt old. There was too much going on; too much he needed to manage; too many problems and not enough answers; too many threats and not enough resources to address them all. He sat back and ran his fingers through his hair. *What a perfect time to rendezvous with a former lover.*

Maybe he shouldn't do it. He had a country to run, a country that was in a state of crisis. A country that might be about to learn that their former President wasn't the only leader to have been murdered on that fateful night nine weeks ago.

More importantly, once he met up with Emma, he would be betraying Morningstar, the man who had been like a father to him. A man he loved...a man he practically worshiped. Morningstar was the man who had stepped in after his parents had died, guiding him through his grief, teaching him about truth, integrity, and the duties of leadership.

But twelve hours ago, the 'father' that he had respected for most of his life had asked – no, *demanded* – that he leave behind the woman he loved...*again.* No matter how much devotion Knight felt for Morningstar, he couldn't do it...not again.

His cellphone vibrated. He looked down at the text. It was from Foster.

"The package has arrived."

She said yes! His throat felt like it was closing; his heart began pounding out of his chest. Emma had accepted his invitation and was now waiting for him in the secret facility outside Falls Church, Virginia. He swallowed; it was like something out of a novel. The most powerful man in the world was about to have an illicit affair with a married woman from Maine. He laughed as he imagined the headlines. "Leader of the Free World caught in a Love Triangle outside Camden."

But those headlines would be nothing compared to Morningstar's reaction. Once he found out, there would be hell to pay.

Knight flinched as he leaned forward and reached for a stack of papers. *Don't think about it.* He stared at the stack. They were mostly either summaries to review, agreements to go over, or emails to answer. Obligations of the President; duties that Judah, a son of Jacob, should be taking care of to cement his role as leader of the free world.

Suddenly, he grabbed the papers and tossed the entire stack to the floor. *To hell with you, Morningstar.* He stood and walked to a corner cabinet. His hands were shaking as he took out a glass, then grabbed a bottle of tonic from a small refrigerator. Though he could have used some gin in that tonic, he couldn't risk it; he had a country to run. *America's President probably shouldn't be drinking before noon.*

He poured the tonic and took a drink, the bitterness a comfort as he tried to battle his uncertainty. He walked to the window, staring out at the branches of a birch tree. The limbs were as gray as the sky, a dusky ash that seemed to extend from the earth to the heavens. The only color came from the flag in the courtyard, its bold red white and blue a stark contrast, a reminder that even in the darkness, there was hope.

He carried his empty glass to the bar, refilled it, and carried it to his desk. He fell into his chair. He was about to defy Morningstar, his mentor, the man who had made him what he was. Was he ready? He sipped the tonic. A battle was brewing, and it was tearing him apart. He sighed and opened his cellphone. He dialed, nearly brought to tears when he heard Foster's chipper Irish brogue. "Yes sir?"

"I'm ready."

The voice on the other end quieted. "Yes sir."

"Can you arrange a team...a trustworthy team?"

"Already taken care of, sir."

"Good. I'll go out the east door...to the Rose Garden. Give me about ten minutes."

Knight ended the call. He walked from the Oval Office to the familiar anteroom that had become his refuge. He gave a quick nod to an agent standing outside the door, then walked in and went straight to the mirror; the same mirror where he had grounded himself so many times over the last nine weeks. *Have I really been President for only nine weeks?* It felt like a lifetime. He shook his head and sighed. There was so much to do; so much that was about to happen. He couldn't be distracted by love. *It won't be a distraction. Emma gives me strength…the will to do what's right.* He took a last look in the mirror and nodded. He would go to her, bring her back with him, and somehow make the nation accept her.

But as he left the anteroom and walked back to the Oval Office, he knew, no matter what, things were about to change…dramatically, and likely not for the better. Not only was he about to put Emma at risk, he was about to put the entire nation at risk. Morningstar could be unpredictable when he didn't get his way.

Knight flinched as he put on his suitcoat, then his overcoat, and walked to the door. *It can be no other way. Either I am the leader of this country with Emma Melnikov at my side…or I am not the leader of anything.*

CHAPTER 83

Outside Falls Church, Virginia

Emma walked up and down in the drafty warehouse, overcome by all that had happened. In less than twenty-four hours, she had gone from a dull, depressed wife and mother, to a woman on the run, about to meet the only man she had ever truly loved in an abandoned warehouse outside Falls Church, Virginia. But not just any man...*the President of the United States of America.*

She shook her head as she looked around the warehouse. Secret Service Agent Jerry Foster – now pretty much her only friend – had done his best to make the site hospitable. Emma was appreciative, though she didn't really care what it looked like. It was a palace as far as she was concerned, and it would soon house the relationship that had transcended time. Foster had told her that it had been used by a former Military Academy to stockpile munitions. Though there were cameras in nearly every corner, Foster had assured her that he had disabled any that might betray her privacy. *"But the important ones are still intact, and they will keep you safe."* She had wanted to ask, *"Safe from what?"* but had said nothing, not sure she wanted to know.

The building was about the size and shape of a football field, and had a small office at one end. Foster had turned the office into a kitchen, and had then divided the remaining warehouse space in half with a sturdy floor-to-ceiling wall divider, giving it the feel of an apartment...with a bedroom, a living room, and a kitchenette. There were two bathrooms, one near the kitchen, the other in the make-shift bedroom at the far end of the warehouse. Foster had gone out of his way to make the bathroom in the bedroom appealing. Though it was small, it had a cabinet with two shelves. He had put fancy soaps on one of the shelves, and a set of decorative towels on the other.

The entire warehouse was without windows, which was the hardest part for Emma, but Foster had addressed it at least to some degree with several well-placed posters that showed the mountains of northern Maine. Those mountains had been a big part of Emma and Romer's life, and the fact that Foster had caught on to that so quickly spoke volumes about him. She had asked him how he had been able to sneak everything into the warehouse without anyone seeing. His reply: *"It was the middle of the night, Ms. Cannon...and the moon was hidden by clouds."*

Emma looked around. To think that she was about to spend time with the President of the United States in an improvised love shack in the middle of nowhere; it hadn't been something she would have ever imagined when she was growing up outside Bangor, Maine. *Then again...is anything the way we imagine it as a child...*

"Emma! Emma Melnikov, get in here and eat your lunch!"

Her mother's stern Russian accent had changed very little over the years, though Galina Melnikov had done her best to always speak English in front of Emma. 'We are American, now, Emma dear, and we will speak the language,' she would always say. Which was fine with Emma; after all, she was ten and had known nothing different. She didn't want to be 'the Russian girl down the street.' No, what she really wanted to be was a dancer; a world-renowned ballerina who would grace the stages of the finest theaters, and make magic with her elegant movements and her weightless leaps in the air.

She had been studying dance for over three years and her teacher, the kind Mrs. Serebrov, had told her that she would someday be great. 'You have moves like Baryshnikov, my dear Emma,' the woman would say, with an accent like her mother's. That was good enough for Emma; Baryshnikov had inspired generations with his magical leaps and turns.

"Emma, I'm not telling you again! Get in here and eat your lunch!"

Emma ran from her room, leaping across the floor in a perfect cabriole. "I'm coming, Mama," she said, as she landed the jump with perfection. Yes, she would be a beautiful dancer someday, she was certain of it. But first she had to eat her tuna fish sandwich...

Emma grinned as she walked into the 'kitchen' and arranged the chairs around a small wooden table in the middle of the room. Pretending that the back of one of the chairs was a plié barre, she put her feet in first position, then second, and finally third, elegantly dipping up and down as she had for years as a child. She gave a final flourish of her hand and chuckled; it was the most she had danced in years. *It's funny how quickly a dream can die,* she thought as she looked around the room. She had gone from dancer to swimmer to wife to mother, and the transformation had been stunning in its rapidity. She pulled out the chair and took a seat, thinking back on the choices she had made. Did she regret them? Did she wish she had worked harder to be a prima ballerina? Did she mourn the fact that she had given it up when things didn't work out the way that she had hoped? Of course she did. *"Regret is for fools"* her mother used to tell her. Emma sighed. *Maybe so...but that doesn't mean we don't feel it...and some of us feel it every single day of our lives.*

She looked around the kitchen. Foster had chosen well; the small, sturdy table had four matching chairs, and he had placed a bowl of fruit in the middle. A dorm-sized refrigerator had been stocked with juice and lunchmeat, along with several cups of yoghurt and a pint of milk. *How long does he expect me to be here?* There was a loaf of bread on the counter, along with condiments, plates, glasses, and silverware. It would appear that Foster had thought of everything.

She walked to the fridge and poured a glass of milk. She checked her watch. *7:30 a.m. in America...2:30 p.m. in Romania. Galina is likely about to perform...*

"Michael, hurry! We need to get inside. Galina is about to perform!"

"I'm coming, I'm coming." Michael Cannon got out of the car and laughed. "I don't know who's more excited; you or Galina!"

They walked into the church, where five-year-old Galina was sitting next to her music teacher in the front row. She was wearing her favorite dress. She looked over her shoulder, spotted her parents, and waved excitedly.

Emma and Michael sat three rows behind her. The music teacher stood and welcomed everyone to the piano recital. After a few announcements, she introduced Galina. Emma's eyes filled with tears as she watched Galina stand and walk to the stairs. Emma had practiced with Galina for as long as she could remember, helping her as she learned the notes and keys, and mastered the scales. It had been clear from the start that Galina was gifted. Yesterday, as Galina had been rehearsing, Emma had sat next to her, ready to once again help her. Galina had looked at her and had shaken her head. She had said determinedly, "I can do it by myself now, Momma."

As Emma watched her climb the stairs to the stage, she tightened her jaw to keep from crying. Michael hugged her. She whispered to the little girl on the stage, "I know you can, baby...that's what makes this so sad..."

Emma began to cry. She wiped at the tears. She didn't want to think about it...about *them,* the family she would soon rip to shreds. And for what? For the sake of a decades-old love? Was it even real? Were she and Romer meant to be together, or were they simply in love with the past... with the young man and woman they had once been...hopeful, eager for a future not yet jaded by life.

She sighed. It didn't matter; she couldn't spend another sleepless night wondering. The ache in her heart for a man she hadn't seen in sixteen years was more powerful than any emotion she had ever known...more powerful even than guilt. And she had felt plenty of that.

She leaned against the cupboard as she sipped her milk. She could turn it around; there was still time. She could find Foster and ask him to take her home. She could leave Romer a note and tell him that she had made a mistake and, though she would love him forever, she was going back to the family that she had dedicated her life to. She pounded the cabinet with her fist. *Do it, Emma. Go back to them.*

She stumbled to a chair and put her head in her hands. She couldn't; her need to follow this through was too great. *What's wrong with me? What sort of woman – what sort of mother – thinks this way?*

She was startled by the ringing of a trac phone that Foster had given her when she had arrived at the warehouse. She answered with a hushed, "Yes?"

"We're leaving now, Ma'am."

"O—Okay." Emma closed the phone and slid it in the pocket of her jeans. It was official; the President was on his way to her.

She had considered dressing up – to look appropriate for the leader of the free world – but had quickly dismissed the idea. It wasn't the President she was about to spend time with; it was Romer, who knew her in jeans and a sweater, her black hair hanging down her back, her face clean and fresh without a trace of make-up. And, though it had been sixteen years and the lines of life had begun to carve their way into her forehead and around her eyes, she had allowed herself only a hint of blush.

She carried her milk to the 'living room,' smiling at an agent who was standing by the only door with a gun in his hand. The gun made Emma nervous, and she quickly walked to a coffee table and rearranged magazines. She was about to grab one of them when she stopped. Sitting next to them was a photo in a copper frame. Taken using the timer on her camera, it showed her and Romer on one of their last days in the mountains. *Where did Foster get this?* Clearly, Romer had given it to him. Which meant that Romer hadn't just kept the picture, but had kept it readily available.

She picked it up and stared at the faces; the young, bright faces that beamed with joy. She touched her fingers to the glass and smiled at Romer's kind, dark eyes. But it was her own eyes which said the most; they were completely, utterly content. There was no hesitancy, no doubt; just the simple joy of life. *I was happy then.*

She sighed and set the photo on the table. She had to do this. To live a lie was to betray the life she had been given. How had her mother put it? *"To pretend to love is the worst sort of lie."* It was done. She would see this through; she had to.

She grabbed one of the magazines and sat down. There was no TV, but there was a small radio sitting on the table. Emma was about to lean over and turn it on, then stopped herself. She welcomed the quiet. It gave her a chance to think.

She wished she had her phone. It held pictures of the life she was leaving behind. Foster had taken the phone almost immediately. As she had placed it in his waiting hand, she had asked, *"What will you do with it?"* He had sighed. *"I'm sorry, Ma'am, but I'll have to destroy it. It's a link that could put you in danger."* Emma had narrowed her eyes. *Danger from what?* she had wondered. He must have sensed her concern. As he had slid the phone in his pocket, he had said, *"There are those who don't want you and the President to be together."* He had then handed her the trac phone. *"This is how I will notify you that he's on his way."*

And that had been the end of it. Her phone and her life…gone. In their place, an untraceable existence. Fifteen years of a lack-luster marriage with one of the kindest men she had ever known was over. She had asked Foster to make it look as if she had been kidnapped. *"Please don't let Michael think that I simply walked out on him,"* she had begged… though that was exactly what she had done. She had walked away, stunned at how quickly, how easily she had made the decision; as if the choice had been considered every day for the last fifteen years. The truth of the matter was it had. She had wanted to explain everything to him, but she knew that she couldn't. *I can't even explain it to myself.*

Foster had told her that he couldn't do that; a kidnapping would bring in the police and the FBI. He had suggested that she simply write a note and state that she had needed time away and was visiting family overseas.

"It's a coward's way out," her mother would have told her. And she would have been right. But Emma couldn't tell him the truth. *I can't hurt him like that.* And what of Galina? Would her daughter forgive her if she knew that Emma had simply walked away? No. It was best that they both think that Emma's disappearance was not only voluntary, but temporary. If someday she learned the truth, Emma could only pray that – by then – she would be old enough, with enough experiences of her own, to understand.

She sighed. *But I didn't even get to say goodbye.*

She set the magazine on the table and carried her glass into the kitchen. She was done reflecting; done battling the merits of the decision she had made...the pain she was about to cause, and the horrific self-interest that had brought it about. Whatever had driven her – be it selfishness or the need to be honest with her feelings – it was bigger than her. The decision had been made sixteen years ago.

She walked into the 'bedroom' at the far end of the warehouse and checked to make sure that everything was perfect. There was an old desk sitting against the wall, and Foster had somehow gotten a full-sized bed into the room. He had been good enough to get Emma some candles; it was one of the few things she had requested once he had dropped her at the warehouse. Candles, a bottle of wine, and two long-stemmed glasses. As she walked into the room, the scent of cinnamon greeted her and she took a breath, imagining the next few hours that would be spent almost entirely in that room.

But he's the President. Would the Secret Service be in there with them? *How did JFK do this?* Would the nation find out? Was some eager reporter waiting outside, ready to snap a picture of Jerome Knight sneaking into an abandoned warehouse in the middle of nowhere just as dawn crept over the horizon? She hoped not, though she couldn't imagine how he would get away with it. She didn't care; all she knew was that she needed to see him; she needed to feel him in her arms.

The phone rang. "Yes?"

"We're ten minutes away, Ma'am."

Her hand was shaking. "Th—thank you, Foster. I'll be waiting."

* * *

The fact that Secret Service Agent Emmett Wilson had somehow missed Emma Cannon's departure from the hotel room in Maine had pissed him off. He had only realized it a few hours later, when he had finally had enough of staring at a dark window and had decided to walk up to her room, knock on her door, and pretend to be a hotel investigator. There was no answer, so he had picked the lock and slid into the room unannounced. She was gone. Other than the unmade bed, there was no evidence that she had even been there...though he knew that she had.

Instead of reporting it to the man who had hired him, Emmett had decided to fix the mistake by tracking the President. *After all, that's who she's after...right?* Fortunately, Emmett had timed it perfectly. He had arrived at the White House and had parked as close as he could to the West Wing, so that he was near the Oval Office. He had just pulled out his binoculars, when he spotted Knight sneaking through the Rose Garden. Emmett was stunned. *What the hell is going on?*

Still in the rental car, he eased away from the White House. As he rounded the corner, he was able to see Knight and an agent sliding into the back of a black sedan. He fell in behind the car as it headed south on I-95. He was three cars back, curious about the fact that there were only two cars in the entire entourage. Whatever Knight was doing, it wasn't sanctioned. Too few agents and too few cars. *What is he up to?*

Suddenly, he frowned. What if Knight was leading him away from Emma Cannon instead of closer to her? He shook his head. It didn't matter. Knight was clearly up to something, and Emmett felt certain that Morningstar would want to know. Though he had insisted that Emmett track the woman, Morningstar would welcome the inside scoop on the President's mysterious journey.

Emmett pulled out his phone and called a Secret Service friend of his who had recently been assigned to the White House. After a bit of small talk, and doing his best to not give too much away, he asked the man how it felt to be so close to the President.

"It's kind of boring, actually. The guy doesn't really go anywhere. He's usually upstairs by ten p.m., then he comes down before sunrise and goes straight to the Oval for the rest of the day. We just stand outside and wait."

Emett thanked him and hung up. Even his own detail wasn't aware that he had left. There was no doubt about it; Knight was up to something. This journey he was on was a secret. And unlike every other secret in DC, this one was being kept.

I'll follow him to his destination, then I'll call Morningstar. Maybe Emmett had stumbled onto something bigger than the antics of a Russian spy. Maybe the higher-ups would take notice and he would be reinstated. He grinned. *Let's hope so.*

He stayed with the motorcade, surprised when it left the highway at the exit to Falls Church, Virginia. He drove on past in order to stay undetected, turned at the next exit, then doubled back. He got off at Falls Church and spotted the motorcade heading southeast. He stayed with them as they turned onto a country road. Majestic, well-kept farmhouses dotted the landscape. The small motorcade drove another ten miles before turning onto an almost imperceptible drive. Emmett drove on past, not turning his head or adjusting his speed, hoping to look like nothing more than an out-of-town traveler. When he had gotten half-a-mile down the road, he stopped and parked behind a thick row of evergreens. He stepped out, buttoned his coat, and pulled on a hat. It was late October; the air was cold and damp. Rain was coming. He grabbed his binoculars and quietly closed the door. He ran through a patch of trees, hoping to get a look at the agents as they stepped out of the cars. He would likely know them, which meant that he would know who was keeping the President's secret.

There were cameras everywhere, so he made sure to stay under the brush. Two feet in front of him was a wire fence that covered the entire perimeter. He could hear a series of beeps; the fence was armed. *What the hell is this place?*

Using the binoculars, he scanned the area. He could see a large building hidden by a row of evergreens about a hundred feet away. He moved closer and tightened the lens. He could see stacks of wood and piles of old crates with the logo from an arms manufacturer printed on the front. *Some sort of munitions storage facility.* There were weeds covering the only door, implying that the facility had been abandoned for some time. *Why would POTUS be driven with an undermanned detail to an abandoned warehouse?*

He focused his lens on the motorcade. They had come to a stop at the weed-covered door. He looked on as four agents and Knight stepped from the two cars. Emmett recognized only one of the agents. He had blond hair and fair skin. Emmett remembered him from a detail they had both been on a few years ago. *Now, what was his name?* He couldn't remember. Emmett never was good with names.

The warehouse door opened and a man with a rifle – clearly Secret Service – walked outside. Emmett frowned. Though there were now a total of five agents watching over the President, it wasn't nearly enough if something went wrong. The Secret Service would never allow such a thing. Whatever was going down either outside or inside that warehouse was clearly off the grid.

It started to rain. Emmett shivered as he held the lens to his eye. He was getting soaked. The wind whipped through the trees, chilling him to the bone. He pulled his cap over his ears, and buttoned the collar of his coat. He continued to watch, hoping to get a glimpse inside the warehouse. He waited. The agent who had originally come out of the warehouse knocked on the door. It was opened partway, and a splash of light covered the area outside the door. He tightened his lens. As the six men filed into the warehouse, he saw her: the very same woman he had been instructed to keep an eye on. *"Track her, Wilson. She's a Russian spy."* "Holy shit!" he said under his breath. The President of the United States was about to have a secret rendezvous with a sworn enemy of the United States Government.

CHAPTER 84

Strongsville, Ohio

Andrew had been on the run for the past two hours. He had gone nearly five miles, making several laps past the downtown square in search of a bus station. He had looked first to the north of town, then to the south, and was now heading west. He was about to make a loop around, when he spotted a terminal next to the exit for Interstate 71. He ran half a mile to the door of the terminal, then stopped to catch his breath. With his hands on his knees, he took several deep breaths, then walked into the station as calmly as he could. He found a seat in the back of the lobby behind a rack of coats. He had a good view of the front door and he kept his eyes glued, just waiting for the poorly dressed Pentagon agent to burst inside waving his gun.

What now? he wondered as he peered out from behind the coats. *Should I get a bus for home?* No, he couldn't go home. Not only was he being followed by two very persistent Pentagon agents, but there were questions that needed answered. His mother hadn't drank herself to death; she had been murdered...by Todd Jackson. And his sister had been targeted by a Pentagon employee, Jacob, who had somehow drafted the son of a man from Maddi's past to help him. For whatever reason, that son, Todd, felt certain that Maddi had killed his father. *Which is just ridiculous.*

He patted the recorder in his pocket. He had yet to listen to the end of the tape, though he doubted there was much more to hear. After all, he had heard his mother being strangled, and had heard Todd drop the recorder sometime during his harried exit out of Jeannie's house.

Suddenly, he frowned. Todd had dropped the recorder. *So why was it right by Jeannie's hand?* Todd wouldn't have left it there; he would have spotted it right away. *So, how did it get there?* He swallowed. *Could it be?* Had his mother maybe found the recorder and left a parting word for either him or Maddi?

He looked around. Though the station was busy, there was no one standing near him; he was more or less invisible behind the coats. He pulled out the recorder and rewound the tape about thirty seconds. With the recorder held close to his right ear, he covered his left ear and pushed play.

He swallowed as he was forced to once again hear his mother being choked to death. Still he kept going. He heard Todd trip, then mumble the comment about Jacob. He waited. Would there be more? Had Jeannie somehow managed to grab that recorder and say a final word? Maybe a clue to explain who the mysterious Jacob was, or why he had been so driven to destroy Maddi?

For about a minute, Andrew heard only silence. He closed his eyes. That tape was an indictment, not only of all that had gone wrong in that lonely house two months ago, but of all that had gone wrong for the last thirty-two years.

Suddenly he tensed. He held the recorder closer to his ear. He could hear her; his mother…the last gasps of a dying woman. His heart broke; she hadn't died…*not right away, anyway.* He held the recorder even closer. His hands began to shake. He felt sick. He could hear Jeannie dragging herself across the floor. She was still gasping. He heard a thud and his heart broke. She had collapsed. He heard the click of the recorder and was about to slam the entire thing against the coat rack, when suddenly, he heard her weak voice say, *"No…Todd…I…I won't say…that Cindy killed…Evan, because…she…didn't."* There was a final gasp, followed by a whisper, *"…it was me…I'm the one who shot Evan Jackson twenty-two years ago."*

CHAPTER 85

Outside Falls Church, Virginia

Emmett shoved his hands in his pockets to try to warm them, but even his pockets were wet. He had been watching the warehouse for over an hour, but now the rain was coming harder and he was soaked. But still he stayed; it was worth it. The President of the United States was having a secret rendezvous in an abandoned warehouse...*and I have a front-row seat!* He had watched, stunned, as Knight had walked to the door and had kissed the Russian spy...*right on the lips!* Emmett knew that he needed to call Morningstar, but he didn't dare leave his post for fear he might miss something. He had started to shake from the cold. Finally, when he could stand it no longer, he scooted from behind the trees and ran to the car. *I'll make it quick.*

He reached the car, slid behind the wheel, and rubbed his hands to try to warm them. He pulled out his phone and dialed Morningstar.

"Hello." The voice sounded more callous than usual.

"Um...sir, it's Emmett Wilson...with the Secret Service. You had wanted me to monitor...the traitor...and call if I saw her try to make contact with POTUS?"

"Yes."

"They have made contact, sir."

There was a pause. "They have, have they. Where?"

"In an abandoned warehouse outside Falls Church, Virginia."

Another pause. "I see."

424

"And sir, it would appear that the two are…rather close."

"What do you mean?"

"Um, they kissed, sir. When he got to the warehouse, he kissed her."

There was a sigh. "How many agents are with the President?"

"I counted four, sir. And there was one at the location when they arrived. What do you want me to do, sir?"

"Listen closely to what I'm about to say, Wilson. That woman is a traitor; an expatriated Russian who is working for the Putin regime. I'm certain that she has involved herself with our President in an effort to steal secrets…maybe even blackmail him as war is breaking out in Eastern Europe."

"Dear god."

"Yes. Now, with five men protecting them, I doubt you're in a position to take her out."

Emmett swallowed and wiped the sweat from his forehead. Even though it was only 38 degrees inside the car, he had suddenly become quite warm. Could he take out five men? Probably not. But he could take out two, if he had the upper hand. He cleared his throat. "I…I could get to her when they leave, sir. If they keep the same arrangement, there will only be one man guarding her."

"Excellent plan, Wilson. You're a good man. But there's something you need to know before you agree to this."

"What's that, sir?"

"You will be on your own. This is not a sanctioned mission. I'll deny any knowledge of it if I'm ever questioned."

It was Emmett's turn to pause. "I see."

"However, if you complete this task successfully, I'll make sure not only that you're reinstated with the Service, but that you receive a commendation."

Wilson grinned. It was music to his ears…to have his role within the Agency restored, and to finally get recognition for his hard work. *Maybe I can even take over for that prick, Sam Allen.* "I understand, sir. I can do this. I'll call you when it's done."

"As I said before, you're a good man, Wilson."

"Thank you, sir." The line went dead. Emmett put his phone in his pocket. In spite of the fact that he was chilled to the bone, he was bursting with pride for the opportunity that had just been given to him. *I will make Morningstar proud.*

He opened a duffel bag, pulled out a pair of rubber-handled wire cutters, and slid them in his pocket. He reached in the back of the car and grabbed a long, narrow bag from under the seat. He slid the bag under his arm and stepped out of the car. He quietly closed the door and ran back to the warehouse, making sure to stay low in the brush. The rain hadn't let up, and he was soaked by the time he reached his spot outside the barbed wire. And he was nervous; he had never shot someone in cold blood. *It's for the sake of the country,* he reminded himself as he laid flat in the mud and pulled his rifle from its bag. *For the country...and a long overdue commendation.*

CHAPTER 86

Washington, DC, and Falls Church, Virginia

Damn you, Judah! Just when I was getting everything in order. Morningstar was pissed. Why had Judah defied him? He had told the man – in no uncertain terms – to stay away from that woman.

He stood and paced his office. *You're an idiot, Knight!* Morningstar had never felt more betrayed. No, that wasn't true. Joseph's betrayal a year ago had felt just as bad. Like Joseph, Morningstar loved Judah. He loved him like a son…a *real* son. He had once loved Joseph like a son, as well. *And now they have both betrayed me.*

But Judah was defying a direct order. Morningstar had specifically told him to stay away from the Russian émigré. *"Emma Melnikov is a traitor, son. You've got too much to lose by associating with such a woman."* He bristled. Knight's rendezvous with that Russian whore had put the entire mission at risk.

He stopped at the window. His hands were shaking; he placed them on the sill. *I should have that bastard killed.* He stared out at the rain. It would be easy enough to do. After all, Zebulun had killed another sitting President just a few months ago. Morningstar could have Emmett Wilson reinstated, assign him to cover the President, then have the man shoot Knight while he slept.

Morningstar flinched. Yes, it would be so easy. He shook his head and sighed. But he couldn't do it; not yet, anyway…he still needed Knight.

But Knight's lack of gratitude was a tough pill to swallow. Morningstar had moved mountains to get Knight where he was. Though Sturgill had been given the more basic tasks of clothing and feeding the boy, it was Morningstar who had raised him. *I made that boy into a man.* Morningstar had shown him the future…he had made him a king.

He felt weak…empty. He turned away from the window and walked back to his desk. He sighed as he fell into his chair. Joseph and Judah… two sons, two boys he had trained to be men, two fools who were willing to toss their birthrights to the wind for their own foolish desires. With a fierce rage, he swept his arm across the desk, shoving his laptop and a stack of files to the floor. "To hell with you, Knight!"

He was glad he had told Emmett to kill Emma Cannon. *And I hope you get to see it, Knight.* But Emmett Wilson wasn't the most capable soldier…he wasn't the most capable man on any front. Could Morningstar count on him?

He frowned as he stood and once again paced the room. *She has to die. I can't complete God's mission if my President is sleeping with a damned traitor!* He raised his eyes to the ceiling. *Okay, God. I need you to ensure that Emmett gets this right.* A clap of thunder filled the silence, shaking the glass of the only window in his small office. Morningstar laughed. "I'll take that as a 'yes.'"

Again, he walked to the window. The rain was coming harder now; it seemed to calm him, to give him clarity. He couldn't have Emma killed in front of Knight; it would destroy him. *And I need him to be strong.* Yes, she needed to die, but not while Knight was watching. *I'll call him. I'll give him one more chance to do the right thing.* Perhaps, if Morningstar was clever, he could convince Knight to leave Emma on his own terms. *Then, once he has left her, Wilson can kill her anyway.*

He checked his watch. *So, what would a President be doing to his mistress at nine-thirty in the morning?* He chuckled as he pulled out his phone. *Whatever it is, I hope I interrupt him.* It was answered almost immediately. "Agent Foster, here."

Morningstar frowned. *Where is that asshole Simmons who usually answers this phone?* He cleared his throat. "Agent, I need to speak with the President."

* * *

428

Emma touched Knight's arm, once again reassuring herself that he was real. It was like a dream, in spite of the agents that were hovering just beyond the divider. But they had given them privacy; in that makeshift bedroom it had been only her and Romer... alone. He had come through the door of the warehouse and she had been unable to hold back. She had embraced him and the two hadn't been apart since. He had carried her past the divider and into the bedroom, and it had been just as it had been sixteen years ago. No, it had been even better. Sixteen years of longing expressed softly, fervently in an eight-by-eight room.

"What are you thinking about?" he asked as he brushed a wisp of hair from her face.

She looked at him and smiled, fighting tears that had come out of nowhere.

He pulled her close and kissed her forehead. "Don't cry, Emma."

She whispered, "I love you too much."

"You can't love me too much," he whispered back.

"Sure I can. Think about it, Romer. You're the President. This can't work."

"Why not?"

"Well, for one thing, I'm a married woman and it would be a huge scandal for your administration."

"That's manageable. Anything else?"

"Yes, you're needed right now." She shook her head. "A lot has happened and your leadership and guidance are required."

"And you'll help me, Emma. You'll be at my side through every step of it."

She shook her head. "I can't be at your side. It would place shame on you at a time when the country is looking to you for direction."

He hugged her. "We'll make it work, Emma."

She hugged him tight; she wanted to believe it. She wanted to think they could somehow get past the obstacles. But she knew better.

He whispered in her ear. "I am ordering you to relax."

She laughed and pulled the covers over their heads. "Yes sir," she said as she reached for him. If she could have frozen a moment in time, it would have been that one. But, like all such moments, it ended abruptly...with a quick knock on the wall outside the divider. Romer pulled the covers from over his head and barked, "What."

"Sir, there's a call for you...on the special phone."

"Shit!" He had said it softly, so only Emma heard, but she knew what it meant. Whoever was calling him on "the mystery phone" would ask him to leave her. The same thing had happened when they were on the mountain in Maine; the phone call had come, he had gone to answer it, and then he had told her goodbye. She didn't think it was personal, but, then again, maybe it was. After all, she was the one he kept leaving. And, unlike typical calls which he had delegated twice already, this call was different; whoever was on the other end of that phone expected him to drop whatever he was doing and answer...at once. And for whatever reason, he did. *But he doesn't want to...that much I can tell.*

"I'll be right there," he said, as he pulled the covers back over their heads. He whispered, "I'll be right back."

"No, you won't."

He kissed her. "Sure I will."

She sighed. "We'll see."

He threw off the covers and got out of bed. She watched him as he pulled on his shirt and trousers. He slid into his shoes, walked to the divider, then gave her a quick smile as he slipped past it. As she watched him leave, she wondered...*So, what happens now? Where does this go?* But she already knew the answer. No matter what, she would never be able to have the President.

* * *

Knight walked out of the bedroom, took the phone from Foster, and said firmly, "This is Knight."

"What the hell are you doing, asshole?"

"Nice to talk to you, too, sir," Knight said as he walked to a corner of the makeshift living room.

"Don't give me that shit. You're in bed with that bitch, aren't you?"

Does he have a camera in my brain? "Sir, I don't know—"

"Cut the crap, Judah. You need to end this and you need to end it now."

He moved into the kitchenette, waving away an agent who was sitting at the table. When the agent was out of the room, he closed the door and said quietly, "Jacob, I assure you, she will not interfere with our plans. I promise you, I can carry on with her at my side."

"You stupid lunatic. She's *Russian!* She's likely a spy, and if she isn't, the minute it's known that you're bedding an expatriated Russian, she'll be approached and either compromised or killed. Is that what you want? You want your Russian whore to be murdered before your very eyes?"

Knight was having trouble focusing. The allegiance he had felt for one man and one man only was suddenly biting back at him, challenging him to defend the tirade he was being forced to endure. "Jacob, are you threatening Emma?"

There was a pause. "Uh...no, son...of course not. I would never hurt a woman you're fond of. I'm just worried for her. I wish I could tell you that she was safe in your arms, but I can't. I know for a fact that you were spotted with her, and I fear it's only a matter of time before she's... taken out."

Knight's legs felt unsteady. He fell into a chair, his hand shaking as he held the phone. He knew what that meant. *Emma has been targeted.* But was it Knight's love for Emma that had put her in danger? *Or does this man simply want to eliminate the only person who holds power over me... besides him?* Suddenly, years of devotion and unquestioned obedience faded away, as he said firmly, "I can handle it."

"No, son...no, you can't."

"Okay, then I have a request."

"What is it, son?"

"I need to finish this on my own terms. I need you to give me a chance to end this the way that I should have sixteen years ago."

"And how is that, my son?"

He whispered, "I need to be the one to kill her."

Knight ended the call before Morningstar could reply, shaking as he folded the phone. *That oughta do it.*

He walked into the makeshift living room, and was about to hand Foster the phone when he thought better of it. He slid it in his pocket. "I'll keep it from now on, Foster."

"Yes sir."

Knight walked into the bedroom. He closed the door and looked at Emma. She was turned away from him, facing a poster of the Katahdin Mountains.

"Do you want to go back there?" he asked.

She turned to look at him and his heart felt like it might explode. Suddenly he knew: his love for her was bigger than the plans he had been a part of since he was a boy…bigger than the Presidency…even bigger than Jacob himself.

She smiled. "Yes. Yes, I do."

"Okay. We'll go."

"When?"

"Soon."

She grinned and turned back to face the poster. He leaned against the door, thinking through the next several minutes that would most assuredly alter his life forever. He walked around the bed and knelt in front of her. "How much do you love me, Emma?"

"What do you mean?"

"How far are you willing to go for us to be together?"

She raised up on one elbow, her hair falling across her cheek, the light from the candles throwing shadows on her pale skin. She brushed her hair back as she smiled and said, "I know now that I would go to the ends of the earth to be with you, Jerome Knight."

He had never felt so much love for anyone, ever. "Good." He reached for her and pulled her close, the feel of her against his chest as natural as breathing. "Because I'm pretty sure that's what we're going to have to do."

* * *

Morningstar was stunned. Had Knight just agreed to kill the woman that he had loved for a lifetime? *Yes, because he holds that much reverence for me.*

And so…that was that. It was over. In a matter of two phone calls, Morningstar had dealt with the sixteen-year-old problem. Either Judah was going to kill the bitch, or Emmett Wilson was going to do it.

He chuckled as he walked to his desk and sat down. He leaned back in his chair and grinned. "Either way, she'll be dead."

CHAPTER 87

Strongsville, Ohio

"A boy's best friend is his mother." The quote by Joseph Stefano had been something Andrew's mother had said to him many times before she lost herself to the alcohol. Of course young Andrew had never heard of Stefano. And, even now, all he really knew about him was that he had written the movie "Psycho." But the quote had stayed with him, mostly because of the irony of it no longer being true. It had been at one time, however…Jeannie and Andrew had been tight. But that was before Jeannie's husband – Andrew's father – was gunned down in the line of duty, and her reaction had been to bury her grief in a bottle of booze. But, as he thought of it now, he knew…Jeannie had still felt it.

And it was clear now that she had felt a similar devotion toward Maddi. Jeannie was claiming responsibility for a murder that Andrew knew she couldn't have done. Had she recorded the last line on that tape to protect Maddi? From what? *Not murder…there is no way Maddi could've killed Jackson; Maddi couldn't kill anyone.* Regardless, for whatever reason, Jeannie was claiming that *she* had been the one to kill Jackson. And, though he could understand why Jeannie might have wanted to kill that man, he couldn't imagine her pulling it off. Twenty-two years ago, Jeannie was drinking heavily. *She could barely get out of bed…let alone have the wherewithal to get a gun, hunt down Jackson, then hold the weapon steady while he did what? Let her shoot him? No way.*

He put his head in his hands. It was too much. Over the course of the last twenty-four hours, he had left his wife and son to the care of a retired cop, had run off to a near stranger's house to hide, and had been forced to listen as Todd Jackson strangled his mother. That had been followed by Todd's offhand comment that Jacob intended to destroy Maddi. Finally, he had heard his mother claim responsibility for the murder of a cop that had taken place twenty-two years ago.

He had never understood how the Pentagon agents had learned of Jeannie's death so quickly. But now he had an idea. Todd must have called Jacob to tell him what he had done. It made far more sense than the agent's claim that Jeannie had been tied to terrorists. Which meant that Jacob had probably sent those agents not only to remove evidence that Todd had been there, but to find the tape that he had so carelessly lost; a tape that clearly incriminated Jacob in a crime. Which implied that Jacob's role at the Pentagon was big...big enough to give him the authority to quickly dispatch two agents to a woman's home in Indiana, make them lie for him, then overrule a coroner and an entire police department to take ownership of the body.

Andrew was still at the bus station hiding behind the coats. He was sitting on a plastic chair, his back against the wall. He pulled out the coin that Jeannie had left for him and laid it in his palm. About the size of a half-dollar, it was faded gold, with rubbed edges and scratches... clearly quite old. He could make out a faint image of a woman with wings. He turned it over, noting letters across the top. He looked closer.

NEATLAIDIBA

He frowned. *What does that mean?* He tried to rearrange the letters in his head to come up with something that made sense, but finally gave up and shoved the coin in his pocket. He couldn't dwell on it now; he had to keep moving.

He was so tired. He missed Amanda. Though he had promised her that he would be home by the end of the week, he doubted he would make it. He couldn't go home until the threat from the Pentagon was over...until he understood how Todd was tied to Jacob...until he learned why Jacob was so eager to destroy Maddi...*and until I know for sure if my mother killed a cop twenty-two years ago.*

One thing he did know: Todd Jackson had murdered his mother. He couldn't let it stand. He needed to find Todd, tell the world what he had done, then make him pay. But there was little on the tape to identify him. All Andrew had gotten was his name, and that he was the son of a dead cop.

Suddenly, his eyes widened. *Yes…but so am I.*

He stood and threw his backpack over his shoulder. There were measures taken when a cop was killed in the line of duty. Measures that involved the identification and documentation of all members of the family, particularly the surviving spouse. Unfortunately, Andrew knew those measures all too well.

He walked to the counter. He knew how to find Todd Jackson. The man had a mother. Was she still alive? Was there still a Mrs. Evan Jackson somewhere back in Evansville, Indiana? He hoped so. *Because a boy's best friend is his mother…and that woman will know where Todd is.*

CHAPTER 88

The Henderson Compound

Henderson stared thoughtfully at Walter sitting across from him in the den. The chair that Walter was sitting in had always been understood to be 'his chair;' an oversized Chesterfield with tufted leather and intricately carved legs dating back to the eighteenth century. It suited him. Even as a boy – especially as a boy – Henderson had seen Walter as someone who transcended time. In Henderson's eyes, Walter was not only the biggest man he had even known, but he was also the wisest and most strategic...about war, about people, about life. It was as if Walter hadn't simply learned the lessons of history, but had come to embody them. In seventy-two years, he had seen – and been a part of – quite a bit of history. Born during the depression, he had learned the value of hard work. A child at the advent of the second world war, he had learned the importance of sacrifice. A teenager when America had dropped atomic bombs on Japan, he had come to understand that sometimes there are no good choices. Coming of age during the Korean War, then volunteering to serve in Vietnam, he had learned how fools in DC made decisions with no appreciation for the hardships of war. As an advisor during the Cold War, he had seen the fall of the Berlin Wall, and had been instrumental in the liberation of Soviet occupied republics, particularly Latvia, which had allowed him to know the gratification that comes when good triumphs over evil. Finally, standing less than a block away when planes attacked New York City on 9-11, he had begun to see the hatred that existed in parts of the world for freedoms that the West often took for granted. Yes, Walter had seen it all; he was a member of the Greatest Generation, and Henderson welcomed his insight as he and Cravens struggled with how to untangle the ramifications of a tragic plane crash that they now understood to have been a planned assassination.

As for Cravens, Henderson guessed that he didn't see Walter in the same light. Though Cravens and Walter had gotten to know one another over the course of Henderson's illness, he hadn't had the chance to understand the wisdom that Walter could bring to the situation. Henderson sat back and sighed. *He'll see it soon enough.*

The trip to Liepaja to retrieve Cravens' "item" had gone off without a hitch. The fact that Dimitri was already leaving the estate at noon had worked in their favor, as it had allowed for no suspicion on either his timing, or the journey itself. It turned out that his appointment in Grobina was to inventory a cache of weapons that had been purchased for the war, and he was able to drop them in Liepaja on his way.

He had let them out at a well-known café just off the highway. *"I'll be back at three."* Cravens had wanted a cup of coffee. Henderson had ordered one, as well, but when he had reached for his wallet, he had remembered that he had left it in his backpack, which was still in the den. Cravens had paid for the coffees, and they had left the diner and made the thirty-minute walk to the bus station. During that time, they had talked…about Cravens' time with the Secret Service, about Henderson's understanding of the Latvian wars with Russia, and about Maddi. The discussion about Maddi had been the hardest, for both of them. But it had felt good to talk about her; to acknowledge the life she had lived, the impact she had had on so many people.

They had reached the bus station just after one, and had quickly found the locker. Cravens had opened it, and had taken out a duffel bag and a briefcase. Henderson had assumed that whatever he was returning to Walter was inside one of the bags. They had left the station and had walked back to the café. They had about an hour-and-a-half before Dimitri was scheduled to come back for them, so Cravens had asked if they could get a sandwich. Henderson had let him know that his wallet was back at the castle. *"How convenient,"* Cravens had joked, then had added, *"Don't worry, I've got it."* They had each ordered a sandwich and a beer. As Cravens had opened his wallet to pay, Henderson had seen that he was taking out his last euro. Henderson had said quickly, *"I'll pay you back when we get to the castle."* Cravens had waved him off, but Henderson had decided then, not only would he pay him back, but he would give Cravens enough cash to get him through the next week or so. He had clearly run out of money; Henderson guessed he had few options to get more.

They had finished their meal and had sat in the café for another hour. Dimitri had come for them soon after three p.m., and had driven them back to the estate. At Henderson's request, he had dropped them outside the gate. *"This time, Cravens, we are walking – not sneaking – through that gate...and you will lead the way."*

Henderson had called ahead and had told Ivor that a good friend of his, Secret Service Agent Tom Cravens, was coming to the estate between 3:30 and 4:00. He had added that Cravens would have a friend with him, a Mr. Aiden Balkus. *"Let them in, Ivor and escort them to the den. I'll take care of letting Walter know they're coming."*

They had walked into the den just as a grandfather clock had rung out the last of four chimes. Henderson had been surprised to hear a phone ringing in his backpack. But it wasn't his satellite phone; he had that phone with him, and it had been programmed to vibrate. The phone had stopped ringing by the time he got to his backpack, but he had been stunned to find a burner phone in the outside pocket. He had tried to see who had called, but the phone had no caller ID. He had shoved it in his pocket, curious how it had gotten into his backpack in the first place.

But he hadn't had time to dwell on it; he and Cravens had needed to prepare for their conversation with Walter. What they were about to tell him would change the landscape dramatically...especially Walter's landscape. A plane crash that had killed a prominent senator had been ruled an accident. Not only would that ruling be called into question, but it was likely that someone with considerable authority had played a role in the crash. Walter was friends with most of the well-heeled leaders in America and in Britain. Which meant that it was quite possible that he would soon be forced to implicate a friend, or at least an associate.

They had spent the next hour reviewing the facts that they were sure of, as well as the theories that they were not so sure of. At five p.m., Henderson had turned to Cravens. *"Are we ready?"* Cravens had nodded, and Henderson had called his father to the den. *"I have something vital I need to share with you, Dad. Come alone, and please don't tell anyone that I'm here."*

Walter had walked in just minutes ago, and Henderson had immediately explained his disguise as Aiden Balkus. *"It's the only way I can get around, Dad…even the Latvian police are working with the Americans to find me."*

He had also made sure to tell him that Cravens knew that Matt was actually Martin. *"Mom told him sometime while we were in Edinburgh."*

Walter had nodded, clearly stunned to see Cravens. He had immediately walked over and reached out his hand. *"It is so good to see you again, Agent."* The two had shaken hands, and he had added solemnly, *"I know that you have been through quite a lot."*

Cravens had merely nodded self-consciously and had taken a seat on the sofa, a Queen Anne from the early 1900's. His oversized frame seemed awkward on the delicate piece of furniture. Walter had taken a seat in his designated chair, and Henderson had elected to stand. That had been a few minutes ago; no one had said a word since.

Henderson could see Cravens squirming on the sofa. He was clearly nervous to give Walter whatever it was he needed to give to him. Henderson sighed. *The sooner he gets this over with, the better.* He cleared his throat. "Dad, Agent Cravens has something he'd like to return to you." He turned to Cravens and nodded. "Go on."

Cravens sighed, then reached behind the sofa and lifted the briefcase from the floor. Henderson had assumed that whatever he was returning to Walter was inside the case, but as he looked at it now, he recognized it. He was surprised he hadn't noticed it sooner. That briefcase had belonged to Henderson's grandfather, Walter's father. Walter had taken it with him on nearly every trip they had ever gone on.

Walter clearly recognized it, too. His eyes narrowed, but he said nothing.

With the briefcase in his lap, Cravens turned to face Walter. He swallowed, then said, "I…I believe this briefcase is yours, sir." He handed the case to Walter.

Walter took it and rubbed his hands tenderly over the leather. Without looking away from the case, he said, "How long have you had it?"

Cravens shifted uncomfortably. "Too long, sir." He tugged at his collar. "I…I found it…in Lyon, in Place Bellecour…back in the spring."

Walter looked at Cravens but said nothing as he resumed his inspection of the briefcase. He used painstaking care to toggle every latch and brush over every inch of the rich brown leather.

Cravens cleared his throat. "I'm…sorry, sir. I never meant to keep it so long."

Walter nodded, but still he said nothing. He came to the insignia at the bottom corner of the case and slowly, carefully ran his fingers over the emblem.

Cravens said, "That emblem, sir, is why I held onto it."

Walter looked at him. "I see. What do you know about the emblem, Cravens?"

Again, Cravens tugged at his collar. "Not much, actually. But my uncle had a medal with the same insignia, and I knew how much that medal had meant to him."

Walter's eyes widened. "Your uncle?"

Cravens nodded. "Yes sir. Uncle Harry." He swallowed. "He had a lot of medals…including five silver arrows which represented five separate beach landings. He had made a point of telling me about each and every one of those landings; when they had occurred, the gunfire he had faced, the men who had died. But whenever I would ask about the medal with the church and star, he would clam up, refusing to say much about it. Only that he had gotten it '…*from the general himself.*'"

Walter narrowed his eyes. He stared at Cravens, then slowly began to smile. "He was the man outside the door."

"Sir?"

Walter nodded. "My father had told me that there was a man – one of America's bravest soldiers, according to Ike – who had stood outside the church the entire time a group of men were holding what would become the first of many secret meetings." He frowned. "He had described him as the only man present that didn't know the purpose of the organization, but had nonetheless become a part of the pact."

Cravens sat up straighter. "I…I am honored to hear that, sir." He looked down at his shoes. "But I owe you an apology for keeping the case for so long."

Walter shook his head. "Nonsense. Better you than some nosy French policeman." He frowned. "But how did you know it was mine?"

Cravens cleared his throat awkwardly. "Well sir, this is where it gets tricky." He shifted on the sofa. "All...all I had was the insignia, which I knew was special."

Walter's eyes began to narrow. "Go on."

Cravens took another deep breath and sighed. "I...I had no idea whose initials were JH, so I had no idea who to give it back to." He hesitated. "I also knew that I couldn't break into the case, so I—" Cravens stopped midsentence.

"Please, go on, Agent."

"I hired a man to open it."

Walter raised an eyebrow. "I see." He leaned forward, holding the briefcase protectively in his lap. "I'm assuming that you felt you could trust this man?"

Cravens nodded emphatically. "Oh yes...yes sir. When I tell you about him, you'll think I'm crazy, but I can assure you, sir, I did my research. Also, I've developed a pretty good instinct for reading people over the years."

Walter said nothing. Cravens went on. "I...I met the guy in a diner."

Henderson sat back, stunned. *"You met him at a diner?"* he wanted to say. But he held back, fully aware that he didn't need to add to Cravens difficulties. He guessed that Walter was about to make it plenty difficult without Henderson's help.

Cravens swallowed. "We...he and I had hit it off. He worked intelligence for the UK, and I sort of did the same for America. It seemed to be a bond between us." Cravens sighed. "I also liked the fact that he had started out as a criminal."

Walter's eyes narrowed even further, but still he said nothing.

Cravens continued. "I...I sensed the sincerity of a man who had changed his ways." He paused. "The only way I know to put it, sir, is that I really liked Shaw. He was quiet, he spoke with candor, and he seemed to value his privacy. There was a considerable amount of depth and honesty in the man."

Walter's brow had creased. "Go on."

"His specialty was safecracking, which seemed perfect for what I needed." He paused. "So, after many nights of talking to the man over coffee, I told him of my dilemma…that I had a briefcase that I needed to return to its owner, but I didn't know who that man was. I also told him that I felt certain that whatever was inside the case was sensitive. *"Beyond top secret,"* was how I think I put it." Another pause. "I asked him if he thought he could break into the case without destroying it or whatever was inside; he said that he had yet to find a lock he couldn't crack. I told him that all I wanted was to learn the name of the man who owned it; nothing more." He paused. "After some deliberation, he agreed to open it, learn the identity of its owner, then forget that he had ever seen the briefcase or its contents, or even me, for that matter."

"And you believed him?"

Cravens took a deep breath. "Yes sir, I did."

"And do you still feel the same?"

Cravens hesitated. He looked first at Walter, then at Henderson. He took another deep breath and nodded. "Yes sir. As I said, one thing I'm good at is reading people." He looked directly at Walter. "And I would stake everything I stand for on the integrity of Shaw."

Walter sat back in his chair. His hands were gripping the briefcase.

Henderson cleared his throat. "May I ask…what's in it, Dad?"

Walter looked at Cravens. "Why don't you tell him, Agent Cravens."

Cravens shook his head. "Actually, sir, I don't know. I didn't want to know. I told Shaw not to tell me…no matter what."

Walter continued to stare at Cravens. After a minute, he turned to Henderson and said, "The truth is, son, that it is merely a collection of drawings. I doubt they would have any value to anyone who didn't understand their purpose."

Henderson knew enough about the Morning Star organization to ask nothing more. He simply nodded.

Cravens said, "I cannot tell you how sorry I am, Mr. Henderson."

The room grew silent. The fire in the hearth had faded, and the sun was sighing a last gasp just beyond the window. A table lamp gave off only a dim light, leaving the room covered in deep, dark shadows. But it seemed appropriate…not only for what had been said, but for what was about to be said.

After several more minutes, Walter leaned forward and set the briefcase on the floor by his chair. He looked at Cravens and nodded. "I understand what you did, Cravens. As a matter of fact, I appreciate it.

To have given it to your boss, or – god forbid – the French police, would have been a disaster." He cleared his throat. "But I will need to know more about this Shaw fellow."

Cravens, who had been staring at the floor, looked up and frowned. "I'm sorry to say, sir, that in spite of my research, I don't know much about him. He worked for MI6, and conducted undercover operations on their behalf in exchange for his freedom. From the sound of it, everything he did was done in secret. He will be tough to find."

Walter frowned. "Is Shaw his first name or his last?"

Cravens flinched. "Actually, I...I don't know, sir."

Walter stared at Cravens in disbelief. "You entrusted this man with a top secret briefcase, but you didn't even know his full name?"

Cravens nodded reluctantly. "Yes...yes sir."

Walter stared at Cravens with an expression that Henderson knew well. He felt a sudden kinship with Cravens, having been at the other end of that unforgiving stare far too many times in his forty-four years.

Finally, Walter sat back and sighed. "I have a friend who is well-acquainted with a high-ranking MI6 operative. I'll have him see what he can find on this Shaw fellow."

Cravens nodded. "Again, I'm sorry, sir."

Walter shook his head. "No apology necessary, Cravens. You did your best with a difficult situation." After another minute or so, he reached over and patted him on the shoulder. "Actually, Cravens, I owe you a debt of gratitude for getting this back to me safely." He sighed. "The letters on the briefcase are my father's initials, Jeremy Henderson. He was a friend of Dwight Eisenhower's. It would appear that Ike was your uncle's tie to the organization, as well. It is quite likely that my father may have known your uncle." He smiled. "Which is quite a remarkable coincidence, if you think about it."

Cravens sighed. "Yes sir, I agree."

"As for the briefcase and its contents, or the insignia on the side, we will say nothing more about it. Understood?"

Cravens nodded quickly. "Yes sir. I will forget I ever the saw the thing."

Walter turned to Henderson. "Was this the vital information that you needed to share with me?"

Henderson shook his head. "No sir." He was about to tell Walter what he and Cravens had learned about the plane crash, when a phone rang in his pocket. It was the trac phone he had put there earlier. He pulled it out and stared at it.

Walter said, "Aren't you going to answer it?"

Henderson opened it and offered a tentative, "Hello?"

"Is this Matt Henderson?" The voice was formal and clearly British.

"Who's asking?" Henderson said.

"My name is Dr. James Samuels. You might remember me, sir, from our time at Dalgety Bay."

Henderson remembered him, or at least his name. They had nearly died together. "I can't say that I actually remember you, Doctor, but I have heard quite a lot about you. I'm curious...how did you get this number?"

There was a pause. "I...I was told that you were...given the phone that you are holding in order to take this call."

"Told by who?"

Another pause. "The gentleman sitting next to me. As it turns out, he was also at the Bay. He actually escorted Nenita and I from Lyon to Scotland. He has asked that I tell you that his name is Gad."

Henderson tensed. "I see. And what is it that he wants?"

"He...he is requesting that you come to Vilnius."

"What for?"

Another pause. "To...discuss strategy regarding Lithuania's role in Latvia's war with Putin."

Henderson frowned. *Gad doesn't give a shit about Lithuania or Latvia.* "I see. And how are you involved, Doctor?"

There was a longer pause. "Actually, Mr. Henderson, this man is holding a gun to my head as we speak."

CHAPTER 89

Outside Falls Church, Virginia

Knight felt sick. The more he thought about it, the more he was able to see what Morningstar had done through the years. Like the script of a play, he had begun to see how each infernal act fit together. Starting with the death of Knight's parents, Morningstar had taken advantage of every situation. He had groomed Knight for the role he was playing, and Morningstar, either through luck or manipulation, had even orchestrated Knight's rise to the presidency. And now that he was there, Morningstar was using him to achieve his goals...not for the country, but for himself.

Knight was also aware that there were others...men like him who had been compromised, either by grief or pain or neglect, and had, over time, become pawns in Morningstar's fiendish plot. He had hired those men as sons in his army; he had molded them into devoted soldiers for his cause. What exactly was his cause? Knight shook his head and sighed. *Does it matter?* Morningstar's goals had seemed noble; they had been Knight's goals, after all...a stronger America that took pride not only in its strengths but in its freedoms, and displayed its success without shame. Though not perfect, the experiment that was America had worked well for over two centuries. But America's role had started to fade; both Knight and Morningstar had felt it.

But now, suddenly, it was as if a shade had been pulled from Knight's eyes, and he had seen the light. Morningstar wasn't after respect for

America, he was after power. *For himself.* And, though Knight was unwilling to accept that the man would actually kill Emma, he had to face the fact that he had implied that it might happen…and soon. *Why imply such a thing unless he has a hand in it?*

Which had led Knight to where he was now…struggling to breathe as he sat hunched over a small wooden desk in a makeshift bedroom at a warehouse outside Virginia. He suspected that what Morningstar had told him was true; that someone was just outside the door, waiting to put a bullet in his beautiful Emma. So, he had spent the last hour trying to come up with a plan for her escape.

Emma was sleeping on the bed beside him. But it wasn't restful; that much he could tell. He could see her brow crease, her eyes flutter. *What have we done?* Not only had they gone down a path that could tear her family apart, but now her very life was at risk. Was it worth it? Only she could answer that question. And he was afraid to ask her; afraid to find out. He was also afraid to let her in on the fact that their love would likely get her killed. He focused on the computer screen in front of him.

The computer belonged to Foster. It was his surveillance laptop that he never went without. The minute Knight had ended the call with Morningstar, he had asked Foster to download the White House surveillance reports from the past twenty-four hours. *How much has Morningstar seen?* Though Knight knew that the reports wouldn't say, "Edward Morningstar is monitoring the President," he was hoping to see something that would indicate the reach of that man into his world. He frowned. *Hell…the reach of that man is infinite…and I have known it for most of my life…*

> *"Stop, Jerome!" The voice was deep, echoing through the quiet bedroom like a gong.*
>
> *Sixteen-year-old Jerome Knight looked up from the bed, where he was about to have his first sexual encounter with a girl, Tammy, from the nearby Catholic school in downtown Bangor. Where had the voice come from? The girl pulled her blouse around her as she, too, scanned the room.*
>
> *The voice spoke again, seemingly from the heavens, the heavy intonation not unlike Jerome's images of God Himself. "There's no time for dalliances with whores. Now get her out of there!"*

But God wouldn't refer to sweet little Tammy as a whore. She was actually a virgin herself, and, though Jerome certainly wouldn't say he was in love with her, he liked her…quite a bit. Wasn't that enough?

Tammy's dark eyes were wide with fear, her white cheeks now fiery red. "I…I need to go, Jerome. This was…a mistake."

"No, wait, Tammy. I'll close the blinds…we'll be fine."

"They're already closed. That…man…must have a camera in here."

She was right. Though Jerome couldn't imagine why or where it would be, it was clearly the case; how else had he seen what was about to happen?

Jerome got up and grabbed his pants from the floor, pulling them on as he scanned the room. The voice came again. "Don't look for a camera, Jerome. You'll never find one. But now you know…I will always see you…I will always know where you are and what you are up to…"

Knight leaned forward and put his head in his hands. Morningstar had spied on him his entire life. What had made Knight think that Morningstar wouldn't find a way to follow him to the hide-away in Virginia? He frowned. *But only Foster knew of the warehouse.* And Knight felt certain that he could trust Foster. So…unless Morningstar had a camera in Knight's head, someone else was watching him. *How many eyes does Morningstar have working for him?* He sighed as he looked at the reports on the screen. They told him nothing. Yes, the White House was being watched by members of the military establishment, but no, that wasn't odd. *"Don't look for a camera, Jerome. You'll never find one."* Morningstar had at his disposal the most highly advanced reconnaissance available. *Maybe there really is a camera in my head.* He flinched. *Or a tracking device!* Had the maniac put some sort of GPS tracker under his skin? He patted his arms and legs, feeling for what he knew wasn't there. *If there was such a device, he wouldn't have let me get this far with Emma.* So, how had he known about her…both at Katahdin and in Virginia. *A spy? A special agent who works only for him?* That seemed plausible, but who?

Knight stood and paced the room. *It could be anybody…even one of the agents in this warehouse.* He stopped and stared at Emma. His heart broke as he looked at her, angry at the thought that he had put her in danger. *If Morningstar wants her dead, she'll be dead.* But how far would the man go? How many would he be willing to kill in order to get to Emma? Would he kill Foster, a decorated agent who had received numerous commendations for his service over the years? *Yes, in a heartbeat.* How about the other agents, both there and in the White House; would Morningstar be willing to kill one of them to get to Emma? He realized now that he would. How about the Vice-President, Bob Harrington? Would Morningstar be willing to take out the second most powerful man in the world for the chance to kill his 'son's' lover?

From nowhere, came the image of the former President, Jim Wilcox, and the assassination that had catapulted Knight, within months, from a little-known Florida senator to the highest office in the land. Knight grabbed his stomach, a sudden bout of nausea forcing him to the bathroom. He leaned over the toilet, spitting as he fought the urge to vomit. His legs were shaking; he put one hand on the back of the toilet and the other against the wall. *Here I am, standing over the shitter...the most powerful man in the world, yet the most vulnerable man alive.* He coughed a few more times, then straightened, staring down at the bile-tinged water as he flushed it away. He hadn't allowed himself to dwell on the murder of the President; he had ordered an investigation but had left it at that. He hadn't dared to think who might profit from such an act. *Me...and Morningstar.* But suddenly, it was all he could think about. It had worked out spectacularly for both of them. Was Morningstar depraved enough to kill a sitting President? Suddenly Knight knew...the answer was at least a firm maybe. He grimaced. *And if he's willing to do that, then how can Emma ever be safe?*

He walked to the sink, rinsed his mouth, and splashed water on his face. How many times had he stared in those eyes, searching for the man he used to be; the man who had climbed mountains and had loved Emma with joy in his heart? *Who am I now?* he wondered, as droplets of water hung from his chin. *Who do I work for?* Though he wanted to say "the people of America," he knew better; he worked for Morningstar. Everything he had done for the past twenty-four years had been done for one man and one man only. Through hours of study and years of sacrifice, Knight had become what Morningstar had wanted him to be; the center cog in an elaborate power grab.

He looked closer, then, suddenly, his eyes grew wide. *But Morningstar is as vested in me as I am in him; his success relies on mine.* He grabbed a towel and wiped his face as he continued to stare in the mirror. *I'm the one man he won't kill…at least not yet.*

He walked back to the bed and stared down at Emma. She was lying on her back, her eyes closed. She almost looked dead. He flinched as he faced the cold hard truth. *She must be with me…always. I am the only one who can protect her.*

But where could they go? Could he hide her in the White House? There were hidden tunnels and secret rooms throughout that building. Again, he thought of the bedroom in Maine and his attempt at sex when he was sixteen years old. Just like that bedroom, Morningstar was probably monitoring every foot of the White House. Knight fought another bout of nausea as he realized that Morningstar had probably seen him at his most vulnerable…in the bedroom lying awake at night, in the bathroom crying under a steaming shower…*in the alcove near the Oval Office, where I stare in the mirror and search for who I used to be.* Morningstar had probably seen him smile as he recalled the days with Emma, or frown as he tried to imagine how he had become President. Yes, the man had probably seen every emotion, every triumph, every weak moment, every aspect of his life…*for the past twenty-four years.*

Emma moaned and turned on her side; he watched her. She would wake up soon. He had to finish his plans.

He walked to the desk, noticing for the first time its solid oak construction and the thick metal knobs. He guessed that the desk had been left in the warehouse when the cadets were moved to Virginia. He rubbed his hand over it. Though the wood had faded and the knobs had become tarnished and scratched, that desk was an imposing piece of furniture. It spoke of history and diligence and decisions that had been made during years of trials and strife. It had character…*and now, so must I.*

He took a deep breath and sighed. One thing was clear: he would need to keep Emma at his side. He was the only one who could keep her safe. He couldn't take her to the White House; Morningstar had eyes and ears everywhere. *So where will we go?*

He thought of his Vice-President, Robert P. Harrington III. The guy wasn't formidable; quite the opposite, he was more or less a figurehead…

perfect for a VP. He would be well-suited for the role Knight had in mind; not as Commander-in-Chief, but as an empty suit, a puppet, the guy who does what he's told by the Man behind the Curtain. Knight shook his head and muttered disgustedly, "Just like I've been all this time."

"What did you say, baby?"

He turned to look at Emma. She was up on one elbow looking at him.

"Nothing," he said as he walked to the bed. There she was; the woman he had dreamed about so many nights for the past sixteen years...*and, finally, she's here.* Knight knew what he had to do. Though it would border on the insane, and might possibly be disastrous in the end, there was no other option.

"So...what comes next, Romer?"

He narrowed his eyes. "I'm going to keep you safe."

She frowned. "From what?"

"I'm not quite sure."

She frowned. "I feel safe with you."

He smiled and knelt down in front of her. She seemed so small, so fragile...*so vulnerable,* he thought, as he pulled her close. "You are safe with me."

She smiled, but then it quickly turned to a frown. "So, what's wrong. What's troubling you?"

Knight sighed. "Not everyone is happy that we're together, Emma."

Emma nodded. "I know. Perhaps we should stop this. I don't want you to lose everything...your goals, your dreams...for this...for me."

He hugged her. "You're my dreams, Emma. You have been my dream ever since the day I met you."

She smiled, seemingly relieved. "And you, mine, Romer. But I've been watching you at that desk, and I mean it; you can't do...whatever it is you're thinking of doing."

He put his hands to her cheeks. "I have to do this, Emma...*we* have to do this. We actually have no other choice." She was about to object again, when he leaned forward and kissed her forehead. "We'll be fine, Emma. The world will be better off...trust me." He could feel her trembling. He added, "But I need to let Foster in on the plan. There's a man outside this warehouse, and he may not wait much longer."

Emma's eyes widened; she sat up in the bed. "For what?"

Knight sighed. "To hurt you."

Again, he kissed her forehead, then walked out of the room.

He found Foster. "Come with me." He took him by the arm and walked him toward the kitchen. He grabbed the radio on the way, and, as they walked to the back of the small room, he set it on the table. He turned it on low in an effort to muffle their voices. With a vibrant Handel opera playing in the background, Knight whispered, "We're leaving...soon, Foster. Emma is coming with us. We'll head back to DC so I can take care of a few things, then we'll leave."

Foster's eyes were wide. "Where are we going, sir?"

"To the mountains, Foster. We're going to the mountains."

Foster shook his head. "I'm going to need time to prepare—"

"There's no time." Knight put his hand on the agent's shoulder. "I'm not coming back, Foster...at least not any time soon."

Foster was unsteady; he tried to find a chair. He fell onto a box instead. He was visibly shaking as he looked up at his boss. "Wh—what?"

"There's something I have to do." Knight combed his hands through his hair. "I love this country, Foster, and I can't do what is about to be asked of me."

"Sir?"

"I can't leave Emma, and... I–I can't carry out The Plan."

"What plan?"

"It doesn't matter, Foster. I've lost my stomach for it. And, though I should now step down, I can't. I am in the unique position of knowing what's coming next."

Foster's jaw tightened. "I...I don't understand, sir. What's coming next?"

Knight shook his head. "There's a Plan...it has been in the works for quite some time, Foster. And I was to play a central role. But I can't do it...not anymore. And I can't step down...not yet. I alone possess the knowledge and the means to stop it, but only if I'm somewhere safe. And Emma won't be safe unless she's with me. She must disappear... which means that I have to disappear, as well."

Foster swallowed. "Sir, I don't understand. How is Emma in danger?"

Knight frowned. "I don't know the details, Foster. But she is. Imminent danger...right now, as a matter of fact."

Foster looked around furtively. "From who, sir?"

Knight stared at Foster. "Do you trust the four agents who are with us in this warehouse?"

Foster nodded. "Yes sir. I handpicked them for this assignment, sir."

Knight nodded. "If that's the case, then I'm guessing that there must be a man outside who's been watching us since we arrived. And I would also guess that he received orders about an hour ago to kill Emma the minute we leave."

"Dear god!"

"I know it's a lot to swallow, Foster, and I'm sorry for bringing you into it."

Foster said nothing as he stared down at his shoes.

Knight went on. "I didn't come up with this plan on a whim. It is all I've been thinking about since I took that call." He paused. "But I can't do it alone. I'll need you to gather three or four good men. They can't be from any agency. Off the grid, if you know what I mean. Men you trust...and who would never be recognized if they were seen on the street. No database history; no run-ins with the law. Can you do it?"

Foster continued to stare at his shoes. Without looking up, he said, "Are you devoted to this country, sir?"

"I am."

"Are you faithful to the tenet that you are here to serve the people of this great land, and not the other way around?"

"I am."

Foster looked up, his eyes meeting Knight's. He nodded. "I know just the men, sir." He paused. "What do you need from them?"

"You must be able to trust them...I mean really trust them...with anything."

Foster nodded. "I can trust them, sir. We are bound by an event...a secret, if you will." He added, "Secrets can be very binding."

Knight sighed. "Yes, they can." He paused. "Their discretion will be vital if we hope to keep this country safe." He frowned. "But first we need to get Emma out of here without the guy outside knowing. She'll need to be disguised...as an agent."

Foster's eyes widened. "As an agent, sir?"

"Yes. The man outside is no fool. I'm sure he counted how many came in, and he will count how many leave. How much do the agents know about Emma and I?"

"They think you're having an affair. Nothing more. It happens, sir."

"Well, I can't pull them in on this; I'd be risking their lives, as I've already done yours. We need to somehow cover her in a suit and hat and get her to the car without the agents or the guy outside knowing what we're up to."

Foster shook his head. "Sir, with all due respect, these men will know. They need to be let in on it."

Knight sighed. "You're right. But we need to leave soon. Any ideas?"

Foster consider it. He nodded slowly. "I'll tell them a newspaper is trying to get the scoop on the affair and that we need to avoid an embarrassing incident. I can disguise Emma as one of the agents and send her out the door with you and three others. It will look like we're leaving the way we came: four agents and you, sir."

Knight nodded. "Sounds good, Foster. You need to be one of the men who leave with us. Two agents will remain here at the warehouse. The guy outside will think there's only one agent and Emma. That's when he'll likely make his move."

Foster nodded. "What then, sir?"

"Tell the agents to do whatever they must to keep the warehouse protected. It is government property, and a trespasser – particularly one with a gun – cannot be tolerated, especially during the shooting epidemic that is facing our country." He paused. "I will also need you to put out an announcement – through the local police – that a woman matching Emma's description was murdered sometime around noon today near Falls Church, Virginia. Don't give them her name."

Foster frowned, then let out a deep sigh. He cleared his throat and nodded. "Okay, I'll do it, sir. What do you need from my off-the-grid friends?"

Knight took a deep breath. "While I'm attending an afternoon tea in the Red Room with the Prime Minister of Japan, you – with the help of your trusted friends – will be preparing a command post for Emma and me."

"A command post, sir?"

"Yes. We need a bunker – a very secure bunker, Foster – somewhere in the caverns of Mount Katahdin."

CHAPTER 90

The Henderson Compound

Henderson hadn't moved. The call from Dr. Samuels had left him speechless. Apparently, the man with the gun had forced Samuels to call Henderson several times before he had finally answered. *And thank God, I did,* he thought. Who knew what Gad might do to that poor man if he were to become angry. Henderson had instantly told Samuels to do whatever he could to get away from him. He had then asked the doctor to put Gad on the phone. Before Gad had been able to say a word, Henderson had said, *"As you know, I'm on the run, and I'm a long way from Vilnius. It's going to take some doing for me to get there."* Gad had smirked. *"Find a way, asshole."* Henderson had said, *"I have something I need to do first. I'll call you when I'm on my way."* To which Gad had replied, *"To hell with that, Joey boy. You either come now, or the doctor dies."* Henderson had merely laughed. *"You touch one hair on that man's head and I'll slit my own throat. I'm guessing you'll be in quite a bit of trouble if that happens, right Gad?"* There had been a pause. Then, *"Make it quick, Joseph."*

The call had ended.

Walter and Cravens had simply stared at him. Though he knew they were eager for an explanation, he had told them very little. He wasn't yet ready to share the sordid details of Gad and Joseph and the detestable Jacob. *"Gad and I met in a previous life. Can we leave it at that?"* Both men had merely continued to stare.

Finally, in an effort to break the tension, and likely to relieve Henderson of the burden of revisiting his past, Walter had arranged for dinner to be brought into the room. *"I've learned that challenging discussions are often aided by a hearty meal,"* he had said as the servant had left the room.

Henderson had eaten only a few bites of a well-prepared filet, his mind consumed with how to save Samuels without losing his own freedom. He had yet to come up with a plan.

"Why do you suppose the man holding Samuels – this Gad fellow – wants you in Lithuania?" Cravens asked as he wiped his chin with a napkin.

In unison, Walter and Henderson said, "Extradition treaty."

Cravens' eyes widened, then he nodded. "I see. So, what're you gonna do?"

Henderson sighed. "I've bought a little time, but I see no way around it, I'll have to go. I can't let…that man…harm Samuels. The poor doctor has been through far too much already."

Walter shook his head. "You'll do no such thing, Martin. There are other ways to stop a man like that." He frowned. "How about you tell us how you know him."

Henderson frowned. To reveal how he knew Gad could lead to questions he wasn't prepared to answer, such as *"Have you ever worked with him?"* or *"Are there others like him?"* Could he simply say that he knew Gad, without revealing his own ugly past with Morningstar and the Sons of Jacob? He rubbed his neck and sighed. "Let's just say that he and I know a lot of the same people."

Walter narrowed his eyes. It looked as if he wanted to say more, but he simply nodded. "I see. So, what *can* you tell us about him?"

Henderson shook his head. "Not much. As you've already learned, he's referred to as Gad, and he is remarkably clever. He is also one hell of a sharpshooter, especially with only one eye."

Cravens stared at him. "What do you mean?"

"He has a glass eye, but can still shoot a gnat off a fence from 100 feet away."

Walter nearly dropped his glass of port. He grabbed Henderson by the arm. "Did you say a glass eye? The guy doesn't happen to be black, does he?"

Henderson frowned. "As a matter of fact, he is. Why?"

Walter shook his head. "Nothing. It's just that I had a driver—"

Cravens and Henderson stared at one another. Henderson said, "Was his name Carlos DeMarco?"

Walter frowned. "Let me think." He nodded. "Ya know, I think it was. Why?"

Henderson cleared his throat. "DeMarco was our original reason for wanting to talk to you." He paused. "We think that he – or a man impersonating him – purposely drove to the site of the plane crash within minutes of it hitting the ground."

Walter frowned. "You're saying that you saw one of my drivers at the site?"

Henderson nodded. "Yes. And I've done some research. DeMarco was the driver that was assigned to the car."

"But what makes you think that he went there intentionally? We're not that far from Liepaja…couldn't he have simply been driving by, and then stopped to help…or maybe out of curiosity? I mean a tragic accident like a plane crash—"

"That's just it, Dad. The crash…wasn't an accident."

Walter stared at him in disbelief; Henderson ignored him. His mind was going a mile a minute. "Which means that the man holding Samuels is quite likely the same man who drove to that crash site." His hands were shaking; he rubbed them on his pants. "Which means that *that man* knows exactly who was behind the crash."

He stiffened. It also meant that Morningstar – the bane of his existence – was somehow responsible for the crash. He could barely contain his anger. *Morningstar killed Maddi…there is no way around it.*

Walter stood and walked to the window. He turned to face them. "I… I don't understand. How do you know this? And why didn't you say something sooner?"

Henderson frowned. "It's a long story, Dad. Cravens has been looking for this guy for the past two months. And now we know…this guy is Gad, and he knows the truth behind the crash. Which means that he knows who's responsible for…for killing Maddi." As tempted as Henderson was to tell them that Gad's involvement meant that Edward Morningstar was surely responsible for the crash, he held back. It wasn't time; he needed more evidence…*evidence that I could definitely get from*

Gad. "I need to go to Vilnius. I, alone, am in a position to get this guy to talk."

Walter shook his head. "I don't know what you mean by that, but the answer is still no." He frowned. "We need to bring in the authorities."

"We can't." It was Cravens. He had stood and was looking down at the fire with his hands against the mantel. Without looking up, he said, "The minute we pull them in, we lose any chance of figuring out who is responsible for the plane crash."

Walter rubbed his forehead and sighed. "Why do you say that?"

Cravens turned to face him. "Because it's quite possible that 'someone in authority' was behind the crash. I mean, who else could sabotage an RAF plane?" He frowned. "We simply don't know who we can trust."

"So, what do you think we should do?"

No one spoke for nearly a full minute. Finally, Henderson looked at both of them and sighed. "We need to know not only what Gad knows about the plane crash, but what his plan is moving forward." He frowned, then nodded solemnly, "…which means that I need to go down there…now."

CHAPTER 91

Vilnius, Lithuania

Samuels hadn't recognized the wiry stranger; not at first anyway. The man had been wearing a hooded sweatshirt, and had pulled the hood low over his forehead. He had also been wearing sunglasses. But the minute he spoke, Samuels had known instantly who he was. He was the same man who had escorted Samuels and Nenita Villamor from Lyon to the Dalgety Bay schoolhouse in Scotland.

And the realization had frightened him. The man whom Cobra had referred to as Gad when they were at the schoolhouse, hadn't actually hurt either him or Nenita during that harrowing journey, but there had been no doubt in Samuels' mind either then, or now, that he wouldn't hesitate to hurt – or kill – anyone who got in his way.

He had approached Samuels in the booth and had said, *"Mind if I join you?"*

At first, Samuels had started to object. After all, he had had quite a bit of work to do. But before he could get out the words, the man had lowered his glasses, and Samuels had seen the glass eye – a memorable sky blue – that he remembered from the journey to Dalgety Bay. *"What...what is this?"* he had somehow managed to say.

The man, Gad, had laughed. He had patted his pocket and had said, *"I have a friend with me, his name is .38 special. We need you to come with us."*

Samuels had swallowed and had somehow found the strength to say, *"To where, young man. I have quite a bit of work to do."* He had looked around

458

the diner, hoping to get the attention of either a patron or a waiter, but there had been no one in sight. Gad had timed the abduction well.

He had grabbed Samuels by the wrist, and had said, *"I don't give a shit about your work, Doctor. Now, let's go."* He had squeezed the wrist even tighter and had added, *"...and if you try anything, I'll shoot you right here, right now, old man."*

Gad had left a twenty-euro bill on the table, then had slowly led Samuels out of the diner and onto the empty street. They had walked for about a mile, until they came to a small hotel which had a lighted vacancy sign over the door. They had walked in, and Samuels had done his best to move his eyes in such a way as to alert the clerk that he was in trouble, but the clerk was quite old, and could barely see his ledger, let alone the silent machinations of a man in trouble.

Gad had purchased a room for the night – with cash – and had led Samuels up a set of rickety stairs to the second floor. It was then that he had told him the plan. *"You're going to call Matt Henderson and convince him to come to Lithuania."*

Samuels had frowned. *"How will I convince him to do that?"*

Gad had shaken his head. *"I don't care how you do it, just do it."*

"I don't know his number."

"Don't worry, I do. You'll use this phone." He had handed him the phone. *"Just push 'send.' I've already plugged in the number."*

Samuels had stared at the phone and had shaken his head. *"No, I won't do it."*

That was when Gad had pulled out his gun, had held it to his temple, and had said, *"I think you will, Doctor."*

Samuels had swallowed and, with a shaking finger, had pushed 'send.' But there had been no answer, and there was no voicemail. *"He didn't answer."*

Gad had cursed and kicked the leg of a divan. *"We'll try again in an hour."*

They had tried three more times, as a matter of fact; Samuels had started to worry that if Henderson didn't answer the next call, Gad would kill him on the spot.

During that time, Samuels had been forced to sit in an old, wooden chair in the drafty hotel room. As the night had dragged on, Gad had been good enough to get Samuels a pot of tea, and then a sandwich sometime the following morning. He had allowed Samuels to use the bathroom, but had made him keep the door open. Whenever Gad left the room, he tied Samuel's feet and arms to his chair with zip ties, and put a gag in his mouth. Memories of being chained to a similar chair at the Dalgety Bay schoolhouse had nearly undone any composure Samuels might have tried to maintain. He had been forced to sleep sitting up, as Gad had taken the bed, and had again used zip ties to keep Samuels attached to the unsteady chair. Needless to say, not only was Samuels fighting to not fall completely apart emotionally, but his head was pounding, his eyes were burning, and his bones ached all the way through.

It had been a full eighteen hours from the time Samuels was abducted to the fifth call to Henderson; the call when he finally answered. The conversation had been short and to the point. Samuels had started by telling Henderson that Gad insisted that Henderson come to Vilnius, and that he was holding a gun to Samuels' head. Henderson had told him that he should try to get away, and had then asked to speak to Gad. From what Samuels had been able to tell, the call had only intensified the anger of the despicable Gad.

That had been over two hours ago, and it was clear that Gad was getting restless. He had paced the small hotel room nonstop since the call.

He stopped pacing and walked to the window. "I don't like waiting." After a minute, he turned to Samuels and sneered. "What if it's a trick?"

"A trick?" Samuels shook his head. "I know Matt Henderson. He wouldn't try to trick you when another man's life is at stake."

Gad smirked. "A noble guy, huh?"

Samuels nodded. "Yes. I've found both him and his uncle to be quite noble." He was about to add, "...unlike you," but guessed that Gad would hit him. He wasn't sure he would survive it.

Gad turned back to the window.

Samuels stared at him, thinking maybe he could use his skills to calm him, maybe even get him to stop what he was doing and let him go. He took a deep breath and sighed. "So, tell me, Gad, why are you so eager to get Matt to Vilnius?"

Gad turned to face him. The hate in his expression sent a chill down Samuels' spine. He smirked. "None of your damn business, old man. You just better pray that he gets his ass down here soon."

Though Samuels was afraid, he found himself intrigued by the man. *Clearly, something horrible has happened in this man's past that has left him bitter and broken.* Nonetheless, Samuels would do exactly what Gad had just told him to do...he would pray that Matt Henderson would get there soon.

CHAPTER 92

Barcelona, Spain

Cobra was tired…and irritated. Morningstar's insistence that he leave Hank – after his valiant effort to find him – and travel all over God's creation just to kill some Chinese minister's son was irksome. But at least he now had a timeline for his takeover of the castle. *I'll get to enjoy the holidays with my dear, delightful family.*

But first he had to take care of the business in China. He couldn't deny that the task intrigued him. Killing a Chinese military leader and a U.S. senator? Not bad. But he was angry that he had to go back to London before flying to America; it was an inefficient use of his time. He didn't understand why the senator, Sturgill, couldn't just meet him in London. Regardless, he had agreed, and now that he was no longer chasing Hank, what else did he have to do. Christmas was a full two months away.

He leaned back in the stiff chair near track seven of the Barcelona train station. His train to Paris wouldn't arrive for another forty minutes. He was still wearing his disguise as Oskar Berg; he would wear it until he reached London, when he would then become Daniel Frisk, also known as 'Viper.'

He laughed as he tried to imagine the look on Walter's face when he saw Cobra waltz through the massive doors of his ostensible castle. Of course, by then, Walter will have been taken prisoner by Morningstar's soldiers; it was the only way it could work. *And I'll still be Daniel Frisk, at least in the beginning.* Otherwise, some eager soldier might try to capture Cobra just for the sheer glory of finally stopping the most notorious killer since Jack the Ripper.

He grinned. How fun it would be to let his father know that his prodigal son would soon be coming home. He felt certain his time at the castle two months ago had left an indelible scar on his father's psyche. *To think that it was I who saved his righteous son, as if I had cut down Christ Himself from that tree.*

He laughed aloud. A poem was coming to mind. He quickly scratched it on a flyer that he had grabbed on his way into the station, the verses coming with remarkable ease. Once he had finished, he laughed aloud. *This poem is one of my finest. I need to share it with my father…he will be so proud of me.*

He pulled out his cellphone – Martin's phone – and found Walter's number under 'Dad.' He sneered as he checked the time. *Eight-thirty in Latvia, he's probably just finishing dinner.* He dialed. The call was answered with a quick, but cold, "Yes?"

"Hello, father…it's me, your favorite son."

There was a pause. "Why are you calling?"

"I have such good news, Father." Cobra chuckled. "I'm coming home! If all goes well, I should be there in time for Christmas! Isn't it wonderful?"

He heard a man's voice in the background. "Who is it, Dad?"

He recognized the raspy voice and he sneered. "Oh joyous delight! There he is, now! The favored one…the savior whose ass I saved not all that long ago." He paused. "Put it on speaker, Father."

"I will not put it on speaker."

Cobra frowned. In his most sinister voice, he said, "Put it on speaker, or I'll kill a dozen whores tonight and make you read it in tomorrow's paper, *Father.*"

There was a pause. He waited. He could hear the phone click to speaker. "Fabulous, Are you both there? Are you both listening?"

Silence.

"I need to know that both of you are on the line, or I'll have to proceed with my heinous, whore-killing plan."

A reluctant voice said, "I'm here." It was Walter.

"And how about you, Martin. Are you there, dear brother?"

Finally, a cold, "Yes."

"Good. I have a poem I'd like to share. But before I do, I thought you might want to know, Martin, that your lovely whore called me just before she died."

Cobra could practically feel the man's wrath through the phone. "Don't you even talk about her, Cobra."

"Don't you want to know what she said?" He chuckled.

Silence.

"She was apparently about to die, and she called this phone, thinking that she was calling you. She told me how much she loved me."

More silence.

Cobra chuckled. "Now for my poem." He looked around. Though the station was crowded, no one was paying attention to the lone traveler near track seven. He laid the paper on his lap, cleared his throat, then said in a hushed, but eloquent voice,

> *"October's chill is in the air*
> *And I must take a brief sojourn*
> *But while I'm gone, please don't despair*
> *As I will soon make my return*
>
> *"But likely not until the snow*
> *Has crested on the evergreen*
> *And skiers shuffle to and fro*
> *As carolers lie about their King*
>
> *"Yes, I'll be there to join you all*
> *As Christendom extols its lord*
> *And feigns a holy cattle call*
> *Put forth by a degraded hoard*
>
> *"So do not fret, I'll be home soon*
> *And then we'll kill the fatted calf*
> *But only if the crescent moon*
> *Is willing to indulge a laugh*
>
> *"The wise moon knows who saved mankind*
> *And no, it's not the One you thought*

For though He healed the sick and blind
He could not stop my juggernaut

"My boldest act? I saved your son
And hence, your future, come what may,
As I, the ill-begotten one,
Will join you there on Christmas Day."

He laughed. "See ya soon, Pops." He ended the call.

CHAPTER 93

Outside Falls Church, Virginia

Damn, it's cold! Emmett was tired…and incredibly bored. He had gotten a phone call from Morningstar soon after 1:00 p.m. asking if he had heard a gunshot, or had seen any commotion from within the warehouse. The question had puzzled him. *"Uh…no sir, but I saw POTUS and four agents leave the facility around twelve-thirty. That leaves only one guy guarding the Russian spy."* Morningstar had paused, then had said, *"Let me call you back. Don't do anything until you hear from me."*

That had been about an hour ago, and Emmett was getting tired of waiting. He was cold, he was wet, and he was getting stiff lying among the trees. He checked his watch. *Two-fifteen…come on, Morningstar.* He adjusted himself in his makeshift lair, doing his best to move his feet so they wouldn't cramp. Fortunately, the rain had stopped, but he was already drenched to the bone, and would soon have frostbite.

He edged his way to a row of hedges closer to the facility and again checked his watch. It was only three minutes later than the last time; he sighed. *Maybe Morningstar changed his mind.* Emmett shook his head. Morningstar wouldn't change his mind; he had had Emmett hunting the Russian traitor for the past forty-eight hours. If anything, the Pentagon official had become even more insistent that she be 'removed'. Which meant only one thing; Morningstar hadn't called him again because he was counting on Emmett to handle it on his own. *A good soldier doesn't need to be reminded of what he's been sent to do.*

A burst of rain came out of nowhere, and Emmett covered his eyes. He was only getting wetter and colder. It was time to act. *Either I kill her, or I get the hell out of here.* He tightened his jaw. Should he do it? *Yes, it's my only way back into the agency.*

He shoved the binoculars in his jacket and pulled his gun from its bag. *Here I come, Russian bitch.* Holding the gun with one hand, he used the other to inch closer to the fence; he was looking for a break in the wire. Not finding one, he pulled the rubber-handled wire cutters from his pocket and touched them against the metal wire, waiting for a shock, or to see if alarms would sound. There was a quick jolt, but no alarms. Using the cutters, he made four quick cuts, which were followed by four more jolts. He widened the opening until he could slide underneath without touching the wire, then crawled to within fifty feet of the door. He had decided that his best approach was to storm the door, kill the agent, then take out the girl. He swallowed, recalling Morningstar's words. *"Once you do this, Emmett, you're on your own."* But then he thought of his reinstatement and the commendation he had been promised. He nodded. *You have no choice, Emmet.*

He positioned himself solidly behind a rock and checked his weapon. It was a Remington 700, and it felt like a part of him. He had spent hours training with that rifle, and – though he had never been forced to use it – he felt qualified and ready. He gripped the stock of the gun with one hand, and the cold wet steel of the barrel with the other. He held his breath as he rose to a squat, ready to run at the warehouse and do his duty to God and country. As much as he hated to kill a fellow agent, he had no choice; he couldn't leave a witness to his killing of the Russian… *even if she is a spy.* He knew some candy-assed lawyer would have a field day indicting the ex-G-man who had taken the law into his own hands. There was no way around it; he had to kill them both.

Holding the rifle in both hands, he crept closer until he was only a few feet from the door. He stood and raised his rifle. Just as he was about to charge the entrance, the door flew open, blinding him with a flood of bright light. "Who's there?" a voice yelled from the doorway.

Emmett fired in the direction of the voice, as a barrage of bullets came at him from two different rifles. He felt a sharp pain in his temple. He grabbed his head and fell to his knees, then onto his back. He looked up, the trees and the sky blurring into one giant fog. As he lay with the rain pelting his face, he grimaced and said aloud, "For God…and… country." And then, Agent Emmett Wilson died.

CHAPTER 94

Washington, DC

Morningstar was tired of waiting. He stared out the window, taking a quick glance at his watch. *Two-thirty. By now that Russian bitch, Emma, should be dead, killed by my loyal son, Judah.* He had sensed that Judah's vow to kill Emma had been sincere, but he found himself wondering how he would do it without at least one of the agents seeing him. *Maybe he convinced the agents to leave without him, so that he could be alone with his woman for an hour or two.* But Emmett had told him that POTUS and four agents had left the warehouse two hours ago. Was one of the agents merely disguised to look like Knight? That could work, though Morningstar found it hard to believe that the agents would ever let Knight talk them into such a thing. And even if he had, how would Knight explain Emma's death when the agents came back for him? He would need to make it seem as if she had died from natural causes. Which meant that a gun was out of the question. *Poison?* he wondered, with a chuckle. But where would Knight get poison? He nodded. *Surely there is rat poison somewhere around that old warehouse.*

He thought about it some more, then shook his head. Not only was it farfetched to think that Knight could convince well-trained Secret Service agents to leave him alone with a woman, but he felt certain that if, in fact, Knight *had* killed Emma, he would have called Morningstar immediately afterward.

He picked up his laptop from where he had swept it to the floor in his rage, and turned it on, relieved to see that it still worked. He typed in 'Falls Church local news.' He was hoping to find something to suggest that Emma Melnikov was dead. He clicked on the news feed and skimmed the page. Nothing in the first few articles, nothing in current events, nothing in the 'midweek roundup.' Then he saw it. Listed as 'breaking news' at the bottom of the screen was a single paragraph that told of an active investigation into a shooting that had been discovered just minutes ago near an abandoned weapons facility outside Falls Church. The victim: a thirty-eight-year-old female. Was it Emma? He chuckled. *It has to be.*

He picked up his cellphone and dialed Knight's private phone. He would praise his son for finally seeing the light. He waited, his anger rising as the call went unanswered. There was only one reason why Knight wouldn't answer him. *Because the bastard didn't do what I asked.*

He dialed Emmett's number, thinking he must have been the one to kill the woman, but he didn't answer either. Morningstar was about to throw his phone against the wall when he tossed it on the desk instead. He needed his phone.

He walked to the window. The rain had stopped, but had left its gray, wet fingerprint over the entire courtyard. He bristled. *Don't sweat it, Morningstar. The news indicated that the woman is dead. What does it matter who killed her?*

He walked back to the desk and picked up his phone. He dialed Levi. "There's been a death outside Falls Church, Virginia. A thirty-eight-year-old woman. Find out who she was and how she died."

He ended the call, then tried again to get through to Knight. Again, it went unanswered. *Why isn't he answering?* Morningstar was furious. He looked at the paperwork he had swept to the floor; he should at least pick it up. *No…it can wait.* He needed to get out of there.

Though it wasn't even three p.m., he grabbed his laptop, slid it in his briefcase, and shut down his office computer. He took his coat from a hook on the door, pulled it on, and stormed out of his office and down the hall.

As he stepped out into the damp, bitter air, he looked up at the gray sky and frowned. *I swear on my life, Judah…if you have double-crossed me, you will feel the rage of the ages…like only God Himself can deliver.*

CHAPTER 95

The Henderson Compound

Henderson had never known such anger. Cobra's words had torn through his mind like hate-filled shrapnel, laying bare whatever was still standing in his bitter, broken soul. Not only the poem, but the fact that Maddi had called Cobra, thinking that she was calling him. But there had been a certain grace in finally knowing it; in hearing her last words, those words that had evaded him. *She still loved me.*

But beyond the heretical, hate filled verse, or the message from Maddi, there was a certain line in the poem that had unsettled him to the point of irrationality, and he had been unable to get it out of his head since the call had come through. *"My greatest act? I saved your son."* What had Cobra meant by those words?

He had asked his father, but Walter had been reluctant to say, so broken was he by Cobra's malicious rant.

Fortunately, Cravens had left the room just moments before the call had come through. He had gone outside to smoke, which is what he had done off and on throughout the evening. No longer needing to hide his presence at the castle, he had simply excused himself, had left the den, and had come back a few minutes later, a much calmer man. But it had left Henderson and Walter with only brief intervals during which they could discuss Cobra's disturbing words. During each of the breaks, Henderson had tried to get Walter to explain the line about saving his son. Walter had yet to do so.

But Walter's demeanor had definitely changed. Though Cravens must have noticed, he hadn't said anything. But the change worried Henderson. How could he leave with his father defeated, and Cobra vowing to come to the castle by Christmas?

But it hadn't changed the fact that – in Henderson's mind, anyway – Walter owed him an explanation for Cobra's toss-away line about saving his son.

Cravens left for another smoke break, and Henderson walked over and stood directly in front of Walter, who hadn't left his chair since Cobra's phone call. Henderson knelt down so that he was looking his father in the eye. The man seemed older, more stooped than he had earlier in the night, and it broke Henderson's heart. Though he hated to press the man, he had no choice. He was running out of time.

He took a deep breath, then softly, but emphatically said, "Am I to go to Vilnius never knowing what that bastard meant by those words?" He checked his watch. "It's almost ten, Dad. I need to leave soon, before Gad kills Samuels."

Walter focused his gaze at him. "You're not going to Vilnius." He cleared his throat. "And it seems to me that, though I might be keeping a secret from you, son, you are also keeping secrets from me."

"Like what?"

"Like your knowledge of what this Gad character is up to." He paused. "For example, your comment earlier that Gad won't kill Samuels until he has you." He frowned. "I think the way you put it was that you could cut your own throat as a way to keep Gad from hurting the doctor." He cleared his throat. "If that's the case, then it seems to me that you have all the time you need to get down there."

Henderson said nothing. Though Walter wasn't wrong, his father had no idea how unhinged Gad could be. In spite of the fact that Morningstar had obviously told Gad to bring Henderson to him alive, he wouldn't put it past Gad to kill Samuels if he was forced to wait too long. Walter had no way of knowing that; he had no way of knowing that the man they were discussing had gunned down an entire village of Argentine aborigines as they were dancing in the moonlight. Actually, there was so much that Walter didn't know. He had no idea, for example, that it was Morningstar who was responsible for all that had gone wrong in the world the past few weeks, the past few months, the past few years. Or how the man had commandeered both of Walter's sons – not just Cobra, but Martin, as well – to do his dirty work. No, there was quite a bit that Walter didn't know...*and hopefully never will.*

Walter cleared his throat. "How about this. I'll tell you what Cobra meant by that line in the poem, if you'll tell me the truth about your relationship with Gad."

Henderson flinched. *It isn't a relationship, Dad,* he wanted to say. But in essence, it was. Both he and Gad had been brothers of sorts; sons of the man who called himself Jacob. Just thinking about it made Henderson sick to his stomach.

He stood and walked to the window. Without looking at Walter, he said, "I honestly don't know Gad all that well. As I said earlier, we crossed paths a time or two, when I was...the Phoenix." He looked over his shoulder at his father. "Truth be told, Dad, you likely know him better than I. After all, he was a driver for the estate."

Walter shook his head. "He was only at the compound for a short time." He frowned. "I will say, however, the first time I saw him I thought I recognized him. And I had this bad feeling about him...right from the start." He hesitated, then looked down at the floor. "As it turns out, he left the night of the plane crash."

Henderson turned back to the window. "Yeah, I determined that from the drivers' logbooks."

Walter cleared his throat. "But before he left, I think he might have helped another man escape the compound."

Henderson turned to face him. "Who?"

Walter sighed. "Cobra."

Henderson's eyes widened. "Cobra...was here...at the castle?"

Walter nodded. "He was. But I didn't realize it was him until he was gone."

"What do you mean?"

Walter hesitated. "He left a poem...specifically for me."

Henderson frowned. "A poem...like the one he just recited?"

Walter swallowed. "Pretty much." He paused. "I got the impression that he had been here for at least an hour or two before he wrote it."

"Why do you say that?"

Walter tugged at his collar, then combed his fingers through his hair. After a minute, he looked at Henderson and sighed. "Martin, it was Cobra who cut you down from that tree."

CHAPTER 96

Evansville, Indiana

Thus far, Claire's journey to Evansville hadn't gone much differently than it had the last time she had gone there two months ago. She had set down in the same airport, had waited in the same line for a cab, and had been dropped off at the same intimidating courthouse in downtown Evansville. And now, as she stared at the steps which led to the daunting double doors, she wondered if maybe this time she would see it through.

She checked her watch. *Three-forty-five.* Her appointment was for four; she was surprisingly early. Claire was rarely early…for anything. *Maybe that's what comes with a firm decision.* She laughed. This decision was anything but firm. But she had finally accepted the fact that – right or wrong – the Vanderburgh County Prosecutor needed to know what happened to a cop twenty-two years ago. Still, it wouldn't be easy. She wondered what the prosecutor would do with the information. *Surely, he won't make it public…now that Maddi is dead.* She frowned. *Of course, he will. Solving a cop-killing cold case in an election year? He'll be a hero.*

The good news: there was no one left who would be hurt by the news. Both Maddi and her mother were dead. Claire had learned of Jeannie Madison's death only days after Maddi's, in an article discussing how unlikely it was that her mother had died at almost the same instant that her daughter was dying thousands of miles away. *Maddi's poor brother was forced to bury them both,* she thought with a sigh.

Suddenly, she frowned *...which means that he can still be hurt by this revelation!* Andrew, who had suffered through the loss of his entire family, would be heartsick as he watched his sister's memory being dragged through the mud.

With one foot on the step, Claire stopped. *I can't do this.* She sighed. *You have to do it, Claire...but maybe you should at least try to call him first.* She shook her head. *No, the last time you tried to warn someone about this horrible thing that you're about to do, the person you tried to warn wound up dead from a plane crash.*

She climbed the next step and stopped again, still battling it in her mind. Was Andrew the only one who would be affected? No, there was Hank Clarkson, and of course, the Hendersons. There were plenty of people who would be affected by what she was about to do. *But only one will have his entire life turned upside down...by newspaper reporters, TV news media, and investigators who will insist that he reveal what he knows about the crime from over twenty years ago: Andrew.*

She continued to climb the steps. She reached the top stair and was about to walk to the door, when she spotted a bench off to the side. It was the same bench she had sat on after she had heard the news of Maddi's death. She walked over to it, took a seat, and set her briefcase beside her. Should she call Andrew Madison and at least try to prepare him? She frowned. She could practically see the Exigent Cardinal waving his bright red wing at her. *"Of course you should, Claire. It is the only decent thing to do."* She sighed. *Perhaps, Mr. Cardinal, but I don't even know how to find him.*

Suddenly she thought of the folder she had brought with her. It was Maddi's chart, and it contained everything they had ever discussed. But in Claire's recollection, Maddi had never told her where Andrew lived. Suddenly, her eyes widened. *Wait a minute, she did!*

She pulled the folder from her briefcase and skimmed the pages, her eyes tearing up as she recalled each of the days when the entries were made. *Maddi's life...scribbled on 8 by 11 sheets of paper.* Maddi's emotions as she had told Claire of the fire that had burned poor Martin Henderson nearly to death. Her guilt over her inability to love Hank Clarkson as much as she loved Martin Henderson. The notes regarding her mother; the poor woman who had drowned her grief in bottles of wine...for over thirty years. Then she saw it; notes about Andrew, the brother who had been closer to her than most. She had written down Maddi's words…

"Though Andrew lives in Columbia with his wife, Amanda, we see each other whenever we can."

And she remembered her response…

"Colombia…as in South America?"
Maddi laughed. "No…Columbia…as in South Carolina. He and his wife work together at an inner-city clinic. They are both such good people…"

She checked the time. *Not quite four…they should still be at work.* She frowned. *And I should be walking into the Prosecutor's office.* Without giving herself time to talk herself out of it, Claire pulled out her phone and dialed information. "I…I need the number for an inner-city clinic in Columbia, South Carolina."

"Do you have the clinic's name, Ma'am?"

"Um…no. But I'm guessing there's not that many."

She waited, tapping her fingers on her lap.

"You're in luck, Ma'am; there's only one. I'll connect you."

Claire tugged at her collar. *I should hang up…right now!*

"Columbia Clinic, how may I help you?"

"Um, yes. I was wondering if I might speak with Dr. Andrew Madison."

"I'm sorry, Ma'am, he isn't here at the moment. May I take a message?"

Darn! "I don't suppose his wife is available," Claire checked her notes, "…Amanda?"

"She is. May I tell her who's calling?"

"Um, yes, just tell her that I was a good friend of her sister-in-law, Senator Madison."

"One moment please."

Claire waited. She checked her watch again. *Two 'til four…two minutes until I'm expected to report this crime.*

"This is Amanda. Lisa said you were a good friend of Senator Madison's?"

Claire was speechless. *This was a bad idea.* "Um…yes. I knew her well. We were DC friends."

"I see. What is your name?"

"Claire Porter."

"What can I do for you, Claire?"

"Actually, I was hoping to speak with your husband, Andrew."

There was a pause. "He's…out of town at the moment."

Drats! "How unfortunate. I really do need to speak to him."

"Can I give him a message?"

Claire sighed. *Yes, tell him that I'm about to ruin his sister's well-earned reputation, and disrupt his life in a way that he may never recover from.* She cleared her throat. "I'm calling to warn him—" she hesitated. Then, quickly, before she could change her mind, she sputtered, "Let him know that I'm in Evansville, Indiana…at the Prosecutor's office, and that I'm about to do something that will…affect his life greatly, and that I am so very sorry."

Claire ended the call before Amanda could ask any questions. Was it enough? She sighed. Of course it wasn't. *But it will have to do…there is nothing left inside me.*

She jumped as the tower clock rang out the first of four rings. She gathered up her things, walked to the door, and put her hand on the oversized handle. She took a deep breath. *Here 'goes.* She opened the door, almost wishing for another catastrophe to stop her dead in her tracks. *Where are you, Jimmy Olsen, when I need you?* She waited. Nothing. No catastrophe…no eager reporter rushing out the door to deliver a scoop to his publisher. *No, this time you are going to have to follow through, Claire.*

CHAPTER 97

Evansville, Indiana

Andrew pulled on his hood as he ran down Sycamore Street in Evansville, Indiana. He was exhausted. He had tried to sleep during the six-hour bus ride from Strongsville, Ohio, but had had little success, certain that the agents he had spotted outside Jenny's house were going to board the bus at the very next stop.

He hadn't wanted to make the journey, but he had no choice. The only way he was going to find Todd Jackson was through Todd's mother. And the only way to find Todd's mother was to go to the Evansville courthouse and locate her name in the file that had been set aside for the family members of deceased cops. He knew from his own experience that the records were kept in the clerk of court's office. At least they used to be, in a file that was regrettably referred to as "The Final Report."

But coming back to Evansville was even harder than going back to McCordsville. At least in McCordsville, he had some good memories. Not so with Evansville. Life there for the Madison family had been nothing but bad.

The bus pulled into Evansville at four p.m. sharp. He dragged himself off the bus and walked toward town. He looked around, barely remembering anything from his days in Evansville. He had done all he could to forget them.

He turned onto Elm Street and was about to cross onto the main road, when the vibration of his burner phone made him jump. He stepped between two buildings for privacy, as he fumbled through his backpack for the phone. He opened it and whispered "Amanda?"

There was a pause. "Andrew, I am so sorry to call, but I couldn't let this go."

"Let what go?"

There was a pause. "I…I just got a call from a woman who claims that she was a good friend of Maddi's. Claire Porter's her name. Have you ever heard of her?"

Andrew frowned. "No. What did she want?"

"She said that she was at the Evansville courthouse – at the Prosecutor's office – and was about to do something that would affect your life…dramatically."

"What was she talking about?"

"I don't know. But she said it was happening right now, and that she was very sorry. I know that you're nowhere near the—"

"Amanda, I have to go. I love you."

He shoved the phone in his pocket and ran down the street. He could see the courthouse less than a block away. He had no idea who Claire Porter was, or what she could do at the Evansville Prosecutor's office that would affect his life dramatically. But he was less than two minutes from that very courthouse, and he had already been confronted by so many unanswered questions, he couldn't help but think that – just maybe – whoever this Claire was, she might be able to shed light on at least a few.

As he sprinted to the courthouse, he realized that he had no idea who he was even looking for. *Claire Porter; who is she? What does she look like? How did she know Maddi? What could this woman – who claims she was a friend of Maddi's – be about to do at the Evansville Prosecutor's office that would affect my life?*

Suddenly, he stopped. *Is Claire with the Pentagon?* He shook his head. *No, they wouldn't bother with a county courthouse.*

He ran on until he reached the building. He ran up the steps and was about to open a massive door, when he stopped again. *Evan Jackson. Does this Claire woman maybe know something about what happened to Evan Jackson twenty-two years ago?*

He opened the door and stepped inside, waiting impatiently as he and his backpack were processed through Security. He grabbed his pack and said, "Where's the Prosecutor's office?"

"Second floor, toward the back."

He ran up a flight of stairs and sprinted to the back of the building. He reached the office and burst through the door. A smartly dressed older woman was seated at a desk. She looked up with a scowl. "I'm sorry, sir, but you can't just—"

"I'm looking for Claire Porter."

The woman shook her head. "I'm going to have to ask you to leave."

Andrew cleared his throat. "I…I just got word that Claire Porter is in with your Prosecutor. She's about to give him…information. I need to talk to her first."

"Sir, I—"

"Just let me talk to her…or to your Prosecutor…please!"

The woman held his gaze as she stood and put her hands on her hips. She narrowed her eyes. "What's your name?"

"Andrew Madison."

Finally, she sighed and said, "Give me a moment." She turned and disappeared into a room behind the desk.

Andrew swallowed nervously. He had no idea what he would even say if he was allowed to speak to the Prosecutor. *I guess it depends on what Claire has told him.*

The woman reappeared. "Follow me."

Andrew was led into a well-appointed office with a large picture window that overlooked downtown. Sitting behind a desk was a man who looked to be in his mid-forties with short brown hair and a goatee. A sign on his desk identified him as Richard Platt, Deputy Prosecutor.

Sitting across from him was a slightly overweight, pleasant-seeming woman with short, strawberry-blonde hair. *Claire Porter?* She was staring at him.

"I can see it," she said with a smile. "You actually look quite a bit like her."

Andrew's eyes began to sting. "I'm…I'm sorry…I don't believe we've met."

"No, but I've heard a lot about you." The woman stood and offered her hand. "I'm Claire Porter…I was Maddi's…therapist."

Andrew frowned. *Maddi was seeing a therapist?* "Andrew Madison," he said as he took Claire's hand. He turned to the Deputy Prosecutor and offered his hand.

The man reached across the desk, shook his hand, and waved him to a chair. "I'm Richard Platt. Please, have a seat, Mr. Madison."

Claire said, "It's actually *Doctor* Madison."

The Prosecutor nodded. "I'm sorry...Doctor."

Andrew sat down nervously.

The Prosecutor said, "Ms. Porter was just telling me a fascinating story about how Senator Cynthia Madison – your sister, I presume?"

Andrew nodded.

"About how your sister killed a police officer twenty-two years ago."

Andrew swallowed and shook his head vehemently. "Maddi? There is no way...no...no, that's not what happened. Not at all. You've got it all wrong."

The man leaned forward and clasped his hands on the desk. "Enlighten me."

Andrew's hands were shaking. He gripped them into fists. *Why does Maddi's therapist think that she was the one who killed Evan Jackson?* He thought of the tape and how Todd had repeatedly made the same claim. Andrew suddenly felt sick. *Maddi must have told her that that was what happened.* He swallowed and turned to Claire. "I...I don't know what Maddi told you, Ms. Porter, but...there is no way she could've killed Evan Jackson."

Claire's eyes were kind as she said, "I feel the same way, Andrew. But I think she was up against some terrible obstacles; perhaps she felt it was all she could do."

He frowned. "But...why do you feel compelled to tell someone – a *Prosecutor* – about all of this." He rubbed his eyes. "I mean...Maddi is... dead."

Claire let out a sigh. "It hasn't been easy, Andrew...trust me. But, it's my job to report any knowledge I might have of a capital crime...even if it's decades old...and even if the perpetrator is...gone."

Perpetrator? Andrew was having a hard time breathing. Why had Maddi told her therapist that *she* was the one who killed Jackson? To protect Jeannie? Why had she felt the need? It wasn't like the story was going to come to light. *Or was it?* Was Claire's appearance at that office related to Todd Jackson's visit to his mother's house? He looked from the Prosecutor to Claire, then back to the Prosecutor. Regardless of why it was happening or what the truth might be, he couldn't let some therapist ruin the reputation that Maddi had earned over a lifetime of good deeds. He felt the recorder in his pocket and thought of his mother's final words. Suddenly he understood. *Those words were Mom's dying act…for a child that she loved.*

He cleared his throat. "I…I know for a fact that it wasn't Maddi who killed that police officer."

Claire's eyes widened. The Prosecutor frowned as he sat back and crossed his arms over his chest. "What are you talking about, Dr. Madison?"

Andrew stiffened. Should he throw Jeannie to the wolves? The poor woman, finally sober after thirty years, had gone to great lengths to protect both Maddi and Andrew from Todd Jackson. *She was willing to give up her reputation…her very life…for us.* He closed his eyes. *It is what she wanted me to do.* With a heavy heart, he said, "My sister didn't kill Evan Jackson…who was a terrible man, by the way."

"Then who did, Doctor?"

Andrew's hands were shaking even more; he shoved them in his pockets. Though he had no idea what really did happen twenty-two years ago, he was certain that his mother had not possessed the strength nor the will to kill a man. *So, who killed Jackson?* He frowned. *Does it matter?*

He stared at Claire, then turned to the Prosecutor. In as commanding a voice as he could pull together, he said, "It was my mother, Jeannie, who killed Evan Jackson twenty-two years ago," he pulled out the recorder, "…and I can prove it."

CHAPTER 98

Madrid, Spain

Hank was tired and his heart was empty. It had taken over four hours for the horse-drawn buggy to reach the coastal town of Valencia, where an ocean liner had been waiting. The journey had taken them over hills and through dense forests. They had said little during the ride. Not only was it loud inside the buggy, but they had both been exhausted. They had mostly just leaned against one another, Maddi's head on his shoulder, his head resting gently on hers. Finally, as the sun had started to fade, Angelo's daughter had stopped the buggy at the edge of town. She had handed Maddi a packet, with a simple *"Boat, Santa Anna, waiting at dock."* Hank and Maddi had hiked into town, and, by the time they had reached the pier, they had had only a few minutes before the boat was scheduled to leave. Hank had run into a nearby shop and had bought Maddi a trac phone. He had written down the number, and had handed her the phone. *"Call me when you get to Corsica…and don't call another soul."* Maddi had agreed, and he had then walked her as far as the footbridge. They had stood there…waiting while the other passengers climbed aboard. They had simply stared at one another. There was nothing to say. Six long years had led them to that moment, and neither one knew what to do. A young man had walked by and said, *"Don't worry, bloke, you'll see her soon enough."* Maddi had started to cry, but then her tears had turned to laughter as she had slapped Hank playfully on the shoulder. *"Yes, bloke. You'll see me soon enough."* He had reached out and hugged her.

He had held her tight, fully aware that he would not see her soon enough…it was quite possible that he might never see her again. She had whispered, *"Be well, my dearest friend."*

With his jaw stiff, he had taken a step back and had watched in silence as she had turned and boarded the ship. She had stopped at the door, thrown him a kiss, and then vanished. She had reappeared on the top deck minutes later with several other passengers. She had waved; he had waved back. *"Goodbye, Maddi,"* he had whispered, as the ship's horn had blared. He had stood there, motionless, watching as the liner inched away from the shoreline. Twilight had set in, and, as the boat had turned and gone out to sea, she had quickly been lost to the shadows. He had kept watching. Finally, when the liner was little more than a speck on the horizon, he had turned away and walked into town. Even the act of moving his feet had required thought; breathing had no longer felt natural. Everything had become an effort. He had loved Maddi forever, it seemed, and, though that love had changed many times over the years, it was never gone. Maddi had never been gone…until that moment.

He had gotten a bowl of soup and a beer, and had then taken a cab to the nearest train station. He had boarded a train to Madrid, and had spent the hour on the train searching for a flight to DC. Every flight had been booked except for an eleven-thirty p.m. flight out of Madrid. He had booked the flight, had arrived in Madrid, and had taken a tram to the airport, which was where he had been ever since. After two long months, it was time to go home.

It was ten-thirty p.m. His flight would leave in about an hour. He put his hand in his pocket, surprised to feel the scrap of paper that Angelo had given him as they had been leaving his home. He pulled it out. It was an address. He frowned. *Maddi's new location?* He stared at the paper, then put it back in his pocket. He would look into it once he had gotten back to the States.

There's someone else I should call first. He had put off calling Jenny, knowing that he didn't have the energy to try to explain where he had been or what he had been doing for the past two months. He was hoping it would be easier to lie to her when he was with her…when he could reassure her with a hug and a smile.

He had also put off calling his boss, Hanover. It would be harder to lie to him…the man had every investigative tool at his disposal. Hank would need to come up with something so convincing that Hanover wouldn't even think to look into it. *Good luck with that one, Hank.*

He leaned back, stretched his legs, and rubbed his hand over his right thigh; the thigh that had been injured when he had tried to stop Maddi's kidnapper at the London hospital back in March. He combed through his hair, his fingers brushing over the scar from the fist fight with Henderson outside the Kauffold estate. Those scars were visible; most of the scars he had acquired over the last six years were not. He had fought a lot of battles for Maddi...*and I don't regret a single one.*

But leaving her on that Spanish coast had been the most painful of all of them...*for both of us,* he guessed. Not because they were in love with one another, but because they loved one another. They had become a part of each other's history, like childhood friends who had never been separated. *I should've gone with her.*

He heard the first boarding call for his flight. He let out a deep sigh. He was leaving; Maddi had already left. He was still Hank Clarkson; she had become Harriett Winthrop. He would be who he had always been; she would become someone else...possibly forever. He tried to imagine Maddi as a Brit. Fortunately, because of her time with her grandparents in Darlington, as well her years at Oxford, she had pretty much mastered the accent. *Maddi will be fine...she's a survivor.*

He rubbed his eyes. Yes, Maddi would be fine...but would he? He took a deep breath, then cleared his throat. *I need to talk to Jenny.*

He pulled the third and final trac phone from his pocket. *Where do I begin?* He thought back to all that had happened starting nine weeks ago. He had been about to leave the Henderson compound to go for a simple ride, when he had overheard a conversation suggesting that Maddi was about to be killed – *murdered* – in a plane crash. Could he tell her that? *No...the world thinks the crash was an accident.*

He continued mulling it over, and, after a few minutes, he had come up with what he would say. He heard the second call for boarding. He opened the trac phone and plugged in Jenny's cellphone number. He waited, suddenly aware of how nervous he was...not because he had been with Maddi for the past nine weeks...no, it was more like the anxiety one feels on a first date. He laughed. He had been married to Jenny for eleven years; they had a child together.

But the minute he heard her voice, his throat tightened and he was finding it hard to breathe. "Hey Jenny."

There was a pause. "Oh my god, Hank…it's you."

"Yes, it's me, Jenny…and I'm ready to come home."

CHAPTER 99

Washington, DC

"Have faith in yourself, Jerome." Knight was holding a crumpled photo in his hands. It was the only picture of his parents that he had held onto over the years. Not that there hadn't been many photos of the distinguished Carlton Knight and his wife. This just happened to be the one he felt portrayed them most honestly. He brushed his fingers over it, then set it on his desk. He walked over to a huge fireplace along the south wall of the White House master bedroom. He stared at the fire, the rising flames and changing colors reminding him of a similar fireplace in his father's study when he was a boy. *"Have faith in yourself."* How many times had he heard it; how many times had his father said the five simple words that had given him so much strength.

The phrase hadn't come from his pretend father, Edward Morningstar, or the stand-in, Charles Sturgill, but had been the words of his real father, the man whose DNA he shared. If young Jerome dropped the ball in Little League or was cut from the play at school, the honorable Carlton Knight from the Fourth District Court of the State of Virginia would be ready with a milkshake and those inspiring words. Knight smoothed back a strand of silver-gray hair. *So, what would you tell me now, Dad?*

It had been so long since Knight had spoken to his father...he barely even remembered him. The man had been tall...*the tallest man in the world.* And his eyes were darker than Knight's...and infinitely kind.

486

Knight felt his own eyes tear up; he missed him…he missed the father he had barely had time to know.

He thought of his mother; the way she would kiss his cheek whenever he was worried. *"Hush Jerome,"* she would say, *"it will all work out just fine."* He didn't remember his parents well, but he suddenly missed them more than he had in years.

He had been only fourteen when they had died in a car crash, and their deaths had devastated him. Within days, he had been whisked to Maine and more or less 'given' to his aunt and uncle, Charles and Beatrice Sturgill. It had taken him years to get past the grief, but, over time, he had learned to embrace his new life. Filled with discipline and inevitability, it challenged him like nothing ever had, and it gave him something to work for…something to look forward to…something to help him forget the pain of having lost his parents at such a young age. Gradually, those real parents faded into the past…like a scratchy old film with scenes missing, sentences blurred. But his father's words had stayed with him. *"Have faith in yourself, Jerome."*

Knight, along with a disguised Emma and three Secret Service agents, had left Falls Church, Virginia at 12:30 p.m., and had arrived at the White House about thirty minutes later. Emma, still dressed as an agent, had been secreted into the bedroom, where she had been hidden behind a divider in the back of the room. Earlier in the day, Foster had arranged for two White House staffers to put up the floor-to-ceiling divider. Aloud, for the sake of a potential listening device, he had said, *"They're remodeling the room next door, Mr. President. The screen should keep you from hearing the worst of it."* Fortunately for Emma, the screen was able to hide a comfortable Chesterfield chair, which is where she had stayed for the next few hours.

Knight had dressed quickly for an afternoon tea that was to begin in the Red Room at 1:30. On his way out the door, he had slid behind the screen and had stopped at the chair to whisper a goodbye to his hide-away lover. She had had a blanket over her head – Foster's idea, so that a stray camera wouldn't pick up the blue in her eyes – and it had been evident that she was crying. Not with sobs that would have forced him to reconsider, but silently, the blanket shaking almost imperceptibly as she tried to hide it. He had let her cry; he had let her mourn the world that she – that they – were bidding goodbye. There was nothing to say;

for better or worse, they had set their path. Both of them would soon be leaving everything behind.

But why was he willing to put her in such a position? Why not just send her home to her loving husband and her simple life? *Because she is only safe with me.* Once Morningstar had seen that Knight's love for Emma was greater than Knight's regard for Morningstar, she had become an even bigger threat than before. And once Morningstar discovered that Knight hadn't killed her, she would become a target.

But that wasn't the only reason he wanted her next to him. Beyond his love for her or his need to keep her safe, Emma Melnikov had always made him a better, stronger man. Sixteen years ago, she had inspired him to be daring and bold. He would need those qualities now if he was to stand tall against the powerful man from the Pentagon.

Fighting the urge to comfort her, he had left the bedroom and had hurried to the Red Room. He had made small talk with dignitaries, participated in a joint speech with Japan's Prime Minister, and had even fielded a couple of questions regarding his administration's efforts to confiscate America's guns. *"We had no other option, I'm afraid. But make no mistake; these shootings and the attempted coup are symptoms of a deadly cancer that is lurking here...a cancer that I will do my best to eradicate."*

Throughout the afternoon, he had received numerous calls from Morningstar on the phone which he now kept with him at all times. He had ignored them, somehow keeping it together as he had chatted with the Japanese Prime Minister about shared alliances and overseas trade. He had also bantered with the press, taking their questions with the ease of the consummate politician. But all the while he kept checking his watch, eager for the moment when he could leave the Red Room and return to Emma.

Finally, at 4:45, he had said goodbye to the last of the guests and had hurried back to the bedroom under the premise that he needed rest before a press conference at seven and a formal dinner at eight. Emma had no longer been in the chair. While Knight had been in the Red Room, Foster had led her to a secret tunnel, its entrance directly behind the divider. The passageway, known to only a few, had hidden lovers, courtesans, and even the occasional spy over the last two hundred years; each of them awaiting their chance to sojourn with the most powerful man on earth. The expression *"if only the walls could talk"* had likely come about from that very corridor. It had been Foster's idea to hide her there; he had assured Knight that he would make her comfortable. *"I'll find her a padded chair, I'll bring in candles to give her light, and I'll even bring in a book or two, sir."* Knight had asked about a bathroom and free-flowing air. Foster had told him that fresh air filtered through a secret door that exited to the outside, and that there was a bathroom at the far end of the hall. *"It's rather small, sir, but it will be suitable for the short time she'll be there."*

Knight had spent the time since making arrangements to leave. But he was struggling as he prepared to leave a job that no man had ever left early, unless by death or shame. He took a deep breath. *So, which will it be, Knight…death or shame?*

He sighed and walked back to his desk. He picked up the letter he had written just minutes ago. It was for his Vice-president, Bob Harrington. He read it through and nodded. *That should do it.* He folded it, slid it in an envelope, and put his seal on the outside. He wrote "For Vice President Harrington only" on the front. He would have Foster call one of the agents to deliver it once they were on their way.

He looked again at the bag he was packing; the backpack he was filling with the few things that mattered. Fully aware that a camera was likely watching him, he had been sure to preface the packing with a comment to one of his aides, saying that he intended to hike first thing in the morning at Boulder Bridge Loop, not far from the White House. *"It's going to be a late night, Simmons; I'll get my backpack ready now. We'll leave at six a.m. sharp."*

He laid the backpack on the desk, and his eyes fell once again on the photo of his parents. *What would they think of what I'm about to do?* Would they disapprove of his plan to run away from the White House? Or would they see, just maybe, that the plan he had been ready to enact on behalf of Morningstar was a destructive one, not only for him, but for the country. Knight had failed to see it…until now. Though he agreed with the premise – America needed to find its strength – he now realized that to achieve the goal with the forced restraint of its citizens was the exact opposite of how it should be done.

But was leaving the White House the answer? After all, he had more power in that house than away from it…didn't he? It was hard to say, and it was hard to know what the Knights of Virginia might have thought of their only son abdicating his responsibilities. He grinned. *But one thing I know...they would have loved Emma.*

He checked the time. *Five-fifty.* The press conference scheduled for seven o'clock had originally been planned so that he could announce that the country was about to be placed under Martial Law. Now it would have a different purpose.

He looked around the room. He had done all he could to ensure that the country would carry on without him. There had been letters to write, documents to secure, and secrets to bury until he could either return to explain them, or vanish forever and hope they never came to light. Periodically, as he had packed and chronicled and packed some more, he had stopped and wondered, *what has brought me to this?* Though he knew that part of it involved his love for Emma, there was more at work than a simple love affair. He had begun to see a chink in the armor of the man he had revered for so long. It was Morningstar who had prepared him to lead, but to what end? Had it been sheer luck that Knight had won his Florida senate seat so handily against the odds? Sheer luck that the Vice-President had resigned when he had? Sheer luck that Knight had been chosen to replace him? Sheer luck that James Wilcox had been assassinated not long after, and that Knight had become President? Suddenly none of those things felt lucky...or accidental. Though he hadn't reached the point where he was willing to believe that Morningstar had actually orchestrated those events, the thought was there...lurking in his mind. For the first time since he had met the man, he was willing to think that Morningstar might not be so noble.

But what was he going to do about it? He had no proof that Morningstar had had anything to do with VP Conner stepping down, or with any of the other 'coincidences' that had catapulted Knight to power. Regardless, he had begun to see that his ascension to the Presidency had never been about his wisdom, his charm, or his steady hand. It was – and always had been – Morningstar's lust for power that had put him there.

What his mentor had failed to predict, however, was that now that Knight had had a taste of ruling the greatest nation on earth, he wouldn't relinquish it easily...*not even for the man who gave it to me.* He *liked* the power...the strength of commanding the most powerful army ever amassed. The pride in overseeing the most vibrant economy in the history of the world. The satisfaction of knowing at the end of every day that it was he, Jerome Knight, who was keeping America safe. *And it is for that reason that I must go.* He was surrendering the most powerful role in the world to save his country. From what? Was it Morningstar…or was it his own hubris? He was no longer sure. For there was one thing that both men shared; a quality that had cursed mankind since the beginning of time…*an addiction to power.* It was like a drug; a poison that through the ages had tempted – and ruined – the greatest of men.

I wish I could leave the role to someone else, he thought as he looked down at the letter he had written to his VP. But he couldn't. The very power he was so eager to let go of was his only tool to stop Morningstar. *So, I will use it.* Once he was safely hidden away, he would investigate Morningstar. And, regardless of what he learned, if the man was responsible for any criminal act; if his motives were anything less than honorable…Knight would bring him to justice. He nodded. *Then I'll step down.*

A clock on the mantle rang out the first of six chimes. *Time to go.* Foster had come to his room just minutes ago, and, after a few perfunctory words regarding the evening's duties, Knight had walked to the other side of the room, while Foster had ducked behind the screen. Though Knight had been assured that his bedroom wasn't bugged, he felt certain Morningstar was watching him. Which was why he and Foster had said nothing that might give away what they were up to. Knight was leaving the Presidency and Foster was leaving his post; the ramifications were mind-blowing.

He started to shake. *What the hell am I doing?* He looked out at the Lincoln Memorial, standing tall in the shadows as the sun sunk low in the evening sky. Jerome Knight was standing in the epicenter of greatness; some of the most powerful men who had ever lived had stood in that very spot. *And I'm about to leave it all behind.* He closed his eyes; there was no other way. He couldn't spend another minute doing the bidding of a man who might be willing to undermine the very country that Knight had sworn to defend.

He zipped his bag and slid the photo of his parents into the outside pocket. He wondered how his life would have turned out if they hadn't died…if he had never met Morningstar. *I wouldn't be President,* he thought with a frown. *But I also wouldn't be running away.*

He set the backpack on the floor by his desk, along with a black hooded sweatshirt that Foster had gotten for both he and Emma. As casually as he could, he nudged the items behind the screen. He then walked over and looked behind the screen. Trying to seem merely curious, he stepped behind it. He put on the sweatshirt, slung the backpack over his shoulder, and fell to his knees. He said a silent prayer that what he was doing was right, then slid a secret panel sideways, and crawled into the tunnel. He closed the panel behind him, waiting while his eyes adjusted to the dark. He crept down the narrow passageway, focusing only on the candlelight in the distance. *"Have faith in yourself, Jerome."*

CHAPTER 100

Washington, DC

"I'm coming! I'm coming!" Vice-President Robert Harrington hated press conferences. Not that he would be the one doing the speaking; the presser had been called by Knight for a 'big announcement,' and, at the last minute, he had insisted that Harrington be there. It was scheduled for seven, but Knight had invited Bob and his wife, Louise, to dinner in his private quarters at six. Bob looked at his watch. *Six o'clock on the nose.* "Louise, are you ready? The boys are here."

'The boys' referred to two Secret Service agents sent by Knight to pick up Bob, his wife Louise, and his Secret Service entourage, consisting of four men and two women. Bob was standing in front of a full-length mirror admiring his suit. He had purchased it several weeks ago, his old suits no longer appropriate now that he was the Vice-President of the United States. They had been fine when he was merely Speaker of the House, but his rise in status had brought about the need for a whole new wardrobe. But in spite of the fact that his new role was impressive, Bob hadn't welcomed it. The Vice-President essentially ran errands for the President. His job was to attend funerals, work the campaign, endure the occasional interview. Not nearly as important as making policy decisions or visiting the Pope.

But it does put me one step closer to the Presidency. The Presidency was his goal. *Isn't it everyone's?* He had been stunned when Knight had chosen him to be his VP. There was no law that said that a new President, replacing a deceased President, had to call on the Speaker of the House to fill the role; it had just worked out that way. Harrington and Knight were from the same party, and they were almost friends. That was as close as two men ever got in DC. Knight had called him personally, and, as many were apt to say, "When the President calls on you to serve, you say yes."

He turned at an angle, admiring the new suit on his tall frame. Though he had gained a few pounds over the course of his two years as Speaker, the paunch in his belly was well-hidden by the cut of the coat as it fell across his waist. He brushed through his silver-tipped hair, tugged at his thin, gray mustache and grinned. His whiter-than-normal teeth glared back at him, and he was glad he had gotten them done. *"For the cameras, Louise...I only did it for the cameras."* His pale eyes gleamed in his sixty-year-old face, the wrinkles well-placed as he nodded favorably at the image before him; he was ready. No, he wouldn't say a word and, no, no one cared what he thought about anything, but he was ready to stand behind the President, smile when appropriate, and nod from time to time. *I might as well look good.*

There was another knock on the door. "Mr. Vice-President, are you ready?"

"I'll be right there," he said through the door. He yelled into the next room, "Louise! Come on! They're here!" A minute later, his short, chubby wife of thirty years emerged from the bedroom wearing a gaudy pink dress with matching shoes. Though Bob wouldn't have chosen the outfit, he had learned long ago to never criticize his wife's attire.

"How do I look, Bobby?" she asked, as she stroked her bleached-blonde up-do with one hand, while tugging at the snug dress with the other.

"Smashing Louise...absolutely smashing. Now, let's go."

He walked to the door with Louise at his heels. He opened it, surprised when one of the agents handed him an envelope. "I've been instructed to have you read this before we go, sir."

Louise ran up behind him and said, "What is it, Bobby?"

He shrugged her away. "I don't know." He pulled a note card from the envelope. The front of the card was etched with the words: "From the President of the United States of America." He opened it and a piece of paper fell to the ground. He picked it up and read the first line, written by hand with a bold, steady stroke.

"Please read this in private."

He moved to a corner of the room and Louise followed him. She was standing on her tip-toes, trying to read the note over his shoulder. He threw her a stern look. "Louise, this is top-secret. Please, leave me be."

"Oh my," she said, with poorly-veiled enthusiasm. She walked to a chair near the door and took a seat. The two agents stood at attention, while Bob crept even further into the corner. He began to read...

> Dear Bob. Something has happened. I've been compromised and you will need to take charge until I can return. My life is in danger, so I would appreciate it if you would keep from sounding any alarms until the very last second before the press conference at 7:00. I have cancelled our dinner, but have arranged to have a meal sent over for you and your wife. I would suggest you use the press conference to indicate that I have been relocated for my safety and the safety of the country. There will be quite an uproar, I'm afraid, and I'm sorry for that. It can't be helped. None of this can be helped. You are in charge of the White House now, Bob, but I won't be far away. I have left a phone in the bottom left desk drawer in the Oval Office. The drawer is locked, but Agent Paulson has a key. He knows nothing of this, however; no one does, but you and me. The phone can't be traced, and no one is aware of it. Carry it with you at all times, and call me if you feel like you want to jump off a cliff. Please – whatever you do – don't tell another soul that I am available to you. There is no other way to say this: not everyone in our inner circle can be trusted. I don't yet know who has been compromised, so, trust no one...only me. I will command the nation from an undisclosed location, but I will do it through you...at least for now.
>
> I have sent memos to both the President pro tempore of the Senate and the Speaker of the House informing them of this situation. They will not get their notes until after you have made the announcement. I've given them no details,

simply explaining that you will now be in charge. It will be your face the nation will see when they turn on their TV sets; your voice they will hear as we march to war. But I'll be here... telling you what you need to know; the things you won't hear from those around you. Listen to them, but then, listen to me. I'll make you aware of what's happening behind the scenes...the things they either don't know or don't want you to know.

Trust me when I say this, Bob: you and I are a team like no other. I need you to help me for the sake of the country and the certainty of our future. I am aware of how hard this will be. There will be many who will tell you what to do, how to feel, and what to think. Be your own man, Bob. I'll be right behind you...the entire time. You can do this. We can do this. I hope to return, but – if I don't – good luck and God speed.

Sincerely, President Jerome Knight.

Bob was speechless. *What the hell?* He read it again, then a third time. It couldn't be. Bob Harrington – only a Speaker just two months ago – had suddenly become the acting U.S. President. *And I can't even tell anybody.*

Louise was staring at him. "Well, Bobby...what does it say?"

His hands were shaking; he shoved them and the letter in his jacket pocket. He looked at her and frowned. "You'll learn about it soon enough." He barely noticed her indignant sigh as she glared at him from her seat by the door. It didn't matter. In little more than an hour, the whole world would know that he, Robert Harrington III from Bedford, Pennsylvania, had just become the most powerful man on earth.

Chapter 101

Washington, DC

Knight had stood in the passageway for a full five minutes, staring at the candles in the distance. This was it. Once he walked down that corridor, there was no turning back. He took a deep breath and sighed. *Just do it, Knight.* He took a few tentative steps, using the sides of the tunnel to guide him. As he got closer to the candles and to Emma, a glimmer of light fell across her face and he smiled. She smiled back and he knew…*this is right.*

Foster was waiting. He whispered, "We have to hurry, sir. Colt is waiting. His boat won't be able to sit at the dock very long without attracting attention."

Emma stood, ran to Knight, and hugged him. Her voice shook as she whispered, "Are you sure about this, Romer? There's still time to turn back."

He hugged her to him. "I'm sure, Emma. Are you?"

She grinned. "Yes. I've been sure for sixteen years."

Foster cleared his throat. "Sir, we really need to get going."

Knight nodded. "Has the note been delivered?"

"Yes sir. Harrington is probably reading it as we speak."

"Good." Knight looked at Emma. "Let's go."

Emma lifted a bag over her shoulder; her entire life in a backpack the size of a grocery bag. She was giving up far more than he was. She was leaving behind a husband and a daughter who had counted on her for fifteen years; a family who had loved her through happiness and heartaches; a man and child who would wonder what had happened to a mother…a wife. He pulled her close, the guilt almost more than he could bear. As if she was reading his mind, she pulled away and put a hand to his cheek. "Don't think about it. We're following a path that was laid out years ago."

"What about—"

She raised a finger to his lips. "Shhh."

Foster whispered, "Colt is waiting, sir…we need to go."

Knight kissed Emma on the forehead, then grabbed her by the hand. They followed Foster to the end of the hall, down a flight of stairs, and along another corridor. They reached the end, which was marked by slivers of light that crept around the edges of a well-camouflaged exit. Foster pushed against it and it opened about an inch. Extending a one-inch camera on a telescopic pole out through the opening, he scanned the area, saying nothing as he moved the lens up and down. Knight didn't know the man they were meeting. He didn't want to. Was Colt his last name, or was it some sort of code name based on the guy's position within the agency? Knight frowned. *Colt isn't likely part of any agency.*

Foster pulled back the camera, folded it, and slid it in his pocket. He shoved against the door, opening it nearly a foot. Cold air rushed into the tunnel. Knight took Emma in his arms, hugging her to keep her warm. The sun had descended behind the buildings of DC, leaving heavy shadows over the hidden door. Foster squeezed through the opening, then took a quick look around. He turned and whispered, "The boat is at the end of the pier. Pull up your hoods," He reached in his pocket and handed them each a pair of wide-framed sunglasses, "…and wear these."

Knight and Emma put on the glasses.

"Now remember, walk calmly; not too fast." Knight nodded as Foster ushered them out of the tunnel onto a barely visible path. He closed the tunnel door, then covered it with evergreen fronds. Knight looked up, noting a tree limb poking through the broken glass of a surveillance camera. Though he felt certain that Foster had been behind it, anyone spotting it would think it had resulted from the heavy winds that had come through earlier in the day. Foster led the way down the path, which was hidden by several rows of evergreens. Knight followed him, but was finding it hard to see because of the sunglasses. He held Emma next to him, focusing on Foster's back as the agent led them out of the trees and down the backstreets of DC. Knight's heart was pounding out of his chest; he could feel Emma trembling. He pulled her closer.

They reached the pier; he could see a fishing boat docked at the end. They ran to it and climbed aboard. An older man with bad teeth – Knight guessed he was Colt – opened a rusted galley door and hurried them down the steps. He locked the door. Knight could hear him running back and forth as he loosened tie ropes and ran to the helm. There was a sudden lurch as the ship pulled away from the dock. Knight and Emma fell against the side of the boat, while Foster clung to a handrail on the wall.

Knight pulled Emma into his arms and smiled. Though he should have been nervous, or at least unsure, he felt neither of those things. "Here we go, Emma."

She grinned, her eyes gleaming as she whispered, "Yes, here we go, indeed."

CHAPTER 102

Washington, DC

Morningstar was alone. It felt odd to be in the hotel room by himself, but Janet had told him that she needed to run a few errands to get things ready for the baby. It seemed like an odd request, but he nonetheless granted it, knowing that she was carrying the future king of the world. But he missed her. Not her good looks, not even her unending allure... he missed the companionship of his lovely, devious Janet.

But I'll never let her know that, he thought as he stared at the fire. He was wearing a silk robe and slippers, and was standing at the bar. He had a cigar in one hand, a glass of brandy in the other. She had promised to get back in time for Knight's speech, so that afterward they could celebrate. *It's not every day that your son the President declares Martial Law on the nation that you are about to control.*

He had tried all afternoon to reach Knight, but to no avail. He hadn't heard from Emmett, either, which meant that he had no idea the status of Emma Melnikov.

Who cares...the plan is still on track. He had been informed that Knight had made it to tea with the Japanese Prime Minister, which meant that he was still on board with the mission. Regardless of what he had been doing a few hours ago, Morningstar felt confident that at seven o'clock sharp, Knight would be standing in front of a lectern in the East Room of the White House, announcing his plans for America.

He checked his watch. *Six-fifty…better turn on the TV.* His private cellphone vibrated, and he answered with a harsh "What!"

"Sir, it's Levi."

"Why are you calling now? There's an important speech about to take place."

"I know sir, but I have something I need to tell you…several things, actually,"

"Hurry up."

"The first is that I intercepted an email regarding a blood vial from the CDC."

"You did what?"

"I intercepted an email, sir. Well, actually you got the email, but I read it."

"You're not making any sense, Levi."

"Okay, because of our…uh…maneuvers…regarding Putin and the war in Latvia, I recently put a tag on all communication that tagged either Latvia or the U.S. Government. Any correspondence would come through you." He paused. "About a week ago, I intercepted an email from an administrator in Sweden. Apparently, a blood sample that had been taken from someone in Latvia two months ago and intended for the CDC, had somehow gotten held up in Sweden. The email was an apology for the delay." Another pause. "I was curious, so I started monitoring the CDC. Three days ago, the vial of blood finally reached Atlanta." He cleared his throat. "The odd thing is, the vial wasn't accompanied by a name; only the initials MH, along with an identification number that reveals next to nothing about the patient from whom the blood was taken."

Morningstar narrowed his eyes. *MH…Matt Henderson?* "Who drew the sample, Levi?"

"Dr. Hank Clarkson."

Morningstar nodded. *Definitely Matt Henderson.* Did it matter? He frowned. *Only if he's tied to Phoenix, which shouldn't happen because there is no way that Phoenix is in any DNA database.* He nodded. "Who all has seen the email?"

"Only me, sir. I set it up that way. I wanted to make sure that I – you, actually – knew what was happening in Latvia before anyone over here became aware."

"Good work, son." He paused. "Keep the email – and the blood – to yourself."

"Um…sir, there's more."

Morningstar sneered. "Get on with it, Levi…I have a speech to watch."

Levi cleared his throat. "Um…the DNA from MH actually triggered a hit on the CDC's database."

Morningstar stiffened. "Go on."

"Whoever MH from Latvia is, he is somehow related to…the Cobra."

Morningstar's eyes widened. He hadn't even considered it. He had been saving that revelation as his final move. *To stun the world with the shocking truth about the Henderson blood line, thereby disgracing one of the most notable families in the world, and removing my only remaining obstacle.* But it couldn't happen yet; not until Martin Henderson was dead…not until he was no longer in a position to tell the authorities what he knew about Morningstar and his operation. He frowned. Without the threat of Morningstar telling the world about Cobra's ties to the Hendersons, Martin Henderson would have no reason not to talk.

He took a deep breath. "Shut it down, Levi. Shut it down…now. I don't care what you have to do."

"Shut it down?"

"Yes, dammit! No one can know what you just told me – not yet anyway – so do whatever it takes to make sure that no one finds out. Do you understand?"

"Um…yes…yes sir…yes, Father."

Morningstar reached for his drink and chugged it. "Is that all?"

"No sir." A pause. "I…I looked into that woman who was murdered earlier today in Falls Church…the thirty-eight-year-old."

"Yes…and?"

"The police department had no idea what I was talking about, sir. They said that whoever filed that report was – and I quote: 'just puttin' out bullshit.'"

Morningstar slammed his fist on the table. *That bastard!* Knight hadn't killed Emma after all. But apparently, Emmett hadn't killed her either. Which meant that Emma Melnikov was still very much alive. He checked his watch. It was 6:58. "I've got to go, Levi."

"There's…there's one more thing, sir."

"Jesus, Levi, get on with it!"

"Sir, I just overheard a conversation between Daniels and the Vice President."

"Go on."

Silence.

"Just tell me, dammit!"

"Um, sir, the President is gone. He has…um…gone into hiding."

CHAPTER 103

Nantucket, Massachusetts

Conner was pissed. "I don't care what he's doing; get Harrington on the line now, dammit!"

The former Vice-President had tried calling the current Vice-President for the past hour but had been told repeatedly that the man was unavailable. Harrington's handlers had used every excuse in the book, and had finally resorted to *"He's at an evening church service with his wife,"* which Conner knew was a lie. *The asshole doesn't even believe in God, for Christ's sake.*

This time, the handler said, "Can I have him call you, Mr. Vice-President? He's preparing for a press conference."

Shit! Conner had forgotten about Knight's press conference. "Yeah, as soon as you can." He checked his watch. *The damn thing's about to start.* "Tell him it's a matter of the utmost urgency, will you?"

"Certainly, sir. I'll take your number and have him call as soon as he can."

"Fine. But if I don't get a call in the next two minutes, heads will roll. Ya got that?"

"Um, yes sir. I will let him know, sir."

Conner tossed his phone on the couch. The press conference had been scheduled out of the blue that morning, with no specifics. The media had spent most of the day speculating on what might be discussed. *Probably just more war talk.*

Conner had spent the last twenty-four hours trying to figure out what to do with the information his former Secret Service Agent, Scott Johnson, had given him the night before. Morningstar, through one of his minions, had possibly concocted faulty intelligence that had spurred what could easily become a world war. Conner needed to discuss it with someone in power, but it wasn't like he could call the President. Knight was the guy who had benefitted most from Conner's removal from office. For all Conner knew, he might be part of the plan. But Conner had to at least tell someone that Morningstar was quite possibly planning something that might destroy not only the United States of America, but the world. He didn't feel he could trust the boys at the Pentagon; no one knew better than Conner how many of them were compromised. *Would they go so far as to betray their own country?* He hoped not. It was one thing to skim a little cash from overseas arms sales; it was quite another to plot against Old Glory.

Conner would need to tread carefully. Morningstar had threatened to bury him when he had forced him to step down from the Vice-Presidency seven months ago; he could certainly do the same thing now. *But I'll be smarter this time.* He would get to Morningstar before Morningstar could get to him. He would align himself with the right players, and he would start with the current Vice-President, Bob Harrington III.

He knew Harrington from their days in Congress, and the man owed him a favor. What he was about to ask wasn't really a favor, but he knew Harrington would at least listen, and then maybe he and Conner could work together to look into what Johnson had uncovered in the secret emails.

Conner stood from his chair on the glassed-in lanai and walked to the window. He opened it a crack and looked out at the bay. He breathed in, the cool, fresh air reminding him of how much he enjoyed his carefree days in Nantucket. His life away from DC was a good one; he didn't want to jeopardize it. But if what Johnson had told him was true, then his way of life was already being jeopardized...*by the overthrow of the very government I pledged to defend.* And, from what he could tell, he was one of the first to know about it. He took a sip of cognac and grinned. *If I play my cards right, I could come out of this smelling like a rose.*

He checked his watch: 7:00. Should he watch the speech? *Hell no... I've watched enough of those speeches to last me a lifetime.*

His phone rang. His frowned; it was his former Secret Service agent. "What's up, Johnson? And make it quick. I'm waiting for a call from Harrington."

"Oh...my god." The man's voice was shaking.

"What's wrong?"

"You're not...watching the speech, are you, sir."

"No, why would I want to hear Knight blather on about a war."

"Sir, it's not Knight who's speaking."

"Who the hell is it?"

There was a pause. "Sir, it's the Vice-President...and he's just announced that Knight...has gone into hiding."

Conner's legs barely held him as he stumbled to a flat-screen TV. He switched it on and then stared in awe as Harrington – who looked like a deer in the headlights – explained to the world that the President had abdicated his position due to *"...threats I cannot elaborate on."* Conner fell into his chair, gulping what remained of the cognac. "What kind of shit is this, Johnson? Presidents don't just...leave."

"Well, this one has. And Harrington's in charge."

Conner was stunned; which was hard to do to a man who had seen the uglier side of Washington more often than he cared to think about. He needed to know more. "Johnson, do you know any of the agents assigned to Knight?"

"Sure, I do. I know every one of them, as a matter of fact."

"But do you know any of them well? Well enough to take them into our confidence?"

Another pause. "One of them. He was kind of a loner, so we hit it off. You probably remember him. The Irish guy; Jerry Foster."

Conner thought back to what seemed like a lifetime ago. He remembered Foster: reddish hair, freckles...too wholesome for DC. "Is he trustworthy?"

"I believe so, sir."

"Good. You need to call him. You need to find out what he knows about the disappearance of the President, and then you need to let him know that you think the country is about to be threatened by a respected member of the Pentagon."

"May I ask what it is you hope to accomplish, sir?"

Conner rubbed the back of his neck. "Johnson, depending on why the President has left the White House, I'm thinking we might be able to enlist Knight's help to stop Morningstar." He paused. "Trust me when I say this, Johnson. It is quite likely the two things are related."

There was silence. "You think Morningstar had something to do with getting rid of President Knight?"

"Maybe." He paused. "Or maybe it's the other way around."

"I'll call him right away, sir. I'll get back to you after I've spoken to him."

They ended the call. Conner muted the TV. He sat in his chair and stared at the screen. He knew his phone would soon be ringing off the hook. His security staff would be doubled, and the normal operations of the United States government would most certainly come to a halt. As he thought about Morningstar – the man he had gotten to know fairly well through the years – he tried to imagine what he might be up to. *So…which is it, Morningstar? Are you after the President…or is the President after you?*

CHAPTER 104

Washington, DC

The shit has hit the fan! Morningstar rubbed the back of his neck, stunned and infuriated by all that had happened. In almost the same instant that he had learned that Judah had betrayed him by lying about killing Emma, he had learned that that same son, his Judah, the President of the United States, had gone into hiding. *Whoever heard of a U.S. President going into hiding!*

Harrington's speech had been brief and to the point. The President, for reasons Harrington couldn't discuss, had felt a need to abdicate his role. Until his return, the feckless Bob Harrington was in charge. Not a word was said about Martial Law.

Morningstar's eye had twitched throughout the ten-minute speech. Afterward, he had switched off the TV and had poured another brandy. He had gulped it down and had poured another. Since then, he hadn't left his chair. He didn't know where to start. Too many bombshells at once. The first was that, unless Levi was able to silence a CDC lab, the world would soon learn that Cobra was a member of the illustrious Henderson clan. And though Morningstar had had every intention of eventually telling the world about Cobra and the Hendersons, he couldn't do it until Henderson was dead…*so the prick can't tell the authorities what he knows about me.*

The threat of the revelation that Cobra was a Henderson was likely the only thing that had kept Henderson from telling the world about

Morningstar and his operation thus far. If that threat was to be removed, then Henderson would have no reason to not tell anyone who would listen what he knew about Morningstar. But hopefully, Henderson was on his way to Vilnius, where a team of U.S. soldiers were prepared to bring him home. Morningstar had to keep the revelation about Cobra quiet until he could get him to America and kill him.

But that wasn't the half of it. His other son, his devoted Judah, had betrayed him with the Russian whore, Emma…*and now the bastard has gone missing!* Had Judah lost his nerve? Had he changed his mind at the eleventh hour? *It's Emma Melnikov's fault!* Morningstar bristled as he thought of the Russian wench with the long black hair. It was clear that she had brainwashed Judah. It was her fault that he had behaved so recklessly. *I'll talk to him. I'll tell him that it's not too late…that he can still come back and make things right.* He slammed his fist on the desk. No, he couldn't talk to him…because Knight wasn't taking his calls.

Morningstar finished off another brandy and lit a cigar. *Where the hell is Janet?* She was supposed to have been back in time for the speech. He checked his watch. *Seven-twenty…the bitch is late!*

His hand was shaking; it pissed him off. He stood, walked to the window, and stared out at the DC skyline. The city, the entire country, had more or less gone into lockdown. Never in the history of the republic had such a thing occurred. It was worse than an assassination; Knight was out there…still alive…somewhere! *What the hell were you thinking, Judah?*

He walked to the bar, refilled his glass, and emptied it in one swallow. He squeezed the glass with his hand, then threw it against the wall. It shattered into pieces; he barely noticed. *I will not let you do this to me, Judah.* He paced the room, growing angrier the more he thought of it. He grabbed a figurine from a side table and threw it at a painting on the wall, hardly flinching when both items fell to the floor in pieces. *Ungrateful son-of-a-bitch…I will kill you for this!*

He was about to exact the same punishment on a bottle of wine, when he stopped. His eyes widened. He had an idea. *I'll solve this entire mess with two simple phone calls.*

He walked to the coffee table, picked up the cellphone he used for work, and scrolled through until he found the number he was looking for. He pushed 'send' and waited. The call was answered with an impatient, "Secret Service. Sam Allen here."

Morningstar cleared his throat. "It's Morningstar...from the Pentagon." He paused. "Sorry to bother you when there's so much going on, Sam, but I think I might be able to weigh in on what's happened to the President."

"What've you got, Morningstar?"

"I've just been informed that an overseas intelligence source has uncovered the name of a woman, Emma Melnikov, who has been working undercover for the Russian government for the past two decades." He paused. "According to the source, she's bad news. He says there is every reason to believe that she is somehow involved with the disappearance of the President."

There was a pause. "Melnikov?"

"Yes," he spelled the last name. "Or she may go by the name Emma Cannon."

"Let me look into it. I'll call you if I find anything."

"Thanks, Sam." He ended the call and chuckled. *That should make things interesting.* But he needed more. He couldn't count on an incompetent government agency to find Knight. He pulled his laptop from his bag, set it on the coffee table, and turned it on. He went to a Pentagon website that could search the background of any U.S. citizen, as well as most non-citizens. He entered Emma's name and waited. He scrolled through information about her mother and father – both Russian emigres, both deceased – then scrolled further down to her family. She was married to Michael Cannon – *straying slut* – and had a child, Galina. He kept going. They lived outside Camden, Maine. He looked for info on Galina. She was a junior in high school, and had recently been selected as a pianist with the internationally acclaimed Maine orchestra. The orchestra had flown out of Portland ten weeks ago to perform overseas in Europe. They were booked to fly back on Saturday morning at ten, for a five-day break before heading to South America. *It's only Wednesday...plenty of time.* He checked his watch. *Two-thirty in the morning in Lithuania...time to wake up, Gad.*

He picked up his private cellphone and dialed.

It was answered after only one ring with a whispered, "Yes Father?"

"What are you doing?"

"Waiting on Matt Henderson to get to Vilnius."

Morningstar's eyes widened. "Are you sure he's coming?"

"I guarantee it. I have leverage. Speaking of which, give me a sec."

Morningstar could hear a door being opened, some mumbled words, and then a door being shut. Gad got back on the line. "Now we can speak freely."

"Who's with you?"

"It's not important. Let's just say that I've found a good way to make sure that Henderson gets down here to Lithuania."

"I assume you have the soldiers standing by?"

"I do, sir."

"Okay, but there's been a change in plans." He paused. "Instead of flying Henderson directly to the States, I need the soldiers to take him to a secret facility located just outside Klaipeda, Lithuania...about ten miles north of the city. It's no longer in use. We'll keep him there until I figure out what to do with him." He added, "Tell the soldiers that the apprehension of this man is to be kept top secret. And whatever you do, don't use his name. Just tell them that he's a valuable asset. Got it?"

"Yes, Father."

"Also, I'll need you to prepare the facility since it hasn't been used in a while. Make sure it's equipped to house a man for at least a few weeks' time."

There was a pause. "But Klaipeda is over an hour-and-a-half away from here."

"So it is. You better go now so you can be back in time to meet Henderson."

A pause, followed by a reluctant, "Yes sir."

"Once Henderson has been handed off to the soldiers, you need to get to the Vilnius airport. I'll have a ticket waiting. You'll fly by way of Warsaw to the U.S. – to Maine, to be exact. Do you have an alias we can use to book the flights?"

"I could use Adrus Sepp from Estonia. That's the ID that I picked up in Riga."

Morningstar considered it. "Can you vouch for its quality? And did you develop any sort of backstory for the ID? Maybe a credit card with the same name?"

There was a pause. "Um...no, not really. I just needed to be able to get around Riga without drawing any red flags."

Morningstar frowned. Scrutiny would be tight, especially in Warsaw. He couldn't risk it. "Have you got anything else?"

Another pause. "How about the ID of the Henderson driver? That guy was an actual person; he'll have plenty of backstory in place. No credit card though."

Morningstar rubbed his chin. As far as the Hendersons knew, their driver had run off the night that Cobra had escaped their compound. He chuckled. *How perfect to tie a former Henderson driver to the chaos I'm about to create.* "Go with that one."

"OK. The name is Carlos DeMarco. The likeness isn't perfect, but fortunately the guy wore glasses. If I wear thick glasses to hide my glass eye, it'll be close enough." He spelled the name, then read off the man's birthdate and home address.

"Perfect. DeMarco it is. I'll have Janet put together a credit card with the same name. It will be waiting for you at check-in, along with some cash." He paused. "Now, I want you to write the rest of this down... you'll need to know every detail."

He waited while Gad grabbed a piece of paper and a pen. "Ready, Father."

"Your brother Judah is misbehaving. He has a woman, Emma Melnikov, who's led him astray." He spelled out Melnikov. "Her husband, Michael Cannon, lives in Camden, Maine. I'm fairly certain that he'll be picking up his daughter, Galina, in three days, Saturday, ten a.m., at Portland's airport." *Since his slut wife won't be able to.* "Michael Cannon is your target." He paused again. "Now, say it back to me."

Gad repeated the information, almost word for word.

"Excellent. Hand off Henderson to the soldiers, and send them on their way. Then fly to Maine and find Michael Cannon," he chuckled, "...and use him to do whatever's necessary to force his slutty wife not only to leave Judah, but to tell you where he's hiding."

CHAPTER 105

Vilnius, Lithuania

Samuels was losing hope. Henderson had urged him to escape. He had had no opportunity. Then again, his small stature, combined with his loathing of violence, had made it impossible for him to even think about overpowering the man. Instead, he had tried to use the gifts that God had given him; he had tried to talk to the troubled young man. But Gad was a reluctant client. Samuels had pretty much given up on getting anything from the man that would persuade him into letting Samuels go.

But then had come the phone call. Samuels was surprised that Gad hadn't been more careful with the call. Though Gad had forced Samuels into a closet soon after he had answered the phone, Samuels had heard the initial salutation, as well as a few words here or there. The call was apparently from the man's father, and Samuels had been stunned. *What sort of father and son would mastermind such a plot?*

It had been clear from Gad's tone that he was receiving instructions. The good news was that Gad had taken notes during the call, and those notes were now sitting on a table by the window. Could Samuels read the notes and maybe learn something that would help him convince Gad to let him go? He nodded. It was worth a try. All he had to do was find a way to get a look at that piece of paper.

Gad had let him out of the closet once he had completed the call, and had sat him in the same chair where he had spent most of the last twenty-four hours. He was about five feet away from the table with the pad of paper, but the writing was angled away from him. *I need to get closer to that table.*

He cleared his throat. "May I have a glass of water, please?"

Gad, who was standing by the window, looked over at him and frowned. "Sure." He walked to a sink, found a glass in the cupboard, and filled it full of water. He walked over to Samuels and handed him the glass without a word.

"Thank you." Samuels sipped the water, never taking his eyes off of Gad, who had returned to the window. Suddenly, Samuels dropped the glass – still half full of water – and let it hit the floor. "Bloody hell!" he exclaimed, as he jumped up and ran to pick up the glass.

Gad just looked at him and laughed. He walked to the sink, grabbed a towel, and threw it at Samuels. "Clean it up," he said as he walked back to the window.

Samuels grabbed the towel, got on his hands and knees, and began to wipe up the water. He moved quietly in the direction of the table. He held up the towel as if trying to find a dry spot, then made a quick glance at the sheet of paper. Through years of study at the university in Vienna, he had gotten good at memorizing a page of words quickly. He was grateful for the skill as he took in the contents of the page in less than five seconds. He did his best to catalogue it, then fell back to the floor.

Gad looked over his shoulder. "Hurry up."

Samuels nodded and made one last swipe across the floor. He stood, walked back to his chair, and draped the damp towel over the arm of the chair. *So, what do I do now?* he thought with a frown. He tried to make sense of the notes he had read. Though they didn't offer Samuels any insight that would assist him in getting away, the words on that page seemed to lay out Gad's assignment for the days ahead. Could that maybe prove useful to Matt Henderson? Samuels nodded. *If I am about to die – which seems likely – the least I can do is stop this man before he does harm to others.* Which meant that he needed to find a way to get the information to Matt Henderson.

Gad had walked away from the window, his frustration evident as he had begun to angrily tidy up the room. He was obviously getting ready to go. Where to; Samuels had no idea. But if he hoped to alert Henderson, he needed to do so in the next few minutes.

He wished he had his phone. Gad had taken it from him soon after they had arrived at the hotel room; it was now sitting on a counter by the sink. But even if Samuels was to gain access to it, he didn't know the number to Matt Henderson's trac phone...only Gad had that number. *So, maybe I can use Gad's phone to make the call.*

He cleared his throat. "I...I need to make a call. May I use your phone?"

Gad looked up from packing his last few items into his backpack and scowled. "Who ya gonna' call."

"Um...my office."

"At two-thirty in the morning?"

"It's seven-thirty at night back home. Betty is expecting to hear from me."

"I don't give a shit what Betty is expecting."

Samuels shifted uncomfortably. "Um...if she doesn't hear from me in the next few minutes, she will contact the Vilnius police."

Gad scoffed. "Why the hell would she do that?"

"Because I nearly died not that long ago in a place called Dalgety Bay."

Gad chuckled. "Oh yeah...you and the skinny bitch." He turned back to the window. "She did die, didn't she?"

Samuels was finding it difficult to keep his cool. "Yes, she did."

Gad shook his head. "Too bad. She wasn't bad looking...a little thin, but some sexy legs." He looked again at Samuels. "I'm not gonna let you make a call. Betty will just have to call the police. We'll be long gone by the time they come lookin'."

Samuels swallowed. *What now?* He cleared his throat. "If you won't let me make a call, may I at least use the bathroom? My intestines are tied up in knots."

Gad grimaced. "I don't care about your intestines, dumbass."

"What I'm saying is that I would like to close the door, if I might."

Gad hesitated. "Fine. But don't take too long. We gotta get movin'."

Samuels stood and looked outside. "Dear me, it's certainly a dark night."

Gad turned his attention once again to the window. "Yeah, and if you try anything, Doctor, it will get even darker."

Samuels trembled at the threat, but moved quickly toward the bathroom. As Gad stayed focused on the window, Samuels was able to move a few steps to his left and grab his cellphone from the counter. He continued into the bathroom and quickly closed and locked the door. He turned on the fan and stared at his phone. He didn't have a number for Matt Henderson, but he did have a number for Walter. Though he doubted they were together, at least Walter could pass on the information.

He found Walter's number and dialed. Just as the call was answered, Samuels flushed the toilet. Without waiting for a hello, he put his lips to the phone and whispered, "Please, write this down and deliver it to Matt." He paused, giving Walter time to get a pen and paper. "A man who calls himself Gad just got a call from his father. As they were talking, Gad wrote down the following: *'Vilnius to Warsaw to America,'* *'Judah, affair with Emma Melnikov,'* and *'Emma + Michael Cannon.'*" Samuels spelled the name Melnikov as he reached over and turned on the faucet. He added, "The message ended with *'daughter, Galina, Saturday, 10 a.m., Portland.'*"

There was a knock on the door. "What are you doin' in there…takin' a bath?"

Samuels whispered, "Goodbye…and good luck," then hung up the phone. He yelled through the door. "I'm…I'm just washing up. I'll be out shortly."

He splashed water on his face and dried it with a towel. At the last minute, he tucked his phone inside the cuff of his shirt sleeve, on the off chance that Gad might search him. He would return it to the counter the second that Gad turned his head.

He walked out of the bathroom and nodded. "I'm ready."

"You better be, old man…we have quite a journey ahead of us."

CHAPTER 106

The Henderson Compound

Cravens had walked back into the room just seconds after Walter had told Henderson that Cobra had cut him down from the tree. Walter had quickly engaged Cravens in a conversation about the driver, DeMarco, sparing Henderson from having to say anything. But the minute that Cravens had left again, Henderson had walked over to his father and, with his voice shaking, had said, *"Why didn't you tell me?"*

Walter had merely shaken his head. *"I didn't think I could say the words."* He had added, *"...and what good would it have done?"* He frowned. *"But I think it's clear now that this Gad character isn't just some run-of-the-mill crook...he risked his own life to save the life of a diabolical killer."*

Though Henderson had wanted to tell Walter that that wasn't the half of it, he had refrained. *There are certain things that that man never needs to know.*

That had been several hours ago. During that time, Cravens had made six more trips outside, leaving Walter and Henderson to try – in five-minute clips – to finish their discussion. And in-between, when Cravens was in the room, Walter had been the one to carry on a conversation with Cravens, leaving Henderson to ponder the fact that his half-brother, Cobra – a brutal and sadistic killer – had saved his life.

Why? he kept saying to himself. But the more thought about it, the more he understood. *That bastard wants to hold it over my – and Walter's – heads...forever.*

But the phone call that Walter had just taken had left both Henderson and Cravens baffled. At first, when Walter hadn't said a word, Henderson had thought that maybe Cobra was calling back. But then, when Walter had grabbed a pen and paper and had started writing, Henderson had known it was someone else.

The call ended and, unable to wait any longer, Henderson said, "Well?"

Walter held up a finger. "Give me a second," he said as he continued to write.

Cravens, who was sitting once again on the Queen Anne sofa, leaned forward, looked at Henderson, and shrugged. Henderson shook his head in reply.

Finally, Walter laid down the pen. He looked at them both and frowned. "That was Dr. Samuels. He called me on his own phone." He paused. "He said that Gad got a call about thirty minutes ago, and that the man took notes during the call. Samuels was able to get a look at those notes."

Henderson narrowed his eyes. "And?"

Walter checked his notes. "Samuels said the call was from Gad's father. His notes started with the words *'Vilnius to Warsaw to America,' 'Judah, affair with Emma Melnikov,'* and *'Emma + Michael Cannon.'* Finally, according to Samuels, Gad had written *'daughter, Galina, Saturday, 10 a.m., Portland.'*"

"Portland...as in Oregon?" Cravens asked.

Walter shrugged. "Maybe, or it could be Connecticut, or even New York."

"Or Maine," added Henderson.

Walter nodded. "Or Maine." He paused. "Wherever it is, there must be some significance to the daughter, Galina, and the time and day."

Henderson nodded. "Likely something scheduled. A train, a plane... or maybe an event that starts at that time."

Cravens stood. "Well, whatever it is, I'm tired of waiting. This Gad fellow knows who's behind the plane crash, and he's only about five hours away. I don't get why the three of us haven't just gone down to Vilnius and made the sonofabitch talk."

Henderson shook his head. "Because he'll kill Samuels the minute he thinks he might be in trouble."

Cravens sighed. "With all due respect, don't you think he'll do that anyway?"

"Not if I can help it. I think if I go down there alone, I can get him to free Samuels, confess to me the name of the man who was behind the plane crash, and then tell me what his overseer is planning to do next."

Cravens frowned. "If that's the case, then what are you waiting for?"

Henderson looked at Cravens. He was right. While Henderson and Walter were stewing over Cobra, the odds that Gad could be hurting, or even killing Samuels was becoming all the more real. "I agree," he said, and made a move to the door.

Walter stopped him. He looked at him and frowned. "I'm curious, son, what makes you think this Gad fellow will confide in you."

Henderson hesitated. "For one thing, Gad and I have…history. For another, over the years, I have, um…acquired…ways of making people do what I want."

Walter shifted uncomfortably, then nodded slowly. "I see." He frowned. "Do you think that Gad's *overseer* had something to do with the plane crash?"

Henderson stared at his father. "I know he did."

"Dammit, Martin…*how* do you know?"

Henderson rubbed his eyes. He had already said too much. As much as he wanted their help to bring down Morningstar, neither Walter nor Cravens could help him. They didn't understand Morningstar like he did. And he wasn't about to tell them how he knew the man…the things that he had *done* for that man. And if he did tell them what he knew about Morningstar, they would be forced to come at the man head on. Morningstar couldn't be brought down with a head-on approach; Henderson had tried that already; he had actually threatened the man's life. But Morningstar had made it abundantly clear that to kill him wouldn't stop his plans. Henderson had gone so far as to threaten him with a video that literally showed Morningstar changing into his disguise before he killed the bus passengers in Laredo, Texas. But even that hadn't intimidated the man. As a matter of fact, Henderson was convinced that it had only made him more determined…*and more careful.* Why was Morningstar so confident that he would never be brought down? Because he controlled all viable levers of power in DC, not just General Daniels, but the entire Pentagon, as well as every corrupt but influential member of the Bentley Group. *Who knows who else the man has a hold over in that infernal city.* No, there was only one way to truly take down Morningstar…*I need to destroy him through his sons.* And all he would need was one of them…one son to work with him to undo the damage that Morningstar had done over the last four years. Only a Son of Jacob had the power to undermine Morningstar's master plan, only a Son of Jacob would be privy to his next moves, *and only a Son of Jacob can take Morningstar's faith in him and turn it into a tool to bludgeon the man to the ground.*

Which meant that Henderson had to go to Vilnius and try to somehow convince Gad not only to leave Morningstar, but to help Henderson stop Morningstar from following through on his plans. But how would Henderson convince Gad to turn on someone he didn't merely see as a father figure, but likely saw as a savior? He sighed. *By making him more afraid of me than he is of Morningstar.*

He frowned. *But what if I fail?* If he was unsuccessful in persuading Gad, then his chance to stop Morningstar was over. Within days, or maybe hours, Morningstar would likely kill him…*which will leave no one to take down Morningstar.*

He turned to Cravens. "I need a favor."

Cravens nodded. "Anything."

"I'm going to try to convince Gad to end his loyalty to his overseer when I get to Vilnius. But if I fail, I'll need you to step in." He frowned. "We know from Samuel's notes that Gad is most likely heading to America. I need you to go there, confront him, and learn what he's planning for the people whose names are written on that piece of paper." He flinched. "I'm almost certain those people are in danger."

Cravens narrowed his eyes, then slowly nodded. "Whatever you need, Henderson." He ran a hand through his thick gray hair. "I'll go to America, track down this Gad fellow, and stop him from doing whatever he's about to do."

Henderson nodded. "Good. Start with Maine. It's your best bet."

Walter looked at Henderson, clearly exasperated. "How do you know that? Do you know these people? Do you know Michael Cannon? Or Emma Melnikov?"

Henderson shook his head. "No, but I know Judah. And I'm fairly certain he has ties to Maine." He cleared his throat. "So, go to Maine,

Cravens. Wait for Gad in Portland at ten a.m. on Saturday. Walter can give you a good description of the guy."

Cravens nodded. "Don't worry; I saw the asshole...up close and personal. I'll know him if I see him again." He frowned. "What are you going to do?"

Henderson ran his hands through his hair. He took a deep breath and sighed. "I'm going to Vilnius...just like I said I would."

Walter walked up and stood toe-to-toe with his son. "No, you can't. I'll go."

"Dad, I have to be the one to go. Samuels' life depends on it."

"Does Gad even know what you look like, son?"

"Not with my disguise. But he definitely knows what you look like."

"That's true. But right now, I think I look more like Matt than you do."

Henderson nodded. "Maybe, but once he realizes that you're not me, he'll kill Samuels."

Walter frowned. "What if I take someone with me?" He hesitated. "I can take Dimitri. He can stay back until I need him."

Henderson shook his head. "No. Gad will kill Samuels before you even have a chance to alert Dimitri." He walked back to the window. Without looking at either of them, he said, "The time has come. I'm going to Vilnius and let that asshole take me into custody. It's the only way." He turned and faced his father. "Don't worry, Dad, I'll be fine." He nodded. "Besides, as you've already heard me say, the man who wants me, wants me alive. Otherwise, I'd be dead by now."

Walter shook his head. "But what will you achieve by giving yourself up?"

"For one thing, it will allow for Samuels to be freed." He paused. "For another, as I said earlier, I'm going to try to get Gad to talk to me...to trust me."

"Let me go with you."

"No, Dad. That's stupid. Gad will shoot you in a heartbeat." He paused. "Someone needs to stay here and manage the war with Putin." Another pause. "Dimitri and I will drive Cravens to the airport in Riga; hopefully they're letting at least a few planes come and go. I'll get a train from there. I'll go to Vilnius, make sure Samuels is freed, then let the soldiers take me."

Walter frowned. "How will you be sure that Samuels is released?"

Henderson sighed; it was a good question. "I'll come up with something."

He rubbed the back of his neck, then pulled out his phone, the trac phone that had been given to him by Gad. He opened it and pushed 'send.' He waited. Gad answered with a snide, "On your way, asshole?"

"I am. It will take me about two-and-a-half hours to get to Riga, and another four-and-a-half for the train to bring me to Vilnius." He checked the time. "It's three a.m. I should be there by ten." He ended the call before Gad could challenge him.

Walter stared at him. "Will you wear your disguise?"

Henderson nodded. "I think I have to. Only as Aiden Balkus do I even make it out of Latvia." He could see that Walter was still struggling. "Listen, Dad, we both know that I should've died five years ago...and that I practically did die two months ago." He had been about to add, *"...and if it wasn't for your other son, I'd be dead now,"* but had held off; Cravens was in the room. He sighed. "Our priority has to be Samuels. The only way to keep him alive is if I let those soldiers take me."

Henderson turned to Cravens. "I have one more request." He paused. "No matter what happens to me, we need proof of what the man responsible for the plane crash has done. Not only the crashing of that airplane, but so many other horrible deeds throughout the last four years." He nodded. "Hopefully, you'll get some of what you need when you confront Gad in America." He reached down and picked up his backpack. He rifled through the pockets and pulled out a key. "You'll get the rest with this key. It opens a lockbox at a Savings and Loan in Boonsboro, Maryland, about an hour north of DC. There's a flash drive in the lockbox that will help you fight back when the powerful who rule our government try to refute your claims."

Cravens frowned. "My claims?"

Henderson nodded. "Against the perpetrator of that plane crash... against the man who killed Maddi."

Cravens narrowed his eyes. "Who is it, Henderson?"

Henderson sighed. He wanted to tell him so badly, but he couldn't. Cravens would want to pull in the Secret Service, and Walter would want to pull in his friends in DC. And they might even succeed in bringing down Morningstar, but that wouldn't stop him; he had made that fact all too clear. The only way to truly stop Morningstar from further destroying the world would be to bring down his entire operation. And the only way to do that, would be to make it fall apart from within.

Henderson cleared his throat. "I'm not ready to say. Cravens, just see what you can learn from Gad," he paused, "…then pick up the flash drive. Once you look at it, you'll know everything." He frowned. "But trust no one, Cravens."

Cravens frowned. "I have to trust someone, Henderson. I'll need help."

Walter said, "I think Jason Hanover is trustworthy."

Henderson nodded. "I agree. And Sam Allen, as well."

Cravens nodded. "Two good men, for sure." He shoved the key in his pocket. "I'll take care of it, Henderson. Don't worry."

Henderson nodded. "I'll join you as soon as I can get away from the soldiers." But even as he said it, he knew that there was little hope that he would get away. Morningstar had gone through quite a bit to finally get him; he wasn't about to let him escape now.

Walter was near tears. It hurt Henderson to see it. The larger-than-life man seemed small and weak as he said, "I'll make a few calls and see what I can do, son."

Henderson nodded. But there would be nothing his father could do. There was nothing anyone could do. Henderson was about to once again come face to face with the man who had ruined his life. And though he knew Morningstar would likely kill him, he was ready. Not only to face the monster…but to die. Perhaps it was why he had been allowed to live in the first place. *Maybe only I can do this…maybe only I can cut the heart out of the snake.*

But it would cost him his life. Which was okay. Better than okay, it was the desired outcome. Henderson had been ready to die for months now…actually years. Since the fire that had scarred him nearly five years ago. *I should've died then,* he thought, suddenly mindful of all the people who would still be alive if he had. Al-Gharsi, Lili, maybe even Maddi. *The world would've been a better place without me.*

He fought back tears as he walked to the door of the den. There would be no goodbyes; the decision had been made. Henderson would leave the castle and go to Vilnius, and – within days – he would be dead. But before he died, he would at least be able to look Morningstar in the eye and say, *"It's over, Morningstar. Your sons are singing as we speak, and we will soon have enough evidence to bury you – and your family – forever."*

CHAPTER 107

Somewhere on the Atlantic Ocean

Knight checked his watch. *Nine o'clock*. The speech from his Vice-President had taken place two hours ago, and the dinner he was supposed to attend with the Japanese Prime Minister had likely been cancelled. The ports had shut down within minutes of the Vice-President's speech, and as if from nowhere, navy vessels soon dotted the entire coastline. Foster had anticipated it and had made sure that Colt had taken them far enough out to sea that the navy ships wouldn't pose a threat. With Foster, Knight, and Emma hidden in the hold of the ship, Colt could claim to be a lone fisherman trying to snare cod before it got too cold. The challenge would come if they didn't believe him, and decided to search his boat. *We'll just have to pray that that doesn't happen*, thought Knight as they sped along the dark sea.

Foster had updated Knight regarding events that had unfolded at the Virginia warehouse after they had left. As Knight had expected, a lone gunman had tried to attack the warehouse. He had been shot and killed. The agents had been stunned to learn that he was a former agent, and that he was carrying a sniper rifle that belonged to the U.S. Secret Service. Knight had bristled at the news. A bullet from that rifle had been intended for Emma; Morningstar had told him as much. The fact that the agent had been former Secret Service was a bad sign. Had Morningstar turned a once-loyal American agent into a killer? Knight didn't want to believe it; he didn't want to think that Morningstar had actually hired a former public servant to kill Emma. *But the man was waiting outside…just like Morningstar had said he would be.*

Knight felt the boat rise sharply, then fall, and he pulled Emma close as they were once again thrown against the wall. Colt, apparently worried about the blockade, had taken the boat even further out to sea. The ride had been rough. Fortunately, neither Knight nor Emma suffered from motion sickness. The same couldn't be said for poor Foster, however, who had vomited three times in the past hour.

Knight stood and walked over to Foster. He helped him to a cot, while Emma grabbed a stack of dampened paper towels. She handed them to Knight, who held them to Foster's forehead. "Some protector you are, Foster."

Foster looked up at him, and did his best to grin. "I could…still take out the first man…who came for you."

"Too bad it's a woman who's got me. You're powerless against women."

Foster chuckled, while Emma went to retrieve more water-soaked towels. Again, she handed them to Knight, who laid them on the man's forehead. "What time are we expected to reach the port, Foster?"

The port he was referring to was Great Kills Harbor, just north of New York City, where an unmarked vehicle would be waiting to drive them to Maine, and then on to the Katahdin Mountains.

"Not until tomorrow afternoon," the agent mumbled. He had told Knight that once they reached the base of the mountain, they would be forced to hike the rest of the way to the bunker. It would require a climb up one of the steeper rises on the back side of the range.

Emma and Knight had scaled that same rise seventeen years ago. Their goal had been to climb the tallest peak of the range. They had reached the top, and had then hiked to a flat area where they could pitch a tent. Emma had stumbled onto a remote cave while looking for a place to set up a bathroom. She had shown it to Knight, and they had explored the cave like kids discovering lost treasure. Replete with everything from food rations to ham radios, they had been curious as to who had occupied the cave. Knight had asked some locals about it, and had learned that in the early seventies a doomsday cult had camped there and had equipped the cave with everything they would need to survive a nuclear holocaust: Food rations, gallon jugs of water, high-tech sleeping gear. There had also been the ham radios, along with video scanners and walkie-talkies. The preppers had gone so far as to wire the cave for electricity, likely intending it to be powered by a generator, though he and Emma had never found one.

Knight had told Foster of the cave just before they had left the Virginia warehouse. *"It might be the perfect place for us to do what we need to do, Foster."*

Foster had called his off-the-grid friends and they had gone to the site. Using money that Knight had wired from a trust fund left to him by his parents, they had spent the last ten hours getting it ready. *"Once we get there, sir, you'll have it all: the latest technology, warm clothes, and good food. Everything you'll need to lead the nation."* Knight had asked Foster how his friends could do so much in such a short amount of time. Foster's reply: *"It's what they do, sir."* That had been the end of it.

Foster finally fell asleep, and Knight grinned as he looked at the agent. That man had sacrificed everything: his position with the Secret Service, any commendations he might receive. He was risking his very life to help Knight escape the White House. *And, in the meantime, he's puking his guts up.*

He looked at Emma, who was coming toward him with another ice-soaked towel, her black hair falling loosely over her shoulders, her blue eyes catching his as he smiled at her and winked. She sat next to him and was about to place the towel on Foster's forehead, when Knight stood and took the towel from her hand. He set it on a nearby table and motioned for her to follow him as he half-walked, half-crawled to what looked like a utility room. It was completely dark inside; he pulled a flashlight from his pocket and shone it around the room. About eight-foot square, it appeared to be a storage closet, though there was little on the shelves other than jugs of water and a few cans of beans. There were no windows; only a ventilation shaft toward the top of the back wall. He spotted a lantern on one of the shelves, with a pack of matches beside it. He lit the lantern, turned off his flashlight, and closed the door.

As the gentle flame filled the small room, he took her in his arms and eased her to the floor. She giggled and he put his finger to her lips. "Shhh…we have to be quiet."

With the roar of the engine and Foster's snores muffling any sound they might make, he kissed her. It was as if no time had passed; as if they were in the tent on the side of the mountain, squeezed together with nothing on their minds but each other. He undid the buttons on her blouse. She looked at him and whispered, "Here?"

He grinned. For the next hour and a half, while the country was panicking over the disappearance of their Commander-in-Chief, and while Foster rested peacefully just a few feet away, Romer and Emma made love in an eight-by-eight closet.

CHAPTER 108

Washington, DC

Janet didn't get to the hotel until after nine p.m. She waltzed through the door, dropped her coat on a chair, and sauntered over to Morningstar, her smile implying that wherever she had been, things had gone well. But, instead of embracing her, he shoved her out of the way. "Where were you? Have you been following the news?"

Unfazed, she walked into the bedroom, stripped out of her clothes, and walked out to the living room wearing nothing but a robe. She sat on the sofa while he paced the room. She said calmly, "Fill me in, baby."

He said nothing for several minutes, simply pacing back and forth in front of her, as she sat quietly. Finally, he stopped and looked at her. "First of all, Judah – our *President* – has disappeared. What kind of horse shit is that?" He resumed his pacing. Janet remained silent. He stopped and looked at her again. "Second of all, he was supposed to kill his Russian whore, Emma Melnikov, but now I know that he didn't."

Janet frowned. "How do you know?"

Morningstar hissed. "Because he put out a bogus police report stating that she was dead, and now he's gone missing…and I'm almost certain that she is the reason."

Janet rubbed her chin. "Interesting."

Morningstar was fuming. "Interesting? You think it's *interesting* that the man I've devoted much of my life to…the man that I put in place to be the most powerful leader on earth…the man who was going to help me save not only this country but this world from its sins…has chosen at this late hour to betray me?"

By now, he was screaming; Janet didn't seem to care. Coolly, she said, "I think it's excellent news."

He stopped and stared at her. Her insolence was infuriating. He walked toward her and pulled back his fist.

She didn't flinch. "Hit me. I dare you."

Morningstar's eyes narrowed. He didn't move. Finally, he lowered his hand. There was something admirable, maybe even erotic about Janet when she dared to defy him. He said evenly, "Tell me, dear Janet, how is that 'excellent news?'"

She crossed her legs, the robe inching to the top of her thigh. He felt his knees weaken as he continued to stand over her. She smiled deviously. "I'm guessing he put Hapless Harrington in charge while he's away?"

Morningstar frowned. "He did." He sneered. "That man's a bumbling idiot!"

Janet chuckled. "Yes…a bumbler and a fool." She nodded. "Fools like Harrington rarely think for themselves. Which makes them easily manipulated…wouldn't you agree?"

"Yes, but—"

She put her finger to his lips. "Which means that a forceful recommendation from someone with authority…say, someone like the Chairman of the Joint Chiefs – or his top aide – could likely control the man's actions without too much trouble."

His eyes widened. *Janet is brilliant.* He fell onto the couch next to her and slid his hand under her robe. She let him fondle her as she slowly rubbed his thigh through his pants.

She whispered, "But you will need to be clever; you can't be too obvious." She leaned over and kissed him, then moved closer so that she was practically sitting on top of him. She whispered, "…but there's more you can do with a man like that."

"What…what do you mean?"

"I would bet Benjamin's inheritance that Knight has made arrangements to stay in touch with Harrington."

Morningstar hadn't even thought of it. Of course, he had. Judah had always been the sort of man who would think about the future, about the consequences of his actions. He would have provided a way to stay in touch with Harrington, if for no other reason than to provide continuity to a broken and besieged country. He smirked. "Not bad, Janet." He kissed her on the cheek, then sat back and nodded. "So, I will simply insist – on behalf of Daniels – that Harrington tell us where Knight is hiding."

Janet smacked him hard across his cheek. "Don't be stupid!" He was too stunned to move. Before he could hit her back, she reached over and embraced him, hugging his shoulders and arms to his side. "He won't tell you," she whispered as she licked his ear, "...he can't tell you, baby." She put her hand once again on his thigh. "My guess is that he was told that Knight's life is in danger, which means that he'll feel a need to protect Knight." She dug her nails into his thigh as hard as she could until he grimaced in pain. She leaned close and whispered, "Besides, silly fool, Knight won't have told Harrington where he's going...your son is too smart for that."

Morningstar was trembling with rage. But never had he wanted Janet so badly. He pried her hand from his thigh, then stood and slid out of his pants. He leaned over her and shoved her against the couch. Ignoring her bulging belly, he fell on top of her and whispered, "So what do you propose I do, my sweet whore?"

She dug her nails into his back. She pulled him to her and said coolly, "You use Harrington to feed Knight information...false information."

Morningstar stared at her. He stood back from her, continuing to stare. *Why didn't I think of that?* Suddenly, he grabbed her by the hair, jerked her head back, and kissed her so hard he broke the skin. He yanked her head harder, ignoring her grimace as he said with a nod, "That is exactly what I'll do." He gave her a shove, then fell onto the couch beside her.

She ran her tongue over her bloodied lip. Unfazed, she turned to him and said, "I don't think you realize how much power Judah has given you."

He narrowed his eyes and looked at her. "What do you mean?"

She leaned into him. "You can use Harrington," she whispered, as she rubbed his thigh, "...to teach Knight a lesson." She moved her hand slowly up his thigh, allowing her fingers to fall softly against his skin. He began to tremble. She licked his ear, then said quietly, "Let him see how far you're willing to go…to get him back."

He had started to shake; he couldn't seem to stop. He was lost to her as he sputtered, "How…how far…am I…willing…to go?"

She chuckled. "Tell him – through Harrington – that you're willing to ignite a…nuclear war." She moved her hand the rest of the way up his thigh and grabbed him. He gasped. She laughed and said, "That ought to get his attention."

EPILOGUE

Henderson stared at the bold gray fortress in the distance. The castle had stood outside the town of Kaunas, Lithuania since the 14th century. Though he knew little of its history, he felt a kinship with the ancient castle. It was nearly as old as the one that Henderson had grown up in...the castle where so much had happened, where so much had gone wrong. Where hope had been high, but where misfortune, followed by treachery, had brought that hope – and him – crashing to the ground. And the crash had been unbearable. The loss of innocence had been far greater than any pain he had ever endured...except for the loss of Maddi. And that loss – the loss of the only woman he would ever love – he now knew was unsurvivable. As the castle faded in the distance, he checked his watch and sighed. *Noon...it won't be long now.*

He didn't know where they were taking him; he didn't care. He was surprised, however, that he wasn't being flown directly to DC. All he knew was that he was traveling west through Lithuania to an undisclosed location. Was it a holding cell until Morningstar could fly over and kill him without the oversight of the U.S. Government? Or was it simply the place where he would be put on a boat or plane to eventually be taken to DC. *Does it matter?* He shook his head and sighed. *No, not at all.*

He thought back over the last eight hours that had brought him to that point, surprised that it had gone as smoothly as it had. Over Walter's protests, he had had Dimitri drive him and Cravens to the Riga airport,

532

where they had dropped Cravens at the door just in time to catch a six-a.m. flight to the UK. Fortunately, limited flight traffic had resumed, mostly to allow for NATO officials to come into the country. The plan was for Cravens to fly from the UK to Maine, where he would lay in wait for Gad, then follow him and do whatever he could to keep Emma Melnikov and Michael Cannon safe. Cravens would then try to persuade Gad to turn on his boss. If things went as planned, Jacob and his Sons would be destroyed by week's end.

Walter had insisted that Henderson take two of their security officers with him to Vilnius. *"No sense not having them with you, at least as you travel out of Latvia."* Henderson had accepted it, though he knew it wouldn't change a thing. One way or another, he was about to face Morningstar, which meant that he was about to die.

He had refused to say anything other than a quick goodbye to Walter, and no goodbye to Dora. She hadn't even known he was at the castle. *"Let her think that I'm still on the run,"* he had said after a quick hug. There had been enough goodbyes, enough pain…on both sides. *Better to just go and let them both get on with their lives.*

They had reached the airport at four a.m., and Henderson had secretly shoved five hundred euros in the pocket of Cravens' soot-ridden coat as they gave one another a quick hug goodbye. Henderson had grinned as he had watched Cravens shuffle through the front door. He had nodded as the oversized man had waved goodbye. Henderson had been sad to see him go. Their journey together had been a short one, but in that time, he had grown fond of the gruff, taciturn agent with the messy hair. He could tell that he and Maddi had been close. Being with him had made Henderson feel closer to Maddi.

Once Cravens was no longer visible through the door, Henderson had had Dimitri drive him and the two soldiers to the train station, where he had booked the three of them on a train from Riga to Daugavpils, then on to Vilnius. The train ride had taken four hours, during which time Henderson had managed to pull together an hour or two of sleep. He was still disguised as Aiden Balkus, and had removed anything from his wallet with the name Matt Henderson, in case he was searched. His identity as Aiden Balkus should work to his advantage. Not only would it get him safely across the border, but he hoped it might give him an edge before Gad was aware of his true identity.

The long train ride to Vilnius had given him time to think. And think he did…about Maddi, about Lili, about all the people he had been responsible for killing, one way or another. And he thought about Cobra, and the irony that the man had saved his life. Though he guessed that Cobra had saved him so that he could inflict his own pain at a later date, it had left Henderson puzzled. What had Cobra been doing at the estate in the first place? And where had he gone from there? Henderson had finally concluded – with a surprising sense of calm – that soon enough, it wouldn't matter. As a matter of fact, nothing would matter in another day or two.

He had spent the last hour of the journey thinking about the fact that Morningstar, rather than have him killed, had been insistent on keeping him alive. He had gotten to know Morningstar well enough over the years to conclude that in Morningstar's deluded mind, he probably felt that God had told him that *he* needed to be the one to actually kill Henderson. Regardless of the reason, Henderson would hopefully be able to use that fact to protect Samuels.

He and the soldiers had arrived at the Vilnius train station at nine-thirty in the morning. He had used the trac phone to call Gad, but he didn't tell him that he was wearing a disguise; he needed to force Gad to release Samuels before Gad was aware of who he was.

He had instructed his two soldiers to go to the downtown library and wait there. *"My hope is to have Dr. James Samuels report to you within the hour. You are to get him out of here at once and take him directly to our estate."* He had given the men a description of Samuels before they had left for the library, and had instructed them to look up his picture once they were there. *"He's a psychiatrist in London…shouldn't be too hard to find."*

He had then waited outside the train station for Gad, who had arrived by way of a military transport vehicle. Gad had had the doctor with him, along with four soldiers dressed in U.S. Army uniforms. Henderson, still disguised, had been able to see the six of them get out of the car. He had called Gad. *"I'm watching you. Put Samuels back in the car, and send him to the local library. Don't try anything. I have a switchblade in my hand. I'll slice my own throat if you fail to do what I've asked."*

Gad had looked around to try to find him, but had looked right past the blond-haired Aiden Balkus. Gad had then asked him what assurance he would have that, once he freed Samuels, Henderson would cooperate.

Henderson had said, *"Believe it or not, Gad, I'm looking forward to seeing our father again. I have something I need to tell him…in person. Besides, I'm tired of running."* He had paused. *"I'll come out the minute I get word that Samuels is safe."*

Gad had said, *"Get word? How will you get word?"*

Henderson had replied, *"I have a team of soldiers waiting for him. Once I know that he's safe, I'll tell you where I am."*

Gad must have believed him, for seconds later he was putting Samuels back in the car. At the last minute, he had sent one of the soldiers with him; likely an insurance policy in case Henderson didn't follow through on his promise. The car had pulled away, and Gad and the other three soldiers had waited outside the train station.

Twenty minutes later, as Henderson had stood with a group of travelers, he had gotten the call from his own soldiers that Samuels was safe. He had called Gad and had stepped away from the group. *"Okay, I'm yours. I have blond hair, I'm wearing glasses, and I just walked away from a group of tourists outside the station."*

Gad had immediately had the three soldiers take him into custody. Without a word, he had been led to the military vehicle. As one of the soldiers had tied his hands behind his back, Gad had laughed. *"That was way too easy."* Henderson had nodded. *"Like I said, I'm tired of running."* He had added, *"What about you? Aren't you tired of running?"* Gad had said nothing. Henderson had added, *"We could take him down together, you know. Stop him from whatever insane path he's on. You could be a hero, Gad."* Gad had paused, then had punched Henderson in the face. *"Shut up, Joseph."* And that had been the end of it. Henderson's bluster about forcing Gad to defy Morningstar out of fear had ended with a quick jab to his own jaw. All Henderson could hope now was that Gad would make the journey to America, and that Cravens would succeed where Henderson had failed.

He sighed as he leaned his head against the seat. With his hands tied behind his back, there was little he could do to alter his predicament, but he didn't care. He didn't have the energy or the desire to try to escape.

And it was doubtful that he could have escaped, even if he wanted to. The two soldiers in the front seat and the one next to him were all carrying military-issue weapons. Henderson wouldn't get two steps without getting gunned down. Though it was tempting to go out with guns blazing, there was one last thing he needed to do…one final thought he needed to share with the man who had ruined his life.

Apparently, Gad hadn't told the soldiers his actual name…probably by design. Morningstar wouldn't want the world to know that he had ties to an international assassin, or a bioterrorist. *Better in Morningstar's mind to leave my identity vague and insignificant for as long as he can…especially if he plans on killing me.* One of the soldiers had frisked him and had found his wallet; he had been referred to as 'Balkus' from then on.

They had been on the road now for about an hour. Henderson looked out at the passing scenery, smiling as he saw a group of children playing on a playground. In spite of the fact that he would most assuredly die in the next twenty-four hours, he felt remarkably at peace. He hadn't been lying when he told Gad he was tired of running. He was tired, period. Exhausted, as a matter of fact. It had been a long five years, and in that time, many good people had died. Some he had barely known; a few he had loved…deeply. He closed his eyes, his anguish nearly unbearable. *Soon it will all be over.*

A phone vibrated and the soldier in the passenger seat answered. "Officer Harold Smith here." There was a pause. "Yes sir." Again, a pause. "Balkus? Why, yes sir. We have him in custody now." There was another pause. "Certainly, sir." The soldier leaned over the seat and handed the phone to the soldier in back. "Hold it to his ear, Owen. Somebody from Homeland Security wants to talk to him."

The soldier sitting next to Henderson held the phone to his ear. Henderson said tentatively, "Hello?"

"Is this Aiden Balkus?"

"Um yes…yes, it is."

"I'm Director Jason Hanover with the Department of Homeland Security. I'm patching through a Latvian military officer. He says he has vital information that he can share only with you."

Henderson frowned. *What the hell?* "Um…okay…sure." He waited. There were a couple of clicks, then he heard the familiar voice of his father.

"Son, I have only a few seconds. I want you to know that I love you and I'm doing all that I can to get you out of this." Henderson started to stay something; Walter cut him off. "Just listen. You need to know

536

this, in case—"

Henderson closed his eyes. "It's okay. There is noth—"

"Son, listen!" There was a pause. "I just learned that Lili Platacis is alive."

The End

ABOUT THE AUTHOR

Dr. Jill Vosler is a family physician whose medical studies took her abroad to the University of Edinburgh in Scotland and on to extensive travel throughout the UK and Europe. Her love for these places has flavored her novels, along with the many years spent as a deputy coroner under the guidance of her father, who was the county coroner well into his eighties. She has a keen interest in geopolitics and a passion for music, but most enjoys traveling the world with family and friends.

NewAtlantianLibrary.com or
AbsolutelyAmazingEbooks.com
or AA-eBooks.com

Thank you for reading. Please review this book. Reviews help others find Absolutely Amazing eBooks and inspire us to keep providing these marvelous tales.

If you would like to be put on our email list to receive updates on new releases, contests, and promotions, please go to AbsolutelyAmazingEbooks.com and sign up.

For sales, editorial information, subsidiary rights information
or a catalog, please write or phone or e-mail

AbsolutelyAmazingEbooks
Manhanset House
Shelter Island Hts., New York 11965, US
Tel: 212-427-7139
www.AbsolutelyAmazingEbooks.com
bricktower@aol.com
www.IngramContent.com

For sales in the UK and Europe please contact our distributor,
Gazelle Book Services
White Cross Mills
Lancaster, LA1 4XS, UK
Tel: (01524) 68765 Fax: (01524) 63232
email: jacky@gazellebooks.co.uk

www.ingramcontent.com/pod-product-compliance
Lightning Source LLC
Chambersburg PA
CBHW070352030726
47504CB00001B/157